FORBIDDEN LONGING

He had not known that he was lonely until Arrian came into his life. She made him yearn for that which he could not have.

"Arrian, are you so unhappy here?"

"I pass my days knowing you will allow me to leave before August."

Warrick took her face between his hands and stared at her parted lips. "What if I asked you to remain?" he whispered.

Before she could reply, he covered her lips with a burning kiss that sent her heart racing.

"No, my lord, I would never willingly stay with you. I must remind you again that I am betrothed to Ian. Nothing you can do will change that."

His eyes had lost their softness. "I was always one to take up a challenge, my lady."

Also by Constance O'Banyon

Forever My Love
Song of the Nightingale

Available from HarperPaperbacks

Highland Love Song

Constance O'Banyon

HarperPaperbacks
A Division of HarperCollins*Publishers*

This is a work of fiction. The characters, incidents, and dialogues are products of the author's imagination and are not to be construed as real. Any resemblance to actual events or persons, living or dead, is entirely coincidental.

HarperPaperbacks *A Division of* HarperCollins*Publishers*
10 East 53rd Street, New York, N.Y. 10022

Cover illustration by Pino Daeni

First printing: August 1993

Printed in the United States of America

HarperPaperbacks, HarperMonogram, and colophon are trademarks of HarperCollins*Publishers*

❖ 10 9 8 7 6 5 4 3 2 1

When I close my eyes I can still hear the sound of sweet baby laughter that brought such joy to each day. You have been a source of pride to me since the day you blessed this family with your presence. You are as beautiful of heart as you are of face. Dearest Kimberly, you are a much loved daughter.

To Jeffrey Gee, who inspired me to create a hero with the same beautiful silver eyes. You are definitely one of my heroes, my wonderful grandson.

AUTHOR'S NOTE

Because of your wonderful response to the DeWinter family in *Song of the Nightingale,* and because of so many requests, I decided Arrian DeWinter's story must be told. Having a dram of Scottish blood in my veins, it seemed only natural to set the story in the Highlands.

Until July 1940, marriage by declaration was legal in Scotland. The couples who wished to wed had merely to declare their intentions before witnesses.

Prologue

Davinsham Castle, Scotland
1818

A storm was gathering over the Lowlands. Thunder
rumbled so loudly that the ground trembled while
bursts of lightning split across the ebony sky like
jagged swords.

As the first raindrops fell earthward, sixteen-year-old
Lord Warrick, Viscount of Glencarin, and heir of the Clan
Drummond, rushed from the stables where he had bedded
down his horse for the night. It was difficult for him to realize that he was actually within the confines of Davinsham
Castle, the stronghold of the MacIvors, his family's lifelong
enemy. So troubled were his thoughts that he was unmindful
of the rain that pelted him, soaking him to the skin.

Only this morning Lord Warrick had been forced to witness his sister, Gwendolyn's, marriage to Gavin MacIvors, a
man twice her age.

It had escaped no one's notice that Lord James had not
attended the wedding, sending instead his son to represent

the family. Though the chief of Clan Drummond had pleaded illness, everyone presumed, and rightly so, that he had been unwilling to watch his only daughter become the wife of a MacIvors.

Warrick remembered how pitifully Gwendolyn had pleaded with their father not to force her to marry the son of a rival chieftain, but her pleas had been ignored. She was being used by both sides in hopes of uniting the two clans. Old hatreds ran deep, though, and Warrick doubted this marriage would heal the wounds from generations of conflict.

Warrick hurried into the castle and up the stairs, his lip curling in distaste. The MacIvors displayed their wealth as one would display a trophy. The walls were decorated with silken wall hangings, and plush rugs covered the floors. Yes, there was wealth here, but not warmth. He thought of his own home, Ironworth Castle, which was shabby in comparison. There had been no woman to take over the household duties since his mother's death. Gwendolyn had cared little for housekeeping, preferring to leave that task to servants. Ironworth was in desperate need of a mistress.

His mouth tightened in anger as he dressed for the wedding banquet. This morning at the chapel, Gwendolyn's beauty had been paraded before the MacIvors clan like a prize. At age nineteen Gwendolyn was lovely, with honey-colored hair and soft gray eyes: Would Gavin MacIvors, who was their father's age and a well-known womanizer, cherish her as she deserved? Poor Gwendolyn could have been married many times over to a more worthy husband than Gavin MacIvors, but their father had insisted on this match.

The tears Warrick had seen in his sister's eyes had been like a knife stab in his heart. With fury he buttoned his black velvet coat and pushed his feet into high black boots. Almost defiantly he wrapped his family plaid about his shoulder and attached it through his belt. He would be glad when the celebration was over so he could leave this place. His only sadness was that he had to leave Gwendolyn behind.

*　　*　　*

It wasn't until Lady Gwendolyn was dressed in a wine red gown that she remembered her new husband had requested that she wear the ruby ring he had given her on their betrothal. Pushing her distaste aside, she picked up the MacIvors's ring. The huge red stone reminded her of blood, and she almost dropped it from her trembling hand. At the precise moment she slipped it on her finger, lightning flashed across the sky, the casement window flew open, and the candle blew out, leaving her in total darkness. She cried out to her maid, only to remember that Cora had gone to her own room.

Stumbling around in the darkness, Gwendolyn felt overwhelming fright. Warrick would be leaving in the morning, and oh, how she wanted to go with him. After he was gone she would be alone among her enemies.

Moments later a servant knocked on the door, carrying a candle to light the room. "Your husband's waiting for ye', m'lady," the woman said churlishly. What would her life be like if even the servants showed their disdain for her? she wondered.

As Gwendolyn followed the surly maid along darkened hallways, the light from the candle caused grotesque shadows to dance across the walls. Gwendolyn tried to gather her courage as they descended the stairs, moving ever closer to the sound of music and laughter. The massive double doors of the banquet hall were thrown open at her approach, and everyone fell silent. Gwendolyn felt her muscles tighten with apprehension.

Aristocratic etiquette was strictly observed in Davinsham Castle. Lord Gavin MacIvors was seated beside his father, Lord Gille, who was chief of Clan MacIvors. Although Gavin was twenty years older than Gwendolyn, he was a fine-looking man with red hair and a red beard. She lifted her eyes to the husband whom she had met for the first time yesterday. Her father had promised her that this marriage would bring peace between the two clans. She saw only hostility in the many eyes that stared at her.

Quickly searching the crowd of faces, Gwendolyn found the person she wanted most to see, her brother, Warrick. Their eyes locked in sad understanding. He realized, as she did, that she had been sacrificed to the devil, and that he could not help her—no one could.

Gwendolyn took a brave step toward Gavin MacIvors. She knew so little about her new husband, except that he had two sons, and the eldest, Ian, was her age. She had heard whispers that Gavin lived openly with his mistress, Lorraine Turnot. Gwendolyn stared at him now and saw something that frightened her. She'd had no mother to prepare her for the night to come, but she recognized desire in Lord Gavin's eyes, and it terrified her.

She trembled as he seated her next to him. How she hated Gavin and all he stood for. When her eyes met his, she blushed at his bold stare.

"Come, my child bride, smile for me," he cajoled.

He reached across her, deliberately brushing his arm against her breasts as he poured her a goblet of wine. Her heart filled with dread for what would happen between them when they were alone.

Miserable and forlorn, it was all Gwendolyn could do to keep from weeping. She tried to catch Warrick's attention, but he was staring transfixed at the blood-red ring on her finger.

Lord Gavin's voice was low and seductive as he offered her the best meats and most tender vegetables from his plate. Lady Gwendolyn knew she would not be able to swallow anything, so she refused him with a shake of her head. He stroked his red beard, his eyes burning into hers.

"I like modesty in a maiden. I am weary of walking plowed fields. It's many years since I've been exposed to virginal pastures."

Gwendolyn lowered her head and clasped her hands in her lap, oblivious to the merriment around her. She had never attended a wedding feast before, but apparently no one thought her behavior strange for a bride.

Lord Gille addressed her directly. "Lady Gwendolyn, it is most unfortunate that you have neither mother nor mother-in-law to advise you in the management of your newly acquired household. As it is a great responsibility for one so young, I believe I shall appoint someone to assist you."

Gavin spoke up quickly. "Father, I have arranged for Lorraine Turnot to continue managing the household until my . . . wife is ready to assume those duties."

"No!" Lady Gwendolyn cried in a sudden show of defiance. She stood and faced her husband, unmindful that clan members looked on in astonishment. "You will not openly place your mistress above me. I did not become your wife today so that I can be shamed and humiliated."

Lord Gavin was enraged. "It is you who shames me, madame. You forget yourself. Perhaps you are fatigued: You will now retire to your chamber."

"No," Lady Gwendolyn repeated. "Not and let that woman be placed at your side in my absence. I did not want to be your wife, but now that I am, you will place no one above me."

Lord Gavin and Lady Gwendolyn stood glaring at each other until Gavin seized her arm and roughly dragged her away from the table. This drew sneers and lewd comments from several of the MacIvors.

"Please continue with your meal. I won't be long," he assured his guests through clenched teeth.

Gwendolyn looked at her brother. "Help me, Warrick," she said.

Warrick jumped to his feet and threw his chair against the wall. "Take your filthy MacIvors hands off my sister."

"Don't interfere in this, young Warrick," Lord Gavin said. "Your sister is my wife, and I'll do with her as I will."

Warrick was beside his sister, prying her hand out of Gavin's grip. "I'm taking my sister out of here, and don't try to stop me," he said. "She didn't come here to suffer your insults and abuse."

Out of the corner of his eye, Warrick saw Ian MacIvors come up behind him. Before he could react, Lord Gavin's son struck him a heavy blow to the head, and Warrick crumpled on the floor.

Gwendolyn cried out for her brother as her husband dragged her off. She wrenched her body and struggled to get away, but his enormous strength made her attempts futile.

"Let me go to my brother, he's hurt."

"He has just learned a valuable lesson. One should never interfere between husband and wife."

She glared at him in hatred. "I'll not be a wife to you!"

By now they had reached Lady Gwendolyn's bedchamber and, kicking and flailing her arms, she had managed to land several painful blows on her husband.

Lord Gavin kicked open the heavy wooden door and thrust his wife to the floor.

She was up again and facing him with the unsheathed knife she carried at her waist. She thrust forward, and the blade pierced his forearm. She stared in horror as Gavin's blood fell on her hand and covered the ruby betrothal ring. She had always been told that the MacIvors were a violent, hot-tempered family, but was it not she who had drawn first blood?

Lord Gavin's expression was murderous. "I'm cursed with a she-devil," he roared. "I'll tame you or kill you."

"I curse you to hell, Gavin MacIvors." Then she fell to her knees and began to sob deep, wrenching sobs that shook her slight body. There was no help for her. She would end her days in misery and despair with a man she despised.

* * *

It was morning before Lord Warrick regained consciousness to find himself in a tower room. Mactavish, who had accompanied him from Ironworth, stood over him with concern.

"Thank God," Mactavish said. "I was fearful you wouldn't wake."

Warrick tore the bandage away from his head and sat up. Pushing Mactavish aside, he hurriedly pulled on his boots.

"How is my sister? Have you heard?"

"I've been with you all night and have heard nothing of Lady Gwendolyn."

With determination in his heart, Warrick decided to go to his sister. The halls were strangely silent, and when he met a servant she merely ducked her head and hurried past him.

He rushed into his sister's bedchamber without knocking, for he felt there was something dreadfully wrong. He found the room empty.

With his head pounding, he bent to examine a blood-splattered rug and retrieved the knife he had given Gwendolyn on her fifteenth birthday.

A shadow fell across his face, and he looked up to see Lord Gavin standing over him. Slowly Warrick rose, staring at the man.

"Where is my sister?" he demanded.

"It's my sad duty to inform you that your sister's dead. As you witnessed last night, she was overwrought. She deliberately threw herself down the stairs rather than bind our marriage." Lord Gavin lowered his eyes, unable to meet Warrick's piercing gaze. "I'm sorry to say her neck was broken in the fall."

Warrick shook his head, unable to believe what he was hearing. "No. Not my Gwendolyn!"

"It was not of my doing," Gavin said, taking a quick step away from the boy with fury in his eyes. "Had I known her mind was so unstable, I'd never have agreed to marry her."

"You are a lying bastard," Warrick said. "If what you say is so, whose blood is on this rug?"

"'Tis mine." Lord Gavin indicated the bandage on his arm. "Your sister objected to my handling of her. It is regretful that she met with such a cruel fate. Had she not been so—"

"Nothing you can say will make me believe my sister took her own life!" Warrick yelled, his grief almost too much to bear. "I'll see her body at once so I may judge for myself."

"Of course. She is laid out in the formal meeting room."

Warrick's eyes widened in horror. "Not in the chapel? MacIvors, if you insist on this lie, my sister will be denied burial in consecrated ground."

Lord Gavin nodded. "Because she did such an evil deed, she deserves no better. I've just spent hours listening to my father rave at me, young Warrick. I don't have to listen to you. Get you home and forget what happened here."

A strange calm settled over Warrick, and he spoke to his sister's husband in a quiet tone. "I'll never forget the wrong you have done my sister. Your life is forfeit, Gavin MacIvors. There is nowhere you can hide that I will not find you."

Gavin looked into silver eyes that were so filled with hatred that it took his breath away.

"Have no concern that I'll take your miserable life now, Lord Gavin, for this day will be spent grieving over my sister's death. I want you to live in dread of the day I'll finally come for you. Always look over your shoulder and sleep lightly, for I may come at you from the darkness."

Warrick was gratified by the fear he saw in the older man's eyes. "When next you see me, Gavin McIvers, it will be the day you die!"

Gavin's face whitened. "Don't threaten me, you whelp of the devil."

"'Tis not a threat—'tis a promise. There can be no peace between our two clans. The blood feud will continue until the last MacIvors is dead!"

* * *

Kilmouris
1819

For over a year, resentment over Lady Gwendolyn's death simmered and intensified between the Drummond and MacIvors clans. There had been several insignificant skirmishes, but so far no deaths had occurred. Suddenly the flame of hatred erupted out of control and was about to flame into full-scale war.

Late that evening word had reached Ironworth Castle that MacIvors clansmen were on the move. It was said that they would attempt to cross Drummond lands to claim Kilmouris, which had come to Gavin MacIvors as part of Lady Gwendolyn's marriage settlement. Warrick's father, feeling remorse for his daughter's death, had decided that the MacIvors had no right to the property or the dowry and demanded it be returned. The MacIvors, however, took issue with this and would neither give up title to the land nor return the money.

Since dawn the Drummond clan had begun to gather in force, and they now blocked the only throughway to Kilmouris, determined to deny the MacIvors entrance to the land.

Warrick drew even with his father, and their eyes met in understanding: Today Gwendolyn's death would be avenged. Pride swelled in James Glencarin's breast as he watched his only son fearlessly await the oncoming battle. He had tirelessly drilled Warrick, knowing he would one day take his place as head of the clan. He would now see if his teachings had spawned a leader of men.

"It's a good day to die, my son."

Warrick glanced at his father, who looked every bit the chief, wearing the belted plaid of Drummond secured to his shoulder by the chieftain's badge. His bonnet sported a fine feather and was set at an angle on his graying head.

"I'd rather die, Father, than allow one grain of Drummond land to fall into the hands of the MacIvors."

"Well said, my son."

Warrick glanced first at the advancing MacIvors, who wore their black, gold, and red plaids, and then at the Drummonds, whose plaids were black, white and red. He laughed as he unsheathed his sword. "It'll be easy enough to recognize our enemy by their colors."

Across the valley the clash of steel and the sound of musket balls exploding mixed with the sounds of battle cries as Drummonds came against MacIvors.

Young Warrick Glencarin wielded his sword with a vengeance, striking an oncoming MacIvors such a stunning blow that the man fell from his horse to be trampled beneath Warrick's steed.

Warrick had no time to dwell on his first act of taking a human life. His motives were of the most noble, the most dangerous. He was fighting to regain family honor and to avenge the death of his sister.

He fought valiantly beside his father amid the savage hordes, swinging his battle sword and mercilessly cutting down the enemy.

But father and son were soon separated, and Warrick found himself facing two MacIvors. He thrust his weapon forward, wounding one in the shoulder, and then turned to the other. Their swords clashed in a struggle for life and death.

Suddenly Warrick saw Ian MacIvors bearing down on his father. He yelled out a warning, but it could not be heard above the noise of battle.

Ian MacIvors's sword plunged forcefully into James Glencarin's heart, mortally wounding him. The chief of Clan Drummond was dead before he hit the ground.

Warrick fought like a man possessed to reach his fallen father, but too many MacIvors separated them. He felt searing pain in his head and he fell from his horse into blackness.

It wasn't until Warrick was being carried from the battlefield that he regained consciousness to learn that the battle was over and his father was dead.

Laden with grief, Warrick realized there had been no winner today, though both sides would ultimately claim the victory.

It was with heavy sadness that Drummonds and MacIvors moved beside each other retrieving their dead and wounded. So many had been slain that only the dead were spared the anguish of mourning a friend or relative. As Warrick was being carried away from the scene of battle, he knew his family's honor had not been satisfied today. Not only had he lost his sister to the MacIvors, but now Ian MacIvors had slain his father. When his men would have lifted him onto his horse, he insisted on standing.

He was so weak from loss of blood, Mactavish had to assist him. Silently the Drummonds watched as their young chief struggled to his feet, striving to remain erect. He took up his father's sword, pointing it toward the heavens, and cried out in agony, "I will see justice done. I swear that from this day forward, I will practice war on all MacIvors!"

Chapter 1

Ironworth Castle, Scotland
1833

Warrick Glencarin, earl of Glencarin, chief of
Clan Drummond, stood tall against the
floor-to-ceiling window of his ancestral
castle. He watched the gray October sea crash forcefully
against the rocks, trailing foamy spray that immediately
ebbed and swelled into another invading wave. The endless
motion of the North Sea was repeated again and again while
he watched with a scowl on his face.

Lord Warrick pondered the unchanging sea and how,
over the centuries, it had eaten at the limestone on which
the castle stood, just as the bitter taste of anger was eating
away at him. He had lived with resentment and hatred for
so long, they were his constant companions.

For years he had brooded over his sister's tragic death.
And when he closed his eyes, he could still see the triumph
in Ian MacIvors's eyes as he delivered the blow that had
ended his father's life.

His dark brows met across his aristocratic nose, and his lips thinned in a severe line. No matter what, he could not throw off his hatred for the MacIvors. So far, he had managed to keep them from taking possession of Kilmouris, but it was only a matter of time until they would occupy the land, as they held the legal deed.

Today Warrick's mood was darker than usual. Forces were at work that would once more pit him against his old enemies. Perhaps this would be the final confrontation. He was so deep in thought that he did not hear Mactavish enter the room.

Standing in the doorway, Mactavish observed his Chief. Warrick had become earl of Glencarin fifteen years ago at the age of seventeen. Now he was a man capable of leadership and admired by his clansmen. His hair was as dark as midnight, and his eyes were silver gray with piercing depths. He was handsome of face and had long ago accepted, without arrogance, the fact that women were attracted to him.

Warrick had inherited a troubled earldom with little money and many debts brought on by years of turmoil and unrest. His feats of daring were legendary. While many clans had been scattered, Clan Drummond was held together by Warrick's force of will. There was not a man who would not readily follow this bold young chief to the death.

Mactavish spoke at last. "Haddy told me I'd find you here. Thought you'd want to join me in the hunt today. I saw two big bucks down by the glen early this morning. One was a twelve pointer."

Warrick didn't bother to turn around. "I'll not be hunting today. Go along without me."

"Come with me, Warrick. You've not been hunting in over a month. What's troubling you, lad?"

Warrick touched the window and traced a line of frost with his finger. "I have duties that require my attention, Mactavish. You know that."

Mactavish walked to the window and studied Lord

Warrick's reflection in the glass. "If you're not of a mind to hunt, I'll not go either. There's always tomorrow."

Warrick turned to the leather chair and sat down, leaning his head against the high back. "Please yourself."

Mactavish stood over him with dread in his heart. "I was told a messenger came this morning from the king. Was it bad tidings?"

Warrick gazed at the man who had once been his father's confidante and was now his own friend. Though it was never spoken aloud, it was whispered that Mactavish was Warrick's grandfather's bastard son. Warrick valued his advice and always put him in a place of honor at his side.

He removed a letter from his breast pocket and thrust it at Mactavish. "Read it for yourself."

"You know I canna read."

"It's from Lord Thorndike, a deputy appointed by the king. In two weeks I'm commanded to attend a meeting at Edinburgh Castle along with Gille MacIvors."

"'Tis not possible that you'd be asked to occupy the same room as a MacIvors," Mactavish said, indignant at such an idea. "You'll not go, of course?"

"I'm to have little say in this matter. I dare not ignore a command from the king. Lord Thorndike states in his letter that any party who does not send a representative to the hearings may have their lands confiscated by the Crown."

"Then send me. I'll meet with The MacIvors in your stead."

"I can't do that, but you may accompany me, my friend. I don't expect it to turn out well. Most certainly Lord Thorndike's decision will not favor me—and you can guess who petitioned for this meeting."

Mactavish nodded. "Who else but that wily old fox, Gille MacIvors." He sat down and studied the scuffed toe of his boot. "We both know he's a cunning old bastard and isn't to be trusted."

"Spoken true."

"And still you'll go?"

Warrick nodded. "I will meet with Lord Thorndike, though little good it'll do me. You're my voice of reason in this, Mactavish. Help me decide what I must do."

The older man looked into troubled gray eyes not unlike his own. "The king'll be wanting you to put the feud aside. There's not been bloodshed between our two clans since your father was killed, there's been only little incidents brought about by the MacIvors's villainy."

"Even though there have been no battles, I've not forgotten what they did to my family."

"Lay the hate to rest, Warrick. Gavin MacIvors was killed many years ago—stabbed with your sister's knife. I'd call that blood justice."

Although they had never spoken of it, Warrick suspected Mactavish had slain Lord Gavin. The deed had been committed with Gwendolyn's own dagger—a dagger that had been in Warrick's keeping since her death, and only he and Mactavish had known where it was kept.

"My sister's death may have been avenged, but there are other matters that will not rest."

"Aye. I'm not forgetting that it was the MacIvors who kidnapped the woman you were to marry."

Warrick stood up, his eyes narrowing with contempt. "No woman is safe from their lechery."

"Then it's well that you're meeting with the king's man, Warrick. You can put your grievance before him and therein may be hope."

"You advised me to petition King William when Lady Helena was abducted before our wedding. The king did nothing, and now she is married to one of those devils."

"Think you Lady Helena was forced to marry against her will? I've heard she went willingly enough into Jamie MacIvors's bed."

"And that," Warrick said in a voice laced with ire, "makes the insult more intolerable."

Mactavish knew the shame Warrick had suffered when

his betrothed had been abducted on her journey to Glencarin. It mattered not that Warrick had hardly known Lady Helena, having seen her on only one occasion. Even the loss of land and the large dowry she brought with her had not been as bad as the insult to Warrick's pride.

"The confrontations between our two clans have brought the English king's wrath down on Drummond and MacIvors alike, Warrick," Mactavish said. "I suspect the old chief distrusts and dislikes the British as much as we do."

"Dislike for the British is the only thing we agree upon. There will be no end to the hatred between us. Not until my honor has been satisfied. We both know that no MacIvors has honor, so how can they recognize it in others?"

"Nothing you do will bring back your sister or your father, Warrick. And you wouldn't want Lady Helena back now—this I know."

"No, I wouldn't take her back, but I owe it to her to find out if she's satisfied with her marriage."

"Then it's decided, you'll go?"

"Aye, I'll attend if for no other reason than to find a weakness in Lord Gille. If there is a way to strike at the heart of that devious bastard, I'll find it. I will have my revenge, Mactavish."

The older man nodded. "Aye, of that I've little doubt."

"My sister's soul calls out to me from her unconsecrated grave. I will not rest until she is honorably buried beside our ancestors!"

Calais, France

Lady Arrian DeWinter, daughter of the duke of Ravenworth, stood on deck of her father's yacht, the *Nightingale,* staring at the storm clouds gathering in the east. The ship, manned by Captain Norris and a crew of seven, was taking Arrian six hundred miles across the North Sea to the shores of

Scotland, where she would be reunited with the man she was to marry. The captain had assured her that if the winds were favorable they would reach Scotland within a week.

A heady sea breeze tossed her long golden hair, and she relished the taste of salt air on her tongue. Happiness burst within her heart as she thought of what would be waiting for her at the end of the voyage, or rather, who: Lord Ian MacIvors.

Did he love her as much as she loved him? Was he counting the days until they would be joined together as man and wife?

Arrian thought about the summers she and her brother, Michael, had accompanied their aunt Mary to Scotland to visit her great-grandfather. In those years, Ian had hardly noticed her at all.

Her mind began to drift back to the occasion of her thirteenth birthday, and the first time she had realized she loved Ian. . . .

He had been so gallant and attentive that day. That night she had walked in the garden and he had found her there, and placed an armload of wild heather in her arms.

"I saved my present to you until we were alone," Ian said, smiling down at her.

Arrian touched a soft blue petal. "It is a wonderful gift," she said, glancing up at him in awe. He was so tall, so handsome.

"Some would not consider it a great gift, Arrian. But to me, it is given with great affection and for a special reason."

Her heart stood still as he took her hand and raised it to his lips. "What is your reason?" she asked, trembling with pleasure at the warm kiss he placed on her wrist.

"I want you always to remember Scotland and me."

Her eyes were shining. "I will never forget either of you."

"You are so young. Can I make you understand how I have waited for you to grow into womanhood? Even now you are a child."

Arrian could not believe her ears. Was Ian confessing his love for her? "I was thirteen today," she said.

He touched her cheek. "That is yet young, Arrian."

She wasn't certain what he was trying to tell her. "I will get older."

"Yes, my young beauty, but will you remember me when you are far away in London with gentlemen competing for a smile from you?"

"Yes," she said, her eyes gleaming. "I'll think of you even then."

He gently pulled her against him, and she thought he might kiss her, but he merely placed heather in her hair. "I will not allow you to forget me, Arrian. I intend to come to England often to make certain you don't."

Ian's eyes spoke to her of love, and Arrian found herself losing her heart to him. . . .

The wind intensified, stinging Arrian's cheeks and bringing her mind back to the present. Ian had been as good as his word. After that night in the garden he had come often to England. On her seventeenth birthday he had declared his love for her, and she had happily agreed to marry him.

She glanced upward at the gathering clouds and wondered if it would storm before the day was over. She pulled her cloak about her and made her way down the companionway, where she rapped softly on a door and entered the darkened cabin.

Great-aunt Mary was perched amid silken pillows, her head rolling back and forth with the motion of the ship. She did not look well at all, and the voyage had just begun.

Arrian sat on the stool beside her aunt, taking her limp hand and lacing her fingers through it. "Is there anything I can do to make you feel better?"

"I never liked sailing, and especially not when the sea is rough," Lady Mary Rindhold said with a moan. "Lord, it's

March. I thought the worst of the storms were behind us or I wouldn't have set out on this voyage."

It had been at Lady Mary's insistence that they sailed for Scotland ahead of Arrian's parents and brother. But Arrian saw no reason to remind her aunt of that fact.

"Would you like me to leave so you can rest?"

"No. Talk to me. Do anything to take my mind off the swaying of this ship."

Arrian's eyes became dreamy. "I was just thinking of Ian. Aunt Mary, do you suppose men feel love as deeply as women? I hope they do."

Lady Mary mumbled something under her breath and then spoke more distinctly. "It's been my experience that men feel love just as deeply as a woman, but far more frequently."

"Not all men, Aunt Mary. Not Uncle George and Father. I want Ian one day to look at me in that special way I see Father looking at Mother."

"Yes, well, what your mother and father have is rare. As you know, I had it with your uncle George." Her eyes softened. "Of course, men like your father and my George are unique." Then Lady Mary added with her usual directness, "I'm not sure Ian is of their cut."

"Oh, you are wrong, Aunt Mary. Ian is wonderful."

"I'm sure you think so."

"Did you know that I was thirteen when I decided I would one day marry him. It was no more than a fanciful dream until last summer when he came to Ravenworth. I still can't believe he loves me."

"Arrian, the man isn't blind. How could he help but love a beauty like you?"

Arrian looked doubtful. "Am I truly beautiful?"

"You don't need me to tell you that. Ian wasn't your only suitor last summer. They were too numerous to count."

Lady Mary looked at her great-niece, seeing her as Ian MacIvors must have seen her. Arrian was a stunning beauty, from the top of her golden head to the tip of her dainty feet.

Heads turned in her direction when she entered a room. Her eyes were light blue and often danced with humor. Many young girls in her circumstances would have been spoiled, but not Arrian. She reflected the modesty and kindness of her adopted mother, Kassidy.

"I only hope Ian is deserving of you, Arrian. That's why I decided to make this journey with you. Even though he is my nephew, I want to see his character for myself. There's still two months until the wedding, and during that time, I intend to watch him closely."

"He knows you watch him," Arrian said. "He's nervous when you are around."

"Why should he be nervous if he has nothing to hide?"

Arrian's musical laughter rang out. "I'm certain those that don't know you as well as I do could be intimidated by your haughty attitude."

"Nonsense. Me, haughty?"

"Perhaps it's the Scottish blood that makes you so."

"Your mother is half Scottish, which makes you part Scottish, Arrian."

"I'm proud of my MacIvors blood."

"Aye, but you have been raised with English traditions, and you may find life hard in Scotland."

Arrian smiled. "I will make Ian a good wife—I know I shall. Do you think he will be waiting for me when we make port?"

"Of course he'll be there. You can be sure of that."

Lady Mary suddenly turned white, and Arrian quickly pushed a basin in front of her. After retching until she was weak, Lady Mary lay back against the pillows while Arrian bathed her face with cool water.

"I'll never make it if the sea doesn't calm. To feel better I'd have to be dead," Lady Mary said.

Arrian felt pity for her aunt and guilty because she had never been the least bit seasick. Of course, she and Michael had practically grown up aboard the *Nightingale*.

"You aren't the only one who's ill. Tuttle is in her cabin feeling just as wretched."

"That doesn't make me feel one whit better. Go on and dream of your wedding. There's nothing you can do to help me."

"Are you certain?"

Lady Mary closed her eyes. "I believe I'll just try to sleep now."

Arrian pulled the cover to her aunt's chin and then watched the waves splash against the porthole. She sat for a while, looking out to sea, remembering how difficult it had been to say good-bye to her family that morning.

What a wonderful holiday they'd had in France. They had spent days in museums, in parks, and on picnics, while at night they had attended the ballet, musicales, and concerts.

The holiday had been her mother's idea, because she had insisted that Arrian's trousseau be designed in Paris. Belowdecks there were dozens of trunks packed with magnificent gowns and accessories.

Arrian would always cherish that time with her family. She would miss them dreadfully after the wedding when they returned to England. And how she would miss dear Aunt Mary.

She thought of Ian, so tall and handsome, the very picture of what a Scottish chief should be. He would someday be an honorable heir to the Clan MacIvors, and she was determined to make him a worthy wife.

Chapter 2

Edinburgh—Two Weeks Later

*T**he morning was overcast,** and only pale sunlight strained through the high window of Edinburgh Castle, adding a dismal air to the council room.

Ian MacIvors, future chief of Clan MacIvors, stood with his hands clasped behind his back, glancing across the volcanic cliffs on which Edinburgh Castle was built. His sandy-colored hair was swept off his wide forehead to expose an arresting face and deep brown eyes. His gaze moved to the three men who had accompanied him and his younger brother, Jamie. Ian nodded in approval when Jamie opened his coat to reveal a concealed pistol.

"Keep that hidden," Ian said. "The king's representative sent word we were to come unarmed."

Jamie quickly straightened his coat. "I don't trust Warrick Glencarin. He's too wild and unpredictable. And I refuse to present myself to him defenseless. Of all of us, he bears me the most ill will."

Ian glanced at Jamie's wife, who was sitting in the shadows near the back of the room. Lady Helena had once been considered a beauty, but now she was not even pretty. Her once flawless complexion was blotched, and her belly was swollen with child. Her extra bulk made her clumsy and awkward.

"I will take great satisfaction in flaunting your wife in Lord Warrick's face and tormenting him with the fact that she is heavy with a MacIvors's child. I want him to hear from her own lips that she preferred you to him."

Lady Helena had been reluctant to come today, knowing she was being used as a pawn in some kind of game between Warrick Glencarin and her husband's family. She looked furtively around the room and twisted her hands anxiously in her lap. Lord Warrick had a fierce temper— would he direct that anger at her today?

"Grandfather wouldn't approve of Helena being here. Unlike me, he is eager to settle the feud with the Drummonds." Ian's eyes narrowed, and he smiled in satisfaction. "When Warrick sees her, he'll become enraged and show himself for the devil he is."

There was movement at the open doorway, and two men entered the room. One was the king's deputy, and the other, the Lord Mayor of Edinburgh.

Ian leaned closer to his brother. "I intend to win the English deputy to our side so the judgment will go against the Drummonds. If we can't defeat Lord Warrick in battle, we'll defeat him with the deputy's ruling."

Jamie's eyes filled with admiration for his older brother. "If anyone can do that, Ian, it'll be you."

Ian watched Lord Thorndike and Sir Brodrick approach, and he whispered to his brother, "All Englishmen are fools. Watch and learn how easily they can be outsmarted by a Scot."

"Gentlemen," Sir Brodrick said, plainly impressed with his role in the day's proceedings, "I'm pleased to present

Lord Thorndike, deputy to the king and mediator between the House of MacIvors and the House of Drummond. Your lordship, may I present Lord Ian and Jamie MacIvors, grandsons of Lord Gille MacIvors."

Lord Thorndike acknowledged the two men with a nod. "I have been informed that you will be representing your grandfather."

"That is so," Ian replied.

Lord Thorndike noticed the men Ian had brought with him. "And who are they?"

"They're my men, who are here merely to make certain there will be no trouble," Ian answered.

"They are not to be part of the proceedings. They can remain only if they keep separate from us."

Ian nodded to his clansmen, indicating that they should move to the back of the room.

Lord Thorndike's gaze now fell on Lady Helena. "Who is the female?" he asked, annoyed by all the uninvited visitors. "You were informed that this was to be a private session, were you not?"

"'Tis only my wife," Jamie said. "Since she is heavy with child, I wanted to keep her near me. She has promised to cause no interruption."

Lord Thorndike bestowed a look of displeasure on the young man. "See that she does not," he said. "Am I to take it that Lord Warrick has not yet arrived?"

"Just what you'd expect from a Highlander," Ian said. "They have no consideration for others. They have no manners and no liking for law and order."

Lord Thorndike was a seasoned negotiator of great insight, which was why he had been chosen by the king to settle the feud between the two clans. He had been warned by King William not to become entangled in a dispute between Highlander opposing Lowlander.

"It is not yet the appointed time for the meeting," Lord Thorndike stated, moving to a desk and placing his satchel on it. "I have papers to read. Perhaps the rest of you can make yourselves comfortable. We'll be in for a long day." His attention turned to Sir Brodrick. "You will no longer be needed. When Lord Warrick arrives, send him in at once."

Ian watched the Lord Mayor's hurried withdrawal. "See how the man scurries to do the Englishman's bidding? It fairly sticks in my throat to witness a Scot taking orders from an English dog."

"No one can force you to do anything against your will, Ian," Jamie said. "You'll have your way today."

There was no time for Ian to reply, because at that moment the door was thrust open, and two men stood in the doorway.

The older man, Ian dismissed as unimportant. The second man was not so easy to ignore. He was dressed all in black, save for the Drummond plaid across his shoulder, which proclaimed him to be the chief. His head was held at a proud tilt, and his gaze swept the room with indifference. Ian had last seen Lord Warrick at the battle of Kilmouris, when he had been only a lad. Now he exuded power and self-assurance. Ian was not a coward, but there was something in Warrick's eyes that sent a chill through his heart.

"That is he?" Jamie asked. For years he had heard much of the chief of Drummond, but until now he'd never seen him.

Warrick Glencarin's features were dark. From a distance it was impossible to tell the color of his eyes, but they were arresting, and there was a look of contempt in their depths. It was apparent that he had no liking for this day's encounter.

"I once clubbed him with the hilt of my sword," Ian said. "It was the time when our father married his sister. I should have killed him when I had the chance. Now he's too powerful to kill. Perhaps I can one day give him a choice between death and dishonor—he'll choose death."

"He has the savage, unkempt look of a Highlander," Jamie observed.

Lord Thorndike moved forward to greet the newcomer just as the mantle clock chimed the appointed hour. "Lord Warrick, I am Lord Thorndike, the king's deputy," he said. "You're right on time."

Warrick gave Ian a sharp glance but spoke to the king's man. "It is not my habit to be dilatory. I value my time as you must value yours." He turned to his companion. "This is my man, Mactavish. He glanced at the group of men who had accompanied Ian. "It would seem we are outnumbered."

"Quite so, quite so," Lord Thorndike said. "Shall we get on with the proceedings? Are you acquainted with Ian MacIvors?"

Warrick glared at Ian, his lips twisted into a grimace. "I know the man only by reputation, and by a fleeting encounter one night at a banquet." His eyes narrowed. "And, yes, he was present the day my father died."

There was a feeling of intense animosity in the room as the two men stared at each other like two predatory animals. They were both remembering that Ian had killed Warrick's father.

At last Ian spoke, pushing his brother forward. "You will have heard of my brother, Jamie? He is the husband of Lady Helena."

Jamie flinched and stepped back a pace as Warrick's cruel gaze was turned on him. He sucked in his breath, unable to look away from the probing intensity of Warrick's slate-gray eyes.

"Ah, yes, the bridegroom," Warrick said. "One can only hope you find happiness in wedded bliss, Jamie MacIvors. When one takes a bride by force, he can never be sure of the woman's true affection."

"I . . ." Jamie's voice trailed off as fear sealed his lips.

Ian stepped forward and spoke for his brother. "Lady Helena carries my brother's child. Their's is a love match."

"Ah, well," Warrick said, with a smile that did not soften his eyes. "No doubt you will breed many little—MacIvors to inhabit the Lowlands."

Lord Thorndike, realizing that the animosity between the two men could quickly turn into a fray, intervened. "Be seated, gentleman. There is much we need to accomplish here today. The king's orders are that we are to remain sequestered in this room until all concerned have come to a satisfactory agreement."

Warrick stared at the Englishman. "Why is Lord Gille not here? Can it be that he is late for the appointed meeting?"

Lord Thorndike looked uncomfortable. "The Lord Mayor advised me that his lordship will be represented by his grandson and heir, Ian MacIvors. Is that acceptable to you?"

Warrick's lip curled in disgust. "I came here today expecting to meet with Gille MacIvors. Surely you don't intend that I deal with an underling who has no power?"

Ian's temper flared at the insult. He reached down where his sword should be, only to find the scabbard empty. "You'll pay for this affront. I'll not stay in the same room with a slovenly Highlander."

Before Ian knew what was happening, Warrick grabbed him by the coat front and jerked him forward.

Jamie rushed to help his brother, but a warning glare from Warrick made him reconsider. He felt the cold metal of the gun against his chest, but his hands trembled so, he dared not draw the weapon.

"Ian MacIvors, return to your grandfather, and tell him not to send an unworthy to speak in his stead. I came on the king's orders, and I assumed your grandfather had received the same command. I had no inkling that a subordinate would be representing the MacIvors."

Lord Thorndike was too wise to restrain physically the angered Lord Warrick, so he spoke quickly. "I was about to inform you of Lord Gille's request. Will you please hear what I have to say?"

Warrick flung Ian away with a force that sent Ian stumbling against a table. "I'll listen, but if I don't like what you say, be warned, I'll not feel obligated to remain."

"I was told that Lord Gille MacIvors is in ill health." Lord Thorndike glanced up at Warrick. "After all, he's a man of eighty-three years."

"He is an old man," Warrick said. "But I also know he still has the faculties and strength of a much younger man." He glared at Ian and Jamie. "I can hardly credit that your grandfather would miss an opportunity to face me. There must be another reason he did not come."

Ian started to speak but was interrupted by Lord Thorndike.

"There is another reason Lord Gille could not attend today. He is making ready to welcome his great-granddaughter, who is Ian MacIvors's betrothed," Lord Thorndike said.

Warrick wasn't placated. "I see no reason why that should have kept him away."

"Lord Ian's betrothed is the daughter of the duke of Ravenworth, and the king expects her to be shown every courtesy. His Majesty has also sent an envoy to welcome the duke's daughter on her arrival. I hope you will agree that Lord Gille's reasons for not being here are legitimate."

Warrick looked quickly at Ian for confirmation and could tell from his self-satisfied smile that Lord Thorndike spoke the truth.

"My felicitations," Warrick said. "I'm sure you and your English bride deserve each other."

Lord Thorndike stepped forward. "I'll not have brawling and accusations. This meeting will be conducted in a manner befitting gentlemen of your stations. Don't force me to return to London and advise the king to send troops to quell this hostility between you."

The Englishman now had both men's attention, and they fell silent. Neither wanted the king embroiled in their age-old feud.

"Say what you will," Warrick agreed. "Just get on with it. I have important matters that require my attention."

Lord Thorndike cleared his throat. "I'll cut right through

the formalities and go straight to the charges—is that acceptable?"

Warrick thought for a moment before he replied, watching Ian, who was straightening his coat. "Lord Thorndike, I'll only remain if I'm satisfied you are not a MacIvors man," he said.

"I'm no one but the king's man," Lord Thorndike declared indignantly. "If anyone believes differently he's at liberty to leave. Otherwise, be seated and I'll begin."

An uneasy peace settled over the room as Lord Warrick and Lord Ian sat down at the table. They both watched Lord Thorndike rifle through papers until he found the documents he needed.

"Starting with the MacIvors's grievances," the king's deputy stated, "you, Lord Warrick, are accused of denying the MacIvors passage through your lands to visit their property, Kilmouris. It further states here that they are often attacked and harassed by your men."

Warrick stared at Ian. "I will never allow them access to Kilmouris, because the MacIvors have no legal right to it. Kilmouris belongs to me."

"Why say you this?" Lord Thorndike asked.

Warrick drew in a deep breath. He was wasting his time talking to the Englishman, who he doubted would be impartial. "In the year 1818, the lands of Kilmouris were deeded to my sister, Gwendolyn, as part of her dowry. Even then my father did not trust a MacIvors well enough to deed the land directly to them." Warrick's eyes hardened. "At that time my sister was in good health. Even so, she died the night of her marriage to Gavin MacIvors under mysterious circumstances."

"I had heard of this, but continue."

"I was informed that my sister deliberately threw herself down the stairs to her death. Knowing how faithful Gwendolyn was to the Church, I realized she would never have taken her own life. She always had a horror of being buried in unconsecrated ground."

"I fear the truth of what happened that night will remain a mystery, since your sister and her husband are both deceased," Lord Thorndike stated.

"Then ponder this, my lord," Warrick continued. "Our land was never returned to us, nor was the body of my sister. For countless years we have petitioned your king—three of your kings, to be exact—but our charge has gone unheard and our claim ignored."

"That's why I'm here today, to listen to all charges, weigh the evidence, and draw my own conclusions to present to His Majesty."

"I wonder if you will be fair."

"After this is finished, I'll allow you to judge that for yourself," Lord Thorndike answered.

Warrick leaned forward, his eyes blazing with distrust. "How would you deal with a man who would forcibly abduct an innocent maid just before her wedding, spirit her away, and force her to marry her abductor? How would you rule in this instance?"

Lord Thorndike had known he would face insurmountable problems in the meeting between the two hostile houses, but he had not come prepared to judge on such an unthinkable infraction. "If your charges are true, Lord Warrick, then the matter will be dealt with as I see fit."

Warrick pointed at Jamie. "Then deal with him, for the charge is indeed true. Jamie MacIvors is the abductor, and the woman he took was to be my bride. Judge him if you want me to believe in your justice."

Lord Thorndike turned on Jamie. "Tell me, is this charge true?"

Jamie stood up quickly and rushed to the back of the room. Taking a reluctant Helena by the hand, he pulled her forward. "May I present my wife, Lord Thorndike. You can hear from her own lips if she was taken away by force or if she willingly became my wife."

Jamie pushed Lady Helena forward, and she lowered her head, unable to meet the Englishman's eyes.

"Speak, my lady, and have no fear of reprisal. I only want the truth," Lord Thorndike said kindly.

Warrick's eyes burned with fury when he saw the woman who had been meant to be his bride, her belly swollen with the seed of a hated MacIvors.

"I . . ." she licked her dry lips. "I . . . came to love my husband." She still could not raise her eyes.

Warrick had to know if Helena was being held captive. "Are you certain that you remain at Davinsham Castle of your own free will, my lady?"

At last she looked at him. "I am content, Lord Warrick. And I have come to realize that you and I would never have . . . dealt well together. I think you frighten me a little. 'Twas not love that was to bind our union. Y—you know this."

Warrick felt rage brewing within him. It did not matter that he did not love Lady Helena. She should have been his wife—it should be *his* child she was now carrying. "I am well rid of you, madam," he told her coldly. "A fickle heart is not what I look for in a woman who would bear the next earl of Glencarin."

Warrick paused and looked at the king's emissary. "You can report what you will to your king, Lord Thorndike. I will no longer stay in the same room with a MacIvors."

As Warrick walked to the door, Mactavish followed at his side. When the door slammed behind them, a satisfied smile curved Ian's lips. "You see how it is, Lord Thorndike. You can't talk reason to a Drummond. It is my grandfather's hope that you order Lord Warrick to open the road and award us uncontested deed to Kilmouris. Perhaps you would also recommend attaching a monetary penalty on Lord Warrick for his actions here today, and even post troops between the properties to make certain that we are not harassed when we go there."

Lord Thorndike crammed papers in his satchel, his eyes snapping with anger. "Do not presume to dictate policy to me or his majesty. As I see it, you were the ones who committed the wrong, Lord Ian. I believe you and your brother deliberately brought Lady Helena here today to provoke an outburst from Lord Warrick. Had I been in his place, I would have acted no differently."

Ian's face hardened. "You cannot take his part against the MacIvors. My grandfather will never allow that. You would be well advised—"

Lord Thorndike cut him short. "Inform your grandfather that the king will make the decisions, not you, not he. As for you, Jamie McIvors, return to your grandfather and tell him the Crown does not sanction abducting women, for whatever reason. If I were you, I'd thank your merciful stars that Lord Warrick was unarmed today. I doubt even I could have restrained him had he seen fit to punish you. You trifled with the man's honor, and he does not appear to be a man who would take an insult lightly."

Jamie drew himself up to his full height. "I am not afraid of him."

"Good day, gentlemen. You'll be hearing from me when a decision has been reached." The Englishman walked across the polished floor, opened the door, and closed it softly behind him.

"Did we do wrong to bring Helena with us?" Jamie asked, not really understanding the consequences.

Ian pushed his brother aside. "You ride home and inform grandfather what has happened." His eyes narrowed. "Be certain you stress the fact that Lord Warrick left the meeting first. And I see no need for you to mention that Helena was here with us."

Jamie looked doubtful. "Why can't you tell grandfather? You know he doesn't like me."

"I have more important matters on my mind. I'm off to welcome my bride. I want to be waiting when her ship docks."

"You are a fortunate man, Ian. Not only is our cousin beautiful, but her father possesses great wealth."

"Indeed I am fortunate, Jamie, for unlike your marriage, mine will be a love match."

Lady Helena heard the brothers' exchange and felt tears sting her eyes. Her marriage was not a love match, and she had a weakling for a husband. Jamie lived in the shadow of his brother and seemed to have no voice of his own. But somewhere, deep inside her, she had a feeling that Jamie would be a better man if he were separated from Ian. There were times when he was kind to her, and he seemed happy about the baby. With an effort, she moved to stand beside her husband.

When Jamie looked at her there was no softness in his eyes. But sometimes at night, when he was far from Ian, he would say sweet things to her and hold her tenderly in his arms until she fell asleep. At those times she almost loved him.

Warrick's face was a mask of fury as he mounted his horse and rode away from Edinburgh with Mactavish at his side. It had been very apparent to him that Lady Helena had no wish to be rescued. With the feeling of betrayal weighing heavily on his shoulders, he turned his mount toward the Highlands. He had lost today. Lord Thorndike would certainly award Kilmouris to the MacIvors, and Warrick was helpless to prevent it.

Chapter 3

The North Sea storm raged with ever-increasing intensity, tossing the *Nightingale* around with the same carelessness it would have a bobbing cork. For three days punishing winds and pelting rain had hammered at the ship, and there was no sign that the storm would abate. It wasn't until the fourth day that the wind diminished and the waves no longer crested over the side of the ship. Lady Mary remained below, too ill to venture from her cabin.

Arrian sat by her aunt's bedside, trying to convince her that the worst of the storm had passed. But poor Lady Mary would not be consoled.

There was a knock on the door, and Arrian opened it to find Captain Norris smiling at her.

"Please come in, Captain. Perhaps you can help me persuade my aunt that the storm has passed."

He was a tall man and had to bend his head to enter the cabin. His face was weather-beaten, and the heavy lines at his eyes crinkled when he smiled. Arrian had known him all her life and had a great fondness for him. He removed his hat and tucked it under his arm.

"Lady Mary, I want to confer with you about our destination."

Lady Mary sank weakly against a pillow. "What are our choices?"

"As you know, we were to put in at Leith, but we are far from that port and in the waters of Moray Firth."

Lady Mary looked taken aback. "Why were we blown so far off course?"

"It was a fearful storm, my lady."

"What do you recommend, Captain?"

"I must be frank with you. It's my opinion that the storm still rages in the direction of Leith, but it has lost most of its strength. If we continue on course it will not be as bad as before."

Lady Mary shook her head. "I will never go through another storm at sea—not ever! I'd rather take my chances on land."

"Does your ladyship realize that the land you see in the distance is the Highland coast?"

"It matters not to me. Just put me ashore at the closest port."

"We are just off Rattray Head, my lady."

"Then make arrangements to put my niece and me ashore, Captain. I'll have no trouble hiring a carriage that will take us to our destination."

"I strongly advise against that, my lady. This is wild country, and a winter snowstorm can hit without warning. You would fare much better at sea."

Lady Mary set her chin in determination. "We'll go ashore today."

Captain Norris looked as if he would like to protest further, but he dared not. "It will be as you wish, my lady. But at least allow two of my crew to accompany you as outriders."

"What good will they do me on land? They are sailors."

The captain smiled. "They can shoot as straight on land as they can at sea, should the need arise."

"I don't need them to accompany us. I'll hire men in the village who know their way about the Highlands. I'll not travel with your men, who are English enough to get their throats cut by the inhabitants."

Arrian felt deep disappointment as she walked on deck and stood at the railing. She had envisioned her reunion with Ian and how they would journey together to their grandfather's castle.

She glanced at the land barely visible through the fog. Wild country, the captain had said. It certainly appeared to be dark and foreboding. She watched as ominous clouds gathered on the horizon, and shivered, wishing her aunt would change her mind and decide to remain on board the *Nightingale*.

It was a cold, blustery morning with only a feeble sun shining through an occasional break in the clouds. Arrian climbed aboard the coach with her aunt, and they set off from the coaching inn at a steady pace.

Much to Aunt Mary's displeasure, both Arrian's and her maids were still feeling ill. She had no intention of nursing the two women across the Highlands, so they had been sent on ahead to Leith with Captain Norris.

A dense fog swirled about the coach, encasing the occupants in a strange eeriness. The only noise they could hear was the muffled sound of the horses' hooves on the snow-packed road.

Arrian smiled cheerfully at her aunt, determined to make the best of the situation. Lady Mary was wrapped in woolen shawls, so only her face was visible.

Dear Great Aunt Mary was indeed unique. If Arrian had to be confined in a coach for days, there was no one she'd rather be with than her. Although a widow, Lady Mary Rindhold was famous for her socials and galas. Invitations to her parties were coveted by London nobility. The years had not diminished her fragile beauty. Her skin was still youthful and unlined, she had charm and intelligence, and Arrian adored her. Arrian reached out, placing her gloved hand on Lady Mary's arm. "Are you comfortable?"

"Not so you'd notice. I have been at sea in a storm, and now my bones are aching, so it will undoubtedly snow. My aches are never wrong when predicting the weather."

Arrian poked her hands into her ermine muff to keep them warm. She decided to attempt to take her aunt's mind off her discomfort. "I'm looking forward to seeing Great-grandfather MacIvors. There was a time when I was frightened of him because he was so brusque. But as I grew older, I saw a softness in his eyes that belied any gruffness."

Lady Mary laughed. "My father has bullied friends and family alike into believing he's a tyrant—and I must confess, in many instances he is. It's my belief that you are special to him because you look so much like my dead sister for whom you were named. Then, of course, he's most fond of your mother. Kassidy was spunky as a young girl, and father loved that about her." Lady Mary smiled. "In that respect, she has not changed."

"I love to hear Mother talk about how she and my father met."

"You know, of course, when she married your father, your mother made the match of the decade. I can tell you that my father did not approve of the marriage because Raile is English. Father often remarks that she would have done better married to a Scotsman, which you and I know is not true."

"Mother has often told me of my real parents, but I cannot imagine them. I have always thought of them as ghostly figures who had no meaning in my life."

"Kassidy and Raile have always cherished you as their daughter. Kassidy fought to keep you with her. You were the daughter of her beloved sister, and she loved you from the first."

Arrian smiled. "I know Mother and Father were brought together by my birth."

"Since Raile was half brother to your real father and Kassidy was your mother's sister, you were already a part of them both. You belonged to them as surely as if you had been born to them. But they still wanted to adopt you so you would always know that they wanted you."

"I have always known that I was loved."

Lady Mary's expression became wistful as if she were remembering something. "Kassidy and Raile overcame great hardships and pain before they found happiness. All you need to remember is that they love you. You're the daughter of their hearts."

At noon the coach stopped at a posting inn. Arrian and Lady Mary were served a light luncheon in a private room. The weather had grown colder, and Arrian lingered before a roaring fire, dreading the thought of getting back in the coach.

Lady Mary insisted, however, that they continue their journey, hoping to make the next village before nightfall.

Once settled in the coach, Lady Mary looked out at the passing scenery. "I must confess, I'm always somewhat uneasy traveling through this part of the Highlands. These are the lands of the legendary Lord Warrick Glencarin. He's the chief of Clan Drummond and has little love for my father's clan."

Arrian had grown up on exciting tales about Scottish lairds and battling armies. Her favorite tale was of Robert the Bruce, who was proclaimed king of Scotland after his victory over his English enemies. Perhaps it was because of her fascination for this wonderful land that she had lost her heart to Ian MacIvors.

"Tell me about this Lord Warrick. Why does he bear the MacIvors ill will?"

"Oh, he's a devil, that one. Of course, I admit that having been born a MacIvors, my assessment of him might be somewhat distorted. Your uncle George helped me see that there had been wrongs on both sides, although I doubt you could convince my father or Warrick Glencarin of the truth of that."

"Warrick Glencarin . . . he sounds like a knight out of some medieval tale. Is he handsome, do you think? Or is he old, and has he outlived many wives?"

Lady Mary pressed her face closer to the window and noticed that it had started snowing. "Don't be such a romantic, Arrian." Her brow knitted into a worried frown. "I doubt you'd find Lord Warrick a knight to rescue maidens from peril—not if that lady has a dram of MacIvors blood in her veins, or if she's English. And you, my dear, are both. Not to mention the fact that you will be marrying the future chief of the MacIvors."

"Surely King William does not allow such feuds to continue in this day and age."

"William has little to say about it. When a Drummond meets a MacIvors, blood is sure to spill. They are sworn to a blood feud. I doubt it'll ever end."

"Tell me more about the clans."

"Old ways are cherished here, Arrian. Honesty and plain speaking is preferred. The Scots remain true to their heritage and their passionate love for Scotland. Sadly, most clans broke apart after our war with France. The great landowners found they could run sheep on their land and make more money than from their tenant farmers. Many of the clan members migrated to the cities or left the country, some going as far away as the Colonies."

"But this Drummond clan survived, and so have the MacIvors. Tell me everything you know about Lord Warrick," Arrian said eagerly.

"It's said that Lord Warrick is a man of the wild north who scoffs at the gentry of the south. I suppose I admire him in many ways. He is a power to reckon with and holds sway over his people. I never met him personally. However, five years ago, he was pointed out to me on the streets of Edinburgh. I admit he was more comely than a man has a right to be, in a dark sort of way."

"What are a chief's duties to his clan?"

"It's a strange relationship, something like a father caring for his children. If he is a noble chief, he visits the old ones in their cottages when they are ill, knows each man and woman, and calls each child by name. My father was like that when he was younger. But you must know, Arrian, that the MacIvors clan is no longer the force it once was. There are few left to work the land. I believe it was Ian's idea to run sheep and let the tenant farmers go."

Arrian missed the criticism in her aunt's voice. Her thoughts were on the faceless chief of the Drummond clan. "Do you think Lord Warrick is a noble chief?"

"I've heard he has the power to fire the imagination of others—especially his own clan. They look to him for guidance and stand ready to carry out his least order, and often his orders are to torment my father. He has been a constant source of irritation to my father for years."

"I have often heard Mother speak of the Highlands and the Lowlands as if there was a great difference."

"To be in the Highlands is like stepping back in time. Highlanders are less refined, have rougher edges, and speak mostly Gaelic. Although many Lowlanders will not admit it, their lives resemble their English cousins. It's a pity neither side will acknowledge that the old life is over and that they are eternally joined to England."

Arrian shook her head. "It must have been a glorious sight when the Scottish chiefs paraded about with their banners flying and their armies dressed in clan colors. 'Tis a pity such a heritage has been lost forever."

"Nay, child, think not what has been lost of the old ways, but rejoice on that which has been saved."

Arrian's mind moved on to other matters. "I hope Ian won't worry about us when he discovers we aren't on the *Nightingale* when it makes port at Leith."

"Captain Norris will inform him of the reason for our delay, if the good captain doesn't sink in the storm. I swear I'll never journey by ship again." She pulled a woolen robe over her shoulders. "Let us talk of more amiable matters." The older woman's eyes twinkled. "Let's speak of your wedding."

Arrian noticed the heavy snowflakes that drifted past the window of the coach. "Ian is everything I could want in a husband. It's no wonder I waited for him to realize he loved me. He was always in my mind, overshadowing all other gentlemen I met."

Lady Mary studied Arrian intently. "Are you certain what you feel for Ian is a deep and lasting love and not a young girl's fanciful dreams?"

"Mother asked me the same thing, but I assured her that I wanted to spend the rest of my life with Ian."

Lady Mary wiped the frost from the glass with her gloved hand, and peered outside. "This storm is getting much worse. We should have put up at the last posting inn. Lord, the snow is so heavy I can't see the side of the road."

It was growing colder, and Arrian pulled the woolen robe across her legs and shivered. It was snowing so hard she could only see a vague outline of the two outriders who were huddled over their saddles.

"Poor men, they must be miserable in this weather." She leaned forward as they disappeared completely in a swirling tide of white. "They will be lost," she said in a worried voice. "Surely they can't find their way in this."

Lady Mary took Arrian's hand. "I have never seen a worse storm. Night will soon be upon us, and I doubt if the poor driver can see the road. If anything happens to you, I'll hold myself responsible."

Before Arrian could answer, the carriage suddenly tilted and then righted itself, spilling Lady Mary to the floor.

Arrian clutched tightly to the door, striving to keep from being thrown about. Then the coach slid sideways and rolled over, slamming into a snowdrift.

Pain exploded inside Arrian's head, and she slumped forward into unconsciousness.

Dazed, Arrian sat up slowly, trying to remember what had happened. It was dark, and she was so cold her teeth chattered. There didn't seem to be a part of her body that didn't ache. Her mind slowly began to clear, and she remembered the accident.

She could hear the sound of the gale-force wind as it shook the coach. She fumbled frantically around in the dark and discovered that the coach was on its side and the door was now above her head, out of her reach.

"Aunt Mary, where are you? Are you hurt?" Panic took over her reasoning. "Why don't you speak to me?"

There was no answer. At last she found her aunt's hand, but it was limp and cold. "Oh, no. Don't worry, Aunt Mary," she cried. "I'm sure the coachman has gone for help."

Still her aunt made no reply. Where were the driver and the outriders? Why hadn't they come to their assistance?

Arrian managed to pull the woolen robe over her aunt. She sat for what seemed like hours, holding her aunt's hand, too stunned to move. Had she heard the sound of voices? Hope sprang within her. Perhaps it was one of their men returning.

The door was wrenched open, and someone thrust a lantern into the coach. Arrian blinked her eyes, blinded by the light, and asked, "Who is it?"

"Be ye all right, miss?" a man asked in a heavy Scottish brogue.

"Please help us!" she cried, groping toward the light. "I fear my aunt has been badly injured."

"Don't you fret, now, lassie. We'll have you out o' here in no time a'tall."

Arrian watched with renewed hope as the man climbed into the upended coach. With a quick assessment of the situation, he gathered Lady Mary in his arms and lifted her up into someone else's arms. Next the man caught Arrian by the waist and hoisted her upward, where she was pulled to safety.

It was bitterly cold, and the snow was still coming down in a white flurry. Someone quickly wrapped Arrian in a fur robe and placed her in the arms of a man on horseback.

"How is my aunt?" she asked when she could not see Lady Mary.

"She's been taken on ahead," a kind voice assured her. "She'll be taken care of, have no fear."

"The coachman?" she asked, straining to see through the ceaseless curtain of white.

"The coachman should'a known not to take to the road in this weather. He's beyond help, lassie—neck's broken."

Arrian shuddered and buried her face against the man's shoulder. "Can you tell me what happened to our outriders? We lost sight of them before the accident."

"Na, they must'a been lost in the storm. Most likely they made it to safety somewhere."

She pressed her body against the stranger, hoping to borrow from his warmth.

"You're no' to worry, little lassie. We'll take you to shelter. Them at the big house, they'll attend to your aunt and see you're made comfortable."

Arrian only knew she was cold and her body ached, but mostly she was worried about Aunt Mary.

Then she thought of Ian. If they had continued with the voyage, she would now be in his arms.

Ian paced the deck of the *Nightingale*. "What do you mean, they left the ship?"

Captain Norris secured a rope while a strong wind

snapped at the sails. "Lady Mary refused to continue after the storm blew us off course," he said. "I made certain that they had a coach and driver and two outriders. More than that I could not do."

"That meddling old woman," Ian mumbled. "I'm of a mind to ride out to meet them."

"I'd not do that, m'lord," Captain Norris said. "The weather was fierce all the way down the coast. I have a notion Lady Mary and Lady Arrian are snugly installed in some inn waiting for the weather to clear."

Disappointment showed in Ian's face. He left the *Nightingale* with Jamie a step behind him. They climbed into a waiting carriage, and Ian angrily tossed his buff-colored coat across the seat.

"Don't worry, Ian, Arrian will come to no harm," Jamie said.

"This isn't the way I planned our meeting. I went to great expense for the ball tonight. I wanted to parade Arrian before Edinburgh and watch the envy in my friends' eyes."

Jamie stared at his brother. "That's where you and I differ, Ian. I would never want to parade Helena before others."

"Helena isn't Arrian."

Jamie hesitated before he asked the question that had been bothering him. "Do you love Arrian or are you merely influenced by who she is?"

Ian was not offended. "I love Arrian passionately, and I'll make her a good husband. Still," he added, "I can't discount the enormous fortune she brings with her, as the only daughter of the duke of Ravenworth. But even if Arrian had nothing, I would want her." A possessive light came into his eyes. "She's mine, like the air I breathe."

Jamie studied the passing scenery, wondering if Arrian was aware of Ian's jealous nature. He turned to his brother and saw that his jaw was clamped tightly. Ian didn't like it when his plans went awry.

Chapter 4

The ride seemed endless as Arrian leaned against her rescuer. It was so dark, and the cold was almost unendurable as the wind whipped up the falling snow and flung it in her face. She squeezed her eyes tightly shut, praying that her aunt had not been badly injured. She tried not to think about the poor coachman, or the missing outriders.

At last the man halted his horse, and Arrian was handed down into other arms. She was assisted up the steep steps into a dimly lit hallway. A woman rushed forward and drew Arrian into a room where a warm fire was blazing.

"Are you the mistress of this house?" Arrian asked, holding her trembling hands out to the fire.

"Och, no," the woman said in accented English. "I'm only the housekeeper. Name's Edna Haddington. Your aunt told me her name and yours."

Arrian was flooded with relief. "Then my aunt is all right?"

"As ta that, I dinna, m'lady."

"Please take me to her."

"She's being tended. God love you, lass, you're near ta frozen. Sit you down by the fire and I'll serve you some nice hot tea and put a warming pan at your feet."

Arrian looked at the white-haired woman who fussed about her with gentle concern. "I must be with my aunt. Take me to her at once."

Mrs. Haddington appeared doubtful. "You'll no' be wise to leave the fire. You'll surely catch your death if you don't first look to yourself. After you're warmed, I'll take you to your aunt."

"I want to see her now," Arrian demanded, her voice trembling because she was shivering with cold.

The housekeeper relented and picked up a candle to light their way. "Very well, follow me. My daughter Barra's help-ful with the ailing, and you can trust her doctoring."

Arrian climbed the stairs behind Mrs. Haddington with dif-ficulty because her legs were numb with cold. Her ribs were sore, and there was pain in her shoulders, but she would not rest until she saw her aunt and knew her condition.

Mrs. Haddington opened a door and bade Arrian to enter. Lady Mary was lying on a bed with a woman bent over her. The housekeeper quickly introduced them. "This is my daughter, Barra, and this is the poor woman's niece, Lady Arrian."

The dark-haired woman merely nodded and continued to tear strips of linen.

Arrian moved forward with dread in her heart. Lady Mary was pale, and her eyes were closed. Arrian reached out to touch her, but Barra put a restraining hand on her arm.

"Have a care, m'lady," Barra said in clearer English than that spoken by her mother. "Her leg's broken, and it's bad. I was about to set it when you came."

Arrian felt tears well in her eyes when she softly touched her aunt's cheek, noting the bluish bruise on her forehead and several deep wounds. She turned pleading eyes to the housekeeper's daughter.

"Why is she unconscious?"

"It's a blessing she's not conscious, m'lady."

"Please help her."

"I'll do all I can, m'lady."

"Have you a doctor?"

"No, m'lady. Not within two days' ride. But even if we could get word to him, he couldn't come in this storm."

Feeling the panic rising in the young girl, Barra spoke with assurance. "I know some about healing, m'lady. I'll give what comfort I can to your aunt." She pulled back the bed clothes to expose Lady Mary's leg. "It must be set without delay if you'll trust me to do it."

Arrian gasped when she saw that her aunt's leg was discolored and swollen. Summoning her courage, she threw off the fur robe she was wearing, no longer mindful of the cold. "Tell me how I can help."

"If you'll just hold the candle, I'll do what needs doing."

Arrian swallowed the sickness that swelled in her throat. She had been protected and sheltered all her life, never having had to face such a difficult, heart-wrenching situation. Closing her eyes, she drew in a deep breath. Aunt Mary needed her, and she had to be strong. She watched as the woman grasped her aunt's knee and foot. There was a quick jerk, and she heard a soft snap.

Arrian fought against the dizziness that threatened to overcome her. I won't faint, she told herself, I won't!

Barra placed a smooth, narrow board under Lady Mary's leg and bound it with clean white linen. "That's all I can do for her. We'll need to keep her warm, and she'll need watching tonight."

Arrian gently brushed a white curl from her aunt's forehead. "Will she . . . recover?"

"I don't know about head wounds, m'lady. And the leg's bad. We'll have to wait and see. I'll just build up the fire

and bring you something nice and hot to eat. I'll send someone for the doctor, though it could take days for him to
arrive."

Arrian sat in the chair beside her aunt's bed, clutching
her hand and trying not to give in to fear. "Dearest Aunt
Mary," she whispered in a trembling voice. "You will be all
right—you just have to be."

Somewhere a clock chimed eleven. The candle had burned
low, and still Lady Mary had not awakened. Arrian heard
voices in the corridor and jumped to her feet as Barra
entered, accompanied by a gray-haired man.

"We're fortunate, m'lady. My son discovered that the doctor
was visiting his daughter in the village, and he agreed to
look in on your aunt."

With a stiff professional manner, the doctor moved
toward the patient. It seemed to Arrian that it took him an
eternity to unwrap and examine her aunt's leg. He gave a
nod of satisfaction at the housekeeper's daughter. "Well,
Barra, you did as well as I could have done under the circumstances."

He then proceeded to examine each of Lady Mary's
limbs. Next he gently touched the bluish swelling on her
forehead. He leaned closer to lift her eyelids and look at her
pupils.

Arrian clasped her hands tightly. "How is she?"

The doctor noticed Arrian for the first time and gave a
quick nod. "Folks hereabouts call me Dr. Edmondson. Is
this your ma?"

"No. She's my aunt. Can you help her?"

"She's had a severe blow to the head, and it's always hard
to tell with this kind of injury. Sometimes all we can do is
wait and see. As for her leg, it's a bad fracture, and it
doesn't look good. If only we could get her to Edinburgh
where the doctors know about such injury."

Her heart skipped a beat. "What are you saying?"

"I'm saying that she may be crippled or even lose her leg or life if she doesn't get the proper care."

"But you are a doctor, you can help her."

The doctor cleansed the head wound and applied ointment. "So I am, but I've never seen a worse break."

"I have money, and I'll pay anything if you'll help her, Dr. Edmondson—anything!"

He looked at her, bristling with indignation. "I'll not take that as an offense since you're obviously distraught, and on account of you being English and not knowing better."

She realized she had insulted the man. "I'm sorry, Dr. Edmondson."

He applied a bandage to Lady Mary's wound before he spoke again to Arrian. "I'd help your aunt the same if you owned the whole of England or if you were without funds."

Arrian's cheeks flushed. "Forgive me. I was impertinent. It's just that I'm so worried about her."

"Can't think why two females would be traveling alone in the worst storm of the season. I should have thought your aunt would be old enough to know it was folly."

"It does seem a bit foolish now, but it didn't when we started out, Dr. Edmondson."

At last he smiled, and his eyes softened with kindness. "Perky little lassie. Were you hurt in the accident?"

"Nothing but bruises."

He hoisted his bag on his shoulder. "I'll be back tomorrow to see the patient, unless her condition worsens sooner. I still strongly advise that she be moved to Edinburgh as soon as weather permits."

"You aren't leaving, are you?"

"I have other patients, and I don't expect to see my bed until morning." He looked at her. "You should get to your bed though, lassie, you look ready to collapse."

"Thank you for your concern, but I'll remain with my aunt tonight."

"You can't do anything for her that Barra can't. And you surely won't be helping her if you become my patient yourself."

Arrian extended her hand. "You have my gratitude for ministering to my aunt. I'll expect to see you tomorrow."

He shook her hand and gave a nod. As Arrian watched him leave, she moved to the fire and held her hands to the warmth, then glanced over her shoulder at her aunt. Lady Mary groaned, and Arrian ran to her. But her aunt didn't open her eyes, and Arrian feared for her aunt's life. At that moment Arrian longed for the strength of her father and the comfort of her mother. She did not realize that she had not thought of Ian throughout this horrible ordeal.

Lady Mary slowly opened her eyes and blinked in confusion at the stranger who bent over her. Where was she, and who was this man?

"I see you're awake." He smiled and patted her hand. "I know, I know. You're wondering who I am. Well, I'm Dr. Edmondson, and you have had me worried till now."

"How did I—" She groaned suddenly, remembering the accident. "What's wrong with me? Why am I so weak? Why is there so much pain?"

His soft Scottish accent was welcome to her ears. "You have a broken leg, m'lady, and a nasty bump on your head. Beyond that, I'd say you also have lesser cuts and bruises."

Lady Mary tried to rise, but weakness pinned her to the bed. "Where is my niece?"

"I sent her to rest. She was with you all night."

"She is uninjured?"

"I can assure you that she is only concerned about you. Your niece is a right spirited lass, going about demanding that we all help you. I'd like to have her on my side if I were ill."

Beads of sweat popped out on Lady Mary's upper lip. "I am in a great deal of pain."

Dr. Edmondson held a glass to her lips. "I'd expect you to be after what you've endured. Drink this."

"What is it?"

"It's opiate."

"I don't want to be drugged."

"'Tis mild, but will take the edge off your pain. You'll need this many times before you heal."

Reluctantly Lady Mary drank the bitter liquid, which began to take effect almost immediately.

"To whom do I owe my thanks for their hospitality?" she inquired drowsily, looking about the room.

"Why, m'lady, you're at Ironworth Castle, home of the chief of Clan Drummond."

Lady Mary's eyes widened in shock. "No," she whispered, trying to fight off the effects of the drug. "I must see my niece at once—at once, do you hear me?"

The doctor nodded at the maid who stood nearby. "Get the young lady. Perhaps she can calm her aunt."

When Arrian rushed into the room a short time later, it was to find her aunt struggling to rise. She hurried to her side and grasped her hand while gently pushing her back against the pillow.

"Dearest Aunt Mary, the doctor assures me that you must not overexcite yourself. You are going to recover. But you must rest for a time so your leg will heal properly."

Lady Mary's eyes were wild, and she gripped Arrian's hand. "Got . . . to tell . . . you . . ."

"Shh. Don't fret. Anything you have to tell me can wait until you are stronger. The doctor has given you something to make you sleep. I'll stay with you."

Lady Mary was helpless against the potion. Her tongue felt thick, and it was hard to keep her eyes focused. "Arrian, you must listen . . . to me. You must . . . That . . . man . . ."

Arrian's brow knitted with concern. "I know what's

bothering you. You want me to send someone to inform Grandfather where we are so he will not worry. I promise you, I'll speak to our host today and ask him to send a message to Davinsham as soon as the roads are passable. Does that make you feel better?"

"No . . . you must not tell—" Lady Mary struggled, but the drug was doing its work. Unable to fight any longer, her eyes fluttered shut with the terrible truth she had been unable to utter still poised on her lips.

Arrian stepped into the dimly lit hallway and stood at the top of the staircase. She had been too concerned about her aunt to notice her surroundings. She now observed the castle, thinking there was nothing extraordinary about it. There were many castles in Scotland, and most of them were more magnificent than this one.

The rugs were threadbare, and it appeared that the housekeeper was lax in her duties, for there was dust on the banisters. Still, she was grateful for the owner's hospitality and wanted to thank him.

The storm had lessened during the night. Perhaps she could keep her promise to her aunt and ask their host if he would send a rider to inform her grandfather that they were safe.

As Arrian descended the stairs, a man came through the front door. He removed his hat and coat and handed them to the housekeeper. Only a single candle glowed on the hall table, and she could not see him clearly. Even so, there was no doubt in her mind that he was the master of this castle.

"Sir," she said, descending the last three steps to stand before him, "if you are lord here, may I speak to you?"

His face was still in shadows, so she could not see his features.

When at last he spoke, it was in a clipped Scottish accent. "I am lord here. Come into my study where it's warm," he said, leading her to a room off the entryway. "I'm told my men have gone back for your trunks and will deliver them shortly."

There was a warm fire crackling in the fireplace and several candles burning in wall sconces. Arrian walked to the fire and turned to the man. "You are most kind. I wish to thank you, sir, for your hospitality. If not for you and the care of your servants, my aunt and I would most probably be dead."

He stepped into the light, and she was surprised to find him so dark. Black hair curled against his tanned cheek, and although he was clean-shaven, his thick black sideburns met at the edge of his high collar. He wore a white cravat and a green frock coat that fell to his knees. His gray trousers were tapered down his long legs to fasten beneath his boots.

He was probably the most striking man she had ever seen. She stared at him for a moment before realizing that he was also assessing her. He had expressive gray eyes that, in this light, looked like liquid silver.

Mrs. Haddington had informed Warrick that the girl his men had rescued was titled and English, but she had not informed him that she was a beauty. His gaze moved down her golden hair that seemed alive as the reflection of the firelight played on each strand. Her eyes were pale blue and had the tranquillity of innocence. She wore a crimson velvet gown that made her skin appear shimmering white.

His gaze dropped to her hand, where he saw, to his shock, a ruby ring on her finger. How well he knew that ring, for there could not be another like it in the whole world. The last time he'd seen that ring it had been on Gwendolyn's finger. It was the MacIvors's ring!

He spoke with practiced control. "I can assure you that no one could be more welcome than you, my lady. In fact, I count myself fortunate that you have come to . . . my home."

"You are most kind."

"Not at all. The doctor has told me of the severity of your aunt's injuries. As soon as she's recovered sufficiently to travel and the roads are passable, we shall discuss transporting her to Edinburgh for the care she requires."

"We are both indebted to you." She thought to offer him money for his hospitality but, remembering the doctor's reaction to payment, decided against it. "I wanted to inquire what happened to the body of our driver."

"He was known by my steward, and his body was returned to his family in Rattray Head."

"I seem even more in your debt."

"Is there anything you desire?" he asked.

Arrian felt overwhelmed by the commanding light in those silver-gray eyes. She looked down, unable to meet his penetrating stare. "You have done so much for me, I hesitate to ask another favor of you."

He bowed slightly, and his voice came out in a deep tone as though he were mocking her. "I'm at your service."

"I would like to send word to my grandfather that my aunt and I are safe. Will that be possible?"

Warrick found himself wishing he could as easily make all her desires come true. "And who would your grandfather be?"

"He is in truth my great-grandfather. Perhaps you know him. He is the chief of Clan MacIvors."

There was a strange silence, and the very air became charged with emotion. Warrick drew in his breath sharply. "Gille MacIvors?"

"Yes, that's my grandfather. My Great-aunt Mary is his daughter."

Warrick's eyes hardened. "How strange it is that fate should deliver you into my hands."

Misunderstanding his meaning, she nodded. "I believe so, too. I don't know what would have happened had your men not found us."

He gazed at her for so long, she began to feel uncomfortable.

"Let me see if I can guess who you are. Is it possible that you are the daughter of the duke of Ravenworth, my lady?"

She was astonished. "But how did you know? Are you acquainted with my father?"

"I only heard his name once, but it's a name that remained in my mind."

Arrian was beginning to feel that something was strange. She had told no one here her identity. "Since you know who I am, may I ask your name, sir?"

He bowed to her. "I, my lady, am Warrick Glencarin, chief of Clan Drummond."

She gasped and stepped quickly away from him, her heart pounding with fear. Arrian had not considered that this might be Drummond land. The accident and worry for her aunt had pushed all other thoughts from her mind. Now she remembered her aunt's fervent attempt to speak just before she fallen asleep. Aunt Mary had tried to warn her that they were in the home of Lord Warrick Glencarin.

His voice was hard, his eyes stabbing. "From your reaction I'd say you have heard of me. I can only imagine how disturbing it must be for you to find yourself under my protection."

She groped for something to say. "I . . . thought you would be older."

There was arrogance in the way he stood and dislike in the tone of his voice. "I also thought you would be older, and not so comely."

She took another hasty step backwards. "You don't know me."

"Ah, but I know your betrothed, my lady. I am acquainted with Ian MacIvors."

There was something in his eyes that made her want to flee into the storm, anything to escape. "Will you send word to my grandfather?" she asked, taking another step backwards. "He . . . will be distressed about us."

Sudden amusement lit his eyes. "Indeed. You can depend

on it that I'll do just that, my lady. But not yet. When the time is right, your grandfather will surely know that you and your aunt are my . . . guests."

Concern for her aunt made her forget her fear. "I will not allow you to do anything that will endanger my aunt's health. I will fight you in every way I can."

He smiled down at her grimly. "So I would expect. But you cannot win, my lady."

Panic took over her reasoning, and her voice trembled. "Will you let us go?"

"In good time, my lady—in good time."

She backed toward the door, each step taking her farther from him. "What will you do with us?"

His laughter was deep and slightly amused. "Why, my lady, I believe you fear me. I wonder why? Could it be that you have heard that I have no love for anyone who is attached to the MacIvors?"

ear sent shock waves through Arrian's body. She whirled around and ran quickly out of the room and up the stairs, half expcting Lord Warrick to pursue her.

When she reached the safety of her aunt's room she found Lady Mary still sleeping. Arrian looked on both sides of the door for a key but found none. In desperation she tugged on a heavy oak chair, sliding it across the room and bracing it against the door, knowing that it would not keep Lord Warrick out should he want to enter.

With a pounding heart she listened for footsteps. Moments passed, and no one came. Perhaps he had not followed her.

"We are prisoners, Aunt Mary," she cried, taking her aunt's hand and gently shaking her. "Please wake up and tell me what to do. Even though he did not say so, I know he will not allow us to leave."

Lady Mary was still under the effects of the drug and did not stir.

"We are in the hands of a devil," Arrian whispered. "It might have been far better if we had perished in the storm. Oh, Father, Mother, what shall I do?"

Her Grace, the duchess of Ravenworth, moved out from the arched doorway of the Hôtel de Ville, pulling her fur-lined hood over her head to keep out the bitter wind. A liveried servant rushed forward to assist her into the carriage, where she joined her husband and son.

Raile took Kassidy's hand and held it in a firm grip. "I'm glad to be quit of Paris. I have little liking for the French."

Kassidy glanced at her husband, trying not to show her amusement. "Thus speaks Wellington's soldier." She reached out her other hand and clasped her son's hand. "Do you think we should tell your father that the war is over and has been for many years? Would he be shocked to hear that the French are now our allies?"

Raile's lip curled in ill humor. "Have your little jest, Kassidy," he said.

Michael smiled at his beautiful mother. "Perhaps we should remind Father that he may be about to take on the Scots and doesn't need a war on two fronts."

Raile almost smiled at his son's humor. "You mistake my intentions, Michael. I have no desire for a confrontation with Gille MacIvors."

"But you must take seriously his dislike for anyone English, Raile," Kassidy said.

"I can assure you, I take it very seriously. But I will not allow him to spoil my daughter's wedding."

"I'm sure by the time we reach Scotland, Aunt Mary will have smoothed the path for you. If anyone can control Grandfather, it's she."

"I was opposed to allowing Arrian and your aunt to sail to Scotland ahead of us. Your aunt has always been head-strong, Kassidy, but when Captain Norris informed me that she left the ship and hired a coach to take her and Arrian to Davinsham, she exceeded all boundaries of common sense."

"You know how she detests sailing. After the storm, she refused to remain on the *Nightingale.*"

"Then why did she insist on sailing to Scotland ahead of us, Kassidy? You know I admire and respect Lady Mary, but I believe she is in her dotage."

"I agree that what she did was not rational, Raile, but her intentions were good. In spite of her fear of sailing, she boarded the *Nightingale,* hoping to convince Grandfather to accept you."

"No one, not even that old man, will keep me from seeing Arrian married. If he does not relent, the wedding will simply take place in England."

"Have you said this to Arrian?"

"I have."

"And what was her reaction?"

A satisfied look came into Raile's eyes. "Our daughter will not marry in Scotland unless I'm with her."

"I agree," Kassidy said. "But you don't know Grandfather."

"We may never meet, Kassidy."

"I wanted the wedding to take place at Ravenworth, but it was important to Arrian that she be married at Davinsham." Kassidy clutched her husband's hand, knowing he would not be pleased when she told him her idea. "I believe, Raile, it would be wise if I went on ahead to join Aunt Mary and Arrian. I will add my pleas to theirs and persuade Grandfather to acknowledge you. I know he'll do it for me."

"I don't like this," Raile said, tightening his grip on her hand. "I'd rather you returned to England with me."

"But don't you see what this means to Arrian? I believe I should try to change Grandfather's mind about you."

"I don't want you to go to Scotland without me, and I must return to England."

"After you have concluded your business in London, you

and Michael can join me." Kassidy leaned her head against Raile's shoulder and linked her arm through his. "Please, Raile."

Their son watched Raile's eyes soften with adoration. His mother would have her way today, of that Michael had little doubt.

Raile shouted up to the coachman. "To Calais, Atkins, to where the *Nightingale* is anchored."

Michael couldn't help but smile at how easily his mother had overcome his father's objections. The coach lurched forward, and the young viscount soon lost interest in his parents. His gaze followed a pretty young woman as she hurried down the street. When the girl disappeared into a shop, Lord Michael's thoughts returned to the family. He was looking forward to being with his sister. Their family would never be the same after her marriage. If their mother was the heart of the family, Arrian was the soul. What would they do without her?

When Raile escorted Kassidy on board the *Nightingale,* his eyes were filled with indecision. "I still think you should come with me."

"I must do this, Raile. And remember you are to speak before Parliament on the twenty-third. You will have to take ship for England no later than Monday next."

"I know, I know."

Kassidy gazed up at him, smiling. "It won't be long until we are reunited, dearest. We must just be patient."

"I don't like to be separated from you."

"But you'll have our son to keep you from being lonely."

Raile hugged her to him. "Take the greatest care of yourself."

A breath of icy wind chilled Kassidy, touching her with a feeling of deep foreboding. Glancing at her son, she saw by his expression that he'd felt it also.

Scots were of a suspicious nature and would call her intuition a forewarning or a bad omen. She only knew that something was dreadfully wrong, and she would not be at ease until she saw Arrian again. But she decided that it would be unwise to share her distress with her husband.

"Good-bye, my dearest," she said, pressing her cheek against Raile's. "I shan't sleep well until we are together again."

"Nor will I," he said, aching to keep her with him.

Michael hugged his mother and smiled. "When next we meet, it will be on Scottish soil."

Kassidy felt the deck pitch beneath her feet as her husband and son left the ship. Already she missed them, but her daughter needed her—she could feel it.

Hours had passed since Arrian had confronted Lord Warrick, but her apprehension had not lessened. She sat before a smoldering fire, startled by every noise. If only her aunt would awaken and tell her what to do.

Hearing a soft rap on the door, Arrian scrambled to her feet. She hurried to press her ear against the door. "Who is it?"

"'Tis Barra. I've come to tend your aunt."

With great relief, Arrian moved the chair away from the door, feeling a bit foolish. Barra greeted her with a quick nod. "Lord Warrick asked if you'll attend him at your convenience. He'll await you in his study."

Fear prickled Arrian's spine. "No. I will not go."

Barra looked amazed at Lady Arrian's refusal. Lowering her eyes, she walked over to Lady Mary. After examining her patient, she turned to Arrian with a worried frown. "The leg's bad. She should have the kind of care I canna give her."

"Dr. Edmondson has also told me this. Are the roads passable?"

"Not yet." The maid walked to the door. "What would you have me tell his lordship?"

Arrian could see the puzzlement in the woman's eyes. "Tell him I . . . don't want to leave my aunt."

Barra merely nodded. "Will you be wanting to take your meals in here?"

"Yes, thank you," Arrian said. "And I will also want a bed brought in, please." In truth, Arrian did not want to be alone. She was too frightened.

"Very well, m'lady."

"Do you think the doctor will come today?"

"No, m'lady, the snow's too deep. Will there be anything else?"

"No, nothing. Only . . . please let it be known that we do not wish to be disturbed by anyone except yourself or the doctor."

Barra nodded. "It'll be as you say. I'll see that your bed is set up before nightfall."

Arrian walked to the window and pulled back the heavy drapery. It was snowing so hard she could not even see the courtyard below. She and her aunt were imprisoned in this icy world, but she had to find a way to get them to Edinburgh.

She traced Ian's name on the frosty window. What must he be thinking? Surely he was worried. Perhaps by now he had initiated a search for her.

Lady Mary groaned, and Arrian rushed to her aunt's bedside to find her awake. She gripped Arrian's hand, her eyes wide with concern. "Do you know where we are?"

"Yes. I have spoken with Lord Warrick."

Arrian didn't know how much to tell her aunt. She didn't think it would be wise to upset her at this time, but Arrian had not reckoned with Lady Mary's sharp perception.

"He won't allow us to leave, will he?"

"I don't believe so."

"My leg is bad, isn't it, Arrian?"

"Yes, dearest, but you must not be concerned. I will find a way to get us out of here. I promise."

"I doubt that man would dare to hurt us physically, Arrian. But don't mistake this, he's our bitter enemy. You are to stay away from him."

"I am frightened."

"And with good reason. If you knew more about Scotland and the feuds that have torn it apart, you would better understand what we are facing."

"Why does Lord Warrick hate the MacIvors?"

"There are many reasons. I fear he will never allow us our freedom until he gets what he wants from my father—whatever that might be. Perhaps I should speak to him."

Arrian laid her hand on her aunt's forehead and found that she was feverish. "You will do nothing of the sort. You must rest and not upset yourself."

Lady Mary closed her eyes and breathed deeply. "I find I am very weary, Arrian, and will be of little use to you." Her eyes opened for just a moment. "You must keep away from that man. Stay by me."

"Don't concern yourself with me. I'm in no danger."

Lady Mary fought against the drowsiness but eventually gave in to it. She was soon locked in a heavy sleep that brought no rest.

That night Arrian lay awake in the small cot that had been placed beside her aunt's bed. She had wedged the chair against the door once more, but still she jumped at every noise.

When a weak dawn lit the corners of the room, Arrian was still awake.

Warrick dismounted and handed the reins to the young stable boy.

"Looks like the snow'll never let up, m'lord."

"So it does, Tam. Give Titus a good rubdown and extra oats. See that the stables are kept warm tonight. I don't want the livestock to freeze."

"What about the sheep still running the bogs, m'lord?"

"We'll lose the youngest tonight, but there is no help for it. We can't find them in this blizzard."

With long strides, Warrick made his way to the castle. At first he had been angry when the girl had refused to come to his study. But the ride had cleared his mind, and he knew what he must do with the great-granddaughter of Gille MacIvors. He would no longer delay their confrontation.

A clock somewhere in the distance chimed four o'clock when the rap came at the door. Arrian moved slowly across the room and opened the door a crack. She was surprised to see the housekeeper and not Barra, who usually served them.

"M'lord's asked that you attend him at once."

"I made it clear to your daughter that I would not see him."

The housekeeper shook her head. "It'll do no good ta deny him, m'lady. He'll have his way in the end. It would be better if you just come along with me."

"Do you . . . know what he wants of me?"

"His lordship doesn't confide in me, m'lady."

Her aunt was still sleeping. She was alone in this and would have to face him eventually. She could not remain in this room forever like some scared little rabbit, but she would see him when she was ready, not when he ordered it.

"Inform his lordship that it isn't convenient for me to see him at this time," she said.

"I'd no' like to be the one to defy him." Mrs. Haddington shook her head and withdrew, closing the door behind her.

Arrian quickly ran a brush through her hair and tied it back with a green ribbon that matched the green velvet gown she wore. Taking a deep breath, she left the room. Standing at the top of the stairs, it took her a moment to gather the courage to descend into the dim hallway.

With determined steps, she made her way to Lord Warrick's study. She would have knocked, but the door swung open, and his tall figure loomed in front of her.

"I was told you ignored my invitation, so I was about to come to you."

Arrian threw her head back and glared at him. "Well, my lord, do we converse in the hallway, or will you offer me the warmth of your hearth?"

He bowed to her and swept his hand toward the fireplace. "Be my guest, my lady. I thought you might be curious as to what I've decided to do about you and your aunt."

Arrian held her hands out to the flames that did little to warm the chill in her heart. She shrugged, trying to pretend indifference. "As soon as the weather permits, my aunt must see a doctor in Edinburgh. We will be happy to be on our way, thus ridding you of our encumbrance."

A smile tugged at his lips. "That's not quite what I had in mind, my lady. Won't you be seated, so that I, too, may sit?"

"No. I'd rather stand."

"Then you force me to stand also. You see, we have been instructed in good manners here in the Highlands, my lady, no matter what you may have heard to the contrary."

She dropped into a chair, as she certainly didn't want him hovering over her. She was glad when he was finally seated.

"Mrs. Haddington made tea and some of her wonderful scones. Will you not partake?" he asked.

Arrian glanced at the table that had been laid with a white cloth and a silver tea set. "No, thank you. I care little for scones."

"I have no doubt you find us primitive," he said. "My home must seem drab to you, since you are the daughter of the wealthy and powerful duke of Ravenworth." The way he said her father's title was not a compliment.

She was silent.

"You do not answer."

"I am merely wondering if I should be truthful as my

father would have me be, or temper truth with decorum as my mother would advise. I will answer you thus. I don't apologize for who I am or who my parents are."

A smile curved his lips. "Spoken like an Englishwoman. You can save yourself the necessity of choosing between your father's or your mother's teachings. I have seen the glory of your grandfather's home, and I can only wonder at the treasures of Ravenworth Castle."

"You mistake me, my lord. I have also been taught not to judge a person by the blood that runs in his veins, or the worldly possessions he has accumulated. I have learned to admire good manners, honor, and truthfulness. If you fall short of these attributes, my lord, then I will not admire you. But if, in your kindness, you would let us go, you will always have my regard."

He examined her closely, trying to decide if she was speaking the truth. After all, she had the contaminated blood of the MacIvors in her veins.

Arrian saw the hardness in his silver eyes and knew that her pleas had not touched his heart. "Let us not play games, my lord. She looked down at the threadbare rug. "I have little doubt you could use money. If you help me get my aunt to Edinburgh, my father will be most generous with you."

The expression on his face was unreadable. "I have no need of your father's money, my lady. And as for allowing you to go to Edinburgh, I think not."

Her eyes widened in anger. "Surely you will not deprive my aunt of the medical attention she needs so desperately."

"I have no wish to take my anger out on Lady Mary, nor of keeping her from proper treatment."

"You just said you wouldn't allow us to go to Edinburgh."

"That's not what I said." His eyes became slate-colored and hard. "I said, my lady, that I would not allow *you* to leave."

"You are pitiless and hateful."

His eyes rested on the ruby ring she wore—the ring that

had once graced his sister's finger. "Aye, that I am. It's good you know that about me."

"Neither my aunt nor I have done anything to you. Why should you want to punish us?"

His eyes narrowed. "Indeed, my lady, your aunt is not my enemy—nor are you. You have unwittingly become a pawn in a game that will soon be played to its finish."

She felt terribly frightened and wished she had not agreed to see this man alone. "What do you want of me?"

"It's quite simple. I want you for my wife."

She stared at him as if he'd lost his mind. When she tried to speak, no sound issued from her lips.

"I see you are overwhelmed by my proposal." There was sudden amusement in his eyes. "Think how I must feel, my lady. I only met you yesterday, and today I will have no one if not you for my bride."

"You are a beast! You know I'm betrothed, and even if I weren't, you would be my last choice for a husband."

"My lady, how you do wound me."

Arrian straightened her spine, knowing that she must appear undaunted by his absurd proposal. "I find myself with a single objective, sir, and that is to get free of you."

"Perhaps you will never be free of me."

"What are you saying?"

"Shall I repeat it?"

"But I don't know you. We don't even like each other."

He laughed softly. "Does that matter, my lady?"

Chapter 6

"*I'll never marry you*. You can't force me!" His eyes didn't waver as he stared at her.

"Can't I?"

"You must think me mad. I'll never agree to be your wife."

"Won't you?"

He was too sure of himself, and that frightened her more than his words. She had a feeling that she was living a nightmare. If she concentrated very hard, would she awaken? No, she was not asleep—it was all too real. Arrian looked into his eyes. "This is laughable, my lord. I can't think why you want me, and I certainly don't want you."

He poured a cup of tea and extended it to her. "Are you certain you wouldn't like tea, my lady?"

She shook her head. "No, thank you." She sat forward in the chair and folded her hands in her lap, hoping he wouldn't notice how they trembled. "I think we have nothing more to say to each other, my lord."

His eyes hardened. "There is much we have to say. We must settle this thing between us."

He picked up a crystal decanter and poured wine into a glass. Then he took a sip and rolled the glass between his hands while she watched, fascinated by his movements.

"Tear the cobwebs from your mind, my lady, and heed my words. You are in my home, and you cannot escape. Don't think you will be rescued, because no one knows you're here except those who are loyal to me."

She shook her head. "I will not listen to you any longer."

"You must not think only of yourself. Consider your aunt and how she will benefit by our marriage."

"Surely you aren't threatening me with my aunt?"

"Not at all. I merely wish to strike an agreement with you." Warrick saw the fear in her eyes, and it made him feel sick. It was not in his nature to treat a woman with such callousness. But when he looked at the ring on her finger, he was reminded of sweet Gwendolyn, and it hardened his heart.

"The way it appears to me, my lady, is that I give something to you, and you give something in return."

She noticed that his gaze kept going to the ring, so she nervously twisted it on her finger. "I will give you nothing, my lord."

"If you agree to my proposal, I will allow your aunt to be transported to Edinburgh."

"I don't understand why are you doing this."

"Perhaps you are the wife I have been waiting for all these years, my lady. Perhaps I cannot live without you."

Warrick was aware of how young and frightened she looked—just as his sister, Gwendolyn, had been young and frightened at her marriage to Gavin MacIvors. His sister had died alone, in fear and hate. Fortune had placed this girl in his hands, and she would be the weapon he would use to strike at the heart of the MacIvors clan.

"Nothing you can do will make me marry you," she said.

He toyed with the glass, staring at the cut crystal so long that Arrian thought she would scream. At last he looked up at her. "You can make it easy on yourself or hard—it's up to you. I will have you, with or without marriage. Consider which way you would prefer it."

Her heart thundered within her. "You aren't saying that you would—that you—that—"

"That's exactly what I'm saying. Decide quickly, my lady, so that I can arrange for witnesses to hear our wedding vows."

She stood up slowly, knowing that if she had to run, her legs would not obey. "You're an evil man. Surely somewhere in you there is a thread of decency. You cannot do this to me. My father will kill you."

"I have no quarrel with your father, and he may indeed try to kill me. But that doesn't affect us tonight."

She shook her head, trying to make sense out of what he was doing. "You are only trying to frighten me. Besides, I'm certain you could not get a minister to come out in this weather. Then the banns would have to be posted. That all takes time."

"This is Scotland, not England. Our laws are quite different from yours. All we have to do is confess before witnesses that we are married and you will be as legally bound to me as if we'd stood in the church at Westminster and had a bishop join us together."

She felt the trap closing on her, but her proud spirit came to her rescue. "I will never say you are my husband."

He shrugged. "Please yourself, but I would carefully consider the alternative."

Warrick placed his glass on the table and stood up, holding his hand out to her. Arrian shook her head and backed away. "Come now, my lady, I will make an admirable husband."

She clasped her hands behind her. "No."

"Either come with me now to my bedroom, or agree to the marriage."

She tossed her golden head. "I'm more afraid of becoming your wife than of anything you can do to me in your bedroom, my lord."

He grabbed her wrist and drew her resisting body to him. He held her so tightly that she could feel every breath he took. Arrian looked up into those silver eyes and saw no compassion, no mercy. She knew he would not relent.

"There are far more dangerous things, my lady, than becoming my wife."

Arrian felt terror well up inside, and it reduced her to pleading. "I beseech you, my lord, please don't do this to me."

"You do want your aunt to receive proper care, don't you? Dr. Edmondson is a devoted man, but his skills are limited at best."

"You promise you will allow my aunt to leave if I agree to this thing?"

"I promise." His eyes were stabbing. "What is your answer?"

She struggled against him, but he held her firm. "I still say no. My aunt would never agree to this."

"Have you thought about the war that will surely come if your family believes that I took you against your will? Many would die in such a conflict—perhaps your grandfather, perhaps Ian MacIvors, perhaps even your own father."

Stinging tears swam in her eyes. He had hit her where she was most vulnerable, her love for her family. "You would let me go before it came to that. You would not want a war."

"I can assure you that if it's to be war, it will not be of my doing. But if they come for you—as surely they will—I shall defend this castle."

She was trembling with anger and fear. "Why are you doing this? Why do you threaten me with those I love?"

"Let us say it is to settle an old debt."

"If you have a grievance with the MacIvors, my father will help you settle it. King William is his friend, and my father has his ear."

"A grievance, my lady?" There was humor in his eyes. "Is that what they call bitter conflict, murder, and betrayal, in the polite drawing rooms of London?"

"King William will listen to my father, I promise you that."

"I have little faith in the justice dispensed by your King William. In the last confrontation between my clan and the MacIvors, there were many men slain on both sides. Your king sent troops to punish those who participated in the battle. Both Drummonds and MacIvors swore to the English that our dead had fallen in friendly competition. We have no respect for your king. In this we are united with the MacIvors."

"But my father—"

He finally released her. "Enough. You have only one thing to decide, my lady. I'm running out of time and patience."

"Have you no heart?"

There was about him a sudden melancholy. "If I once did, it has long since deserted me. Perhaps you can help me find it again." Warrick raised his eyes to Arrian, sending a shiver down the back of her neck.

"I will not remain under your roof one moment longer than is necessary. I insist that you ready a coach to take my aunt and me away from here at once!"

He reached forward, but she pulled away from him. But when he held out his hand, she reluctantly laid her hand in his.

He held the ruby ring up to the chandelier, and the light danced on the stone as if it were on fire. "I saw this ring on the finger of another young girl." He dropped her hand. "'Tis of no importance. I will replace it with my own ring."

"I'll never take this off." she declared, clasping her hands in a show of defiance.

"Perhaps you do not understand the gravity of the situation. My sister was about your age when she married a MacIvors. She died on her wedding night."

"Are you threatening me with death?" she asked in horror.

"It is not my custom to harm a lady. That would be more the practice of a MacIvors. No, I want no harm to come to you. I want you to live to be a very old woman." Warrick lightly touched her cheek and let his hand drift up to her golden hair. "Ian MacIvors cannot help but love a beauty like you. I want him to suffer every day of his life, knowing that what he desires most belongs to me."

"I will never belong to you. I love Ian—I will always love him."

He drew in an impatient breath. "I weary of this conversation. If it's not to be marriage, then you will come to my bed."

Her eyes glistened with anger. "I will not."

He swung her easily into his arms. Without a word he carried her out of the room and toward the stairs. Frantically she fought him, but his grip only tightened.

"Be still," he said. "You cannot fight me."

Arrian stiffened as he climbed the stairs, and she looked around desperately for anyone that might help her.

"If you think to call out, save yourself the trouble. My servants will not help you."

She tried to think of what her mother would do in such circumstances. Suddenly she knew. "Do with me what you will, my lord. I'll still not marry you."

At the top of the stairs he turned and carried her down a long, dark hallway, in the opposite direction of the room she shared with her aunt. Without warning he opened a door and carried her inside.

Arrian knew instantly that this was not his bedroom. The bed had a lace canopy with a matching coverlet. A warm fire blazed in the hearth, and the room smelled strongly of lemon oil as if it had been recently cleaned.

"No," he said, answering her unspoken question. "'Tis not my room—mine's across the hall. This was my sister's, and I have had it prepared for you." He set Arrian down on her feet but kept a hand on her arm. "Your trunks are already in the dressing room. If you require anything you have only to inform a servant."

"I don't like this room. I insist on staying with my aunt."

"Until we have settled our dispute, you will either occupy this room or you will share mine. Which is it to be?"

She freed her wrist and moved to the fire. Her heart was thundering with fear, but he mustn't suspect it. "You have me confused. I can't think clearly."

"It's very simple. If you will swear before witnesses—and one of the witnesses must be your aunt—that you take me as your husband, then you may occupy this bedroom . . . alone. And I'll allow your aunt to leave for Edinburgh."

"And if I don't?"

"I already told you, my lady, you'll share my bed."

"I've never wronged you."

His eyes grew cold. "We've been over this ground. The decision is yours, my lady. You have one hour to decide."

"Are you certain the ceremony will consist of nothing more than a confession of intent before witnesses?"

"Quite certain."

"And you will let my aunt leave after I do this?"

"I have said so." He moved closer to her, and she felt as if she might faint from fear. He slid his hand around her neck and pulled her face forward. "A taste of what you can expect if you do *not* marry me."

Before Arrian could resist, his mouth crushed against hers. She could not breathe, and her heart was beating so hard that it hammered in her ears. She pushed against him, but to no avail. She twisted and turned, but he held her fast, his lips bruising and punishing hers. Then, just as suddenly as he had taken her, he released her.

Arrian was trembling, and a sob was building within her. She stared into his silver eyes, thinking to see triumph but saw instead puzzlement.

"You are a rare prize indeed, my lady. I almost pity Ian MacIvors his loss."

Arrian stood shivering from fright. She wilted against the bed, too weak to bear her own weight.

Warrick moved away from her and stood in the open doorway. "Think hard on what I have said. I'll be back in one hour." He closed the door behind him with a snap.

There was no doubt that this man had meant every word he said. She glanced up at the mantel clock and noted the time. He'd given her an hour to make up her mind.

Her head was aching, and she felt as if she were going to be ill. She moved to the water pitcher, dampened a cloth, and placed it on her pounding forehead. She had to keep a clear head or she would be lost.

Arrian went to the door, turned the knob, and found to her relief that it was unlocked. She wanted to tell her aunt what had happened, but Aunt Mary was in no condition to advise her. In this she must act alone. She would get no help from anyone in this man's domain.

She moved to the fire and stared at the dancing flames. What would her mother do? The duchess of Ravenworth would gain the upper hand and come out the winner in this game. But how? What could she do against Lord Warrick?

If she could make her way to the stable and take a horse, she could ride into the first village and beg for help. Surely someone would come to her aid.

For some reason an old saying Aunt Mary was fond of reciting came to her mind. When you are forced to dance with the devil, make certain it's to your tune.

Arrian knew what she had to do.

Mactavish looked at Warrick with a frown. "I've seen you grow from a lad into a man. I've seen you struggle against an unloving father to become a man of honor who cares about the clan that depends on you for their survival. I've seen you take food from your table so they wouldn't go hungry. I've also seen your grief when your sister died, and I grieved with you. But until today, I've never had a reason to be ashamed of you, Warrick Glencarin. You must let them both go as soon as possible."

"I didn't bring them here," Warrick said, "but I'll take advantage of the fate that placed them in my hands."

"You'll not force the lass to marry against her will, Warrick. That's unworthy of you."

"Why not? Jamie MacIvors forced Lady Helena to marry him. It's my right."

"Your fight is not with Ian MacIvors's betrothed. She's innocent. Let her go. If you do this thing, who can say you are more noble than the MacIvors?"

"If she agrees to the Irregular Marriage, she'll come to no harm from me."

Mactavish looked doubtful. "And you'll let her go?"

Warrick took a moment to answer. "After a time, when it suits me."

Frustration showed on the older man's face. "I'll have no part in this, Warrick."

"Have you forgotten my sister?"

A deep intake of breath expanded Mactavish's wide chest. "I've not forgotten."

"As my friend, will you stand beside me as my witness?"

"What'll you do if the lady refuses?"

"Let her go, even though she thinks she's my prisoner. I could never force myself on a woman—not even for revenge. I'd like to think my hate for the MacIvors hasn't brought me that low."

Mactavish nodded. "Aye, lad. I'll stand beside you. But you must be prepared for the disastrous backlash that'll surely come. At that time, you'll need me more than ever."

"I'm depending on you."

Arrian stood by the window watching snowflakes drift slowly earthward. She did not reply to the knock on the door or turn when Lord Warrick entered. He moved to stand beside her, took her by the shoulder, and turned her to face him.

"Have you decided?" He could tell nothing from her expression.

She wanted to strike out at him. He was hateful and demanding, but she had to remain calm and pretend to be passive. "You must understand that I love Ian. In my heart, I'll never belong to you."

He laughed. "You are assuming that I want your heart—I assure you I do not."

"If I agree to this farce, I don't want you ever to touch me."

Warrick released her and stepped back a pace. "I will not touch you unless you ask it of me, my lady . . . and perhaps you will."

She raised her head, her eyes flaming with indignation. "Never!"

"Enough of this. Have you made up your mind?"

Arrian appeared to waver, as if she were considering the alternatives anew.

When he saw her indecision, he spoke. "You will have your own room with the only key. You have my word."

"I don't know if your word can be trusted."

"I haven't broken it as of yet."

She swept him a haughty curtsy. "It would seem that you have the whip hand, my lord."

"Just so you remember that."

"I think you will live to regret this."

His eyes burned into hers. "I have many regrets, my lady. One more will not trouble me overmuch."

"Just when will you expect me to participate in this mockery of a marriage?"

"Tonight at nine. Since your aunt is so ill, I thought we would have the ceremony in her room so that she can bear witness. I'll send Mrs. Haddington to help you dress for the occasion."

"No, I do not wish the ceremony to take place until tomorrow. I need time to prepare."

He was silent for a moment as he pondered her words. "Agreed. What's one day more?"

Arrian pretended to accept him while planning her escape. "I want you to know that I will never, never consider myself your wife."

He smiled for the first time. She had expected to see him gloat because he had gotten his way, but there was only humor in his eyes.

"It will be at best an uneasy alliance, my lady."

Chapter 7

rrian waited by the fire, fearfully listening for the sound of Lord Warrick's footsteps. When he did come, she heard him pause at her door. She felt relief when he left and went to his own bedroom.

The clock struck midnight, and still Arrian waited. She would allow another hour to pass. By then surely everyone would be in bed, and she could make her escape.

She had dressed in a warm woolen gown and slipped into her riding boots. Scooping up her gloves and fur-lined cape, she slowly opened the door. The hallway was silent and dark. She picked up a single candle and moved quickly in the direction of her aunt's bedroom.

Lady Mary was clearly restless, and she moaned as Arrian approached her. Taking her hand, Arrian saw her aunt's eyes slowly open.

"Where have you been, child? I have been so worried about you."

Arrian wanted to throw herself into her aunt's arms and blurt out all her fears. But knowing how ill Lady Mary was, she dared not burden her. She would tell her as little as possible.

"Aunt Mary, I have decided I must go for help. We are not safe here."

"I blame myself for this," her aunt said. "If I hadn't been a stubborn old woman who was set on having her own way, none of this would have happened."

"Don't blame yourself. You are not to think of anything that will upset you. Just conserve your strength, and I'll be back for you."

Lady Mary's eyes widened with concern. "What has happened? Has that devil laid his hands on you?"

Arrian fought against the tears that swam in her eyes. "He is making demands that I cannot tolerate."

Lady Mary closed her eyes while she gathered her strength. When she looked at Arrian there was desperation in her gaze. "You must get away now—tonight!"

Arrian leaned forward and pressed her cheek to her aunt's. "I wish I didn't have to leave you."

Lady Mary's mind seemed to clear. "He will not harm me. It's you I'm worried about. Go—hurry!"

"I will attempt to make my way to the stables without being discovered."

"Is it still snowing?"

Arrian ran to the window. "No. The moon's out, and it's as bright as daylight." She did not mention to Aunt Mary that there were dark clouds gathering in the distance.

"It grieves me that you have been forced into this position." Lady Mary gave Arrian an encouraging smile. "You can make it safely away—you must."

They looked at each other in understanding. "I would rather freeze than give in to Lord Warrick's demands."

"Yes, dearest," Aunt Mary said, "it would be the lesser evil." She shook off her gloom. "But you are a fine horsewoman, and you'll make it. When you are mounted, take the road south. Have you money?"

"Yes."

"I curse this weakness that keeps me from going with you." Lady Mary tried to ignore the pain in her leg. "You must ride for Aberdeen. When you get there, go directly to the house of the Lord Mayor. He'll help you, because he's a friend of my father's."

"How far is it?"

"I can't be sure. Perhaps you will have to ride all night and most of the day. When you come to a village, buy a fresh mount. Keep going even if you are weary." Her words were urgent. "You must leave now."

"Don't despair, dearest aunt. I will get help and come back for you."

Lady Mary gripped Arrian's hand. "Don't come back. I will deal with Lord Warrick. You must go now. If you are lucky, they won't miss you until morning."

Arrian slipped her cape around her and put on her gloves. "Pray for me, Aunt Mary."

"I shall, child. Now leave while it's still dark. That will be your one advantage."

Arrian walked quickly to the door and turned back to her aunt. "I'm loath to leave you. It is the hardest thing I have had to do in my life."

"You are not leaving me, Arrian. I'm sending you away."

She went quietly out the door and closed it behind her.

Lady Mary lay staring at the fire and listening to the settling of the house. "God go with you, dearest child, and take you in His keeping."

Arrian quietly descended into the darkness of the entry-way, keeping well into the shadows. As she opened the front door it creaked on its hinges, and her heart stopped. Moments passed, and no one came to investigate, so she rushed outside, closing the door behind her.

Since Aunt Mary's bedroom faced the back of the castle, her view had been of the sea. Arrian was therefore not familiar with the grounds, and it took her a moment to locate the stable. She ran across the courtyard and down the snow-packed path. When she reached the stable, she stopped to catch her breath and turned back to make certain no one was following her.

She was grateful that the stable door swung open on well-oiled hinges. There was no light inside, so she paused long enough to allow her eyes to become accustomed to the dark.

Moonlight streamed through a window, helping her locate the stalls. She passed the first stall and stopped at the second, where she found a spirited animal that looked as though he could make the arduous journey.

In the shadow interior she found a saddle and threw it over the horse's back. It was a man's saddle, but what did that matter. Tightening the cinch under the horse's belly, she led him outside. The night was awash with moonlight glistening off the snow. She had hoped for darkness to aid in her escape, but the storm clouds still loomed against the distant horizon.

With resolve Arrian slipped her foot into the stirrup and climbed into the saddle. She urged the horse into a walk and moved along slowly until she topped a hill and rode down the other side. Then she kicked him in the flanks, and he shot forward.

Apparently she had chosen well, for the animal's long strides quickly took them away from the castle. When she topped another hill, she drew rein and looked back at Ironworth. The view took her by surprise, for it was a picture of beauty and tranquility. The gray castle dominated the landscape, and in the background she could see waves splashing on the shore. The whole scene was bathed in mystical white snow, making it appear illusory.

For Arrian this was the time of reckoning. Should she go back to face Lord Warrick and stay with her ailing aunt? Or should she ride on, seeking assistance? But her choice had been made. There was no turning back.

With the wind whipping at her cape and her cheeks stinging from the cold, she turned the horse southward. She prayed Lord Warrick would not pursue her and hoped she would not lose her way before she could find help.

Mrs. Haddington entered the dining room with a clatter of dishes. She slammed the platter down on the table and glared at Lord Warrick.

He glanced up at her and saw the look of displeasure on her face. "Go ahead, Haddy, speak your mind. We both know I'll not have my breakfast in peace until you have told me what's bothering you."

"Well, m'lord, if you're asking me if I approve of this marriage between you and the English girl, I'd have ta say not. I've looked after you since you were a wee bairn, and I say this is wrong."

"What would you say if I told you this English lady's grandfather was the chief of the MacIvors, Haddy?"

"Then I'd say it's double reason for you not ta marry her. Everyone knows the MacIvors have tainted blood and are children of the devil."

His lips curved into a smile. "Who is everyone, Haddy?"

"Everyone's folks hereabouts."

"I have heard that most MacIvors share the same view about Drummonds, Haddy."

"There'll never be a MacIvors, born or bred, that can stand up in a fair fight with a Drummond. They dinna ken the meaning of honor." She removed his plate from the silver server and slid it before him. "You've had little enough happiness in your life. I'd see you married to the right woman before I die."

Warrick watched her pour steaming tea into his cup. "I have come to believe that happiness for me is an elusive dream. What is happiness, Haddy? You can't hold it in your hand or taste it on your lips. I will find satisfaction in knowing I have wounded Ian MacIvors and deprived him of his happiness. You see, Haddy, this lady was to be his bride."

The housekeeper's face paled. "God help us—'tis more reason to send her on her way."

"I will marry her, Haddy."

Before she could reply Tam appeared in the doorway, his young face creased with worry. "M'lord, someone came right into th' stable last night and made off with Titus."

Warrick jumped to his feet. "Are you certain he didn't break out by himself?"

"His stall gate was closed, and he couldna' done it."

"How could this have happened?"

The young boy looked befuddled. "I don't know, m'lord. With me sleeping above the stable, you'd think I'd a' heard something."

Warrick hurried out of the room with Tam keeping pace with him. "Were there tracks we can follow?"

"If there were, the snow's covered them, 'cause it came a real blow late last night."

Warrick rushed out of the house and into the stable. His saddle was missing too. He looked around for some trace left by the horse thief. He bend down and traced a small muddy boot print with his finger. It's obvious our thief is a lad or—" His eyes narrowed with speculation. "Or—a woman!"

Warrick raced back to the house and up the stairs. He threw open the door to his sister's room and saw that the bed had not been disturbed. Then he hurried down the hallway to Lady Mary's room.

He rapped on her door and, not waiting for an answer, entered to find her ladyship awake as if she had been waiting for him.

She smiled at him with satisfaction. "Yes, Lord Warrick, my niece has escaped. She is an excellent horsewoman, and you can't overtake her. She's safe from you at last."

"My God, woman, do you know what she's done? It's snowing harder now than it was the night your coach overturned. She'll lose her way and freeze to death."

Tears rolled down Lady Mary's colorless cheeks. "You left her no choice."

"My lady, I would not have harmed the girl. But now she will surely die unless she's found."

Lady Mary searched his eyes and saw only concern there. "You made impossible demands on her, and she had to get away."

"With me, she would be alive and not buried in some snowbank."

Lady Mary held out her hand to him. "You must find her, my lord. It's my fault that she is not safely with our family at this moment. I will not have her death on my hands."

Warrick felt pity for the woman. It was clear that she loved the girl and was desperate in her concern. "I'll do what I can. Have you a notion of which direction she would have taken, my lady?"

Lady Mary hesitated for only a moment. "She will be traveling south toward Aberdeen."

She watched Lord Warrick leave, feeling like a foolish old woman and wondering how she would ever explain to Kassidy and Raile that she was responsible for their beloved daughter's death. Her good intentions had ended in disaster.

The howling of the wind was a reminder of nature's fury. Arrian urged her tired mount onward in the driving snow. At last the horse stopped, and no amount of urging could make the exhausted animal move.

Dismounting, she laid her face against the horse's sleek neck and cried bitter tears. The snow had covered the road, and she was lost. Surely they would both perish.

She led the horse behind a rocky projection where she hoped to find some shelter against the wind. Shivering and cold, she patted the magnificent animal that had aided her in her escape.

The storm that had hit just before morning had now

become a blinding blizzard, fierce and merciless. Since there was no sun to gauge the direction, Arrian could not even be certain that she had continued south as her aunt had instructed.

In total misery, she leaned against the horse, borrowing from his warmth and hoping to lend warmth to him at the same time. After a while her legs became numb with cold, and she sank to the ground, too weary to stand.

Arrian weakly raised her head to protest against fate. "Father, Mother, Michael, I'll never see you again," she cried. Her cry mingled with the howling sound of the wind and was lost. Now she would never know what it would be like to be Ian's wife, to have his children, to grow old with him.

With stiff fingers she pulled her cape around her and brought the hood over her head. Perhaps it was her destiny to die here in the land of the enemy.

The horse seemed only tired and not suffering from the cold. Arrian remembered her aunt explaining that the animals of the Highlands had thicker coats than those in England, to protect them from the harsher climate.

She was so weary, perhaps she would rest for only a short while and then continue her flight. Perhaps the storm would blow itself out and she would be able to find the road to Aberdeen.

Arrian didn't know how much time had passed when she awoke in bewilderment. She stood up slowly and cried out when she discovered that the horse had run away. Leaning her head against the boulder, she moaned in misery. Night was encroaching, and she would surely freeze. Even now her legs were so numb that she could hardly feel them as she slumped to the ground.

As time passed, Arrian realized her situation was desperate. She closed her eyes, knowing that sleep was about to claim her, perhaps a permanent sleep. She was freezing, her life was inching away, and she didn't even care. She only wanted to give herself over to the lethargic feeling that was enveloping her so she would feel no more pain. . . .

Mactavish grabbed Warrick's reins and yelled to be heard above the wind. "It's no use. We'll no find her in this. She must be frozen by now, unless she found someone to take her into their home."

Warrick wrenched his reins from Mactavish's hands. "I'll not stop. She's lost and alone and it's my fault. I'll find her."

On they pushed, with Tam riding just behind them. By late afternoon the wind had died down and the snow had stopped. Warrick was beginning to feel the futility of their mission. The girl must be dead by now. How could anyone who was unaccustomed to the Highlands survive in such a storm?

It was Tam who spotted Titus first. The tired horse limped toward them on his homeward trek. Warrick urged his mount forward and caught the reins. He bit back his anger at seeing the magnificent animal in such a state.

"Tam, take Titus back to the stable. MacTavish and I will continue to search for the girl. Titus's prints should lead us to her, if they're still visible."

Arrian awakened as she felt hands pulling at her, trying to make her stand against her will. She was floating in a shadowy world where she no longer felt the cold. "Leave me alone," she murmured.

Against her weak protest, she was lifted into strong arms and wrapped in a fur robe. Was she dreaming, or was she being carried on horseback?

She heard mumbling voices, but nothing they said mattered to her. She just wanted to sleep.

"Mactavish, ride back and inform Lady Mary that we found her niece. It will be better if I take her to the hunting lodge. In her condition, I don't think it's wise to make the long ride home. Assure her aunt that I'll bring her back tomorrow when she is well enough to travel."

Arrian snuggled against the hard body, reveling in the warmth. Then for a moment she opened her eyes and looked up at Lord Warrick in sudden fright. He tightened his arms around her and whispered in her ear, "Don't be frightened, my lady, you're safe now."

Warrick guided his horse down the familiar path, knowing he had to get to his lodge as soon as possible. The horse stumbled on a slippery incline and almost lost its footing, so Warrick had to slow his pace.

He held the girl close to him, feeling agony because he was responsible for her flight. He had pushed her too hard and too soon, and it must have terrified her.

The moon drifted out from behind a cloud and washed the countryside with its light. He glanced down at the sleeping girl. She was so lovely and helpless. A strange yearning came over Warrick—one he neither understood nor welcomed.

Out of the darkness he spotted the hunting lodge and nudged his horse to a faster pace. The girl had been exposed to the elements for hours. He had to get her inside.

She was so limp and pale, even now it might be too late to save her.

Chapter 8

arrick placed Arrian on the bed and piled woolen coverlets on her. After he had a roaring fire going he boiled some water and made tea, which he laced with sugar. He went to the girl and lifted her head.

"Here, drink this. It'll help warm you."

Arrian pushed the cup away, but he was insistent. Thinking to satisfy him so that he would leave her alone and let her sleep, she took a sip. Finding it to her liking, she drank more.

Her eyes fluttered open, and she saw Lord Warrick's face. "No," she groaned, "not you. I have to get away from you. Leave me alone."

"Not quite yet, my lady. I have to make certain you don't have frost bite. Your body is so cold, we have to warm you up slowly."

He pulled off the covers and removed her wet cloak.

"What are you doing?" she asked. "No, don't."

"You may not like what I must do, but it's for your own

good. You were near frozen. I must remove your wet clothing."

She had no more strength to fight him as he slipped her gown over her head and stripped her down to her underclothing.

When she protested weakly, he hushed her with a command, "Be still."

Arrian decided it took too much strength to fight him, so she gave in to his ministering hands.

Warrick wrapped her arms and legs in hot towels with practiced detachment. He paused when he saw the black and blue marks on her shoulders and back. She must have been hurt in the carriage accident. Why hadn't she informed Dr. Edmondson of her injuries?

At last he felt she'd had enough moist heat and wrapped her in a fleece blanket. He carried her over to the fire and sat down with her in his lap.

Arrian, dreaming that she was warm and protected, nestled into the comforting arms that held her. "Ian," she whispered. "Ian."

Warrick trembled with loathing at the sound of the hated name on her lips. He was more sure than ever that this young girl was the one person in all the world he could use to wound his enemies.

Long after Arrian had fallen asleep, he held her in his arms, staring into the fire. If she had come to harm, her death would have been on his soul for all eternity. She mystified him. Why hadn't she complained about her injuries from the carriage accident? Didn't most women like to be fussed over and treated like helpless adornments?

With a sigh, Arrian turned her face to rest against his chest, and he looked down at her. He caught his breath at the sight of her loveliness. She was like a delicate flower. There was an innocence about her and an untouched beauty.

His gaze went back to the fire. He did not want to examine the guilt he was beginning to feel.

But he could not keep his eyes from straying to her face.

Silken lashes lay against her creamy skin. He remembered well how those blue eyes could flame with indignation and anger—would he ever see them sparkle with happiness? He had never heard the sound of her laughter—would it be as musical as her speaking voice?

With angry resolve, he stood and carried her to the bed, where he laid her down and pulled the covers over her. Only when he was certain that she was sleeping peacefully did he go outside and unsaddle his horse. He led the animal to shelter and gave it water and oats.

When Warrick returned to the lodge, the girl was still sleeping. After standing over her a moment, he turned away. He could not allow pity to weaken his resolve. He still had a vendetta to settle with the MacIvors, and she was the perfect weapon to use against them.

Arrian snuggled into the warmth of the blankets, not knowing that her fate still lay with the brooding chief of Clan Drummond. She was dreaming that she was back at Ravenworth, safe in her own bed.

Arrian awoke feeling warm and rested. She burrowed her face into the pillow and relished the softness. Her mind was halfway between a dream world and reality, and she preferred the dream world.

Suddenly she became aware of the smell of food and realized she was hungry. Stretching her hands over her head, she sat up and looked around her in total confusion. Where was she?

It appeared that she was in a cabin built of rustic logs. Several stag and boar heads stared down at her from the walls.

Arrian heard someone outside the door stomping snow from his boots. When the door opened, she stared dumbfoundedly at Lord Warrick. She pulled the covers up and pushed her tumbled hair from her face.

"Why couldn't you let me die?"

Warrick dropped an armload of wood in the bin, ignoring her question. "I trust you're hungry."

She folded her arms across her chest. "No, I'm not. And you can't make me eat."

"Pity. I'm starved. Mactavish was here this morning and delivered a bounty of food from Haddy."

"Haddy?"

"To you she would be Mrs. Haddington. You see, she was once my nurse, so I call her Haddy."

"I can't fathom that you were ever a baby."

He smiled. "I'll wager you were your parents' little darling. I can see them parading you about for all to admire."

"I'll wager you caused your father and mother no end of trouble," she said.

Warrick smiled. "No doubt."

She watched him drop two fish into a hot pan, and soon a delicious aroma wafted through the room. Arrian tried to ignore the smell, but she was so hungry.

"Nothing like fresh salmon," he said. "I can taste it already."

Arrian watched out of the corner of her eye while he unloaded a basket of food. "Let's see . . . there's oatcakes, raspberry sauce, honey, cheese, and butter."

"I'm not interested."

He arched his brow at her. "No?"

"No," she stated emphatically.

"For someone who almost froze to death last night, you made a quick recovery. I'm glad to see your spirit is intact, even if your temperament is not."

She watched him remove his coat and toss it across a chair. On his face was the shadow of a beard. He had apparently not shaved. He seemed to fill the whole room with his presence, and she found herself wondering why he wasn't already married. He certainly was handsome.

"Where is this place?" she asked when the silence became heavy.

"My hunting lodge."

"Oh. My father has a hunting lodge. It has nine rooms."

His lips twitched, but he did not smile. "I can't think why anyone would need nine rooms in a hunting lodge."

"That's really quite small. Our country home at Ravenworth has over a hundred rooms," she said.

He speared one of the fish, turning it in the pan. "Are you trying to overwhelm me with your father's wealth?"

Arrian shook her head. "Not at all. I'm trying to make you understand that my father is a very important man. When the king goes hunting, he often comes to my father's lodge. He eats at our table and allows my father to call him William."

Warrick removed the fish from the fire and placed them on a plate. "I am impressed." He didn't sound as if he was.

"You don't understand. I don't want to impress you, my lord. I want you to know that you can't hold me against my will. My father won't allow it, and neither will the king. You can surely see this is futile."

"Do you prefer raspberry on your oatcakes, or honey?"

"I said, I'm not hungry," she told him in exasperation.

He paused. "Raspberry, I think."

She glared at him.

Warrick took his plate and sat in a chair near Arrian's bed. He stabbed a flaky chunk of fish and put it in his mouth, smiling at her. "Mmm . . . delicious."

She turned her face from him. "I suppose you disrobed me."

"I did."

"I don't think a proper gentleman would have been so bold, my lord."

"Perhaps a proper gentleman would have let you freeze. I'm beginning to wish I had. You can be most disagreeable, can't you?"

She wouldn't let him see that he'd hurt her feelings. "Not usually. Not until I met you. I have always been told that I had a good disposition. I believe that's no longer true."

"I can only judge by what I've observed."

"Perhaps I shall have just a bit of salmon, and honey, not raspberry, on an oatcake."

Without showing his triumph, he nodded. After spreading honey on an oatcake and placing fish on a plate, he handed it to her.

"Eat heartily, you'll need to regain your strength."

She looked at him again. "Do I smell tea?"

He laughed as he poured her a cup. "Indeed you do, my lady."

Arrian devoured the fish and swallowed the last crumb of oatcake. Sipping on the hot tea, she felt quite fit.

"What are you going to do with me?" she asked at last, hoping he would agree to let her go. "You can see, I'm nothing but trouble to you."

"You would be trouble to any man, my lady. It's a wonder you ever got anyone to agree to marry you."

"Apparently you had no hesitation in asking me to marry you," she said. "Of course, if you would like to reconsider . . ."

He stood at the window with his back to her. "My plans for you have not changed."

She came to her knees, clutching the blanket to her. "I don't want to be with you. Don't you understand? I love Ian. I want to be his wife. I will never help you hurt him. He loves me a great deal and must be out of his mind with worry by now."

Warrick turned to her. "I'm counting on that."

She wrapped the coverlet about her and moved across the cold stone floor to him. "Please let me go."

He scooped her up in his arms and carried her back to the bed, where he tucked the covers around her. "I'll not let you go, my lady. You may as well know that my mind is set on this marriage, and it will not change."

She caught his hand. "But it would not be a real marriage. Surely there must be another woman you would have for your wife."

"There was."

"Will she not object to me?"

"She is married to Jamie MacIvors."

Arrian was puzzled. She had paid little attention to her cousin Jamie, because he had been overshadowed by Ian. She remembered him as being surly and complaining.

"I can't think why any woman would prefer cousin Jamie to you. Jamie is not as handsome as . . ." Her voice trailed off. "How could Jamie have won a woman from you?"

"Are you sure you want to know, my lady? You may not like what you hear."

"I want to know."

"I wonder if you will recognize the truth when you hear it."

"I'll know if you speak the truth."

His expression seemed reflective. "Lady Helena was on her way to Glencarin to marry me when she was abducted."

"How horrible. Was it highwaymen?"

"Those who were witness to the kidnaping said Jamie MacIvors was one of the men."

Arrian shook her head. "I cannot think why he would do such a thing."

"But there is more, my lady. Jamie not only abducted her, he insisted that she marry him, which she did. I wonder if she resisted as vehemently as you have?"

"Is that why you—"

"She now carries within her body his child. Or perhaps she has delivered the child by now."

Arrian realized in that moment why Lord Warrick had such hatred for her family. "But surely you will not punish Ian for his brother's sins."

He swung around to face her. "Did I forget to mention that your Ian was among the kidnapers that day?"

"No. Ian could not commit such an atrocity."

Warrick moved to the bed and stood over her. "I thought you might not believe me."

Arrian shrank away from him. She refused to consider

his lies. He would say anything to make her think ill of the man she loved. "Ian would not abduct an innocent woman on the way to her wedding."

"Wouldn't he? I told you, my lady, that you might not believe me."

She looked into his eyes, which were glowing with discontentment. How had she become caught in this web of hatred?

"Will you ever let me go, my lord?"

"Perhaps when you carry the seed of my child within your body."

She gasped and scooted to the far side of the bed. "Never!"

"I told you before, the choice is still yours."

"It's done then. I'll agree to your plan." Her heart was beating wildly. "I don't believe you will ever allow me to leave."

He took her hand and stared at the ring on her finger. "I have no reason to keep you. After a time, when I have tired of the game, I will send you back to Ian."

"Perhaps he will not want me then. Perhaps you place too much importance on how he feels about me."

"You said yourself he loves you." He touched her hair. "How could he not?"

She shivered at his soft touch, and he let his hand drop away.

"I'll leave so you can dress. I believe you are strong enough to travel today." His eyes hardened. "But first I would ask a promise of you."

"What is it?"

"That you will never try anything as foolish as this again."

"I won't make that promise. You may be certain that I shall try every possible means of escaping from you."

He smiled. "So it's to be a contest of wills. It's been too long since I have been offered such a charming challenge, my lady."

Chapter 9

rrian reluctantly allowed Warrick to place her on his horse while he climbed on behind her. Her attempt to hold herself rigid so she wouldn't come in contact with his body only brought laughter to his lips.

The journey back to the castle took them past a frozen stream that twisted and meandered through the valley.

"My lord," she said, feeling ungracious, "your Highlands are cold, damp, and cheerless. They appear to be a barbaric country devoid of comforts."

Warrick halted his horse and glanced at the wide panorama, as if trying to see the land through her eyes.

"Have you been to the Highlands in the spring or in high summer, my lady?"

"No, this is my first time. I wish I had forgone the pleasure altogether."

"On my land there are majestic mountains, streams teeming with salmon and trout, and several mysterious lochs. There are valleys that in the summer are dotted with purple heather, and in high summer there are breathtaking crimson sunsets."

She glanced down at the hands that held the reins. They were strong hands, capable hands, and yet he had been gentle with her. Could a man be all bad when he had such a love for his land?

"The Highlands, my lady, is not an easy land. Our women are hearty and healthy, not puny and weak like Englishwomen."

"Hearty, perhaps, but I would not discount the strength of an Englishwoman."

Her hood had fallen back, and she tossed her hair into a silken swirl, which drew a look of admiration from Warrick. "I will allow that you might be the exception, but I would attribute your strength to the Scottish blood that runs in your veins."

She looked back at him with triumph in her eyes. "MacIvors blood, my lord."

He suddenly scowled and urged his horse forward. She was far too clever for his liking.

Lord Warrick was a complicated man, Arrian thought. One moment he was ruthless, and the next he could be gentle. If only she had never met him and become involved in his scheme.

She felt his breath tickle the back of her neck and jumped as if he had struck her. He was a man intent on having his own way, and for the moment he seemed to want her.

In the distance Arrian saw Ironworth Castle standing gray against the whiteness of the snow. To her it would be a prison from which she might never escape. But she would try—oh, yes, she would definitely try.

"You will soon grow accustomed to our climate," he told her, watching how the ermine lining of her hood lay softly against her cheek.

"I won't be here that long," she replied.

* * *

With a heavy heart Arrian climbed the stairs and went directly to her aunt's room. She was surprised to find Dr. Edmondson adjusting a bandage around her aunt's forehead, even though her aunt was asleep.

"How is she, doctor?" she asked.

"Her leg was giving her great pain, so I gave her a dose of tincture of opiate."

"I want very much to talk to her. Will she awaken soon?"

"She should sleep for two or three hours."

"I'm so worried about her. Do you think the delay in treatment will have damaged her leg?"

"I'm a country doctor, m'lady, and I can only tell you that your aunt's leg is not healing properly."

Arrian picked up Lady Mary's hand and held it to her cheek. "When can she be moved?"

Dr. Edmondson scratched his chin thoughtfully. "I believe she should be taken to Edinburgh as soon as possible. But I have no say in the matter."

"Could you impress upon his lordship the seriousness of my aunt's condition?"

"I have already done so. He says your aunt will leave tomorrow, weather permitting."

So Lord Warrick would keep his word and allow her aunt to go free if she complied with his wishes. Arrian saw no way out of her dilemma.

She became aware that the doctor was staring at her strangely. "I was surprised to hear that you'll be marrying him. Never thought I'd see the day when the blood of a MacIvors would again mingle with a Drummond, not after what happened to Lady Gwendolyn."

"If you are talking about the sham that will take place here tonight, I will never consider it a real marriage."

He looked taken aback. "You have not consented to the marriage?"

"Oh, I'll stand up with Lord Warrick and say what he demands of me, but I will not be his wife."

His weathered face creased in a smile. "Better look to the laws of Scotland, lass. You could be more married than you'll be wanting to be."

Her blue eyes snapped with anger. "Scottish laws do not apply to me—I'm an English citizen, Dr. Edmondson."

He walked out of the room, shaking his head. The lass must have overlooked the fact that Scotland was tied to England. Well, it was not for him to interfere in matters of the heart. Apparently his lordship knew what he was about.

Arrian walked to the window and threw it open. Ignoring the icy blast of wind, she stared at the churning sea. How bitterly she regretted the storm that had blown the *Nightingale* off course and landed her in this harsh land.

In just four weeks time, she was to have become Ian's wife. Now she would be forced to pretend marriage to a man she detested.

She shivered and closed the window, but not before a gust of wind blew out the candle, leaving the room in shadows.

Arrian picked up her shawl and pulled it around her shoulders, feeling as if she were being drawn into a dark abyss from which there was no escape. The time was approaching for the mock wedding, and she was frightened.

What would Ian think when he learned she had given in to Lord Warrick's demands? Surely he would understand that she would not willingly dishonor him.

Arrian could not find an appropriate gown among her trousseau, so she borrowed a plain black dress and a black veil from her aunt. She had trouble hooking the back, but at last she stood before a mirror and observed her appearance with satisfaction.

The stark black gown would show everyone how she felt about this wedding. She arranged the veil over her face, feeling pleased with her cleverness. Surely Lord Warrick would be displeased by her attire. He'd not have everything his way tonight. In a final defiant deed, she picked up her ruby betrothal ring and slipped it on her finger.

"Well, my girl," she told her own image, "you look more like a woman going into mourning than a bride." She smiled behind the veil. She would show that arrogant lord the contempt with which she viewed him.

There was a knock at the door, and she wrenched it open, expecting to find Lord Warrick. Instead Mrs. Haddington greeted her.

The housekeeper was clearly shocked by Arrian's appearance. "I'm ta take you to Lady Mary's room, m'lady." There was something cold and distant in the housekeeper's eyes that had not been there before.

"I'm ready, Mrs. Haddington," Arrian said, raising the veil and putting a brave foot forward.

As they walked down the hallway, the housekeeper spoke in a hurried whisper. "May I ask, m'lady, if you are truly related to Lord Gille MacIvors?"

"I am proud to be his great-granddaughter. My aunt Mary is his daughter."

The housekeeper sucked in her breath. "It would have been far better if you'd no ha come here. Nothing good has ere come from joining a Drummond to a MacIvors."

"I will not be joined to your chief—it's all playacting for Lord Warrick's benefit. He seems to derive some pleasure in demonstrating his hold over my aunt and me."

"I'm sure his lordship has his reasons."

By now they had reached Lady Mary's room, and Arrian rushed to her aunt. She had hoped to prepare her aunt for the ceremony earlier but had not found her awake. Lady Mary's eyes were still closed.

Barra looked at Arrian with the same coldness her mother had shown. "Her ladyship comes and goes. 'Tis the drug," she said.

Arrian was almost glad her aunt would not have to witness her humiliation. But she felt so alone in a hostile world. She touched her aunt's cheek, and the older woman's eyes fluttered open.

"Arrian, my dear, why are you dressed in my black gown? No one has died, have . . . they?" She tried to sit up but fell back. "We must . . . leave this . . . place."

"Aunt Mary, you see—"

Her aunt's eyes closed, and Arrian brushed a tear from her cheek. "Sleep, dearest," she whispered, "and don't weep for me. You will soon be safely away from this place."

There was a knock on the door, and Arrian's heart filled with dread. Pulling the black veil into place so he wouldn't see her face, she turned to see Lord Warrick enter with a gentleman she had not met.

Warrick approached her and smiled ironically. "Your manner of dress doth stab at my heart, my lady."

"It reflects my feelings of the moment, my lord."

Warrick turned to the tall man beside him. "May I present my most trusted friend, Mactavish. He, along with your aunt, Mrs. Haddington, and Barra, will witness our joining."

Was there a look of compassion in the older man's eyes, Arrian wondered? No, surely if he was a friend of this devil he would feel no pity for her plight. She acknowledged the introduction with the merest nod. Then a terrible suspicion came to her. "You are not an ordained minister are you?"

"No, m'lady. I'm no more than Lord Warrick's steward and friend," Mactavish said.

Arrian was glad her face was hidden behind the veil, because she knew her eyes would reflect the terror she was feeling. Her hands trembled so that she clasped them behind her back.

"I'd sooner see this evening's work come to a hasty end, my lord," she said. "Could we not go on with this ritual?"

Warrick bowed stiffly to her. "As you wish, my lady." He extended his hand to her, and she reluctantly placed hers in his grasp. Something within her rebelled against this heinous deception. But she was trapped and had no alternative but to see it through to the end.

Lord Warrick moved forward until he stood beside Arrian while the others in the room closed in around them.

"Lady Mary," Warrick said in a soft voice, "can you hear me?"

To Arrian's dismay her aunt opened her eyes. "I hear you, you Drummond devil." Her gaze fell on Arrian. "What has happened?"

"I only want you to hear a pledge between myself and your niece," Warrick said.

"Well, do it and be done with it," Lady Mary said sleepily.

Before Arrian could protest, Warrick reached out and removed Arrian's veil and tossed it on the floor. "I don't even know your Christian name," he said with a smile twisting his lips. "Amazing, is it not?"

She stared at the crumpled veil and then into his silver eyes. "Arrian—Arrian DeWinter."

Warrick suddenly became serious. "Lady Arrian DeWinter, I take you as my lawful wife."

Arrian suddenly felt like laughing. This was indeed not to be a proper wedding. She was almost lighthearted when she answered him. "Lord Warrick Glencarin, I take you as my lawful—"

"No, Arrian, no!" her aunt protested in a weak voice. "Do not speak it—"

"Say the words," Warrick insisted forcefully.

Arrian saw the fear in her aunt's eyes. She then looked to the housekeeper and her daughter and saw hostility reflected on their faces. She would have done with this nonsense as soon as possible.

"I take you as my husband," she answered through stiff lips. "And there's the end of it."

There was a gleam of victory in Warrick's eyes as he took her hand and quickly removed the MacIvors betrothal ring. Before Arrian could object, he slid the Drummond wedding ring in its place.

"You give me back my ring," she said. "Give it to me at once!"

Warrick turned to Mrs. Haddington. "I believe you can all leave now. The deed is done."

Without a word the three witnesses filed out the door, then Warrick turned back to Arrian. "Now, what were you saying? You want what?"

Arrian held out her hand. "I told you to return my ring."

"Nay, my lady. I'll not have it on your finger. It will be returned to Ian MacIvors."

"You are hateful," she cried, wanting to strike out at him. "I despise you for the villain you are."

"Tut tut, my lady wife," he said, "married such a short time and our first quarrel."

Lady Mary reached out to Arrian. "Do you know what you have done, child? The deed cannot so easily be undone."

"You need not be concerned, Aunt Mary. This will not be a real marriage. Lord Warrick demanded this imitation wedding to fuel his own arrogance."

"Arrian, Arrian, what will your father say?"

"But you don't understand, Aunt Mary. There was no minister to sanction the marriage, so it isn't legal."

"Oh, my poor, dear child. In Scotland you need no minister. You are bound to this man as surely as if you had been married with your parents' blessings and with all the trappings."

Arrian's face whitened, and she turned to the man who

was apparently her legal husband. "You tricked me! You let me believe—"

"I was never anything but honest with you, my lady. It was you who chose to ignore the importance of a Marriage by Consent."

Arrian looked at her aunt for help but saw the expression of finality on Lady Mary's face. "You are a beast, my lord, and I do not honor you."

Warrick shrugged. "I had so hoped marriage would calm you, my lady—apparently it has not."

Anger boiled inside her, but she had no retort. "You will still allow my aunt to leave in the morning?"

"What's this?" Aunt Mary asked. "What are you saying, Arrian?"

Warrick answered in a kind voice. "Your leg needs medical attention, Lady Mary. You will be sailing to Edinburgh tomorrow morning."

"I'll not leave without my niece. And there is no way I'll step foot on another ship. I'd rather walk."

"You have no choice in this, my lady. I will not be responsible for your losing a leg, and you are not well enough to travel by coach."

"Then Arrian must accompany me."

"No, Lady Mary, she will not." He thrust the ruby ring at her, and she clasped it in her hand. "You will deliver this into the hands of Ian MacIvors with my wife's regrets. Tell him she now wears the wedding ring of a Drummond—and is the first lady of Clan Drummond."

Lady Mary stared at the young chief for a long moment. He was most certainly a handsome rogue, but haughty and decidedly too sure of himself. "It seems I have no say in this matter," she said at last. "But there will be grave consequences from this deed. Arrian is not some little unknown. Her father wields more power than you can imagine. I beg you to allow her to accompany me. You have what you want. She is legally your wife."

"If the duke of Ravenworth is as powerful as you say, he could easily have the marriage annulled. No, Arrian will remain with me to prevent such an action."

Arrian would have spoken, but her aunt silenced her with a glance. "How long do you intend to keep her a prisoner in your castle?"

"She will not be a prisoner. But I shall keep her until it suits me to let her go."

"I will expect you to honor her and not lay a hand on her."

Warrick smiled at Lady Mary, liking her in spite of the fact that she was Gille MacIvors's daughter. "You have my word that she will have a separate bedroom from mine, and a door that locks."

"Locked doors only keep out those who want to stay out," Lady Mary stated.

"I will not intrude on your niece. In marrying me, she has given me what I want from her."

Lady Mary stared into gray eyes and found herself believing him. "I'll hold you to that."

"Your niece will be safe from me, my lady—but who will save me from her?" He smiled at Arrian, who only glared at him. "I have found her to have a fierce temper, and she has demanding ways."

Lady Mary reached for Arrian's hand. "If that is so, you are the first person to evoke those distasteful emotions in her. Her temper was always sweet and her nature loving."

"It will be blood hate between us, my lord," Arrian said. "We are locked in a contest of the strongest."

His silver eyes looked cruel. "Your understanding is exceptional, my lady wife." He bowed slightly to Lady Mary and then to Arrian. "I'll bid you both good night. I know you'll have much to talk about since you are departing in the morning, Lady Mary."

After he'd left, Arrian could not stop the tears from

falling down her cheeks. She could not imagine what life would be like after her aunt was gone.

This world was cold and unbearable, a hostile place where she had no friends.

Chapter 10

rrian stood silently, battling the conflicting emotions that ran through her mind. She wanted to rage at the man who had tricked her into marriage and had taken away her future with Ian. She so desperately wanted to leave with her aunt, but that would not be possible.

Trying to disguise her sadness, she turned to Lady Mary. "You're so pale. I fear this evening has been a strain on you. Shall I get your medicine?"

"That would be nice, child," Lady Mary said, wanting to be lost in forgetfulness. "I find the pain is almost more than I can endure."

Arrian picked up the vial and poured the liquid into a spoon. "I will be glad to have you in Edinburgh where you can receive proper care."

Lady Mary took the medicine and then caught Arrian's hand. "You did this for me, didn't you?"

Arrian avoided her aunt's eyes, hoping she could hide the truth from her. "Why would you think that?"

"Because it's my leg that's damaged, Arrian, not my mind.

You came to Scotland to marry Ian and would never have agreed to marry a man you hardly know unless there was a good reason. I heard the exchange between you and Lord Warrick. You didn't marry him out of love. You only agreed to this marriage because I need medical attention."

"I never thought the marriage would be binding. I believed it was only a way to try to humble me and humiliate Ian."

"It is most certainly binding, Arrian."

"I know that now." She plumped up her aunt's pillows and tried not to cry. "I can only imagine what my parents will say when they hear what I've done."

"Dear child, why didn't you come to me before you agreed to go through with the wedding? I could have warned you."

"You were ill, Aunt Mary. I made the decision on my own, and I'm prepared to live with the consequences."

"I don't know how I will explain this to your mother and father. I fear there will be a terrible backlash. Raile will come thundering in here with a vengeance, you know he will."

"Aunt Mary, that's exactly what Father should not do. You must try to keep this from him as long as possible. Meanwhile, I shall try to escape, or perhaps Lord Warrick will release me. I don't want anyone to be hurt."

"If your father is in Scotland, no one will be able to stop him from coming to Ironworth." Lady Mary's eyes grew sad. "I don't know how this will all end, but there's bound to be much sorrow. I can't endure to leave you, Arrian."

"You heard Lord Warrick, he won't allow me to go with you—and you must go."

Lady Mary held out the ring she had clutched in her hand. "I can't think what Ian will do when I give this to him."

Arrian was tempted to take back Ian's ring, but she no longer felt that it belonged to her. "I pray he will not turn away from me because of what I've done."

The drug was already beginning to take effect, and Lady Mary was becoming drowsy. "The blame lies with Warrick and Ian, this is their fight. You have innocently become entangled in their feud."

"But I still love Ian and want to be his wife. Impress upon him that I will come to him as soon as I'm able."

"I will do that. But have a care, Arrian. Don't provoke this man, and don't forget for a moment that he is the enemy."

"I shan't forget that."

"I curse this weakness that prevents me from helping you. In days gone by, no young upstart would have gained the upper hand with me."

"Don't think about that, just go to sleep now. But try to send word of how you are doing, for I shall be worried until I know you are well."

"I will write." Lady Mary said, her mind growing unclear. "I find I am very sleepy now. You must rest also."

Arrian watched her aunt drift off to sleep. She would remain with her tonight. There was no way of knowing when they would meet again. She touched a white curl that lay against her aunt's cheek, praying that the doctors in Edinburgh would save her leg.

She went to the hearth to place wood on the fire and drew up a chair. She was so lonely, a tear trailed down her cheek. She had often dreamed of her wedding night, but Ian had always been the man in those dreams, not his enemy.

Warrick slid his booted foot into the stirrup and mounted Titus. He needed to put distance between himself and his new bride. Guilt lay heavily on his shoulders, but given the same choice again, he would have behaved no differently.

He headed Titus down the rutted bridle path on his way to the hunting lodge. Victory was his! He had struck at the heart of Ian MacIvors. But where was the feeling of elation he had expected? Was Mactavish right about him—was he no better than a MacIvors in forcing a woman into marriage against her will?

He halted his horse and turned back to the castle, which was barely visible under the cloudy sky. The act he had committed was vile and unworthy of the chief of Clan Drummond.

He nudged Titus forward, unmindful of the cold wind. Lady Arrian had conveniently fallen into his hands. What he would do with her, he did not know. But he would not free her until he was ready.

The moon shed its light on the solitary rider. There was torment in his eyes and heaviness in his heart. He could not forget the vision of tears in Lady Arrian's eyes. He had caused her a great deal of pain, and for that he was sorry. He had nothing against her—she had merely been useful to him.

When he reached the lodge he was surprised to find lights shining from the windows. Dismounting, he saw Mactavish standing in the doorway.

"Thought you'd be here, so I came ahead of you to lay a fire." Mactavish picked up a bottle of whiskey and poured a liberal amount into two goblets. "Thought you might also need a good friend and a strong drink."

"You know me too well, my friend," Warrick said, throwing off his coat and taking the offered glass. "Let's celebrate. I want to drink myself into oblivion so that I won't think about blue eyes swimming in tears."

Mactavish raised his glass in a toast. "To the new Lady of Glencarin. May she not live to regret this night, or you either, m'lord."

Warrick's expression hardened. "I thought you came as a friend, not as my accuser."

Mactavish downed his drink, and poured another. "So I did."

Warrick took a deep drink of the burning liquid. "To my bride," he said raising his glass. "May she and God forgive me."

Lady Mary tied a silk scarf around her head turban style. She fumbled through her jewels until she found a huge sapphire brooch, which she pinned to the middle of the turban.

"Just because one is ill doesn't mean that one should neglect one's appearance." Holding the hand mirror, she nodded in satisfaction. "Exotic, don't you think, Arrian?"

Her aunt was dressed in a white brocade gown with black velvet on the collar. "You look elegant as always. Does your leg pain you overmuch?"

"I could tell you it didn't, but in truth it never stops throbbing."

Arrian bent and kissed her aunt on the cheek and then slid her arms around her neck. "I shall miss you desperately, but I'll take comfort in knowing that you will have the best of care."

Lady Mary dabbed at the tears in her eyes. She had always taken pride in her strength of character, and crying was not in her nature. She knew that Arrian was putting on a brave face, so she could do no less.

"Highlanders like Lord Warrick are driven by stubborn pride, Arrian. I would beseech him to let you accompany me, but we both know it would do no good."

Arrian's jaw set in a stubborn line. "We shan't beg him for anything, Aunt Mary."

Lady Mary tried to find something hopeful to say. "I have learned from the housekeeper that my nephew Jamie kidnaped Lord Warrick's bride. Perhaps now his lordship will feel that his honor has been satisfied, and release you."

"Do you really believe Jamie is capable of such a deed?"

"I'd believe anything of Jamie."

"And Ian—do you think he was involved?"

Lady Mary saw the uncertainty in Arrian's eyes. "Has he been accused?"

"Y—es."

"I don't know if I can answer that, Arrian. But I'll find out."

Arrian placed her aunt's jewelry chest in a trunk and closed the lid, snapping it shut. "I'll never believe Ian capable of dishonor," she said.

There was a knock on the door and Mrs. Haddington entered. "It's time for your medicine, m'lady. Otherwise you'll not be bearing the pain when they take you to the ship."

Lady Mary took the offered medicine. "I'd never thought to find myself aboard a ship again. After this, I travel only by land."

Warrick appeared at the door. "If you will allow it, I will carry you downstairs, Lady Mary."

"Little say I have in the matter, I'm sure," Lady Mary said, resigned to her fate.

"I want to accompany my aunt as far as the ship," Arrian said, pulling on her leather gloves.

Warrick lifted Lady Mary gently in his arms. "I had anticipated that."

Lady Mary moaned in pain, and she was surprised to see Lord Warrick's silver eyes fill with compassion. "I'll be as careful as I can, my lady. Your ordeal will soon be at an end."

"What is the condition of the sea?" Lady Mary asked with concern.

"I am told by the captain that you should have smooth sailing all the way to Edinburgh."

"That's a blessing, anyway."

"If you will allow it, Barra has agreed to travel with you and remain until she is no longer needed," Warrick told her.

"It seems you have thought of everything, my lord."

By now they had reached the carriage, and Warrick

placed Arrian's aunt gently inside and pulled a woolen robe over her legs. When he would have left, she clasped his hand.

"Tell me, Lord Warrick, would you have allowed my niece to leave if she had not consented to the marriage?"

He smiled. "We shall never know the answer to that, shall we?"

"Be good to her. This is her first time away from those who love her. Arrian is a rare jewel. Treat her as such."

There was sudden anger in his eyes. "I don't harm women, Lady Mary. I'll leave that to your nephews."

Arrian came down the steps, carrying her aunt's medicine, and Warrick helped her into the carriage beside Lady Mary.

The coach pulled away with Mactavish in the driver's seat, while Warrick, mounted on Titus, rode beside them. Arrian and her aunt were silent, partly because Barra accompanied them and partly because their emotions ran too deep to express in words.

Too quickly it was time to say good-bye. With a hurried hug, Arrian watched Warrick place her aunt in the longboat that would transport her to the waiting ship.

Arrian refused to cry as the small craft moved out to sea. Warrick stood beside her, but she refused to acknowledge him. In the distance her aunt was being helped onto the ship, and Arrian held her breath, knowing the pain Aunt Mary must be feeling.

"I pray the doctors in Edinburgh will be able to heal her."

"As do I, Arrian. I found much to admire in Lady Mary."

"I'm sure she does not return your feelings."

He laughed. "Nor would I, were I in her place."

After Arrian watched the anchor rising out of the sea, she returned to the coach. "I am ready now, my lord."

Warrick had expected, at the last moment, that Arrian would beg to go with her aunt. But she had not. He was discovering a strength in her he had not expected in one so pampered. Arrian would continue to fight him, and she would be a worthy adversary, but he would not want to see her wonderful spirit crushed.

He helped her inside the coach and noticed the circles under her eyes. She must not have slept the night before.

"Arrian, would you like me to ride in the coach with you?"

"No, my lord. I prefer my own company." Even while her lips trembled with the effort she was making not to cry, her eyes defied him.

Arrian was so bored, she wandered through the castle, inspecting the unoccupied rooms. Most of them were dusty and neglected, but the furnishings must have been grand at one time.

She was elated when she discovered steps leading to the battlements. Quickly she climbed to the top and stood with the wind in her hair, awed by the magnificent view of the valley. She watched as a brilliant sunset reflected against the iron gray mountains in the distance.

Suddenly she was overcome with a loneliness so intense, she cried out, "Mother, help me."

Arrian heard someone come up behind her and thought it might be Warrick. She turned to do battle with him, but her anger faded when Mactavish appeared.

"I was in the courtyard below and saw you, m'lady. I brought your cloak, thinking you might be cold."

She allowed him to place the cloak around her shoulders and was glad for its warmth. "Thank you for your thoughtfulness."

"It was my pleasure."

"This is a harsh country, isn't it, Mr. Mactavish?"

"Aye, that it is. You already know about the hazardous winters. But you will presently be surprised with the arrival of spring."

There was misery in the depths of her blue eyes. "Do you think I'll be here that long?"

He lowered his gaze. "It's not for me to say."

She knew he was blameless in her situation. "Mr. Mactavish, was it you who brought me to the castle that night the carriage overturned?"

"Aye, m'lady. You rode upon my horse."

Deep in thought, she leaned her elbows against the containing wall and glanced at the courtyard below. "Why do you suppose the Highlanders and the Lowlanders don't get along—or for that matter the Scottish and the English?"

"There are many reasons. Speaking of the Highlanders and Lowlanders, anytime you put two Scots together they'll argue on the amount of salt to put in their porridge. As for the English, we Scots object to their lacing their porridge with sugar, or for that matter, breathing air."

She turned to him and couldn't help smiling. "There's more to it than that, Mr. Mactavish, and you know it."

"My name's just Mactavish, m'lady. And aye, it's more than that. I always liken our alliance with England as living next door to a giant—when the giant takes a step, the rumble can be felt from Highland to Lowland."

"I've learned some of the reasons the MacIvors and the Drummonds fight. If only they could come to an agreement. They are all Scots."

"The trouble goes back many years, and it isn't up to me to tell you all the reasons. You may want to ask him," Mactavish said, referring to Warrick.

"I have always been proud of that part of me that was Scottish. My mother instilled that pride in me. Now I don't know how I feel."

A gust of icy wind struck, and Arrian shivered.

"We should go in, m'lady. The weather grows bitter with the setting sun."

She nodded and entered the castle while he held the door for her. "His lordship was wondering if you would like to take dinner with him tonight."

"So he sent you to ask me?"

Mactavish smiled. "I believe he is a little afraid of you, m'lady."

She returned his smile. "What? He, a big man, and I, a wee lass. Whatever can he be thinking?"

"I canna guess."

"You may tell his lordship I shall take dinner with him tonight. But it is not to become a habit."

Mactavish grinned at her. "I'll be glad to relay both messages."

She laid her hand on his. "Thank you for being so kind to me, Mactavish."

"Haddy and Barra have not been unkind to you, have they?"

"I understand their resentment, but I also think it should be aimed at Lord Warrick and not at me. I didn't ask to stay here."

"I'll speak to them."

"No. Please don't. It will only make matters worse." Her eyes danced. "I have found at least one friend in the enemy camp."

"I hope you will always feel that I am your friend, m'lady."

Chapter 11

t took Arrian a long time to dress because she was accustomed to her maid performing that task. She wore a sapphire blue velvet gown with long puffed sleeves. Her shoulders were bare, and she wore no jewelry, no adornment. Because the castle was drafty, she pulled her white cashmere shawl over her shoulders. Her hair, she braided and wrapped around her head, securing it with a golden comb.

When she entered the dining room, Warrick came to his feet, his eyes filled with admiration. With a smile, he held a chair for her.

"I was not certain you would come."

"I never break my word. If I'm here long enough, you'll learn that about me, my lord."

His gaze moved over her creamy neck and the swell of her breasts that were just visible from the cut of the gown. "You are lovely." He had not intended to compliment her, but the words were spoken before he realized what he'd said.

"It would be the gown, my lord. My mother has impeccable taste in clothing." Her voice became icy. "The gown is part of my trousseau. It was intended for Ian's eyes, not yours."

He made no reply but merely sat down at the head of the table and unfolded his napkin, placing it across his lap. "You will feast tonight. Cook has prepared her best."

Arrian looked around the large formal dinning room. Mrs. Haddington certainly set a splendid table. The silver gleamed beneath a crystal chandelier. The lace tablecloth must have been very old and precious, and Arrian was certain it was only brought out on special occasions. The china was gold rimmed and engraved with a golden *G* for Glencarin. Since the table was so long, Arrian had been placed at Warrick's right.

Arrian had never seen Warrick in formal dress. His powder blue coat fit snugly across his broad shoulders. The white ruffle of his shirtsleeve fell across his tanned hands. She raised her eyes to his face and thought how proud and aristocratic he looked. He would be a sensation in London. The young ladies of nobility would compete for his attention.

"I admire your china, my lord, it is rather beautiful."

"Although I cannot be certain, I believe I once heard it was a gift to my great-grandmother from her family when she married my grandfather."

"I wonder if you have heard of Ravenworth China. It is world famous," she said. "After the war with France, our villagers were having a difficult time, so my mother helped them market their china. Today, even the Czar of Russia has on occasion dined on Ravenworth China."

"Your mother must be a most remarkable woman."

Arrian warmed to his praise of her mother. "I would challenge you to find anyone more beautiful. There are many who have benefited from her kindness."

"It would seem beauty runs in the DeWinter family."

Arrian didn't want Warrick to think she was seeking compliments, so she turned her attention to the meal.

Dipping her spoon into the cock-a-leekie soup, Arrian took a bite of tender capon.

Warrick shrewdly questioned her so that he could learn more about her. "Your life has been happy, hasn't it?"

"I've never known sorrow except the day Uncle George died. He was Aunt Mary's husband, and I adored him. He was a man of great power in the House of Commons."

"Have you any brothers or sisters?"

"I have a younger brother, Michael. He's my best friend, and I miss him desperately."

"And your father—what about him?"

Her face brightened and her eyes glowed. "Father is the most exceptional of all. Aunt Mary told me that until my mother married him, my father was considered the best catch in England."

"So you have the perfect family."

She glanced at him quickly to see if he was being sarcastic, but there was only genuine interest in his eyes. "I believe my family has faults as any family does, but they are honorable and trustworthy. If my father tells you something, it will be the truth."

She fell silent, but already his curiosity was piqued. "I would hear more about your family."

"Everyone loves my mother. As for Michael, I very much admire him."

"I suppose you live most of the year in London, attending parties and galas?"

She wrinkled her nose. "None of my family is fond of London. We prefer to live a simple life in the country. Aunt Mary is the exception. She thrives on London society."

"So you live simply, in a hundred-room castle."

She searched his eyes. "Do you mock me?"

"Not at all. I'm merely trying to draw a picture of your life." A sudden thought occurred to him. "I suppose Ian MacIvors was offered a handsome dowry as your future husband."

Arrian's eyes clouded, and she pushed her soup aside. "I suppose. I don't know the details. I hope you don't think the dowry will be coming to you."

He pressed his lips together in a thin line. "No. I would not touch your father's money. I was only wondering if Ian had yet received the dowry."

"My father did not tell me about the arrangement between them." She leaned closer to him. "When will you allow me to leave, my lord? I don't belong here."

He stared into her blue eyes, made bluer by the color of her gown. "I wonder, had we met under different circumstances, if we might have been friends?"

"We will never know. In truth, my lord, I might have liked you, but I believe you would always have despised the MacIvors blood in me."

"I can assure you that I don't despise you, my lady. Quite the contrary. Do you think me so base that my only feelings revolve around hate and revenge?"

"I have only seen the side of you that hates. I would not know if you are capable of love—nor do I wish to find out."

Mrs. Haddington came in to remove the soup bowls, and Arrian and Warrick fell silent while she served the main course and then withdrew.

"Arrian, suppose you and I declare a truce. I see no reason why we should quarrel."

"I have many reasons to take exception to you, and as for a truce between us, it would depend upon what it was based."

"Suppose we become nothing more than friends. We will spend time together, get to know each other. I'll show you Glencarin as you have never seen it. Would you agree to that?"

"What would I gain from this friendship?"

"Eventually, your freedom."

"When would I have my freedom?"

He took her hand and was surprised when she did not

pull away. "I have not yet decided, but until I do, it would be more pleasant if we were cordial."

Arrian thought of the long hours of loneliness that stretched before her. He could be pleasant when he wanted to. "You would expect nothing more than friendship?"

"You have my word. I have no wish to fight with you, Arrian. I don't want your memories of Glencarin to be unhappy."

"How could they be otherwise? I cannot forget that you disrupted my life and made me marry you. I only want to be with Ian, and I probably never can be. . . ."

"We both know that marriages can be annulled, Arrian. If you stay with me willingly until I decide to let you go, I will give you your freedom."

"Out of spite you might decide to keep me until I am old."

He laughed. "I can assure you that I shall release you before high August."

"Then I would be free to marry Ian?"

"You would be free to do as you will."

"You are a puzzlement to me, my lord. On the one hand you can be kind, and then suddenly change and become demanding and threatening. If I didn't know better, I'd think you were two different men."

"Perhaps when you come to know me better, the puzzle will be solved."

"If I do as you say, I'll soon be free to go to my great-grandfather?"

"You will." He glanced down at her hand and noticed her finger was bare. "I see you don't wear my ring."

"I don't feel as if it belongs to me. I only wait for the time when I shall have Ian's ring back on my finger."

He sat back in his chair, observing her quietly. When he spoke, it was on a different subject. "Do you like to hawk?"

"Indeed I do. But I will not fox hunt. To me, hawking is sporting, but when several dozen men with twice as many hounds ride after one little fox, I see no sport in that." She cut into a piece of veal and savored the delicate taste. "It occurs to me, my lord—"

"If we are to be friends, you should call me Warrick."

"Very well. But it seems to me, Warrick, that you know a great deal about me, while I know little of your life. It's only fair that I ask you questions and that you answer them as honestly as I have answered you."

His face was transformed by a smile. "I yield to your curiosity. Ask what you will."

Mrs. Haddington served the tea and a lemon tart while Arrian and Warrick talked. "You never mention your mother, Warrick."

"She died when I was seven."

"Someone taught you manners."

He stared at her for a moment. "You assume that all Highlanders are savages."

"I had heard that," she replied with candor. "But you prove that assumption false."

He chose not to become embroiled in an argument about the Highlands and the Lowlands. "I have happy memories of my mother. As I recall, my sister looked very much like her. There is a portrait of her in the east wing. I'll show it to you one day."

"I know your sister died. Were there no other sisters or brothers?"

"No, there were only the two of us."

Arrian took a sip of tea and laid her napkin on the table. "Were you close to your father?"

Warrick rose and pulled back her chair. "Shall we retire to the salon where we can continue our conversation, Arrian?"

She placed her hand on his proffered arm and allowed him to lead her forward, but she watched him out of the corner of her eye, not quite ready to trust him.

A fire burned brightly in the hearth, and soft candlelight

disguised the shabbiness of the salon. There were beautiful and valuable masterpieces on the walls, but the castle had been allowed to fall into disrepair.

Arrian sat beside Warrick on the settee, with her hands folded in her lap.

"Where were we?" he asked, crossing his long legs and resting a hand on his polished boot.

"I had asked about your father."

"My father was a hard man, Arrian, not at all the way you describe your father. He forced my sister to marry Gavin MacIvors against her wishes. Being a proud man, he insisted that she not be shamed by going to the MacIvors without a large dowry. To obtain the funds he sold herds of cattle and flocks of sheep. He took all the money we had and presented it to Gavin MacIvors."

Warrick looked up at a portrait hanging on the wall. "We were fortunate that the estate was entailed, or my father might have stripped Ironworth of its treasures."

She suddenly felt sad for him. "How terrible for you."

"Not for me. For my sister, Gwendolyn. She was young, like you, at the time of her marriage and very frightened of Gavin MacIvors."

"Gavin was Ian's father."

"Yes, and at that time he was your grandfather's heir."

"As Ian is now?"

"That's right. Had my sister and Gavin MacIvors been well suited, and had she found love with him, how different my life might have been." His eyes touched upon her golden head. "Think about it, Arrian, perhaps we would have met one summer at your grandfather's castle and become . . . friends."

"Are you certain your sister died on her wedding night?"

"Yes, quite sure. I attended the wedding and I also witnessed the cruelty inflicted on her by your cousin, Gavin."

"You must have been young then."

"Not so young that I didn't know what was happening.

My sister pleaded with me to help her. Mactavish told me later that it was Ian MacIvors who struck me from behind when I went to her aid."

"I can't believe Ian would do that unless he thought his father was in danger."

"His father was in danger—yes, I suppose he was. I would have killed him that night if I could have got my hands on him. If I had, Gwendolyn would be alive."

Arrian didn't want to believe him, but somehow she sensed that he was telling the truth. "What happened then?"

"I knew nothing until the next morning. When I went to see my sister, I was informed that she was dead. It was said she threw herself down the stairs to save herself from Gavin MacIvors. I don't know if we will ever know the real truth of what happened. But even now it haunts me."

"It isn't inconceivable that a young woman could be so distraught from an unwanted marriage that she would throw herself down the stairs. Not if she loved another, as I love Ian. I can only imagine your sister's despair."

Warrick fell silent. It was clear that he didn't like the comparison she had just pointed out to him. His voice was cold when he spoke. "Perhaps you are weary and wish to retire now."

She rose, convinced she had driven her plight home to him by using the love he had for sister. "I will wish you a good night, my lord."

He watched her sweep from the room, knowing he had lost a battle. She was young but clever. She was a wife to be proud of, but she didn't really belong to him. At every opportunity, she reminded him that she belonged to Ian MacIvors.

While Arrian dressed for bed she thought of the young girl whose room she occupied. They had much in common.

Poor Gwendolyn, so frightened and alone. Arrian vowed to discover the truth about her death one day.

Warrick was in a dark, brooding mood when he went to his bedchamber. He did not like to be compared to the MacIvors, and yet, was not his sin worse? At least his sister had been given in marriage by her father. But what about Lady Helena—surely she had been forced to marry against her will? No, he had been right to marry Arrian. He would soon see his honor satisfied.

He removed his shirt and draped it over a chair. He sensed that Arrian had begun to trust him tonight. Perhaps he would woo her, make her fall in love with him. It would be easy enough—she was innocent and ripe for a man's touch.

He closed his eyes, remembering the sweetness of her smile. He had promised not to touch her, but he had not promised he wouldn't try to win her affections.

Pain ripped through his heart as he remembered his sister's face as she called out to him for help.

The muscles in his jaw tightened. He would make Arrian beg for his touch. He would use her and then send her back to Ian MacIvors.

Chapter 12

On reaching the harbor, the *Nightingale* had been met by a messenger bearing news that Lady Mary's was in Edinburgh. Kassidy stood by her aunt's bed now, shaking with anger, unable to believe what she was hearing.

"And you say this Lord Warrick forced my daughter to marry him against her will?"

"It was not done at sword point, but he forced her all the same. Handsome devil that he is, he could have any woman he wanted—but he wanted Arrian for revenge."

Kassidy felt as if her heart would break, and there was desperation in her voice. "I felt something was wrong. I must go to her at once. Do you think he has done her harm?"

"I have no fear for her, Kassidy. For all he has done, I believe he has a strong code of honor. No, he will not harm her. And I have to say, if what I heard at Ironworth is true, the young chief had reason for bitterness. He was not treated well by our family."

"I don't care about him, Aunt Mary. I only want to see Arrian and know she's safe. She must be so frightened."

"You would have been proud of the way she conducted herself."

"I must get to her as soon as possible."

"I fear you'll not be allowed in, dearest. The castle is surrounded by Drummonds. You have heard stories of how they protect their own, and I believe it to be true."

"But she's alone and friendless."

"I know. Yesterday I tried to convince Tuttle to go to Ironworth, but the poor woman became so distraught, I had to give her coach fare back to England."

Kassidy rubbed her hands together in thoughtfulness. "I wonder. Your leg is healing nicely and I'm told grandfather will be sending a coach for you, so you don't need me as much as Arrian does."

"What are you thinking?" Aunt Mary asked suspiciously.

Kassidy dipped into a curtsy and imitated a Cockney accent. "M'lady'll be wanting her own maid with her, to be sure. I don't think his lordship'll deny her that small comfort."

Lady Mary shook her head. "No, Kassidy, you wouldn't. I have enough to explain to Raile when he arrives, without having to tell him you also fell into Lord Warrick's hands."

"What concern would I be to Lord Warrick, ducks? I'm just a 'umble serving wench, Tuttle by name. I only live ta do my mistress's bidding, and see ta her wants."

"Lord save me from the DeWinter women. It must be the English side of your blood that makes you behave so rashly. Don't do this, Kassidy."

Kassidy leaned over and kissed her aunt. "Don't fuss, dearest. I'm going after my daughter and I'll not come back without her."

Lady Mary knew there would be no stopping Kassidy. "Lord help the poor man with both of you making his life miserable. He'll get what he deserves."

"I hope Raile doesn't leave London before I have Arrian

out of there. It would mean disaster. If he arrives too soon, I'll depend on you to tell him anything but the truth, Aunt Mary. I don't want my husband to become embroiled in a war if I can get Arrian out without him."

"You and Lord Warrick are a matched pair," Lady Mary said. "There'll be the devil to pay over this."

Kassidy plumped her aunt's pillow. "You're right about that. If that man's harmed my daughter, he'll rue the day."

Aunt Mary frowned. "Indeed he will. But you should wait for Raile."

"Let's keep Raile out of this if we can, Aunt Mary. I can deal with that young man."

Lady Mary knew when she was defeated. "I'm sure you can, Kassidy. I'd give half a year of my life to be there when you take the earl of Glencarin to task."

Arrian rushed down the stairs with a light heart. She would be free of this dismal room, if only for a few hours. Warrick had invited her to go riding.

When she reached the stable she found Warrick already mounted, and the stable boy led her horse forward.

"I see you located a sidesaddle," she said, pleased.

"It was my sister's and hasn't been used in years. Tam worked on it into the night so it would be ready for you this morning."

She smiled at the redheaded, freckle-faced lad. "Thank you, Tam. It was most thoughtful of you."

"It wasn't nothing, m'lady." He led the horse to the mounting block and helped her onto the sidesaddle.

She straightened her jaunty little hat and nodded at Warrick. "I'll race you up the hill."

A bright sun was shining, and a warm wind touched her cheeks. They rode for several moments before Warrick reined in his horse. "I wanted you to see this view. As a boy I would spend hours staring out at the North Sea, wondering what was on the other side of the waters' end." His eyes softened as they fell on her. "How could I have known that the sea would one day bring you to me?"

Arrian turned her face from him and looked at the beautiful spectacle. They were atop a hill where she could see the mountains to the east and the sea to the west. In the far distance she saw the spine of even larger mountains. Their valleys dipped into streams that were full to their banks with melting runoff. Her eyes followed one stream on its path to the sea. Although it was not in her view, she could hear the thundering sound of a waterfall.

Warrick pointed to her left, toward a village where the soft snow powdered the cobbles. Even though most of the ground was covered with a thin layer of snow, there were patches of green peeping through where the sun shone.

Arrian reached over her head, broke an icicle off the branch of a tree, and held the point out to Warrick.

"En guarde, Drummond," she said. "Face your fate at the hands of a DeWinter."

He watched her take a bite of the icicle, then threw back his head and laughed. "I surrender. I have known from the start that I was no match for you."

He dismounted and held his arms up to her. "Arrian, to be precise, you are no longer a DeWinter, you are Lady Arrian Glencarin of Clan Drummond."

She wrinkled her nose as he encircled her waist and swung her to the ground. "My great-grandfather would be in a terrible temper to hear you say that."

He slid his arm around her shoulder and turned her to face the North Sea. "Look there just beyond the breaker, Arrian. There is a cave where my sister and I used to dig for buried treasure. We were certain some marauding Vikings had left their booty in the caves."

She turned to him and her lips brushed accidently against his cheek. For a long moment she looked into his eyes and felt a tightening in her stomach. She felt she could not breathe.

He suddenly released her and moved to the edge of the hill, his steps leaving deep impressions in the snow. Arrian placed her small foot where he had stepped as an even stranger feeling took possession of her. Before God and man she was Warrick's wife. She felt as if his presence enveloped her, just as his footprints enveloped hers.

"It's rather cold, but would you like to walk beside the sea? The tide won't be in for several hours."

"I'd like to see the cave," she said.

"Come," he replied, holding his hand out to her. "The horses are well trained and will remain here until we return."

She slipped her hand into his and walked beside him down the hill. All the while she was wondering why she no longer resented his touch, but in fact welcomed it.

Arrian was so confused by her new emotions that she pulled her hand free, feeling as if she were betraying Ian.

When they stepped onto the beach, she ran toward the lapping waves that rushed forward in a flurry of creamy foam. She removed her hat and tossed it aside, relishing the piercing cry of the seabirds.

Warrick could only stare at the girl whose golden hair had been ripped from its tight coil to swirl around her face. She was beautiful and high-spirited, and he wanted to be the one to tame her. No—not tame her, he thought, for she should never be tamed. He wanted to be close to her warmth, to bask in her sweet fire, to be loved by her.

That was a sobering thought that brought him up short. He raised his face to the sun, trying to calm his thundering heart.

"We had best explore the caves another day. The wind has shifted, and a pervading southwest wind inevitably brings rain to the Highlands."

She tried to hide her disappointment as they retraced their steps.

Warrick retrieved her hat and placed it on her head. In a

move that startled her, he traced the outline of her lips with his gloved hand.

"Your mouth has become a source of fascination for me, but more so now that I've seen you smile."

Arrian had never had such words spoken to her, and it took her breath away. The sunlight glistened on Warrick's midnight-colored hair. She was transfixed by those silver eyes.

At last she found her voice. "There has been little to smile about lately, Warrick."

His lips thinned in a grim line. "Then we shall just have to remedy that. What are some of the things you enjoy?"

She shifted her gaze away from him to stare in the distance at the flat gray sea. "As I told you, I like hawking. I'm particularly good at archery. I like to ride and dance."

Warrick and Arrian talked as they walked toward their waiting mounts. "I suppose, Arrian, that you are versed in all the accomplishments befitting a lady of your station."

She smiled and dipped into a curtsy. "I am, my lord. I can embroider and do needlepoint adequately. I play the harp and piano reasonably well. I am proficient in French, Latin, Italian. Alas, I do not speak Gaelic at all, and speak only enough Russian to get myself into trouble, forcing my brother, Michael, to cover for any affronts I utter out of ignorance. I once thought I was telling a Russian noblewoman that she had a lovely gown. Michael quickly apologized to her and begged her to forgive my limited knowledge of her language."

"What had you said to the woman?"

"It seems I said something about her gown being fit only for a swine."

Warrick was finding himself drawn more and more to her intelligence and wit. "I bow to your many accomplishments. Did you attend a school for young ladies in London?"

"No. I refused to leave Ravenworth, so I had tutors."

"Of course."

"What about you, my lord? Since we are learning about each other, tell me of your accomplishments."

"I fear they are far inferior to yours. I play neither the piano nor the harp. I have no knowledge of embroidery or needlepoint. Like you, I know only a few words in Russian, and I know French and Latin, but not Italian. I, of course, am proficient in Gaelic."

"Did you attend a university?"

"Yes. In Edinburgh."

"That's why you speak English with very little accent," she observed. "You must have studied English."

His eyes suddenly hardened. "I would not adopt the language of the Thames Valley by design. If my English is satisfactory, it can be attributed to the Englishman who taught at the Royal School in Edinburgh."

She laid her hand on his. "Surely you can see there is a rift as wide as a river between us, Warrick. We cannot even get through a conversation without a confrontation."

He clasped her hand and drew her slowly toward him. His face was very near, and she could feel his warm breath stir her hair.

"Don't you know, Arrian, bridges are built over rivers every day. Shall I build a bridge between us? I could, you know—with very little effort."

She shook her head, her heart too full to speak.

"Shall I show you how easily we could cross a bridge to find each other, Arrian?"

Again she shook her head, but she did not pull away when he lowered his dark head and his lips brushed against her cheek and his arms tightened about her.

"Oh, yes," he murmured, "it would be so easy. You would relent, Arrian."

When his mouth touched hers, she ached to be closer to him. As a sunflower worships the sun, she followed those elusive lips that now brushed against her brow, her ear, her cheek again, trying to entice them back to hers. Arrian could not have known how her provocative move trapped the breath in Warrick's lungs, fanning his desire.

Warrick stared into confused blue eyes and saw something that pleased him—the awakening of desire. He did not have to be told that this was a new emotion for Arrian, he knew it instinctively. There was a prickle of remorse as his lips settled firmly on hers. He knew, with his experience, he could easily take advantage of her innocence.

Against her will, Arrian melted against him, her arms gliding around his waist.

Warrick applied pressure to her lips and positioned her closer to his body. She felt his hands moving across her back, caressing, circling. A burst of sensation exploded within her as he traced her lips with his tongue. Like churning tides in a storm, a wild yearning rippled through her body.

Suddenly frightened, she pulled away from him, staring at him with new eyes.

"I . . . don't know why that happened. I'm so ashamed that I betrayed Ian."

His quicksilver eyes reflected anger, not passion. "Did Ian MacIvors ever kiss you like that?"

She hoped he hadn't noticed how her hands trembled. She welcomed the cool breeze on her cheeks. "No. Not like that. He would never have taken such liberties." She turned her back to him, her emotions now under control. "Ian is a gentleman, my lord."

He reached for her, swung her onto her horse, and handed her the reins. "I'm not a gentleman, Arrian, and it's best you remember that about me."

They rode back to the castle in silence. Arrian went immediately to her room, glad for the solitude. She needed time to think about what had happened to her today. She felt so guilty and wondered how she could ever face Ian.

* * *

Warrick turned his horse away from the castle and rode across a wooden bridge and down a well-worn path. In the distance he could hear the roar of a waterfall, and he galloped Titus in that direction.

He dismounted and stood at the edge of a cliff, watching water rush over the high embankment. Sprays of mist settled on his face and hair, and he closed his eyes, hoping the cleansing water would heal his soul.

For so long he had felt no emotion other than hatred and revenge. Now a door had opened within him, and a tide of feelings he did not welcome overwhelmed him.

He had to force himself to forget how soft Arrian's lips had felt beneath his. He did not want to think about the silkiness of her hair or the clean scent of her velvet skin.

She must not become too important to him. She was a tool, a means to an end. Perhaps he would make her love him and use her newfound desires to bind her to him. Only then would he send her back to Ian, who would be cheated of her love.

His eyes closed against the light rain that had begun to fall. He must take care not to become a victim of those innocent blue eyes.

The next morning, when Arrian came downstairs, she found Warrick waiting for her in the breakfast room. She had been dreading the thought of facing him after what had happened between them the day before.

But he smiled at her and held at her chair while she sat down. "Try the muffins, they're delicious."

She picked up a teacup, staring at it because she could not look at him. How could he act as if nothing had transpired between them?

He placed a scone dripping with creamy yellow butter on her plate. "Did you sleep well?" he inquired.

"I . . . yes, I did."

"I wondered, Arrian, if you would like to go riding again today."

She would have liked nothing better than to go riding with him. "I'm not sure if that would be wise," she said.

"I thought you might like to go into the village with me."

Before she could reply the door opened, and a woman dressed in a yellow riding habit entered, looking first at Warrick and then at Arrian.

Warrick came to his feet. "Louise, I hadn't heard that you'd returned."

Louise moved up to him, standing so close her breasts brushed against his chest. "I missed . . . home."

Arrian looked at the woman who, though not beautiful, was certainly striking. Her hair was brown, and she was dressed in the latest fashion. Her yellow habit was just the right color to call attention to her soft brown eyes.

Warrick turned the woman to face Arrian. "May I present Mrs. Louise Robertson, a neighbor and longtime friend. Louise, this is my . . . er . . . wife, Lady Arrian."

With rage in her eyes, Louise Robertson stared at the young beauty, but she managed to smile at Warrick. "So it's true. You have taken a wife—and so young." She touched his arm and spoke in a familiar tone. "I was sure you would wait for me—apparently you have not."

His smile was reserved. "Now, what would have given you that notion, Louise?"

She ran a gloved finger across his chin. "I can think of several reasons."

Arrian quickly came to her feet, unwilling to sit through such wanton behavior. "If you will both excuse me, I'll leave you to your reunion."

Warrick caught her hand. "No, don't go. There is nothing we have to say that you can't hear."

Louise pouted. "I had hoped you would lend me your expertise. A gentleman will be arriving this afternoon with several horses he wants me to purchase. I know so little about good horseflesh, I need a trained eye so that I won't be cheated. Could you not come to Longwood and help me?"

Arrian moved to the door. "Yes, go with her, Warrick. Anyone who doesn't know good horseflesh when they see it would surely need help."

Louise Robertson stared after Lady Arrian as she went out the door. She wasn't certain, but she might have just been insulted.

Warrick smiled to himself. "I'll go with you, Louise, but I cannot stay past noon."

Louise gazed into his eyes. "Are you really married, Warrick?"

"Very married."

"But they say the lady is a MacIvors. Can that really be true?"

"No, Louise," he said with some satisfaction, "she is a Glencarin."

Arrian paced the length of her room, venting her anger. How dare that woman carry on so brazenly in front of her, and how dare Warrick allow it? After all, he was her husband and—

She dropped down on a chair, trying to gather her thoughts. Why should she care what Warrick did with that woman? He was nothing to her.

Why then did she feel this restlessness of spirit—and why was it tinged with a sense of betrayal?

or five days Arrian did not see Warrick. She imagined him with Louise Robertson, and for some reason she didn't like the thought of the two of them together. She spent her time walking around on the grounds, visiting the stables, and gazing off into the distant rippling waves of the North Sea.

Today she was feeling particularly restless as she walked through the courtyard to the back of the house. She was appalled at the neglect of the gardens. At one time Ironworth must have been a magnificent castle, with its beautiful view of the mountains and sea. How could Warrick care so little for his property?

She saw Mrs. Haddington doing the wash and walked in her direction. Since the wedding the housekeeper had been respectful but distant.

"The snow has all melted and the weather is warm, Mrs. Haddington," Arrian said, trying to make polite conversation.

The housekeeper paused at her task and wiped the soap suds from her hands. "It seems so, m'lady."

Arrian sat on a wooden bench, thinking how good the sun felt beating down on her. "Have you heard anything from your daughter? I'm worried about my aunt."

"Barra'll not write. We'll know what's happened when she returns, and I don't know when that'll be."

"I was just wondering what Ironworth Castle must have been like at one time, Mrs. Haddington."

"'Twas once grand, m'lady, but it fell to ruin when the old chief settled most of his money on Lady Gwendolyn."

"Warrick had told me about that."

"Now my lord toils ta hold us together. Those who canna go out on the fishing boats become shepherds. All his lord-ship's money goes ta buy sheep and help them in the village."

Arrian remembered her aunt telling her about the duties of a chief. It seemed that Warrick cared more about his villagers than his own comforts. That thought touched her heart. "I have not yet visited the village, but I hope to soon."

"Meaning no disrespect, m'lady, but you'll no' find our village ta your liking."

"You don't like me very well do you, Mrs. Haddington?"

"It no for me to say if I like or dislike you. I have'na' found you to be of a bad nature, but I dinna like what you're doing to his lordship."

"Mrs. Haddington, I would say I was more sinned against than sinned."

"Well, as to that I dinna ken." Her eyes became accusing. "Ye're a MacIvors."

"Mrs. Haddington, my name is DeWinter. I did not ask to be brought here, and I do not want to stay."

"Like as not you'll tear his heart out before ye're done."

Arrian realized she should not talk so intimately with a servant. The woman didn't seem to care that she had been forced to marry Warrick. Of course the housekeeper would know that they didn't share the same bedroom and had no real marriage.

With a resigned sigh, Arrian turned to walk away.
"M'lady?"

Arrian glanced back at the woman. "Yes, Mrs. Haddington?"

"I have found ye to be of a sweet nature. And no'
demanding. I shouldn'a be saying this, but I like ye better
than that Louise Robertson."

Arrian smiled. She had just received high praise indeed
from the housekeeper. "Thank you, Mrs. Haddington."

"If that one had her way, she'd stand in ye're place."

Arrian walked away, not wanting to think about that.
Perhaps Warrick was sorry for their hasty marriage. Well,
she thought angrily, it served him right. All he had to do
was let her go, and he could have Louise Robertson.

Arrian had eaten a solitary dinner in her room, and loneliness lay heavy on her heart. She was still worried about her
aunt, and she wondered what her parents and Michael were
doing. Surely by now they would know that she was a prisoner at Ironworth Castle.

There was a soft knock on the door, and Mrs.
Haddington entered. The woman's eyes seemed to have lost
much of their hostility.

"His lordship asks if you'd join him in the sitting room."

Arrian came quickly to her feet, seething with anger.
"Indeed I shall."

"If you'll go right down, m'lady, he's waiting."

Warrick watched Arrian enter in a flurry of cranberry-colored
taffeta. Her cheeks were flushed, and her eyes bright. It was
obvious that she was angry with him. So, his waiting game
had worked.

He slowly walked toward her, took her hand, and raised
it to his lips. "Each time I see you, you grow more beautiful.
How can that be?"

Her eyes flickered. She was accustomed to receiving tributes to her beauty. Most of the time she laughed them off, but it was different now. She had a feeling Warrick was true to his convictions and never offered a woman his good opinion unless he meant it.

She turned away from him. "I suppose you and Mrs. Robertson spent the last five days together."

His eyes flickered. "No. I have not seen Louise since that day I helped her select horses."

"I have been restless, and too much in my own company."

"Dare I hope you missed me, Arrian?"

"I merely said I was lonely, my lord. There is very little here to occupy my time."

He clasped her hand. "Then we shall just have to remedy that. Do you play chess?"

"I have played on occasion."

He led her to the chess board and seated her on a chair. She picked up a wooden pawn and touched several medieval lords and ladies.

Warrick seated himself across from her. "I'll have to warn you, Arrian, I mastered chess at age twelve, and my game has steadily improved since then."

She sighed. "I can only hope you will be merciful with me, my lord."

He generously offered her the white, so she made the first move.

Warrick smiled indulgently at her. "It isn't wise to move your knight and leave him unprotected, Arrian."

He moved a pawn forward, his eyes challenging her. "You wouldn't like me to take your knight with a pawn would you?"

She smiled at him. "No, my lord." She moved her queen, offering it to him as a temptation.

"I suppose chess is much like war, Arrian. That's why it's a man's game. I don't believe a woman is capable of stratagy. A man would never sacrifice his queen." He moved his bishop forward, taking her queen.

"You are far too pompous, my lord. How shall I punish you?"

Three moves later, Arrian slid her knight into place with mischief dancing in her eyes. "Checkmate, my lord."

Warrick stared at her in astonishment. Then his eyes danced with humor. "You little devil. You deliberately offered me your queen as bait."

Her eyes were shining with triumph. "But Warrick, you pointed out that chess was a man's game. Will you surrender to a mere woman, my lord?"

"Yes, my little trickster—I yield the game to you. But you were naughty to let me believe you were only a novice at chess."

"I never said so."

He took her hand and raised her to her feet. "You have taken the day, Arrian. I don't believe I'll play chess with you again until I find out how you did that."

She walked with him to a table where Mrs. Haddington was laying out tea and brandy. When the housekeeper withdrew they sat on the wide sofa.

"Truth to tell, I'm not really an expect chess player, Warrick. As a matter of fact, my brother beat me so often that my father took me aside one day and showed me those moves. Most people don't expect the sacrifice of a queen or to be checkmated by a knight. It's a ploy that will work only once. If we played again, you would surely win, for I do not play well."

He laughed at her earnestness. She was so young and enchanting, he could only imagine what joy she brought to her family. There was no weeping and wailing as he had expected—she was everything that a wife should be.

He watched her pour brandy into a glass and hand it to him. She then poured herself a cup of tea.

"What other talents do you have that I don't know about, Arrian?"

She placed her cup on the table and leaned forward as if

she feared someone would overhear her. "I once rode the winning horse at a race in Ravenworth."

He pretended to be shocked. "Surely you jest. Not a lady such as yourself—for that matter, not any female."

"I can assure you it's the truth. My uncle George had a horse entered for he had long coveted a win. The morning of the race my brother and I went to the stall to inspect his horse."

"You were allowed to do that?"

"Of course. It's our village. I am allowed freedom there that I wouldn't be allowed in London."

"Go on."

"Well, as my mother's maid, Elspeth, would say, the rider was in his cups. He couldn't stand, much less ride. Michael and I debated whether to tell Uncle George, because he had such high hopes."

"I can see your dilemma."

"Well, I determined that the jockey and I were about the same size. Against Michael's pleading, I donned the jockey's garb and shoved my hair beneath a cap. To my surprise, I won, which I had not counted on because I had to be led to the winner's circle, and I was afraid everyone would recognize me."

The little charmer had Warrick completely entranced. "Then what happened?"

"Well, I could tell that my uncle knew it was me right away. After recovering from the shock, he silently accepted the trophy and the twenty pounds prize money."

"Did he give you away?"

"Not he. In fact, Uncle George never mentioned it to me. However, for my birthday the next year, my mother and father could not understand why he gave me his trophy. Of course Michael and I laughed at his generous gesture, knowing how long Uncle George had coveted that win."

Warrick found himself being drawn more and more under Arrian's spell. She had no notion how adorable she was as she spoke of her misdeeds.

He had not known that he was lonely until Arrian came into his life. She made him yearn for that which he could not have, made him restless and dissatisfied.

"Arrian, are you so unhappy here?"

"It has been difficult, Warrick. But I pass my days knowing you will allow me to leave by August."

He took her hand and raised it to his lips. "What if I asked you to remain?"

She looked into his eyes, wondering if he were speaking the truth or playing some kind of cruel game.

He pulled her against him and held her for a long moment. He half expected her to move away, but she didn't. Was she beginning to fall in love with him? His plan was to break down her resistance, but he had to go slowly so that he wouldn't frighten her.

Warrick took her face between his hands and stared at her parted lips. "You have not answered," he whispered. "If I asked it of you, would you stay with me?"

Before she could reply, he dipped his head and covered her lips with a burning kiss that trapped her breath and sent her heart racing.

Arrian could not speak as his hot hand drifted down her neck to move lightly across her breasts. She trembled with emotions she did not understand. Then she pushed his hand away, feeling the need to escape.

"No, my lord, I would never willingly stay with you. I must remind you again that I belong to Ian. Nothing you can do will change that."

His eyes had lost their softness. "I was always one to take up a challenge, my lady."

"I issued you no challenge. I merely entreat you to let me go free."

"That I cannot do."

"I don't want you to touch me again."

Warrick pretended seriousness, while thinking how desirable she was. "You didn't like my kiss?"

"You have no right to take liberties with me. I don't belong to you."

He decided to take another tactic. "How would you like to ride with me in the morning?"

Her eyes brightened. "I would like that, my lord."

"Then I shall wish you a good night."

For some reason Arrian didn't want to leave him, but he had definitely dismissed her. "Good night, my lord."

Warrick walked her to the door and raised her hand to his lips, his mouth lingering on her wrist. "Until tomorrow, my lady."

Arrian felt warm inside. Her feet seemed to glide up the stairs. Each time she saw Warrick her resentment of him lessened. When he kissed her tonight she should have slapped his face. He was slowly wearing down her resistance, and she was slipping further into his grasp. Was she in peril?

When she reached her bedroom she locked the door, wondering if she was locking Lord Warrick out, or herself inside.

Chapter 14

*A*rrian *was thinking* of Ravenworth and how different this land was from her home. This was a wild
land, untamed and challenging, not unlike the
man who rode beside her.

As they neared the village she watched the smoke that
curled from the chimneys. She looked around with interest
as their horses clopped along cobbled streets.

They rode past shops and cottages of drystone walls with
roofs of thatch and heather. Soon laughing children surrounded them, their windburned faces showing evidence of
nature's wrath and a harsh sea.

"Morning, m'lord," one precocious little dark-haired girl
called out. "Is this your lady?"

"Yes, she is, Laura. Why aren't you children in school
today?"

"We saw ye out the window, m'lord, and the Mr. Dickerson
wasn't in the room, so we ran out to give ye greetings."

Arrian had never seen this side of Warrick. He laughed
with the children, calling each one by their name and

inquiring about their families with genuine concern. The children looked at him with respect and an easy affection.

"Duncan, how's your arm?" Warrick asked.

"It's right as new, m'lord." To demonstrate, the blond-haired lad proudly flexed his arm and held it out for inspection. When Warrick nodded in approval, the lad's eyes danced with delight.

Warrick tossed a few coins their way, and when they scrambled to retrieve them his features became stern, his voice reproachful. "After school you can each go to the shop and buy candy. Until then, it's back to school with all of you."

They pocketed their coins, smiled at him, and quickly retreated in the direction of the school.

"The little scamps don't realize how difficult it was to get a schoolmaster who was willing to come to the village, since we are so far north."

"So you pay for the teacher?"

"The villagers are poor and have trouble just eking out a meager existence. They have been fishermen for generations and are dependent on the run of the fish. They could hardly be asked to pay wages for a teacher. Many of the lads take to sea at a young age, without an education. I've insisted they have at least two years of school and can read and write before they take up their father's trade."

"You care a great deal about your villagers don't you, Warrick?"

He glanced at her. "Of course, they are my responsibility. Some of them are like children, waiting for me to tell them what to do."

"I've heard they are very loyal to you."

"Not to me as Lord Glencarin, but surely to me as chief of Clan Drummond. Traditions run deep and last for generations."

"Aunt Mary said much the same thing to me."

"You see, Arrian, here time is measured by the wind and sea. Changes come slowly. These people sprang from clansmen who lived in my village for many generations. There has never been a question of loyalty."

"It's different at Ravenworth. While the people love and respect my father, they are not governed by his decrees."

He frowned. "There are many differences between Scotland and England."

Arrian decided to change the subject. "What is that strange aroma I smell?"

"That would be the peat fires. Since so few trees thrive here, because of the wind and rocky ground, the villagers gather peat, sometimes mixing it with heather stalks. It makes a most admirable fire."

When the villagers realized their chief was among them, they came out of their houses to gather around him. Arrian listened to them speak, but she didn't understand what they were saying, because they spoke in Gaelic and Warrick answered them in kind.

Since the only males seemed to be elderly, Arrian assumed the younger men were fishing or tending the herds of sheep and cattle.

She realized that she was the object of many curious glances. Warrick said something to the people in Gaelic, and that seemed to satisfy them. He turned to her and said, "I just explained to them that you are my wife."

She realized that she was becoming more and more a part of his world. There seemed to be no escape.

With a wave of his hand, Warrick led the way out of the village. For a time they rode silently, and Arrian thought they were heading for the sea. But suddenly he changed direction, following a rushing stream.

As they rode along, the sun played tag with high, fluffy white clouds, while in the distance iron gray mountains rose like church steeples. The snow had melted but for the highest peaks and the evergreen heather awaited for summer to burst into full purple blooms.

Warrick paused for a moment and pointed to the highest

spine of mountains, where the tops were shrouded in mystical clouds. "I wonder if you can see the beauty as I do when you look at this land, Arrian."

"Yes, it is beautiful." She had a feeling the land could no more be tamed than could the chief who ruled it.

"How did you like my village?"

"It's very isolated, but I like that. My father's village has become a bustling hamlet since the Ravenworth China became so famous. I sometimes wonder how Ravenworth must have been before so many strangers tramped the streets."

"I doubt your villagers have known what it's like to have their bellies so empty they cried out for food and went to bed hungry."

"I am told that before my mother came to Ravenworth, the village had suffered harshly. My father had been with Lord Wellington's troops in France. When he returned it was to find that his uncle and cousin had died, making him the duke. He was faced with a suffering duchy."

"Your mother must have liked playing the bountiful duchess. Did it satisfy some charitable feeling for her to help the poor unfortunate villagers?" he asked bitterly. "Neither you nor she could have ever known hunger."

The insult went straight to Arrian's heart. "You can say what you will about me, but don't ever insinuate that my mother aided the suffering for some personal satisfaction. You cannot know how she suffered, or you would regret your words. She was locked up in . . . a place where she had only gruel and water for months and was close to death. If she helped our villagers, it's because she loves them and they love her. I'm sorry if I'm less perfect in your eyes because I have never known hunger—perhaps you would respect me more if I had."

"I'm sorry, Arrian. I do always seem to be finding fault with your family. I wanted this to be a pleasant day for you."

This was as near as he had ever come to an apology, but she was still annoyed with him. "I saw no sign of malnourishment in your village."

"No, not now. But they have known hunger. Bringing sheep into the valley has rectified the problem. It gives them wool to sell and meat for their tables."

Warrick turned his horse away from the stream, and Arrian had no choice but to follow. At last they were in sight of the hunting lodge, and Warrick dismounted and turned to her.

By now her temper had cooled a bit, but she wasn't ready to forgive him. "Why did we come here?"

His eyes appeared fathomless as he turned to her. "I wanted to be alone with you."

She felt excitement stirring within her and knew she should not stay. "I have no wish to be alone with you." The lie came hard to her lips.

"I only hoped we could talk uninterrupted."

She silently assessed the situation. He had never given her reason not to trust his conduct. "Very well." She allowed him to assist her to the ground. "But I don't want to be away for long."

While Warrick turned away from her and led the horses into a pen, Arrian looked around with interest. When she had been here before she'd taken little notice of her surroundings. The lodge was located in a beautiful glen that was cut in half by a stream. It was early afternoon, and already the mountains cast a shadow across the land. She could see that the sun would set early in this valley.

Warrick guided her toward the lodge and opened the door, allowing her to precede him inside. A warm fire was glowing in the hearth, and an inviting feast had been laid out on the table. She could see it was still hot and wondered had provided the meal.

"Mactavish was here, but he left," Warrick said, answering her unasked question.

"You had everything planned, did you not?" she asked, feeling a prickle of uneasiness.

"I thought only of your comfort," he said with a hint of mockery.

She moved to the table and pointed at the meat swimming in a yellow sauce. "What's that?"

"Red grouse. It's commonplace in the Highlands, and you will find it very delicious."

She dropped down in a chair and removed her gloves. "I will talk to you while we eat, and then we must be getting back. It really isn't proper for me to be here with you alone."

He sat across from her, a smile playing on his lips. "I forget that you English are always worried about what's proper."

"I don't believe a properly brought up Scottish lady would behave any differently, Warrick."

"Perhaps you are right. But don't forget, Arrian, you and I are husband and wife."

"You know as well as I that our marriage is nothing but a sham."

"Why don't you forget for a day what is considered proper and concentrate on enjoying yourself?"

"I'm not sure I can do that."

He laughed deeply, his eyes fastened on her face. "So you see me as having some devious design in bringing you here?"

"I see in you a danger, my lord. I don't know if I can rely on your honor."

Again there was a hardness in his eyes. "You would do well to look out for me, Arrian. I'm overcoming my sense of guilt where you are concerned. I may well be a danger to you."

She reached for his hand, hoping she could make him understand her feelings. "It isn't where a person was born, or the name they bear that makes them what they are. It's their kindness toward others that counts—and their pride and sense of honor must not be discounted. But none of this is important if the person does not have a loving heart."

He pressed her hand against his chest. "Can you feel how my heart beats beneath your fingertips?"

She sucked in her breath. "Yes."

"That is the heart of a Scot, Arrian—the heart of a Drummond."

She pulled free, staring at him. "I'm surprised to find you have a heart."

"You think I'm without honor, don't you, Arrian?"

"What you have done to me would not recommend you for a commendation—but the reasons for your actions might temper judgment for the crime."

Warrick stood, pulling her to him. "With you beside me, perhaps you could make me see my mistakes. You could forge me into the man you want me to be."

"I don't want to take on that responsibility, Warrick. Are you forgetting Ian?"

His eyes stabbed hers, and his grip on her tightened. "I never forget him. He's always in my thoughts, standing between us." Warrick pulled her tightly against him, while the light in his silver eyes held her prisoner. "I want you to forget him—and by God, you will!"

"No, I—"

His lips ground brutally against hers, and she struggled against him, trying to wedge her hands between them. Her hand mistakenly slipped inside his shirt and brushed against the furry mat on his chest. She quickly drew back at the intimate touch.

He smiled at her. "I see you don't like my kisses. I wonder if I could make you want them?"

She slipped out of his arms. "No, I can assure you that you could not."

He smiled and pulled her toward the fire. "Your hands are cold. Let me warm them for you." He pressed her hands inside his. "Do you despise me so much, my lady?"

"No. I don't despise you. But sometimes I don't like you very much."

His arm slid around her shoulders, and when she would have moved away he whispered against her ear. "I still want only to warm you."

She stood stiffly, not knowing what to expect. For some reason she no longer feared him, but she couldn't guess his intentions.

His hands moved to her cloak, which he unfastened and tossed across a chair. When she would have protested he drew her once more against his warm body. "I'll warm you as you have never been warmed, Arrian."

She didn't want to move out of his arms. When his hands moved up and down her back, she laid her head against his shoulder. She could not see him smile or see the look of triumph in his eyes.

"I'm sure many men have told you that you are beautiful, Arrian."

"I have not been left alone in the company of many gentlemen."

"Ah, yes, you have been in the country."

His hands moved to her neck, where he gently caressed her tense muscles until he felt her relax.

She tried to think of something to say that would take her mind off the masterful hands. Only her mother came to mind. "You should see how the gentlemen stare at my mother when she enters a room. My father is none too pleased when some overzealous gentleman tells her how lovely she is. They seldom repeat the deed more than once."

"So your father is possessive of your beautiful mother?"

"Yes, he is, but without reason. She loves only him."

Warrick could understand the jealousy that could haunt a man who was married to someone as lovely as Arrian. He was filled with anger because she belonged to Ian MacIvors. That realization only hardened his heart and strengthened his resolve to send her back to Ian with his mark upon her.

"I wonder if you know the torment I have been through

since you became my wife. You are legally mine, and yet I have no right to touch you."

"You gave me your word you wouldn't," she reminded him. "I expect you to keep that word."

"Does holding you in my arms go against my word?"

She was bewildered. She wanted him to hold her, she wanted to feel his lips on hers, but wasn't there danger in becoming too intimate with him?

He swept the silken hair aside, and his mouth hovered over the nape of her neck. A shiver went through her.

He brushed his lips against her ear. "If only I could have some small part of you to keep with me—to remember you when you are gone."

He raised his head, looking deeply into baffled blue eyes. "I wonder if I might have just one last kiss."

She wasn't certain if she should allow him to kiss her, although the thought of his lips on hers spread a warmth throughout her body. She decided it would do no harm, so she closed her eyes and offered him her lips.

He smiled at her childlike gesture. Clasping her shoulders, his lips came down gently on hers. His hands moved to the front of her gown, and he unfastened the top hook. When she would have resisted, he deepened the kiss.

Arrian tried to press her mouth tighter against the hard lips that were draining her of all resistance. She had not known a kiss could be so pleasurable and evoke such a strong longing that it left her breathless.

Her innocence was no match for Warrick's expert skills. He unfastened the other hooks, slid her gown off her shoulders, and let it drop to the floor. His thigh rubbed against her while his lips plundered hers, robbing her of protest.

He was still kissing her when he lifted her in his arms and carried her to the bed. He knew what he was doing was wrong, but that would not stop him.

Arrian fought against her body as it betrayed her. Everywhere he touched it tingled, leaving her begging for more.

Warrick had not expected to feel this deep burning need for his captive. At that moment he could not have said whether he was seducing her to hurt Ian or because he desperately wanted her. He had dreamed of the moment he would make her blue eyes smoulder with desire.

He wanted to be the one to stir within Arrian the first realization of what it was like to have a man touch her. He would not take her all the way—no, only to the brink, and then pull away.

As he stared into her soft eyes there was in him such a strong yearning, it was almost like pain. He knew then that he would not stop until he had all of her.

Warrick brushed hot kisses against her silken neck and Arrian threw back her head.

He lay back against the pillow and pulled her on top of him. Hot desire kindled in his bloodstream. He trembled with yearning as her soft lips opened to his probing tongue.

He knew that she would soon be his. Victory was within his grasp.

Chapter 15

*A*rrian *could feel the heat* of Warrick's body through her thin chemise, and she knew that what was happening between them was wrong.

Pressing her hands on the bed, she raised her body from his and managed to stand on shaky legs. "I know what you are trying to do, Warrick. You are breaking your word to me. I'll not give you what you want."

He swung to his feet, towering over her, his hand lightly touching her. "I would not be breaking my word if you consent, Arrian." His gaze moved over the swell of her breasts. "I can make you beg for me, Arrian. Shall I do that?"

"N . . . o."

His hand drifted down her neck to the tie that held together her chemise. She looked into his eyes, the hot words of denial dying on her lips.

Slowly he pulled the tie and exposed her breasts to his hands. With a soft groan she threw her head back, and his lips touched her neck, sliding downward to sprinkle kisses on first one breast and then the other.

She tried to speak, but his plundering mouth closed over hers, and she went limp in his arms.

Arrian felt herself going backward onto the bed with his arms cushioning her fall. A small voice within her mind warned her that she was in danger, but it didn't matter, nothing did except that mouth that made her a willing captive of his desire.

Arrian had never known a man's body was so hard. She was aware of each breath he took, for she matched it with her own breathing.

Warrick pulled up her chemise and allowed his hands to drift up her leg and spread across her rounded buttocks. With pressure he pushed her tightly against his thighs and slid her up and down against his throbbing desire.

"Warrick," she said in a breathless voice, "this is wrong. I will never consent."

"No," he whispered against her lips, "not yet."

"I'm not thinking of you," she said through trembling lips, trying to gain control of her emotions. "I'm thinking only of Ian." Even as she said the words she could not remember what Ian looked like, she could only see silver eyes.

An angry cry escaped Warrick's lips, and he stared at her. She tried to turn her head away but could not. In a move that surprised her, he quickly removed his clothing. When she turned away, he only laughed.

Warrick rejoined her, and taking her hand, he placed it on his chest. When she tried to pull it away he held her fast. "Feel me, Arrian. I am flesh and blood. Look at me. I am not Ian MacIvors, I am your husband."

Her voice came out in a painful cry. "No, no."

"At this moment you belong to me. You will never forget this day no matter how old you grow, or how much you think you love Ian MacIvors."

He rolled over so that she was beneath him and lowered his body to hers. A tremor shook her. "Feel my body, Arrian, and say my name."

"Warrick," she whispered, feeling a deepening need building within her virginal body. There was no thought of Ian, no feeling of guilt, only a need to draw closer to the flame that stirred her heart.

His hands moved over the full magnificence of her breasts, and she thought she would die with longing, and yet she had never felt so alive. She was conscious of his every move, his every touch, for each brought a new discovery.

When his mouth moved across her breasts, Arrian thought she would faint from the joy that surged through her body.

Warrick looked at her, his flintlike eyes softening, and in that moment she knew he was as moved by the experience as she was.

She was not prepared for the hand that slid across her stomach and downward to spread her legs.

"Now is the time to ask me to stop, Arrian," he whispered against her ear. "If you wait much longer, I will not be able to control myself."

"I don't want you to stop," she said as he hovered above her, his lips parting as he lowered his head to take hers in a deepening kiss.

"Release me from my promise," he said in a raspy voice. "Give me leave to take you to a world of pleasure and delight."

"Yes," was all she could manage to say.

He slid into her, filling an emptiness she never knew existed. A gasp escaped her lips, and she would have moved away but for the heat of his moist mouth, making her light-headed.

Fear entwined with burning pleasure at his invasion. There was a stinging pain as he jabbed through the narrow barrier of flesh. With another thrust he came to rest deep inside her.

Warrick's hungry mouth devoured Arrian's lips, smothering the cry in her throat. She languished between pain—oh, such sweet pain—and lingering desire.

His mouth moved down her neck to burrow between her breasts. Arrian slipped her fingers into his thick black hair and groaned.

Warrick's body trembled with consuming need. He strained to hold his desire under control while he cupped her face and looked deeply into her eyes. "Who am I, Arrian?"

Her body became a traitor as he slid back from her and then forward, making her feel she would faint. "You are Warrick," she groaned.

"Every time Ian takes you, you will remember only me."

She stared at him, her mind clearing. What had he meant? But before she could protest, he moved inside her again and she gasped with pleasure.

Warrick felt as if he were wrapped in silk. Was he possessing her or was she possessing him? Her softness was driving him mad with passion. Her sweetness was filling his very being, and he knew he would never forget the enticing aroma of her satiny hair.

His pleasure built with raw urgency, but he held back, wanting to make love to her slowly and lingeringly. He wanted to savor each consuming moment of desire.

Arrian stared into his silver eyes, which were softer than she had ever seen them. Then he closed them as if he wanted to block out her face.

Giving a forceful thrust, he plunged into her with a driving passion.

Arrian could no longer resist. She was his to do with as he willed. His lips were brutal as he ravished hers, but she clung to him, begging for more.

"Now," he whispered, "I have you, my lady."

When he pressed her against his chest she instinctively began to move with him, her passion matching his as it raged wilder and wilder until it ignited into an inferno of pleasure.

She heard him groan and whisper in her ear. "Do I have you, or do you have me?"

Her body quaked, and she heard him take a gasping breath. Together they trembled, fusing as one. They were left breathless.

For a long moment they lay in each other's arms, lingering over the feelings that neither could understand. As his hand slid across her breasts, she wondered how she would explain to her family that she could never leave Warrick. He had truly become her husband today, and she his wife.

She wanted to hear him say that he felt as she had. But she was shy of the newfound love and could not ask it of him.

He gathered her close, feeling the need for her once more. He took her softly this time, wanting to create a lasting memory in her heart.

For hours he caressed her, made love to her, whispered endearments in her ear.

Night fell, and shadows crept across the room. The fire had gone out and was replaced by a chill in the room. "We should be getting back," Warrick said.

She moved reluctantly out of the comfort of his arms. "I never knew it could be like this between a man and a woman."

A sadness filled her whole being as she thought of Ian and how she had betrayed him. She realized she would have to tell him about Warrick.

He saw tears in her eyes and pulled her to him. "Did I hurt you?"

"No. I was thinking of Ian."

He wanted to hold her in his arms and never let her go, but her words brought him back to reality. She had just reminded him that her heart belonged to Ian MacIvors, a fact he had forgotten. Well, he would never forget it again.

Closing his eyes, he tried to remember why he had brought her here today. "Ian may thank me for the lessons I have taught you here today, Arrian," he said.

She stared at him in anguish, not understanding why he

had suddenly turned cruel. A sob was building deep inside her, but she clamped her hand over her mouth so it would not be uttered. He could not have hurt her more had he plunged a knife into her heart.

Warrick turned from her and began to dress. He bent to build up the fire, allowing her time to digest what he had said. When he heard her sob, he resisted the urge to go to her. Ian stood between them and always would. Warrick wanted only to remember the hate he felt for the MacIvors. He must not think of the love that she had planted in his soul.

Arrian dressed quietly, thinking what a fool she had been to fall into Warrick's trap. Oh, he had been clever. He had wooed her with honeyed words. He had known just where to touch her to make her come alive. She had been hurt by his harsh words, but she wiped her tears away and straightened her back. She would not give him the satisfaction of seeing her cry.

Warrick walked to the window and propped up his foot on the low window seat. "What would you do in my place if our roles were reversed, Arrian? If you came upon the perfect object to use against your enemy—would you not take advantage of that object?"

"You are referring to me as an object?"

"Perhaps that was a bad choice of words."

She spoke through trembling lips. "I cannot answer you as you would like, Warrick, for I have never felt the ugly enmity that seems to possess you. But I think I would never use an innocent . . . object to strike at the heart of my enemy. My mistake today was in forgetting that we are enemies. I will not forget again."

"Perhaps we both forgot for a time. But, like you, I shall not forget again."

His eyes were probing as he looked for some trace of the Arrian who had surrendered to him. He saw only a cold, beautiful woman whose eyes defied him.

She pushed her tumbled hair out of her face. "I have never known what it felt like to hate until today, Warrick. Now you have drawn me into your blood feud, and I resent you for making me betray Ian."

Her eyes were glistening with the tears she was too proud to shed. "I fell in with your well-laid plans today. How you must have laughed at me. I gave you everything you need to wound Ian to the heart. Now will you let me go?"

He held his hand up to silence her and moved to the door. "Finish dressing while I see to the horses. I'll take you back to Ironworth."

When he left, Arrian ran to the water pitcher and splashed cold water in her face, trying to regain some of her composure. With trembling hands she pulled on her clothing and tied her hair back with a ribbon. An unwelcome tear slipped down her cheek, and she brushed it away angrily.

When Warrick returned, she was still pale and shaken. "I feel pity for you, my lord, because you use people for your own aim and then act as if they should thank you for it."

"Don't pity me, my lady. I got what I wanted from you, and it took very little effort on my part. You were an easy conquest, Arrian."

She wanted to cry out at the coldness of his words. She wanted to run at him, pound him on the chest, and make him hurt as she was hurting.

She walked to the door and yanked it open. "I'll never allow you to touch me again, Warrick."

He followed her outside and placed her on her horse. "Never is a long time, Arrian. And just remember, I didn't take you by force. You were quite willing."

She turned from him, feeling as if her heart would break. "I will be happy to be rid of you, my lord. Should the chance present itself, I'll escape."

"I would expect you to try, Arrian."

They were both silent on the ride back to the castle. Arrian gazed at the first stars of the evening that twinkled against an ebony sky. How cold and faraway they seemed, and how devoid of warmth—just as there was no warmth in her heart.

When they halted their horses at the castle, Arrian allowed Warrick to help her from her horse. He held her hand for a moment, but she jerked it free and ran inside and up the stairs to the safety of her room.

Warrick stared after her, wondering why the sight of her tears had struck him like a knife. Why did he feel lower than the vilest creature on earth?

Arrian didn't bother to light a lamp. She stood looking at the sea that was no more then a darkened shadow creeping toward shore. She was filled with self-loathing. How easily she had allowed Warrick to use her. She had wanted him to touch her, to make love to her. She had to admit that she had thought she loved him. How could she love a man who was consumed by hate? Revenge had been his motive tonight, and that was what hurt most of all.

She pressed her hand over her mouth, but it didn't stifle her loud sob. She buried her face against the curtains and allowed the tears she had held back to flow freely.

Tomorrow she would feel anger, and perhaps remorse, but tonight she felt only betrayed by a love that had seemed beautiful and unique.

Soon she would find a way to escape her prison. Then she would never have to see Warrick again.

Chapter 16

wo days passed and Arrian remained in her room, fearing that if she left she would meet Warrick. Now she was Warrick's prisoner more than ever. Her meals were served by a maid from the village who was taking Barra's place until she returned.

On the third day of her self-confinement there was a knock on the door and Arrian opened it, thinking it would be the maid, but it was Mrs. Haddington.

"I've been worried 'bout you, m'lady."

"I thank you for your concern, Mrs. Haddington. I'm just not feeling well and have kept to my room."

The housekeeper looked her over carefully. "You look pale. His lordship's asked if you'll join him for dinner, m'lady."

"No. Tell him I most certainly will not!"

The housekeeper looked surprised. "He'll want ta know why."

Arrian realized it would not be proper to involve a servant in her quarrel with Warrick. "Tell him I'm not feeling myself."

"If that's your wish, m'lady."

After the housekeeper had gone, Arrian wondered at Warrick's daring in asking her to dine with him. Did he think she would forget what had happened between them?

Another day went by, and again Mrs. Haddington appeared at Arrian's door with the same request from Warrick, and once more Arrian gave the same response.

Later in the afternoon Arrian heard a heavy knock on the door. She opened it to find Warrick standing there.

Her eyes met his defiantly. "I wasn't expecting you, my lord. Apparently you didn't get my message."

"Oh, I got it, Arrian. That's why I'm here. You look healthy to me."

"If I had wanted to shame you in the eyes of your housekeeper, I could have told her the true reason I didn't wish to dine with you. I could have said no woman is safe in your company. I have no wish to dine with you."

Warrick stared at her for a long moment. "It wasn't a request, Arrian, it was an order. I'll not allow you to close yourself off in this room."

She glared at him. "I will not come downstairs."

"Very well. I'll have Haddy serve us dinner in here."

"You don't seem to understand, I don't want to be with you!"

"I'll try to make it as painless as I can. We'll speak only of frivolous matters and forget what passed between us."

"I'll never forget—or forgive."

"I asked for neither. But I expect obedience. Which is it to be? Do we dine here, or will you come downstairs?"

He would have his way again, she thought, raising her head and bestowing her haughtiest glance upon him. She was so angry she could hardly choke out the words. "I'll come downstairs, my lord, but you will not find me a very entertaining dinner companion."

He reached out to her. "I have always found you to be delightful."

She spun away from him. "Don't touch me."

There was sadness in his eyes, or had she been mistaken? He turned away. "I'll see you at seven."

Arrian came down the stairs wearing an emerald green gown with a high neck and long sleeves. When Mrs. Haddington heard her approach she came from the dining room to greet her. "His lordship is waiting for you in the salon."

Arrian gathered her courage and moved through the door. Warrick stood up from the settee. He looked at her with approval.

"I'm delighted you decided to be my guest tonight."

She waited until the housekeeper left to reply. "Let us have no more pretense between us. I am not your guest, my lord, I'm your prisoner."

He smiled slightly. "I don't consider you my prisoner, Arrian, but rather a very beautiful companion."

Their eyes locked, and they both remembered what had happened between them.

Arrian tore her gaze away, her face flushed. "I will not stay if you persist in making pretty speeches, Warrick—nor will I trust you."

"Pity," he said, moving away from her. "I believe I would treasure your trust above all else."

"Could we not eat now, my lord? I would have this evening over so I can return to my room."

He offered her his arm, but she only stared at him. At last he laughed. "Shall we dine, Arrian?"

She walked beside him to the dining room and sat down. "I don't suppose you have thought more about allowing me to leave Ironworth?"

He lowered his eyes and studied the hand she had placed on the table. "You do wound me sorely, my lady. I'll not let you go just yet. I find I'm loath to part with you."

Arrian hardly tasted the food, because she was all too

aware of Warrick's eyes on her. He tried to make polite conversation, but she would answer him only with a nod of her head. She was relieved when the dessert dishes had been removed and Warrick stood. When he pulled out her chair, she rose quickly.

"I believe I'll retire now, my lord."

He towered above her. "Not just yet. You said you played the piano. I thought you might play for me."

Arrian didn't even wait for him but made her way to the salon, knowing he was right behind her. She sat down at the piano and ran her hands over the keys, noticing it was slightly out of tune.

She chose an old Scottish lullaby her mother had sung to her as a child. As the melody spun around in her head, she was overcome with homesickness.

Warrick stood at her side, watching her play. "Do you sing as well?"

"A little."

"Please sing for me."

Warrick was not prepared for the lovely golden voice that filled the salon. The tone was so clear that each note vibrated through his heart.

Arrian was unaware that the servants had gathered at the door, listening to her song.

When the morning sun doth rise
and the heather meets the skies,
I'll be waiting for you, sweet, bonny baby,
for there's magic in your smile.
So help me forget, sweet, bonny love,
that the world is a cold, cold place,
ere I look upon your face.

With the candlelight shining on her golden hair, Arrian looked so beautiful that it brought an ache to Warrick's heart.

When the last note had died away she raised her eyes to Warrick's. "May I leave now, my lord?"

Before he could answer, Mrs. Haddington caught his attention from the doorway.

"Yes, Haddy, what is it?"

"Begging your pardon, m'lord, but my daughter's returned from Edinburgh."

Arrian came to her feet. "Has she news of my aunt?"

"I wouldn't know, m'lady, but your maid's come back with her."

Arrian suddenly felt elated. "Tuttle is here? Where is she?"

Mrs. Haddington stepped aside, and Arrian watched the maid enter. A gasp escaped her lips as she stared at the woman dressed in a simple gray-striped gown and a stiff mob cap covering her glorious golden hair.

"Lord love you, m'lady," the woman said hurriedly, "it's your Tuttle come to see you're being properly cared for."

Warrick paid little attention to the maid, but he was glad she had come. Now perhaps Arrian would be better satisfied.

"Tut . . . tle," Arrian said, stumbling over the name. "I wasn't expecting you."

"You should'a known I'd come, m'lady. I see I've not come a moment too soon. Ye've been out too much in the sun and your skin's brown. And when did you start wearing your hair down? That just won't do."

Arrian bit her lower lip to keep from laughing aloud. She wanted to run into the comforting arms of her mother, but she dared not. "Oh, Tuttle, you are most welcome."

"I'm sure you'll have much to talk about, Arrian," Warrick said. "You'll want particulars about your aunt." He looked up at the maid. "I trust Lady Mary is well?"

"That she is, m'lord. And she told me all about you. We'll just have to keep an eye on you, won't we?"

Warrick thought he heard a warning in the woman's voice, but she had lowered her head and turned away, so he couldn't be certain.

"Go along, Arrian. You'll want to see your maid settled."

Arrian wanted to run up the stairs, but she forced herself to walk slowly while Kassidy followed. When they were in the bedroom with the door closed, Arrian was immediately drawn into her mother's arms.

"Oh, my dearest, I feared I'd never see you again."

Arrian closed her eyes, feeling safe at last. "Oh, Mother, I've needed you so badly."

For a long moment they embraced, then Arrian asked, "Is Aunt Mary really all right?"

"She's as saucy as you'd expect. I believe she should be with Grandfather by now. Her leg is far from well, but the doctor has assured me that in time, it will heal properly. He has cautioned her to stay off the leg, but when last I saw her she was hobbling about, defying his orders."

"Poor dear. She can't stand to be confined."

Kassidy smiled. "I'm sure when she gets back to London, her injury will be a great diversion at her dinner parties. Her adventure will be envied by all."

The questions tumbled from Arrian's lips. "Have you seen Ian?"

"I have not seen Ian, nor has Aunt Mary. He wasn't in Edinburgh when she arrived. It seems for some reason Grandfather ordered Ian home, and he awaits you at Davinsham. I'm sure he must be very concerned by now."

Arrian wondered how she would tell her mother all that had occurred. "Ian will have to know everything."

"I'm happy to report that your father and brother are still in England and they believe you to be safely with our MacIvors relatives. I pity us all when your father finds out differently. Let's pray he remains in London until I can get you out of here."

Kassidy took Arrian's face and turned it to the candle-light. "There is something different about you I can't define. A new maturity, perhaps."

Arrian clasped her mother's hand, unable to speak of her remorse.

"I despaired for your safety," Kassidy said. "Has that man harmed you?"

Arrian was unable to answer. She buried her face in her hands. She sobbed and was enfolded in her mother's arms.

"What has happened? Why are you so distressed?"

"Oh, Mother, I'm so sorry I allowed Lord Warrick to use me to hurt Ian."

Kassidy gripped her daughter's shoulders and looked into her eyes. It tore at her heart to see the misery there. "Are you saying that he seduced you, Arrian?"

Arrian laid her head against her mother's shoulder. "The pity is that I was willing enough, Mother. At the time it happened I could only think how right it was because I'm his wife."

Kassidy was angry at the man who had so cruelly used her daughter. She resisted the urge to storm downstairs and demand satisfaction. But Lord Warrick must not know that she was Arrian's mother, or they would never escape—retribution would come later.

"My dearest, you did nothing wrong. It is he who will have to answer for enticing an innocent."

"If only we could leave."

Kassidy lifted Arrian's face and gently brushed the tears away. "Never fear, we will leave when the time is right. I didn't come here without a carefully laid plan to get you to safety. Meantime, I don't want you to be alone with Lord Warrick as you were when I arrived."

Arrian moved away to stand by the window. "Mother, it hurts so badly. I believe the unforgivable has happened."

Kassidy came up beside her. "What, dearest?"

"I believe . . . I know I love him, but I don't want to love him."

Kassidy caught her daughter in her arms and allowed her to sob out her misery. Tears ran down Kassidy's face, too, but her eyes were gleaming with anger. She and Raile had protected this precious charge so that nothing could harm her. Lord Warrick would pay mightily for what he had done to Arrian.

Arrian dried her eyes. "I'm sorry our reunion was spoiled by my tears. I'm so happy you're here."

"You must have felt so alone. It took a great deal of courage to stay behind so that Aunt Mary could leave."

"I didn't feel brave at the time." They clasped hands, and Arrian's face paled with a sudden agonizing thought. "You should not have come, Mother. Now you are also his prisoner."

"No, I'm not, Arrian. I told you I didn't come after you without a plan. Captain Norris is just off the coast waiting for a chance to take us away."

"Do you think we can make it to the *Nightingale?*"

"Yes, I do. Are you allowed to go about without being accompanied?"

"Yes, of course."

"Good. That's what Aunt Mary told me. Captain Norris will be watching for us every day."

Arrian twisted her hands. "Will I ever be the same again, Mother?"

"Yes, you will. I know how deeply you have been hurt, but it will pass. I will see to that."

Again tears brightened Arrian's eyes. "I am unfit to be Ian's wife. He won't even want me now."

"Don't think about that. We shall just take one day at a time. Things are not as hopeless as they seem, Arrian." Kassidy looked around the room. "I suppose I should begin acting as your maid. We don't want anyone to become suspicious."

"What will you do?"

Kassidy walked over to the door that led to a small dressing room and glanced inside. "I'll go below and demand to have a bed set up in there."

"But Mother, you can sleep with me."

"No, I can't. Arrian, I must warn you to be on guard and make certain no one suspects who I am. If we are going to escape, we'll have to be very careful. We don't want to do anything that will put Lord Warrick on alert."

Chapter 17

It was early morning when Barra knocked on the door and entered carrying a breakfast tray. She gave Arrian a sour look. "I had little contact with that English maid of yours, m'lady. But it appeared to me she's caught up in her own importance."

Arrian sat up in bed, looking over Barra's shoulder at her mother. "You are right, Barra, Tuttle can indeed feel her importance. You'll have to overlook her ways. I'm afraid I've been too lenient with her."

Barra placed the breakfast tray on a side table and turned to the maid. "Here's her ladyship's breakfast. If you want anything, you'll have to go to the kitchen."

Kassidy unfolded a napkin and handed it to Arrian while they both tried not to laugh. "Yes, Tuttle," Arrian said with mischief dancing in her eyes, "go along to breakfast."

"I'd rather not," Kassidy said.

"There you have it, Barra, she is too obstinate. But I am accustomed to her and will keep her as long as she doesn't test me too far."

Barra sniffed. "It seems to me, m'lady, that she's far too disrespectful."

As Barra sailed out of the room, Arrian fell back against her pillow in a fit of laughter. "She doesn't seem to approve of you, Mother. I wonder why?"

"Eat in the kitchen, indeed," Kassidy said. "What kind of a household is this? If I asked Elspeth to eat in the kitchen, she'd let her views be known."

"Ironworth is in bad repair, Mother, and Warrick has no one capable of helping him. Most of the rooms are closed off and covered with dust. Although Mrs. Haddington tries, she is too fragile for the responsibility of a home this large."

Kassidy took a muffin from the tray and bit into it. "The cook is to be complimented. This is delicious." Then she looked at Arrian. "Lord Warrick's troubles are not yours, Arrian."

"When I sailed for Scotland, Mother, I thought I knew exactly what I wanted. All I could think of was Ian and our life together. Now, I'm sorry to say a whole day can go by and I don't think of him. Is that wicked, Mother?"

Kassidy thought of the handsome young lord she had seen with Arrian the previous night. "No, you are not wicked, Arrian. But you must remember that Warrick Glencarin is only using you to hurt grandfather and Ian. Remember how he tricked you into marriage."

"Is it inconceivable that he could love me?"

Kassidy shook her head. "No, my dearest daughter, it is not inconceivable that he could love you. But you don't understand what you have fallen into here. These blood feuds are stronger than any emotion—even love. Make no mistake about this, Arrian, Lord Warrick would use you, even if he did love you, to hurt a MacIvors."

Arrian let out a shuddering breath. "I know what you say is true, Mother."

"Take a long look at him, Arrian. I learned much about the feud between the Drummonds and the MacIvors in

Edinburgh. I will admit that my family is much at fault. But that doesn't give Lord Warrick the right to use you. I'll never allow that to happen again."

"What will we do if he demands to see me again, Mother?"

"Just leave that to me."

"Will we get through this?"

"Yes, we shall."

"I can only hope Grandfather and Ian will understand when they learn the truth."

"Arrian, I have learned some things that make me ashamed of my MacIvors relatives."

Arrian's eyes widened. "What did you learn, Mother?"

"You know that Lord Warrick's sister married my cousin, Gavin?"

Arrian nodded. "I have learned of it since coming here."

"Well, it seems that my grandfather asked for a large dowry and land besides. Apparently the girl died under suspicious circumstances. It's a sad business, and I don't think the MacIvors were totally innocent."

"I know something about that. In a way, I can understand why Warrick is so bitter. You can see, can't you, Mother, that he would want to regain his honor?"

"Of course I see. But I'll not have him regain it at your expense. The feud has nothing to do with you. Don't pity Lord Warrick too much, Arrian."

"But I am involved, whether I want to be or not."

"Only as long as it takes for me to get you out of here," Kassidy said.

Arrian's eyes were sad. "I want to go, and yet I think he will be lonely if I leave."

"I am furious with that man for preying on your emotions. He knows exactly what he's doing. As for him being lonely, Arrian, it's well known he has many women to comfort him. I heard in Edinburgh that the ladies flock around him. It's said he could have married several titled and wealthy women. We know why he chose you."

Arrian lowered her eyes. "Yes, I suppose you are right." She had forgotten for the moment that she had reason to detest Warrick.

There was a knock, and Kassidy quickly swallowed the muffin and went to answer the door. Barra was standing there with a sullen expression on her face. "His lordship wants to see you at once in his study."

"Me? He wants to see me?" Kassidy asked.

"That's his order."

"Tell him I'll be right down."

"I wouldn't dawdle if I were you."

Kassidy closed the door with a puzzled look on her face. "I wonder what this is all about?"

Arrian took a sip of tea and spread butter on a muffin. "I can't guess. Will you go?"

"Of course." Kassidy made certain her hair was tucked beneath the cap and walked to the door. "I shall just have to see what he wants with me."

Warrick was going over a ledger when Kassidy appeared in the doorway. "You asked to see me, m'lord?"

"Yes, come in, Tuttle."

Kassidy shuffled forward, keeping her eyes downcast.

"I wanted to inquire about Lady Mary's health. I know you said she was well, but I was concerned that there might have been lasting damage to her leg."

"She's faring nicely," Kassidy said in clear Cockney. "She's a strong one."

"I'm glad to hear that. I liked Lady Mary and was concerned about her."

Kassidy could see how charming he could be. "Her ladyship didn't speak too highly of you, m'lord."

Warrick looked quickly at the maid and for the first time noticed the golden hair that had escaped from her cap. She was as obstinate as Barra had said, and she always looked at her feet rather than the person to whom she was speaking.

"How long have you known the Lady Arrian, Tuttle?"

"All her life, m'lord. Mine were the arms that comforted her since she was a baby. I wouldn't like to see anyone hurt her—again. I'll see that don't happen."

"Tuttle, has anyone complained that you are far too recalcitrant and forward to be a proper maid?"

"Oh, no, m'lord, not me. I live only to serve m'lady."

"Very well, go back to your lady and ask her if she would like to ride this morning at eleven."

"She won't, m'lord. She didn't sleep well last night, and a ride would be too much for her."

He came to his feet with a rush of impatience. "Tuttle, suppose you tell your lady what I said and allow her to make that decision. Wait, tell her I insist that she ride with me today."

Kassidy clamped her lips together to keep from making an angry retort. "Yes, m'lord, I'll tell her."

Warrick watched the maid shuffle out of the room. He never thought he would tolerate an English maid in his house. Although this one behaved humbly, she was far from it. Of course, as the woman had been with Arrian since birth, that would give her the right to speak plainly. God knew Haddy never spared him her opinions.

It was almost an hour later when Kassidy came downstairs with word that Lady Arrian would ride with his lordship. She had agreed with her daughter that they dared not refuse, lest it make Lord Warrick suspicious.

The air was crisp, and the sun was warm as Warrick led the horses out of the stable with Mactavish beside him.

"I don't understand women, Mactavish."

"I don't doubt it—not this one, anyway. You force her to stay with you against her will, and then you expect her to thank you for the privilege? I don't like what you're doing to her—she doesn't deserve it."

"Have a care that you don't say too much, Mactavish. I do what I must."

Mactavish draped the reins over the horse Lady Arrian was to ride. "I feel responsible for her since I'm the one who brought her to Ironworth. I say let her go."

Warrick set his lips in a unyielding line. "That's my decision to make."

"Aye, it is. But this goes beyond injured pride and a need to right an old wrong. I say no good can come of this. There's going to be bad trouble."

"Mactavish, you worry like an old woman. After I let her go, she'll forget about Ironworth, and I can assure you I'll put her out of my mind."

The old man looked as if he'd like to oppose Warrick, but he said nothing.

"Suppose I asked her to stay of her own free will?"

"Then you would have to bury the past and make a life with her. Knowing you as I do, I don't think you can do that."

"I have a long memory."

"Then you have your answer, Warrick. You must allow her ladyship to leave as soon as possible."

"What about the marriage?"

"It is a farce and can be easily annulled."

"You like her, don't you, Mactavish?"

"Aye, I do. She's a bonny lass. If you don't see her worth, I certainly do. She's what you need, if you'd but admit it."

Warrick frowned. "I don't understand you, Mactavish. You tell me to let her go, then in the next breath you say she's what I need. Which is it?"

"There we have the problem. I doubt she'll have you, Warrick. She has no reason to think well of you."

By then they had reached the front of the house, where Arrian stood on the steps with her maid. Warrick circled her waist and placed her on the horse. "I believe we shall make a day of it, my lady."

Arrian was strangely silent and acknowledged Mactavish only with a nod of her head.

As they rode away, Mactavish stood beside Kassidy. "You're her ladyship's maid?"

"Yes, I'm Tuttle," she said absently, never taking her eyes off Arrian.

He could sense she was troubled. "Don't worry about your charge. He'll not harm her."

Kassidy spoke before she thought. "I think we both know he's already harmed her."

"I'd not like to think so."

"Why should you care?"

"Have you thought those two might bring the Drummonds and the MacIvors together after generations of hate?"

She glared at him. "I will not see her sacrificed to settle an old blood feud."

Mactavish watched the woman enter the house. He had a suspicion that she was more than she seemed. Her speech was refined, and there was nothing about her that would make one think she was merely a maid. He must warn Warrick to watch this woman.

Arrian said nothing as she rode beside Warrick. After the horses had galloped across the sandy beach for a while, he halted his and looked at Arrian.

"I've been worried about you," he said. "Are you well?"

She refused to look at him. "I am well."

"I have wanted to talk to you to—"

"Look," she said, pointing in the distance. "A sailing ship, probably bound for France."

"Will you not look at me, Arrian?"

She turned to look directly into his eyes. "Satisfied?"

"I wish it had been different between us, Arrian."

"Are you feeling guilty, my lord?"

He shifted in his saddle. "Perhaps."

"I'm glad. I hope you feel so remorseful that your sleep is disturbed. I hope you—"

He held up his hand. "Spare me. You probably wish I would fall off Titus and break my neck."

"Your words, not mine," she snapped, wondering how she could appear detached when she was so aware of his presence.

"Will you never forgive me?"

She blinked her eyes, wondering if this was another of his tricks. "I don't believe so, my lord."

He looked at the sailing ship that was little more than a tiny dot against the horizon. "Perhaps we should leave. It's turned quite cold here by the sea."

She whirled her horse around and raced toward Ironworth. She had to escape. How could she bear to be near a man she had every right to hate? But then, could she deny the love that was as consuming as a raging fire?

Chapter 18

*T*he spacious coach bounced over the rutted
road, and inside, with her leg propped up on
satin cushions, Lady Mary let out a muttered
oath. Her eyes were blazing as she motioned to her maid.
"Agnes, inform that coachman to look to the road or I'll
have him lashed to the lead horse."

As the coach clattered along, Lady Mary closed her eyes,
wondering if this journey would ever end. They were now
traveling through familiar countryside, and she knew they
were on her father's land. If they didn't encounter trouble,
they would reach Davinsham Castle by nightfall.

Absently she stared at the ancient pine forests. Spring
was in the air, and the ground was sprinkled with primroses
and ferns. This was where she had been born and had
grown to womanhood, but she felt no kinship with the land.
She now belonged to England where her beloved George
was buried.

"M'lady, perhaps you should not have made this journey
so soon. Your leg's not yet well."

"You know I have to get to Davinsham, Agnes. I can tell you for certain I'm not looking forward to being the bearer of bad tidings. Ian, I fear, has a malevolent personality and is apt to strike out for Glencarin with armed men."

"These Scots are a fighting lot, m'lady. But I doubt it would be prudent for them to wage a war. His Majesty would never allow it."

Lady Mary sighed. "No doubt my father will view the incident as reason for a fight. There is likely to be a bloody confrontation if cooler heads don't prevail. If only Raile were here, he'd know what to do."

"M'lady, I'm most distressed to think of Lady Arrian and Her Grace in the hands of that devil."

"Don't fret about them. My niece can hold her ground with Warrick Glencarin. I'm more concerned with the consequences that will come from Lord Warrick's actions."

As the sun slipped behind the darkened woods and painted the sky with bright streaks of crimson, the coach entered the gates of Davinsham Castle.

A cortege of servants rushed from the castle to aid Lady Mary. She was carried upstairs to the bedroom that had been hers as a girl. Her leg was propped on pillows, and her maid went below to get her something light to eat.

There was a knock on the door, and Ian MacIvors entered. He stood silently watching the servants make his aunt comfortable, then ordered them to withdraw so that he could talk to Lady Mary in private.

"Your messenger arrived only yesterday morning, Aunt Mary, and he was a bit vague." His eyes snapped with anger. "I have been damned patient, but I demand to know why Arrian isn't with you. Has she decided she no longer wants to marry me?"

Lady Mary looked at her nephew with calm disdain. She had been dreading this moment. "I would have thought you might inquire about my health, Ian."

He sat down beside her, his eyes boring into her. "How

careless of me. But you see, I deduced that if you were well enough to make the odious journey from Edinburgh, you would most likely be recovered."

Lady Mary tried to postpone the inevitable for as long as possible. "Never mind about that. Where is my father and why wasn't he present to greet me?"

"Then you don't know?" Ian leaned back and shoved his hands in his pockets. "My messenger must have passed you on the road."

"I saw no messenger."

"Then I'm afraid it falls to me to tell you that Grandfather is gravely ill. The doctor is with him now. It's his heart again, only this time it's much more serious."

She eased her legs off the bed. "Help me up. I must go to him at once."

"First I want to hear about Arrian and why she isn't with you."

Lady Mary didn't want to contend with Ian's questions, not until she saw her father. It would be better if she told them both together. "Lend me your arm. I'll go to my father now."

Reluctantly Ian stood and helped her to rise. She leaned heavily on him as they walked along the hallway.

"I asked you before if Arrian had decided against marrying me. She's returned to England, hasn't she?"

"No, she hasn't. She's with her mother. I said I would tell you about Arrian later. Your love life will keep until I've seen my father."

Ian had never liked his aunt. She had a way of ordering people around, and she always got her way. But it wouldn't be long until he was head of the MacIvors clan. Then he would have the power and have to answer to no one.

She gripped his arm, hobbling toward her father's room. Ian hoped her leg pained her with each step she took.

The room was dark, and there was only a single candle burning near Gille MacIvors's bed. Lady Mary limped to her father's bedside and stared down at him. His eyes were open, but she could not be sure he saw her.

She glanced up at the doctor, who shook his head sadly.

"Well, Mary," Lord Gille said in a weak voice, "I might have known you wouldn't let me slip away without instructing me on how the deed should be accomplished."

It hurt her to see that her father was only a shell of the man he once was. He had been a great hulk of a man whose mere presence overpowered lesser men. He had held the family together with pure strength and determination. Now his breathing was labored, and his arms looked so fragile and brittle it appeared they could be snapped like dry twigs. His skin was stretched tightly across his face and resembled old parchment.

She smiled through her tears. "You're too stubborn to die unless you choose the time and place, Father."

He rolled his eyes at her with some of his old fire. "This is the place, and it's nearing the time. Will you grieve for me, Mary?"

"Nay, Father—I'll miss you, but I'll not grieve. You've had a good long life and had everything your way. I hope when it comes my time I can say the same, then I'll be glad to go."

He laughed so hard that it turned into a spasm of coughing. The doctor picked up a bottle, trying to poke medicine down his throat, but Lord Gille pushed his hand away.

"Get out. I don't need a doctor."

Lady Mary sat on the edge of the bed holding her father's hand. "Had I known you were so ill, I would have been here sooner."

"Where's Kassidy?" the old man asked, looking around the room. "Where's my favorite grandchild?"

Ian hung back with a scowl on his face. It had always been Kassidy his grandfather favored. His eyes narrowed. Even now the old man hadn't asked to see him.

Lady Mary held back her tears. "Father, Kassidy doesn't know you are ill, or she'd be here."

"I want to see her again. I won't die until I tell her she did right in marrying that Englishman. He's been good to my Kassidy, and that's all I ever wanted for her."

"She'll be glad to hear that, Father. She has always wanted the two most important men in her life to approve of each other."

Lord Gille noticed Ian standing impatiently by the door and motioned for his daughter to lean closer. "Watch over Arrian," he whispered in a raspy voice. "I'm not so certain Ian is the husband for her. He has a cunning about him. I thought he would grow out of it, but he hasn't."

Lady Mary had thought she was the only one who had sensed something sinister about Ian, but apparently her father had felt it also. He would die without ever knowing that Arrian and Kassidy were, at this moment, prisoners in the home of his enemy. "I'll watch over Arrian. You can be certain of that, Father."

Ian heard his name mentioned but couldn't hear what was being said. With anger boiling inside him, he stalked out of the room and down the stairs. His aunt was keeping something from him about Arrian, and he intended to find out what it was.

Lady Mary stayed with her father until he fell asleep. It was after midnight when she got back to her room. To her displeasure, she found her nephew waiting for her.

"I'm bone weary, Ian. I haven't seen a real bed in three days. Anything you have to say to me can surely wait until morning."

Agnes fussed about disapprovingly, unfolding woolen blankets and placing a warming pan in the bed. "I told him as much, m'lady. But he insisted he'd see you tonight."

"Leave us alone, Agnes. What I have to say to my aunt is private."

Lady Mary turned on Ian. "You'll not take it upon yourself to order my maid about. Agnes takes orders from me, and only me—you might want to remember that in the future."

Ian's eyes hardened. "I'll remember."

"See that you do. Now, what would you like to know about Arrian?"

"Surely you can guess that I've been out of my mind with worry about her. I was told that she would be landing at Leith and I rushed there to meet her. But when the *Nightingale* docked she wasn't aboard. Because of Grandfather's failing health I was ordered home. I thought Arrian would then be coming by coach with you, but you arrived alone. What am I to think? If you're trying to spare my feelings, don't bother. If she's changed her mind about our marriage, tell me now."

Lady Mary sank down on the bed and leaned her head back against the pillows. "Agnes, bring me my jewelry chest."

The maid quickly complied and stepped back a respectful pace while Lady Mary searched among her jewels. At last she found what she was looking for and held the ring out to Ian.

He took it and stared at the bright ruby for a long moment. "So, she's returned the ring."

"No, she did not. The ring was returned to you by Lord Warrick Glencarin. He sends regrets and says I am to tell you that she wears the Drummond wedding ring."

The color drained from Ian's face as he leapt to his feet. "By, God, I'll see him dead for this! How dare that bastard take my Arrian." The veins stood out in his neck, and he balled his fists. "She belongs to me. I know she'll never allow him to defile her with his touch. She'd rather die."

Lady Mary stared at Ian as if seeing him for the first time. She had known him to torment the other children when he was small, and he had often been called to task for mistreating animals. But the man who stood before her now was incapable of rational thought.

"Leave me now, Ian. I am very weary, and I'm worried about my father."

He turned on her with hatred blazing in his dark eyes. "How could you have allowed this to happen? She was under your protection. You are responsible for this."

"As it was, I had very little control over the situation."

"I want to hear every detail," he demanded.

She nodded to Agnes and the maid walked to the door, holding it open. "Tomorrow, Ian," she said firmly. "I will talk to you no more tonight."

Ian knew it would do no good to press his aunt further. She was a stubborn old woman who would have her own way. "I trust you'll have a pleasant sleep, Aunt Mary. I will call on you early, for I will not close my eyes until I know everything."

He stormed out of the room, slamming the door behind him while Lady Mary and Agnes stared at each other.

"There's sure to be a fracas, m'lady."

"Yes, there will be, Agnes, and God help us all."

A week had passed since Arrian had gone riding with Warrick. Every day he sent word that he would like her to ride with him again, but each time her maid came with the message that Lady Arrian refused his invitation.

Finally Warrick knocked on Arrian's door. When her maid answered, she blocked his entrance. "M'lady has a headache," she said.

"I'll hear that from her own lips. Stand aside, you obstinate creature."

Kassidy kept a firm grip on the door and continued to block the entrance with her body. "Mayhaps you'll come back tomorrow and she'll see you."

Warrick's eyes clashed for a fraction of a second with the maid's angry green eyes before she lowered her head.

"Out of my way, Tuttle."

Kassidy entertained the notion of slamming the door in his face but decided against it, fearing it might arouse his suspicion. She moved out of his way and dipped into a quick curtsy. "As you wish, m'lord."

Arrian was seated on the window seat with a book in her lap. She warily watched Warrick cross the room to her. When he sat down beside her she stiffened, resisting the urge to run into the safety of her mother's arms.

"What is this?" he asked, taking the book from her hand. "*Childe Harold's Pilgrimage.* So you are an admirer of Lord Byron? I suppose most women appreciate him because he romanticized life."

Arrian's voice was stilted but her eyes flaming. "Yes, Warrick, I admire Lord Byron. And I grieved for the world when he died."

"While I have never admired his poetry, I'm sure his wit is missed."

Arrian wondered how they could be having this casual conversation when so much had happened between them. Her heart was beating fast, and she had difficulty drawing a deep breath.

"You certainly didn't find this book in my library," he said, turning it over in his hand. "So, therefore, you brought it with you."

"I borrowed it from my mother before I left France." Her eyes met Kassidy's. "My mother and father met Lord Byron on a visit to Italy, Warrick. Lord Byron had a particular fondness for my mother. You will see the book is signed to her by Lord Byron's own hand."

Kassidy had tried to distract her daughter to keep her from showing Lord Warrick the inscription. But it was too late, for already Warrick was reading it aloud.

To you, Kassidy, with hair the color of a golden sunset and eyes as green as the most precious emerald. Do you think Raile will mind if I adore you from afar?

Warrick stared at the inscription for a long moment, feeling like a fool. He laid the book aside and stood. With a deep bow, his eyes went to the maid. "Do I have the pleasure of addressing Her Grace, the duchess of Ravenworth?"

Kassidy stood up to her full height with a proud tilt to

her head, her defiant green eyes meeting his silver ones. She removed her cap and tossed it aside, and shimmering gold hair tumbled down her back.

"You will have to forgive the deception, Lord Warrick. But you see, you have something that belongs to me and I have come to get her back."

Warrick stared at the golden-haired beauty, understanding very well why Lord Byron had praised her loveliness. "I must say, you have gone to great lengths to deceive me, Your Grace—a duchess posing as a lowly maid. No wonder my household thought you too obstinate."

"I will not play word games with you, Lord Warrick," Kassidy said. "The day will come when you will be called to task for what you have done to my daughter."

"Perhaps, Your Grace. But that day has not yet come."

"Oh, but it will. You will answer to me and her father, and if that isn't enough to keep you awake at night, you will also answer to the king."

He smiled. "Your Grace, I believe I would be more frightened of you than any crowned head."

"I have come to take my daughter away, Lord Warrick, and I intend to do just that."

He turned to Arrian. "And is it still your wish to leave?"

"I want to leave more than I have ever wanted anything in my life, Warrick."

He moved to the door and wrenched it open. "I will think on the matter. I'll let you know my decision at dinner tonight." His eyes went to Kassidy. "I would ask to dine alone with your daughter, Your Grace."

Kassidy stood face to face with him, her eyes burning like green fire. "That will not be possible." Hundreds of angry words ached to be spoken, but Kassidy did not want to provoke the man too far. After all, they had to lull him into passivity so they could escape. "Arrian does not want to be alone with you, and you can guess why."

"What if I give you my word that no harm will befall her?

I only want to talk to her. There is much I need to settle in my mind."

"I'm sure you will understand if I'm not too concerned whether your mind is settled or not. I'm slow to trust your word, my lord," Kassidy said.

"Would you trust me if I should offer my word as the earl of Glencarin?"

"Not good enough."

"What if I give you my word as chief of Clan Drummond?"

Kassidy thought for a moment. The word given by a chieftain was not to be broken. "Then that would suffice, my lord. But you should first ask my daughter if she is willing to dine with you."

Arrian laid the book on the window seat and stood. "I have nothing to say to you, Warrick."

His eyes were almost pleading. "But I have many things to say to you."

Kassidy nodded her head only slightly to indicate that Arrian was to accept.

"Very well," Arrian said. "But only in the company of my mother."

Kassidy smiled at him. "You have my daughter's answer."

"She told you about what happened between us, Your Grace?"

"Of course she did. Did you think my daughter would keep such a thing from me?"

His eyes were hard as they probed Arrian's. "I had hoped that what happened between us, Arrian, would remain between husband and wife."

Arrian glared back at him. "Not true husband and wife, my lord."

Warrick turned to Kassidy with a touch of humor in his smile. "I will be a most fortunate host tonight, Your Grace, with two lovely ladies at my table."

"I'm glad we understand each other, my lord," Kassidy said.

"I'll look forward to this evening. Until then, there is something in the village that requires my attention."

"Tonight, my lord," Kassidy said, "all will be settled between you and my daughter."

Warrick's eyes sought Arrian's, and she thought she detected pain in the silver depths. But, no, surely she had been mistaken.

"Until we meet again, Arrian."

Chapter 19

*A*fter the door had closed behind Warrick, Kassidy sprang into action. "Hurry, Arrian, dress warmly and sensibly so that it will appear we are merely going for a stroll. We haven't much time."

Arrian's eyes were wide. "Are we leaving now?"

"Yes, as soon as possible. You heard him say he would be in the village most of the day. We may never get another chance like this one."

Arrian flew to her trunk and sifted through its contents until she found a gray woolen gown. She quickly changed, and Kassidy fastened the hooks for her while nodding in approval.

Kassidy changed her own clothing while Arrian slipped her feet into boots and tied her unruly hair back in a ribbon.

"Wait here until I return," Kassidy said, picking up the breakfast tray. "I'll watch below until I see him leave. Be ready when I return."

Arrian looked around the room that had been her prison for so long. She touched the lace on the canopy, thinking of the other girl who had occupied this room. In a way they had been kindred souls. Warrick's sister had also been forced into a marriage she hadn't wanted. But poor Gwendolyn's life had ended in tragedy, while Arrian was about to escape.

She tried not to think of Warrick or of her feelings for him. It still hurt too badly, and the wound was too raw and deep.

She closed the trunk, knowing she would have to leave her beautiful gowns behind. Her jewel chest was on the dressing table and she opened the lid, selecting those that had special meaning—the pearls her father had given her on her fourteenth birthday, a diamond brooch from Aunt Mary, a golden locket that had been her mother's.

She picked up the ring Warrick had slipped on her finger the night they were married. She had removed it and put it away without looking at it. Now she saw that it was very beautiful, a large diamond surrounded by sapphires. She slipped the ring into her pocket—she would keep it as a remembrance.

Carefully she picked up the book that Lord Byron had given her mother and tucked it inside her cape.

She picked up a quill, dipped it in ink, and scribbled a quick letter to Warrick. When she was finished she propped it against the mirror so he would find it.

Kassidy rushed into the room. "Lord Warrick and his steward have ridden away, so we must act quickly. I informed Mrs. Haddington that you needed fresh air and we would be walking on the beach."

Arrian picked up her cape and threw it over her shoulders. "She didn't suspect anything?"

"No. She has been worried about you and agrees that fresh air will do you good."

Arrian took a last look around the room and followed her mother into the hallway.

They walked leisurely out the front door, hoping to allay

any suspicion, should someone be watching. They hastened their steps as they walked in the direction of the sea.

Arrian took her mother's hand and led her to the steps that had been carved into the stone. Descending quickly to the beach, they began to sense that freedom was within their grasp. Soon they were both running as they followed the path away from the castle.

Arrian kept looking over her shoulder. Suppose Warrick returned early and discovered her letter before they were safely away? Oh, why had she written that letter?

Arrian pulled her cape around her more tightly. The sea fostered a cold wind, and she shivered. "What do we do now, Mother?"

"We walk southward and hope Captain Norris is watching for us."

Arrian glanced up at the imposing castle that towered high atop the rock-faced cliff. Why was she feeling such heavy sadness? If Providence had not brought her to these shores, she would never have known Warrick. In another month she would have become Ian's wife. But would she have been happy? Could she have ever truly loved Ian if she had so readily given her heart to Warrick Glencarin? These questions haunted her as she raced farther away from the man who had won her heart.

Kassidy stopped to catch her breath, and Arrian pulled her against the cliff wall. "Mother, is it possible to love a man and hate him at the same time?"

Kassidy clasped Arrian's hand, knowing she had to answer her question as honestly as she could. "I would think it's possible to love a man and think you detest him. But knowing you and the values you respect, the man you choose to love would have to be honorable or you would not respect him. Without respect there can be no love."

Arrian was pondering her mother's words. It was true. She could never love a man she didn't respect.

They came to what looked like an impassable rock formation

that projected across the water. Kassidy stopped for a moment, gripped her daughter's hand, and began to climb.

At last they dropped on the other side. Arrian began to feel elated. They were going to make it! When she rounded a corner she was quickly grabbed and dragged into the shadows.

"At last you have come, my lady," Captain Norris said, smiling. "I'm so happy to see you. We began to despair that you would never escape."

"Let us leave at once," Kassidy said, hurrying toward the boat that would take them to the *Nightingale,* which lay at anchor inside the cove.

Arrian and her mother were placed in the boat, and several men pushed it into the swelling waves.

Arrian felt a sudden rush of happiness, until she glanced up at Ironworth Castle. Then fires of uncertainty smoldered in her heart. If she was so happy to be free, why did she have this strong urge to leap from the boat and run back to Warrick?

Tears choked in her throat, and her mother pulled her into her arms. "Don't cry, dearest. It's all behind you now. You will never have to see him again."

Arrian turned her face against her mother's rough cape, and a shudder went through her body. Never see him again? Oh, why did those words tear at her heart?

High above the cliff two riders watched the longboat fight against the incoming tide to reach the yacht anchored nearby.

"You were right, Warrick, they lost no time in leaving," Mactavish said.

Warrick's gaze was fastened on the small figure huddled in her mother's arms. "When you told me that a ship lay off the coast, I knew it waited for Arrian and her mother."

"So you let Lady Arrian think she escaped."

"It was the only way. I was certain if I told them I would

be away from the castle today, they would make their way to the ship."

Mactavish studied his chief's face and saw the misery Warrick tried to hide. "You did the right thing."

"Yes, you convinced me of that. But somehow I had hoped she might decide at the last moment to stay."

"I thought I saw something between the two of you that—"

"You saw nothing," Warrick said angrily, spinning Titus around and riding toward Ironworth.

The loud call of the sea birds and the rhythmic splashing of the waves against the face of the cliff were soon drowned out by the pounding of Titus's hooves as he raced the wind.

Warrick couldn't bring himself to go into Arrian's bedroom until she had been gone three days. At last he gathered his courage and opened the door. Everything was neat and in its place as if she had just stepped out and would soon return.

He closed the door and stood in the middle of the room for a long moment, feeling somehow like an intruder.

Finally he walked into the small dressing room to find the trunks containing all of her clothing. He remembered Arrian telling him she had gone with her family to Paris to buy a trousseau. All had been left behind.

Warrick raised the lid of the trunk and ran his hand across the soft pile of the crimson velvet gown she had worn the first day he'd seen her. He lifted it against his face and closed his eyes, breathing in the sweet lingering scent that still clung to the fabric.

A quick pain stabbed his heart. He neatly folded the gown and replaced it in the trunk. On the floor he found a red satin shoe that must have been purchased to match the gown. He held it in the palm of his hand, thinking how tiny she was, how defenseless.

Like a man in a trance he walked back into the bedroom. First he picked up her brush, where strands of golden hair still clung to the bristles. He touched it lightly and then placed it back on the dressing table. A large chest caught his attention. The key was in the lock, so he turned it and stared at magnificent diamond, ruby, and emerald jewelry. He wondered why Arrian would have left it behind—it had to be worth a king's ransom.

When he closed the lid, his eyes fell upon the letter that was propped against the mirror. He was reluctant to read it, for he knew it would be her last message to him.

His hand trembled as he stared at the neat handwriting.

My lord,

By the time you read this I will be gone from this prison you created for me. However, I am not unsympathetic to your plight and that of your villagers. The jewels in this chest belong to me, so I give them to you to use as you see fit. Since it was the MacIvors branch of my family who wronged you, it is only right that the jewels should come to you. It is unlikely that our paths will cross again and I cannot find it in me to wish you ill. Perhaps the feud between our families is over at last. Let it die with us, my lord. I have seen what hate has done to you. Let it go, Warrick. I have.

He stared at his image in the mirror, feeling as if his life's blood was spilling out of him. Arrian was right. For so long, revenge had been his only reason for existing. Too late, he realized it was time to let the blood hate die.

The voyage had been uneventful as the *Nightingale* sailed down the Scottish coast. Arrian kept mostly to her cabin and lay on the bed for most of the day. Kassidy had remained with her daughter, silently lending her strength.

Arrian would cry herself to sleep at night, thinking her mother wouldn't know, but of course she did. Kassidy knew there was nothing she could say to make her daughter's pain lessen. Later, when Arrian felt less hurt, they would talk.

Arrian stood on deck beside Captain Norris as the ship neared land. He seemed troubled so she knew he was bothered.

"You want to ask me something, Captain?"

"Yes, my lady. I've been worried about you. I've heard much about the fierce fighting between these two clans. Will there be more bloodshed over this incident?"

"There's been too much bloodshed already. I intend to see that this feud dies."

"You know I stand ready to help in any way I can, Lady Arrian. You used to toddle around my legs and climb on my lap. I have a particular liking for you."

She smiled. "You are kind, as always. If you will excuse me, I'll go below now."

Kassidy joined the captain, and they both watched Arrian disappear down the companionway.

"I suppose His Grace will have to be told what happened," Captain Norris said.

Kassidy and Captain Norris exchanged looks, both knowing Raile would be a power with which to be reckoned. "Yes, he will have to be told," Kassidy replied. "Did you call on the Lord Mayor in private, as I asked?"

"I did, Your Grace. He regrets that he can do little to annul the marriage between Lady Arrian and Lord Warrick unless both parties agree to the act."

"I see. Well, perhaps my husband can persuade Lord Warrick that it would be advantageous to his health to sign the paper, Captain Norris."

He was silent, and Kassidy knew he was wondering what Raile would do when he learned what had happened to his daughter. She was wondering how she would have the courage to tell him.

It was a dull, misty day when the *Nightingale* dropped anchor in the port of Leith, a tiny fishing village that stood in the shadow of Edinburgh. The yacht sailed to the docks and lowered her sails.

Arrian stood beside her mother, who gave her an encouraging smile.

"Nothing is so bad, dearest, if it's shared with someone. I promise you'll not be alone. I'll stand beside you."

"I need your strength, Mother. Especially when I see Ian."

"If it is your wish to leave for Ravenworth now, Arrian, I'll instruct Captain Norris to put out to sea at once."

"I have to face Ian—I owe him that."

Kassidy recognized a new strength in her daughter. She would stand back and wait to see if she was needed.

Suddenly there was the sound of a dear, familiar voice calling out. "Your Grace, my lady, I thought you'd never get here." The maid waved up to them. "I'll see to the trunks, then I'll come to you."

Arrian smiled at her mother. "It would seem Elspeth is our greeting party. I should have known she would meet us as soon as we docked."

Arrian thought of her mother's maid, who was more like a member of the family. The sound of Elspeth issuing orders brought a feeling of normality to her life.

"Careful with Her Grace's trunks, she had them made special in Paris, France. Don't scare a one of them."

When Elspeth had climbed to the upper deck, she rushed to Arrian and hugged her tightly. "Lord, but I thought we'd never see you again, m'lady. If you hadn't come when you did, I was ready to storm that castle myself."

"Elspeth," Kassidy asked, "is Aunt Mary still in Edinburgh?"

"No, Your Grace. She said I was to tell you she's gone on to her father."

"Has there been any word of my husband and son?"

"I heard they're still in England waiting for the *Nightingale* to come for them."

Kassidy instructed Captain Norris. "Sail directly for

London and deliver this letter to His Grace. I have asked him to come to Scotland with all haste."

Captain Norris took the letter and nodded. "I'll pray for a swift wind, Your Grace."

Arrian turned her face upward and closed her eyes. She felt the warm sun, but there was no warmth in her heart. She had started her voyage as a young woman looking forward to marrying the man she loved. Now she doubted that Ian would want her, and she wasn't certain how she felt about him.

She wasn't the same innocent girl who had fallen in love with Ian when he'd come to Ravenworth.

Kassidy took Arrian's hand, and they walked down the gangplank together to the carriage where Elspeth was waiting for them.

"We must first visit the shops, Arrian, to find you suitable attire. Then we shall go directly to Davinsham. I have a feeling we should make haste."

Arrian nodded. "After I've talked to Ian and seen Grandfather, I'll want to go home."

Chapter 20

he carriage rolled along at a steady pace, and Arrian became aware that it was a glorious spring day, with leaves sprouting on the trees and wildflowers dotting the countryside. She thought of other times when she had joyously made this journey with Michael and Aunt Mary. There was no joy in her heart today.

She glanced at Elspeth, who slept in the corner, her head rolling back and forth with the motion of the coach.

"Look, Arrian," her mother said, trying to cheer her, "you will be able to see Davinsham Castle from the next rise."

Arrian pretended interest. "The castle always reminds me of Great-grandfather . . . strong, sturdy, and defiant."

"Yes, that's a good description of him. But I learned long ago that Grandfather was not as gruff as he would have people believe."

"Aunt Mary says that you're his favorite."

"I believe he has a great fondness for you also, Arrian. But he can be harsh with those who do not find favor with him. I always thought he was a bit stern with Ian."

At last Arrian put into words what they had both been pondering. "I want to be alone with Ian when I tell him what happened, Mother. I have decided to tell him I won't marry him."

Kassidy studied her for a long moment. "If that's your decision. Don't allow Ian or Grandfather to press you, because you know they both want the marriage. I've sent Captain Norris for your father, so he'll be here soon."

"I need Father. I want to lay my head on his shoulder and have him to tell me that everything is well."

"Arrian, when you were small and a favorite doll got broken, your father could mend it for you. And when someone had been unkind to you, your father could make you smile. But I fear your father cannot make this disappear for you, Arrian. Your healing will have to come from within yourself."

"I know for certain that I love Warrick even though what he did was wrong. To leave him was like tearing out my heart."

"But you also thought you loved Ian," Kassidy reminded her. "You must examine all your feelings carefully."

"What I felt for Ian was a childish emotion when compared to the love I feel for Warrick. My love for Warrick is consuming, and I can only think of him. After all that's happened between us, I don't want to see him hurt. Is that not love, Mother?"

Kassidy closed her eyes, willing herself not to cry. "How well I remember what it feels like to know true love for the first time, Arrian. Like you, I did not believe he returned my love, and yet I still wanted him."

"You speak of Father?"

"Yes."

"But your story has a very different ending than mine."

Kassidy remembered the haunting look she had seen in the eyes of the young lord of Glencarin. Had he been feeling love or remorse? She did not believe they had seen the last of him. She knew he had deliberately allowed them to leave, although she had not said this to Arrian.

Arrian leaned back against the seat. "I shall love him until I die."

Kassidy was silent, wondering if the pain Lord Warrick had inflicted on Arrian had wounded him as severely. Perhaps he was not the villain she had first thought.

Ian sent riders to the far reaches of his grandfather's land with instructions for the clan to gather at Davinsham. Slowly they began to arrive at the castle, where they were armed. They waited only for word to ride for Glencarin.

Hate coiled inside Ian like a poisonous snake. This time he would not stop until he saw Warrick Glencarin dead, but not before he was tortured. He wanted to hear him beg for mercy, and cry out for death to release him.

Ian had just come from the stables when the carriage pulled up to the front of the castle. Thinking it would be more members of the clan, he was shocked to see Kassidy step down.

"Cousin Kassidy, I'm so distressed by what has happened. You should know that I have called the clan together and we will ride on Glencarin within the hour. I will rescue Arrian—"

Ian was struck silent as Arrian stepped to the ground. For a long moment he could only stare at her. There was an air of uncertainty about her, and she had not yet met his eyes. With one big step he grabbed her and hugged her to him.

"Arrian, Arrian, you are safe. You have been returned to me."

Kassidy saw the misery in Arrian's eyes and came to her rescue. "I'm sure you will understand, Ian, that my daughter has been through a great deal. She will need to rest before she talks to anyone."

He released Arrian and saw the paleness of her cheeks. "Of course you must rest, my dear. And don't worry, we will soon make Lord Warrick regret what he's done."

Arrian shook her head. "You must do nothing, Ian. I

demand that you send the clan members away until we have had time to talk."

"This is men's business, Arrian. I must do what I know is right."

Kassidy intervened. "I ask you to do nothing until I have spoken to Grandfather."

"The men are restless, but I'll hold them here for a while."

Arrian's eyes were pleading. "Please don't let there be bloodshed because of me. I could not live with that."

"When can we talk?" Ian asked. "I'll want to hear all that's happened. I must know what he did to you."

"Tonight after dinner," she said, moving to stand beside her mother.

Kassidy looked at her nephew, reading anger and confusion in his eyes. She would not allow him to turn his anger into a war. "Is Aunt Mary here?" she asked.

Ian nodded, his eyes still on Arrian. She had changed. She had not seemed happy to see him. "Yes, Aunt Mary's here. I'm afraid there is sorrow here, Kassidy. Grandfather is gravely ill."

Kassidy turned and ran up the steps with Arrian right behind her. They hurried straight to Gille MacIvors's room and found family and clan members gathered around his bed.

Everyone moved aside when they saw Kassidy and Arrian. Kassidy approached her grandfather with pain in her heart. His eyes were closed, and she dropped down on the floor beside him and laid her head against his bed. She took his hot hand in hers and raised it to her cheek. Arrian knelt beside Kassidy to lend her strength, knowing that her mother loved the grizzled old man.

"I'm here, Grandfather. It's Kassidy."

His dull blue eyes stared at her from a sunken face, and his hot fingers clasped hers. "Now that I have looked upon your dear face, I can die," he whispered in a trembling voice.

"I told them I would not go until you came. You, my dearest granddaughter, with golden hair so like your grandmother's."

He smiled slightly and took a deep breath that came out like a hiss. Kassidy knew the exact moment Lord Gille died, because his hand fell away from hers and dangled lifelessly over the side of the bed.

The doctor came forward and shook his head. "The chief's gone."

Lady Mary, Kassidy, and Arrian stayed at his side while the others filed sadly out of the room. The three women who had loved him hugged one another and cried tears of grief.

The bagpipes played a mournful tune as they had all day. Ian stood at the window of the study, staring out at the rain that had begun to fall. When he turned to his brother, Jamie, he was frowning. "Can't someone stop those damned pipes? They are beginning to annoy me."

Jamie shook his head. "They're a tribute for our grandfather. You know that."

Ian sat down in a chair and ran his hand through his tousled hair. "I thought that old man would outlive us all." His voice was bitter. "Look around you, Jamie, and tell me what you see."

"I see Grandfather's study."

"No, not Grandfather's. Not anymore. Everything you see here is mine. I'm the chief of Clan MacIvors."

"Yes, you are. But for now I feel only sadness at Grandfather's passing."

"You can't tell me you cared for that old man? My God, Jamie, he never gave you a passing thought."

"I respected him. I can't imagine a life without him. Didn't you love him, Ian?"

"No. I only waited for the day when I could stand in his shoes. I had my life planned for a very long time. Did you know that I had decided to marry Arrian when she was only a child? I only waited for her to grow up. There were many times I could have married, but I wanted the best—Arrian's the best."

Jamie stared at Ian. "Why are you ungrateful for all Grandfather did for you? He taught you everything and made you his heir."

"He taught me nothing, and I would have been his heir in any event."

Jamie shook his head. "I once admired you, Ian. But lately I'm not so sure you are worthy of the trust Grandfather placed in you."

"It matters little what you think, Jamie. I'm chief and will answer to no one. I'll need your help, and damn it, you will do as I say."

"You didn't plan on Warrick Glencarin spoiling your plans, did you? You know why he did it, don't you? To lash out at me for taking Helena away from him." Jamie was silent for a moment. "I'm not sorry I married Helena, for she is a gentle soul and has given me a fine son. But I do rue the way I forced her to marry me—she deserved better."

Ian looked at Jamie in disgust. "You're getting soft."

"Perhaps, but you're getting hard, Ian. How can you not grieve at Grandfather's passing?"

Ian wasn't listening to his brother. "Lord Warrick will pay for what he's done to my Arrian." He shuddered, wondering if the man had touched her in any way. "I'll see him rot in hell."

"You should feel some satisfaction, Ian. Arrian and Kassidy escaped from that man. So his revenge on you was not quite a total victory."

"Yes. He didn't expect me to get her back. I'll petition the king and we'll have that mockery of a marriage annulled, and then Arrian and I shall be married. Lord Warrick has dug his own grave this time. The punishment will come swiftly from the king because of Arrian's importance. She's not just some little Scottish noblewoman, and this is not just another feud."

"Aunt Mary says there can't be a wedding or any celebrating for a year because of Grandfather's death. You'll have to bide your time."

Ian slammed his fist down on the desk. "Will you stop telling me what Aunt Mary says! She isn't chief here—I am. It's my word that will be obeyed, not hers."

Arrian had been dreading the meeting with Ian, but it could no longer be delayed. She was prepared to face his displeasure and recriminations.

She chose to meet him in the garden where she had often played as a child. When she approached him, he was standing with his back to her. She felt pity for him, knowing how he must be grieving for their grandfather and that she must add to that grief.

"Ian," she said, watching him turn around to face her. "Are you all right?"

"I'm holding up." He took her hand and raised it to his lips. "I have been thinking of you."

"Ian, I'm so sorry about Great-grandfather. Will you accept my condolences?"

He lowered his dark eyes. "We shall console each other, Arrian, for he was dear to us both."

"I didn't know Grandfather as well as you did, but I loved and admired him."

"Grandfather was a hard man, Arrian, although you would not have seen that side of him. He expected much out of his family, and more from me."

"Yes, I can believe that."

"He loved your mother more than anyone. I believe Kassidy could have asked anything from him and he would have given it to her."

"Mother is very distressed. She loved him a great deal. I'll be glad when Father arrives so he can comfort . . . us all. He can help you put your affairs in order if you wish."

"I want you to know that your father will always find a welcome at Davinsham Castle. Unlike my grandfather, I respect him and will welcome his advice in many matters."

She knew they were both talking of trivial things to keep from saying what was on their minds. Now that she stood before Ian, she knew that whatever she had felt for him had been only a young girl's fancy. But she could not tell him this. She could not hurt him any more than he'd already been hurt.

She gathered her courage. "You know that I agreed to a marriage with Warrick Glencarin?"

"Yes, and I understand why. Aunt Mary explained it to me. It wasn't your fault, Arrian, and it isn't a real marriage."

"I am told that it is legally binding."

"Yes, but I'll deal with that." He searched Arrian's face. "Aunt Mary assured me that you didn't share Lord Warrick's bedroom."

She felt laden with guilt. "No, Ian, I didn't share his bedroom." She lowered her head, feeling as if her heart would break at what she must tell him.

He forced her to look at him. "Something happened between you, didn't it?"

She took a deep breath. "I want to be honest with you, Ian. I am no longer a maiden."

Arrian watched Ian's eyes fill with rage before he turned away from her. She watched his shoulders droop, and she felt such remorse for hurting him.

At last he turned back to her, his face contorted in fury. "How dare that bastard touch what belongs to me! You were to be mine, pure and sweet, untouched by any man. I waited for years for you. There were times when I wanted you so badly I ached. But I controlled the urge, knowing that you would one day belong to me alone."

She felt his anguish. He loved her, and she could not return his feelings. "I'm sorry, Ian."

"Sorry . . . sorry!"

"Yes, of course I am. You act as if I deliberately set out to hurt you, and you know that is not true."

"You should have taken your own life rather than allow your name to be linked with our enemy."

She could not believe the things he was saying to her. She thought of poor Gwendolyn, who had done just that. "It was not only my life I was worried about at the time. I also had concerns about Aunt Mary."

"Damn Aunt Mary. That meddling old woman has caused nothing but trouble."

Arrian was shocked and felt the need to defend their aunt. "Aunt Mary is—"

"Did you find Lord Warrick handsome, Arrian? Was he hard to resist? Do you think I hadn't heard how he attracts women to him? Did he attract you, Arrian?"

She backed away from him. "Why are you asking me these things?"

"Because I have the right to know." He grabbed her wrist and pulled her against him. "Did he stir within you the flames of desire that only I should have stirred?"

"Ian, let me go." She tried to pry his fingers loose from her wrist. "You're hurting me."

At that moment they heard someone coming down the path, and he released Arrian reluctantly. "Is there nowhere we can be alone? Every time I try to talk to you someone interferes."

Arrian was relieved to see Lady Helena walking toward them. She had met her only this morning and had found something sad and lonely about the woman. Arrian wondered if she still loved Warrick.

"Ian, Arrian, isn't it a lovely spring morning?" Helena pulled back when she saw the scowl on Ian's face. "I'm sorry. I suppose the two of you want to be alone."

"No. Wait," Arrian said, moving quickly toward Helena. "I'm coming with you." She glanced at Ian. "I'm sorry. We will talk about this later."

Arrian turned her attention to Jamie's wife. "I hear you have a son. I would like very much to see him."

Jamie's wife looked pleased. "He is a delight, and so like his father."

Arrian refused to look back at Ian, but she could feel his eyes burning into her. She couldn't blame him for being angry. He didn't deserve to be hurt, and she had hurt him dreadfully.

Lady Helena chattered on, and Arrian tried to follow her conversation. But her mind was far away at a castle by the sea. She wondered what Warrick was doing at this moment.

igh scattered clouds occasionally blocked out the sun, and a brisk wind blew out of the south on the day Gille MacIvors was laid to rest in the family crypt. Hundreds of clan members, friends, and family gathered to pay their last respects.

The chief of Clan MacIvors had ruled with might rather than benevolence, but still he'd commanded great respect.

Arrian stood with her arm around her grieving mother while the pipes wailed a forlorn strain. It was the passing of an era and the finish of a man who, if he had not gained a name in history, had at least touched the lives of those who knew him.

While the minister painted a flowery tribute to her great-grandfather, Arrian looked at the people around her. Her mother and Aunt Mary were genuinely grieving. As new head of the clan, Ian stood in a place of honor, his head bowed, obviously saddened by Lord Gille's passing. Arrian saw a tear slide down Jamie MacIvor's face, and his wife Helena was sobbing loudly.

She felt her mother take a faltering step, and Arrian's

hand tightened on her arm. "Have courage, Mother, and lean on me."

"Good-bye, Grandfather," Kassidy said. "This world will not see your like again."

Kassidy and Arrian turned back to the castle, while two clan members helped a distraught Lady Mary up the grassy pathway.

Ian stood alone, his thoughts not touching the crowd around him. He followed Arrian with his eyes. She had changed toward him. He now had everything he wanted, everything except her, and he would have her too—nothing would stop him.

There was a strained intensity in the formal dining room as the servants silently went about the task of serving dinner to the many guests who had remained after the service. Ian took his rightful place at the head of the table, placing Kassidy on his right and Arrian on his left.

As the new chief surveyed the faces of the fifty people at the table, he stood up, wineglass in hand.

"I ask you all to drink with me to acknowledge that the torch of power has been passed from my grandfather to me. There will be many changes in the old ways, for we are a new generation. I want you to know that I take up that torch with confidence in the future and with assurance that we can overcome our enemies. If any of you have troubles, you will come to me as chief of the clan and I shall endeavor to help you."

There was a raising of glasses from the guests, but there were also hostile glances from many of them. An uncomfortable silence passed as the ladies and gentlemen took a sip of their wine, their eyes fastened on their new chief.

Arrian swallowed the food without tasting it. There was something about Ian that was different and somehow disconcerting, yet she could not have said what it was that disturbed her. It was as if she saw him for the first time. He seemed somehow like a little man sitting in a big man's chair.

Kassidy watched her daughter's face and read much of her thoughts. Ian was feeling his power and expressing that power with pompous arrogance. Accustomed to her father's quiet strength, Arrian was not stirred by Ian's swaggering show of importance.

Aunt Mary had difficulty rising because of her leg, but she managed to stand, drawing everyone's attention. "I, too, wish to give a tribute—not to my nephew, who is so newly become chief, and who has not yet proved himself worthy— but to my father, who proved his worth many times," she said, her eyes blazing. "Ladies, gentlemen, I give you a salute to Gille MacIvors. He was a man who stood taller than most. His enemies feared him, and his family cherished him. He will be missed."

With an uproarious shout, the family members rose to their feet and drank to her toast. Lady Mary took a sip of her wine and placed the glass on the table. "Now if you will all excuse me, it has been a tiring day."

The company gathered at the table watched in shock as Lady Mary left the room, for what she had done amounted to a slap in Ian's face.

Kassidy laid her napkin aside and stood up. "You will excuse me also, Ian. I must see to Aunt Mary. This has all been very difficult for her."

Anger smoldered in Ian's eyes. He had thought to use this large gathering of clan members to his advantage and firmly establish himself as chief. Now others were leaving. Too late he realized he had blundered by pressing his claim too soon.

As the moments passed, there were only Jamie and Helena and Arrian left at the table with him.

"Well, it would seem we are to have our dessert alone," Ian said, trying to hide his fury.

"You shouldn't have done it, Ian," Jamie said in a rare show of defiance against his brother. "The family and friends were here to pay their last respects to Grandfather. This was not the time for you to establish your claim as head of the family."

Arrian's heart went out to Lady Helena, whose face was puffy and red from crying. The woman was obviously not happy. Could she possibly still be grieving over Warrick?

Ian came to his feet. "At least you didn't desert me, Arrian. Come with me to the library. There is much we have to discuss."

"I would prefer we have our conversation another time, Ian. We only buried Grandfather today, and I need time to grieve for him alone."

"Ah, rebuked by my bride-to-be. Perhaps you will be the one to refine my rough manners and save me from being too impetuous as I was today."

Before Arrian could reply, his hand fastened on her wrist, and he led her from the room. She said nothing until they were in the library, and then she turned on him furiously.

"I am not accustomed to being handled in that manner, Ian. When I said I didn't want to talk to you tonight, I meant it!"

His jaw clamped shut tightly. "Perhaps if I had been the handsome chief of the Drummonds, you would have come readily enough with me."

She stared at him, thinking she must have misunderstood his words. "I can assure you this has nothing to do with Warrick."

He spun around. "So, you call him by his Christian name. Did that man force you to his bed, or did you go willingly?"

"How dare you!"

"I knew he would have you—he had to, because it was his twisted way of hitting at me. He did wound me this time, Arrian."

"Ian, I'm sorry if I hurt you. I don't know what to say except to ask you to forgive me."

He caught her arms and pulled her close to him. "I doubt a man has ever loved a woman as I love you. No man has waited as long or as patiently as I've waited for you. I will not let you go, Arrian."

She pushed against him. "I am not property, Ian, nor am I one of your clan that you can tell me what to do."

He saw resentment in her eyes and quickly released her. This was not the way he wanted it to be between them. "Now I must ask pardon, Arrian. I allowed my adoration for you to make me speak rashly. Can you not be a little charitable toward me, for I have suffered greatly?"

"I know you have," she said kindly. "Let's not think about it, Ian. We are all under a strain because of our grief for Grandfather."

"Yes, his death has left us without direction. That's why I'm trying to establish my leadership. The clansmen need to know that I'm capable of standing in his place."

She felt pity for him. He had a great deal of responsibility on his shoulders, for which their Grandfather probably hadn't prepared him. "It will come to you in time, Ian. After the clansmen have grieved for Grandfather, they will be ready to listen to you."

"With you beside me, I could rule the world, Arrian. I know the MacIvors clan has been drifting apart, and I want to bring it together in a reunion of spirit and purpose."

She saw his dream through his eyes and felt sorry that he would never see it fulfilled. "Many of your people have moved away, Ian. Aunt Mary told me that MacIvors have settled in different parts of Scotland and some have even gone as far away as America seeking a new life. She says there is nothing for them here. The land will no longer support them as it did in the past."

"Aunt Mary is not all-knowing. I will live to see the day when we McIvers will crush our enemies and break the shackles of England! The day will come when we shall again rise to power."

She realized he was not speaking rationally. "You must not say that, Ian. Surely you know that's impossible."

His eyes flamed with passion. "Does not the Scottish blood in you cry out to be free of English domination?"

"I am English, Ian. You must try to remember that when you speak of crushing my country."

Ian tried another approach. "Don't you want to bring Warrick Glencarin down from his lofty perch, to slam him to his knees and make him beg for mercy?"

"No. I only want to see an end to the conflict, Ian. Unlike Clan MacIvors, Clan Drummond is still intact and they greatly outnumber you. Ian, you could not win a war against them, for they are loyal to their chief. If you continue, you'll surely bring King William's wrath down on your head—then you'll lose everything."

He didn't seem to hear her words, or he chose to ignore them. "Will you see the sham of a marriage between you and Lord Warrick set aside?"

"Yes, at the proper time."

He moved away from her and stood looking out the window. "Your pain is too new. I will give you time to regain your footing, Arrian. Then we shall talk more of this."

She moved to the door. "Good night, Ian."

He neither turned around nor acknowledged her departure.

Instead of going to her room, Arrian walked out into the garden, needing a breath of fresh air after her confrontation with Ian. Davinsham was a grand castle. Her grandfather had made money in many endeavors. He, like Warrick, had put money in sheep and cattle. But unlike Warrick, he had dispersed most of his tenants to turn the farms into grazing land.

As she moved down a dark path, Arrian thought of Ironworth Castle, which was not so grand as Davinsham. But the master of Ironworth stood like a sentinel to his people who dwelled in that beautiful and peaceful domain by the sea.

Through the branches of a tall pine tree she could see the twinkling stars. Was Warrick standing beneath the same sky looking at the same stars and thinking of her? she wondered. Did he miss her?

Arrian closed her eyes, picturing Warrick riding Titus across heather-covered hills. She could see him standing with the wind in his dark hair, gazing out to sea.

She felt a deep yearning much like a physical pain. She

was not sorry she had met Warrick, for without him she would never have known love. She was only sorry that life had cast them on opposite sides in this blood feud.

Her mind was clear and she knew what she wanted to do. With a heavy heart, she returned to the castle and climbed the stairs. She wanted to go home to England. There was nothing for her in Scotland.

Haddy set a plate of steaming salmon before Lord Warrick, but he pushed it aside and reached for the brandy bottle. "You shouldna' be drinking without eating a bite, m'lord."

"Don't bedevil me, Haddy. I'm a man grown and don't need a nursemaid to suckle me."

"I know what a man needs when he growls at those that would help him."

He glared at her. "Since when did you become an expert on what a man needs?"

She smiled at him, undaunted by his petulance. "Oh, I've had me time. Barra didn't just happen, you know. And don't be forgetting she has four brothers. I had me a good man 'til I lost him to the sea."

Warrick poured a glass of brandy and took a deep drink. "What I need, Haddy, is not to feel anything. I want to drink myself into numbness so I won't dream."

The housekeeper's eyes saddened. "She'll no' be coming back to you, m'lord. She's not for you. You knew that from the start."

"Are you certain, Haddy?" He drained the glass and refilled it. "I'm not so sure."

"When first I knew who the lady was, I had no liking for her. But I soon saw her sweetness and liked her well enough. If the truth be told, m'lord, she's too good for you *or* Ian MacIvors."

His eyes clouded as he refilled his glass and drank once more. "She made me see that my life was a wilderness, and I was a man without direction. I now know that hate can eat away at a man and make him unworthy to be with others. As you observed, Haddy, I'm not worthy of Lady Arrian."

Haddy motioned for her daughter to come forward. Between the two women they managed to help Warrick stand. He was a big man, and it took all their strength to hold him upright. Slowly they moved him out of the dining room, with Haddy mumbling, "Where's Mactavish when you need him?"

"Where are you taking me?" Warrick protested, as he allowed them to lead him toward the stairs.

Haddy told him in the same scolding voice she'd often used on him when he had been a mischievous lad, "You're not used to drinking, m'lord, and ye're a bit in your cups. We're putting you ta bed, and that's the end of it."

Warrick pushed them away and staggered back to the dining room, picking up his bottle. His steps were uneven as he climbed the stairs, warding off Haddy's efforts to help. "I can make it on my own. Don't coddle me."

Mother and daughter exchanged sad glances.

"He'll no' recover from this, Ma. This time the MacIvors tore the heart right out o' him."

"No, lass, it weren't the MacIvors that done this. This wound was self-inflicted. He did it to himself."

"He shouldna' let Lady Arrian go."

"Aye. But you can't make a woman love you by keeping her prisoner. He woulda' been more unhappy if she'd stayed hating him."

Warrick fell on his bed, the bottle dropping out of his hand. "Damn you, Arrian, your eyes haunt me. I wake up at night calling your name. My salvation lies with you. Without you I'll continue to hate until I'm consumed with bitterness."

Chapter 22

A week had passed since Gille MacIvors had been laid to rest. By now most of the guests had returned to their own homes, and a gloom hung over Davinsham Castle.

Kassidy and Arrian helped direct the footmen who were loading Aunt Mary's trunks onto a coach.

Lady Mary had her maid and seven outriders in attendance. "I can't get home soon enough to please me." She looked at Kassidy. "You and Arrian should be coming with me."

"We have much to settle before we can leave," Kassidy said, tucking the robe around her aunt. "Besides, we're waiting for Raile and Michael."

"They'll be shocked when they arrive since they believe they are coming for a wedding. But put it out of your mind," Lady Mary advised. She leaned forward and kissed Arrian. "Hurry back to England, dear, I think you know you don't belong here."

"Soon," Arrian said.

Kassidy pressed her cheek against her aunt's. "We wait only for Raile to arrive. Are you certain you don't want to take the yacht with us?"

"Never! I'll not set foot on any kind of boat, not even a small one. I'll return home at my own pace and be glad when I reach London."

Ian stepped forward. "You will certainly be missed, Aunt Mary," he said.

Lady Mary saw no sincerity in his eyes, nor did she expect any. "I doubt I shall ever return to Scotland now that my father is dead."

"I hope you will reconsider," he said, taking Arrian by the hand and holding her possessively at his side. "You will surely return to see Arrian, if not me."

Lady Mary saw that her niece was very uncomfortable. "I'll expect Arrian to make up her own mind as to whether she leaves or remains in Scotland."

The coach started off with a jerk, and Kassidy and Arrian waved until it was out of sight.

"There is always a heavy emptiness when Aunt Mary leaves," Arrian said. "I miss her already."

"She's a power to reckon with," Kassidy said. "She makes her presence known."

"I have always found her to be nosy and an ill-tempered old woman," Ian said.

Arrian pulled away from him and moved to stand by her mother. "Then why did you ask her to return if you feel that way, Ian?"

He looked annoyed at having to explain his actions. "Merely out of politeness."

"When do you think Father will arrive, Mother?"

"Soon, I should think. I look for him any day."

Ian's brows came together in a frown. "I'm certain His Grace will agree with me that the marriage between Arrian and Lord Warrick should be terminated as soon as possible. That's why I've already taken steps to bring this about."

"You had no right to do that," Arrian said. "We can discuss this when my father arrives. Until then, we will not speak of it, Ian."

"Yes, of course. If you ladies will excuse me, I have much that needs my attention. Grandfather was not one to keep good accounts. I'll be going over them for several days. I shall, however, see you at dinner."

Arrian forced a smile before she went into the house. Why was she finding Ian's presence so offensive? She was now more certain than ever that even if her marriage was dissolved, she would never marry him.

Arrian and her mother spent the morning riding. When they returned to the stable, Kassidy remained with the groom. One of the horses had developed a limp and she wanted to make certain it was not serious.

It was a glorious day and Arrian was reluctant to go into the house, so she opened the gate and entered the garden, where flowers and herbs merged together in harmony. The scent was wonderful.

Arrian walked down a path lined by blooming shrubs. She had just bent to smell an early spring rose when she heard someone crying. She listened until she located the sound and then moved slowly around the corner to find Helena huddled under the vine-covered arbor, her face buried in her hands.

Arrian sat down beside Helena and offered her a handkerchief. "May I help?"

Helena shook her head. "No one can help. I am so miserable and lonely."

"I would like to be your friend, Helena. You can trust me to keep your confidence."

Helena dabbed at her eyes. "Is it true that you were forced into marriage with Lord Warrick?"

"Yes, it is true."

"Like you, I had no choice in my marriage, either. Were you aware that I was to have been Lord Warrick's wife?"

"Yes, I did know that. Are you crying because you still love him?"

"I never loved Lord Warrick," Helena said in a shocked voice. "We were hardly acquainted. I believe I was a little frightened of him because he was so dark and scowled at me on our first meeting. I was certain he was not happy about our impending marriage, and neither was I."

"But you agreed to the marriage. Surely you had some feelings for Warrick."

"It was my father who made the arrangements. Although I found Lord Warrick handsome, I found it difficult to look into his eyes because there was no softness there. Don't you think he had unusual eyes?"

Arrian thought of those silver eyes, remembering when she'd seen them soften and even flame with passion. "Yes, he has most unusual eyes."

"Surely you must have been terrified of him, Arrian?"

"At times I was, but I'm free now." Arrian felt such pity for this woman who had been so ill-used by everyone. "Let us talk about you, and the reason you're so unhappy. If you didn't love Lord Warrick, then I suppose you are crying because you were forced to marry my cousin, Jamie?"

"I first met Jamie when he and several others captured my coach. It was frightening when they subdued my two outriders, and abducted me. My maid swooned dead away and my sister, who was my companion on the journey, fought the men to keep them from taking me."

"You were the only one abducted?"

"Oh, yes. Jamie took me upon his horse while I cried out for help. There was no one able to come to my rescue."

"Why did you finally agree to marry him? Surely you didn't love him."

"I didn't love him at first, in fact I didn't even like him. But he's a different person when he's away from Ian. Now I love my husband, even though he seems only to tolerate me."

"You gave Jamie a son. That must count for something."

"He is proud of Patrick. But that does not mean he loves me."

Arrian was pensive. "If you love him, why don't you set out to win his heart? I would think if you have to spend the rest of your life with a man, he should at least admire you."

"I'm not clever or beautiful like you. And I cry easily, which always seems to irritate Jamie."

Arrian noticed Helena's hair was a beautiful brown color, but it was tangled and not well groomed. Helena had not taken care of her complexion and she definitely needed help in choosing her wardrobe. The dress she wore was suitable for a much older woman, and the color was all wrong for her.

"You are very pretty." Arrian looked into soft blue eyes. "All you need is the right gowns and to wear your hair differently, then you would be beautiful."

Helena gripped Arrian's hand. "Do you think so? Could you help me?"

"Yes, I certainly will. The two of us have much in common. It's time we stood our ground and did something about our situations."

Helena looked puzzled. "What will we do?"

"First we will do something about your hair. Also I will want you to go riding with my mother and me every day. It's wonderful exercise and it gets you out into the fresh air. You will soon make it your daily regimen and your complexion will benefit. A man likes to be proud of his wife and her accomplishments."

"I don't like to ride."

"If you want to win that husband of yours, you will have to do many things you don't like. First of all, no matter what Jamie says to you, you will not allow him to see you cry—even if you have to go off by yourself to shed your tears.

Next, you will not always be available to him when he wants you. Do you read?"

"No. I hate books."

"I'll pick out several of my favorites for you to read. It never hurts to know more than a man. Jamie has never struck me as a man who went about improving his mind."

Helena giggled and then excitement danced in her eyes. "I'll do whatever you say. I just want Jamie to notice me."

"Oh, he will." Arrian laughed. "When you have two women against one man, he has no chance. Perhaps we'll also enlist my mother's aid."

"Could we? Her Grace is always so lovely."

"Mother will help you all she can."

Helena's eyes brightened with hope. "I'll do whatever you say. I'll even learn to ride and read books if it'll help get Jamie to notice me."

Arrian and Kassidy watched Elspeth deftly loop Helena's dark hair around her head and secure it with three mother-of-pearl combs.

"Now remember, m'lady, you are to cleanse your skin every night. I have mixed the cream that Lady Arrian uses. See how her skin glows?"

Helena stood up and twirled around. Arrian had given her several of her own gowns and Elspeth had let them out at the waist to fit her. Of course until the mourning period had been observed, Helena could wear only black. Arrian had added a lacy white collar to the black gown, which brightened Helena's complexion.

"You look wonderful, Helena," Arrian said. "Jamie will be overwhelmed by you."

"I did what you suggested, Arrian. Last night when Jamie was ready for bed, I told him I was going to remain in the library to read. I didn't go to bed until after midnight."

Arrian smiled. "What was my cousin's reaction to that?"

"He pouted like a little boy. But he was awake when I slipped into bed beside him. He asked me what I had been reading, and I told him the geography of Europe. He asked me questions and I was able to answer them. I think I'm going to enjoy reading immensely."

"I'm delighted."

"In the past, Arrian, Jamie would spend every morning with Ian. But this morning he came to the nursery and played with the baby and stayed to talk with me."

Kassidy studied her daughter. She was glad Arrian had taken on the task of uniting Jamie and Helena. It gave her a diversion and helped her forget, for a while, her own troubled life.

Arrian dreaded the evenings most of all, especially when the whole family gathered for dinner and then afterwards migrated to the sitting room. These were the times that Ian would seek her out, and tonight was no different. He sat beside her and slid his arm possessively around her shoulders.

"How did you spend your day, Arrian?"

"My mother and I rode with Helena this morning. Then this afternoon we took a long walk about the grounds."

"We shall have to arrange a ball for you so I can show you off to all the neighbors. How would you like to have a masquerade ball?"

The thought of being paraded before Ian's neighbors was not to her liking. "I don't believe it would be proper to have any festivities since Grandfather has so recently died."

"No, I suppose not." He was silent for a moment. "How else can we entertain you?"

"I need no entertaining, Ian. I only wait for my father's arrival so that I can return to England."

"I don't want you to leave." He took her hand and held it tightly. "You are committed to me and I shan't so easily let you out of that commitment, Arrian." He raised her hand to his lips. "You will always belong to me, no matter what."

"Let go, Ian," she said, trying to break free of his grasp.

He dropped her hand. "I demand to know how you feel about me. I have been patient long enough, Arrian. You owe me that much."

"Yes, I do, Ian. I know I'm not being fair to you, but I don't know what my feelings are."

"You knew well enough how you felt about me last summer."

"I thought I did. Now I'm not so sure you and I are suited to each other. I believe you would do far better marrying a woman who shared your interests."

"You're what I want."

"Ian, give me time. As soon as I know my feelings I'll tell you."

His eyes were searching, his voice laced with the merest threat. "Don't make me wait too long, Arrian. I want a family and I want you."

Helena slid in between Arrian and Ian, for which Arrian was grateful. "I have the most wonderful news. Jamie has suggested that we go to Edinburgh for a week. Can you imagine that—just the two of us!"

Ian scowled at his brother's wife. "You have him mooning after you like a lap dog, Helena. Next you'll be asking him to take up needlework."

Arrian patted Helena's hand and leaned over to whisper in her ear, "If Ian has noticed Jamie's actions, then you are indeed making progress."

"Arrian, will you walk with me in the garden?" Helena asked, drawing Ian's further displeasure. "There is something I would like to discuss with you."

Arrian was only too glad to leave the sitting room. She ignored Ian's look of disapproval. "Of course. Will you excuse us, Ian?" She gave him no chance to reply.

They stepped into the garden, where only a pale moon lit the path. "I feared you would be gone when I returned from Edinburgh," Helena said. "And there is something you need to know."

Arrian stared at the woman, who was five years older than she. "I will miss you. I feel that we have become friends. I also believe Jamie will make you a good husband, in time."

"I have come to believe this also. But that's not what I wanted to talk to you about. First I must know how you feel about Ian."

Arrian didn't want to answer. "I'm not certain. So much has happened to confuse me."

"I've been watching you for some time, and I don't mean to pry, but I believe you love Lord Warrick."

Arrian was shocked that Helena could have read her so well. "Why would you say that?"

"Just from your actions. You are not happy when you are with Ian. That's why I want you to know what Jamie told me about Lord Warrick's sister. It's a closely guarded secret, so please don't let Ian know I told you."

"Of course I won't. Lady Gwendolyn didn't throw herself down the stairs, did she?"

"No, she didn't. It was an accident. Lady Gwendolyn was trying to flee from Gavin MacIvors, and they struggled. She lost her footing and fell to her death. Lord Gavin convinced everyone it would be best to claim that Lady Gwendolyn took her own life. Later, Gavin died under strange circumstances, but no one knows who killed him. However, he was stabbed with Lady Gwendolyn's own dagger. Do you not think that strange? There are those who say Gwendolyn's ghost killed him, and others who believe Lord Warrick committed the deed."

"If Warrick had killed Gavin, he would certainly have made sure everyone knew. He would have viewed it as a victory."

"Jamie doesn't think Lord Warrick did it, either."

Arrian took in a deep breath. Warrick needed to know that his sister had not taken her own life. He wanted Gwendolyn buried at Ironworth. If she did nothing else, she would see that Lady Gwendolyn's body was returned to her brother. Perhaps that would help him put some of his hatred aside.

"Thank you for telling me this, Helena. And I know you are going to be happy with Jamie and your son."

"I am, Arrian. I know the exact moment when I first began to love Jamie. It was strange the way it happened. I had been feeling ill every morning and I had no notion I was with child. But Jamie knew at once, because he recognized the symptoms. The love was just a small thing at first, but it grew with each passing day."

Arrian was no longer listening to Helena. She leaned against the garden gate for support. For several weeks now she had been feeling sick to her stomach just before breakfast. She had attributed it to the constant strain. This morning the sickness had been much worse. Was it possible that she was carrying Warrick's child?

Arrian wanted to cry out in agony. Gathering all her courage, she turned to Helena and gave her a quick kiss on the cheek. "You and Jamie must have a wonderful holiday."

Arrian walked quickly down the path, but instead of entering through the sitting room she went through the front door, hoping to avoid Ian.

Hurriedly she went up the stairs and down the hallway to her room.

Arrian waited for her mother. They always talked before they went to bed, but her mother was late that night. She moved to the ewer and dashed water on her face. She felt sick, or was it only her imagination?

There was a light tap on the door and Kassidy entered. Unfastening her jeweled necklace, she dropped it on Arrian's dressing table. "I can't stand many more of these nights. It's just not the same without Grandfather's bright conversation. I can't imagine what can be keeping your father."

"Mother, come and sit beside me. I want to talk to you about something serious."

"It's Ian, isn't it? I know he's urging you to make a decision. But short of insulting him, I don't know what to do, Arrian."

"No, it's not about Ian, Mother." Arrian twisted the sash at her waist. "How can a woman know if she is . . . is . . . with child?"

"It's not always apparent at first. Why, does Helena suspect she's having another baby?"

"No, Mother. Not Helena."

Kassidy's face paled and she stared at Arrian. She placed her hand on her daughter's forehead to see if she was feverish. "Why? Do you feel ill?"

"Each morning for several weeks I have felt sick, but as the day progressed, it would pass. I didn't mention it because I didn't think it was important."

"You're probably just coming down with something. We shall have to take better care of you."

"Mother, there are other signs. I just didn't think it was important until Helena mentioned how she felt sick before she had her baby." Arrian swallowed a painful lump in her throat. "Is it possible that I am going to have Warrick's baby?"

Tears glistened in Kassidy's eyes as she gathered Arrian to her. "Oh, my dearest, I sincerely hope not. Pray it is not so. You have already suffered enough."

Suddenly Arrian imagined what it would be like to have Warrick's child. In a burst of happiness she smiled and hugged her mother. "I wouldn't mind, Mother. By the law, I'm his wife."

Kassidy shook her head. "You can't mean that you're happy about this?"

"I wasn't until this moment."

Kassidy stood up and began pacing the floor. "It never occurred to me that this would happen."

"If it's so, Mother, I'll always have some part of Warrick with me. Do you suppose he would be happy if he knew about the baby?"

Kassidy leaned her head against the mantle of the fireplace, trying to clear her mind. Here was a snarl that she would need Raile to untangle. One thing was certain, Arrian did love Warrick.

"We could be mistaken, Arrian."

Arrian held out her arms to her mother. "Be happy for me, because I can assure you I am very elated."

"Oh, dearest, I cannot find it within me to feel happy about a situation that is only going to cause you pain."

Kassidy did not mention the trouble this news would bring. There would be Ian to consider, and there was no knowing how he would react. Then there was Lord Warrick, who might not be pleased about fathering a child by Arrian.

Tensions and tempers were high at Davinsham, and Kassidy hoped Raile would come before everything exploded.

Chapter 23

The sky was darkening along the horizon, but Arrian hardly noticed. As always, whenever she was troubled, she went for a long walk. She moved along the grassy pathway at the front of the castle and paused by a large fountain where two lovebirds were entwined around the statue of a winged cupid. She vaguely wondered what distant relative had erected such a garish sculpture. Certainly it had not been her great-grandfather, for there had been no romance in his heart, and he had better judgment.

Continuing down the path, her mind returned to her own troubles. Now she was sure she was with child, and Ian had to be told. She glanced up at the sky, trying to think how best to approach him. It would have to be when they were alone—she owed him that much.

Her footsteps lagged when she saw Ian in the distance. Apparently he hadn't seen her, for he was headed in the direction of the kennel.

Arrian gathered her courage. She would tell Ian about the baby today. Perhaps now he'd agree that they could have no future together. He would not want a wife who was carrying a child fathered by Warrick Glencarin.

As she neared the kennel, Ian glanced up and smiled at her. "Grandfather's prize Gordon setter, Musky, had a litter last night." He shook his head. "I suppose I must stop thinking that everything still belongs to Grandfather. Musky is mine."

Arrian placed her hand on the head of a frisky two-year-old setter from Musky's previous litter. She was rewarded when the dog greeted her with a lick on her hand and a wagging tail.

"It's hard to believe Grandfather's gone," she said. "He was such a strong presence, I still expect to see him walking down the path with Musky at his heels."

Ian watched her closely. "Did you come to visit the kennel, or did you want to see me?"

The sun shone on his sandy-colored hair, and his dark eyes sparkled as he looked at her. Today he was more like the old Ian. Perhaps now was not a good time to speak of the baby.

"May I see the new litter?"

He opened the gate, leading her inside where Musky was confined with her pups. The dog greeted her with a wag of its tail.

Arrian bent to pick up a furry black pup, which snuggled against her cheek. "I'd forgotten how sweet puppies can be. This one is very precious."

"As soon as she's weaned, she's yours," Ian said. "You can train her as you wish."

She returned the pup to its mother. "Oh, no. I couldn't take one of Musky's pups. I know her bloodline is impeccable. Grandfather once told me that he had a list of patrons who waited for her to drop a litter."

Ian smiled and took her hand. "Arrian, everything I have is yours. I want you to be mistress of my home, to have my children, to sit across from me at the dinner table." He raised her hand to his lips. "I'll be the envy of everyone."

Arrian realized she could no longer delay telling him the truth. "I can't be your wife, Ian. And you wouldn't want me to be."

He led her out of the kennel and fastened the gate. "I won't pretend I'm happy about what happened to you at Glencarin. But I've been thinking, and I still want you for my wife. I'm willing to wait until you are free to marry me."

They walked down the path toward the castle and she stopped by the fountain. "It isn't that, Ian. It's much more." She dipped her hand in the pond and watched the water ripple.

He turned her to face him. "I don't care what your feelings are for that man, Arrian. I'm willing to overlook everything. That's how much I love you."

Her eyes locked with his. "Even if I am going to have Warrick Glencarin's child?"

She watched the softness in his eyes harden into intense anger. His face whitened as if he were ill. "No," he choked out. "You'll not have this bastard, do you hear me, Arrian? I'll not permit it!"

She backed away, for the first time feeling afraid of him. "The baby will be legitimate, Ian. I am Warrick's legal wife and that cannot be disputed."

He grabbed her wrist and yanked her to him. "There are ways a woman can rid her body of an unwanted child. Magda, in the village, can rid you of it."

She covered her mouth with horror. "You are mad, Ian. Do you think I would do anything to harm my unborn baby?"

"You will do what I say—and I say you will be rid of this Drummond bastard."

She jerked her hand free and ran a few steps away from him. "I told you before, Ian, I am not of your clan and you can't order my life."

He caught up with her and swung her around, slamming her into the fence. "We would have been married by now and I would have had sway over every aspect of your life, had it not been for that man. You will go to Magda, if not today, then tomorrow."

At that moment, to Arrian's relief, a housemaid hurried down the path toward them. "Lady Arrian," she called out, puffing to catch her breath. "There's someone asking to see you."

Ian shoved her away from him. "Go, it's probably your mother. But don't forget what I said. We aren't finished with this, Arrian. I'd rather see you dead than to give birth to that man's whelp."

Arrian backed away from him, her heart pounding with fear. She turned and ran to meet the maid, glad to be rescued. This was still another side of Ian that she had never seen—a violent side—and it frightened her.

"There's a gentleman asking to see you, m'lady. He says his name is Mactavish."

Arrian glanced back to see if Ian was listening, but he had returned to the kennel. "Is he alone?"

"But for his driver, m'lady."

"Where is he?"

"He said he'd wait for you at the front of the house. I told him no proper lady would meet a gentleman under such a condition, but he insisted I inform you he's here."

Arrian practically flew down the path, her heart beating like thunder. At least she would have some news of Warrick. Was it possible he had sent Mactavish for her? Would she go to him if he had?

Mactavish stood beside the coach with his hands clasped behind him. When he saw Arrian, his eyes lit up with genuine pleasure.

"M'lady, it's good to see you looking so well."

She offered him her hand and he touched it lightly. "I'm happy to see you, Mactavish. Are you . . . is everyone faring well?"

"Indeed. Indeed."

"Would you like to come inside? I'm sure you must be hungry and thirsty."

He grinned at her. "I'm taking a chance coming here as it is. I'll not test Providence by entering the lion's den."

"Did Warrick send you?"

"That he did, m'lady." He opened the coach and withdrew her jewel chest and placed it in her arms. "He's returned these and all your trunks."

"Oh." Her heart hit bottom. "Did he send me a message?"

Mactavish looked into the shiny blue eyes. It was apparent that Lady Arrian missed Warrick.

A shadow fell across Arrian's face, and she looked up to see Ian standing beside her.

"So the watchdog comes for his master," Ian said icily. "I would have thought you too wily to put yourself so conveniently into my hands, Mactavish."

"I came to see Lady Arrian. My business is with her and has nothing to do with you."

"Oh, does it not? Everything that concerns Lady Arrian concerns me. All I have to do is call out and you will be surrounded by my men. Unless I say the word, you'll never leave here alive."

"Now I'm truly scared," Mactavish said.

"Leave him alone, Ian," Arrian said. "He only came to return my belongings. You will not harm him."

"I happen to know this man is Lord Warrick's right arm. Perhaps the chief himself will come if he knows his dog is locked in my dungeon."

Several men had begun closing in around them, and Arrian moved to stand in front of Mactavish. "If you don't let him go, I'll never speak to you again. His reason for being here has nothing to do with you, Ian."

Ian moved closer. "He's a Drummond and that concerns me."

Kassidy suddenly appeared beside her daughter and quickly assessed the situation. "How good of you to bring my daughter's clothing, Mactavish. Tell Lord Warrick it was most thoughtful of him to return them."

"He won't be going anywhere, to tell anyone anything," Ian said, stepping closer to Mactavish.

Kassidy moved past Ian, ignoring his threat. "You, there." She motioned to Ian's armed men. "Help unload my daughter's trunks so this man can be on his way. Hurry, he'll want to be off before dark."

Ian glowered at Kassidy, but he said nothing as his men moved forward to do her bidding.

Ian's voice came out in a growl. "We'll settle this at a later time, Mactavish. A time when you aren't hiding behind a woman's skirt. As it is, my men and I will escort you from my land."

For some reason Arrian didn't trust Ian. "You'll not harm Mactavish, will you?"

"Not if you ask it of me, Arrian," Ian answered smiling. But there was something sinister in his gaze—or was she mistaken?

Kassidy's eyes issued the huge man a warning. "I would suggest you leave at once. It doesn't seem to be healthy around here for you." Still not trusting Ian, she felt compelled to speak to him. "Please remember this man is our guest. I'll expect you to treat him accordingly."

Ian was sulky as he waved several men forward. "Your guest is about to be escorted off my land."

Arrian smiled. "Thank you for bringing my trunks."

Mactavish politely touched his hat, bowing first to Kassidy and then to Arrian. "I'll wish you both well," he said, swinging to the top of the carriage and nodding for the driver to pull away.

Ian and his men closed around the coach. Arrian moved closer to her mother and they both watched her trunks being carried up the steps.

"Ian won't harm Mactavish, will he, Mother?"

"I would think he'll not break his word. I can't see what purpose it would serve to hurt Lord Warrick's servant."

"Warrick sent no word to me, Mother."

"I didn't think he would, Arrian. I'm sure he feels he had no right to say anything to you."

"I left a letter telling him to keep the jewels. I wonder why he didn't?"

"He's a proud man, Arrian. And honor seems to be important to him. That's why he returned the jewels." Kassidy changed the subject. "Did you tell Ian about the baby?"

"Yes, and he was furious. I have never seen him like that." She shivered. "I don't want to talk about it. I want to go home," Arrian whispered. "If we could make time go backwards and I could do it all over again, how different the outcome would be."

"You can never go back," her mother told her.

Kassidy watched her daughter turn away sadly and walk up the steps, knowing she could not help her. If only Aunt Mary had not left, she would know how to advise Arrian.

Mactavish kept his eyes on Ian MacIvors. He knew what Lady Arrian and her mother did not—that the new chief of Clan MacIvors was not going to let him go as easily as they thought.

After riding for an hour, Ian motioned the coachman to pull over. When the horses came to a halt, Ian ordered Mactavish to step down, while one of his men held a rifle on the driver. Ian ordered another of his men to tie Mactavish's hands behind him. He then ordered Mactavish dragged into the woods where they would not be disturbed.

Mactavish was tied to a tree, and he watched Ian toy with the silver handle of his whip.

"You know what I'm going to do to you?" Ian taunted.

"Little I care," Mactavish said. "Do your worst and get it over with."

Ian circled him. "If you beg, I might let you off with just a warning."

Mactavish stood tall, his eyes straight ahead. "I'll beg nothing from a MacIvors pig."

Ian reacted violently, bringing the whip handle hard against the side of Mactavish's head. The man slumped against the ropes.

Ian circled him again, and with all his strength slammed the handle into Mactavish's midsection. The big man's knees buckled.

"I have changed my mind, Ian MacIvors—you aren't a pig, you're a bastard. If you'll untie me, I'll show you who's the best man."

The handle came down with force against Mactavish's temple, and this time he did fall forward, sagging against the ropes that cut into his wrists. There was blood running down his face, and into his eyes.

Mactavish pulled against the rope that restrained him, but he could not break the bounds. "Kill me and get it over with, MacIvors. I have no fear of you," he said, staggering to his feet.

"I don't want you dead." Ian prodded his chest with the whip handle. "I want you to deliver a message to your chief for me."

"I'm not your messenger."

"Oh, I think you'll want to tell him this."

"If you're not the coward you appear to be, come with me to Glencarin and you can tell Lord Warrick in person. I'm sure he'll give you the same welcome you gave me."

This time the leather whip lashed out, cutting deeply through Mactavish's shirt and slicing through his skin. He gritted his teeth to keep from crying out.

"Listen to me because I want every word repeated to Warrick Glencarin."

Mactavish shook his head to clear the blood from his eyes. "I told you I'm not your messenger."

Ian grabbed a handful of Mactavish's hair and jerked his head up. "Tell your master that his mockery of a marriage to Lady Arrian will soon be set aside."

"He expected that, so it will come as no surprise to him."

"Perhaps he expects the annulment, but what I have to say may come as something of a shock to him. Tell him that Lady Arrian carries his child." He gave Mactavish time to absorb his words. "Tell him before he goes to sleep at night, to think of his son or daughter—whichever it turns out to be—in my hands. I will raise the child, teach it to think as a MacIvors. Tell him if it should be a son, I will not recognize it as my heir, but I shall make the child a servant to my own son."

"Be damned with you."

"You fail to see the humor in this, don't you?" Ian laughed bitterly. "Imagine the heir to the Drummond clan subservient to the heir to the MacIvors clan. The humor goes even deeper when you consider that they will both have the same mother."

Mactavish tried to see the face of his enemy so he could determine if the man was telling the truth. It would strike at Warrick's heart to know that Lady Arrian was carrying his child.

"I don't believe you, dog, and neither will Lord Warrick."

"I wouldn't expect him to believe me. But when the child is born, I'm sure he'll know it for his own flesh and blood."

Ian pushed the whip handle against Mactavish's face. "Imagine, if you will, a Drummond growing up within my power. Even if it turns out to be a daughter, I'll still have control of her future."

Ian cut the ropes and Mactavish fell forward on his face, as blackness engulfed him. Ian kicked him in the side and then called his men to carry Mactavish back to the coach. Once they pushed him inside, Ian waved the driver forward. He watched the coach disappear with a satisfied smile on his lips.

This could turn out better than he'd planned. Warrick would live in torment for the rest of his life.

Ian threw back his head and laughed, drawing confused glances from his men. "At last I have Glencarin where I want him. He'll never be free of me now."

Chapter 24

*A*rrian *sat at the dressing table* while her mother ran a brush through her long, golden hair. By observing her mother's reflection in the mirror, Arrian could see the anger that smoldered in her eyes.

"Ian said what to you?"

"He insisted that I go to this woman he knows in the village and have her . . ." Arrian shuddered. "It's too horrible. I can't bear to think about it."

"Ian has gone too far this time." Kassidy lifted Arrian's chin. "Are you certain you have no tender feelings for him?"

"I don't know why I ever thought I did, Mother."

Kassidy was relieved. She had seen many sides of Ian that she didn't admire since their grandfather's death. "We'll leave as soon as your father arrives. Until then, stay close to me."

"Mother, why do you suppose it's taking so long for Father to arrive? Aunt Mary will have reached London days ago. I had thought Captain Norris would bring Father and Michael right away."

"I don't understand, myself, Arrian. But it must be something unavoidable or your father would be here. We'll wait for one more week and if he doesn't come, then we'll leave by coach."

Kassidy laid the brush aside. "Where did you disappear to this afternoon, Arrian? I searched for you but you weren't to be found."

"I was at the small graveyard outside the church walls where Warrick's sister is buried. When I first located the grave it was sadly overgrown, so I pulled the weeds, and now I place flowers on the grave every day."

"I had forgotten Lord Warrick's sister was buried here at Davinsham. It's said the poor woman took her own life."

"Lady Gwendolyn didn't kill herself, Mother. Helena told me that she and Gavin were struggling and she fell down the stairs."

Kassidy looked surprised. "Are you sure?"

"Helena gave me leave to talk to Jamie about it and he confirmed what she had told me. They all allowed the world to believe that Lady Gwendolyn took her own life."

"What a monstrous thing to do. I wouldn't have thought Gavin capable of such a deed. I can't think Grandfather would have sanctioned such deception."

"Jamie doesn't think Grandfather knew, but he can't be sure. He said at that time the Drummonds vastly outnumbered the MacIvors and Grandfather didn't want another clan war. Of course, there was one anyway."

"Yes, I recall. Many on both sides were slain. That brought the king's wrath down on them."

"Mother, I wish Ian would send the body of Warrick's sister back to Glencarin so she could be buried beside her family. Warrick is haunted by the fact that she was not buried in consecrated ground. I would also like to see her dowry returned."

"Ian would never agree to that."

"I must find a way to persuade him."

"Arrian, you knew Grandfather as a loving man, but he could be hard when dealing with his enemies. What he did to Lord Warrick's family wasn't right. But what Warrick did to you was an act of revenge and was not right either."

"I know, Mother, but perhaps it will be different now with the baby—"

"I don't think so, Arrian. These two warring clans will never be friends. I fear Ian and Warrick will both try to use you and the baby to their own advantage and I'll never allow that to happen."

"Mother, you have a certain power of persuasion over Ian. Could you not convince him to return Warrick's land and the body of his sister to him?"

"I will not interfere in this, Arrian, and neither should you. You already know the consequences of becoming involved in their hate. If you ask a favor of Ian, he'll expect something in return."

"Mother, I have been doing a lot of thinking and I have reached a decision. Even when we are back in England there can be no annulment of my marriage. To do so would leave my baby without a legitimate father."

Kassidy knew that there should never be any doubt about this child's parentage. "You're right, the marriage must stand. But that doesn't mean you'll have any contact with Lord Warrick. I'm taking you back to England with me where no one will ever hurt you again."

Arrian smiled. "I pity the person who gets in your way, Mother."

"Come, my lovely daughter, let us go for a walk. I'm a firm believer that when a woman is with child she should get plenty of fresh air."

Mother and daughter walked arm in arm through the park, enjoying the afternoon sunset.

Suddenly Arrian raised her eyes to the end of the path

and saw two figures walking toward them. She paused, her hand at her throat. Then she started running, her black gown flying out behind her.

"Father, Michael, you are here!"

She was smothered in Raile's arms as he hugged her tightly to him.

"We had trouble with the yacht and had to put in for repairs, or we would have been here sooner."

Arrian glanced over her father's shoulder and saw her brother Michael. He seemed to have grown since their last meeting. She moved into his embrace and he hugged her tightly.

"I know some of what has happened to you. But I'll want to hear everything. I think it's time we took you out of this wild country, dear sister."

She laid her head on his shoulder. "I missed you, Michael, and I'm ready to go home as soon as possible."

Raile gathered his wife in his arms and held her to him, absorbing her nearness. "I came too late. I was just informed about your grandfather's death. I'm so sorry."

Kassidy dreaded what she must tell Raile, but for now it was glorious to be held in his arms. What a relief it would be to place all of Arrian's troubles in his capable hands.

Warrick watched, guilt ridden, while Barra and Haddy dressed Mactavish's wounds. There was a gash on the side of his head and one above his eyes. It appeared several ribs were broken and he was in a great deal of pain.

"He's got to have stitches over his eye, m'lord," Barra stated. "We'd best give him whiskey before I start."

"I'll no' be drinking anything but good scotch, thank you," Mactavish said. "And you'll no sew on me till I'm too drunk to care."

Warrick poured a liberal amount of scotch in a glass and handed it to the giant, who swallowed it in one gulp and then held the glass out to be refilled.

"I should have gone to Davinsham instead of you, Mactavish. I blame myself for your injuries because I knew about Ian's temper. He'll regret this offense. I'll not rest until he pays dearly for this insult."

Mactavish groaned as Haddy tightened a wide bandage around his ribs. "Don't be blaming yourself, lad. I wanted to go and there was no stopping me."

"I should have known a MacIvors couldn't be trusted. I hope Ian feels proud of himself, since it took four of his men to do this to you while you were tied to a tree."

Mactavish didn't seem to be listening to Warrick. After five glasses of straight scotch, Haddy nodded to her daughter.

"I think he'll be ready."

Warrick stood at Mactavish's head and held him still while Barra took several stitches. Other than a few groans and several grimaces of pain, Mactavish didn't complain. After Barra had finished, she bandaged his head.

Barra picked up the utensils she had used, and Haddy followed her out of the room. Warrick handed his friend another glass of scotch.

"No, I'll not be needing more. I want to keep my head clear for what I have to tell you. Already the room seems to be turning."

"After all you've been through, you need to rest. Anything you have to tell me can wait until tomorrow."

"This . . . can't wait." Mactavish slurred his words. "Too important."

"You saw the Lady Arrian?"

"I did, and a sweeter lady you'll no' find. She don't know what Ian did to me. She made him promise he'd not harm me. 'Course I knew what he'd do when he was out of her sight."

"Is she well?"

"She was as pretty as the morning in spring. And as sweet as a primrose."

"Did she send me a message?"

Mactavish remembered the Lady Arrian asking the same thing of him. "No, m'lord. There was no word from her—but I got plenty from Ian MacIvors."

"I care not what he had to say."

Mactavish struggled to sit up. "You'll care about this, laddie."

Warrick dropped down in a chair and studied his lifelong friend. "I see you won't rest until you have your say. What message did the new chief send to me?"

"He was kinda' like taunting me. If my hands hadn't been tied, I'd have torn in to him."

Warrick's eyes fell on the angry red marks that circled Mactavish's wrists. "I have no doubt of that. Next time you meet him, your hands won't be tied."

"For first time in my life I wanted to kill a man with my bare hands. I'd a' done it too, if I coulda' got at him. I may yet."

"Mactavish, will you just tell me what he had to say?"

The older man rubbed his forehead, wondering how he could say the words. He couldn't just blurt them out. "He . . . Ian MacIvors, said to tell you that . . . her ladyship was going to have your . . . wee bairn."

Warrick's breath became trapped in his chest and he let it out slowly. "It's one of his tricks. He only wants to torture me."

"I donna think so. He was too pleased for it not to be true."

"I hardly think he would be pleased if the woman he wants to marry is carrying my seed."

"You dinna know how his twisted mind works. He said to tell you that your marriage to Lady Arrian will soon be ended—he'd see to that."

Warrick flinched. "It is as I expected."

"Ian MacIvors said he wants you to think about this every night before you sleep. He wants you to know that whether it's a son or daughter it'll be in his hands. He'll teach the child to become a MacIvors. If it's a son he'll not recognize it, but the child will be servant to his own son."

A painful yell echoed through the room. "I'll see him in hell for this! He will not make a child of mine a bastard."

"He says he will."

"I'd not have thought Arrian would allow it. Even if it is my child, it is also of her flesh. The woman I knew had spirit and a loving nature—she would not sentence her child to a life of degradation."

Mactavish's eyes grew sad as he thought of his own life as the illegitimate son of Warrick's grandfather. "Aye, I could tell you something about that. You have no sense of worth when you have no name."

"It's been a hard life for you, hasn't it, Mactavish?"

"I've had my moments of glory, lad. The world may not see me as your uncle, but I've always known I was. And I think you've known it, too."

"I have wanted to acknowledge you as my uncle for a long time."

"Nay, lad, I'll not have it."

"You and I, Mactavish, will always know that we have a blood tie."

"Aye, that's all that matters. But what are you going to do about Lady Arrian and the bairn?"

Warrick stared at his trembling hands. "The idea is still too new to me. I never considered becoming a father." He turned to his friend. "Does she hate me so much that she would punish me through our child?"

"The words were not from her, Warrick, but from the mouth of Ian MacIvors. I have only his word that there is a child."

"Oh, there's a child. That fact must be sticking in his throat like bitter brine. I'll not allow him to have control of any child that has my blood in its veins."

"You canna stop it, Warrick."

"My inclination is to ride to Davinsham and take her out of there, but that's not the solution."

"I've ne'er known you to think before you acted, laddie.

There comes a time to put the old ways aside. That time could be now."

"This time I must think carefully before I act." Warrick looked with satisfaction at Mactavish. "I'm learning patience. But I have not learned to turn away from a MacIvors affront. Ian MacIvors and I must meet—it's been coming for a long time."

"Thig latha choindui fhatbast," Mactavish said, reciting an old Gaelic saying.

"Yes, the black dog's day will come yet," Warrick echoed in English.

"Go now and think on what I have told you. I'm not fit company for anyone and I want to drink alone."

"I'll stay and we'll drink together."

"Nay, lad. You're not a drinking man. I'll no' have Haddy flogging me for leading you astray."

Warrick stood up. "You should get some rest now. You will be abed until those ribs heal."

"Aye, but I'll not be liking it."

Warrick climbed the stairs to his bedroom. Until he met Arrian, he hadn't known loneliness. When she went away, he had been left with an aching void that could never be filled.

He thought of the child Arrian carried and felt an immediate possessiveness. He would not allow a child of his body to grow up beneath the roof of a MacIvors. Nor, for that matter, would he allow his child to be born on MacIvors soil!

Chapter 25

rrian knocked on the door, knowing Ian would be at his ledgers this morning. It had taken courage for her to come to him, because she had to tell him she was returning to England and at the same time ask a boon of him.

When she entered the room at his invitation, she found him not at his desk but sitting before the portrait of their grandfather with a glass of wine in his hand. When he saw Arrian, he came to his feet with a pleased smile on his face.

"Arrian, what a pleasant surprise. You have never visited me here."

She stood beside him and glanced up at the portrait of Gille MacIvors in his younger days. The old chief's eyes were piercing and seemed to dominate the atmosphere.

"I often came here to visit Grandfather," Arrian said. "He kept hard candy for me in his drawer."

Ian's voice came out cold and bitter. "He never gave me anything but the benefit of his unsolicited advice and criticism."

"I'm sure he had to impress upon you the magnitude of

the responsibilities you would be facing when you took over for him."

"He impressed them on me right enough. I never did anything that pleased him. He never gave me rock candy. But I have it all now that he's dead. That's my satisfaction."

Arrian looked into small, greedy eyes and noticed the cruel twist to his mouth. She wished she had not sought him out today, but she was here, and she would ask her favor of him.

"You are aware that my family is leaving within the week?"

"Yes, your father told me." He looked regretful. "You will, of course, be going with them. It would not be proper for you to stay here until our year of mourning is over."

Ian was taking her departure more calmly than she had thought he would. "It wouldn't be right for me to remain under the circumstances."

"As I just pointed out to you." Now his tone was biting, and she realized he'd had too much to drink. "You will give me credit for knowing the proper way to behave."

She was puzzled by his attitude. Had he decided they were not meant to be husband and wife? She hoped it was so.

"I have also come to ask a favor that only you can grant."

He smiled down at her. "You should know that anything you ask of me will be granted. What is your wish?"

"I—" She met his gaze. "I would ask you to return the body of Lord Warrick's sister to Glencarin."

She would have thought him unaffected by her request had it not been for the balling of his fists. "And why should you care where Lady Gwendolyn is buried?"

"Because a great wrong was done to her. I believe she should be laid to rest with her ancestors. Hers is a sad story, and I like happy endings."

"The dead don't care where they spend eternity."

"No, but those who love them care."

"So, you do it for him." Ian stared for a long moment at his grandfather's likeness and then turned back to her. "And just who would escort the remains of Lady Gwendolyn to

Glencarin? I don't believe you could pay any MacIvors enough money to go onto Drummond land."

"My brother, Michael, has agreed to escort the body, if you will allow it."

He looked down at her, his eyes cool and calculating. "How badly do you want this?"

"I have come to care a great deal about Lady Gwendolyn's plight. I visit her grave every day with fresh flowers."

Ian was silent. If they were married, and he still had not given up hope on that, he did not want there to be any reminders of Warrick Glencarin here at Davinsham. He certainly didn't want her making a pilgrimage every day to put flowers on Lady Gwendolyn's grave.

It felt good to have the power to grant her a favor. "I will allow it, but only on one condition."

"And what would that be?"

"It would mean your postponing your departure for two weeks. Do you think you could convince your father to agree to that?"

"There would have to be a good reason to do so. He's anxious to return to Ravenworth."

"I can assure you it is the best of all reasons. I petitioned the king again to hear my grievances against Lord Warrick when I learned that you had been . . . shall we say, detained by him."

"You had no right to do that, Ian. My father will do what needs to be done when we get back to England."

"I have every right, and it's already done. I have only to appear with Lord Warrick to hear the king's judgment. There is little doubt that the ruling will be in my favor this time."

Arrian was angry that Ian had taken it upon himself to petition King William. "I don't believe my father and mother will want all the facts made public."

"They won't be. I'll see that the evidence is sealed so that only the parties involved will know about it. All I'll need from you, Arrian, is for you to testify how Lord Warrick held you prisoner. That will ensure his doom. Of course, the meeting will take place whether or not you return to England. I just thought you might like to be here when the outcome is decided."

Arrian was so angry she could hardly speak. Did he really believe she would testify against her baby's father? "When will this meeting take place?"

"I received a letter only today from the king's deputy, informing me that the meeting would be in Edinburgh two weeks hence. I have no doubt, since your name is DeWinter, the matter was brought immediately to the king's attention."

"Is this blood feud destined to go on forever, passed from one generation to another?"

"Let us hope it will soon be over. Do I have your agreement to talk to your father?"

Arrian lost the last bit of respect she had for Ian. "I'll speak to my father."

He took her hand and stared down at the finger where his ring had once rested. "I will only be happy, Arrian, when you again wear my ring."

She pulled her hand from his grasp. "An absurd notion, since I carry another man's child."

He dropped his gaze. "I will raise your child as if it were my own. No one need ever know that I'm not the father."

She could not forget that he had wanted her to be rid of the baby. "But you and I would always know, Ian."

Arrian and Michael stood beside the black-draped coach that was waiting to begin its sad journey. The coach would be returning a daughter of the Highlands to her final resting place.

"Michael, please beseech Warrick to let the feud die with the return of his sister's body."

Michael took a long look at his sister. "I may be younger than you, Arrian, but I know you well enough to sense when you are troubled."

Arrian tucked a golden strand of hair behind her ear and

met her brother's eyes. "I wonder if there is anything but sadness in this cursed country. I'll be glad when I'm back at Ravenworth. I'll never again leave, I can promise you that."

"Will you be happy there, I wonder?"

"I . . . what do you mean?"

"You love him, don't you?"

She chose to misunderstand him. "I thought I did. But what I felt for Ian was merely a young girl's fancy for an older man."

"I wasn't referring to Ian and you know it, Arrian. I was asking about the Highlander."

"I am no longer certain what love is, Michael. But I do know this, I don't want to see Warrick suffer any longer."

Michael gave her a quick peck on the cheek, thrust his foot into the stirrup, and threw his leg over his prancing horse. He waved his hand, and the coach moved away. "Don't despair, sister. One never knows what might happen."

Arrian wiped a tear from her eyes and whispered, "Rest in peace, Lady Gwendolyn."

Raile DeWinter glared at his wife. "I demand to know what is happening here. Damn it, Kassidy, why are we delaying our return to Ravenworth? I have little liking for this place and even less for Ian MacIvors. If your grandfather had not died, our daughter would have been married to him by now. I'm aghast at that thought."

"Don't be such a bear, Raile. Arrian is going home with us. Isn't that what you wanted?"

"What I want is to know what scheme you have buried in that beautiful head of yours. You aren't telling me everything about our daughter."

"Let's talk about that later."

"I've been too long away from you," he said, tugging at the gathered neck of her gown and forgetting for a moment what was troubling him.

"I missed you, too, Raile. Everything goes wrong when you aren't with me."

He loosened the pins in her hair. "I can't think why you stopped me from riding to Glencarin and thrashing Lord Warrick. That man has little time left on this earth, because I will bring him down, Kassidy, and not you or anyone will stop me!"

Her arms inched around his neck. "Everything is not as it seems, Raile."

"Then tell me how it is? Why has my son gone off to deliver a dead body to Glencarin? Will you tell me when in hell did I lose control of my own family?"

Kassidy pressed his face between her hands. "As I told you, there is more to it than you know, Raile. In fact, it's quite complicated."

"I have time," he said, dropping into a chair and studying her with a scowl on his handsome face. "So tell me everything."

Kassidy knelt down in front of him, her apricot-colored gown billowing out about her. She tried twice to say the words, but they stuck in her throat. "Raile, Arrian is going to have Lord Warrick's baby."

She watched emotions play across his face—first anger, then denial, and then a deep sadness. "By God, I'll kill him for this, Kassidy!" He stood up so fast he almost knocked her on the floor. "Why didn't you tell me so that I could have gone with Michael?"

"Because I want to explain to you how it happened, Raile."

"I know how such things happen, Kassidy. What I don't know, in my daughter's case, is why."

"I have explained to you that they are legally married. What I haven't told you is that I believe Arrian loves him."

Raile shook his head. "No. No you don't, Kassidy. I'll never give her over to that man. He has no honor and he took advantage of her innocence. As far as our daughter is concerned, he's a dead man!"

"There is nothing you or I can do to stop her from loving him, Raile. No more than anyone could have stopped me from loving you. I will love you for the rest of my life, and I believe Arrian will be miserable if we don't help her in this situation. She is very troubled, Raile, and she needs us to understand."

His eyes did not soften, but his voice was calmer. "How can you know she loves him? She thought she loved Ian, remember?"

"I remember. But there is a difference between being in love with an ideal and loving a man."

Raile still glared at her. "Don't expect me to understand the workings of a woman's mind. I haven't been in control of my life since I met you."

She went to him and pressed her cheek against his. "Don't understand me, Raile—just love me."

His arms tightened around her, and he held her next to his heart. "I could sooner stop breathing than stop loving you, Kassidy. But damn it—"

She pressed her lips against his, cutting off his speech. There would be time later to convince Raile that Arrian belonged with Warrick Glencarin.

Barra entered the dining room with a puzzled expression on her face. "M'lord, there is the strangest sight outside. A coach bedecked in black. I told the gentleman, who insisted on seeing you, that you was dining. He said you'd want to be disturbed for this."

"Who is it?"

"I never saw the likes of him before. But he'll be a proper gentleman, and English, I'd say from the sound of him."

Warrick left the room and hurried to the front door. He stared at the tall young man who stood, hat in hand, beside his horse.

"I'm Warrick Glencarin. You wanted to see me?"

"Yes, my lord. I have come from Davinsham precisely to see you."

Warrick stood eye to eye with the young English gentleman. "You can just return to Davinsham and tell Ian MacIvors that I want nothing from him."

"What I have for you was not sent by Ian MacIvors." Michael opened the door of the coach so Warrick could see inside. "My lord, I will not haggle with you over something so important as your sister's body. You see, I have brought Lady Gwendolyn to you."

Warrick hurried forward, his hand touching the stone coffin with his sister's name carved deeply into the granite. His eyes probed the young man's. "Is this some cruel jest?"

"I can assure you it is not, my lord. It is indeed the body of your sister."

Lord Michael watched Warrick take a staggering step backwards and witnessed the pain that played across his face. "I know how you must feel, my lord. Believe me, if this were my sister, I would not rest until she had a proper burial."

"You said this isn't Ian MacIvors's doing?"

"Ian allowed it after being persuaded that it was the right thing to do."

Warrick stepped to the carriage and ran a trembling hand over the cold stone. "At last, Gwendolyn, you have come home." He glanced up at the young man, whom he judged to be no more than sixteen. "I don't know who you are, but I'm grateful to you."

"If you have no objections, my lord, I would like to remain for your sister's burial."

"May I ask your name?"

"Let's just say I'm someone who wants to see justice done."

Warrick nodded. "Reason enough. Yes, you may attend my sister's burial."

"I have a message for you. There is proof that Lady Gwendolyn did not take her own life. She died by accident."

A tremor shook Warrick's body, and he looked quickly toward the horizon as his eyes misted. "Praise be to God, it is as I'd hoped."

His gaze moved back to the young gentleman. "Whoever you are, you have my eternal gratitude."

Warrick then turned to the stable boy, who looked on in puzzlement. "Ride as fast as you can, Tam, and alert the clan that today we bury my sister."

Warrick knelt while Gwendolyn's body was placed in the stone vault along with untold numbers of Glencarins who had gone before her. The villagers gathered around, their heads bent in prayer.

Michael stood apart from the clan as it buried one of its own. He had purposely asked to stay so he could study Lord Warrick. He saw much to admire in the man Arrian loved. He also thought it was right that they should be together, especially since she was having his baby.

When the ceremony was over and the clan members dispersed, Warrick came to Michael. "You have come a long way. Will you sup with me?"

In truth, Michael wanted to know more about this man, but he dared not remain longer. He'd promised his mother he would return immediately. "I have a long journey ahead of me and I must leave at once."

Warrick ordered Tam to saddle his horse because he wanted to ride alongside his mysterious guest to make certain that no well-meaning clansman took it into his head to harm the lad.

They rode together in silence until they came to the crossroad, then Warrick reined in his horse.

"At first I couldn't think who you were, and then I realized you had to be Arrian's brother, Lord Michael."

"I am."

"I can't say that you favor your sister, but you have the same green eyes as your mother."

"I'm told I favor my father."

Warrick used his powerful leg muscles to control Titus. "Is your sister well?"

There was a serious expression on Michael's face. "As well as one would expect since she is with child."

"So it's true."

"I can assure you it is."

"Is it also true that she works to set aside the marriage?"

"As to that, you will have to find out Monday next in Edinburgh. I understand you will be meeting with Ian and Lord Thorndike."

"Will your sister be present?"

"I shouldn't think so. I don't believe my parents would allow it."

"Well, young Michael, I haven't met a member of your family thus far that I haven't liked."

"I'll carry the message to my mother and sister."

"Arrian was the one who convinced Ian to return my sister's remains, wasn't she?"

"Yes, she was."

"She was also the one who discovered how Gwendolyn died, wasn't she?"

"Arrian can be most persuasive when she feels strongly about something."

"So I've learned."

Michael held out his hand. "It's been a pleasure meeting you, my lord."

They shook hands. "It has indeed, Lord Michael."

"Is there anything you wish me to convey to my sister?"

Warrick's eyes took on a sudden sorrowfulness, but he only smiled. "No. I have nothing to say to her, except to thank her for what she has done on behalf of my sister."

"Is that all, my lord?"

"I will have a proposal to put before your sister after the meeting with Ian MacIvors and Lord Thorndike. But not knowing what the outcome will be, I can't approach her at this time."

Michael turned his horse onto the road. "Good-bye, Lord Warrick. I believe we shall meet again."

Chapter 26

U *nlike the first meeting* with Lord Thorndike, where Ian arrived first, Warrick was there an hour before the others. He sat at the council table, his hands folded, his eyes reflecting nothing of what he was feeling.

He had little doubt that today he would be stripped of title and land, and his clan would scatter to the winds. One did not expect the king to overlook a transgression committed against the daughter of the duke of Ravenworth.

No matter what happened today, Warrick had decided to take his sentence without comment. He would make no excuses and would beg no pardon of anyone.

Ian MacIvors sauntered in, followed by his brother, Jamie. Ian's eyes were hard when he looked at Warrick.

"Today is the day I have waited for with great relish, Glencarin. I didn't have to do anything to bring you down." Ian beamed with satisfaction. "Fool that you are, you brought about your own destruction this time."

Warrick stood slowly, his eyes cold and threatening. "I

came here today because I was commanded to—but I don't have to listen to the croaking of a bastard."

Ian laughed. "I, a bastard? No, Warrick, you have it wrong. You were surely speaking of your—"

At that moment the door was thrown open and Lord Thorndike entered, carrying his leather satchel. He said nothing as he settled his spectacles on the bridge of his nose and fumbled through his papers until he found what he needed.

"Lord Ian, Lord Warrick, I didn't expect to see the two of you again this soon. It seems nothing will stop this feud between the two of you except His Majesty."

Ian put himself between the mediator and Warrick. "Did the king read my complaint? Is he prepared to act upon it today?"

"With a matter of this great import, you can be sure it was brought to His Majesty's attention as soon as it came to me. You made very serious charges indeed, Lord Ian. I went to Ravenworth to confer with the duke to authenticate your charges. Unfortunately His Grace was not at home."

"The duke of Ravenworth is a guest in my home this very moment, Lord Thorndike."

The mediator looked startled. "Was it not the duke's wish to appear here today?"

"This is Scotland, not England." Ian said, strutting to the table and sitting down. He hooked his thumbs in his belt and leaned back. "His Grace preferred to leave these proceedings to me, and of course to your good judgment."

Lord Thorndike's attention turned to Lord Warrick, who had stood silent and brooding. "Are you aware of the new charges against you, my lord?"

"I can imagine."

"Shall we all be seated around the table so we can get on with the proceedings? I have no liking for this and would see it to its conclusion today."

Ian smiled at Warrick but spoke to Lord Thorndike. "All

you have to do is hear the circumstances and you'll quickly decide that Lord Warrick has committed a grievous wrong."

Lord Thorndike's expression was serious. "The charges against you, Lord Warrick, are serious indeed. You are accused of abducting Lady Arrian DeWinter."

Warrick leaned forward and folded his arms across the table. "The charge is false as it stands. Lady Arrian was traveling through Glencarin with her aunt, Lady Mary Rindhold, when their carriage overturned and they were brought to Ironworth Castle in a snowstorm. Had they not been rescued by my people, they would both have died in that storm."

Lord Thorndike exchanged glances with Ian. "Is that the truth?"

Ian traced the pattern of velvet on the cuff of his coat. "When I wrote you the letter I believed that my bride-to-be and her aunt had been taken by force. I have since learned that the carriage did indeed overturn."

"I see."

"But that does not alter the facts of what this man did to Lady Arrian while she was under his protection," Ian said.

Warrick held up his hand, realizing for the first time that what he had done to Arrian might cause her shame in England. "Can I assume anything that is said here today will not go outside this room? I would not like Lady Arrian's name sullied."

"I'm glad you are concerned for Lady Arrian's welfare," Lord Thorndike said. "As it is, Lord Ian has already petitioned me to keep these proceedings sealed so that no damage will be done to Lady Arrian's reputation. I take it that is agreeable with you, Lord Warrick?"

Warrick nodded.

Lord Thorndike cleared his throat. "I shall go on with the charges." He raised his eyes to Warrick. "As I previously stated, the charges herein are most serious, Lord Warrick. I warn you beforehand that, should they prove true, you will be stripped of your title by order of His Majesty. There might even be criminal charges brought against you if the parties involve deem it to be appropriate."

"I understand," Warrick answered, his voice devoid of feeling.

"Did you or did you not force the Lady Arrian into a marriage that was not of her choosing?"

"Why don't you ask me, Lord Thorndike?" a woman's voice spoke up. "I can tell you exactly what happened."

All eyes turned to the doorway, where Arrian stood casually removing her gloves. The man behind her helped her out of her cape and draped it over a chair.

Warrick watched Arrian move gracefully across the room, followed by the tall, aristocratic-looking man who could only be her father, the duke.

Lord Thorndike scrambled to his feet. "Your Grace, I did not expect to see you here today."

"Why not, Thorndike? This meeting involves my daughter," Raile said, his eyes falling for the first time on the man who had caused his daughter so much unhappiness.

Raile and Warrick stared at each other until Lord Thorndike spoke up. "I don't know if the two of you are acquainted. Lord Warrick, may I present His Grace, the duke of Ravenworth."

Each man acknowledged the other with the slightest nod.

Lord Thorndike offered Arrian a chair. "Is it your wish to bear witness here today, my lady?"

Arrian had not yet looked at Warrick. "It is. I'm sorry if I have caused any inconvenience."

"No, not at all, my lady."

The duke sat beside Arrian, his presence overshadowing everyone else. "When my daughter makes up her mind about something, Lord Thorndike, she's like her mother. Arrian insisted on being here today and I agreed that she should be heard."

The king's representative was puzzled as to what to do next. "How is Her Grace?"

"She is well and sends her regards." Raile's eyes became hard. "I want you to know that this meeting was none of my doing. Had I heard about it in time, I would have put a stop to it." His eyes bore into Ian. "I will not have my daughter's good name tarnished in any way."

Ian squirmed beneath the heated gaze of the duke.

Lord Thorndike spoke up. "I'm glad you've come, Your Grace. Now we can get the problem solved in short order. When I received the complaint from Lord Ian, I took it right to His Majesty, and he instructed me to act upon it immediately. If I'd found you in residence when I called on you, the hearings would not have gone this far."

"I would have preferred that William had consulted me before engaging you in this action," Raile said. The fact that he had called the king by his first name was lost on no one in the room. Again his eyes met Ian's. "I learned of the meeting only this morning when my daughter came to me."

"What would you have me do?" Lord Thorndike asked.

Raile gazed at his daughter and then at Lord Warrick. "I'm not pleased with either Lord Ian or Lord Warrick. And especially not Lord Warrick."

Warrick had been staring at Arrian, and his gaze moved to the duke. "I care little about your goodwill, Your Grace."

Now Raile's words were hard. "You should, because I'll deal personally with you later. But for now, will you and my daughter explain why you couldn't wait to be married until her mother and I arrived? Did it not occur to you that, as a father, I would want to attend my only daughter's wedding?"

Warrick was struck dumb. He had come here expecting to see his world collapse about him. Until now, he'd hated all Englishmen. But this one, for reasons unknown to him, had just saved him from the English king's harsh judgment.

Ian jumped to his feet. "Surely you aren't going to pretend that you approve of this marriage when we all know it to be a farce, Your Grace. I'll not have it!"

Raile glared at Ian, but his words were for the king's

mediator. "Lord Thorndike, I will never understand the young people of today. They are so impulsive. And as for young women," he gazed at Arrian, "they can never quite make up their minds whom they want to marry. It seems first she wants one and then marries another. It wasn't that way in our day, was it?"

"No, it wasn't, Your Grace. We were all aware that Lady Arrian was coming to Scotland to marry Lord Ian."

"And so she was. Can you explain the workings of a woman's heart? I certainly cannot."

Lord Thorndike shook with laughter. "No, Your Grace, I can't either. I have five daughters of my own, and I never know what mischief they will get into next."

Raile looked down at Arrian. "Thank the good Lord I have only one daughter."

Ian was furious. "I will not stand here and listen to lies. We all know what happened and what that man did to Arrian. She belongs to me and I won't give her up!"

"Ian, I would advise you to control yourself. I am going to assume that you are overwrought because my daughter chose Lord Warrick over you. It's understandable, and you will be forgiven for the insults you spoke."

Ian shrank away from the dark look in Raile's eyes. "She still belongs to me, Your Grace." Ian turned to Warrick, who had not spoken a word. "We have not finished, Glencarin. We shall certainly meet again." He turned toward the door and stalked out, leaving Jamie to hurry after him.

"I'm sorry you were inconvenienced, Lord Thorndike," Raile said, slapping the king's man on the back. "Lord Ian is suffering from rejection. I believe that after he's had time to reconsider, he'll come to realize his petition to you was a mistake."

Arrian stared into Warrick's eyes and saw only confusion.

Warrick stood up, his mind unable to grasp the significance of the moment. He watched Raile DeWinter and Lord Thorndike move across the room, deep in conversation.

"I never expected you to be here today, Arrian."

Her eyes were shining as she looked at him. He looked thinner and haggard, as if he had not been sleeping. "I had to come, Warrick."

"But why? You owed me nothing."

"No matter the reason, you are the father of my unborn child, and I don't want my baby to grow up knowing its father is in prison. My mother and father agreed that you should not be judged and punished by His Majesty or Lord Thorndike."

"So it's true about the child." His eyes dropped to her stomach. She wore a full gown, so it was impossible to see if she was with child. "I haven't the words to tell you how I feel, Arrian."

Uncertainty reflected in her eyes. "And there's the pity. Between us we created a life, Warrick, and still we have nothing to say to one another."

He stared at the ceiling until he could bring his emotions under control. "I want to say so much." His voice came out in a raspy whisper. It seemed that at the most important moment of his life he had no words to express his true feelings.

Arrian had hoped he would at least be happy about the baby, but apparently he was not. She wanted only to make a hasty departure, but first she had to close the door on this part of her life forever.

"I'll say it for you, Warrick, and save you the trouble. What happened between us is over. Our lives touched for a brief moment in time. The only lasting effect is the new life we created."

"I still don't understand why you came here today."

"Surely you didn't think I would let our marriage be put aside and leave my child without a legitimate name."

Warrick swallowed hard. "Yes, of course." His voice came out in an even tone. "That's why you did this. I can see the legitimacy of the child would be a great concern to you and your family."

"Of course it is. Does it not matter to you, Warrick?"

"I've thought of little else."

There was a long, uncomfortable silence until Arrian spoke. "I must be leaving now."

"Will you one day want to marry Ian?"

"No. I have found we are not suited."

Warrick let out his breath. "Arrian, I want to thank you for having my sister's body returned to me."

She made a great show of working her fingers into her gloves. She wished her hands would stop trembling. "It was little enough to do, Warrick."

"Will you be returning to Davinsham?"

"No. My family and I sail tomorrow at first light for England. I'm going home."

He took in every detail of her face, wanting to burn it into his memory. "You will let me know about the child?"

She wanted him to hold her and tell her he was happy about the baby, but of course he didn't. "I'll send you word when the child is born."

There was concern in his eyes. "You are feeling well?"

"My health is good."

He reached out to her but then dropped his hand to his side. "I don't suppose you would agree to—no, you wouldn't."

Her heart was thundering with excitement. Had he been trying to ask her to return to Ironworth with him? When he said nothing further, she held out her hand. "Good-bye, Warrick. I hope you will find peace in your life."

He met her eyes, feeling very unsure of himself. "Are you happy about the child?"

She could have told him that she was happy to have this child because it was a part of him that she would always have with her. But instead she said, "A child should be born from love, not through hate."

He nodded and released her hand. "You have every reason to feel that way."

"Yes, I do."

"I believe a child should know its father."

"I will tell the child about you, Warrick, omitting of course, many truths."

He quickly masked his pain. "Will I ever see you again?"

Her eyes were heavy with sadness. "I don't think so. But I wish you well, Warrick."

He watched her leave, still unable to understand all that had happened in this room.

Arrian and her father said good-bye to Lord Thorndike, and Warrick watched them leave before he moved to the window. The sun had just come out from behind a cloud to bathe the land with its golden light.

Suddenly it came to him. Hate was what destroyed lives. God only knew it had destroyed his family.

He had been given a child, a reason to turn away from darkness into the light.

How could he allow Arrian to walk out of his life forever? He could not give her up without a fight. His jaw set in determination. He would go to her and ask her—no beg her, if he had to—to come home with him.

Raile handed Arrian into the carriage, and the horses clipped along on the cobbled streets in the direction of the *Nightingale*.

"This has been the most difficult day of my life, Father."

"No, there will be others, Arrian. But you took the first step of ridding yourself of this cursed land."

She turned to look out the window. "I long for Ravenworth," she said, slipping her hand into her father's and leaning her head against his shoulder. "Please take me home."

Chapter 27

ord Michael met Warrick as he stepped onto the deck of the *Nightingale*. "I thought you might come, but I expected you earlier, Lord Warrick."

Warrick stared at Arrian's brother. There was no dislike in the boy's eyes, only humor and a searching look.

"Is your sister aboard?"

"She is, as are my mother and father. You see, my lord, no one but I expected you to come. I've been waiting for you for over two hours."

He motioned Warrick to follow him. "The family is below. I must say, I admire your bravery in coming here. My mother and father will not welcome you."

"And your sister?"

"I'm not certain, but only because she doesn't yet know herself. For what it's worth, I'll advise you not to allow my father to intimidate you."

"No one will make me leave until I know your sister's true feelings."

"Then come with me, my lord. This will surely prove to be entertaining."

Warrick would have thought Lord Michael's attitude flippant, were it not for the serious expression on the boy's face. They crossed the deck and went down a brightly lit companionway.

Michael led Warrick into a roomy salon, complete with thick rugs and polished furnishings. Warrick had not expected such comforts on board a ship.

He searched the room for Arrian but saw only the duke and duchess. From their grim expressions, he knew Lord Michael had been correct: He was not welcome.

Kassidy was the first to speak. She stood and walked slowly toward him. "Lord Warrick, I had not anticipated your visit."

"You should have known I'd come."

Raile's face was stoic as he looked at the young lord. "I can't imagine why you thought you'd be welcome here," he said at last. "After I accompany my daughter home, I had every intention of returning to Scotland. You and I have something to settle between us."

"Arrian and I had little chance to talk this morning, Your Grace," Warrick said. "I will not leave until I've seen her."

"My daughter does not wish to see you. Don't you think you've already done enough to her?" There was no mercy in Raile's eyes. "I want you to know that when I helped you this morning, it was for Arrian's sake and not for yours."

Warrick and Raile were of the same height and stood facing each other. "I realized that, Your Grace. I would not expect you to have any liking for me."

"I care little what happens to you. If I had my way I'd throw you overboard right now and leave you for fish bait."

Warrick didn't flinch. "If I were in your place I'd feel the same."

"I only agreed to talk to Thorndike this morning because I couldn't fight both my wife and daughter when they asked me to intercede on your behalf."

"You and I both know there was another reason you helped me."

Raile's eyes bored into Warrick's. "Yes, the child was also my concern. I do not want there to be any gossip about my daughter, and for that reason, I agreed that the marriage could not be set aside—not yet."

"Whatever the reason, I'm grateful for what you did, Your Grace," Warrick said. "But I didn't ask for your help, and I didn't want it."

Raile's voice was cold. "Humility isn't one of your strong points, is it, Lord Warrick? Nor, perhaps, is genuine gratitude."

"I have never been accused of being humble. But I have thanked you, Your Grace."

Raile nodded toward his son. "It seems you have a friend here to champion your cause. My son seems to endow you with characteristics you probably don't possess, such as loyalty and honor."

Warrick's face whitened as he looked from father to son. "My honor has never been in question."

"I would not have called you an honorable man. Not after what you've done to my daughter."

"Your Grace, I care not about your opinion of me. I have come to take your daughter away with me, if she will come."

"The devil you will!" Raile yelled, taking a threatening step closer to Warrick. "You will live the rest of your life without ever seeing my daughter again. And you will wish to God you had never heard of me."

"Hello, Warrick."

Everyone turned to Arrian, who stood in the doorway. The black mourning gown she still wore for her grandfather was most becoming. Her hair hung down her back in curls, making her look very young and vulnerable.

Kassidy rushed to her daughter. "You don't have to be here if you'd rather not."

"This concerns me." She took a hesitant step closer to Warrick. "I will hear what you have to say."

Warrick's eyes swept her face. Only now, seeing her in these surroundings, could he understand the life to which she had been born. How could he expect this beautiful woman to give up everything and go with him? Still, he had to try. "I have come to ask you to return to Ironworth with me. I hope you will consider it."

There was silence as they all waited for Arrian's answer. "Why would you want me to come with you, Warrick?"

"Because you carry my child. If it is a son, he will one day be chief of the Drummonds. The child should be born at Ironworth."

"By God!" Raile said, striding toward Warrick. "I'll break you with my bare hands."

Kassidy came between her husband and Warrick. "For Arrian's sake, Raile, allow him to have his say."

Raile's eyes burned with anger, but his wife had a calming effect on him. "I'll allow him to state his reasons before I toss him over the side."

Warrick would have preferred to speak to Arrian in private so he could make his true feelings known, but her family would never allow that. He reached for her hand, and she didn't pull away. "Arrian, come with me." He was good at masking his feelings, and he did so now. "I ask it of you for the child's sake."

She searched his eyes for softness or some sign of love but she saw none. Even so, Arrian didn't hesitate in her answer. "I'll go with you, Warrick."

She saw joy shining in his eyes. His grip tightened on her hand. "Your Grace, I'm taking your daughter with me. Don't attempt to stop me."

Kassidy put a restraining hand on Raile's arm. "Arrian, are you certain this is what you want?" she asked.

"Yes, Mother." She looked at her father. "Try to understand. I'm having Warrick's baby and the child should not be denied a father."

There was anger and sadness in Raile's heart. "I wanted more than this for you, Arrian."

"This is what I want, Father."

Michael had been watching the confrontation with interest. Yes, it was clear to him now that Arrian loved Warrick. He wasn't so sure of Warrick's feelings, however.

"Don't try to pretend," Raile said, "that you don't know my daughter is an heiress of considerable fortune. You can't deny you know nothing about the seventy thousand pounds I set aside for her."

"You're the one that seems to be obsessed with money, Your Grace. I want nothing that doesn't belong to me. I didn't marry Arrian's money or her family. This is not England, but Scotland. You cannot bend me to your will as you did Lord Thorndike today."

"Upstart," Raile mumbled.

Kassidy caught her husband's hand. "Perhaps we should all take a deep breath and calm down. Raile and Warrick, you have both said many cruel things. We are Arrian's family and want only what is best for her. It is only right that we question your motives, Lord Warrick."

There was remorse in Warrick's eyes when he looked at Kassidy. "I do apologize, Your Grace. I did not come here to insult your family. I only came for Arrian."

"You may as well cede, Father," Michael said. "Arrian is determined to return to Ironworth with Lord Warrick."

Raile pulled Arrian to him, looking deeply into her eyes. "Are you certain this is what you want?"

"Oh, yes, Father, very certain."

Kassidy and Michael came to Arrian and hugged her. Warrick felt like an outsider, a spoiler, and suddenly he had an aching need to gain the respect of the DeWinter family.

At last Kassidy came to Warrick and took his hand. "You will be taking our most precious jewel, Warrick. I beg you to treat her with gentleness."

"You have my word on that."

"Michael has expressed a wish to go to Ironworth and remain with Arrian until the baby is born. I will also be sending my maid, Elspeth. Is this satisfactory to you?"

Warrick could hardly contain his elation. He had not expected Arrian to agree to go with him, or her family to relent so easily. What did it matter if others came also? "That is acceptable."

"Raile and I must return home at this time. But we will come to Ironworth before the birth of the baby."

Warrick nodded. "I'm sure Arrian will want her family around her at such a time."

Raile was not so easy on Warrick. "In my eyes you don't deserve any consideration. However, my wife and daughter seem to feel differently. Perhaps they know a side of you I haven't yet seen. But be warned, Warrick, if Arrian isn't treated with kindness and respect, I won't need His Majesty to pass judgment on you—I'll do that myself."

Warrick's face seemed carved out of stone. "I'll do my duty by Arrian. But I will not answer to you for anything, Your Grace. You cannot buy me with your money, and you cannot impress me with power."

Raile's eyes hardened with anger, but there was also a growing admiration for the young Scottish chief. Certainly he was more impressed with this man who spoke his mind than he'd been with Ian MacIvors, who was secretive and cunning.

"Now," Michael said, "I'm going to rescue my new brother-in-law and show him the workings of the *Nightingale*. We get underway within the hour. We'll just go above and tell Captain Norris to chart a new course."

"I won't be sailing with you," Warrick said.

"You must," Kassidy told him. "A long carriage ride would not be good for Arrian at this time."

"I cannot go with you," Warrick explained. "My men are waiting for me in Edinburgh." He turned to Arrian. "We will next meet at Ironworth. It is a three-day ride, so you may arrive ahead of me."

Kassidy drew Warrick's attention. "Come with us and

allow my husband this time to get to know you better. He is a father who loves his daughter. Surely you can cede on this one point—you won all the others."

"I'm sorry, Your Grace, but I must decline. I believe Arrian would benefit by these few days alone with her family."

"Perhaps you are right," Kassidy said.

"I would like to see Arrian alone now, if you don't mind," Warrick said.

"I'll walk with you on deck," Arrian said.

He wished her family a pleasant voyage and followed Arrian up the companionway.

They stood on the deck of the *Nightingale,* watching the sun as it appeared to sink into the sea. Neither seemed able to put their thoughts into words until Warrick spoke. "I never dared hope you would come home with me."

The sun hit her golden hair with a halo of light. "I have little choice, Warrick. We have to put our feelings aside and think of the baby."

"Yes, the child."

She gripped the railing, unable to look at him. "My family was very hard on you."

"It was to be expected. I deserved their contempt and distrust." He looked down at her. "Arrian, I have known little softness in my life, and certainly not the love and affection you have with your family. All I have known is how to fight and how to hate. I don't know if I can change."

Oh, how she wanted him to take her in his arms and say he loved her, that she would soften him and teach him to love. "I will try to make you a good wife," she said.

"I am ashamed of many things I have done to you. I can't tell you how I felt today when you came to my rescue with Lord Thorndike. You should have hated me and wanted to see me suffer. I have never met anyone like you."

Arrian managed to smile. "I have always been the champion of lost causes."

He returned her smile. "Am I a lost cause?"

"I don't know," she admitted in all honesty. "I hope not."

"Now that I have met your family, I can see the extraordinary bond you have with them."

"Did you know that I was adopted?"

He stared at her in shocked surprise. "You never told me that."

"My mother died the day I was born. You see, she was Kassidy's only sister, so she and I already had a bond almost from the first. My real father was Raile's half brother."

"I never suspected."

"Before I had reached my second birthday, my real father died, unexpectedly and rather heroically. I won't go into the details because I still don't like to think about it. I have always known that I belonged, and I never doubted that I was loved."

"I'll be good to you, Arrian."

Arrian wanted to take his face between her hands and kiss away the sadness she saw there. "I believe this child may teach you to love, Warrick."

There was a tightness in his throat, and his voice was deep with emotion. "I feel very humble, Arrian. I'm not worthy of a second chance, since I got you by trickery."

She was quiet for a moment, and when she spoke her voice came out in a whisper. "Sometimes, Warrick, we are guided by Providence, and we have little control where our lives will take us. I still have doubts about you. But it took a lot of courage for you to come here today, and I admire that."

It was painful being so near her and feeling as if he had no right to touch her. "I hope I never give you cause to regret your decision today."

She laced her fingers together and stared at the distant lights of Edinburgh. She knew he would be leaving soon, and she didn't want to be parted from him. "Are you sure you won't reconsider sailing with us on the *Nightingale*?"

"I must decline. But tell me, why is the ship called the

Nightingale?" he asked, wanting to delay his departure.

"That is a secret shared only by my mother and father. It's something personal between them that they don't seem inclined to share with anyone, not even Michael and me."

"I have never seen more love and respect between a husband and wife than there is with your mother and father, Arrian. As I remember, it wasn't that way between my parents."

"Having grown up under the protection of that love, I cannot imagine it being otherwise." She raised her face to him and saw the dying rays of the sun played across his dark hair. "I wish the same for this child, Warrick."

"Do you think you would have had a good marriage with Ian? Did I cheat you of the life you wanted with him?"

How could she make him understand that Ian was not the man she had supposed him to be. "I can never know. Mother says one must take the hand life deals them."

There were words he wanted to say to her, but he could not give them voice. "I want to make everything beautiful for you. I wish we could go back to that first day we met. How different it could have been."

Warrick's face was half hidden by the shadow cast by the rippling canvas sail. Her hand was clasped in his, and Arrian wished she could move into his arms and have him hold her. She wanted to hear how he truly felt about the baby—and about her.

"We cannot go back, Warrick. But what would you do if we could?"

He didn't even hesitate, although the words brought him pain. "I would have let you go without planting my seed in your body."

That was not what she had wanted to hear. "It's too late for that, isn't it? I don't feel pity for you because you are bound to a wife and baby you don't want. This was your doing, Warrick."

He released her hand and gripped the railing so hard his knuckles whitened. "Arrian, I don't—"

She felt the cold wind against her cheek and pulled her shawl closer to her for warmth. "I believe you should leave now, Warrick. We will soon be getting underway."

He stared into her eyes for a long moment and then turned away. As he stepped onto the gangplank a man was boarding the *Nightingale,* and Warrick moved aside to allow him to pass.

Arrian watched Warrick leave the ship without a backward glance. Her attention was drawn to the newcomer, whom she recognized as Ian's valet.

"Lady Arrian, I have come with a message from Lord Ian."

Absently she took the packet from the man and went below to her cabin, where she laid Ian's message aside, unopened.

That night Warrick stood in the shadow of a warehouse watching the *Nightingale*'s sails catch the wind. With Mactavish at his side, he turned his horse homeward. If he rode hard perhaps he would reach Ironworth before Arrian arrived.

I *t was an overcast day* when the *Nightingale*
dropped anchor off the coast of Glencarin.
Raile and Kassidy had decided not to accompany
Arrian ashore.

They both watched Michael hand Arrian into the longboat with tenderness and then tuck a wrap about her. "Our
son will watch over her," Kassidy assured Raile.

"Are you so sure Lord Warrick is the right man for her?
Arrian could have chosen from dozens of suitors from the
best of families."

"But she wants this man, Raile. In many ways Warrick
reminds me of you when we first met."

"Do you suppose our daughter will smooth his rough
edges the way you did mine?"

Kassidy laughed. "I didn't smooth your rough edges,
dearest, I merely clipped your wandering wings."

Raile watched the figures in the boat grow smaller and
smaller. "I pray to God he's good to her."

"He will be," Kassidy said. "He loves her desperately. I only hope he finds the courage to tell her."

Warrick watched from the castle while Arrian and Michael stood on the cliff to wave to their parents as the *Nightingale* caught the evening tide. Even now he couldn't believe she had actually come to him. He had feared she might change her mind at the last moment.

His boots were mud splattered, and he needed a shave. He had ridden day and night so that he would arrive ahead of Arrian. Now that she was here, he could rest.

"Haddy, welcome Lady Arrian and her brother, Lord Michael. Tell them I will see them at dinner."

Wearily, he went to his room. Without undressing or removing his muddy boots, he lay on the bed and immediately fell into an exhausted sleep.

Arrian was sad to see her mother and father leave, but this was where she belonged—to this land and to the man who was its laird.

As the sun set, the sea and sky seemed to merge as one. Arrian turned her gaze to the heather-covered mountains that looked as if nature had splashed them with a purple paint brush. She breathed in the fresh, crisp air and smiled at her brother.

"Isn't it wonderful here? The beauty is such that it takes my breath away."

Elspeth's feet sank into the sand, and she looked disgruntled. "I never liked Scotland."

"I believe it's different from anywhere we've traveled," Michael said. "I have this urge to see many places, Arrian."

"You are growing up, Michael. Soon Father will be giving you more responsibilities."

"I know." He hugged her. "But that's not today. How shall I pass my time here?"

"I'm told the hunting is good. And," she smiled with mischief, "you might want to challenge Warrick to a game of chess. I defeated him."

"Arrian, surely you didn't use those moves Father showed you, did you?"

She laughed. "He was far too arrogant and needed to be taught a lesson."

At that moment Tam and several servants arrived to transport their trunks to the castle. Elspeth directed them with her usual sternness.

"Do you wish ta ride, m'lady?" Tam asked.

"No," she told him. "It's such a glorious day, my brother and I shall walk."

"Not I," Elspeth said, climbing into the wagon.

Taking Michael's hand, Arrian pulled him up the stone steps that led up to the castle.

"When we were children I thought our family would always be together. Now we are about to be scattered to the four winds. Aunt Mary in London. Mother and Father at Ravenworth, and I in Scotland. Where will you be, Michael?"

"Times change, Arrian, and people change with it. But it matters not where our family goes, we will always be bound together by a special bond."

"Yes. I believe that also."

Arrian found, to her surprise, a warm reception from Mrs. Haddington and Barra. She had not expected Warrick to arrive ahead of them, but she was told that he was in his bedroom. She wondered why he had not come down to welcome her.

Arrian no longer occupied Gwendolyn's room but had been moved into the master suite, where her bedchamber and Warrick's were connected by a sitting room.

It had been a long day, and Arrian slipped between crisp, white sheets, aching with weariness.

Elspeth placed a tray on Arrian's lap and then went to stoke the fire. "You need to eat a bit before you sleep."

Arrian groaned. "I don't want to, Elspeth, take it away. When will this sickness pass?"

"In a few weeks, m'lady. Would you want me to sit with you for a time?"

"No. I just want to sleep. I realize now how miserable Aunt Mary must have felt when she was seasick."

"I'll just go below and speak to the housekeeper. She's ranting that I'm taking her place and I want to assure her I'm doing nothing of the kind. I only told her she should employ some of the women from the village. You'll be needing more help to run this place properly."

"Mrs. Haddington is nice when you get to know her, Elspeth."

"I'll soothe her and make certain she knows I'm only here to help."

"You'll do well with her. It's the English and MacIvors she doesn't like."

"She has a liking for you, m'lady."

Arrian yawned, burying her head in the pillow. "Does she? I would have thought otherwise."

Elspeth left the room, closing the door softly behind her.

Arrian's eyes fell on the packet Elspeth had placed beside her bed. She had forgotten all about the message that had been delivered to her on board the *Nightingale*. She reached for it now and tore it open, not really wanting to read anything from Ian. To her surprise the ruby betrothal ring fell into her hand. She stared at it now, feeling as if it were almost a thing of evil. Her hand trembled as she read his scrawled words.

My dearest love,

I return my ring to you, wanting you to keep it as a reminder of the love we once shared. I am confident you will one day slip the ring back on your finger and we will be husband and wife as God intended us to be. Until that day, I remain the man who loves you more than life.

There was a light rap on the connecting doors. She knew it would be Warrick.

She ran her fingers through her tangled hair, excited that he had come to her at last.

He entered, looking strangely uncomfortable. "Do you mind if I sit and talk to you for a moment?"

Her gaze ran over him. His dark hair was wet as if he'd just bathed. "No, of course not."

"I trust you had a smooth voyage. I apologize for not welcoming you on your arrival."

There was a heavy silence.

"You must have ridden hard to arrive so soon," she finally said.

"Yes, I did. I hope you find these rooms comfortable." He looked around, for the first time realizing how shabby they must seem to her.

"I find them very pleasant, Warrick."

He saw the letter she clutched in her hand. "Correspondence so soon?" he asked, assuming it would be from her mother.

She opened her hand and the MacIvors betrothal ring glittered in her palm. "It's from Ian. It arrived just after you left the *Nightingale*."

He stared at the ring he detested. There was coldness in his voice when he spoke. "I'm sorry if I've intruded on your memories of Ian MacIvors. Does he pour out his heart to you in the letter? As for the ring, I'd rather you wore it for all to see than have you cry over it in private."

"Ian is having a difficult time—"

He came to his feet with fury in his eyes. "Spare me. It's apparent that you sleep with his letter and his ring. Do you also sleep with your memories of him?"

"Warrick, you don't understand. I—"

"Oh, I understand. Don't worry that I'll intrude on your private memories. Deliver my child, then you can go back to the man you love, or to hell for all I care."

She struggled for something to say that would clear up

this misunderstanding. She held the ring out to him. "I don't want—"

Warrick walked to the door and stood looking at her for a long moment. "I forced you to marry me, and I implored you to return because of the child. Have no fear, I will not force my company upon you. You will be left alone with your memories."

He hesitated at the door, as if reluctant to leave. But she turned away from him. "I just want to be alone," she said.

Arrian watched him leave the room and close the door behind him.

He had assumed the worst and had not even allowed her to explain. She had envisioned this reunion quite differently. In her foolish heart she had thought he would come to her with words of love. Instead he had been hard and accusing.

What demons were driving him? Would he ever be able to put his distrust aside and accept her love?

The weather turned gloriously warm.

Arrian went down the stairs to join Michael, who was waiting for her with the horses for their daily ride. As she passed the salon, she noticed that workmen were rolling up the tattered rug.

"Mrs. Haddington, what are they doing?" Arrian asked the housekeeper, who was watching the workers to make certain they didn't break anything.

"We're having a housecleaning. Taking all the rugs and draperies up and having women from the village come in to help clean." Mrs. Haddington looked disapprovingly toward the library. "His lordship's engaged that Mrs. Robertson to help oversee the villagers' work."

Arrian felt her temper rising. "And why is that?"

"I don't rightly know, m'lady."

At that moment the library door opened and Arrian saw Louise Robertson carrying an armload of draperies. Mrs.

Haddington sniffed and mumbled under her breath. "She reaches above her station. Thinks she's lady of the manor."

Louise Robertson approached. "Lady Arrian, I'm sorry you haven't been well. I wanted to call on you, but Warrick insisted you weren't to be disturbed. I felt honored that he wanted me to take your place here at Ironworth."

Arrian stared at the woman. "Whatever do you mean?"

There was a slight smile on the woman's lips. "I merely meant that you are too ill to take on the household duties, so I'm doing your part."

"I'm not ill, Mrs. Robertson."

"Perhaps not. But I have been led to believe you are of a delicate nature."

Arrian was seething inside. "If you will excuse me, Mrs. Robertson. I won't keep you from your appointed task."

Louise Robertson blocked Arrian's path. "Warrick has said the rugs are to be replaced. I was wondering if you have a preference in color."

Arrian was startled to see such dislike in the woman's eyes. "I'm sure my husband and I will decide on that. You indicated you were only to supervise the cleaning."

"I had hoped to convince you to speak to Warrick on my behalf."

"For what reason?"

"I have asked him if he would like me to oversee the decorating of Ironworth, and he mentioned that he would have to consult you. I'm sure you don't want to be bothered with such a menial task."

"That will be up to my husband." Arrian moved around the woman. "In the future, Mrs. Robertson, if you want to speak to me, consult my maid."

By the time she reached the front door, her anger had still not cooled. Elspeth handed Arrian her gloves. "The few times I've come against that one, I've found her cold and distant. I might also add, she has eyes for your husband."

"Perhaps he admires her," Arrian said, angrily working

her fingers into her leather riding gloves. "All I could think about while that woman talked was how beautiful Ravenworth is at this time of year."

Elspeth caught Arrian's hand. "If it was me, m'lady, I'd not let the fox in the stable."

"What's that supposed to mean?"

"Mrs. Haddington says that woman has had her eyes on his lordship for years. She said they might have married after her husband died. But Lord Warrick married you instead."

"I'm surprised you listen to idle prattle, Elspeth. I'm not concerned with that woman's interest in my husband. I'd rather know about her suitability for decorating. She seems to want to make Ironworth over for Warrick."

"Well, I'm keeping an eye on her. There's something about her that I don't trust," Elspeth said, going back into the house and leaving Arrian to ponder her warning.

Arrian's face lit up when she saw Mactavish talking to Michael. She hurried down the steps toward them. "Hello, Mactavish," she greeted him with genuine pleasure.

"M'lady, I was hoping to see you this morning." His eyes brightened as they rested on her face. "If you don't mind my saying so, you're prettier than ever."

"Thank you, Mactavish." On studying him closer, she saw a deep, raw scar across his forehead, and there were circles under his eyes as if he'd been ill. "What has happened to you?"

He touched the scar and smiled at her. "It's just a reminder of Ian MacIvors's hospitality."

"Do you mean he did this the day you brought my trunks to Davinsham?"

"'Tis of little matter. It's all but healed."

"That's not all our cousin did, Arrian," Michael spoke up with indignation. "He broke Mactavish's ribs and beat him with his whip."

Before Arrian could voice her horror at what Ian had

done, the big Scot picked her up and placed her on her saddle. "Don't fret about me, m'lady. It's in the past."

She stared at him in disbelief, angry that Mactavish had been hurt because of her.

With Michael at her side, Arrian raced across the hills and toward the sandy beach. Once she reached the sea, she galloped her horse through the splashing waves, trying to cool her temper.

Michael caught up with her and grabbed her reins, bringing her to a halt. "Do you want to break your neck, Arrian?"

"I don't care. No one is what I thought they were, and nothing makes sense anymore. There are undercurrents and intrigues everywhere. What kind of country is this?"

"I like the Highlands."

"I'm not so certain I do, Michael. There is a hardness about the people here. I had this romantic image in my mind about this country. Dreams die hard, I suppose."

Michael's attention was caught by a flock of geese flying across the sky. "Arrian, people are much the same here as they are in England. Unfortunately, you became caught in a feud and saw the worst of both sides. As for dreams, put them aside and live in this world."

"I have come to believe that Ian is evil." She shivered. "When I think how close I came to marrying him, it frightens me. Even from a distance he has been able to reach out to me and destroy my happiness."

"What about Warrick?"

Arrian slid down from her horse and walked along the beach. "He's a complicated man with deeply rooted anger and distrust. I had hoped I could somehow help him, but now I know I cannot."

She still wondered what Louise Robertson meant to Warrick, but she did not mention it to her brother. "Let us shake off our mood, little brother. Let's ride to the meadow where the heather is in bloom."

Michael was glad she was distracted. "I'll race you."

Her eyes brightened by his challenge. "You could never beat me. Remember, I won the Ravenworth race."

Warrick was supervising the roofing of a cottage when he glanced up to see Arrian and her brother racing across the hill. He envied the closeness they shared.

When Arrian and her brother disappeared over a hill, Warrick went back to work. He invented reasons to stay away from the castle to give Arrian time to adjust to her new life.

He would do anything to keep her near him, even if it meant staying away from her.

Chapter 29

A stern-faced Mrs. Haddington served dinner in the small informal dining room.

"Is his lordship not to join us?" Michael inquired.

"As to that, I don't know, m'lord. He's no' come home, and he's sent no word."

Arrian lowered her eyes so Michael wouldn't see how hurt she was. "The fish is delicious, Haddy," she said, trying to sound unconcerned. "I have become partial to salmon since coming to the Highlands."

The housekeeper paused in the doorway. "Cook wants particularly ta please you, m'lady, with the wee one coming on."

Michael waited until Mrs. Haddington withdrew before he spoke. "I wonder what can be keeping Warrick? We've hardly seen him since we arrived."

"I'm sure I don't know," Arrian replied, wondering if he was with Louise Robertson.

After dinner, Arrian went upstairs to her bedroom and Elspeth helped her undress and get into bed. "You look weary, m'lady. I don't think you should ride horseback until after the baby comes."

"Yes, I suppose you're right. From now on I'll go about in the carriage."

After she was in bed and Elspeth withdrew, Arrian stared out the window at the darkened night. She had thought Warrick was happy about the baby, but now she wasn't too sure.

Her eyes were heavy. Quiet fell over the castle and she drifted to sleep. Arrian didn't know what time it was when she heard the sounds from the connecting room of someone bumping into furniture, followed by a muttered oath.

She lit a candle, slid out of bed, and went to the sitting room. The light of the candle spilled into the darkened corners and she saw Warrick standing by the window.

He turned to her with an apologetic look. "I'm sorry if I disturbed your sleep. I know how you need your rest."

"I'm not a doll that will break, Warrick." She glanced down at the glass in his hand and saw he was drinking.

"I don't usually drink alone, but you see I have a problem I can't solve and this helps dull the pain."

"Pain, my lord—are you ill?"

He stared at her. "Perhaps I used the wrong choice of words."

"May I help?"

"No, you can't help, Arrian. You are the problem."

She blinked, not understanding his harsh words. "Are you drunk, Warrick?"

"Yes, I am, but I'll be a lot drunker before I'm finished."

"I know you are having regrets because of me."

He took another drink before looking down at her. "Well, you will soon be out of my life and you can have your precious Ian, though God only knows why you'd want him."

"Warrick, if it weren't for my baby, you wouldn't have come to the *Nightingale* that day, would you?"

He took the candle from her and placed it on a table. He

then moved to the window and motioned for her to join him there. "Tell me, Arrian, what you see out there?"

The bedroom she had occupied before had faced the seaward side of the castle. Here she saw the view of the mountains and valleys. He stood behind her, his breath touching her cheek.

"I see that the night hides the beauty of the countryside. I suppose what you want me to say is that I see only Drummond land, Warrick."

"That's right, Arrian." He turned her to face him. "Now what do you see?"

"I see the chief of the Drummonds."

"Yes, and you love the chief of the MacIvors. In a moment of weakness I forgot you were a distant daughter of the MacIvors clan. I should never have brought you back among us."

She swallowed painfully and her eyes stung from his cruel words. "The fault lies with you, Warrick. It was you who came storming onto my father's ship demanding your rights."

"I could do no less—I had to give your child my name. I owe much to you and your family, because you saved me from Lord Thorndike's judgment, which would surely have gone against me. It's a bitter thing to be indebted to one's enemies, Arrian."

"You see no enemy here, Warrick. There is only a woman who is a fool. I thought we could at least be amiable to each other. It seems I was wrong. Why did you ask me to return and allow me to think you wanted the baby?"

He turned away from her to gaze out the window. "I didn't want your lover to raise a child of Drummond blood."

"Your child," she reminded him.

It seemed he hadn't heard her words. "If the child is a boy, shall I proudly parade him before my people? 'Here,' shall I say, 'is your future chief. Forget that within him flows the blood of MacIvors.'"

She stared at his rigid back while trying to keep control over her emotions. She turned toward her room, not wanting to hear more.

Before she reached the door Warrick caught up with her and grabbed her arm. "Don't leave yet. There is more I'd say to you."

"You have said quite enough. You think by punishing me that you are striking out at Ian. Your acts are like a doubled-edged sword, my lord. You have had your revenge."

He pulled her forward, bringing her face up to his. "When I touch you, do you think of him? What eats away at me is that even now I want you." He closed his eyes for a moment. "If there were a way, I would drive all thoughts of him from your mind. Then perhaps I could find peace, Arrian."

"You have created your own torment, Warrick. Only you can find your release."

His arms circled her, and he pulled her tightly against his body. "I'll drive Ian MacIvors out of your mind."

His mouth crushed against hers with a grinding force. Arrian could taste the brandy on his lips. His kiss was meant to punish rather than to show affection. She struggled to be free of him, but he grabbed her head and held her still, thus deepening the kiss.

Warrick released her so suddenly that she staggered backward, bumping into a chair. He shook his head as if to clear it. "Forgive me. It was not my intent to force myself on you."

"I've forgiven you many things, Warrick, but I'll not be so quick to forget what you have said tonight. You are cruel and heartless. I wish I never had to see you again."

She rushed into her room and slammed the door behind her. She almost wanted him to come after her, but there was only silence on the other side of the door.

Arrian flung open her trunk, wildly rummaging inside until she found her royal blue riding habit. She was more angry than hurt as she dressed in the darkness. She had to get out of here so she could think clearly.

She met no one on her way out of the house, but when she reached the stables, she found Tam giving the horses fresh oats.

He looked startled when he saw Arrian at this time of night. "Can I help ye, m'lady?"

"Yes, Tam, saddle a horse for me. I'm going riding."

He thought it strange that Lady Arrian should be riding so late at night, and alone, but it was not for him to question. He obediently did as she asked. "Looks like it might rain," he observed, hoping to dissuade her.

She merely smiled. Silently Tam helped her onto the saddle and watched as she rode away, her horse's hooves striking sparks against the cobbles.

Unknown to Arrian, Warrick watched her from the window. When he saw her ride into the night, he muttered under his breath and ran downstairs. "Saddle my horse," he barked at Tam, "and make haste about it."

Arrian had no direction in mind as she urged her horse into a swift gallop. The night was black, without moon or stars to guide her. On she rode, her mind feeling as if it were shattering into millions of pieces. She could remember every cruel word Warrick had uttered to her tonight. She had been such a fool to return to Ironworth. Her father had tried to warn her, but she had been insistent on having her own way.

Thinking it would be too cool to ride toward the sea, Arrian turned the horse in the direction of the mountains. She splashed through a stream and raced up the steep embankment.

The wind struck suddenly, and drops of rain pelted her face. Still she rode onward.

In the distance Arrian could hear the sound of another rider, and she set her chin with determination. No one had to tell her that Warrick had come after her. She slapped the reins, and the horses's long strides took her up a hill. So desperate was her need to escape Warrick, she did not see the stone wall that lurked in the darkness. She heard Warrick call a warning, but it was too late.

Arrian saw the outline of the wall and pulled back on the reins. The horse came to a quick halt, but she plummeted through the air, hit the wall, and crumpled to the wet ground.

She cried out in pain as she tried to rise.

Warrick was beside her immediately, feeling her body for broken bones. "You little fool. Did you want to kill yourself?"

"I don't care," she moaned, doubling over as another pain ripped through her body. "But the baby," she gasped. "I have harmed my baby."

"Oh, God," he cried out in anguish, lifting her into his arms and trying to shield her against the driving rain. "What have I done?"

Arrian's tears of pain mixed with the rain as he carried her to his horse and mounted, holding her tightly against him.

He nudged Titus forward, racing toward the castle. "My horse," Arrian managed to say between pains.

"I'll send Tam for him."

He wrapped his arms around her and rested his face against hers. "Do you know where you are hurt?"

"The baby," she groaned. She bit her lip to keep from crying out. "Get me to Elspeth. She'll know what to do. Hurry, please!"

Warrick rode like a madman. When he reached Ironworth, he dismounted and carried her into the house and up the stairs, hating himself for the pain she was suffering. She had ridden into the night to escape him.

Arrian stiffened as another pain tore at her insides.

Warrick laid her gently on the bed while Elspeth appeared at his side. "What have you done to m'lady?" she asked, already beginning to strip off Arrian's wet riding habit.

Warrick looked on Arrian's pale face. "Will she lose the child?"

"I don't know. Leave me to look after her. Later I'll want to know what happened."

Reluctantly Warrick left the room. He would keep the long vigil throughout the night. To him, this was God's punishment. It would be his fault if Arrian died. He picked up the brandy bottle and flung it into the fireplace, where it smashed against the iron grate. Never had he felt such helplessness and anguish.

One hour passed, and then two. He was conscious only of the ticking of the clock and the moans of pain that came from Arrian's room.

Elspeth came through the connecting doors to find Warrick sitting by the window staring into the early dawn. The eyes he raised to the maid were red rimmed, and he had the stubble of a beard on his face.

"She lost the baby, didn't she?"

Elspeth's eyes were filled with compassion, for it was obvious that Lord Warrick had suffered greatly. "Yes, she did, m'lord. I'm sorry."

"Arrian's going to die, isn't she?"

"Of course not." Elspeth went to him and poured him a steaming cup of coffee from the pot Haddy had brought in earlier. "Here, drink this."

Obediently he raised the cup to his lips. "It's my fault, you know. I'm responsible for the death of the child. She was trying to get away from me."

"M'lady said you'd be blaming yourself, m'lord, and I'm to impress on you that you are not to blame."

He buried his face in his hands. "Even after this, she thinks of my feelings."

"That's the way she's always been, m'lord. I'm wondering why you don't know this about her."

"Did she ask to see me?"

"No. Lord Michael is with her now. It's best you leave them alone. He'll comfort her."

Warrick nodded and went silently to his own room. Shortly afterwards he left the house and rode into the hills. He did not come back that day or the next. Alone, with no one to comfort him, he grieved for the baby that was lost to him.

Michael sat beside his sister, wiping her tears and talking to her soothingly. "You'll have other children."

She rolled toward the window, watching the sun bathe the room in its glory, feeling empty inside. "I don't want another child. I wanted this one."

Michael could do no more than clasp her hand and wait for her tears to dry.

It wasn't until three days later that Warrick knocked on Arrian's door, but Elspeth sadly sent him away because Arrian refused to see him.

Each day he came to her door, but the answer was always the same—Arrian would not see him.

After a week he no longer went to her room.

Arrian's health improved, and she was able to come downstairs. Michael watched her move from a chair to the window and back.

"You are restless. I believe that's a sign that you are fully recovered."

"I have something I've been wanting to say to you and I only now gathered the courage."

"You want to return to Ravenworth."

"Yes, as soon as I can travel."

Michael caught her hand and forced her to look at him. "Are you certain this is what you want? You know if you go through with this you may never see Warrick again. Can you live with that?"

"I want to go home and forget any of this ever happened." Her eyes were bright with tears. "Please, Michael, take me home!"

"If that's what you really want, I'll make all the arrangements. But make sure before we leave that you'll have no regrets, Arrian."

"Thank you for understanding, Michael, and for not asking too many questions."

"When you're hurt, the whole family is wounded, Arrian. But I have to tell you, I like Warrick. I have never known a man could suffer so from the loss of a baby. I wish you could be a little kinder to him."

"I will not be unkind," she said, picking up her cashmere shawl and placing it about her shoulders. "I just don't know what to say to him. Besides, it seems Louise Robertson is here almost every day. I suspect she's been a great comfort to him."

"Perhaps the least said about her, the best," was Michael's enigmatic reply.

Chapter 30

*M*ichael and Arrian were seated in the library with a large tapestry-covered tome opened across their laps.

"This book contains drawings of Ironworth, Michael, and it would seem the book was done by a family member." She traced the name that had been signed in a feminine hand. "'Lady Brendolyn Glencarin, 1566.' It says here that she's the one who brought the Glencarin title to the Drummond family. If I were redoing Ironworth, I'd use her drawings for my guide. Look how she had detailed the furnishing and colors of each room."

"Why don't you show this to Warrick and make that suggestion to him, Arrian?"

"I don't think so."

At that moment Mrs. Haddington came bustling in with their tea and placed it on the table before them.

"Look, Mrs. Haddington," Arrian said, turning the book so the housekeeper could see. "These are drawings of Ironworth."

The housekeeper merely glanced at the book and grunted, turning her attention to Michael. "Would you be wanting brandy, m'lord?"

"No, I'll have tea with my sister. I hope you have some of those delicious raspberry tarts, Haddy," he said, using the familiar name he'd heard Warrick use with the housekeeper.

"I do, m'lord, and lemon, too." Haddy smiled, pleased with Lord Michael's friendliness. Arrian thought no one could resist Michael's genuine charm.

"You spoil me," he said, reaching for one of the confections and biting into it. "Mmm, this is what I'll miss most when I leave Scotland, Haddy."

That reminded Arrian that she wanted to talk to Warrick about leaving. She had been dreading this moment. "Is his lordship in this evening, Mrs. Haddington?" She hated to ask a servant where her husband was, but it could be no secret to anyone that she and Warrick had not seen each other since she'd lost the baby.

"He'll be in his study with Louise Robertson. I believe she's having her way in the house."

Arrian closed the book and stood up. "I'll return shortly, Michael. I'm going to talk to Warrick now."

Both Michael and Mrs. Haddington watched her leave, and the housekeeper clicked her tongue. "There'll be trouble with those two, and it saddens my ol' heart."

Michael silently agreed with her but said nothing. He might lightly banter with servants but he was too well brought up to discuss personal matters that concerned his family.

Arrian tapped lightly on the door and heard Warrick's voice bidding her to enter. She stared for a moment at the sight that met her eyes. Warrick and Louise Robertson sat at a small table spread with a bounty of food. She had not expected to find Warrick having an intimate dinner with that woman. She was so hurt that for a moment she could only stare at them.

"Arrian, what an unexpected surprise," Warrick said, coming to his feet.

She glanced at Louise Robertson, who was looking very attractive in a bright green low-cut gown that would have been more properly worn at a ball. The woman wore her brown hair loose, in a style suitable for a much younger woman, Arrian thought spitefully.

"Excuse me," Arrian said loftily. "I see you are otherwise occupied, Warrick. I'll talk to you another time."

He walked toward her, his face unreadable. "Louise and I were just going over plans for the second floor. We thought it would be pleasant—er, easier to discuss them over dinner."

"You owe me no explanation, Warrick. Go on with whatever you were doing."

She turned to leave, but he caught her arm. "You were just leaving, weren't you Louise?"

"Of course, Warrick. I believe we've finished for the day. Any other decisions can wait until tomorrow." She rushed across the room and stopped before Arrian. "I believe you are going to like the changes in your bedroom." Louise smiled. "I'm decorating it just the way I'd like it if it were my room." Her innuendoes were not lost on Arrian, but went unnoticed by Warrick.

Arrian stared at the brazen woman until she left.

"You had no reason to be rude to Louise, Arrian. She is always kind when inquiring into your health and has worked tirelessly on your behalf."

Arrian could not prevent the rush of jealousy that took possession of her. Was Warrick a fool that he didn't see Louise Robertson was devoted to him? Of course he knew, and probably encouraged her. It was very apparent that Louise was assuming the role of mistress of the house, and had already increased her authority.

"I suppose you dine with her every night?" Arrian despised herself for sounding shrewish.

"No, Arrian, this is the first time I have dined alone with Louise. I arrived home late and was told that you had already dined. Louise was still working in the salon and since she hadn't—"

"Please spare me your excuses. I'm not interested in what you do with that woman. You are free to dine with her, or do whatever you please with her."

"Arrian, I know what this looks like, but you're mistaken. I had not eaten since morning and she wanted me to see the plans for the second floor. I thought that combining the two would save time."

Arrian shrugged and moved over to the table to toy with a silver dessert spoon. "Warrick, I've come because I need to talk to you."

He pressed his hand into her back and guided her to a chair where he seated her. "You are well?"

"I'm completely recovered."

"Arrian, about that night you lost the child—"

"I don't want to think about that night. It's over and I only wish to put it behind me."

He sat in a chair and stared at her. "I need to ask you something that I have not had the courage to ask until now. You don't have to answer if you don't want to. Was the child a son or daughter?"

"It was to early to tell."

He seemed to shrink visibly. "Since the moment we met I've always done the wrong thing with you. That night was no exception."

"What happened was not your fault."

"You are being kind."

"Then I hope you will be equally kind, Warrick, for I have come to ask something of you—not that I need your permission, but I would like leave without incident."

He leaned back and stared at the ceiling. "I have been

wondering how long it would take for you to get around to that."

"I only delayed my decision until I felt well enough to make the long journey."

"I don't suppose there's anything I can say to make you change your mind?"

"I don't think so, Warrick."

"You do blame me for the loss of our child."

She stood and walked to the window. "It wasn't the loss of the baby, Warrick, that made me decide to leave. It was discovering how you felt about me and our child. You will always remember what I am, Warrick, and not who I am."

"I know I was cruel to you that night, although I don't remember everything I said."

"It's of no importance."

He had come up behind her and turned her to face him. "It's important to me."

She moved away from him. "I thought Michael and I would leave on Monday next."

His silver eyes dulled. "You don't have to leave."

She turned to him. "A true gentleman could have said no less. We both know our marriage was for the wrong reasons. And because of that, innocent people were hurt, Warrick."

"Arrian, I never meant to hurt you. I'd rather die."

She turned to the door. "I'll be gone before you start on the second floor. Have Louise Robertson decorate the bedroom in colors that please her. She is better suited to you than I ever was, since she's neither a MacIvors nor English."

Arrian left before Warrick could reply and climbed the stairs to her room. When she entered, she was shocked to find Louise Robertson going through her jewelry chest. Her anger exploded when she saw the Drummond wedding ring on her finger.

"Take that off at once!" Arrian demanded.

Louise slowly slid the ring off and dropped it on the dressing table. "No matter. I'll have it one day." Louise moved around Arrian, eyeing her up and down. "I was here long before you arrived, m'lady, and I'll be here long after you're gone. I'm told his lordship sleeps alone. When he belongs to me, he'll never be alone in bed."

Arrian picked up the ring and clasped it so tightly in her hand that the diamond cut into her palm. "Get out of my room, it's not yours yet."

Louise laughed. "I'll leave for now. But I'll be back."

Arrian raised her head and said in her most imperious manner, "Do not come in this room as long as I reside here. I care not what you do after I'm gone."

Arrian watched Louise pick up a fan her father had brought her from the Orient. Grabbing the fan from her, she pointed to the open door. "As I said—leave."

Louise's taunting laughter followed her out of the room. Arrian glanced down at the ring, her eyes blazing with fury. That woman would never wear the ring—Arrian would take it with her!

That night Arrian did not sleep well. She wondered if Warrick was with Louise and hated herself for caring.

She awoke during the night with the awareness that someone was in her room. She did not need to open her eyes to know that Warrick stood watching her. After a moment, she heard him leave quietly.

Michael found Warrick in the study, staring out the window. When he came up beside him, Michael discovered that Warrick was watching Arrian walking toward the beach.

"Are you just going to do nothing while she goes out of your life?"

Warrick looked down at Michael. "I have no right to expect her to stay with me."

"You're her husband—I'd say that gives you a right."

"I'm her husband by trickery."

"You fathered a child by her."

"I don't care to think about the child I lost."

"Warrick, why in hell did you bring Louise Robertson here?"

"I know now that it was wrong. Her husband was a friend of mine and she was in need of money. I thought to help her by allowing her to work at Ironworth. I don't think Arrian and Louise have much in common."

"Oh, I think they have something in common."

"Haddy told me how Louise goaded Arrian. Again, I was at fault." There was sadness in Warrick's eyes. "Everything I do regarding your sister seems wrong. I don't know how to please her."

"Arrian is not as complicated as you might think. She likes the same things other young ladies like—to be courted, to be told she's beautiful, to have a man tell her he loves her. You do love her, don't you?"

Warrick stared at the young lad he had come to respect. It was hard for him to speak, but he had to know. "When do you leave?"

"Early tomorrow morning."

"I will want to talk to Arrian before you go."

Michael shook his head. "I'll never be able to understand you where my sister is concerned. Why don't you go to her now?"

Warrick walked quickly toward the beach. After tomorrow he would again find life the meaningless void it had been before she had entered his domain.

Arrian was seated atop a huge rock that jutted out into the sea. Her legs were drawn up, and her head rested on her knees. She was unaware that she was being observed.

"Do you want to come down, or shall I join you?" Warrick yelled to be heard above the roar of the sea.

"I'll come down," she said, wondering if he'd just happened by or if he'd sought her company.

He offered Arrian his hand and helped her down to the beach. "You like the sea, don't you, Arrian?"

"It's timeless and everlasting, never changing unless a storm comes along. But when the storm passes, it again goes back to being calm and peaceful. The sea is beautiful here at Ironworth."

A lock of golden hair blew across her face, and he resisted the urge to touch it. "You are like the calming sea, Arrian. I have never known a woman like you, and I don't know how to deal with you."

She was caught by the magic of his silver eyes. "You are like a summer gale. You stormed through my life leaving only destruction."

He flinched as if she had struck him. "Will you be glad to be quit of us, Arrian?"

"I love it here, Warrick. And I'll miss Haddy, Mactavish, and Barra. I have come to respect them. I believe they also have a liking for me."

His voice was deep. "There are many here who will miss you."

"I'm sure Louise Robertson isn't one of them."

He shifted uncomfortably under her accusing gaze. "I should never have brought her to Ironworth, I know that now. You might like to know she's gone and won't be returning."

Arrian shrugged. "That's of no concern to me now."

He gripped her shoulders. "Damn it, Arrian, she meant nothing to me. I don't even think of her as a woman."

Their eyes locked. Her expression was cold, his was one of confusion. "I don't want to talk about her."

"Perhaps not, but I wanted you to know." He turned to look up the incline. "Would you like to see the waterfall before you leave?" he said, wanting to prolong their last moments together.

"Yes, I would."

Warrick took her hand and led her up a footpath over moss-covered rocks and then down to the rushing Fee River. Arrian stared up at the waterfall that tumbled across craggy rocks.

"The source of the water comes from the mountains, Arrian. Even if it hasn't rained, the river still runs full to its banks because of the rain in those mountains."

She felt the soft spray on her face and closed her eyes. "It's not unlike the feeling one gets at sea."

"It is said that one of my ancestors, who had been in a battle defending Queen Mary against those who would have seen her dethroned, was blinded from a blow on his head. Lost in the mountains in a snowstorm, he followed the river here to the waterfall and was rescued by Drummond clan members."

"Poor luckless queen, to become the victim of treachery from her own people."

Warrick glanced down at her, noting the beads of water that had peppered her face. "Aye, betrayed by her countrymen and beheaded by your queen."

"I had heard that the MacIvors also supported Queen Mary."

Warrick frowned. "Must we talk of your clansmen today?"

"No. I suppose not."

He watched a shimmering rainbow that arched behind her head. His gaze dropped to her lips, which were wet with mist from the waterfall. Without being aware of it, he gravitated toward her and felt a shock when his lips touched hers.

Blissfully Arrian melted into him, her arms twining around his shoulders, her mouth eager for his kiss. How she had ached for his touch. If only—

Suddenly he tore his lips away from hers and stepped back. "Come," he said, taking her hand. "It's time to leave. It's getting late."

"Will you think of me, Warrick? Or when I'm gone, will it be as if I never existed?"

"I can worship the sun, even knowing I can never touch or possess it. I was able to hold you in my hand for a moment, but I always knew you could never belong to me. Will I forget you? I think not in one lifetime."

She wanted to reach out to him, but he had withdrawn from her into that secret place where he always retreated. Already he walked ahead of her. Arrian wanted to call after him, to beg him to hold her one more time.

"Warrick."

He paused. "Yes?"

"I . . . wish you well. I will often think of you standing here with the wind in your hair." There was a catch in her throat and she struggled to continue. "Or riding Titus over the moors."

"Shall I think of you at a reception for the king, dancing with dozens of admiring gentlemen?"

"No. I'm going home to Ravenworth and there I'll stay until I heal in mind and spirit."

He took her hand and rested it against his chest. "Arrian, if only I could tell you of the regrets that are in my heart."

"I know of some of them. You told me the night I lost the baby."

He blinked and glanced up at a sea bird that was gliding on a gust of wind. "I want more than anything for you to be happy."

"I wish the same for you."

He stood back and looked at her for a long moment. "Allow me to hold you in my arms this last time?"

She moved forward hesitantly, and he slid his arms around her. They had shared so much, and yet their hearts had never joined. They had begot and lost a baby, and yet they had never exchanged one word of love.

Arrian rested her cheek against his rough coat, wishing she could stay with him forever. But they were star-crossed lovers, and it had not been meant for them to be together.

Warrick's arms tightened around her, and he buried his face against her velvet hair.

"When I am feeling particularly lonely, I'll remember this moment, Arrian. It's the first time you came to me willingly, even if it is only to tell me good-bye."

Chapter 31

t was a cloudy day as the coach pulled away from Ironworth. Arrian sat beside her brother, refusing to look out the window and resisting the urge to glance back at the castle. She was going home to England, and she told herself she was glad to quit Scotland. Elspeth was seated across from them, already nodding off to sleep.

Michael watched Arrian's face, knowing she would never be the same carefree girl who'd come to Scotland with such hopes for the future. He wanted to talk to her of frivolous matters and hear her laugh again.

"Is there anything you want to talk about, Arrian?" he asked at last.

She laid her head on his shoulder, and he held her tightly. "I feel so empty inside, Michael. My arms ache to hold the baby I lost. My heart aches to hold a love that can never be mine."

"I believe we gather strength from the pain, just as we learn patience from love."

She smiled up at him. "You always make the wisest

observations. I don't believe I could have endured these last weeks without your strength."

"I only wish there was something I could do to help you, Arrian. I want my sister back."

She buried her face in his shirtfront and cried the tears that she had been holding in for so long. Michael held her without saying a word until there were no more tears. There was no need for words between them.

It was high August, and Warrick rode Titus across the sweeping valley. The wild heather was in harmony with the vivid blue sky, and trout were jumping in the stream he crossed.

Hearing hoofbeats, he turned to see Mactavish riding in his direction. The older man drew even with Warrick, and they rode silently together.

"There's dark clouds out to sea," Mactavish said at last.

"Yes. I suppose we are in for a blow."

"It'll be a gale."

"Yes, I should think so."

Mactavish moved forward in his saddle. "When do you come home? Don't you think you have stayed away long enough? Haddy's beginning to worry about you."

"I've grown accustomed to the hunting lodge. It suits my mood."

"You stopped the repairs on Ironworth."

"Yes. I saw no reason to continue."

"Damn it, Warrick, I feel as if I'm talking to myself. When are you going to realize that life is to be lived? You no longer take an interest in anything."

"To say I do nothing is incorrect, Mactavish. I hunt, I fish, I help the villagers with menial tasks, I've even gone out twice in their fishing boats."

"It's time you became chief again. I can't hold the clan together, Warrick. We need you."

* * *

Ian MacIvors crouched low to the ground, his eyes riveted on the man he hated most in the world. He had been stalking Warrick for days, staying out of sight and waiting for the right moment to end the feud forever.

Ian smiled maliciously. Warrick Glencarin was the last of his line. Without issue from him, the title would end, and the land would revert to the Crown.

With hatred burning in Ian's brain, he braced his rifle against his shoulder, took careful aim, and fired.

Mactavish heard the shot, and turned to Warrick in time to see him fall forward and slide from his horse.

Mactavish leapt from his mount and bent down beside Warrick, who was lying face down. He turned him over to see blood flowing from a head wound. The handkerchief he pressed against the wound was soon soaked.

"Warrick, lad, speak to me!"

There was no reply, only the distant call of a circling hawk.

Hearing a rider approach, Mactavish leapt quickly to his feet, his senses alert. Even from a distance he recognized the sandy-colored hair of Ian MacIvors gleaming in the sun. Mactavish made a dash for his gun when another shot rang out, and he tumbled to the ground, grabbing his chest.

Unmindful of the pain, he inched himself forward to lie beside his fallen chief. His last conscious sight was of Ian dismounting and coming toward them.

Ian stood with his rifle poised inches from Warrick's head. He landed a heavy kick to Warrick's ribs. There was so much blood, Lord Warrick must be either dead or mortally wounded.

"At last, I have you, you bastard. Another bullet in your brain will put an end to your miserable life."

"Don't do it, Ian," a warning voice called out.

Surprise registered on Ian's face when he swung around

to find that Jamie had ridden up behind him. "Did you come to witness our last triumph, little brother?"

"Is he dead?" Jamie asked.

"If he isn't, he soon will be."

"Put the rifle down, Ian. I will not have you commit murder."

Ian's face reddened, and his eyes narrowed. "Would you defend this Drummond dog against your own brother?"

"I don't know who you are, Ian, but you aren't the brother I once admired." Jamie raised his own rifle and aimed it at Ian's heart. "I don't want to hurt you, but I won't allow you to kill him."

Ian sneered. "You aren't a man, Jamie. That woman you married has made you her lap dog. You won't shoot me—you don't have the nerve."

"Toss your gun down, and back away from Lord Warrick. If you don't, I'll shoot you, Ian—I swear I will."

By now several villagers had heard the commotion and had come to investigate. They stood silently watching the exchange between the two brothers. Their worried glances were for their fallen chief. Several men had gone to the village for weapons. Until they returned they could do no more than watch from a distance.

"How did you find me?" Ian asked, stalling for time.

"I realized what you were going to do when you left Davinsham. I've been following you, hoping you'd change your mind."

Ian inched his gun closer to Warrick's head. "You wouldn't choose our enemy's life over mine. I know you wouldn't Jamie."

Ian cocked the hammer of his rifle, and a shot rang out.

Jamie ran forward, throwing his gun aside. He fell to the ground and gathered Ian in his arms. "Damn you for making me do that. I told you I'd not let you kill Lord Warrick."

Ian's eyes were clouding over. He licked his lips and stared at the darkening sky. "Is the Drummond chief dead, Jamie? Who would have thought the chief of the MacIvors and the chief of the Drummonds would both die on the same day?" Ian said.

"I'm sorry," Jamie cried, staring at his brother's blood spilling onto the ground. He was vaguely aware that the villagers had come forward and were lifting Lord Warrick's limp body.

Mactavish staggered to his feet and stood over Jamie. "Your brother'll not live."

"I know."

Ian blinked his eyes. "Why is it so dark, Jamie? Is it going to storm?"

Jamie watched with heavy sadness as Ian's eyes widened and then went blank. His head fell sideways, and he was dead.

Jamie struggled to lift his brother and was surprised when Mactavish helped him. After Ian was secured to his horse, Jamie turned to the big man. "I had to do it."

"I know, lad—you did right. We'll all say you had no choice."

With heaviness in his heart, Jamie mounted his horse and Mactavish handed him the reins of Ian's horse.

"You are also wounded, Mactavish."

"'Tis no more than a shoulder wound. Ride for home. If Lord Warrick dies, even I couldn't answer for your life if you remain on Drummond land."

Jamie nodded and rode away without a backward glance.

After Barra cleaned the blood from Warrick's face she found to her relief that his wound wasn't serious. The bullet had only grazed his scalp, knocking him unconscious. She applied a bandage and smiled when he groaned and opened his eyes.

"What happened?" he asked, shaking his head and trying to stand, but dizziness overcame him and he lay back.

"You've had no more than a grazing, m'lord. Mactavish's shoulder is more serious than your wound."

Barra moved to the giant Scot. "The bullet's still in you and I'll have ta take it out."

"I demand to know what happened. Who did this?" Warrick staggered to his feet. "Damn it, I want some answers."

Haddy pushed him back to the bed. "You'll get your answers after we've tended to Mactavish, and no sooner."

A month had passed since the day Ian died. Warrick and Mactavish had both recovered, though Mactavish still wore his arm in a sling. As they strolled around the grounds, a horseman approached.

Mactavish looked at Warrick in surprise. "Isn't that Lord Jamie?"

Warrick's eyes narrowed. "I believe it is. What can he want?"

Jamie brought his horse alongside the Drummond chief. "Greetings, Lord Warrick."

Even though this man had saved his life, Warrick still didn't trust him. "I can't think why you would come on my land uninvited."

"If you'll hear me out," Lord Jamie said, "I believe you'll approve of my reason for being here today."

"You had better talk quickly. I have no wish to spend my day with a MacIvors."

"As you know, my brother, Ian, is dead."

Mactavish and Warrick exchanged glances. "Of course we know," Warrick said impatiently. "His blood was spilled on Drummond land."

Jamie knew Lord Warrick was trying to provoke him, but he would not be deterred from his mission. "Ian was wrong to try to kill you. As for myself, I'll have to live the rest of life with the guilt of knowing I killed my own brother to save you."

"That would make you chief," Warrick said.

"I am that, though I would have wished it otherwise."

"I won't pretend to grieve over your brother's death. But we do owe you for our lives, and for that I thank you," Warrick said.

"Why have you come, m'lord?" Mactavish asked.

Warrick could see the sadness in Jamie's eyes. "I have come to right an old wrong," the young chief said.

Warrick looked skeptical. "Now, how could you do that?"

Jamie dismounted and stood beside Warrick. "I would like to end this feud between our families. It's gone on too long."

Warrick was puzzled. "I have no hatred for you, Jamie MacIvors."

"I am here today to show my good intentions." Jamie reached into his breast pocket and withdrew a document, which he handed to Warrick. "I signed the lands of Kilmouris back to you. Also, I'm returning the thousand pounds that came to my family as Lady Gwendolyn's dowry."

Warrick was speechless as he stared at the yellowed document. It was the Kilmouris deed. Still suspicious, he looked at Jamie. "Why would you do this?"

"I would like to tell you it was my own conscience that urged me to make restitution. But in truth, it was the letters of pleading I received from my cousin, Arrian, that influenced my actions. She can be very persuasive."

Warrick's mind was whirling. Here before him stood the enemy, and yet he was reaching out his hand in friendship. It was no trick, for the deed was genuine.

Mactavish shook his head. "All the years of feuding and killing, and it's all over because of Lady Arrian's persistence."

"Arrian has a great influence on my wife, and Helena has a great influence on me," Jamie said. "I wanted to please them both, so here I am. You might also like to know that Arrian has returned the MacIvors betrothal ring, and Helena happily wears it."

Warrick stood stiffly, still unconvinced. "I assume you are happy with Lady Helena?"

"She's the only thing I'll not return to you, Warrick. Not that you'd want my Helena. You have the love of Arrian, and that should be enough for any man."

"You are mistaken, Lord Jamie. Your cousin Arrian does not love me."

"I have it straight from my wife that Arrian has been miserable since returning to London. I'm also told she wears your ring and refuses to remove it, even when she retires at night. Arrian begs for news of you. I am instructed by Helena to beseech you to go to Arrian. She is most unhappy."

Warrick searched Jamie's earnest blue eyes. "I thought Arrian would have had our marriage set aside by now."

Jamie pushed his foot into the stirrup and slung his leg over the saddle. "Even though her father has urged her to do so, Arrian has refused to have the marriage annulled. Make what you will out of that." He touched his cap. "I wish you both a good day."

Warrick stood for a long time as if he had turned to stone. Then he glanced at Mactavish, who was grinning widely.

"What are you going to do?" Mactavish asked.

Dark clouds had blocked out the sun, and the wind hit with a sudden force, so that Warrick had to yell to be heard.

"I'm going to England to bring my wife home where she belongs. God help anyone who gets in my way!"

Chapter 32

A *unt Mary's autumn ball* had drawn only the most aristocratic of London society.

Arrian was seated with her aunt as they watched dancing couples whirl merrily around the polished floor. She had come to London to be with Aunt Mary, hoping to cheer the dear lady and to forget her own unhappiness for a while.

"It's hard to think of frivolity when so many of my contemporaries are dying," Lady Mary said. "That's what happens when one reaches my age."

Arrian patted her aunt's hand. "It's not like you to be morose. I have always looked to you as my inspiration."

Lady Mary shook her head. "Here I am going on about my troubles, and you are the one who needs cheering."

"I am happy enough."

"How would you like to go to Paris?"

Arrian smiled. "Aunt Mary, you know you hate sailing, and unless you can sprout wings and fly, I know of no other way to get there."

"Perhaps I can walk on water."

"I would not be in the least surprised, but alas, you would have to carry me."

"If you don't want to go to Paris, how about Venice?"

"You would still have to sail."

"I'd do it for you, dear."

"No, Aunt Mary. When the season is over, I'll be returning to Ravenworth. Perhaps you would like to spend the winter with us in the country."

"Yes. Perhaps I shall. It's so bleak here in winter."

A young gentleman stopped before Arrian and bowed politely. "Would you do me the honor of being my partner for the next dance?"

Arrian wanted to say no, but she nodded, knowing that Aunt Mary would expect it of her. As she was whirled around the dance floor, her mind was on a pair of silver eyes that could rip a woman's heart apart. Warrick was never far from her thoughts. He was, after all, her husband.

The dance ended, and Arrian's partner returned her to Aunt Mary, who was surrounded by several young ladies all buzzing excitedly. "Tell me who is he, Lady Mary? If you know him I insist on being introduced to him at once."

Arrian was curious. "To whom are they referring?"

"That handsome man who stands near the door." One of the girls pointed with her fan. "I'll just die if I don't get to meet him. I've never seen him before."

Arrian still couldn't see the object of their curiosity because the dancers were blocking her view.

Lady Mary smiled, her eyes dancing with mischief. "That, my dear young ladies, is a man who has come to see only one woman. If I introduced him to you, he wouldn't even see you."

One girl was insistent. "But who is he, and who has he come to see?"

"He is Lord Warrick Glencarin, chief of Clan Drummond, and he has come to see only Arrian."

Arrian's face paled as she turned around to see the man who now stood behind her. Her heart stopped beating as she stared into those wonderful silver eyes.

He was dressed in a formal black suit with a white ruffled shirt and diamond studs.

Warrick smiled down at Arrian, and she wanted to run into his arms. She had not realized until this moment what it felt like to be truly alive. The music was sweeter, the laughter merrier.

Warrick held his arm out to her. "Will you dance with me, my lady wife?"

She dipped into a curtsy and placed her hand on his arm. "It would be my pleasure, my lord."

The other young ladies gaped at Arrian as Warrick guided her into a smooth dance step, his eyes never leaving her face.

"I didn't know Arrian was married," one of Lady Mary's companions said. "None of us did," another girl remarked.

"Indeed, she is married." Lady Mary laughed, her gloom all but disappearing. "Don't you think they make a wonderful couple?"

Arrian stared into eyes that looked right into her soul. "You are a long way from home, my lord."

His voice was deep. "Indeed, I am."

"And you dislike England so much. I'm surprised to find you on our soil."

There was laughter in his eyes and a lightness of manner that she had not seen before. "I have come to appreciate many things that are English."

"Is it permitted to ask why you are here?"

"It's very simple, Arrian. You see I've come for something that belongs to me."

She was breathless as she asked the next question. "And what would that be, my lord?"

"You, my lady wife. I have come to take you home."

Tears swam in her eyes, dimming her vision. How wonderful

it felt to be enclosed in his arms. "Are you certain this time, Warrick?"

"More than anything in my life. I am only half alive without you. Come home with me, Arrian. You don't have to love me. You don't even have to share the same bedroom with me if it's not your desire. Just be near so I can see you every day and talk to you."

The music stopped, and Arrian realized that she and Warrick were standing in the middle of the floor and everyone was staring at them.

Lady Mary appeared at their side and kissed Warrick's cheek. "It's about time you came." Then she raised her hand, calling for attention. "Ladies and gentlemen, may I introduce my nephew by marriage, Lord Warrick Glencarin of Scotland."

Soon Arrian and Warrick were surrounded by a curious crowd who plied them with questions. Eventually they were swept away from each other by well wishers.

Again Lady Mary interceded. She rescued Warrick from one of the young ladies who had wanted to meet him earlier. Pulling him off the dance floor, she quickly whispered, "Go upstairs and turn right. Her bedroom is the third door. Wait there and I'll send her to you."

Warrick beamed at her. "Have I told you that you are wonderful?"

She laughed softly. "Go on, you devil. It's not an old woman you need to charm. Save your compliments for your wife."

Arrian hurried up the stairs and entered her bedroom. She was immediately caught in Warrick's arms, and he smothered her with hot kisses.

"I need to touch you, to know you are real," he breathed against her ear. "I can live again—feel again."

She held his face between her hands, hardly able to speak. "I still can't believe you are here."

"Be warned, Arrian, I won't leave without you."

"There will be no need for that, my lord."

He searched her eyes. "Can it be that you are glad to see me?" He lifted her hand, and when he saw his ring circling her finger his heart swelled with pride.

"Indeed," she said, pressing her face against his. "But I never thought I'd see you again."

"You should have known I would come for you one day. Can you ever forget about the pain I put you through?"

"It's all but forgotten," she said, surrendering to his burning lips.

Arrian was surprised when Warrick broke off the kiss and moved away from her. "Before I lose my head over you, I want there to be a clear understanding between us."

She folded her hands demurely in front of her and smiled. "If that is your wish."

He moved back a few paces, as if he didn't trust himself not to touch her. He tried to appear calm, but Arrian saw his knuckles were white from clasping his hands together so tightly.

"There is no reason you should ever trust me, Arrian. I'm not proud of what I did to you." He took a deep breath. "I didn't love you then, but I desired you more than any woman I had ever known. The fact that I wanted you fueled my anger."

"And now, my lord?"

"I . . . love you, Arrian. I have never said this to another person in my life."

She moved to him and gently touched his face. "Will you say that to me often?"

"Every day for the rest of our lives." He pressed her hands in a warm grip. "I cannot say the hour or the day I came to love you, because I would not even admit to myself how I felt about you. I was in my own secret hell, loving you and thinking you loved Ian. I now know that was not the case."

"Are you sure you want me, Warrick?"

He spoke in a painful whisper. "With all my heart, Arrian."

Happiness rushed through her like a gathering tide. "And you have put pride aside and come to me with humility. Knowing what a proud man you are, I can only guess how difficult that was for you."

He raised her hand to his lips. "I would have borne anything just to look upon your face again—to touch you—to ask you to forgive me."

Her eyes shimmered with joy. "I loved you that day in the lodge," she said. "I gave myself to you with no regrets."

Warrick studied her hands before he looked into her eyes. "I had never met anyone like you. The more I was with you the more I felt my control slipping. One look into those blue eyes made me question everything, because I could see myself as you saw me. You will have to understand, Arrian, that I had lived with hatred for so long I had trouble setting it aside."

"I also saw so much good in you, Warrick. You were unselfish in your devotion to your clansmen. Mother believes you allowed us to escape that day she and I left Ironworth. Did you?"

He closed his eyes. "Aye, I allowed you to leave. It was the hardest deed I have ever done, to watch you leave, knowing I was losing the best part of myself."

"Oh, Warrick, I have been miserable without you. I would never have left you if you had told me that you loved me. I thought you loathed me because of who I am."

"Dearest Arrian, I could never hate you. Your sweetness touched a part of me that I thought was dead. You made me feel alive. You made me think of the future instead of looking back at the past. For better or worse you have made me a changed man. You know Ian is dead?"

"Yes. I'm sorry for him. I remember a time when he was gallant and I'll try to remember that about him."

"You loved him?"

"What I felt for Ian was a young girl's fantasy. I discovered true love only from you, Warrick."

He stared at her as if he could not believe her words. "You have no reason to love me. But I shall cherish you, dear Arrian. I hope never to hurt you again and will strive to be worthy of your love."

"The blood feud is ended?"

"I can promise you it died with Ian MacIvors. We'll join the best of both bloodlines, and hope that our children will never know hatred."

She touched his hair so tenderly. "Oh, Warrick, I would like that."

He laughed and pulled her against him. "With you and me ends the blood hate. Do you agree?"

"It was never in me to hate you, Warrick. Perhaps because I was far removed from Scotland and was not caught in this ugliness that you had lived with all your life."

"I want to put that behind me. With your help I believe I can."

He stared at her for a moment as if he wanted desperately to say something and didn't know how. At last it came out in a rush. "I haven't done anything in my life to deserve you. But I love you with each breath I take. I need you to be with me to fill the emptiness in my life." He softly touched her lips. "Let me hear again that you love me."

"I love you, Warrick Glencarin. I always will."

He hugged her tightly. "I will need you to tell me that often."

She glanced up at him. "What made you come after me?" she asked woman-like.

"I got an inkling that you might have affection for me when you convinced Jamie to return my sister's dowry and the lands of Kilmouris." He raised her small hand and kissed the ring on her finger. "But what really convinced me was when Lord Jamie told me that you wore this ring for all the world to see."

He pressed her hand to his rough cheek. "With you beside me, there's nothing I can't do. I want sons and daughters. I want you in my bed, where I only have to reach out for you." His eyes softened. "I'll change into whatever you want me to be."

She pressed her cheek to his, and her arms slid around his waist. "Don't change too much. I like my wild, arrogant Scot, who commands the world to bow before him."

He shook with laughter. "Except you, Arrian. I could not command you."

"That which you could not command, Warrick, you won with honeyed words. You have the gift to turn a woman's head, you know." Her blue eyes danced. "But be warned, you will have only one woman in your life and it is to be me."

"Pray God that I can make you happy."

"I thank God for allowing you to love me, Warrick."

In the distance they could hear music from Lady Mary's gala. But the sound was soon drowned out by the beating of the lovers' hearts.

She pressed against him, her heart overflowing with love. "I have needed you so desperately, Warrick."

"Arrian, Arrian, never leave me again. I could not live without you."

Arrian seemed to float back onto the bed as Warrick came down beside her. "You have so much, Arrian, what can I give that you don't already have?"

She laughed. "I would like a silver-eyed son. And that, Warrick, only you can give me."

"It would be my greatest pleasure, my lady." His laughter was deep. "I find myself wanting to start now."

Locked in each other's arms, Warrick was only aware of the pleasures that awaited him when he took his wife to bed.

Arrian's thoughts were of the future when she and her dark husband would build a new world together—a world where Drummond blood would freely mingle with MacIvors blood to create a new generation.

Lady Mary was happy, her gloominess suddenly gone. She glanced up the stairs, where the two lovers had sought refuge. A distinguished gentleman who had been a friend of her husband's bowed before her.

"You are still more beautiful than all of them," he said gallantly. "May I have the pleasure of this dance?"

She nodded. "Indeed you may. Tell me, Donald, have you heard how I almost lost my leg?"

He looked at her with concern. "No, I haven't."

"Well," she said, "it all began in Scotland. . . ."

AVAILABLE NOW

COMING UP ROSES by Catherine Anderson
From the bestselling author of the Comanche trilogy, comes a sensual historical romance. When Zach McGovern was injured in rescuing her daughter from an abandoned well, Kate Blakely nursed him back to health. Kate feared men, but Zach was different, and only buried secrets could prevent their future from coming up roses.

HOMEBODY by Louise Titchener
Bestselling author Louise Titchener pens a romantic thriller about a young woman who must battle the demons of her past, as well as the dangers she finds in her new apartment.

BAND OF GOLD by Zita Christian
The rush for gold in turn-of-the-century Alaska was nothing compared to the rush Aurelia Breighton felt when she met the man of her dreams. But then Aurelia discovered that it was not her he was after but her missing sister.

DANCING IN THE DARK by Susan P. Teklits
A tender and touching tale of two people who were thrown together by treachery and found unexpected love. A historical romance in the tradition of Constance O'Banyon.

CHANCE McCALL by Sharon Sala
Chance McCall knows that he has no right to love Jenny Tyler, the boss's daughter. With only his monthly paycheck and checkered past, he's no good for her, even though she thinks otherwise. But when an accident leaves Chance with no memory, he has no choice but to return to his past and find out why he dare not claim the woman he loves.

SWEET REVENGE by Jean Stribling
There was nothing better than sweet revenge when ex-Union captain Adam McCormick unexpectedly captured his enemy's stepdaughter, Letitia Ramsey. But when Adam found himself falling in love with her, he had to decide if revenge was worth the sacrifice of love.

HIGHLAND LOVE SONG by Constance O'Banyon
Available in trade paperback! From the bestselling author of *Forever My Love,* a sweeping and mesmerizing story continues the DeWinter legacy begun in *Song of the Nightingale.*

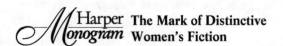 **Harper Monogram** **The Mark of Distinctive Women's Fiction**

COMING NEXT MONTH

ONE GOOD MAN by Terri Herrington

From the author of *Her Father's Daughter*, comes a dramatic story of a woman who sets out to seduce and ruin the one good man she's ever found. Jilted and desperate for money, Clea Sands lets herself be bought by a woman who wants grounds to sue her wealthy husband for adultery. But when Clea falls in love with him, she realizes she can't possibly destroy his life—not for any price.

PRETTY BIRDS OF PASSAGE by Roslynn Griffith

Beautiful Aurelia Kincaid returned to Chicago from Italy nursing a broken heart, and ready to embark on a new career. Soon danger stalked Aurelia at every turn when a vicious murderer, mesmerized by her striking looks, decided she was his next victim—and he would preserve her beauty forever. As the threads of horror tightened, Aurelia reached out for the safety of one man's arms. But had she unwittingly fallen into the murderer's trap? A historical romance filled with intrigue and murder.

FAN THE FLAME by Suzanne Elizabeth

The romantic adventures of a feisty heroine who met her match in a fearless lawman. When Marshal Max Barrett arrived at the Washington Territory ranch to escort Samantha James to her aunt's house in Utah, little did he know what he was getting himself into.

A BED OF SPICES by Barbara Samuel

Set in Europe in 1348, a moving story of star-crossed lovers determined to let nothing come between them. "With her unique and lyrical style, Barbara Samuel touches every emotion. The quiet brilliance of her story lingered in my mind long after the book was closed."—Susan Wiggs, author of *The Mist and the Magic*.

THE WEDDING by Elizabeth Bevarly

A delightful and humorous romance in the tradition of the movie *Father of the Bride*. Emma Hammelmann and Taylor Rowan are getting married. But before wedding bells ring, Emma must confront not only the inevitable clash of their families but her own second thoughts—especially when she discovers that Taylor's best man is in love with her.

SWEET AMITY'S FIRE by Lee Scofield

The wonderful, heartwarming story of a mail-order bride and the husband who didn't order her. "Lee Scofield makes a delightful debut with this winning tale . . . *Sweet Amity's Fire* is sweet indeed."—Mary Jo Putney, bestselling author of *Thunder and Roses*.

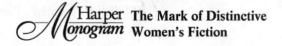 **Harper Monogram** The Mark of Distinctive Women's Fiction

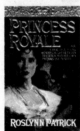

YESTERDAY'S SHADOWS
by Marianne Willman

Bettany Howard was a young orphan traveling west searching for the father who left her years ago. Wolf Star was a Cheyenne brave who longed to know who abandoned him—a white child with a jeweled talisman. Fate decreed they'd meet and try to seize the passion promised. 0-06-104044-4

MIDNIGHT ROSE by Patricia Hagan

From the rolling plantations of Richmond to the underground slave movement of Philadelphia, Erin Sterling and Ryan Youngblood would pursue their wild, breathless passion and finally surrender to the promise of a bold and unexpected love. 0-06-104023-1

WINTER TAPESTRY
by Kathy Lynn Emerson

Cordell vows to revenge the murder of her father. Roger Allington is honor bound to protect his friend's daughter but has no liking for her reckless ways. Yet his heart tells him he must pursue this beauty through a maze of plots to win her love and ignite their smoldering passion. 0-06-100220-8

THE NEW GROVE
SCHUBERT

THE NEW GROVE
DICTIONARY OF MUSIC AND MUSICIANS
Editor: Stanley Sadie

The Composer Biography Series

BACH FAMILY
HANDEL
HAYDN
MOZART
SCHUBERT

THE NEW GROVE

SCHUBERT

Maurice J. E. Brown

WORK-LIST
Eric Sams

W. W. NORTON & COMPANY

NEW YORK   LONDON

First published in
The New Grove Dictionary of Music and Musicians,
edited by Stanley Sadie, 1980

First American Edition 1983

Reprinted 1988

FPT ISBN 0-393-30087-0

Printed in Hong Kong

3 4 5 6 7 8 9 0

Contents

List of illustrations

Abbreviations

Preface

1.	Background and childhood	1
2.	Beginning of career	7
3.	Growing reputation	16
4.	Vienna friends and patrons, 1819-20	22
5.	Events of 1821-2	29
6.	Illness	37
7.	Schubert's circle of friends	42
8.	1825-6	46
9.	Period of 'Winterreise'	54
10.	The last year	61
11.	Posthumous publication	72
12.	Posthumous performance	75
13.	Music for the theatre	77
14.	Church and other choral music	82
15.	Songs	86
16.	Song cycles	93
17.	Mature instrumental music	98

Work-list   106

Bibliography   166

Index   181

List of illustrations

1. Autograph MS of part of 'Szene aus Goethes Faust'
   D126 (Bibliothèque Nationale, Paris)   9

2. Page from Schubert's diary of 10 June 1816 containing
   references to Mozart (Gesellschaft der Musikfreunde,
   Vienna)   14

3. Drawing of Schubert, Anselm Hüttenbrenner and
   Johann Jenger by Josef Teltscher (private collection)   27

4. Charade at Atzenbrugg: watercolour by Leopold
   Kupelwieser (Historisches Museum der Stadt Wien)   31

5. Autograph sketches for the proposed scherzo of
   Symphony no. 8 D759 ('Unfinished') (Gesellschaft der
   Musikfreunde, Vienna)   35

6. Watercolour portrait by Wilhelm August Rieder
   (Historisches Museum der Stadt Wien)   44

7. Schubert Abend bei Joseph von Spaun: sepia drawing by
   Moritz von Schwind (Historisches Museum der Stadt
   Wien)   52

8. Title-page of 'Gesänge aus Wilhelm Meister von Göthe'
   D877   56

9. Schubert's death mask (Curtis Institute of Music,
   Philadelphia)   70

10. Autograph MS of the end of 'Am Meer' and beginning
    of 'Der Doppelgänger' from 'Schwanengesang'
    (Pierpont Morgan Library Mary Flagler Cary Music
    Collection, New York)   91

11. Part of the autograph MS of String Quartet in G (D887)
    (Österreichische Nationalbibliothek, Vienna)   101

GENERAL ABBREVIATIONS

A	alto, contralto [voice]	org	organ
acc.	accompaniment	ov.	overture
add, addl	additional		
add, addn	addition	perf.	performance
arr.	arrangement	pr.	printed
aut.	autumn	pubd	published
		pubn	publication
B	bass [voice]		
b	bass [instrument]	qnt	quintet
bc	basso continuo	qt	quartet
bn	bassoon		
		R	photographic reprint
cl	clarinet	*r*	recto
conc.	concerto	rec	recorder
cont	continuo	recit	recitative
db	double bass	red.	reduction
		repr.	reprinted
edn.	edition	rev.	revision
f. ff.	folio(s)	S	soprano [voice]
facs.	facsimile	str	string(s)
fl	flute	sum.	summer
Fr.	French	sym.	symphony
frag.	fragment		
		T	tenor [voice]
gui	guitar	timp	timpani
		tpt	trumpet
hn	horn	tr	treble [instrument]
		trbn	trombone
inc.	incomplete	transcr.	transcription
inst	instrument		
		U.	University
kbd	keyboard		
		v, vv	voice(s)
lib	libretto	v., vv.	verse(s)
		v	verso
tmovt	movement	va	viola
		vc	cello
ob	oboe	vn	violin
obbl	obbligato		
orch	orchestra		
orchd	orchestrated		

BIBLIOGRAPHICAL ABBREVIATIONS

AcM	*Acta musicologica*
AMw	*Archiv für Musikwissenschaft*
BMw	*Beiträge zur Musikwissenschaft*
GfMKB	*Gesellschaft für Musikforschung Kongressbericht*
JAMS	*Journal of the American Musicological Society*
JMT	*Journal of Music Theory*
Mf	*Die Musikforschung*
ML	*Music and Letters*
MMR	*The Monthly Musical Record*
MQ	*The Musical Quarterly*
MR	*The Music Review*
MT	*The Musical Times*
NZM	*Neue Zeitschrift für Musik*
ÖMz	*Österreichische Musikzeitschrift*
PMA	*Proceedings of the Musical Association*
PRMA	*Proceedings of the Royal Musical Association*
RBM	*Revue belge de musicologie*
ReM	*La revue musicale*
RIM	*Rivista italiana di musicologia*
SH	*Slovenská hudba*
SM	*Studia musicologica Academiae scientiarum hungaricae*
SMw	*Studien zur Musikwissenschaft*
VMw	*Vierteljahrsschrift für Musikwissenschaft*
ZIMG	*Zeitschrift der Internationalen Musik-Gesellschaft*
ZMw	*Zeitschrift für Musikwissenschaft*

Preface

This volume is one of a series of short biographies derived from *The New Grove Dictionary of Music and Musicians* (London, 1980). In its original form, the text was written in the mid-1970s, and finalized at the end of that decade. For this reprint, the text has been re-read and modified by the original author (or in some cases his representative) and corrections and changes have been made. In particular, an effort has been made to bring the bibliography up to date and to incorporate the findings of recent research.

The fact that the texts of the books in this series originated as dictionary articles inevitably gives them a character somewhat different from that of books conceived as such. They are designed, first of all, to accommodate a very great deal of information in a manner that makes reference quick and easy. Their first concern is with fact rather than opinion, and this leads to a larger than usual proportion of the texts being devoted to biography than to critical discussion. The nature of a reference work gives it a particular obligation to convey received knowledge and to treat of composers' lives and works in an encyclopedic fashion, with proper acknowledgment of sources and due care to reflect different standpoints, rather than to embody imaginative or speculative writing about a composer's character or his music. It is hoped that the comprehensive work-lists and extended bibliographies, indicative of the origins of the books in a reference work, will be valuable to the reader who is eager for full and accurate reference information and who may not have ready access to *The New Grove Dictionary* or who may prefer to have it in this more compact form.

✳

As Maurice J. E. Brown had, unhappily, died before the article appeared in print, the revisions undertaken by the late Mr Brown's friend and colleague, Eric Sams, for this publication in book form draw on Mr Brown's other writings on Schubert, in particular his critical biography (published by Macmillan).

S.S.

We are grateful to the following for permission to reproduce illustrative material: Bibliothèque Nationale, Paris (fig.1); Gesellschaft der Musikfreunde, Vienna (figs.2, 5); Historisches Museum der Stadt Wien (figs.4, 6, 7, cover); Richard Macnutt, Tunbridge Wells (fig.8); Curtis Institute of Music, Philadelphia (fig.9); Pierpont Morgan Library (Mary Flagler Cary Music Collection), New York (fig.10); Österreichische Nationalbibliothek, Vienna (fig.11).

Cover: Watercolour portrait by Wilhelm August Rieder
(Historisches Museum der Stadt Wien)

1. Background and childhood

Vienna, in Schubert's day, consisted of an inner city bounded to the north-east by the Danube Canal and enclosed by a rampart; these enclosing walls were to give place to the wide boulevards of the modern Ringstrasse. The real life of the capital was passed in this small and crowded area. Franz Peter Schubert was born in the district of the Himmelpfortgrund, lying to the north-west of the city, on 31 January 1797.

Schubert's father, Franz Theodor Florian, was a schoolmaster. He was a man of probity, a devout Catholic, industrious in his profession and undeniably successful. His ancestors were Moravian peasant farmers: he was born in Neudorf, near Märisch-Schönberg in the Altstadt district of Moravia. He migrated to Vienna to become an assistant to his brother Karl, who had a school in the Leopoldstadt suburb, and in 1785, when he was 25, married Maria Elisabet Katherina Vietz, the composer's mother. We know little of her except that she was born in Zuckmantel, in Austrian Silesia, and before her marriage was in domestic service. Soon after his marriage, Franz Theodor was appointed master of a school in the Himmelpfortgrund district of Vienna and in June 1786 he moved into a house there called 'Zum roten Krebsen'. In the years that followed, no fewer than 12 children were born, of whom only four survived infancy: Ignaz (b 1785), Ferdinand (b 1794), Karl (b 1795) and Franz Peter. A daughter, Maria Theresa (b 1801), was the last of the family. The house was later renumbered and the street renamed: it is now 54 Nussdorferstrasse, and

since 1912 has been maintained by the city authorities
as a Schubert museum. In 1969 it was reopened, after
several years, fully restored to its original condition as
the boy Schubert knew it.

Soon after the birth of Maria Theresa, the family
moved into a new house in the nearby Säulenstrasse
(now no.3), which Franz Theodor had bought a few
months earlier. It was a smaller house, but more rooms
were at his disposal for the growing number of his
pupils. We learn from the memoirs of Schubert's father
and of his brother, Ferdinand, of his boyhood in the
Säulengasse schoolhouse. Franz Theodor's position
offered no social standing and was ill-paid. It is not
difficult to see that when he induced his sons, as they
grew old enough, to become his assistants in the school,
the primary aim was to save money. But the relations
between father and sons were clearly affectionate, as their
extant letters reveal; and Schubert as a boy experienced
neither harsh discipline in his training nor exploitation
of his obvious musical gifts. His father taught him the
violin, his eldest brother Ignaz the piano, and he quickly
outstripped them both. Ignaz wryly admitted that the
boy told him as much, and that he intended to make his
own way in the future. When he was nine or ten his
father placed him under the tuition of Michael Holzer,
organist at the parish church of Liechtental. Holzer is
sketched amusingly by Anton Holzapfel (a schoolfellow
of Schubert's) as somewhat bibulous but a sound
contrapuntist. In addition to lessons on the piano and
violin, young Franz was taught the organ, singing and
harmony, and under Holzer's care both his singing and
violin playing earned him a local reputation. Holzer said
of his pupil: 'If I wished to instruct him in anything
fresh, he already knew it. Consequently I gave him no

actual tuition but merely conversed with him and watched him with silent astonishment'.

Schubert's extraordinary aptitude for music enabled him to absorb with ease this elementary instruction, and no further progress was possible on that road. But another lay before him, and was to lead him to an environment which awakened his genius and showed him the full possibilities of self-realization. Towards the end of 1808 he was accepted as a choirboy in the imperial court chapel, and this meant admission as a scholar to the Kaiserlich-königliches Stadtkonvikt (Imperial and Royal City College). His examiners were the court musical directors, Antonio Salieri and Joseph Eybler, and the choirmaster, Phillip Körner; Schubert also distinguished himself in general subjects. The college was the principal Viennese boarding-school for commoners. The tutors were men in holy orders (although the college was not a religious foundation) and the boarders, about 130 in number, were either scholars at the grammar school or students at the university. Music was a compulsory subject for the choristers, but the principal, Dr Innocenz Lang, was an enthusiastic musical amateur and he encouraged all scholars to practise the art. A young university student, Josef von Spaun, had formed a students' orchestra, which was conducted by a visiting music master, Václav (Wenzel) Růžička, and by the time the young Schubert came to the college, its standard was excellent. Schubert's violin playing greatly impressed Spaun and in a short time he was promoted to be leader of the first violins. The friendship between Schubert and this student, some eight years his senior, was to be one of the happiest things in his life, and it lasted until his death. Schubert was composing in those years, and some of the music has survived (he confessed to Spaun that he was too poor to buy all the music manuscript paper he needed, and Spaun's first act of kindness was to provide it).

When Růžička was absent, Schubert conducted the orchestra – a rare opportunity for a boy such as he to master orchestral techniques. The orchestra played overtures and symphonies by Mozart and Haydn and the first two symphonies of Beethoven. Růžička, like Holzer before him, was nonplussed at the rapidity with which Schubert absorbed his instruction. To him the explanation was simple: 'He has learnt everything from God, that lad'. Eventually Salieri took over the supervision of Schubert's work, a supervision which extended beyond the college years. The association is interesting: it was, indeed, fitting that Salieri, friend of Haydn and rival of Mozart, in a small way a pupil of Gluck and in a smaller way tutor to Beethoven, should have supervised the work of Schubert, the last of these Viennese masters.

The supposition that Schubert neglected other studies to devote himself to music is contradicted by the extant records from Dr Lang of his progress in these years. All subjects are rated 'good' or 'very good' and the comment 'a special musical talent' occurs year after year. Schubert impressed everyone at the college by his musical gifts and an equally deep impression was made by his moral qualities; he was privileged to leave the building for his lessons with Salieri because of his general reliability. The compositions which date with certainty from these years are the Fantasie in G for piano duet (D1; 8 April–1 May 1810), the Six Minuets for wind instruments (D2*d*; 1811, recovered in 1969) and the song *Hagars Klage* (D5; 30 March 1811). It was this song, in Schubert's scena form, which is said to have aroused Salieri's interest. On 8 July 1811, Spaun took Schubert to his first opera, Weigl's *Die Schweizerfamilie*, at the Kärntnertor-Theater (which was to figure in Schubert's own operatic ventures). His first settings of Schiller date from this time, *Des Mädchens Klage* (D6) and *Leichenfantasie* (D7).

In the following year, on 28 May 1812, Schubert's mother died. That he and his father had quarrelled and were reconciled at her graveside is purely fictitious; so is the assertion that he composed the wind nonet *Eine kleine Trauermusik* (D79) to her memory. The eight undated and incomplete numbers of his first operatic composition, *Der Spiegelritter* (D11), to a text by August von Kotzebue, were completed in 1812. In the summer that year his voice was breaking; after the performance of a mass by Peter von Winter, he scribbled on his part, 'Schubert, Franz, crowed for the last time, 26 July 1812', though he remained a pupil at the college for another year or so. There were two terms in the college year, the main holiday occurring in early autumn. It was during Schubert's holidays that a family string quartet was formed, with the composer playing the viola, his brothers Ignaz and Ferdinand the violins, and his father the cello. For this family quartet the early string quartets of 1811–14 were composed.

The compositions of 1813 are numerous and their variety indicates the wealth of his musical experience. Salieri's tutelage is apparent in the many vocal canons, which are primarily contrapuntal exercises, and in the varied settings of verses by Metastasio. Songs of the year include settings of Schiller, Hölty and Matthisson, and a translation by Herder of Pope's *Vital Spark of Heavenly Flame* (*Verklärung* D59). There are German Dances (*Deutsche*) for strings (D90) and six string quartets. The finest of these, in E♭ (D87), with a finale of true

Schubertian quality, was published in 1840 as op.125 no.1.

On 25 April 1813, Schubert's father remarried. His wife, Anna Kleyenböck, was a kindly woman who in later years helped Schubert with loans from her house-keeping money. For his father's name day, 4 October, Schubert wrote the words and music of a trio (D80). The finest of these early works was finished on 28 October, the First Symphony, in D (D82). It is the consummation of those years of absorption in music at the college and of his vital contact with its orchestra; it was his justification for the future. Two days after its completion he began work on a three-act opera *Des Teufels Lustschloss* (D84), to a libretto by Kotzebue. He is said to have stayed away from his lessons until the opera was finished in the following year, and then to have presented the fully scored work to his astonished master. Salieri's criticisms were heeded, for a revised, second version of the opera is dated five months after the completion of the first.

2. Beginning of career

At the end of 1813, probably late in October, Schubert left the Kaiserlich-königliches Stadtkonvikt; unable to withstand family persuasion, he entered a training-school for elementary teachers in the Annagasse, near St Stephen's Cathedral. By autumn 1814 he was teaching in his father's school. It is not true that he adopted the profession of schoolmaster to evade military conscription: assistants, in any case, were not exempt. He was rejected by the military authorities because he was shorter than the minimum height of five feet. His sight was defective, too; by then he was wearing the spectacles familiar from his portraits.

Although he continued to take lessons with Salieri until the end of 1816, his musical tuition was finished. In those years at the college he was able to draw in abundance on the rich resources of orchestral practice and church choral singing, of piano playing and song and chamber music with his fellows, of string quartet playing in his own home, and of frequent visits to some of the finest opera in Europe. These powerful stimuli were about to produce a staggering result. He was on the threshold of an outburst of composition without parallel in the history of music: the means of self-expression had been acquired and his genius sought utterance.

The early months of 1814, however, produced little work of significance: some string quartet sketches, a few songs, and the arrangement, including a new trio (D96) for the minuet, he made in February of a *Notturno*

1. Autograph MS of version a of Schubert's 'Szene aus Goethes Faust' ('Wie anders, Gretchen, war dirs') D126, composed December 1814

op.21 by Wenzel Matiegka, for flute, guitar, viola and cello – it is called the 'Guitar' Quartet, and its attribution as a whole to Schubert is unfortunate. Between 17 May and 22 July he composed his first Mass, in F (D105). Another string quartet, in B♭ (D112), followed in September. The first movement was written in four and a half hours, as Schubert indicated on the autograph.

This was the period of the Congress of Vienna, and it coincided with the centenary celebrations of the Liechtental Church. Schubert's Mass in F was performed in the church as part of these celebrations on 14 October 1814; Holzer's choir sang, Ferdinand played the organ and Schubert himself conducted. The soprano solos were sung by Therese Grob, a young girl with a delightful lyric soprano voice. Ten days later the mass was repeated, in the court church of St Augustine, and both performances brought the young composer a welcome public acclaim. But something took place after those ten days more significant than the adulation surrounding the performances of his mass: he had been reading Goethe's *Faust*, and on 19 October 1814 he set the verses now universally known as *Gretchen am Spinnrade* (D118). It was his first masterpiece. The figure in the piano accompaniment represents the spinning-wheel, but as the song proceeds it gathers into itself all Gretchen's changing emotions as she recalls her lover, and the greatest moment is when, under the transported spirit of the suffering girl, the wheel comes to a standstill, falteringly beginning its motion again as she recovers. It is a song which, unlike several others, has never suffered eclipse during the passing years but rather has grown in stature. Another popular song to a Goethe text followed later in the year, *Schäfers Klagelied* (D121). In December, the song *Am See*

(D124) was composed to verses by Johann Mayrhofer. Spaun had given the poem to Schubert, and soon afterwards he took him to Mayrhofer's lodgings in the Wipplingerstrasse and introduced him to the poet. There began a friendship that was to affect Schubert deeply. Mayrhofer's poetry reveals the conflict between the idealism of the spirit and the actualities of life; it was, in later years, to evoke noble and profound music from the composer.

Schubert was, in 1815, a schoolmaster, feeling the irksome duties of the classroom as an intolerable barrier between him and the freedom to compose. But he evidently found time to put down on paper the music which, throughout that year, welled ceaselessly in his mind. There can have been scarcely a day when his pen was idle, and no other year in his life approached this one for its sheer volume of work. His Second Symphony, in B♭ (D125), begun the previous December, was finished in March. The Third, in D (D200), was written between 24 May and 19 July. There were numerous dances for piano solo, two sonatas, a set of ten variations on an original theme in F, and a sturdy little string quartet in G minor. Besides much varied choral music of secondary value, there were two masses. The first, in G (D167), was performed in spring 1815, soon after its completion. Depths are sounded in the Agnus Dei unknown to the earlier Mass in F. It is a *lento* movement in E minor, and solo passages for soprano and bass alternate with the chorus quietly intoning 'miserere nobis' to gracious, falling phrases. The violas are used expressively to link these solos and choruses. The second mass of the year, no.3 in B♭ (D324), looks to the later Schubert in page after page. The use of short, lyrical episodes, picturesquely orchestrated, between the vocal phrases foreshadows *Lazarus* of five years later; the use of descant-like melodies in violin or oboe hints at the slow movement of the 'Unfinished' Symphony. Above all, there are bravura passages, for example in the Gloria and Benedictus, which suggest the 'Wanderer' Fantasy and the finale of the 'Great' C major Symphony. This is the most consistently interesting of his four early settings of the Mass. The story put forward by Josef Doppler that the style of this work caused a break between Schubert and Salieri is a fabrication.

In the course of the year, Schubert set four dramatic texts to music. No doubt the successful production of an opera in Vienna appeared to him as the gate to freedom. Since Vienna possessed four theatres at which operas and plays with music were produced, he must have felt confident of eventual success. The four stage works are: *Der vierjährige Posten* (D190), to a one-act play by Theodor Körner, the music composed between 8 and 19 May; *Fernando* (D220), to a one-act play by Albert Stadler, composed 27 June to 9 July; *Claudine von Villa Bella* (D239), to a three-act play by Goethe, which was begun on 26 July, and survives in only an incomplete form, since the manuscript came into the possession of Josef Hüttenbrenner, whose servants, in 1848, unwittingly used the pages of Acts 2 and 3 to light fires; *Die Freunde von Salamanka* (D326), to a two-act play by Mayrhofer, which occupied the composer from 18 November to 31 December. The last of these four is the finest and, although Mayrhofer's text is lost, it is perfectly easy to follow the story from the extant musical numbers and so provide the necessary dialogue.

In addition to these larger musical forms, he composed in 1815 145 songs. The range is tremendous and the accomplishment outstanding. There are tiny songs like *Die Mainacht* (D194) and *Der Traum* (D213) on the one hand, and very long ballads such as *Adelwold und Emma* (D211) on the other. The poets include Schiller, Klopstock, Ossian and Kosegarten. He set 30 poems by Goethe, and some of these are among his finest and most famous songs: *Heidenröslein* (D257), *Erster Verlust* (D226), *Wandrers Nachtlied* (D224) and *Rastlose Liebe* (D138). The last of the Goethe settings, the song by which the year will always be remembered, is *Erlkönig* (D328), composed in late autumn 1815. The story of its composition as told by Spaun and others is full of incredible details; it is, in fact, impossible to separate what is factually correct from subsequent accretions. Spaun called on his friend one afternoon (he wrote) and found him excitedly reading Goethe's ballad. Schubert then wrote the song out in the shortest possible time, and the two of them (possibly with Mayrhofer) hurried to the college and gathered a few congenial spirits to hear the composition. The enthusiasm of the students was tremendous and Růžička justified his pupil's use of the discordant minor 9ths at the cry 'Mein Vater!'. When the song was eventually published, some six years later, it spread Schubert's fame far beyond his native city. In his own lifetime and for generations afterwards it was considered his greatest song. Today, perhaps, some of the more subtle songs of his final years spring to mind before *Erlkönig*, but the wealth of harmonic resource, its masterly structure and the mounting tonal climaxes of the threefold lure will always keep it high among his masterpieces of song.

During the autumn Schubert became acquainted with Franz von Schober, who had come to Vienna to study law. He had heard some of Schubert's songs and now came to seek out their composer. According to his own account, he found Schubert in the classroom correcting pupils' exercises. Of the same age as Schubert, he was a cultured, worldly young man and it was typical of his easy-going nature and wealthy upbringing that he urged Schubert to abandon the drudgery of teaching and devote himself to composition. It was not for another year that the composer could bring himself to make the break, but after his encounter with Schober, the step was inevitable. He attempted to do so in April 1816 by applying, unsuccessfully, for the post of music master in a training school for elementary teachers at Laibach (now Ljubljana), some 65 km north-east of Trieste. In the same month he completed his Fourth Symphony, in C minor (D417); the title 'Tragic' is his own. While he was engaged on this work, Spaun sent to Goethe, at Weimar, a group of Schubert's settings of the poet's verses. It included all the finest of the Goethe songs of the previous two years. The attempt to interest the poet in Schubert's work failed. In musical matters, Goethe was greatly influenced by Zelter. Both men shared the feeling of the north German musical world that in 'true German song' the accompaniment should be subordinate to the vocal part; all extravagances of harmony and modulation were categorized as 'bizarrerie' and eschewed. Schubert's songs were returned, and his appeal for recognition ignored. After Schubert's death, Goethe again heard *Erlkönig*, which was sung to him by Wilhelmine Schröder-Devrient on 24 April 1830; he told her: 'I have heard this composition once before, when it did not appeal to me at all; but sung in this way the whole shapes itself into a visible picture'.

In May 1816 Spaun took lodgings with his friend Josef Witteczek, who later became a devoted Schubertian and amassed a superb collection of

2. Page from Schubert's diary of 10 June 1816 containing references to Mozart

Schubert first editions, manuscripts and press cuttings. The house, in the Erdberggasse, was the scene of many of those domestic evening concerts devoted to the music of Schubert which came to be known as *Schubertiade*.

They were symptomatic of a new and vigorous social phenomenon, the cultivation of music by the educated middle class; though altogether humbler than the aristocratic employment of quartets and orchestras in the 18th century, its energetic growth is apparent from the ubiquitous piano and the vast mass of suitable music which poured from the publishing houses. A cantata, *Prometheus* (D451), was composed on 17 June for private performance; it was Schubert's first commissioned work and earned him a fee of 40 gulden. The music was given in the garden of the Erdberggasse house on 24 July 1816 and impressed its hearers profoundly. Whether or not this impression was deserved we have no means of knowing, as the score was lost without trace just before Schubert's death. Leopold von Sonnleithner sang in the chorus and thereby made Schubert's acquaintance; the composer was to be fortunate in this contact with so influential and musical a family as the Sonnleithners.

Several pages of a diary which Schubert kept that year have survived. The entries for June have some interest, since they contain references to Mozart and Beethoven. If anything were needed to demonstrate that music was his only medium of self-expression, we have only to turn from the diary pages of September to the work on which he was engaged at this time – the Fifth Symphony, in B♭ (D485), the best and most popular of his six early symphonies. It was finished on 3 October and performed soon afterwards by a private orchestra which had developed from the family string quartet and which met in the house of its conductor, Otto Hatwig.

3. Growing reputation

In October 1816, after a four-month visit to his birthplace in Sweden, Schober returned to Vienna, and he persuaded the composer to make a move towards independence. There was no clean break with teaching, but by December Schubert was installed in rooms in the house of Schober's affluent mother – a temporary respite. 1816 had been almost as prolific as the previous year. In addition to the compositions already mentioned there was a further Mass, in C (D452), composed during June and July and published nine years later with a dedication to Michael Holzer. The three sonatas for violin and piano (D384, 385, 408), published by Diabelli in 1836 as 'Sonatinas', and the String Quartet in E (D353) were composed that year. The songs, over 100, include *Der Wanderer* (D489), after *Erlkönig* the most popular of his songs for many years, and masterpieces to poems by Goethe such as the three Harper's Songs from *Wilhelm Meister* (D478–80) and *An Schwager Kronos* (D369). It is one of the enigmas of his music that these songs so richly reveal his personal style, whereas in his contemporary instrumental works it appears only fitfully. A few months after Schubert was installed in his new house, Schober prevailed upon the operatic baritone, Johann Michael Vogl, to visit him and make the acquaintance of the composer and his songs. Vogl was well-to-do, a man of culture with a distinguished, even stately bearing. Schubert was overawed and painfully embarrassed, but the singer, very much at his ease, took the proffered songs: the newly composed

Ganymed (D544) was one of them. His parting remark was to the effect that, although there was much fine stuff in the songs, it was ill-presented; Schubert, he said, was too little of the charlatan. But he was more impressed than he admitted. Shortly afterwards he revisited the composer and the two men soon became the delight of the Viennese drawing-rooms. Vogl, his days in the theatre nearly over, was not averse to the plaudits of the salons and initially he looked upon the songs as vehicles for his voice. Occasionally he altered them, adding flourishes and introducing wide skips in voice parts. He once embellished a new song of Schubert's, also transposing it to suit his voice, and on presenting the copy a fortnight later was greeted by the composer with 'A good song. Whose is it, then?'. Generations have chuckled over this anecdote, seeing only the 'clairvoyant' genius (Vogl's word) who forgets his own production when the trance is over; they have missed Schubert's implied protest.

An effort was made during the spring of 1817 to publish *Erlkönig*. The song was sent to the Leipzig firm of Breitkopf & Härtel. Knowing only one Franz Schubert, a musician in Dresden, they sent him the manuscript for confirmation. He replied:

With the greatest astonishment I beg to state that this cantata was never composed by me. I shall retain the same in my possession to learn, if possible, who has so impertinently sent you that sort of rubbish and also to discover the fellow who has thus misused my name.

The manuscript was returned to Schubert without comment.

The spring and summer of 1817 were devoted to the composition of piano sonatas. The wide range of piano styles and the use of unusual keys show that Schubert was experimenting in both form and medium during his months of freedom. Three of the sonatas were published posthumously: the one in A minor (D537) as op.164 (*c*1852); the one in E♭ (D568) as op.122 (1829); the one in B (D575) as op.147 (1846). A work in E minor (D566 and 506) has an extraordinary history of publication: each movement appeared separately over the years between 1848 and 1929, and the whole work, edited by Kathleen Dale, was published only in 1948. The Sonata in E♭ (D568) was first planned in the key of D♭; Schubert himself decided on the transposition and he completed the work probably by June 1817. By November he had returned to the parental home and resumed his teaching duties; he had been obliged to vacate his rooms in Schober's house the previous August. The autumn of 1817 saw the composition of the Sonata in A for violin and piano (D574) and the String Trio in B♭ (D581). Both works show clear evidence of the establishment of his style in the growing harmonic complexity, the exuberant melody and (more subtly) in the spontaneity of the modulations and the obvious delight he took in expanding a new rhythmic or melodic idea.

Vienna at that time was in the grip of one of its furores, this time for Rossini, whose operas had been received in the city with frantic enthusiasm. Schubert himself was not unmoved, and signs of the genial Italian's style appear markedly in the work he was then writing, his Sixth Symphony, in C (D589), which was begun in October. It is a transitional work and shows him attempting to express his mature vision, while still using, and being inhibited by, the language of his earlier symphonies. Two overtures 'im italienischen Stile' (D590–91), finished in November, set out to imitate, almost parody, Rossini. They are attractive and tuneful works; Schubert later re-used material from the introduction and the coda of the first in the work now known as the overture to *Rosamunde*. In December, he arranged both overtures for piano duet (D592 and 597). Besides settings of Goethe and Schiller, whose *Gruppe aus dem Tartarus* (D583) evoked one of Schubert's grandest conceptions, there are songs that year to words by his own friends, among them the immortal *An die Musik* (D547) to Schober's text. Two famous songs of 1817 are *Der Tod und das Mädchen* (D531) and *Die Forelle* (D550), which from the first won all hearts. Both melodies later served Schubert as themes for equally beloved instrumental variations. Of the Mayrhofer settings, the finest is *Memnon* (D541); a slighter song is *Erlafsee* (D586), printed in January 1818 as a supplement to a periodical – Schubert's first published work.

In December 1817, Schubert's father was appointed master of a school in the adjoining district of Rossau. The family, augmented by two sons and two daughters of the second marriage, had moved to the new house by early 1818. Schubert remained there as a teacher until the following July. It must have been doubly irksome to him, this resumption of a task he hated after a year of freedom from routine, and a return to the family circle in which he must have felt deep affection but no true kinship after his recent contact with congenial spirits. No wonder he was to say of himself during this period, 'I should have become nothing but a thwarted [*verdorbener*] musician'. His work of that spring reflects his depression. A sonata in C (D613) and a symphony in D (D615) were both left unfinished. Only a little Rondo in D for piano duet from that period (D608) has any sparkle; it was a tribute to his new friend Josef von Gahy, an excellent pianist with whom Schubert loved to play duets. (The title on the first edition, 'Notre amitié est invariable', does not, however, derive from Schubert.) The second 'Italian' overture, in C, was performed in the hall of the Zum römischen Kaiser restaurant on 1 March and again in May – his début in the concert room. These performances secured press notices in Vienna, Dresden and Leipzig.

In July he was able to leave the Rossau school. He was offered and accepted the post of music master to the children of Count Johann Esterházy: his pupils were the young princesses Marie and Caroline. The count's summer residence was at Zseliz, then in Hungary, about 480 km east of Vienna. Schubert resigned from his father's school and never returned to teaching.

The first weeks at Zseliz were very happy. On 3 August he wrote to his friends in Vienna:

I am quite well. I live and compose like a god, as though that were as it should be. Mayrhofer's *Einsamkeit* is ready, and I believe it to be the best I have done, for I was without a care . . . Thank God, I live at last, and it was high time . . .

Einsamkeit (D620) is a long, discursive ballad of mixed value, and few people would endorse the composer's opinion of it. Other compositions reveal the fact that he was in charge of two young pianists, for they are almost all for piano duet: a Sonata in B♭ (D617), a set of variations (D624) and a fine but little-known set of polonaises (D599). The variations, on a song called *Reposez-vous, bon chevalier*, were published in 1822 as his op.10 and dedicated to Beethoven 'by his admirer and worshipper, Franz Schubert'. As time passed, Schubert grew discontented with life at Zseliz. He felt that none of the people he met there really cared for music, and his existence began to seem unendurably empty compared with the society he had enjoyed in the capital and the stimulus of his Viennese friendships. He wrote to Schober on 8 September:

At Zseliz I am obliged to rely wholly on myself. I have to be composer, author, audience and goodness knows what else. Not a soul here has any feeling for true art, or at the most the countess now and again (unless I am wrong). So I am alone with my beloved and have to hide her in my room, in my pianoforte and in my bosom. Although this often makes me sad, on the other hand it elevates me the more. Have no fear, then, that I shall stay away longer than is absolutely necessary.

While at Zseliz Schubert composed the *Deutsches Requiem* (D621) for his brother Ferdinand who, possibly to enhance his reputation as a music teacher, passed off the work as his own. In a letter of October he referred to this 'sin of appropriation'. Schubert's reply is one of the most affectionate and sweet-natured letters he wrote: he made nothing of Ferdinand's act, saying only that it was his greatest reward for composing the *Requiem*. It was only with the discovery of this letter by Grove on 26 October 1880, announced in his article 'Schubert' in the first edition of this dictionary, that the true author of the *Deutsches Requiem* was revealed. His Sonata in F minor (D625, ?505) was composed at Zseliz in September 1818; it is not quite complete, and of very different quality from the unfinished and inferior sonata of the previous April. In November the Esterházy family returned to Vienna for the winter, Schubert with them. The association was not broken, however, and he continued to give the children lessons during the winter months. There was no return to school-teaching, although for some years he was officially designated 'school assistant at the Rossau'.

4. Vienna friends and patrons, 1819-20

On his return to Vienna, Schubert went to lodge with Mayrhofer in the Wipplingerstrasse. Relations between the two artists were cordial, and even happier was their association in the songs of that year, for Mayrhofer's verses drew from Schubert a music whose grandeur is surpassed only by his settings of Goethe and Schiller. It is moreover an interesting facet of Schubert's work in lieder to find how the greater Mayrhofer settings often led to even greater Goethe settings – as though Mayrhofer had tapped the springs in Schubert from which Goethe could draw a finer music.

Schubert next began work on Georg von Hofmann's one-act play *Die Zwillingsbrüder* (D647); the overture is dated 19 January 1819. Vogl, for whom the leading roles (the twin brothers) were designed, secured its performance at the Kärntnertor-Theater the following year. On 8 January, a performance of the *Prometheus* cantata was given in the house of Ignaz von Sonnleithner, the father of Schubert's friend Leopold. The elder Sonnleithner was a rich patron of music and in his rooms in the Gundelhof regular and lavish concerts were given. In private circles Schubert's name was becoming widely known, and in public circles, too; an overture of his (probably that in E minor, D648, composed in February 1819), was played at Müllers Hall on 14 March, and a tenor of the Theater an der Wien, Franz Jäger, sang the *Schäfers Klagelied* several times during the spring; the performances received favourable notices in the press, one even in Berlin.

Anselm Hüttenbrenner, who had made Schubert's acquaintance when they were both pupils of Salieri's, had left Vienna for his home in Graz during autumn 1818. Schubert's relationship with him was cordial and his letters very friendly; on 19 May 1819 he wrote: 'In spite of Vogl it is difficult to outwit such *canaille* as Weigl, Treitschke etc. That is why instead of my operetta, they give other rot, enough to make your hair stand on end'. The younger brother, Josef Hüttenbrenner, remained in Vienna and gave Schubert the slavish devotion which frequently provokes snubs; Schubert's earned him the nickname 'The Tyrant'.

The summer of 1819 was one of the happiest periods of Schubert's life. He accompanied Vogl to Steyr at the beginning of July and spent nearly three months in a district which he described as 'inconceivably lovely'. Steyr, some 145 km west of Vienna, was Vogl's birthplace and whenever possible he spent the summer there. The popular 'Trout' Quintet (D667), for piano and strings, was begun there, commissioned by the town's most eminent music patron, Sylvester Paumgartner, a cellist. By the following autumn in Vienna it was finished and despatched to Paumgartner; the variation movement which gives the quintet its nickname owed its inception to Paumgartner's love of the song. It has been well suggested that the Steyr countryside was a secret collaborator in the quintet; it is even fortunate in its nickname, with its suggestion of cool, sun-flecked water.

The friends departed for Vienna in the middle of September. The record of the next six months is a chronicle of composition. Schubert rejoined Mayrhofer and in October set three of his friend's poems, including *Nachtstück* (D672). Two Goethe songs followed: one of them, *Prometheus* (D674), is the finest of his lyrico-dramatic songs. A charming song to verses by Schiller is *Strophe aus Die Götter Griechenlands* (D677, 'Schöne Welt, wo bist du?'), written in November. The fifth mass, in Ab (D678), was begun in November, but set aside and not completed until September 1822. Another work, unfortunately, was also left unfinished, and Schubert never returned to this fragmentary score. It is the setting, dated February 1820, of August Niemeyer's sacred poetic drama *Lazarus, oder Die Feier der Auferstehung* (D689). Although a little too full of Schubert's softer, more easy-going lyricism, it is written in a style which is endlessly fascinating; it contains hints of leitmotif, and the orchestral web which forms the accompaniment, colourful and inventive, hints at Wagnerian practice.

Die Zwillingsbrüder was staged on 14 June at the Kärntnertor-Theater with Vogl doubling the roles of the twin brothers. It had only a moderate success and was withdrawn after five further performances. But these performances did bring Schubert's name into greater prominence, and in July he was commissioned by the management of the Theater an der Wien to compose music for a three-act play, *Die Zauberharfe* (D644). It is an extravaganza, full of mechanical stage effects and burdened with a complicated plot. The text was also by Hofmann. Schubert is said to have been as little interested in *Die Zauberharfe* as he had been in *Die Zwillingsbrüder*. The music was composed in a fortnight and the work presented on 19 August 1820. The overture, now known as the *Rosamunde* overture, is Schubert's finest work in this genre and deservedly popular (the reason for its misnaming will be discussed later). The music of *Die Zauberharfe*, entirely unknown to the public, is often very beautiful and had a profound effect on Schubert's development. He was compelled by the nature of the work to write *Melodramen* (i.e. music to accompany spoken words), and for the first time in his operatic pieces was obliged, as it were, to think instrumentally rather than vocally, to develop his themes and thematic figures according to symphonic rather than to lyrical demands. We owe the 'Unfinished' Symphony to *Die Zauberharfe*. That the music was beyond the understanding of the conservative musicians of the day is clear from the words of the critic of the Leipzig *Allgemeine musikalische Zeitung*: 'most of it is much too long, ineffective and fatiguing, the harmonic progressions are too harsh, the orchestration redundant, the choruses dull and feeble'. There were eight performances, the last on 12 October 1820. A poem written by Schubert during September 1820 entitled *Der Geist der Welt* is an enigmatic piece of writing, attacking 'those ... who with wrangling fill these days'. Many attempts have been made to explain the contemptuous dislike Schubert expressed in these words. Rudolf Klein has convincingly suggested that it was the composer's response to the philistine reception of the music he had written for *Die Zauberharfe*.

Through his association with the Esterházy family, Schubert met Baron von Schönstein in 1820. The possessor of a fine baritone voice, Schönstein was, after Vogl, the most notable interpreter of Schubert's songs during the composer's lifetime, and he later introduced them to Liszt. The poet Matthäus von Collin, a cousin of Spaun, introduced Schubert to Ignaz von Mosel and Count Moritz Dietrichstein, two important officials at the imperial court, and also to Ladislaus Pyrker, Patriarch of Venice. In December 1820, at one of Sonnleithner's concerts, August von Gymnich, accompanied by Anna Fröhlich, sang *Erlkönig*. It was received with overwhelming enthusiasm. The performance was to have far-reaching results. The immediate outcome was that Schubert made the acquaintance of the four Fröhlich sisters, Barbara, Kathi, Josefine and Anna, a cultivated and musical family; through them he met Franz Grillparzer, Austria's most eminent dramatist.

Mayrhofer is the poet of several fine songs written during the autumn of 1820; one is the little-known *Freiwilliges Versinken* (D700), which reveals Schubert's growing power of subtle yet picturesque comment in the accompaniment. The year ends with an outpouring of music of the finest quality. The sketch in C♯ minor of Goethe's *Gesang der Geister über den Wassern* (D705), of superb promise, remained unfinished. Its stormy piano accompaniment, which recalls *Gruppe aus dem Tartarus*, might have been Schubert's finest exposition of this passionate style; the choral work is contrapuntal yet transparently clear. The same exalted mood is recaptured in the extended song *Im Walde* (D708), to words by Friedrich von Schlegel (it is sometimes called *Waldesnacht* to distinguish it from the similarly entitled song of 1825 to words by Ernst Schulze). *Im Walde* is almost impracticable in the concert room, but the Schubertian turns again and again to its outpoured splendour. The setting of Psalm xxiii for female voices (D706) was composed in December 1820 for the singing pupils of Anna Fröhlich, who taught at the Vienna Conservatory. Finally that month there was the first movement of an unfinished String Quartet in C minor, known as the 'Quartettsatz' (D703), in which Schubert

3. Franz Schubert (right) with Anselm Hüttenbrenner and Jenger: drawing by Josef Teltscher

achieved the lyrical radiance of the 'Trout' Quintet with the dramatic intensity of his finest songs. It is the first of the instrumental masterpieces of the 1820s. 41 bars of the slow movement, an Andante in A♭, are extant.

5. Events of 1821-2

In the early part of 1821, Schubert decided to leave Mayrhofer and he moved into a house nearby in the Wipplingerstrasse. He became very friendly with a young painter named Moritz von Schwind, some seven years his junior, who was in after years to paint the most famous of the Schubert pictures: it was called *Schubert-Abend bei Joseph von Spaun* and enshrines for ever the Biedermeier atmosphere of the Schubertiads. The settings of Goethe which he composed that spring have become famous: the songs range from the delicacy and charm of *Geheimes* (D719) to the grandeur of *Grenzen der Menschheit* (D716). A new treatment of *Gesang der Geister* for double male chorus with accompaniment for low strings (D714) was finished in February 1821. The poem held a great attraction for Schubert and this finished setting is a sublime work, though the earlier sketch holds even greater promise. At a public concert in the Kärntnertor-Theater on 7 March 1821, Vogl sang *Erlkönig*; it was a masterly performance which created a profound impression.

The continual performances of Schubert's songs and vocal quartets that year and their enthusiastic reception make it difficult to understand why publishers were so reluctant to issue his work. Songs, string quartets and piano pieces by such people as Anselm Hüttenbrenner, Benedikt Randhartinger, Franz Volkert, Ignaz von Moscheles and hosts of other minor composers were readily accepted and published, and one has to accept the fact that, at this period in Vienna, fame as a performer was the key to publication, not merit as a composer for one as obscure as Schubert. Leopold von Sonn-leithner and other friends took matters into their own hands and determined to issue *Erlkönig* by private sub-scription. The response was overwhelming; not only was the cost of the song covered, but also that of engrav-ing *Gretchen am Spinnrade*. The firm of Cappi & Diabelli was commissioned to engrave the works. In this manner 20 songs were published, as opp.1–8, by the end of 1821. *Erlkönig* appeared on 31 March, dedicated to Count Dietrichstein, *Gretchen* on 30 April, dedicated to Moritz von Fries. The other songs include *Der Wanderer*, *Heidenröslein*, *Rastlose Liebe* and *Der Tod und das Mädchen*; dedications were offered to Pyrker, Vogl and Salieri. Schubert did very well from some of these carefully directed dedications; he wrote to Spaun at Linz: 'but I must now tell you that my dedications have done their work; that is to say, the Patriarch has forked out 12 ducats, and, through Vogl's intervention, Fries 20, which is a very good thing for me'.

He composed two supplementary numbers, an aria and a duet (D723), for a performance at the Kärntnertor-Theater on 20 June 1821 of Hérold's *Das Zauber-glöckchen* (originally *La clochette*). Their almost symphonic stature is ill-fitting in such a light work, and they made little impression. Soon after this luckless operatic venture, Schubert went to Atzenbrugg with Schober. The property was managed by an uncle of Schober's, and each summer a party of young people met there and spent a holiday together with excursions, concerts, dances and charades. The 1821 visit is the most notable of the three which Schubert made, since it is recorded pictorially by three drawings made by a new friend, the painter Leopold Kupelwieser. Two of these

are charming watercolours depicting activities of the
holiday party (see fig.4), and the third is a pencil drawing of the composer, signed and dated by him 'July
1821'. The half-dozen waltzes known as the
'Atzenbrugger' Dances (D145 nos.1–3, D365 nos.29–31)
were written during this holiday. Back in Vienna he
began, in August, the seventh of his symphonies, in E
(D729), completing a part of the first movement in score
and sketching, sometimes in detail, the remainder of the
four movements. No hint of the standard reached in the

*4. Charade at Atzenbrugg: watercolour (1821) by
Leopold Kupelwieser; Schubert is seated at the piano
with Philipp Karl Hartmann to his left, Schober,
Kupelwieser and Jenger (left and right) in the doorway,
and Josef von Spaun seated second from the right*

Quartettsatz can be found in this slender production. The symphony has been 'realized' by J. F. Barnett (1883) and Felix Weingartner (1934) but neither attempt is convincing.

During September 1821 Schubert accompanied Schober to St Pölten; they stayed nearby at the castle of Ochsenburg (owned by the Bishop of St Pölten, a relative of Schober's), seeking in this rural retreat the peace and seclusion necessary to embark on the work they were undertaking together, the composition of a full-scale opera, *Alfonso und Estrella* (D732). In later years, Schober wrote that they undertook this opera 'in a state of happy enthusiasm but with great innocence of heart and mind'. The first act was written between 20 September and 16 October. They returned to Vienna towards the end of October, and Schubert finished the second act in November; the opera was completed by 27 February 1822. Schober's libretto has been too readily accepted in the past as the reason for the total neglect of this work. The music is first-rate, full of Schubert's most endearing lyricism and dramatic genius.

The well-known set of waltzes op.9 (D365) was published in November 1821, and shortly after that Schubert began the first of his settings of the poet Rückert, *Sei mir gegrüsst* (D741). From the beginning of 1822 Schubert lodged with Schober in his house in the Spiegelgasse. There Schwind introduced him to Eduard Bauernfeld, later famous as a playwright and translator of Shakespeare and Dickens. Bauernfeld greatly admired Schubert's music and had ardently wished to meet him. These three young men, Schubert, Schwind and Bauernfeld, unlike in character yet united in their artistic ideals and love of music, became inseparable.

During February, Schubert met Weber, who was in Vienna to conduct the first full performance in the city of *Der Freischütz* at the Kärntnertor-Theater. The theatre had just come under the management of the famous Italian impresario Domenico Barbaia, who later leased the Theater an der Wien. These moves did not promise particularly well for Schubert's new opera, on which he was placing high hopes. His published songs, however, were making their mark. They were favourably reviewed in January by the Vienna *Allgemeine musikalische Zeitung*, and in March a long, sympathetic and comprehensive criticism by Friedrich von Hentl appeared in the *Zeitschrift für Kunst*. The variations op.10 (D624) were published in April. Schubert himself is supposed to have taken a copy to Beethoven, but the accounts of this event are so contradictory that it is doubtful whether they have any factual foundation. On 3 July Schubert wrote the strange document describing the dream of a quarrel and reconciliation with a father. It is embroidered with sentimental descriptions of a mother's death and burial, and the entombment of a 'gentle maiden'. The title *Mein Traum* was added years later by Ferdinand. Attempts to look upon the tale as autobiographical have given rise to the fiction of a rupture with his father and a reconciliation at his mother's graveside.

A letter from Spaun's brother Anton, written to his wife on 20 July, gives an unpleasant account of Schubert's relations with Schober and Vogl during summer 1822. Schubert seemed to be behaving in a manner at odds with his true nature; he aped the man of the world, became offhand to his friends (discourteously so to Vogl) and extravagant and loose in his way of life. Vogl considered the libretto of *Alfonso und Estrella* to be thoroughly bad; the absence of his backing, together with the fact that Barbaia was engrossed with Rossini, led to its rejection. Apparently Schubert and Vogl were reconciled by the autumn. 12 of his songs were published in Vienna during the year, the three Harper's Songs (op.12, D478–80) and *Geheimes* (op.14, D719) appearing on 13 December. The songs of 1822 include settings of Mayrhofer, composed in the spring, one of which is the charming *Nachtviolen* (D752); towards the end of the year there were settings of Goethe, not of the stature of *Prometheus*, but containing such sublime specimens of his lyric art as *Der Musensohn* (D764) and *Am Flusse* (D766). The Mass in A♭ (D678) was finished in September, and November saw the first example of his maturity in piano composition, the 'Wanderer' Fantasy (D760).

The outstanding work of that autumn is the eighth of Schubert's symphonies, the 'Unfinished' in B minor (D759). Only one other work among his instrumental compositions up to that time, the Quartettsatz, is not dwarfed by the two movements of the symphony. They were composed during October and the scherzo set aside for the composition of the 'Wanderer' Fantasy.

Many theories have been evolved to account for the fact that Schubert never finished the symphony. That he intended it to be a two-movement work is disposed of by the existence of a substantial part of the third movement. It has been suggested that the symphony was in fact finished: T. C. L. Pritchard put forward the idea in 1942 that Anselm Hüttenbrenner had lost the manuscript of the last two movements, but more recent documentation and discoveries leave no ground for this theory; more recently Gerald Abraham has suggested that the finale of the symphony is the movement used by Schubert as

5. *Autograph sketches for the projected scherzo of Schubert's Symphony no.8 in B minor* D759 *('Unfinished'), composed October 1822*

the B minor entr'acte of the *Rosamunde* music, but his arguments are slender and are contrary to the weight of palaeographic evidence. The truth about Schubert's failure to complete the symphony may lie in psychological factors, and particularly in the tragic event which occurred at the end of 1822. He then contracted syphilis, and by the late spring of 1823 he was desperately ill. To a sensitive man like Schubert the association of the composition of his symphony with the events which led to his illness might have made a return to it repugnant. The fate of the manuscript has also been bedevilled by theorizing on scanty facts. The recent disclosure of documents from the Hüttenbrenner family archives shows that Schubert gave the manuscript of the 'Unfinished' Symphony, in its incomplete state, to Josef Hüttenbrenner some time in 1823, to pass it on to his brother Anselm as a private gift (not, as long believed, as an acknowledgment of his election to the Styrian Music Society). This was probably in payment for a debt or an obligation; Anselm had a perfect right to retain the score. It was eventually, in 1865, handed over to the conductor of the orchestra of the Vienna Musikverein and performed in December that year.

6. Illness

The onset of his unpleasant illness forced Schubert to leave Schober's home. By the end of 1822 he was living in his father's house in the Rossau. In the early weeks of 1823 he was too ill to leave the house, as we learn from a letter which he wrote to Ignaz von Mosel asking him to send *Alfonso und Estrella*, with a letter of recommendation, to Weber at Dresden. On this same day, 24 February, the 'Wanderer' Fantasy was published as op.15.

The pressing need for money forced Schubert into a bad business move that winter. He sold to Cappi & Diabelli, for a lump sum, all his rights in the publication of opp.1–7, and in February offered them the remaining opp.12–14. He suspected the publishers of dishonest dealing with him, and not only in the strict account of sales. He broke with the firm in a letter of 10 April 1823, a letter with an edge which is new in Schubert. His first publication from another house was op.20, issued by Sauer & Leidesdorf; it included *Frühlingsglaube* (D686) and *Sei mir gegrüsst* (D741). His next piano sonata, in A minor (D784), was written in February 1823; it is the first of his mature sonatas, restrained and economical compared with the 'Wanderer' Fantasy, and breaking completely with the graceful, ornamental style of his earlier sonatas. A one-act operetta, *Die Verschworenen* (D787), to a libretto by Ignaz Castelli, was completed in April (in deference to a touchy political censorship the title was changed to *Der häusliche Krieg*). It was not performed in Schubert's lifetime, but has proved to be thoroughly stageworthy, as well as melodious, witty and delightfully scored.

By now, Schubert's condition had grown so serious that he was admitted to the Vienna general hospital. A poem of his, written on 8 May, makes painful reading; it ends:

> Take my life, my flesh and blood,
> Plunge it all in Lethe's flood,
> To a purer, stronger state,
> Deign me, Great One, to translate.

Yet during this depressing period the first songs of the *Schöne Müllerin* cycle were composed; they grace this unhappy year, in truth, like 'a sunny archipelago of songs'. The author is Wilhelm Müller, and the story told in the sequence of poems originated in a family charade.

On 25 May 1823 Schubert turned once more to the composition of a full-length opera, *Fierabras* (D796). The original play had a complicated plot, set in the time of Charlemagne although its ideas and atmosphere are medieval. The libretto was by Josef Kupelwieser, brother of Leopold. Schubert's inability to visualize how ineffective this play would be as a theatrical proposition suggests that there was no genuine theatrical urge behind his repeated operatic ventures. It can never have occurred to him that to earn a living in this way would be as arduous a task as routine class-teaching. He spent the weeks from the end of July to mid-September revisiting Linz and Steyr, where he met Spaun, Mayrhofer and Vogl. His life was regular and quiet; that and the summer air of this idyllic countryside restored him somewhat, though even there he suffered a bout of severe illness. He was elected an honorary member of the Linz Musical Society and met the president,

Friedrich von Hartmann, whose two sons, Fritz and Franz, later came to Vienna and kept copious diaries which contain many references to Schubert and his friends. *Fierabras* was finished on 26 September, and the overture completed on 2 October. The rejection by Barbaia was inevitable: no discerning manager could have accepted the play, in spite of the excellence of its music – music which haunts the mind more than that of *Alfonso und Estrella*, which Schubert is supposed to have preferred to all his other operas.

Weber was in Vienna that autumn for the first performance of *Euryanthe* on 25 October. In Schubert's opinion its bad reception was justified, and when he met Weber at the Zur ungarischen Krone inn he told him so, adding that he preferred *Der Freischütz*. Relations between the two men cooled, but there is no trustworthy evidence that this frankness on Schubert's part led to a quarrel between him and Weber. In November Schubert was again seriously ill; but he rallied, and wrote on 30 November to Schober (who was at Breslau attempting to make a name as an actor) that his health seemed to be firmly restored at last. In those days, of course, a cure was out of the question; the disease never again racked him outwardly, but it steadily undermined his central nervous system. His temperament, too, was altering. With his resilient good humour there would always be periods in which he knew no care; but he had also to contend with pain and giddiness which understandably induced fits of irritability and depression. He told Schober that he had composed more *Schöne Müllerin* songs; the cycle was completed soon afterwards. The remaining Rückert songs, including the celebrated *Du bist die Ruh* (D776) and *Dass sie hier gewesen* (D775), were also probably composed that autumn.

In spite of the object-lesson of *Euryanthe*, he accepted in October a commission to write incidental music to a romantic drama by the same author, Helmina von Chézy. The drama, *Rosamunde, Fürstin von Zypern*, is lost, but a synopsis of the plot, surviving in contemporary records, shows its worthlessness. Fortunately most of Schubert's music is instrumental (D797). Produced on 20 December, *Rosamunde* was a failure, and it achieved only two performances. The orchestral parts for the vocal numbers lay in oblivion until 1867, when they were rescued by Grove and Sullivan. Today the entr'actes and ballet music, although written in an incredibly short time, are among Schubert's most popular orchestral works. The fact that he wrote no overture to *Rosamunde* has led to two of his other overtures' being wrongly attributed to the play. For the actual performance he used the overture to *Alfonso und Estrella*, possibly in revised form; it is this work, in D (D732), which was wrongly printed in the Breitkopf & Härtel complete edition at the start of the *Rosamunde* incidental music and so was looked upon as the authentic *Rosamunde* overture. The second misnamed work, now universally performed as the *Rosamunde* overture, is actually the overture composed for the performance of *Die Zauberharfe* in 1820.

Although Schubert never abandoned his ambition to write a successful opera, *Rosamunde* is his last completed dramatic work. He then turned again to purely instrumental forms, and in them achieved masterly success. At the beginning of 1824 he composed his first chamber works for over three years. On 13 February Schwind wrote to Schober: 'Schubert now keeps a fortnight's fast and confinement. He looks much better and is very bright, very comically hungry and writes quartets and German dances and variations without number'. The quartets were the favourite one in A minor (D804), finished in March 1824 (published the following September as op.29 no.1), and the one in D minor (D810) with variations on the song *Der Tod und das Mädchen* as its slow movement, also finished in March 1824; because of a mistake by Franz Lachner the date 1826 is still often assigned to it. Among the variations mentioned by Schwind is the set for flute and piano (D802) on *Trockne Blumen* from the *Schöne Müllerin* cycle, which Schubert composed for Ferdinand Bogner, professor at the Vienna Conservatory. During February he was also at work on the Octet in F for wind and strings (D803) which had been commissioned by Ferdinand, Count Troyer, a clarinettist and a member of the Archduke Rudolph's musical establishment. The Octet, deservedly popular, was modelled (at Troyer's request) on Beethoven's Septet, and although the work is highly characteristic of Schubert there are links, both obvious and subtle, between the two. The theme of the variation movement is from the duet 'Gelagert unter'm hellen Dach der Bäume' in *Die Freunde von Salamanka*. On 14 March a quartet led by Ignaz Schuppanzigh gave a public performance of the A minor String Quartet; three days later the first part of *Die schöne Müllerin* was published as op.25. Schubert dedicated neither of these works to a rich patron, who might have made some financial return, but instead paid tribute to two fine artists: the first was dedicated to Schuppanzigh, the second to Baron von Schönstein.

7. Schubert's circle of friends

Letters exchanged between his friends often touch on Schubert or his activities; Schwind wrote to Schober on 6 March: 'If you go to see him during the day, he says, "Hullo, how are you? – Good" and goes on writing'. Reading parties, instituted by Schober in autumn 1822, had become so swollen with new and uncongenial acquaintances that not even custom could prolong their existence. Doblhoff wrote to Schober on 2 April: 'Yesterday our reading circle was formally suspended. It had grown so much that in the end it devoured itself . . . Schubertiads are hardly mentioned any more. Schubert himself cannot sing, and Vogl will sing only in agreeable and respectable society'. Schubert's circle had disintegrated and another one was in the process of forming. While we cannot altogether regret the departure of Schober, it is quite another matter to consider Spaun's absence in Linz, Kupelwieser's departure for Italy and the estrangement of Mayrhofer (which occurred that spring). With Schwind he was on terms of affectionate intimacy, and soon Bauernfeld came into prominence; but in the composer's mind the breaking of his friendships and the wreck of his health became associated, and with almost unbearable misery he wrote to Kupelwieser on 31 March 1824:

In a word, I feel myself to be the most unhappy and wretched creature in the world. Imagine a man whose health will never be right again, and who, in sheer despair over this, ever makes things worse and worse, instead of better; imagine a man, I say, whose most brilliant hopes have perished, to whom the felicity of love and friendship have nothing to offer but pain . . . Thus joyless and friendless I should pass my days, did not Schwind visit me now and again and turn on me a ray of those sweet days of the past.

Schubert went that summer to Zseliz for a second time as music master to the Esterházy family, leaving Vienna on 25 May. It was a grudging move on his part, for he wrote to Schober on 21 September: 'Now I sit here alone in the depths of the Hungarian country whither I unfortunately let myself be enticed a second time without having a single person with whom I could speak a sensible word'. In this letter we again have that aching cry for the past: 'I want to exclaim with Goethe: "Who will bring me back an hour of that sweet time?"' (an allusion to *Erster Verlust*, which he had set in 1815). Family letters survive from 1824 as from 1818. Ferdinand and Franz were always devoted brothers, and the composer's illness had drawn them even closer. On 3 July Ferdinand wrote to his brother that a musical clock in the Zur ungarischen Krone inn had played several of his (Franz's) waltzes, and that hearing them he was moved to ... but he could not finish the sentence. Schubert replied, 'Did all the tears come to your mind which you have seen me weep?'. To Schwind, during August, Schubert wrote:

I am still well, thank goodness, and should be quite comfortable here, if only I had you, Schober and Kupelwieser with me, but as it is, I often long damnably for Vienna, in spite of the certain attractive star. By the end of September, I hope to see you all again. I have composed a grand sonata and variations for four hands, which latter are having a great success here.

Both works mentioned are for piano duet. The 'grand sonata' was composed in June and published post-humously under the title 'Grand Duo' as op.140 (D812). The variations are those in A♭ (D813), pub-lished the following spring as op.35. Another piano duet

*6. Franz Schubert: watercolour portrait (1825) by
Wilhelm August Rieder*

of the period is the famous *Divertissement à l'hongroise* (D818) whose best moments are among the most superb passages in Schubert's music for piano duet. The 'attractive star' of his letter is certainly Caroline Esterházy, then nearly 20 years old, with whom he was believed to be in love. The vocal quartet *Gebet* (D815) was written for her during one September day, Schubert receiving Fouqué's words after breakfast and presenting the finished composition for rehearsal that evening.

He arrived back in Vienna, with Baron von Schönstein, on 17 September, and once more went to live in the Rossau. He was considerably better for having spent those quiet summer months in Zseliz, and Schwind wrote to Schober on 8 November: 'Schubert is here, well and divinely frivolous, rejuvenated by delight and pain and a pleasant life'. The Sonata in A minor (D821) for piano and arpeggione (a six-string cello-like instrument with frets) was composed in November and played shortly after by the man for whom it was written, Vincenz Schuster; it is a secondary work compared with the giants of the year, but not to be despised. Anna Milder-Hauptmann, whom Schubert in his youth had revered for her operatic singing, wrote to him on 12 December from Berlin. She had come to know and admire his songs, and asked whether she might use her good offices to secure the performance of one of his operas in Berlin. Schubert sent her the score of *Alfonso und Estrella*, but without success.

His growing intimacy with Schwind led him in February 1825 to move into the suburb of Wieden, where he occupied rooms in a house close to Schwind's home. Schubert was fond of the volatile young painter and called him his 'beloved'; Schwind, for his part, idolized the composer and daily sought his company. In his own sphere as painter and illustrator, Schwind was to achieve notable work, but through Schubert we encounter him in his turbulent youth, and he shows a tiresome strain of adolescent gracelessness, particularly in his childish quarrels. According to Bauernfeld he behaved with studied rudeness to Vogl. Bauernfeld's close friendship with Schubert began during February. It is easy to see how attractive to Schubert was the company of this lighthearted youth, who chaffed him over his love affairs, fraternized with him in taverns and promised him a new operatic libretto.

8. 1825-6

Schubert's reputation grew steadily. Songs and vocal quartets were given in Vienna by the Gesellschaft der Musikfreunde (the Musikverein) and at the Vienna Conservatory. Schubertiads, with Vogl once more supreme, were more popular than ever, taking place in the houses of Witteczek or Weintridt and, on one occasion, in the house of Katherina von Lászny, a former soprano at the Kärntnertor-Theater, courtesan and patron of the arts. To her Schubert dedicated op.36, containing *Der zürnenden Diana* (D707). Another famous singer whom Schubert met that spring was the popular and much loved Sofie Müller. Extracts from her diary tell of frequent visits by Schubert and Vogl to her home in Hietzing, a district which includes the Schönbrunn estate. She herself sang many of his songs, including *Die junge Nonne* (D828) on 3 March 1825, soon after it was composed.

Anna Milder-Hauptmann wrote from Berlin on 8 March and quickly dispelled any hopes Schubert may have had that his opera would be done there. It is evident, reading between the lines, that she had hoped for an opera with a big leading role for herself and had looked upon Schubert as a possible provider of congenial show-pieces. At her concert in Berlin on 9 June she included *Erlkönig* and the second Suleika song (D717). The *Berlinische Zeitung* commented appreciatively on the music, and Anna sent the cutting to Schubert, then on holiday in Gmunden. In both Berlin and Dresden, Viennese correspondents reported favourably on his songs. The publications in Vienna during 1825 make an impressive list, both in quantity and in quality. They include, besides such songs as *An Schwager Kronos*, *Ganymed* (both op.19, D369, 544) and *Die junge Nonne* (op.43, D828), the C major Mass (op.48, D452) and the A♭ variations for piano duet (op.35, D813). Quite as interesting is the variety of publishers. Schubert still had no dealings with Diabelli; the works issued by that firm had been acquired before the break in 1823. But Cappi & Co., Sauer & Leidesdorf and Pennauer published his work and before the end of the year Artaria was negotiating with him.

In spring 1825, the fine Piano Sonata in A minor (D845) was composed; but a potentially even finer one in C, known as the 'Reliquie' (D840) was left unfinished. We may regret this the more deeply since the magnificent first movement is accordingly little known. Some of the songs from Scott's *The Lady of the Lake* were composed that month, in a translation by P. Adam Storck; Schubert hoped that the addition of Scott's original text, when the songs were published, would help to make his name known in England.

Towards the end of May he left Vienna for a holiday with Vogl in Upper Austria; the summers of 1824 and 1825 thus parallel the summers of 1818 and 1819. He spent over four months in this district, a supremely happy period in his life; everywhere he found new friends and old admirers of his songs and piano pieces. To facilitate reference, it may be well to list his movements during the period:

Steyr (20 May–4 June; there was a short visit to Linz during this period); Gmunden (4 June–15 July; including a visit to Ebenzweier); Linz (15–25 July; a visit to Steyregg); Steyr (25 July–13 August); Gastein (14 August–4 September; via Werfen and Lake Traun); Gmunden (10–17 September); Steyr (17 September–1 October); Linz to Vienna (1–3 October).

According to a letter of 19 July to Spaun from Anton Ottenwalt, Schubert's host at Linz, the composer 'worked at a symphony at Gmunden'. This is the first mention of the supposedly lost work of 1825, called the 'Gastein' or 'Gmunden–Gastein' Symphony (D849). Interpretations of the documents vary, but certainly a symphony was sketched (Reed, 1972, believed that the work was practically completed), and the sketches probably became the Symphony in C (D944). There is no evidence, however, to connect the 'Gastein' Symphony with the Grand Duo of 1824.

The songs of *The Lady of the Lake*, particularly *Ellens Gesang III* (popularly known as *Ave Maria* D839), frequently featured in the song recitals which Schubert and Vogl gave for their friends that summer. The performance of these two men, playing and singing as if they were one, was something new and unheard of, and they had tremendous success (so Schubert wrote to his brother Ferdinand in September). His letters to his family are long and interesting, coloured as they were by his journeyings through this lovely region, and by the warmth of his reception at the hands of people who were strangers, but who looked upon him, because of his music, as a valued friend. He wrote to his parents on 25 July:

In Upper Austria I find my compositions everywhere, especially at the monasteries of Florian and Kremsmünster, where with the aid of a gallant pianist I produced my four-hand variations and marches with notable success. What pleased especially were the variations in my new sonata for two hands, which I performed alone and not without merit, since several people assured me that the keys became singing voices under my hands.

At Gastein he finished another piano sonata in D (D850), a work full of the overflowing romanticism so typical of that summer; we find it again in two magnificent songs to words by Pyrker, composed in August: *Das Heimweh* (D851) and *Die Allmacht* (D852), Schubert's rapturous creation in music of the summer beauty of the landscape about him, which had so fortified him in spirit and body during these months.

On 3 October Schubert arrived in Vienna, accompanied by Gahy. He found awaiting him not only Bauernfeld and Schwind, but also Schober, returned from Breslau, and Kupelwieser from Italy. Schober quickly assumed his old place in the centre of the stage, and Bauernfeld recorded in his diary that the reunion led to celebrations in inns and coffee houses, often until 2 or 3 a.m. An acknowledgment of Schubert's growing reputation that year is the fact that his portrait was on sale in December at the house of Cappi & Co. An 'extremely good likeness', the firm called it; it is an engraving by J. H. Passini of the best-known portrait, the watercolour by Wilhelm Rieder made from sketches in May 1825 (fig.6).

In January of the following year, Schubert produced the last of his settings of Goethe, the Songs from *Wilhelm Meister* (D877). All are to lyrics of Mignon which he had set before, but which he now supplemented with more mature if not necessarily more endearing settings. The following month the String Quartet in D minor (D810) was performed at the residence of Josef Barth; it was published posthumously in 1831. The publication, early in 1826, of the A minor Piano Sonata (D845) as op.42 by Pennauer widely established Schubert's status as a composer for the piano; there were favourable notices in Leipzig (1 March) and Frankfurt (26 August). The Zurich publisher Hans Nägeli mentioned Schubert in a series of lectures, purely as a piano composer; he also wrote to

Carl Czerny on 18 June saying that the A minor Sonata was a 'capital piece' and asking him to invite Schubert to contribute to a projected series of piano works by contemporary composers. On 4 July Schubert accepted the invitation, but did nothing further in the matter – unless it is to Nägeli's offer that we owe the composition of the Sonata in G major (D894) in the following October.

The publications of the year are more numerous and impressive than those of 1825, and among his publishers Artaria and Thaddeus Weigl make their appearance. The former published the *Lady of the Lake* songs (op.52), the D major Sonata (op.53, D850) dedicated to the pianist Karl von Bocklet, and the *Divertissement à l'hongroise* (op.54, D818). Weigl, in addition to songs, published as op.63 no.1 a Divertissement for piano duet on supposedly French motifs (D823); Schubert intended this to be the first part of a three-section work, the other two parts being an *Andantino varié* and a *Rondeau brillant*. These two, through a mistake, were published as op.84, and the work has remained in this dismembered state ever since. Op.51, from Diabelli in August, contains the favourite *Marche militaire* (D733). On 12 August Schubert wrote to Breitkopf & Härtel and to H. A. Probst, offering to the two Leipzig firms songs and instrumental pieces. Both replied courteously, but there the matter ended. On 7 April 1826, Schubert petitioned the emperor to be appointed as vice-director of the imperial court chapel; it was a move clearly directed by financial need, but equally clearly he genuinely wanted the post and was disappointed when he heard of his failure to secure it.

Bauernfeld spent the summer in Carinthia, and at Villach he wrote *Der Graf von Gleichen* as a libretto for

Schubert. Once again we are faced with the extraordinary inability of the composer to assess the merit of
opera texts: *Der Graf von Gleichen* (D918) is a lifeless
hotch-potch of stock stage situations with, moreover, a
bigamous marriage as the central theme. It was
prohibited by the censor, but Schubert continued to
make sketches, often in considerable detail, for the
music. Spaun had returned to Vienna during April and
resumed his friendly relations with Schubert; we see the
two friends at a new haunt, the inn Zum grünen Anker,
near St Stephen's Cathedral. To the composer's closer
acquaintance with the poet Johann Seidl we owe a group
of songs including *Das Zügenglöcklein* (D871) and the
Vier Refrainlieder (D866) and two vocal quartets,
Nachthelle and *Grab und Mond* (D892–3). There was
also a fine series of songs in 1826 to poems by Ernst
Schulze, among them *Über Wildemann* (D884) and the
ever fresh *Im Frühling* (D882). During July, while staying at the Schober house in Währing, he composed the
three Shakespeare songs (the German versions were cast
in the original metre, and neither Shakespeare nor
Schubert needs to be modified when the songs are sung
in English). The well-known story of Schubert's composing *Hark, hark the lark* on the back of a menu card,
where a resourceful friend had pencilled staves to
accommodate his sudden inspiration, derives from
Doppler and is fictional, as are most of his reminiscences of Schubert. If other familiar Schubert anec-
dotes are missing from these pages, it is because of
similar dubious provenance.

His last String Quartet, in G (D887), was finished on
30 June. He had written to Bauernfeld the previous
month: 'I am not working at all'; when the period of
inactivity passed it was followed by a burst of creation,

7. *Schubert Abend bei Joseph von Spaun: sepia drawing by Moritz von Schwind; Schubert is at the piano, with Vogl on his right, and Spaun on his left*

and the quartet was begun and finished in ten days. In spite of the publications of this year, he had no money for a holiday; a journey with Vogl was out of the question: the aging singer had married on 26 June. Kupelwieser, too, married that year, on 17 September. Schubert improvised dance music during the wedding celebrations; we read that he would not let anyone else go near the piano. A curious sequel to the wedding ceremony has come to light. One of the waltzes he improvised (AI/14) was remembered by the bride, Johanna Lutz. It was handed down in the family, and successive descendants of Johanna learnt the waltz-tune by ear. Eventually, in 1943, it was heard by Richard Strauss, who wrote it down and arranged it for piano.

For a short time in autumn 1826 Schubert lodged with Schober, but at the end of the year was again in rooms of his own. There is an almost day-to-day account of his doings during December in Franz von Hartmann's diary. He was surrounded by his friends, able to meet them at the Zum grünen Anker or Bogner's café, where more often than not they heard the chimes at midnight. There were Schubertiads at Schober's home or at Spaun's, culminating in the imposing event of 15 December. Here, in Spaun's house, a large and distinguished company gathered and heard Vogl, during the course of the evening, sing about 30 songs (Schwind's famous sepia drawing of 1868 was inspired by this concert; see fig.7). On 2 December the overture to *Alfonso und Estrella* was performed at the Kärntnertor-Theater; the performance was reported in the London *Harmonicon* the following June (1827).

9. Period of 'Winterreise'

Schubert and his friends met in 1827 at the inn Zum Schloss Eisenstadt, but he felt himself bound by no social obligations. Schwind, Sonnleithner, Ottenwalt and even Schober suffered from his neglect, and the Hartmann brothers recorded that in March Schubert invited them to his rooms at Schober's but never put in an appearance. A hostess, writing to a friend in June, said: '[Schubert] was most amiable and talkative, but escaped suddenly before anyone had an inkling'. Engrossment in the work of composition was frequently the cause of this non-compliance, though not always. According to Bauernfeld, he would fail to keep engagements if an evening walk or the chance of a sociable gathering with his friends tempted him to do so. He heard in January of his failure to secure the court chapel appointment. The successful applicant was Josef Weigl; Schubert's comment was generous: 'Much as I would have liked to receive the appointment, I shall have to make the best of the matter, since it was given to so worthy a man as Weigl'. The first part of the song cycle *Winterreise* (D911) was composed in February. The poems are by the author of *Die schöne Müllerin* and there is no need for the evidence in letters and memoirs by his friends to make us realize how eagerly Schubert seized this renewed opportunity to treat Müller's picturesque and limpid verses. Soon after the composition of these songs he rejoined Schober, who had moved into a new house, 'Unter den Tuchlauben'. In March of that year, Beethoven, ill and near to death, may have been given some of Schubert's songs to read while on his deathbed. The story is told by Anton Schindler, who related that among the songs were such masterpieces as *Die junge Nonne*, *Die Allmacht* and *Grenzen der Menschheit*, besides the lyrics of *Die schöne Müllerin*. He was impressed by the songs and, if we are to believe the untrustworthy Schindler, said: 'Truly in Schubert there is a divine spark'. Schubert, in the company of the Hüttenbrenner brothers and other friends, visited the dying Beethoven on 19 March, and for the first and last time the two men, who had lived for years as strangers in the same city, met for a brief moment. A week later Beethoven died and was buried in the Währing cemetery. Schubert was one of 36 torch-bearers in the funeral procession.

He resumed negotiations with Diabelli in spring 1827 and the firm published the Mignon songs of 1826 (D877) as op.62 on 2 March. Together with the re-appearance of this old name in the list of his publishers is a new one, that of Tobias Haslinger, who published several sets of songs, the *Valses nobles* (op.77, D969; 22 January) and the G major Sonata (op.78, D894; 11 April), dedicated to Spaun. Haslinger gave op.78 the spurious title 'Fantasie, Andante, Menuetto und Allegretto'; the name 'Fantasy' has ever since haunted the work, one of Schubert's noblest essays for the piano.

The Viennese press continued to report on performances of his songs and to review his publications, but there was in 1827 a remarkable and widespread increase in similar reports and reviews in the provincial press of Germany in Frankfurt, Leipzig, Berlin, Mainz and Munich. Not all were favourable, but those that were spoke of the composer with high praise. The Leipzig *Musikalische Zeitung* (26 December) devoted nearly

8. *Title-page of the 'Gesänge aus Wilhelm Meister von Göthe'* D877, *published by Diabelli on 2 March 1827*

2000 words to a discussion of op.78; the criticism is still readable and convincing. The numerous press notices belie the 19th-century view of Schubert as a composer with a tragically limited reputation; but their isolation from the context of contemporary documentation produces an equally false view of his fame in Austria and Germany. Its shallowness is proved by the decades of neglect and oblivion which followed his death.

Schubert spent a few weeks in the early summer, possibly with Schober, in the village of Dornbach; he stayed at the inn Zur Kaiserin von Österreich. Vienna was within easy reach, and there were occasional convivial evenings at Zum Schloss Eisenstadt. The only composition known to belong to the period is the lovely *Das Lied im Grünen* (D917), written in June, but probably some of the short piano pieces, later published as 'Impromptus', were also composed then. His election as a representative to the Vienna Gesellschaft der Musikfreunde was made that month, his own city honouring him as Linz and Graz had already done. An opportunity to visit the latter town in the coming autumn arose through his friendship with Johann Baptist Jenger, which dated from 1825. Jenger was a prominent member of the Styrian Music Society; he and Schubert were invited to spend a few weeks in the home of Dr and Frau Pachler at Graz. Schubert wrote to this lady on 12 June: 'I cannot forbear to accept an invitation whereby I shall not only set eyes at last on much vaunted Graz, but have the privilege, moreover, of making your honour's acquaintance'. The first performance of *Ständchen* (D920), to Grillparzer's words, was given by Anna Fröhlich's pupils on 11 August at Döbling. The occasion was the birthday of one of the pupils, Louise Gosmar, who later married Leopold von Sonnleithner. Anna received the poem from Grillparzer and asked Schubert to set it to music. He did so, for contralto solo and male-voice chorus; the mistake was pointed out to him and he quickly rewrote the chorus parts for female voices. The performance, in the garden of the Gosmar residence on that summer evening, would no doubt have delighted the composer, had he troubled to attend it. The new haunt that summer was the inn called Zum Wolf, der den Gänsen predigt; Schwind's and Bauernfeld's names are missing from the records of the meetings. Both were out of touch with Schubert that year; in fact, Schwind left in August for a visit to Munich, and Bauernfeld wrote in his diary:

'What is to become of us all? Shall we stick together?'.

Schubert and Jenger arrived in Graz on 3 September. Their hostess, Marie Pachler, was an accomplished woman, an excellent pianist, who had known Beethoven. She sought to entertain at her home in Graz any notable artist who was visiting the town. The days were spent in excursions to various places in the lovely neighbourhood of Graz, including the castle of Wildbach. Anselm Hüttenbrenner was an old friend, of course, and he, Jenger and Schubert were responsible for the Schubertiads held in the evenings. Schubert's famous nickname of the period, 'Schwammerl', Viennese dialect for 'little mushroom', is an allusion to his diminutive stature, not to his stoutness (which was denied by Spaun); it may still explain, perhaps, why he preferred to improvise dance music for his friends rather than to dance himself. The dances he composed that holiday were published as the *Grazer Galopp* (D925) and the *Grazer Walzer* (op.91, D924). The two songs of the month, *Heimliches Lieben* (D922) and Herder's translation of the Scottish ballad *Edward* (D923), were both composed at the instigation of Frau Pachler, to whom Schubert dedicated op.106, which contains *An Sylvia* (D891) and settings of the poet Leitner (a personal friend of the Pachlers). Later in the year, their small son, Faust, received from Schubert a *Kindermarsch* for piano duet (D928).

The return to Vienna came on 20 September; in his letter of thanks to Frau Pachler, Schubert wrote of his happiness at Graz, and of his difficulty in settling down to life in Vienna. He was, in fact, in poor health, suffering from severe headaches and frequent suffusions of blood to the head. Both Spaun and Mayrhofer wrote of his depression and drawn looks during October, but they were misguided in associating them with the composition of the concluding songs of *Winterreise*. The sombre depths of these songs are the response of his genius to the moods of Müller's verses, not a reflection of his own sufferings. When Schubert sang the *Winterreise* songs to his friends they were nonplussed, and Schober confessed to liking only *Der Lindenbaum*. His preference is illuminating: he cared only for the straightforward, melodious side of Schubert's art, and almost quarrelled with Spaun, earlier in the year, after expressing his dislike of the sonatas opp.42 and 53 (D845 and 850). When Vogl, however, familiarized the friends with *Winterreise*, it was as Schubert had confidently foretold. Their indifference changed to keen admiration. The exact date of composition of the Piano Trio no.1 in B♭ (D898) is not known; it was probably early in 1828. The second, in E♭ (D929), was begun in November 1827. The latter was first performed on 26 December 1827, by Bocklet, Schuppanzigh and Linke. Many years after his death several of Schubert's friends alleged that he had used a Swedish tune in the work; although accounts differ, the tale may have some foundation.

Most of the short piano pieces published under the titles *Impromptus* and *Momens musicals* (sic), as opp.90 and 142, and op.94 respectively, were composed in the autumn of that year. They were in the tradition of Tomášek's similar short lyrics, the 'Eclogues' and 'Dithyrambs', but Schubert owed little to Tomášek; nor has the influence of his own piano pieces of this kind been as great as simplifying historians have claimed. Two pieces from the *Moments musicaux*, D780 nos.3 and 6, belong to earlier years, the first to 1823 and the second to 1824. The last work of 1827 was the Fantasy in C for piano and violin (D934), published in 1850 as op.159. Like the Rondo in B minor of 1826 (D895), for the same combination, it was designed for and played by the Bohemian violinist Josef Slavík. During the course of the Fantasy the song *Sei mir gegrüsst* is used as the basis for virtuoso variations which are not among Schubert's most successful essays in this genre.

10. The last year

The remarkable accomplishments of the year 1828 give to Schubert's death an overwhelmingly tragic aspect. His health was broken, and the feverish rate of production of these unparalleled 11 months before his death undoubtedly exhausted him. The work of 1828 is the *ne plus ultra* of his achievement. At the beginning of the year, and for the last time, his friends were all with him; even Mayrhofer was reconciled and made a brief appearance. The Schubertian circle has occasioned surprised comment on its predominantly non-musical character, but the musicians of that circle were so much less remarkable and articulate than the others that Schubert's quiet friendships with Gahy, Jenger, Lachner and the Hüttenbrenners tend to be overlooked. Under Schober's influence, the reading circles came into existence again, and there in January Schubert made the acquaintance of Heine's *Reisebilder*. Spaun was engaged on 6 January to Franziska Röner; at an evening concert on 28 January to celebrate the occasion – the last Schubertiad to be held at Spaun's house – the B♭ Trio was played by Bocklet, Schuppanzigh and Linke. The marriage took place on 14 April. Schubert's last letter to Anselm Hüttenbrenner, written on 18 January, asks for Anselm's good offices to procure for his brother Karl an appointment as drawing master in the training-school at Graz. He also inquired about two of his songs (*Im Walde* D834 and *Auf der Bruck* D853) which were being lithographed for publication at Graz by Josef Kreiner. They appeared the following May as op.90

(*recte* op.93). In January there were two public performances of his works: Slavík and Bocklet played the C major Fantasy on 20 January, and four days later, under the auspices of the Gesellschaft der Musikfreunde, the Grillparzer *Ständchen* was given; Schubert was present this time and remarked afterwards to Anna Fröhlich: 'Really, I never thought it was so beautiful'. The plan to give a full-scale public concert consisting solely of his own works, which had been maturing so long in his mind (the first mention of it had been in 1823) was put into effect at the end of March. The use of a room in the house Zum roten Igel, belonging to the Gesellschaft, was petitioned and granted, and on the evening of 26 March the concert was given to a packed and fervently partisan audience. The compositions and their performers were as follows:

1. First movement of a string quartet [? in G]: Böhm, Holz, Weiss and Linke;
2. Songs, *Der Kreuzzug* (D932), *Die Sterne* (D939), *Fischerweise* (D881), *Fragment aus dem Aeschylus* (D450): Vogl, accompanied by Schubert;
3. *Ständchen* (D920*b*): Josefine Fröhlich and her sister's pupils from the conservatory;
4. Trio in E♭ (D929): Bocklet, Böhm and Linke;
5. *Auf dem Strom* (D943): Ludwig Tietze, with horn obbligato by Josef Lewy;
6. *Die Allmacht* (D852): Vogl and Schubert;
7. *Schlachtlied* (D912): double chorus for male voices.

The event was called 'Franz Schubert's Invitation Concert', and it may be seen from the Deutsch numbers that nearly all the compositions were late ones. The programme gave no key for the string quartet but called it 'new'; the song with horn obbligato was written for the occasion. The concert received hardly a line in the press; it was eclipsed by the advent of Paganini. The great virtuoso threw Vienna into a frenzy greater than that which attended the advent of Rossini a dozen years earlier. Schubert, for a while prosperous (the concert had brought him 320 florins), went to hear Paganini in April and again in May, when he took Bauernfeld.

The 'Great' C major Symphony – probably, as we have seen, the work sketched at Gmunden in 1825 – was finished by March. It is likely that it was finalized for performance by the Gesellschaft der Musikfreunde; Schubert rarely composed without a performance of some sort in mind. The society, it is said, found the work too difficult, whereupon Schubert offered the earlier C major Symphony, no.6 of 1817–18. The manuscript of his last symphony, which came eventually into the possession of the Gesellschaft, shows more signs of revision than is usual in Schubert's fair copies, and all the alterations tend to give greater melodic significance to the work.

A more modest but likable work of the same month is his setting of Grillparzer's *Mirjams Siegesgesang* (D942), for soprano solo and chorus with piano accompaniment; it must originally have been intended for his concert (hence the piano rather than orchestral accompaniment). The repeated requests of his publishers for short and not too difficult piano works, coupled with his desire to find a market in Germany, may be the reason why he produced so many such pieces that year. In April the magnificent F minor Fantasy for piano duet (D940) was finished; it is the only work which he dedicated to the young Countess Caroline Esterházy (tradition has it that he once declared to her that such dedications were unnecessary, since all his work was dedicated to her). Two other piano duets are the sonata movement in A minor (D947), a superb essay, published as op.144 in 1840 and given the absurd, catchpenny title of *Lebensstürme*, and the very attractive Rondo in A (D951), finished in June and published as op.107 in December 1828. The *Drei Klavierstücke* (D946) were composed in the same year, but not published until 1868.

The few publications of 1828 were chiefly songs. Haslinger published the first part of *Winterreise* (D911) as op.89 on 14 January; the second part, beginning with *Die Post*, appeared in December after Schubert's death. Diabelli published on 14 March, as opp.85 and 86, settings of Andrew MacDonald's *Lied der Anne Lyle* (?1825, D830) and of Walter Scott's *Gesang der Norna* from *The Pirate* (1825, D831) and *Romanze des Richard Löwenherz* from *Ivanhoe* (?1826, D907). On 13 August Weigl announced the publication of *Vier Refrainlieder* (op.95, D866) as a new departure for Schubert: the composer in comic vein (though it is difficult to see how no.2, *Bei dir allein*, fits into this scheme). The *Moments musicaux* were published by Leidesdorf (11 July; op.94, D780).

Both in Berlin (25 June) and Munich (28 July) the *Winterreise* songs received lukewarm comment. Berlin was a stronghold of reaction where songs were concerned: it is a little difficult to see exactly what type of song they considered the 'true German song', but Schubert's did not come into that category and the Berlin journal was derisive in tone. Earlier that year a similar attitude had been adopted towards op.83 (D902), Schubert's three Italian songs dedicated to Luigi Lablache. But as usual the Leipzig *Musikalische Zeitung* was generous in its praise. Johann Rochlitz, the journal's founder, was very favourably disposed towards

Schubert, and had written to him on 7 November 1827 proposing his poem *Der erste Ton* as deserving of the composer's attention (it had already been set by Weber); his suggested treatment aroused no response in Schubert. Other letters from distinguished acquaintances, all expressing sincere pleasure in his work, reached the composer in 1828 and must have given him great satisfaction. Johann Schickh, who as editor of the *Wiener Zeitschrift* had initiated a series of song supplements with *Die Forelle* in 1821, wrote on 3 April, in the name of a number of admirers, urging Schubert to repeat his concert. Johann Mosewius, an opera singer and, in 1828, a lecturer in music at Breslau University, sent a glowing appreciation of the songs on 4 June. Later in the month, Karl Brüggemann, a publisher at Halberstadt, asked very deferentially for piano pieces. A letter which would have been of more interest to us than any of these was unfortunately never sent to him: it was written by Robert Schumann, then a boy of 18.

A bulky correspondence survives from 1828 between Schubert and two publishers, H. A. Probst of Leipzig and B. Schott of Mainz. Schubert was clearly doing his utmost to obtain recognition outside Vienna; the steady decline during these last two years in the amount and variety of work issued by the Viennese publishers showed that the market for his music needed some outside stimulus. By a strange coincidence, both publishers wrote to him on the same day, 9 February. Schott asked for piano compositions or songs, pointing out that the firm had an establishment in Paris and publications would be made known there too. Probst, who had already met Schubert in spring 1827, wrote a more personal letter, suggesting that it would be easy 'to disseminate your name throughout the rest of Germany and in the north, in which I will gladly lend a hand, considering talent like yours'. He replied to Schott on 21 February offering chamber music, impromptus and partsongs; eight days later the publisher expressed interest in several of these works. On 10 April Schubert, elated by the success of his concert, wrote again to both firms. To Schott he offered the E♭ Trio for 100 gulden, the second set of impromptus and a five-part chorus, *Mondenschein* (D875), for 60 gulden each; the same offer was made to Probst, except that the trio was unpriced and the other two works were not specified by name, although the same price was asked for each. It is exasperating to see the subsequent sharp practice of the two publishers, so offhandedly generous in their introductory letters. Schott, for example, accepted the smaller works for 60 gulden (the two); Probst accepted the trio for 60 gulden. The negotiations with Schott came to nothing; the Paris establishment rejected the impromptus as too difficult, and Schubert refused to sell *Mondenschein* for 30 gulden. Under protest, he accepted Probst's offer for the trio, and his two subsequent letters to the publisher (of 10 May and 1 August) are worth quoting:

The cuts indicated in the last movement are to be most scrupulously observed. Be sure to have it performed for the first time by capable people, and most particularly see to a continual uniformity of tempo at the changes of time signature in the last movement. The minuet at a moderate pace and *piano* throughout, the trio, on the other hand, vigorous, except where *p* and *pp* are marked.

The second letter was in reply to Probst's requests for the opus number and a dedication:

The opus number of the trio is 100 . . . This work is to be dedicated to nobody, save those who find pleasure in it. That is the most profitable dedication.

There was no holiday that year; ailing and wretched as he was, a few weeks outside Vienna would have been a godsend. But he had no money. Ferdinand Traweger, his former host at Gmunden, wrote on 19 May offering him a room and board at a nominal price; there was an invitation from Frau Pachler to spend the summer at Graz. Both had to be refused. Jenger, declining the second invitation in his friend's name, mentioned to Frau Pachler that Schubert was 'working diligently at a new mass'. This was the setting in E♭, begun in June (D950). Other church works were composed during the year, all rather superficial in expression and of no great moment. 13 songs of the group known as *Schwanengesang* (D957) were composed in August. The first seven are to poems by Rellstab; there follow six settings of poems by Heine, which Schubert had encountered at the reading circle. Another song, *Die Taubenpost* (D965*a*), with words by Seidl and composed in October, was added by the publisher. *Schwanengesang* is a rich and masterly epilogue to the long series of his songs: whether purely lyrical as in Rellstab's *Ständchen*, or creating unheard-of atmospheric effects as in *Die Stadt* or *Der Doppelgänger*, Schubert's hand was never more sure nor more powerful.

At the beginning of September he went to live with Ferdinand in the Neue Wieden suburb (the street is known today as the Kettenbrückengasse). His doctor, Ernst Rinna, hoped that his health would benefit from the semi-rural surroundings. He was suffering from acute headaches and giddiness. Unfortunately, the house was damp and unsanitary; far from having the desired beneficial effect, the move hastened the end. The last three sonatas, in C minor, A and B♭ (D958–60), were completed by 26 September; Schubert played from them the next day at the house of Dr Ignaz Menz. He had intended to dedicate them to Hummel, but when Diabelli published them, in 1838, Hummel was dead and they were dedicated to Schumann. His last instrumental work was the Quintet in C for strings (D956), using an extra cello rather than the more common extra viola and thus allowing of a more sonorous effect. The work may be ascribed to autumn 1828, since in a letter to Probst of 2 October Schubert mentioned the sonatas and the Heine songs, and went on to say that he had 'finally turned out' a quintet. As with the songs of *Schwanengesang*, the last instrumental works have a splendour in which there is no sign of decline; no sinking glow as of autumn or sunset lights these vigorous masterpieces. The song with clarinet obbligato *Der Hirt auf dem Felsen* (D965) was composed in October for Anna Milder-Hauptmann and sent to her the following year by Ferdinand. Either this or *Die Taubenpost* is the last song he wrote. Early in October he went on a three-day walking tour with Ferdinand and two acquaintances into Lower Austria, and on as far as Eisenstadt where Haydn was buried. It is doubtful whether, in Schubert's exhausted condition, the excursion was of any value. A cordial letter from Schindler, who was living in Pest, reached him on his return, inviting him to attend the first performance of Lachner's opera *Die Burgschaft* and suggesting that while at Pest he could give a concert of his songs. But by then any such visit was out of the question.

As the month of November drew to a close, Schubert's condition weakened. It used to be thought that his terminal illness was typhoid, known on the Continent as 'typhus abdominalis'; but it now seems beyond doubt (see Sams, 1980) that syphilis, from which

Schubert had suffered since 1822, was the cause of death. Signs of serious deterioration appeared on 31 October, when at the tavern Zum roten Kreuz he tried to eat fish and was nauseated by it. From then until he finally took to his bed he ate nothing. On 4 November he arranged to take lessons in counterpoint from Simon Sechter; whether he had lessons or not is uncertain, but a batch of his exercises was discovered in Vienna in 1969; they had been written for Sechter. A week later he was too ill to leave his room; on 12 November he wrote to Schober: 'I am ill. I have eaten nothing for 11 days and drunk nothing, and I totter feebly and shakily from my chair to my bed and back again. Rinna is treating me. If ever I take anything I bring it up again at once'.

His last occupation was the correction of the proofs of part 2 of *Winterreise*. On 16 November there was a consultation at his sick-bed between two doctors. Josef von Vering and Johann Wisgrill, Rinna himself being ill. There were now professional nurses in attendance, but Ferdinand gave him ceaseless care and Schubert's small stepsister, Josefa, was devotedly attentive to his needs. Randhartinger and Spaun visited him during those days, but Schober, for whatever reason, kept away. His last visitors were Bauernfeld, and Lachner who had returned from Pest. He was delirious, but during a lucid interval talked of Bauernfeld's *Graf von Gleichen*. On Tuesday, 18 November, the delirium persisted; Ferdinand recorded his brother's broken sayings, but no significance can be attached to them. He died the following day, 19 November, at 3 p.m., turning from Ferdinand with the words: 'Here, here is my end'.

The funeral took place two days later. Schubert's body was borne from the Neue Wieden by a group of

9. Schubert's death mask

young students and laid in St Joseph's Church in the Margareten suburb. A chorus based on the 1817 song *Pax vobiscum* (D551), to new words by Schober, was sung. The interment was in the Währing cemetery, Ferdinand having interpreted Schubert's deathbed utterances as his desire to lie near the body of

Beethoven; the graves of the two composers are separated by three others.

In the valuation of his property an item labelled 'some old music' was priced at 10 gulden. This does not refer to his manuscripts, most of which were still with Schober, but to various items of printed music. His effects, as a whole, were assessed at 63 gulden. The expenses of his illness and funeral, and his debts, were together far more than the estimates usually given, amounting in fact to nearly 1000 gulden. All were discharged by the following June through posthumous publication fees.

His death was a blow, not only to his family, but also to his friends and acquaintances; they expressed their grief in diaries and letters. Memorial poems were written by Bauernfeld, Mayrhofer, Baron Schlechta and by many obscure admirers. On 23 December a memorial service was held at St Augustine's Church, at which a requiem by Anselm Hüttenbrenner was sung. A number of his friends, under the guidance of Grillparzer, Jenger and Schober, collected money to erect a monument for him; part of the fund came from a concert given by Anna Fröhlich, on 30 January 1829, at the Musikverein. It included Schubert's *Mirjams Siegesgesang* and the E♭ Trio, and also the first finale from Mozart's *Don Giovanni*. The monument, with Josef Dialer's bust of Schubert in bronze, was erected in the autumn of 1830 and inscribed with Grillparzer's epitaph: 'Die Tonkunst begrub hier einen reichen Besitz, aber noch viel schönere Hoffnungen' ('The art of music here entombed a rich possession, but even fairer hopes').

11. Posthumous publication

The wealth of unpublished work left at Schubert's death eventually came into the possession of Ferdinand, who made unremitting efforts to secure its publication. On 29 November he offered to Diabelli & Co. (later Spina & Co.) a large quantity of manuscripts comprising 'all the songs for solo voice with piano accompaniment', piano music (solo and duet) and chamber works. The offer was accepted. The songs appeared between 1830 and 1851 in 50 instalments under the general title 'Nachgelassene musikalische Dichtungen' (often abbreviated to 'Nachlass'). The masterpieces of chamber music lay unheeded on Diabelli's shelves until the 1850s: the String Quartet in G (D887) appeared as op.161 in 1851; the first three movements of the Octet (D803) as op.166 in 1853; the String Quintet in C (D956) as op.163 in 1853. Diabelli's bulk purchase still left Ferdinand with nearly all his brother's operas, symphonies and masses; the works not in his possession were *Alfonso und Estrella* (the original at Graz, the copy with Anna Milder-Hauptmann in Berlin) and the B minor Symphony in Anselm Hüttenbrenner's possession at Graz. In 1835, he appealed to Schumann, as editor of the *Neue Zeitschrift für Musik*, and on 26 April a paragraph appeared in that journal giving a list of the works available to publishers. There was no immediate result, but a few years later, when Schumann went to Vienna, he visited Ferdinand (on New Year's Day, 1837) and saw the piles of manuscripts for himself. The outcome of this famous visit was a performance, in a heavily cut version, of the 'Great' C major Symphony at the Leipzig Gewandhaus, under Mendelssohn, on 21 March 1839. The Leipzig firm of Breitkopf & Härtel published the work (parts, 1840; score, 1849), paying Ferdinand 180 gulden for it. Projected performances of the symphony in Paris under Habeneck (1842) and in London under Mendelssohn (1844) were brought to nothing by the blank refusal of orchestral players to master its difficulties at rehearsals. There are no records extant of a supposed first performance at Windsor by the private orchestra of Prince Albert. The publication of a complete edition of his works was inspired by the great Schubertian Nicolaus Dumba and carried out by Breitkopf & Härtel between 1884 and 1897. Their Kritisch durchgesehene Gesamtausgabe contained 39 volumes in 21 series, the last a supplementary volume. The operas, the early symphonies, over 200 songs and the smaller, unpublished piano and choral works appeared in print for the first time in three volumes. The editorial commentaries contain all Schubert's sketches then available for instrumental and vocal music; of outstanding interest are those for the 'Unfinished' Symphony of October 1822. In June 1967 the Internationale Schubert-Gesellschaft was founded in Tübingen, with the chief object of preparing the Neue Schubert-Ausgabe, a complete and authentic edition of the composer's work, to be published by Bärenreiter. Like the original Gesamtausgabe of 1884–97, it consists of series of classified works, eight in all, the last (entitled 'Supplement') including fundamental bibliographical works such as O. E. Deutsch's documentary biography and the thematic catalogue. The first volumes appeared in the late 1960s. The Neue

Schubert-Ausgabe has been in the care of a group of
senior editors, including Walther Dürr, Arnold Feil and
Christa Landon, and many Schubert scholars are also
responsible for the production.

12. Posthumous performance

Schubert's fame as a songwriter was high in Austria and Germany, and it soon spread to France and England; for many years it seemed as if it were to be the only reputation allowed him. One recalls Spaun's words to Bauernfeld in 1839: 'For all the admiration I have given the dear departed for years, I still feel that we shall never make a Mozart or a Haydn of him in instrumental and church compositions, whereas in song he is unsurpassed'. This was an opinion which, happily, Spaun abandoned as the years passed and he grew more and more familiar with the instrumental masterpieces as they were published. There were occasional performances of the choral and chamber works in Vienna, chamber music in Berlin (the E♭ Piano Trio D929 and the 'Trout' Quintet D667) and in Paris (the B♭ Piano Trio D898). Schumann was indefatigable in his praise and propaganda for works for which he had a preference, such as the 'Great' C major Symphony or the Piano Trio in E♭; but even he was strangely unresponsive to the three fine sonatas of 1828, dedicated to him on publication, indeed almost flippant about them. The operas were ignored; the performances of *Alfonso und Estrella* under Liszt at Weimar (24 January 1854) and of *Die Verschworenen* at Frankfurt am Main on 29 August 1861 were travesties, although the latter opera was well received and reviewed. Not until the impact of the Johann Hellmesberger chamber concerts in Vienna in the 1860s, when the Octet and several string quartets were given, and of the performance of the 'Unfinished' Symphony, through Johann Herbeck's enthusiasm, in Vienna in 1865, was the musical world of mid-19th-century Europe forced to the conclusion that in Schubert there was an instrumental master of the front rank. The impression was of slow and by no means unopposed growth; even as late as the 1920s it was possible for a critic to write of the 'dreary passage-work' of the 'Great' C major Symphony. The new respect for Schubert in the 20th century is in part due to the realization that Beethoven's way with sonata form is not the only, Heaven-ordained way, and with that realization Schubert need no longer be considered as a mere offshoot from his great contemporary. It was not until broadcasting extended the orchestral repertory that Schubert's first six symphonies ever reached performance after their initial hearing: they began to be played during the 1930s and no.5, in B♭, quickly became popular. The sonatas were slower in making their way into public esteem. Artur Schnabel's attitude towards, and his performance of, these works proved to be a revelation. Nowadays the last of the sonatas, in B♭ (D960), is frequently played and has taken its place with the foremost examples of the Classical sonata. His operas still await discovery, and thus need to be discussed in more detail.

13. Music for the theatre

The failure of Schubert's operas to hold the stage, or even to win a hearing, is usually attributed to his librettos. Except for *Die Verschworenen*, these are somewhat pedestrian affairs, and their plots are complicated, often requiring elaborate stage machinery. Schubert matched these plays with music which is mainly of secondary value, though frequently, particularly in the later work, thoroughly characteristic. There is endless resource, and an astounding assurance in his balance of stage mood and movement against the development of his orchestral themes. As we proceed from *Des Teufels Lustschloss* (D84) to the final operas, there is the clear evolution of his own operatic style: the music grows in colour, fluidity and scope. It is unlike the evolution in his songs or instrumental work; it belongs entirely to this unknown sphere of his music. There is an extended use, for example, of richly accompanied recitative, which is quite his own; figuration grows more complex and weaves between voice and orchestra, as in the duets for Florinda and Maragond (*Fierabras*, no.9), or for Alfonso and Estrella (no.12), in a manner quite unlike anything in the songs. The exordia and ritornellos, negligible in early work, achieve the same individuality and importance as in the late songs, until in *Fierabras* there is a movingly sensitive moment where an A major passage, heralding the scene between King Karl and his daughter Emma, is beautifully modified in the orchestra when Fierabras enters and gazes in enraptured silence on the princess.

His handling of the orchestra, competent in *Lustschloss*, grows in skill and boldness until it has the true Schubertian quality, known chiefly from the *Rosamunde* music and the last two symphonies, a quality which was no 'clairvoyant' visitation but the outcome of his endless experimentation and exploration of possibility in the operas. Unlike the orchestra of his early symphonies, which was ordained by college or domestic resources, the orchestra of his operas acknowledged no limitations; he scored for full woodwind and from the first used three trombones. There is much 'nature' music in the operas: winds, storms, floods, birdsong, night and morning scenes, and in all of them the orchestral painting is vivid. *Alfonso* opens in the morning, before daybreak: soft shakes on flute and strings, with phrases on the oboe, depict the scene deliciously. One of the loveliest passages in the whole of his operas closes Act 1 of *Fierabras*: it is night, and Emma appears on a lighted balcony, while Eginhard serenades her from below. The whole of the music is fragrant with the atmosphere of this night in a garden of Spain, with the clarinet breathing its love-song above the plucked strings.

The device, so well known from his songs, whereby a striking word is translated into apt musical figuration for his accompaniments is found in the operas too. For example, the word 'schleiche' ('creep') in Olivia's aria (no.4) from *Die Freunde von Salamanka* (D326) is depicted by a slow chromatic rise and fall in the strings, ostinato, a vivid musical suggestion of slow footsteps. To come upon this aria in going through the early operas is like coming upon *Gretchen* among the early songs; it is the first appearance of the authentic voice amid efficient mediocrity. Mayrhofer drew Schubert to finer issues and this two-act Singspiel is full of interesting work; there is even a *Winterreise*-like pathos in the D minor duet for Olivia and Alonso (no.14).

Adrast, also by Mayrhofer, was not finished; of all the dramatic works before 1821 this is the finest. Noteworthy points of orchestration are the use of two cellos to accompany Croesus's air (no.2) and the use of four trombones in the following chorus. Accompanied recitative, characteristically rich in harmonic nuance, pervades the work. *Die Zwillingsbrüder* (D647) and *Die Zauberharfe* (D644) can be seen as transitional works, between the fruitful experimental work of the earlier operas and the individual fulfilment of the later ones. The benefit to Schubert, in the development and perfecting of his own orchestral style, brought about by the particular nature of the libretto of *Die Zauberharfe*, has already been touched upon. The Romance in the Act 2 finale (no.9, 'Was belebt die schöne Welt?') is a marvellously beautiful aria, which should not be allowed to remain in obscurity; it would grace any orchestral concert and repay an enterprising singer. Both works have worthy overtures: the second is famous as the '*Rosamunde* overture', and the other, which uses a theme appearing in the String Quartet in G minor (D173), also deserves revival.

Alfonso und Estrella was said to be Schubert's favourite opera; its period, 1821–2, is sufficient guarantee of its consistently good level, and many of its numbers rise above even that. The music associated with Adolfo, the conventional villain, is the best, his impassioned aria in E♭ minor (Act 2, D732 no.8*b*) being one of the finest things in the work. One intriguing fact connected with this opera is that six years later Schubert, perhaps unconsciously, took over the melody of Troila's song at the opening of Act 2, 'Das Lied vom Wolkenmädchen' (no.11), as no.19 of *Winterreise* (*Täuschung*). The words of Troila's song clearly show the link:

> Er folgte ihrer Stimme Rufen
> und stieg den rauhen Pfad hinan.
> Sie tanzte über Felsen-stufen
> durch dunkle Schlünde leicht ihm vor.

The words of *Täuschung* which provoked this reminiscence are:

> Ein Licht tanzt freundlich vor mir her
> Ich folg' ihm nach die Kreuz und Quer.

The one-act Singspiel *Die Verschworenen* (D787) is dramatically effective, with music that subtly reflects the atmosphere of this cynical text (based on Aristophanes' *Lysistrata*). A group of ladies, tired of their husbands' insatiable appetite for war-mongering, vow to withhold from them all matrimonial rights until they promise to abandon their exploits. The intrigue, the breaking of vows and the final resolution of the problem are all excellently wrought by the author, Castelli, and Schubert's music is tuneful, witty and colourful as occasion demands. The sad little Romance of Helene (no.2), the ensemble where Udolin tells the knights of their wives' vow (a delicious finger-to-lip quality in this passage), the puzzlement of the ladies (symbolized by a sinuous melody on the violins), and the vivacious play on 'für dich' and 'für mich' in the parallel arias for the Count and Countess – all these warrant an occasional performance of this sparkling operetta.

In *Fierabras*, there is little negligible work: page after page reveals the greater Schubert. One or two of the fine things in the opera have been mentioned. Others are the unaccompanied chorus 'O teures Vaterland' (no.14), also used in the overture, and the outstanding arias for Fierabras (no.6*b*) and Florinda (no.13), both of which could find a place in the concert repertory.

His last finished work for the stage, the celebrated *Rosamunde*, is mainly instrumental; had it been otherwise, the feeble libretto would have entombed it, excellent though the music is. The melodies of these ballets and entr'actes, and their poetic orchestration, so completely individual, are additional revelations of the Schubert of the B minor Symphony. Together these works herald the first period of his maturity which culminated in *Winterreise*. One point requires comment. Examination of the score of the B♭ entr'acte (D797 no.5) shows that the interlude in B♭ minor was drawn from an early song, *Der Leidende* (D432*a*), written as early as May 1816. By some strange chance, the first entr'acte, in B minor, one of the composer's masterpieces, seems to have disappeared from the concert room (Abraham suggested in 1971 that this was the original finale of the 'Unfinished' Symphony, as we have seen).

14. Church and other choral music

All Schubert's choral works, both sacred and secular, were written within a closely defined tradition of practical music-making. There was thus little place for innovation, and the established norms were not conducive to masterpieces. But the works were popular in every sense. The partsongs were frequently performed by friends; several were published in Schubert's lifetime. When in 1826 he applied for a post at the court chapel he testified that he had written five masses, all of which had been performed in various Vienna churches; one (D452) had already been published. In these genres Schubert was often content to satisfy demand, and his writing is accordingly sometimes routine, even perfunctory. But when his interest is aroused and his emotions are engaged, great music can result.

His partsongs begin in 1813 with male-voice trios (TTB). In 1815–16 these gradually give way to quartets (TTBB), and for the next ten years he composed only quartets or quintets, with an increasing use of women's voices. Most are *a cappella* or with unobtrusive piano accompaniment, though other instruments may be added for expressive effect or local colour, e.g. horns in *Nacht-gesang im Walde* (D913). The first tenor usually predominates; the idiom is mainly harmonic with little or no counterpoint. Impetus is maintained by bold key-change and emphatic rhythms. The settings, as in the typical example mentioned, are mainly of poems depicting feelings of solitude or invigoration aroused by Nature, which is imagined as embodying the moods of the poet.

The supreme example is the setting of Goethe's *Gesang der Geister über den Wassern* (D714*b*) for double male voice chorus and lower strings; here the poetic fusion of pictorial and philosophical aspects, concrete and abstract together, is masterfully matched in music. Elsewhere it is more often the element of experimentation that elevates the style into such peaks of achievement as *Nur wer die Sehnsucht kennt* (D656), *Ruhe, schönstes Gluck der Erde* (D657), *Nachthelle* (D892) and *Grab und Mond* (D893). The Grillparzer setting *Ständchen* (D920), though perhaps overlong for its iterative thematic material, deserves special mention for its melodic charm and motivic scene- and mood-painting. Here the partsong form comes closest to the more characteristically Schubertian style of the solo lied, while such quasi-dramatic effects as the assembly and dispersal of a serenading chorus recall his most evocative operatic writing.

The sacred music more rarely arouses any such immediate feelings of presence or participation. Schubert's brother Ignaz was a notorious freethinker. The composer himself was highly heterodox; a letter to him from Ferdinand Walcher in January 1827 begins with a musical quotation above the words 'Credo in unum Deum' and continues 'You don't, as I very well know'. Further, Schubert went so far as to omit, from all of his masses, the words 'et in unam sanctam catholicam ecclesiam'. It is hardly surprising then that the church music can be plainly unconvincing, as in the harmonic clichés and conventional melodies of the *Hymnus an den heiligen Geist* (D948). Other works equally uninspired have enjoyed an abiding popularity, such as the vernacular *Deutsche Messe* (D872), eight separate religious songs for the intervals between the stages of the Office. Even in the Masses, some of which attain great heights of grandeur

and passion, there is much reliance on traditional for-
mulae, especially in the four early settings (D105, 167, 324
and 452). The Credo texts tend to be disposed of in brisk,
business-like sequences that sound like stock responses.
The Kyrie is typically in ternary form; the Gloria is
vigorously rhythmic, usually with a fugal treatment at
'Cum sancto spiritu'; the Benedictus employs solo voices;
and so on. As in the partsongs, which developed in
parallel with the liturgical settings, the texture is mainly
homophonic and the music is kept going by bold harmonic shifts rather than by contrapuntal procedures. But
the liturgical music too is often much redeemed by grace
of melody, as in the Mass in G (D167). And whenever the
words of the Mass take on a special meaning for the more
mature Schubert, the music attains a new spiritual stature,
as in the A♭ and E♭ Masses. Predictably, his response
remains essentially humanist. 'Crucifixus' and Agnus Dei
inhabit the everyday world of the suffering flesh; even the
'Et incarnatus' offers the human tenderness of the
Bethlehem story rather than any special sense of transcen-
dental mystery. But in the A♭ Mass (D678) in particular
the harmonies add a new grandeur to the 'Et incarnatus'
and a new poignancy to the 'Crucifixus' which suggest
that the sacred and the secular strains in Schubert could
have achieved a masterly synthesis. The late E♭ Mass
(D950), though arguably lacking in the universal qualities
that make the great Bach and Beethoven masses acts of
worship as well as works of art, is nevertheless rich in the
new sensibilities, both intellectual and emotive, that had
been stimulated and released by the composition of
Winterreise.

An earlier fusion of sacred and secular had informed
such fine works as the *Stabat mater* (D383) and the setting
for women's voices of Psalm xxiii (D706); and these

same qualities appear in the masterly Easter cantata *Lazarus* (D689). Most of Schubert's other essays in this form were occasional pieces composed for the purpose of honouring various individuals, and performed on an anniversary. These works, though rarely without their moments of attraction, are for the most part negligible. *Lazarus*, composed in 1820 but left unfinished, is in a quite different category. In 1863 the manuscript came into the hands of Brahms, who was deeply impressed; but despite his advocacy and that of other Schubertians the work still remains all but unknown, no doubt because of its unusual form. It consists mainly of richly accompanied lyrical recitatives for the six solo voices, a framework within which the formal aria is not a break or a contrast but a heightening of the musico-dramatic progress. Much of the music is characterized by devices found in the songs and ballads of this period, e.g. a deliberate restriction of the harmony to diatonic chords, and long-flighted melodies within which a short lyrical pattern is repeated. The orchestra has brief modulating figures flexibly used to emphasize the meaning of the words, to interconnect contrasting sentiments and to underscore powerful climaxes, in ways clearly evocative of the Wagnerian music-drama. The embellished recitative accompaniments of this unique work expand Schubert's song-writing techniques into those used in the non-lyrical sections of the operas, that is, those parts of the text where, by dialogue or ensemble, the action of the plot is urged forward. In *Lazarus* the long recitatives that precede and follow each of the four arias embody the best of Schubert's achievement in this style; only the greatest passages in *Alfonso und Estrella* and *Fierabras* surpass them in power and beauty.

15. Songs

One of the reasons for the abiding popularity of Schubert's songs is simple: whatever other elements may or may not be present, the primary essential, the melodic element, or (to put it plainly) an attractive and singable tune, is rarely absent. A second and deeper reason for their appeal is that they are firmly grounded, in idiom and procedure, in the 'Viennese symphonic' period of music, say from 1770 to 1830. One has only to think of such songs as *Halt!* from *Die schöne Müllerin* (D795 no.3), *Auf dem Flusse* from *Winterreise* (D911 no.7), or *Der Zwerg* (D771), with their exposition and development of thematic fragments, to realize that as long as this period remains the most congenial to a large number of listeners, so will his songs with it.

From the first the Schubert song was practically without ancestry; even before *Gretchen am Spinnrade* he was writing passages which have no precedent. Songs there certainly were before his, and in his youth he modelled his own efforts on those of men such as Zumsteeg and Zelter. Many of Beethoven's and Mozart's songs, considered as music, are equal to his own earlier efforts. The miracle he achieved was to match with a reality of music poetry whose depths of human emotion would have appeared to the older composers as rendering it unsuitable for song. Two factors are said to have helped Schubert: the late 18th-century outburst of lyric poetry, whose outstanding exponent is Goethe; and the establishment of the piano accompaniment with its inexhaustible possibilities of picturesque comment. These factors are trifling compared with the power of his genius: otherwise one might ask why Beethoven and Weber, to whom these two possibilities were equally available, composed no masterpieces of song comparable to Schubert's.

The songs, more than 600, fall into four main groups: the simple strophic song in which each verse is sung to the same music; the modified-strophic song in which his endless variety defies classification (examples are *Lachen und Weinen*, D777 and *Das Zügenglöcklein* D871); the *durchkomponiert* (through-composed) song in which various melodies and interpolated recitatives are welded together by the same, basically unchanging accompaniment, like *Die junge Nonne* (D828) and *Auflösung* (D807); and finally the 'scena' type of song, such as *Der Wanderer* (D489) or *Kriegers Ahnung* (D957 no.2), containing separate episodes of different tempo and mood, of which his own scena, Käthe's aria from *Der vierjährige Posten* (D190 no.5), may be cited as a prototype. The poets range from Goethe, Schiller and Heine at one end of the scale to versifying friends like Mayrhofer and Schober at the other. This catholic choice is sometimes taken to indicate that Schubert had no literary taste; when he chose to set a poem to music, however, he did so not to show his literary judgment but because of its musical possibilities. The ready and sympathetic audience of the Schubertiads must not be overlooked in this connection. Schubert obviously favoured the poem with a 'bite' in the last stanza, even in the last line; as for instance in *Erlkönig*, *Der Wanderer* and *Der Doppelgänger*. The way in which he absorbed the quality of a poem and produced an analogous quality in music can best be appreciated when one turns the pages of his poets – of Goethe or Heine, for example. The swift lyricism and movement of the one, the pith and imagery of the other, are perfectly paralleled in the music.

The refinement of later composers in their attention to the poet's text, and in their balance of interest between voice and piano, is instinctive, but not unconscious, with Schubert. His lyric and harmonic vitality and his spontaneous reaction to the stimulus of the poet's emotional or visual appeal give an almost abandoned quality to the music he poured out. Sometimes, as in *An Schwager Kronos* (D369), the result is overpoweringly convincing; elsewhere, as in *Die Gebüsche* (D646) or in *Fülle der Liebe* (D854), the result is less happy. But always there is the firm grasp of the essential. Schubert's periphery may sweep beyond, or not quite reach out to, that of the poet, but it always encircles the same central point. One perceives it in that quality of his famous songs which can only be called 'atmosphere'. The very first bars of *Im Abendrot* (D799), *An die Musik* (D547) or *Nacht und Träume* (D827) take us to the heart of the poem. Nor need the atmosphere be one of abstraction or rapture: the lighthearted *An die Laute* (D905), or the comfortable *Der Einsame* (D800), illustrate the point equally well.

Schubert's melodies, particularly in his songs, are the most individual and revealing of all the factors in his work. Of infinite variety and grace, they have a quality of pathos, of direct appeal to the listener, which is a reflection of the sweetness and sensitivity of his own nature. They are often based on a juxtaposition of tonic and dominant chords as in *Wohin?* (D795 no.2) and *Der greise Kopf* (D911 no.14). The phrase built on a falling dominant 7th is associated in his mind with weariness or grief, so it is used in *Wandrers Nachtlied* (D224) and in the first of the Harper's Songs (D478). The little figure sung at the start of *Frühlingsglaube* (D686) appears repeatedly in his songs whenever blissful contemplation of nature engrosses both poet and composer. The use of sequence is discreet and flexible, as is shown in *Ungeduld* (D795 no.7) and *An Sylvia* (D891); in the latter song the sequential treatment of the opening phrase is exquisite.

The most familiar characteristic of Schubert's harmony is his passing from minor mode to major and, less frequently, from major to minor; the change may be smooth or abrupt, but it always represents an emotional change. Another characteristic, equally important but insufficiently noticed, is his use of the Neapolitan 6th and relationships based upon it. A third is his fondness for passing, with little or no preparation, into the key a major 3rd below his tonic, as for instance in *Nacht und Träume* (D827; B major to G major). An awareness of these three fundamental processes gives an insight into the masterly way in which he handles his harmonic material, for example in the song *Stimme der Liebe* (D412). This flexible use of harmonic changes had its direct influence on his melody and modulation, but the processes were reversible: melody and modulation affected his harmonic spectrum. In addition to these personal harmonic characteristics, Schubert took over from the normal harmony of his day the augmented 6th (in both the 'German' and 'French' forms) and the diminished 7th, using both chords frequently and often with the most poetic effects: consider the use of the diminished 7th in its form C–E♭–F♯–A throughout the song *Die Stadt* (D957 no.11). Arpeggios based on the chord softly sweep the keyboard to depict Heine's 'feuchter Windzug' and are tenuously resolved at the end of the song by a single held *C* in the bass.

Schubert's accompaniments are celebrated for their graphic reinforcement of the inner meaning of the poem or of the external details of the poet's scene. He seems inexhaustible in contriving graceful pianistic figures to illustrate moving or glinting water or the shimmer of stars. Again and again he devised in his accompaniments a music which derives from both aspects of the poem and achieves thereby a powerful synthesis of which the poetry alone is incapable – the ranging arpeggios of *Auflösung* (D807) or the heartbreak in the gusty diminished 7ths of *Die Stadt* (D957) demonstrate such powers. The preludes of his songs can be remarkably apt: the most beautifully poised entry in them all is in *Ganymed* (D544); how the opening bars depict the glory and contentment of morning! The introductory chords of Goethe's *An den Mond* (D296) cloud the A♭ tonality and prepare the listener for the 'Nebelglanz' of the poet's address to the moon. But the last word has not been said about the Schubert song when its melody, accompaniment, atmosphere – all the beautiful externals of his music – have been surveyed. There yet remains the ineffable quality of textual illumination to which purpose all these factors are bent. Consider Heine's *Der Doppelgänger* (D957 no.13). 'The night is still', says the poet, 'the streets are deserted', but there needs no ghost to remind him of his anguish on 'so many nights long ago'. Schubert set the opening words to a falling B minor phrase, low in the compass of the voice; the final agony is implicit in this phrase, and it rings out at the end in a florid version an octave higher. Similar examples abound in the mature songs. There is the way in which the pure diatonic harmony at the start of *Du bist die Ruh* (D776) is tinged with colour as the poet turns from

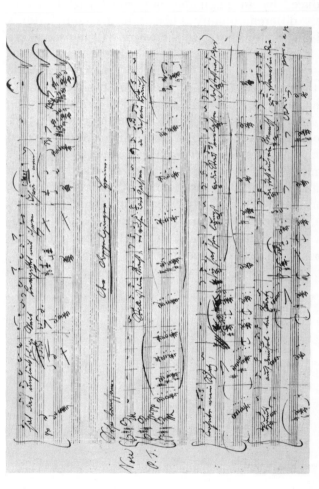

10. Autograph MS of the end of 'Am Meer' and the beginning of 'Der Doppelgänger' from book 2 of Schubert's 'Schwanengesang', composed August 1828

'du bist' to 'ich weihe'. The high opening phrase of *An die Entfernte* (D765) poses a question, 'Have I lost thee?', introduced by an enigmatic diminished 7th; it has an entirely different quality when it recurs later, after a decisive C major chord, to the words 'All my songs cry unto thee'. The refinement by which the main key of *Dass sie hier gewesen* (D775) is held back to coincide with the main statement of each stanza is well known, but this device is just as notably used in *Gruppe aus dem Tartarus* (D583), in which the whole discordant opening prepares for C major and the awesome word 'Eternity', and in *Grenzen der Menschheit* (D716), where the main key of the song is reserved for the declaration of Man's humility. On songs such as these his fame rests; but his stature is as surely revealed in innumerable tiny songs, page-long creations, few without touches of sublimity where with the most modest means he can encompass greatness in a score of bars.

16. Song cycles

Schubert created and perfected not only the lied form but its further development, the song cycle; here too his masterpieces *Die schöne Müllerin* (D795) and *Winterreise* (D911) were practically without ancestry and have never been surpassed. Again this music grew from the German poetic renaissance, this time the original work of Wilhelm Müller in the form of the narrative lyrical sequence. Though there is no direct evidence, it seems likely that Schubert was familiar with Beethoven's *An die ferne Geliebte* (Vienna, 1816), a set of love-lyrics composed in continuous cyclic form, essentially an extended song beginning and ending with the same music. Schubert wrote a masterpiece of this new genre also, in his *Viola* (D786, 1823). But his musical treatment of Müller's versified story eschews all such overt structural devices. The poetry's naive but effective realism, with its depiction of simple and powerful human emotions mirrored in external nature, also includes elements of dramatic conflict, even character study, which seized Schubert's imagination more strongly and held it more consistently than any of his opera librettos. The cycle of poems had been written under the influence of Goethe, and contains much of his scenic and dramatic quality that had already so inspired Schubert in the solo song. Indeed, the verses had begun as a form of domestic literary charade or playlet, and the five-part publication of Schubert's musical setting was not an arbitrary subdivision but a deliberate attempt to present the work in five small 'acts': I, the arrival at the mill (songs 1–4); II, the falling in love (5–9); III, brief happiness (10–12); IV, jealousy and despair (13–17); and V, resignation and death (17–20). As a complement to this objective approach, the composer's own state of mind was perhaps especially receptive to the idea of youthful passion blighted by tragedy. Schubert found Müller's sequence of 24 poems (four of which were left unset) in the summer of 1823, at the very period when he must have realized that his own recently contracted syphilis was certainly grave and possibly mortal. There is an undocumented but perhaps not unfounded tradition that some of the Mill songs were written in the Vienna general hospital during the time of Schubert's emergency treatment there. Whatever the reason, Müller's poems are given, here and in *Winterreise*, a musical universality and power that they could never have attained unaided. The verses need not be decried on that account. Their many felicities of metre and onomatopoeia, their direct and vivid imagery, their limpid diction and versification, their deep roots in traditional folksong, all help to inspire music of mythopoeic quality (see Reed, 1978) with a strong structure articulated far more by verbal narrative and description than by any manifest musical device. No Schubert songs have ever been so consistently beloved and popular; but their apparent simplicity distracts attention from their exquisitely wrought variety of structure, from strophic verse repetition (as in *Mit dem grünen Lauten-bande*) via added refrain (*Trockne Blumen*) or recitative (*Am Feierabend*) or other modification (*Pause*) to the 'scena' song (*Der Neugierige*) or the wholly through-composed *Eifersucht und Stolz*. In *Die schöne Müllerin* the pastoral sound-language of walking, flowing and flower-ing so well defined by Richard Capell (1928) reaches a new pitch of expressiveness. This cycle dominates the lieder of Schubert's middle years, even though, considered as separate songs, none may be thought to equal the settings of Goethe in 1821 or those of Rückert in 1822–3. Their strength derives from their inseparable unity, which adds a new dimension of sustained drama and narrative to the song form.

In *Winterreise* (D911) of 1827, the whole is even more compellingly greater than its parts. It affords fewer occasions for overt musical characterization or dramatic conflict; the tragic themes of coldness and rejection are less varied than *Die schöne Müllerin*, and so are the modified-strophic song structures. But the identification of nature with human suffering is even more intense, and the central character is even more strongly mythopoeic in its union of three Romantic ideals – the wandering youth, the isolated artist and the unrequited lover. The opening words of Müller's verse-tragedy, 'fremd bin ich eingezogen,/fremd zieh ich wieder aus' ('I arrived here a stranger, a stranger I depart'), are designed from the outset to convey a sense of cosmic significance, to say with King Lear that men must endure their going hence even as their coming hither, and that ripeness is all. Schubert's music again reaches the poet's thought and expresses it far more trenchantly and poignantly than Müller himself; but the expressiveness undoubtedly owes some of its power to the poetry both in general outline and in particular detail. Thus the simple phrase 'Vom Abendrot zu Morgenlicht' (from sunset to dawn) in its context suggests the wider horizons of life and feeling, and inspires a great arching theme that traverses 12 slow beats and nearly two octaves. On a smaller scale, impressive effects are attained by a remarkable simplicity of means, as when the wanderer's climactic cry of 'Oh, were the whole world dark' in *Einsamkeit* is driven home with a steely point in a phrase of just two falling semitones. In such ways the verses, once lifted to the height of the composer's genius, are given new and continuing universality. It seems that Schubert himself was aware of a corresponding development in his creative powers. In the well-documented year of 1827, when the Hartmann brothers for example kept full diaries, Schubert's appearances in the journals and letters of his friends have a ghost-like and unreal quality. He seems so quiet and controlled, almost insignificant, whereas we know that all the time he is striving towards, and urging his powers to reach up to, his vision of the *Winterreise*.

Some of this triumph must be ascribed to pure chance. The song cycle was composed and published in two parts, each of 12 songs. The first part, dated February 1827 (though no doubt begun some weeks earlier), corresponds exactly to the order and text of Müller's poems as published in the Leipzig yearbook *Urania* of 1823. Presumably an old copy had come into Schubert's hands in early 1827. As Capell says, 'one can imagine his joy at the beauty of the chance that had brought him his collaborator back, at the countless fresh images provoked by this poetry of fire and snow, of torrent and ice, of scalding and frozen tears'. The eagerness with which he started composing these songs, and the exhausted state in which their composition left him, show how congenial Müller's verses were to his tastes and gifts. He was indeed evidently overjoyed to find another series of lyrics by the poet of *Die schöne Müllerin*, and he did not spare himself as poem after poem stimulated the creative power within him and extorted musical scene after musical scene from his imagination. Then, in the late summer of the same year, Schubert encountered Müller's complete and final version of the cycle, this time in book form as published in 1824, containing 24 poems; an extra 12 had been interpolated at various points throughout the text. Schubert set these also, with unabated enthusiasm and inspiration. By that time however his first set was already in the publisher's hands; and instead of intercalating the extra songs as Müller had done, Schubert simply added them *en bloc* as a second instalment. As John Reed says, had Schubert discovered Müller's poems in the first place in their final 1824 form, he would no doubt have kept to that order – for reversion to which in performance a cogent case can accordingly be made.

This second song cycle, like the first, dominates the lieder of the period. Further, it heralds a new phase in Schubert's work as a whole, one which he did not live long enough wholly to fulfil. But the music of *Winterreise*, once realized, revealed to the composer newer potentialities in his genius. For the first time in his music we find tragedy, not the wistfulness or luxuriating sadness of previous work but the darkness of the genuine emotion; we find it, numbed, in *Gute Nacht* and *Der Wegweiser*, whose threnodic progressions are related to the slow movements of the 'Great' C major Symphony and the E♭ Trio (D929), despairing and passionate in *Erstarrung* and *Der stürmische Morgen*, whose anguish is found again in the slow movement of the String Quartet (D956). Side by side with this tragic utterance is a profound serenity first voiced in *Der Lindenbaum*, which is so characteristic of his later work, but neither *Im Abendrot* (D799) nor *Du bist die Ruh* (D776) has quite the dream-like quality of the works just cited. Technically his music gained from *Winterreise* a greater harmonic piquancy, a discovery of wider yet subtler uses of Neapolitan relationships, and a newer, one might say a more intellectual, manner with thematic development.

17. Mature instrumental music

The 'Trout' Quintet (D667) is the climax of Schubert's approach to maturity in instrumental music, and the Quartettsatz (D703) begins the last phase in his work here. With the exception of the sketched symphony in E of 1821 (D729), the next eight years produced a series of masterpieces marked by an intense lyricism, a chromatic modulation which, for all its spontaneity, moves within an inherent tonal system, an absorbed attention to textural detail and an imagination which moulds its own formal structures. Academic devices such as fugato, elaborately worked canon or invertible counterpoint, all of which can be found dutifully appearing in his early work, are quickly abandoned; but his treatment of subject matter grows more powerful and attains a poetry and an emotion unknown in the years before 1820. As a typical movement, the Quartettsatz stands fittingly at the start of these years. The key scheme of the exposition shows, for the first time, that tonal structure which Schubert was to find so congenial: the C minor and G major tonalities which bracket the section are fairly orthodox, but they enclose a second-subject stretch in A♭ major. His use of the string quartet medium in which cello and first violin have predominant interest is first seen in this movement, and in the demands which are made on the players Schubert is clearly no longer bound by the limitations of the family quartet (particularly in the case of the cello, which was the task of the modestly equipped Schubert *père*).

The next work of importance is the Symphony in B minor (D759), another unfinished essay. The affinities of the symphony's first movement with that of the quartet are remarkable: in the singing quality, the passionate contrasts and the pathos they are obvious, but two technical points have interest. The first is the withholding of the main theme at the start of the recapitulation, in order to use it with greater force for the coda of the movement; the second is in the choice of key for the second subject. In the case of the 'Unfinished' Symphony this has occasioned much comment, but it has precisely the same relationship with the main key as in the quartet: B minor–G major, C minor–A♭ major; and both are instances of Schubert's favourite shift of a major 3rd downwards.

Between the quartet and the symphony appeared the first important composition for piano, a work of an entirely different character. The 'Wanderer' Fantasy takes its name from the *adagio* section, which is based on a theme from the song *Der Wanderer* (D489), of 1816. It is the first of a series of works in C major which have the epic quality thenceforth associated in his mind with that key, and its massive structure, new to his keyboard writing, is rarely absent from his later compositions for the piano. There is an interesting and deliberate use of cyclic form, one aspect of which derives from the dactylic rhythm of the song theme. This rhythm pervades his mature work and is an indication of the profound impression made upon him by the Allegretto from Beethoven's Seventh Symphony. The three chamber works of 1824, the Octet for wind and strings in F (D803) and the string quartets in A minor (D804) and D minor (D810), have much in common. They were written in the short space of only two months, in February and March 1824. They are full of typical melody; all three contain movements based on themes which Schubert had composed for other media from past days, and this fact seems to reflect his mood. In a letter written at this time to Kupelwieser he spoke of a ray of sunlight from past sweet days; the emotion shades from cheerful good humour to pathos, and occasionally, in the D minor String Quartet, to a shuddering terror. Even the cheerful pages, those in the minuet of the Octet, or the finale of the A minor String Quartet, have that characteristic Schubert patina of near-pathos; he was, unlike Haydn or Beethoven, incapable of pure comedy, of Rosalind's 'holiday mood'.

The six piano sonatas (five for solo and one for duet) which belong to the mid-1820s constitute a unified group. To begin with, the main theme of the first movement is invariably the basis of the development section, with supreme effect in the two A minor sonatas (D784 and D845), in the 'Reliquie' Sonata (D840) and in the G major Sonata (D894). The slow movements, with one exception, are in rondo form, the opening songlike theme alternating with dynamic interludes; an attractive example is the Andante of the duet sonata in C (D812). The exception is the slow movement of the Sonata in A minor (D845), a set of variations on an original theme, one of the most successful of his essays in this genre. It contains a delicate use of those chains of suspensions which he had used to good effect in the song *Versunken* (D715) and which are found again in the slow movement of the 'Great' C major Symphony (D944) and in the C minor Impromptu (D899 no.1). The period closes with two magnificent pieces of chamber music. Of the first movement of the String Quartet in G (D887) it is difficult to write without extravagance: the quintessence

11. Autograph MS of the first page of Schubert's String Quartet in G (D887), composed 20–30 June 1826

of every Schubertian virtue is found in its pages. The slow movement (in E minor, though his manuscript shows that it was originally planned in B minor) contains his most daring harmonic adventure, where violin and viola persistently utter a figure in one key, while the music moves more and more remotely from it (bars 52–6, repeated in bars 131–5). The finale is sometimes alleged to show the influence of Rossini; there is as little justification for this as for the so-called 'Hungarian' influence in the finale of the A minor String Quartet.

The Piano Trio in B♭ (D898) nowhere reaches the heights of the G major Quartet, but its humanity (and hence its popular appeal) is greater. The remark that

Schubert's lyrical subjects are unsuitable for development is refuted by the first movement of this trio, as
indeed it is by the first movement of the G major
Sonata; nothing could be more songlike than these
themes, yet each forms the basis of a superbly con-
structed movement. The instrumentation of the trio is
admirable, particularly in the controlled use of the
piano, which is neither overwhelming nor over-modest
in its partnership with the strings. Its soaring flights in
the finale are among the most picturesque of Schubert's
touches in his chamber music.

Before the next important work, the Piano Trio in E♭
(D929), came the completion of *Winterreise* (D911); and
the significance (already discussed) of that song cycle for
Schubert's development can be seen by comparing the
temper of the E♭ Trio with that of its predecessor. This
closing period is also distinguished by signs that Schubert
was concerning himself with two sections of his
large-scale works which he had hitherto treated somewhat lightheartedly, the trio of the third movement and
the finale. Another feature of these final works comes
from his changed attitude to the development section of
his first movements; no longer invariably based on the
opening theme, as was the case in every one of the works
between the 'Unfinished' Symphony and the B♭ Trio,
they may derive from the introduction (C major Symphony), from subsidiary matter in the exposition (the
Quintet) or even from a codetta phrase (E♭ Trio, A major
Sonata). In the E♭ Trio the much maligned finale deserves
a kindlier, more informed, judgment; as with other
finales, the easy-going start leads on to better and greater
things, and the introduction of the theme from the slow
movement is a superb moment, and for Schubert a unique
one.

We come to what is widely admitted to be his greatest masterpiece, the 'Great' C major Symphony. From any viewpoint the work bears the stamp of greatness, but the chief impression left by a study of it is of tremendous rhythmic vitality. No sketches are extant (this is usually the case with Schubert's finished work) and the manuscript suggests that some of the symphony was composed in full score as fast as the pen could travel. The development section of the first movement displays a remarkable synthesis of elements in the exposition section with the opening bars of the horn theme from the introduction. The Andante con moto can fairly claim to be his loveliest slow movement: in the duet for cellos and oboe, after the big climax; in the soft, repeated notes of the horn (a passage made famous by Schumann's eulogy) which lead to the recapitulation; in the varied string accompaniments to the melody of the A major section: all these have poetry and imagination which he never surpassed and never more ardently expressed. The Scherzo and Finale, the former in full sonata form, have a lively rhythmic energy which sweeps all before it: the first has great lyric beauty, the second a splendour of thematic development. In all four movements the use of the trombones, delicate or authoritative, is perhaps the most notable feature in an orchestration that abounds in felicities.

The last group of works for solo piano consists of eight impromptus, the Three Piano Pieces (D946) and three sonatas. Four of the impromptus (D899) were published as op.90 (nos.1 and 2 in December 1827; no.3, transposed from G♭ to G by the publisher, and no.4 in 1857), and four others (D935) as op.142 by Diabelli in 1839. The Three Piano Pieces appeared in 1868, anonymously edited by Brahms. The 11 pieces are realizations of various moods, dramatic, thoughtful or passionate, and all are supremely lyrical. As the first departure by a major composer from the dominance of the sonata over piano forms, and as the modest fore-runners of the Romantic composers' work in this field, they are historically important apart from their own intrinsic worth. But to rank them more highly and to play them more frequently than the sonatas is a folly of which this age is less guilty than the preceding one. And it is ill-informed to consider them as dismembered sonata movements: not only do they, for all their charm, lack the 'grand style' of his sonatas, but a study of their crude transitional passages is convincing of their lesser stature. Schubert's transitions in his sonatas have the vitality and magic which proclaim the master of the form, as may be seen at once in his last three sonatas. This group closes his long series of piano compositions and fittingly contains his finest work. The level of attain-ment rises in each sonata to the heights in the third, in B♭. In the first movements of all three, the development sections show the features already mentioned; the second subjects are many-sectioned and have pic-turesque codas. The slow movements are like richly accompanied songs; they have deeply tranquil opening and closing sections with a dramatic interlude which, in the A major Sonata, has an astonishing complexity and vigour. There is point and significance in the trios of the scherzos, and in the finales an extensive and admirable development of the main theme of the movement. This is especially fine in the finale of the A major Sonata, whose theme is derived, no doubt unconsciously, from the slow movement of the A minor Sonata of 1817 (D537).

Schubert's last great work was the String Quintet in C (D956). It is filled with magnificent moments: the duet for cellos in the first movement; the richness and intriguing instrumentation of the Adagio; the elegiac trio of the third movement (a true pointer to the future); the wonderful rhythmic variants of the finale theme. His subtler blending of the major and minor modes can be seen in the themes of the first and last movements; who, looking at them in isolation, would dream that movements in major keys are being announced? The whole work, as a study of Neapolitan relationships, is without equal.

WORKS

Editions: *F. Schuberts Werke: kritisch durchgesehene Gesamtausgabe*, ed. E. Mandyczewski, J. Brahms and others (Leipzig, 1884–97/*R*1964–9) [SW, ser./vol., p.]

F. Schubert: Neue Ausgabe sämtlicher Werke, ed. W. Dürr, A. Feil, C. Landon and others (Kassel, 1964–) [NSA, ser./vol., p.]

Items are ordered by D number as enumerated in W. Dürr, A. Feil, C. Landon and others: *Franz Schubert: thematisches Verzeichnis seiner Werke in chronologischer Folge von Otto Erich Deutsch*, Neue Ausgabe Sämtlicher Werke, viii/4 (Kassel, 1978); where, exceptionally, numbers have been changed in this edition, a cross-reference is given. Numbers in parentheses following a title refer to separate settings of the same text.

Numbers in the right-hand column denote references in the text.

77ff

THEATRICAL

D	Title	Genre	Text	Composed	First production	Published	SW: NSA	
11	Der Spiegelritter	Singspiel, 3, only ov. and 1st act complete	A. von Kotzebue	Dec 1811–1812	Swiss Radio, 11 Dec 1949	1893	xxi, 1, xiv/7, 109; ii/11	5
84	Des Teufels Lustschloss version a / version b	opera, 3	Kotzebue	30 Oct 1813–15 May 1814 completed 22 Oct 1814	Vienna, Musikvereinsaal, 12 Dec 1879 (as pubd in 1888)	1888	xv/1; ii/1	6, 77, 78
137	Adrast [see ov., 648]	opera 2, unfinished	J. Mayrhofer	?1817–19	Vienna, Redoutensaal, 13 Dec 1868	1893	xv/7, 317; ii/11	79
190	Der vierjährige Posten	Singspiel, 1	T. Körner	8–19 May 1815	Dresden, 23 Sept 1896	1888	xv/2, 1; ii/2	11, 87
220	Fernando	Singspiel, 1	A. Stadler	27 June–9 July 1815	Vienna, 13 April 1907	1888	xv/2, 111; ii/2	11
239	Claudine von Villa Bella	Singspiel, 3, only ov. and 1st act complete	Goethe	begun 26 July 1815	Vienna, Gemeindehaus Wieden, 26 April 1913	1893	xv/7, 1; ii/12	11
326	Die Freunde von Salamanka	Singspiel, 2	Mayrhofer	18 Nov–31 Dec 1815	Halle, 6 May 1928	1888	xv/2, 171; ii/3	11, 78
435	Die Bürgschaft	opera, 3, 1st and 2nd acts complete	—	begun 2 May 1816	Vienna, 7 March 1908	1893	xv/7, 203; ii/12	
644	Die Zauberharfe	melodrama, 3	G. von Hofmann	1820	Vienna, Theater an der Wien, 19 Aug 1820	1891	xv/4, 1; ii/4, 3	24, 35, 40. 79

D	Title	Forces		Composed		Published	SW;NSA	
647	Die Zwillingsbrüder	Singspiel, 1	Hofmann	Jan 1819	Vienna, Kärntnertor, 14 June 1820	1889	xv/3, 1; ii/5	24, 79
701	Sakuntala	opera, 3, sketches for 1st and 2nd acts only	J. P. Neumann, after Kalidasa	Oct 1820	Vienna, 12 June 1971	—	—; ii/13	
723	Duet and aria for Hérold's Das Zauberglöckchen (La clochette)	—	E. G. M. Théaulon de Lambert, trans. F. Treitsche	spring 1821	Vienna, Kärntnertor, 20 June 1821	1893	xv/7, 365; ii/14	30
732	Alfonso und Estrella	opera, 3	F. von Schober	20 Sept 1821–27 Feb 1822	Weimar, 24 June 1854	1892	xv/5, 1; ii/6	32, 33, 37, 39, 40, 45, 53, 72, 75, 77, 78, 79, 85
787	Die Verschworenen (Der häusliche Krieg)	Singspiel, 1	I. F. Castelli, after Aristophanes: Lysistrata	March–April 1823	Vienna, Musikvereinsaal, 1 March 1861	1889	xv/3, 115; ii/7	37, 75, 80
791	Rüdiger	opera, sketches for nos. 1–2 only	?I. von Mosel	begun May 1823	Vienna, Redoutensaal, 5 Jan 1868	1867	—; ii/14	
796	Fierabras	opera, 3	J. Kupelwieser	25 May–2 Oct 1823	Karlsruhe, 9 Feb 1897	1886	xv/6, 1; ii/8	38, 39, 77, 78, 80, 85
797	Rosamunde, Fürstin von Zypern	incidental music to romantic play, 4	H. von Chézy	autumn 1823	Vienna, Theater an der Wien, 20 Dec 1823	1891	xv/4, 345; ii/9	40, 78, 79, 81
918	Der Graf von Gleichen	opera, 2, sketches only	E. von Bauernfeld	begun 19 June 1827	—	—	—; ii/14	50, 51
966	[see 11]	orch interlude to 11/3, frag.						
981	Der Minnesänger	Singspiel, unfinished, lost						
982	—	opera, sketches, 3 nos. only		after 1820			—; ii/14	

SACRED *82ff*

D	Title	Forces	Composed	Published	SW;NSA
24e	Mass, ?F, frag.	SATB, orch, org	?1812	—	—; i/5
27	Salve regina, F	S, orch, org	28 June 1812	1928	—; i/8
31	Kyrie, d	S, T, SATB, orch, org	25 Sept 1812	1888	xiv, 175; i/5
45	Kyrie, B♭	SATB	1 March 1813	1888	xiv, 226; i/5

D	Title	Forces	Composed	Published	SW; NSA	
49	Kyrie, d	S, A, T, B, SATB, orch	April 1813	1888	xiv, 189; i/5	
56	Sanctus, canon with coda, B♭	3vv	21 April 1813	1892	xix, 89; i/8	
66	Kyrie, F	SATB, orch, org	12 May 1813	1888	xiv, 203; i/5	
71a	Alleluja, F, canon	3vv	?July 1813	1956	—; i/8	
105	Mass no.1, F [see also 185]	S, S, A, T, T, B, SATB, orch, org	17 May–22 July 1814	1856	xiii/1, 1; i/1	8, 10, 84
106	Salve regina, B♭	T, orch, org	28 June–1 July 1814	1888	xiv, 47; i/8	
136	Offertory: Totus in corde langueo, C	S/T, cl/vn, orch, org	?1815	1825, op.46	xiv, 1; i/8	
167	Mass no.2, G	S, T, B, SATB, str, org	2–7 March 1815	1846	xiii/1, 121; i/1	10, 84
175	Stabat mater, g	SATB, orch, org	4–6 April 1815	1888	xiv, 101; i/8	
181	Offertory: Tres sunt, a	SATB, orch, org	10–11 April 1815	1888	xiv, 23; i/8	
184	Gradual: Benedictus es, Domine, C	SATB, orch, org	15–17 April 1815	c1843, op.150	xiv, 29; i/8	
185	Dona nobis pacem, F [alternative movt for 105]	B, SATB, orch, org	25–26 April 1815	1887	xiii/1, 931; i/1	
223	Salve regina (Offertorium), F version a version b	S, orch, org	5 July 1815 28 Jan 1823	— 1825, op.47	—; i/8 xiv, 9; i/8	
324	Mass no.3, B♭	S, A, T, B, SATB, orch, org	begun 11 Nov 1815	c1837, op.141	xiii/1, 157; i/2	10, 84
379	Deutsches Salve regina (Hymne an die heilige Mutter Gottes), F	SATB, org	21 Feb 1816	1859	xiv, 215; i/8	
383	Stabat mater, oratorio, F/f	S, T, B, SATB, orch	begun 28 Feb 1816	1888	xiv, 109; i/7	84
386	Salve regina, B♭	SATB	early 1816	1833	xiv, 224; i/8	
452	Mass no.4, C [see also 961]	S, A, T, B, SATB, orch, org	June–July 1816	1825, op.48	xiii/1, 209; i/2	16, 47, 82, 84
453	Requiem, c, frag.	SATB, orch	July 1816	—	—; i/5	
460	Tantum ergo, C	S, SATB, orch, org	Aug 1816	1888	xiv, 39; i/8	
461	Tantum ergo, C	S, A, T, B, SATB, orch	Aug 1816	1935	—; i/8	
486	Magnificat, C	S, A, T, B, SATB, orch, org	15 Sept 1815	1888	xiv, 77; i/8	
488	Auguste jam coelestium, G	S, T, orch	Oct 1816	1888	xiv, 59; i/8	
607	Evangelium Johannis VI, E	1v, bc	1818	1920	—; i/8	
621	Deutsches Requiem (Deutsche Trauermesse), g	S, A, T, B, SATB, org	Aug 1818	1826	—; i/6	21
676	Salve regina (Offertorium), A	S, str	Nov 1819	1845, op.153	xiv, 17; i/8	
678	Mass no.5, A♭ version a version b	S, A, T, B, SATB, orch, org	Nov 1819–Sept 1822	1875 1887	—; i/3 xiii/2, 1; i/3	24, 34, 84

D	Title	Forces	Text	Composed	Published	SW; NSA	
696	6 antiphons for Palm Sunday: Hosanna filio David; In monte Oliveti; Sanctus, sanctus, sanctus; Pueri hebraeorum; Cum angelis et pueris; Ingrediente Domino	SATB		March 1820	1829, op.113	xiv, 218; i/8	
730	Tantum ergo, B♭	S, A, T, B, SATB, orch, org		16 Aug 1821	1926	—; i/8	
739	Tantum ergo, C	SATB, orch, org		1814	1825, op.45	xiv, 37; i/8	
750	Tantum ergo, D	SATB, orch, org		20 March 1822	1888	xiv, 43; i/8	
755	Kyrie, a, sketch	S, A, T, B, SATB, str, org		May 1822		—; i/5	
811	Salve regina, C	TTBB		April 1824	1850, op.149	xiv, 220; i/8	83
872	Deutsche Messe			late summer 1827		—; i/6	
	version a	SATB, org			1870	xiii/2, 325; i/6	
	version b	SATB, orch, org			1845	xiii/2, 340; i/6	
	Appx: Das Gebet des Herrn					i/6	
950	Mass no.6, E♭	S, A, T, B, SATB, orch		begun June 1828	1865	xiii/2, 167; i/4	67, 84
961	Benedictus, a [alternative movt for 452]	S, A, T, B, SATB, orch, org		Oct 1828	1829	xiii/1, 247; i/2	
962	Tantum ergo, E♭	S, A, T, B, SATB, orch		Oct 1828	1890	xiv, 227, xxi, 269; i/8	
963	Offertory: Intende voci, B♭	T, SATB, orch		Oct 1828	1890	xxi, 277; i/8	
992	[sketches for 383]						

MIXED VOICES

(NSA nos. refer to vol. in series 3 unless otherwise stated)

D	Title	Forces	Text	Composed	Published	SW; NSA
17	Quell' innocente figlio		Metastasio	c1812		—; viii/2
	version 3	S, A, T			1940	
	version 4	S, A, T, B			1940	
	version 5	S, A, T			1940	
	version 6	S, A, T			1940	
	version 7	S, A, T, B				
	version 8	S, A, T, B			1940	
	version 9	S, A, T, B			1940	
33	Entra l'uomo allor che nasce		Metastasio	Sept–Oct 1812		—; viii/2
	version 3	S, A, T				
	version 4	S, A, T, B				
	version 5	S, A, T, B				
	version 6	S, A, T, B				

D	Title	Forces	Text	Composed	Published	SW; NSA	
34	Te solo adoro	S, A, T, B	Metastasio	5 Nov 1812	1940	—; viii/2	
35	Serbate, o dei custodi version 1	S, A, T, B	Metastasio	Oct 1812	1940	—; viii/2	
	version 2	SATB					
47	Dithyrambe (Der Besuch), frag.	T, B, SATB, pf	Schiller	29 March 1813	—	—; ii	
168	Nun lasst uns den Leib begraben (Begräbnislied)	SATB, pf	F. Klopstock	9 March 1815	1872	xvii, 241; ii	
168a	Osterlied [formerly 987]	SATB, pf	Klopstock	9 March 1815	1872	xvii, 244; ii	
232	Hymne an den Unendlichen	SATB, pf	Schiller	11 July 1815	1829, op.112/3	xvii, 167; ii	
294	Namensfeier für Franz Michael Vierthaler (Gratulations Kantate)	S, T, B, STB, orch		27 Sept 1815	1892	xvii, 142; i	
329a	Das Grab (1), sketch	SATB	J. Salis-Seewis	?28 Dec 1815	—	—; ii	
439	An die Sonne	SATB, pf	J. P. Uz	June 1816	1872	xvii, 218; ii	
440	Chor der Engel	SATB	Goethe	June 1816	1839	xvii, 245; ii	
451	Prometheus, cantata, lost	S, B, chorus, orch	P. Dräxler von Carin	17 June 1816	—	—	15, 22
472	Kantate zu Ehren von Josef Spendou	2S, B, SATB, orch	J. Hoheisel	Sept 1816	1830, op.128	xvii, 109; i	
609	Die Geselligkeit (Lebenslust)	SATB, pf	J. K. Unger	Jan 1818	1872	xvii, 225; ii	
642	Viel tausend Sterne prangen	SATB, pf	A. G. Eberhard	?1812	1937	—; ii	
643a	Das Grab (5)	SATB	Salis-Seewis	1819	1972	—; ii	
665	Im traulichen Kreise [part of 609]						
666	Kantate zum Geburtstag des Sängers Johann Michael Vogl (Der Frühlingsmorgen)	STB, pf	A. Stadler	10 Aug 1819	1849, op.158	xix, 37; ii	
689	Lazarus, oder Die Feier der Auferstehung, oratorio, 3, only 1st act and part of 2nd complete	3S, 2T, B, SATB, orch	A. H. Niemeyer	Feb 1820	1865	xvii, 1; ii/10	11, 24, 85
748	Am Geburtstag des Kaisers, cantata	S, A, T, B, SATB, orch	J. L. F. von Deinhardstein	Jan 1822	1822; 1849 as op. 157	xvii, 138; ii	
763	Des Tages Weihe	SATB, pf	Fouqué	22 Nov 1822	1842, op. 146	xvii, 212; ii	
815	Gebet	SATB, pf	? K. Schnitzer von Meerau	Sept 1824	1840, op.139	xvii, 198; ii	44
826	Der Tanz	SATB, pf		early 1828	1892	xvii, 228; ii	
875a	Die Allmacht (2), sketch	SATB, pf	J. L. Pyrker von Felsö-Eör	Jan 1826	—	—; ii	

D	Title	Forces	Text	Composed	Published	SW; NSA	
920	Ständchen version a [for version b see 'Female or unspecified voices'] [formerly 921]	A, TTBB, pf	Grillparzer	July 1827	1891	xvi, 108; iii	
930	Der Hochzeitsbraten	S, T, B, pf	Schober	Nov 1827	1829, op.104	xix, 14; ii	
936	Kantate für Irene Kiesewetter	2T, 2B, SATB, pf 4 hands	anon. It. text	26 Dec 1827	1892	xvii, 231; ii	63, 71
942	Mirjams Siegesgesang	S, SATB, pf	Grillparzer	March 1828	c1839, op.136	xvii, 170; ii	
953	Der 92. Psalm: Lied für den Sabbath	S, A, T, Bar, B, SATB	Heb. text	July 1828	1841	xvii, 247; ii	
954	Glaube, Hoffnung und Liebe	2T, 2B, SATB, wind insts/pf	F. Reil	Aug 1828	1828	xvii, 152; i, ii	
985	Gott im Ungewitter	SATB, pf	Uz	?1827	1829, op.112/1	xvii, 156; ii	
986	Gott der Weltschöpfer	SATB, pf	Uz	?1827	1829, op.112/2	xvii, 164; ii	
987	Osterlied [see 168a]						

MALE VOICES

(NSA nos. refer to vol. and p. in series 3)

D	Title	Forces	Text	Composed	Published	SW; NSA
37	Die Advokaten [based on a previous setting by Anton Fischer]	TTB, pf	Baron Engelhart	25–27 Dec 1812	1827, op.74	xix, 2; iii
38	Totengräberlied (1)	TTB	L. C. H. Hölty	?1813	1892	xix, 76; iv, 3
43	Dreifach ist der Schritt der Zeit (1)	TTB	Schiller	8 July 1813	1897	xxi, 337; iv, 4
51	Unendliche Freude (1)	TTB	Schiller	15 April 1813	1897	xxi, 330; iv, 8
53	Vorüber die stöhnende Klage	TTB	Schiller	18 April 1813	1892	xix, 61; iv, 10
54	Unendliche Freude (2), canon	BBB/TTB	Schiller	19 April 1813	1873	xix, 78; iv, 12
55	Selig durch die Liebe	TTB	Schiller	21 April 1813	1892	xix, 67; iv, 14
57	Hier streckt der wallende Pilger	TTB	Schiller	29 April 1813	1897	xxi, 331; iv, 15
58	Dessen Fahne Donnerstürme wallte	TTB	Schiller	May 1813	1892	xix, 63; iv, 18
60	Hier umarmen sich getreue Gatten	TTB	Schiller	3 Oct 1813	1892	xix, 65; iv, 33
62	Thronend auf erhabnem Sitz	TTB	Schiller	9 May 1813	1956	xxi, 334; iv, 22
63	Wer die steile Sternenbahn	TTB	Schiller	10 May 1813	1892	xix, 68; iv, 24
64	Majestätsche Sonnenrosse	TTB	Schiller	10 May 1813	1897	xxi, 335; iv, 26
65	Schmerz verzerret ihr Gesicht, canon, sketch	TTB	Schiller	11 May 1813	1892	xix, 94; iv, 180

6

D	Title	Forces	Text	Composed	Published	SW: NSA
67	Frisch atmet des Morgens lebendiger Hauch	TTB	Schiller	15 May 1813	1897	xxi, 335; iv, 27
70	Dreifach ist der Schritt der Zeit ('Ewig still steht die Vergangenheit') (3), canon	TTB	Schiller	8 July 1813	1928	—; iv, 177
71	Die zwei Tugendwege	TTB	Schiller	15 July 1813	1892	xix, 69; iv, 32
75	Trinklied ('Freunde, sammelt euch im Kreise')	B, TTB, pf	F. Schäffer	29 Aug 1813	1850	xvi, 128; iii
80	Zur Namensfeier meines Vaters	TTB, gui	F. Schubert	27 Sept 1813	1892	xix, 48; iii
88	Verschwunden sind die Schmerzen, canon	TTB	Schubert	15 Nov 1813	1892	xix, 77; iv, 35
110	Wer ist gross?	B, TTBB, orch	Hölty	24–5 July 1814	1891	xvi, 205; i
129	Mailied ('Grüner wird die Au') (1)	TTB		c1815	1892	xix, 72; iv, 37
132	Lied beim Rundetanz, 1 part only	? TTB/TTBB	J. von Salis-Seewis	1815 or 1816	1974	—; iv, 177
133	Lied im Freien, 1 part only	? TTB/TTBB	Salis-Seewis	1815 or 1816	1974	—; iv, 178
140	Klage um Ali Bey (1)	TTB, ?pf	M. Claudius	1815	1850	xviii, 32
147	Bardengesang	TTB	Ossian, trans. E. de Harold	20 Jan 1816	1892	xix, 70; iv, 42
148	Trinklied ('Brüder! unser Erdenwallen')	T, TTB, pf	I. F. Castelli	Feb 1815	1830, op.131/2	xix, 59; iii
236	Das Abendrot	TTB, pf	L. Kosegarten	20 July 1815	1892	xix, 57; ii
242	Trinklied im Winter	TTB	Hölty	?Aug 1815	1892	xix, 74; iv, 48
243	Frühlingslied ('Die Luft ist blau') (1)	TTB	Hölty	?Aug 1815	1892	xix, 75; iv, 50
267	Trinklied ('Auf! jeder sei nun froh')	TTBB, pf		25 Aug 1815	1872	xvi, 131; iii
268	Bergknappenlied	TTBB, pf		25 Aug 1815	1872	xvi, 133; iii
269	Das Leben version a [for version b see 'Female or unspecified voices']	TBB, pf	J. C. Wannovius	Aug 1815	—	—; iii
277	Punschlied ('Vier Elemente, innig gesellt')	TTB, pf	Schiller	29 Aug 1815	1892	xix, 58; iii
330	Das Grab (2) version b [for version a see 'Songs']	4 vv, pf	Salis-Seewis	28 Dec 1815	1895	xx/3, 231; iii
331	Der Entfernten (1)	TTBB	Salis-Seewis	c1816	1866	xvi, 194; iv, 56
337	Die Einsiedelei (1)	TTBB	Salis-Seewis	c1816	c1860	xvi, 195; iv, 58

D	Title	Scoring	Text	Composed	Published	References
338	An den Frühling (2)	TTBB	Schiller	c1816	1891	xvi, 196; iv, 60
339	Amors Macht, 1 part only	? TTB/TTBB	F. von Matthisson	1815 or 1816	1974	—; iv, 178
340	Badelied, T2 only	? TTB/TTBB	Matthisson	1815 or 1816	1974	—; iv, 178
341	Sylphen, T2 only	? TTB/TTBB	Matthisson	1815 or 1816	1974	—; iv, 179
356	Trinklied ('Funkelnd im Becher')	TTBB, lost pf acc.		1816	1844	—; iii
364	Fischerlied (2)	TTBB	Salis-Seewis	c1816–17	1897	xxi, 320; iv, 63
377	Das Grab (3)	TTBB, pf	Salis-Seewis	11 Feb 1816	1872	xx/4, 6; iii
387	Die Schlacht (2), sketch	solo vv, chorus, pf	Schiller	March 1816	1897	xxi, 341; ii
407	Beitrag zur fünfzig jährigen Jubelfeier des Herrn Salieri, [no.1 also in version for TTB, see 441]	T, TTBB, pf	Schubert	by 16 June 1816	1891–2	xvi, 211; iii
422	Naturgenuss (2)	TTBB, pf	Matthisson	?1822	1823, op.16/2	xvi, 76; iii
423	Andenken ('Ich denke dein, wenn durch den Hain') (2)	TTB	Matthisson	May 1816	1927	—; iv, 66
424	Erinnerungen ('Am Seegestad') (2)	TTB	Matthisson	May 1816	1927	—; iv, 68
425	Lebensbild, lost	TTB		May 1816		—
426	Trinklied ('Herr Bacchus ist ein braver Mann'), lost	TTB		May 1816		—
427	Trinklied im Mai	TTB	Hölty	May 1816	1892	xix, 73; iv, 70
428	Widerhall ('Auf ewig dein') [= TTB version of 407/1]	TTB, pf	Matthisson	May 1816	1927	—; iv, 73
441	Der Geistertanz (4)	TTBBB	Schubert	by 16 June 1816	1892	xix, 53; iii
494	La pastorella al prato (1)	TTBB, pf	C. Goldoni	Nov 1816	1871	xvi, 173; iv, 77
513	Gesang der Geister über den Wassern (2)	TTBB	Goethe	?1817	1891	xvi, 134; iii
538			Goethe	March 1817	1891	xvi, 175; iv, 81
569	Das Grab (4)	unison vv, pf	Salis-Seewis	June 1817	1895	xx/5, 122; iii
572	Lied im Freien	TTBB	Salis-Seewis	July 1817	1872	xvi, 180; iv, 89
598	Das Dörfchen	TTBB	G. A. Bürger	Dec 1817	1891	xvi, 223; iii
	version a, a sketch	TTBB, pf		1818	1822, op.11/1	xvi, 41; iii
	version b [formerly 641]	TTBB		c1819	1906–7	—; iv, 97
635	Leise, leise lasst uns singen	TTBBB		April 1819	1867	xvi, 185; iv, 98; 83
641	Das Dörfchen [see 598]					
656	Sehnsucht ('Nur wer die Sehnsucht kennt') (4)	TTBB	Goethe	April 1819	1871	xvi, 187; iv, 102; 83
657	Ruhe, schönstes Glück der Erde	TTBB	Goethe		1897	
704	Gesang der Geister über den Wassern [see 714]					
705	Gesang der Geister über den Wassern (3), sketch	TTBB, pf	Goethe	Dec 1820	1897	xxi, 313; iii; 26
709	Frühlingsgesang (1)	TTBB	F. von Schober	before April 1822	1891	xvi, 169; iv, 106

D	Title	Text	Forces	Composed	Published	SW; NSA	
710	Im Gegenwärtigen Vergangenes	Goethe	TTBB, pf	?March 1821	1849	xvi, 119; iii	29, 83
714	Gesang der Geister über den Wassern (4)	Goethe					
	version a, sketch [formerly 704]		TTTTBBBB, 2 va, 2 vc, db	Dec 1820	1891	xvi, 215; i	
	version b		TTTTBBBB, 2 va, 2 vc, db	Feb 1821	1858, op.167	xvi, 24; i	
724	Die Nachtigall	J. K. Unger	TTBB, pf	by April 1821	1822, op.11/2	xvi, 50; iii	
740	Frühlingsgesang (2)	Schober	TTBB, pf	Jan–April 1822	1823, op.16/1	xvi, 65; iii	
747	Geist der Liebe ('Der Abend schleiert Flur und Hain') (2)	Matthisson	TTBB, pf	Jan 1822	1822, op.11/3	xvi, 59; iii	
778b	Ich hab in mich gesogen, sketch	Rückert	TTBB	?1823	1978	—; viii/3	
809	Gondelfahrer (2)	J. Mayrhofer	TTBB, pf	March 1824	1824, op.28	xvi, 83; iii	
822	Lied eines Kriegers	H. Hüttenbrenner	B, unison vv, pf	31 Dec 1824	1842	xx/8, 32; iii	
825	Wehmut		TTBB	before summer 1826	1828, op.64/1	xvi, 141; iv, 121	
825a	Ewige Liebe	E. Schulze	TTBB	before summer 1826	1828, op.64/2	xvi, 144; iv, 126	
825b	Flucht	K. Lappe	TTBB	by early 1825	1828, op.64/3	xvi, 148; iv, 133	
835	Bootgesang	Scott, trans. D. A. Storck	TTBB, pf	1825	1826, op.52/3	xvi, 89; iii	
847	Trinklied aus dem 16. Jahrhundert	F. Gräffer	TTBB	July 1825	1849, op.155	xvi, 29; iv, 139	
848	Nachtmusik	K. S. von Seckendorff	TTBB	July 1825	1849, op.156	xvi, 166; iv, 143	
865	Widerspruch version a [for version b see 'Songs']	J. G. Seidl	TTBB, pf	?1826	1828, op.105/1	xvi, 93; iii	
873a	Nachklänge, sketch		TTBB	?Jan 1826	1974	—; iv, 187	
875	Mondenschein	Schober	TTBBB, pf	Jan 1826	1831, op.102	xvi, 153; iii	
892	Nachthelle	Seidl	T, TTBB, pf	Sept 1826	1839, op.134	xvi, 98; iii	
893	Grab und Mond	Seidl	TTBB	Sept 1826	1827	xvi, 197; iv, 148	66
901	Wein und Liebe	J. C. F. Haug	TTBB	before June 1827	1827	xvi, 190; iv, 150	51, 83
903	Zur guten Nacht	J. F. Rochlitz	Bar, TTBB, pf	Jan 1827	1827, op.81/3	xvi, 91; iii	51, 83
912	Schlachtlied (2)	F. G. Klopstock	TTBB, TTBB	28 Feb 1827	1844, op.151	xvi, 157; iv, 156	
913	Nachgesang im Walde	Seidl	TTBB, 4 hn	April 1827	1846, op.139	xvi, 1; i	62
914	Frühlingslied	A. Pollak	TTBB	April 1827	1897	xxi, 321; iv, 166	82
916	Das stille Lied, sketch		TTBB				
941	Hymnus an den Heiligen Geist [see 948]	J. G. Seegemund	TTBB	May 1827	1978	—; iv, 188, viii/3	

D	Title	Forces	Text	Composed	Published	SW; NSA
948	Hymnus an den Heiligen Geist version a [formerly 941] version b [formerly 964]	2T, 2B, TTBB 2T, 2B, TTBB, wind insts	A. Schmidl	May 1828	1891 1849, op.154	xvi, 199; i/8 xvi, 11; i/8
964	Hymnus an den Heiligen Geist [see 948]					
983	Jünglingswonne	TTBB	Matthisson	?1822	1823, op.17/1	xvi, 137; iv, 112
983a	Liebe	TTBB	Schiller	?1822	1823, op.17/2	xvi, 138; iv, 115
983b	Zum Rundetanz	TTBB	Salis-Seewis	?1822	1823, op.17/3	xvi, 139; iv, 116
983c	Die Nacht	TTBB	? F. W. Krummacher	?1822	1823, op.17/4	xvi, 139; iv, 118
984	Der Wintertag	TTBB, lost pf acc.	?	?	c1865, op.169	—; iii

FEMALE OR UNSPECIFIED VOICES
(NSA nos. refer to vol. and p. in series 3 unless otherwise stated)

D	Title	Forces	Text	Composed	Published	SW; NSA
17	Quell' innocente figlio, version 2	2S	Metastasio	c1812	1940	—; viii/2
33	Entra l'uomo allor che nasce, version 2	S, A	Metastasio	Sept–Oct 1812	1940	—; viii/2
61	Ein jugendlicher Maienschwung	3vv	Schiller	8 May 1813	1897	xxi, 333; iv, 20
69	Dreifach ist der Schritt der Zeit (2)	3vv	Schiller	8 July 1813	1892	xix, 80; iv, 30
130	Der Schnee zerrinnt (1), canon	3vv	Hölty	c1815	1892	xix, 82; iv, 38
131	Lacrimoso son io, canon, 2 versions	3vv		?Aug 1815	1892	xix, 87; iv, 40
169	Trinklied vor der Schlacht	2 unison choruses, pf	T. Körner	12 March 1815	1894	xx/2, 68; iii
170	Schwertlied	1vv, unison chorus, pf	Körner	12 March 1815	1873	xx/2, 78; iii
183	Trinklied ('Ihr Freunde und du gold'ner Wein')	1vv, unison chorus, pf	A. Zettler	12 April 1815	1887	xx/2, 97; iii
189	An die Freude	1vv, unison chorus, pf	Schiller	May 1815	1829, op.111/1	xx/2, 102; iii
199	Mailied ('Grüner wird die Au') (2)	2vv/2 hn	Hölty	24 May 1815	1885	xix, 91; iv, 44
202	Mailied ('Der Schnee zerrinnt') (2)	2vv/2 hn	Hölty	26 May 1815	1885	xix, 91; iv, 44
203	Der Morgenstern (2)	2vv/2 hn	Körner	26 May 1815	1892	xix, 92; iv, 45
204	Jägerlied	2vv/2 hn	Körner	26 May 1815	1892	xix, 92; iv, 46
205	Lützows wilde Jagd	2vv/2 hn	Körner	26 May 1815	1892	xix, 93; iv, 46
244	Willkommen, lieber schöner Mai, canon, 2 versions	3vv	Hölty	?Aug 1815	1892	xix, 85; iv, 51
253	Punschlied: im Norden zu singen	2vv	Schiller	18 Aug 1815	1887	xx/3, 30; iv, 54

D	Title			Composed	Published	SW; NSA	
269	Das Leben version b [for version a see 'Male voices']	Wannovius	SSA, pf	25 Aug 1815	1849	xviii, 31; iii	
357	Gold'ner Schein, canon	Matthisson	3vv	May 1816	1892	xix, 81; iv, 64	
442	Das grosse Halleluja version b [for version a see 'Songs']	Klopstock	chorus, pf	June 1816	c1847	xx/4, 110; iii	
443	Schlachtlied (1) version b [for version a see 'Songs']	Klopstock	chorus, pf	June 1816	1895	xx/4, 112; iii	
521	Jagdlied version b [for version a see 'Songs']	F. Werner	unison vv, pf	Jan 1817	1895	xx/5, 3; iii	
706	Der 23. Psalm	trans. M. Mendelssohn	SSAA, pf	Dec 1820	1832, op.132	xviii, 3; iii	26, 84
757	Gott in der Natur	E. C. von Kleist	SSAA, pf	Aug 1822	1839	xviii, 10; iii	
836	Coronach (Totengesang der Frauen und Mädchen)	Scott, trans. Storck	SSA, pf	1825	1826, op.52/4	xviii, 1; iii	
873	Canon, a. sketch	—	6vv	?Jan 1826	1974	—; iv, 187	57, 62, 67, 83
920	Ständchen [formerly 921] version b [for version a see 'Male voices']	Grillparzer	A, SSAA, pf	July 1827	1840, op.135	xviii, 20; iii	
988	Liebe säuseln die Blätter, canon	Hölty	3vv	?1815	1873	xix, 83; iv, 172	
988a	—	—	pf acc. only	?after 1820	1969	—; iii	

ORCHESTRAL

(NSA nos. refer to vol. and p. in series 5)

D	Title	Composed	Published	SW; NSA	
2a	Overture, D, frag. [formerly 996]	?1811	—	—; iv	
2b	Symphony, D, frag., 1st movt only [formerly 997]	?1811	—	—; iv	
4	Overture D, for Albrecht's comedy Der Teufel als Hydraulicus	?1812	1886	ii, 1; iv	
12	Overture, D	1811 or 1812	1897	xxi, 23; iv	
26	Overture, D	by 26 June 1812	1886	ii, 13; iv	
39a	3 minuets and trios, lost	1813	—	—; v	
71c	Orch frag., D [formerly 966a]	Aug/Sept 1813	—	—; v	
82	Symphony no.1, D	by 28 Oct 1813	1884	i/1, 1; i, 3	6
94a	Orch frag, B♭	c1814	—	—; v	
125	Symphony no.2, B♭	10 Dec 1814–24 March 1815	1884	i/1, 65; i, 71	10
200	Symphony no.3, D	24 May–19 July 1815	1884	i/1, 143; i, 153	10

D	Title	Composed	Published	SW: NSA	
345	Concerto (Concertstück), D, vn, orch	1816	1897	xxi, 46; iv	13
417	Symphony no.4, c, 'Tragic'	by 27 April 1816	1884	i/1, 191; ii	
438	Rondo, A, vn, str	June 1816	1897	xxi, 73; iv	15, 76
470	Overture, Bb [possibly for cantata 472; arr. str qt 601]	Sept 1816	1886	ii, 31; iv	
485	Symphony no.5, Bb	Sept–3 Oct 1816	1885	i/2, 1; ii	18, 63, 102
556	Overture, D	May 1817	1886	ii, 47; iv	18
580	Polonaise, Bb, vn, orch	Sept 1817	1928	—; iv	18
589	Symphony no.6, C	Oct 1817–Feb 1818	1885	i/2, 49; ii	19
590	Overture, D, 'im italienischen Stile' [arr. pf 4 hands, 592]	Nov 1817	1886	ii, 63; iv	21
591	Overture, C, 'im italienischen Stile' [arr. pf 4 hands, 597]	Nov 1817	1865, op.170	ii, 83; iv	
615	Symphony, D, pf sketches for 2 movts	May 1818	—	—; v	
648	Overture, e [possibly for Adrast, 137]	Feb 1819	1886	ii, 101; iv	31
708a	Symphony, D, sketches	after 1820	—	—; v	11, 25, 34, 35, 72, 73, 76, 81, 99, 102
729	Symphony [no.7], E, sketched in score	Aug 1821	1934	—; v	
759	Symphony [no.8], b, 'Unfinished'	Oct 1822	1867	i/2, 239; iii	48
849	'Gmunden–Gastein' Symphony ['?identical with 944]	June–Sept 1825	—	—; v	
936a	Symphony, D, sketches	?mid-1828	1978	—; v	11, 48, 63, 73, 75, 76, 97, 100, 103
944	Symphony [no.8] no.9, C, 'Great'	?1825-8	1840	i/2, 117; iii	
966a	Orch frag, D [see 71c]	1820 or later	—	—; v	
966b	Orch sketches, A, frag.				
996	Overture [see 2a]				
997	Symphony [see 2b]				

CHAMBER

(NSA nos. refer to vol. and p. in series 6 unless otherwise stated)

D	Title	Forces	Composed	Published	SW: NSA	
2c	String Quartet, ?d/F, frag. [formerly 998]	2 vn, va, vc	?1811	1978	—; iii	
2d	6 Minuets, C, F, D, C, d, Bb [formerly 995]	2 ob, 2 cl, 2 hn, 2 bn, trbn	1811	1970	—; ix	4
2f	Trio of a minuet, C, sketch	? wind insts	1811	—	—; ix	
3	String Quartet, C, frag.	2 vn, va, vc	?summer 1812	1978	—; iii	
8	Overture, c	2 vn, 2 va, vc	29 June 1811	1970	—; ii, 3	
8a	Overture, c [arr. of 8]	2 vn, va, vc	after 12 July 1811	1970	—; iii	
18	String Quartet, g/Bb	2 vn, va, vc	1810 or 1811	1890	v, 1; iii	
19	String Quartet, lost	2 vn, va, vc	1810 or 1811	—	—	
19a	String Quartet, lost	2 vn, va, vc	1810 or 1811	—	—	
20	Overture, Bb, lost		1812	—	—	
28	Trio (Sonata in 1 movt), Bb	pf, vn, vc	27 July–28 Aug 1812	1923	—; vii, 3	71

D	Title	Forces	Composed	Published	SW;NSA	
32	String Quartet, C movts, 1, 3 movt 4 movts 1–4	2 vn, va, vc	Sept–Oct 1812	1890 1897 1954 1890	v, 11 Rev. 53 —; iii v, 19; iii	
36	String Quartet, B♭	2 vn, va, vc	19 Nov 1812–21 Feb 1813	1890	v, 37; iii	
46	String Quartet, C	2 vn, va, vc	3–7 March 1813	1890	v, 53; iii	
68	String Quartet, B♭, 1st movt and finale	2 vn, va, vc	8 June–18 Aug 1813	1890		
72	Wind octet, F	2 ob, 2 cl, 2 hn, 2 bn	by 18 Aug 1813	1889	iii, 69; i, 3	
72a	Allegro, F, unfinished	2 ob, 2 cl, 2 hn, 2 bn	1813	1897	Rev. 41; i, 151	
74	String Quartet, D	2 vn, va, vc	22 Aug–Sept 1813	1890	v, 71; iv	
79	Wind nonet, e♭, 'Franz Schuberts Begräbnis-Feyer' (Eine kleine Trauermusik)	2 cl, 2 bn, dbn, 2 hn, 2 trbn	19 Sept 1813	1889	iii, 81; i, 25	5
86	Minuet, D	2 vn, va, vc	?Nov 1813	1886	ii, 154; ix	
87	String Quartet, E♭	2 vn, va, vc	Nov 1813	1840, op.125/1	v, 147; iv	5
87a	Andante, C	?2 vn, va, vc	Nov 1813	—	—; iv	
89	5 minuets and 6 trios, C, F, d, G, C	2 vn, va, vc	19 Nov 1813	1886	ii, 141; ix	
90	5 Deutsche and 7 trios with coda, C, G, D, F, C	2 vn, va, vc	19 Nov 1813	1886	ii, 147; ix	5
94	String Quartet, D	2 vn, va, vc	? 1811 or 1812	1871	v, 93; iii	
94b	5 minuets and 6 Deutsche with trios, lost	2 vn, va, vc, 2 hn	1814	—	—	
96	Trio, G, added to Schubert's arr. of W. Matiegka's Notturno op.21 [replaces orig. 2nd trio]	fl, va, vc, gui	Feb 1814	1926	—; viii/2	7
103	String Quartet, c, frags, Grave and Allegro	2 vn, va, vc	23 April 1814	1939	—; iv	
111a	String Trio, B♭, frag., lost [? sketch for 112]	vn, va, vc	5–13 Sept 1814	—	—	
112	String Quartet, B♭	2 vn, va, vc	5–13 Sept 1814	1863, op.168	v, 109; iv	8
173	String Quartet, g	2 vn, va, vc	25 March–1 April 1815	1871	v, 129; iv	
353	String Quartet, E	2 vn, va, vc	1816	1840, op.125/2	v, 165; iv	16
354	4 komische Ländler, D	2 vn	Jan 1816	1930	—; ix	
355	8 Ländler, f♯	?vn	Jan 1816	1928	—; ix	
370	9 Ländler, D	?vn	Jan 1816	1930	—; ix	
374	11 Ländler, B♭	vn	?Feb 1816	1902	—; ix	
384	Sonata (Sonatina), D	vn, pf	March 1816	1836, op.137/1	viii, 26; viii, 3	16
385	Sonata (Sonatina), a	vn, pf	March 1816	1836, op.137/2	viii, 40; viii, 17	16
408	Sonata (Sonatina), g	vn, pf	April 1816	1836, op.137/3	viii, 56; viii, 33	16

D	Title and remarks		Composed	Published	SW; NSA	
471	String Trio, Bb, 1st movt and frag. of 2nd	vn, va, vc	Sept 1816	1890–97	vi, 1, Rev, 84; vi	
487	Adagio and Rondo concertante, F	vn, va, vc, pf	Oct 1816	1865	vii/1, 52; vii, 157	
574	Sonata (Duo), A	vn, pf	Aug 1817	1851, op.162	viii, 100; viii, 47	18
581	String Trio, Bb	vn, va, vc	Sept 1817	1897	xxi, 93; vi	18
597a	Variations, A, sketches, lost	vn	Dec 1817	—	—	
601	Overture, Bb, frag. [arr. of orch ov. 470]	2 vn, va, vc	c1816	—	—	
667	Piano Quintet, A, 'Die Forelle'	pf, vn, va, vc, db	?autumn 1819	1829, op.114	vii/1, 52; vii, 185	23, 27, 75, 98
703	String Quartet, c (Quartettsatz), with frag. 2nd movt	2 vn, va, vc	Dec 1820	1870–97	v, 183, Rev, 76; v	26, 98
802	Introduction and variations (on Trockne Blumen from Die schöne Müllerin), e/E	fl, pf	Jan 1824	1850, op.160	viii, 120; viii, 67	41
803	Octet, F movts 1–3, 6 movts 1–6	cl, hn, bn, 2 vn, va, vc, db	Feb–1 March 1824	1853, op.166 1889	iii, 1; i, 27	41, 72, 75, 99, 100
804	String Quartet, a	2 vn, va, vc	Feb–March 1824	1824, op.29/1	v, 191; v	41, 99, 100, 101
810	String Quartet, d, 'Der Tod und das Mädchen'	2 vn, va, vc	March 1824	1831	v, 215; v	41, 49, 99, 100
821	Sonata, a, 'Arpeggione'	arpeggione, pf	Nov 1824	1871	viii, 142; viii, 89	45
887	String Quartet, G	2 vn, va, vc	20–30 June 1826	1851, op.161	v, 251; v	51, 72, 100, *101*
895	Rondo, b (Rondo brillant)	vn, pf	Oct 1826	1827, op.70	viii, 1; viii, 107	60
897	Piano Trio movt, Eb, 'Notturno'	pf, vn, vc	?1828	1846, op.148	vii/2, 106; vii, 143	59, 75, 101, 102
898	Piano Trio, Bb	pf, vn, vc	?1828	1836, op.99	vii/2, 2; vii, 91	
929	Piano Trio, Eb	pf, vn, vc	begun Nov 1827	1828, op.100	vii/2, 46; vii, 17	59, 62, 75, 97, 102
934	Fantasy, C	vn, pf	Dec 1827	1850, op.159	viii, 70; viii, 131	60, 62
956	String Quintet, C	2 vn, va, 2 vc	?Sept 1828	1853, op.163	iv, 1; ii, 19	68, 72, 97, 105
995	6 Minuets [see 2d]					
998	String Quartet [see 2c]					
AI/3	Fugue, C, frag., va part only	? 2 vn, va, vc	?1812	—	—; viii/1	

SONATAS, FANTASIES AND SHORTER WORKS FOR PIANO
(NSA nos. refer to vol. in series 7/ii unless otherwise stated)

D	Title and remarks	Composed	Published	SW: NSA
2e	Fantasie, c [formerly 993]	1811	—	—; iv
13	Fugue, d	c1812	—	—; iv
14	Overture, sketch, lost	c1812	—	—
21	6 variations, Eb, lost	1812	—	—
24	7 variations, F, frag., lost	?summer 1812	—	—

D	Title and remarks	Composed	Published	SW; NSA	
24a	Fugue, C, ? for org	?summer 1812	1978	—; iv	
24b	Fugue, G, ? for org	?summer 1812	1978	—; iv	
24c	Fugue, d, ? for org	?summer 1812	1978	—; iv	18
24d	Fugue, C, frag.	?summer 1812	1978	—; iv	18, 104
25c	Fugue, F, frag.	?summer 1812	—	—; viii/2	18
29	Andante, C [arr. of Str Qt, 3]	9 Sept 1812	1888	xi, 136; iv	
37a	fugal sketches, Bb [formerly 967]	?1813	—	—; iv	
41a	Fugue, e, frag.	1813	—	—; iv	
71b	Fugue, e, frag.	July 1813	—	—; iv	
154	Allegro, E [sketch of 157]	11 Feb 1815	1897	xxi, 136; i	
156	10 variations, F	15 Feb 1815	1887	xi, 112; iv	
157	Sonata, E, inc.	begun Feb 1815	1888	x, 2; i	
178	Adagio, G, 2 versions [2nd version frag.]	8 April 1815	1897	xxi, 244; iv	
279	Sonata, C [minuet = 277a with alternative trio; ? finale = 346]	Sept 1815	1888	x, 16; i	
346	Allegretto, C, frag. [? finale of 279]	?1816	1897	xxi, 222; iv	
347	Allegretto moderato, C, frag.	?1813	1897	xxi, 230; iv	
348	Andantino, C, frag.	?1816	1897	xxi, 233; iv	
349	Adagio, C, frag.	?1816	1897	xxi, 242; iv	
459	Sonata, E, frag. (nos.1, 2 of 'Fünf Klavierstücke')	Aug 1816	1843	xi, 170; i	
459a	'Fünf Klavierstücke', C, A, E (nos.3–5)	?1816	1843	xi, 178; iv	
505	Adagio, Db [orig. slow movt of 625; adapted (? by publisher) as introduction to 506]	?Sept 1818	1897	Rev, 4; iv	
506	Rondo, E [? finale of 566]	?June 1817	1848, op.145	xi, 105; iv	
537	Sonata, a	March 1817	c1852, op.164	x, 60; i	
557	Sonata, Ab	May 1817	1888	x, 30; i	
566	Sonata, e [? finale = 506]	June 1817			18
	Moderato		1888	x, 40; i	
	Allegretto		1907	—; i	
	Scherzo		1928–9	—; i	
567	Sonata, Db, inc. [1st version of 568]	June 1817	1897	xxi, 140; i	
568	Sonata, Eb	?June 1817	1829, op.122	x, 74; i	
570	Scherzo, D, Allegro f#, inc. [? intended as movts 3–4 of 571]	?July 1817	1897	xxi, 236; i	18
571	Sonata, f#, frag. of 1st movt only	July 1817	1897	xxi, 160; i	18
575	Sonata, B	Aug 1817	1846, op.147	x, 44; i	
576	13 variations on a theme by Anselm Hüttenbrenner, a	Aug 1817	1867	xi, 124; iv	
593	2 scherzos, Bb, Db	Nov 1817	1871	xi, 190; iv	
604	Andante, A [? slow movt of 570/571]	1816 or July 1817	1888	xi, 138; iv	
605	Fantasia, C, frag.	1821–3	1897	xxi, 214; iv	
605a	Fantasy, C, 'Grazer Fantasie'	?1818	1969	—; iv	
606	March, E	?1818	1840	xi, 198; iv	

D	Title and remarks	Composed	Published	SW; NSA	
612	Adagio, E [? slow movt of 613]	April 1818	1869	xi, 142; iv	
613	Sonata, C, 2 movts, frag. [? slow movt = 612]	April 1818	1897	xxi, 164; ii	
625	Sonata, f, 2 movts, frag. [slow movt = 505]	Sept 1818	1897	xxi, 172; ii	
655	Sonata, c♯, frag. of 1st movt	April 1819	1897	xxi, 186; ii	
664	Sonata, A	1819 or 1825	1829, op.120	x, 134; ii	19
718	Variation on a waltz by Diabelli, c	March 1821	1824	xi, 134; iv	21
759a	Overture to Alfonso und Estrella, D [arr. from 732]	Nov 1822	c1839, op.69	—; iv	
760	Fantasy, C, 'Wandererfantasie'	Nov 1822	1823, op.15	xi, 2; v	34, 37
769a	Sonata, e, frag. [formerly 994]	c1823	1958	—; i	
780	6 Momens musicals [sic] C, A♭, f, c♯, f, A♭	1823–8	1828, op.94	xi, 88; v	59, 64
784	Sonata, a	Feb 1823	1839, op.143	x, 94; ii	37, 100
817	Ungarische Melodie, b [? 1st version of pf duet, 818]	2 Sept 1824	1928	—; v	
840	Sonata, C, 'Reliquie', movts 3–4 inc.	April 1825	1861	xxi, 190; ii	47
845	Sonata, a	before end May 1825	1826, op.42	x, 110; ii	47, 49, 50, 59, 100
850	Sonata, D	Aug 1825	1826, op.53	x, 146; ii	48, 50, 59
894	Sonata, G (formerly known as Fantasie, Andante, Menuetto und Allegretto)	Oct 1826	1827, op.78	x, 178; iii	50, 55, 100
899	4 Impromptus, c, E♭, G♭, A♭ nos.1–2 nos.3–4	? summer–autumn 1827	1827, op.90/1–2 1857, op.90/3–4	xi, 28; v	59, 100, 103
900	Allegretto, c, frag.	? after 1820	1897	xxi, 220; v	
915	Allegretto, c	26 April 1827	1870	xi, 146; v	
916b	Piano piece, C, sketch	? summer–autumn 1827	1978	—; v	
916c	Piano piece, c, sketch	? summer–autumn 1827	1978	—; v	
935	4 Impromptus, f, A♭, B♭, f	Dec 1827	1839, op.142	xi, 58; v	103
946	3 Klavierstücke, e♭, E♭, C	May 1828	1868	xi, 150; v	64, 103
958	Sonata, c	Sept 1828	1839	x, 204; iii	67
959	Sonata, A	Sept 1828	1839	x, 232; iii	67, 76
960	Sonata, B♭	Sept 1828	1839	x, 264; iii	
967	fugal sketches [see 37a]				
980f	March, G	?	—		
993	Fantasie [see 2e]				
994	Sonata [see 769a]				

DANCES FOR PIANO

(NSA nos. refer to vol. and p. in series 7/ii)

D	Title and remarks	Composed	Published	SW; NSA
19b	Waltzes and march, lost	? 1812 or 1813	—	—
22	12 minuets with trios, lost	1812	—	—
41	30 minuets with trios, 10 lost	1813	1889	xii, 137; vi
91	2 minuets, D, A, each with 2 trios, 2 other minuets lost	22 Nov 1813	1956	—; vi

D	Title and remarks	Composed	Published	SW: NSA	
128	12 Wiener Deutsche	?1812	1897	xxi, 248: vi	
135	Deutscher, E, with trio [see 146]	1815	1930	—; vi	
139	Deutscher, C♯, with trio	1815	1930	—; vi	
145	12 Waltzes [no.7 = no.2 of 970], 17 Ländler, 9 Ecossaises [no.5 = no.1 of 421; no.6 = no.5 of 697], incl. 3 Atzenbrugger Tänze (nos.1–3)	1815–July 1821	1823, op.18	xii, 14; vii	31
146	20 Waltzes (Letzte Walzer) [no.3 = 135 with new trio]	1815	1830, op.127	xii, 66; vii	
	nos.1, 3–11	1815			
	nos.2, 12–20	Feb 1823			
158	Ecossaise, d/F	21 Feb 1815	1889	xii, 136; vi	
277a	Minuet, a [used in Sonata, 279], with trio	?Sept 1815	1925	—; iv	
299	12 Ecossaises [no.1 = Ecossaise no.1 from 145]	3 Oct 1815		xxi, 264; vi	
	nos.1–8		1897		
	nos.9–12		1912	—; vi	
334	Minuet, A, with trio	c1815	1897	xxi, 256; iv	
335	Minuet, E, with 2 trios	c1813	1897	xxi, 258; vi	
365	36 Originaltänze (Erste Walzer), incl. Trauerwalzer (no.2) and 3 Atzenbrugger Tänze (nos.29–31)	1816–July 1821	1821, op.9	xii, 2; vii	31, 32
366	17 Ländler [no.17 arr. from 814 no.1]	1816–Nov 1824		xii, 88; vi	
	nos.6 and 17		1824		
	nos.1–17		1869		
378	8 Ländler, B♭	13 Feb 1816	1889	xii, 102; vi	
380	3 minuets, E, A, C, each with 2 trios, 2nd trio of 3rd minuet lost	22 Feb 1816		xxi, 262; vi	
	nos.1 and 2		1897	—; vi	
	no.3		1956	xii, 94; vii	
420	12 Deutsche	1816	1871	xii, 132; vi	
421	6 Ecossaises, A♭, f, E♭, B♭, E♭, A♭ [no. 1 = Ecossaise no.5 of 145]	May 1816	1889	—; vi	
511	Ecossaise, E♭	c1817	1924		
529	8 Ecossaises	Feb 1817			
	nos.1–3, 6, 8, D, D, G, D, D		1871	xii, 134; vi	
	nos.4, 5, 7, D		1897	xxi, 267; vi	
600	Minuet, c♯ [? trio = 610]	?1814	1897	xxi, 261; iv	
610	Trio, E [? minuet = 600]	Feb 1818	1889	xii, 157; vi	
640	2 dances [see 980a]				
643	Deutscher, c♯, and Ecossaise, D♭	1819	1889	xii, 117; vi	
679	2 Ländler [see 980b]				
680	2 Ländler [see 980c]				
681	12 Ländler, nos.1–4 lost	c1815	1930	—; vi	
697	6 Ecossaises, A♭	May 1820		xii, 134; vi	
	nos.1–4, 6		1889	—; vi	
	no.5 [= no.6 of 145]		1823		
722	Deutscher, G♭	8 March 1821	1889	xii, 115; vii	

D	Title	Date	Year, op.	References	
734	16 Ländler and 2 Ecossaises (Wiener-Damen Ländler)	c1822	1826, op.67	xii, 48; vii	
735	Galop and 8 Ecossaises	c1822	1825, op.49	xii, 119; vii	
769	2 Deutsche			xii, 114; vi	
	no.1, A	Jan 1824	1889		
	no.2, D	by Dec 1823	1823		
779	34 Valses sentimentales	c1823	1825, op.50	xii, 34; vii	
781	12 Ecossaises	Jan 1823		xii, 125; vii	
	no.1 [= Ecossaise no.2 of 783]		1825, op.33		
	nos.4, 7		1824		
	nos.2–3, 5–6, 8–12		1889		
782	Ecossaise, D	c1823	1824	—, vii	
783	16 Deutsche and 2 Ecossaises [no.2 = no.1 of 781]	Jan 1823–July 1824	1825, op.33	xii, 28; vii	
790	12 Deutsche (Ländler)	May 1823	1864, op.171	xii, 82; vi	
816	3 Ecossaises, D, D, Bb	Sept 1824	1956	—, vi	
820	6 Deutsche, Ab, Ab, Ab, Bb, Bb, Bb	Oct 1824	1931	—, vi	
841	2 Deutsche, F, G	April 1825	1930	—, vi	
844	Waltz, G (Albumblatt)	16 April 1825	1897	xxi, 268; vi	
924	12 Grazer Walzer	?Sept 1827	1828, op.91	xii, 60; vii	58
925	Grazer Galopp, C	?Sept 1827	1828	xii, 123; vii	58
944a	Deutscher, lost	1 March 1828	—		
969	12 Waltzes (Valses nobles)	by end 1826	1827, op.77	xii, 54; vii	55
970	6 Ländler, Eb, Eb, Ab, Ab, Db, Db [no.2 = no.7 of 145]	?	1889	xii, 106; vii	
971	3 Deutsche, a, A, E	by end 1822	1823	xii, 108; vii	
972	3 Deutsche, Db, Ab, A	?	1889	xii, 110; vi	
973	3 Deutsche, E, E, Ab	?	1889	xii, 111; vi	
974	2 Deutsche, Db	?	1889	xii, 113; vi	
975	Deutscher, D		1889	xii, 116; vi	
976	Cotillon, Eb	by end 1825	1825	xii, 118; vi	
977	8 Ecossaises	?	1889	xii, 129; vi	
978	Waltz, Ab	by end 1825	1825	—, vii	
979	Waltz, G	by end 1826	1826	—, vii	
980	2 waltzes, G, b	by end 1826	1826	—, vii	
980a	2 dances, A, E, sketches [formerly 640]		1956	—, vi	
980b	2 Ländler, Eb [formerly 679]		1925	—, vi	
980c	2 Ländler, Db, frag. [formerly 680]		1930	—, vi	
980d	Waltz, C	by end 1827	1828	—, vii	
980e	2 dances, g, F, sketches [? for pf]	?	—	—, vi	

PIANO FOUR HANDS
(NSA nos. refer to vol. and p. in series 7/i)

D	Title and remarks	Composed	Published	SW; NSA	
1	Fantasie, G	8 April–1 May 1810	1888	ix/3, 189; i	4
1b	Fantasie, G, frag.	1810 or 1811	—	—; i	
1c	Sonata, F, frag., 1st movt only	1810 or 1811	—	—; i	
9	Fantasie, g	20 Sept 1811	1888	ix/3, 224; i	
48	Fantasie, c ('Grande sonate')	April–10 June 1813			
	1st version [without finale]		1871	ix/3, 234; i	
	2nd version [complete]		1888	—; i	
592	Overture, D, 'im italienischen Stile' [arr. of orch ov., 590]	Dec 1817	1872	ix/2, 26; v	19
597	Overture, C, 'im italienischen Stile' [arr. of orch ov., 591]	Nov or Dec 1817	1872	ix/2, 14; v	19, 20
599	4 polonaises, d, B♭, E, F	July 1818	1827, op.75	ix/3, 160; iv, 126	20
602	3 marches héroïques, b, C, D	1818 or 1824	1824, op.27	ix/1, 2; iv, 3	
603	Introduction, 4 variations on an original theme and finale [see 968a]				
608	Rondo, D				19
	version a	Jan 1818	—	—; i	
	version b (Notre amitié est invariable)	c1818	1835, op.138	ix/2, 136; i	
617	Sonata, B♭	summer–autumn 1818	1823, op.30	ix/2, 40; i	20
618	Deutscher, G, with 2 trios and 2 Ländler, E	summer–autumn 1818	1909	—; iv, 167	
618a	Polonaise and trio, sketch [trio used in 599]	July 1818	1972	—; iv, 180	20, 33
624	8 variations on a French song, e	Sept 1818	1822, op.10	ix/2, 150; i	
668	Overture, g	Oct 1819	1897	xxi, 106; v	
675	Overture, F	?Nov 1819	1825, op.34	ix/2, 2; v	
733	3 marches militaires, D, G, E♭	? summer–autumn 1818	1826, op.51	ix/1, 56; iv, 20	50
773	Overture to Alfonso und Estrella [arr. from 732]	1823	1826; 1830 as op.69	—; v	50
798	Overture to Fierabras [arr. from 796]	late 1823	1897	xxi, 120; v	
812	Sonata, C, 'Grand Duo'	June 1824	1838, op.140	ix/2, 66; ii, 5	43, 100
813	8 variations on an original theme, A♭	summer 1824	1825, op.35	ix/2, 168; ii, 27	43, 47
814	4 Ländler, E♭, A♭, c, C [no.1 arr. as 366 no.17]	July 1824	1869	ix/3, 172; iv, 176	
818	Divertissement à l'hongroise, g	?autumn 1824	1826, op.54	ix/3, 2; ii, 38	43, 50
819	6 grandes marches, E♭, g, b, D, e♭, E	?autumn 1824	1825, op.40	ix/1, 20; iv, 33	
823	Divertissement sur des motifs originaux français, e	c1825		ix/3, 38; ii, 621	50
	1 Marche brillante		1826, op.63/1		
	2 Andantino varié		1827, op.84/1		
	3 Rondeau brillant		1827, op.84/2		

D	Title	Composed	Published	SW: NSA	
824	6 polonaises, d, F, Bb, D, A, E	1826	1826, op.61	ix/3, 136; iv, 140	
859	Grande marche funèbre, c, on the death of Alexander I of Russia	Dec 1825	1826, op.55	ix/1, 70; iv, 74	
885	Grande marche héroïque, a, for the coronation of Nicholas I of Russia	1826	1826, op.66	ix/1, 78; iv, 82	
886	2 marches caractéristiques [see 968b]				
908	8 variations on a theme from Hérold's Marie, C	Feb 1827	1827, op.82/1	ix/2, 194; iii	58
928	March, G, 'Kindermarsch'	12 Oct 1827	1870	ix/1, 116; iv, 124	63
940	Fantasie, f	Jan–April 1828	1829, op.103	ix/3, 112; iii	64
947	Allegro, a, 'Lebensstürme'	May 1828	1840, op.144	ix/3, 88; iii	64
951	Rondo, A	June 1828	1828, op.107	ix/2, 118; iii	
952	Fugue, e, pf/org	3 June 1828	1848, op.152	ix/3, 176; iii	
968	Allegro moderato, C, and Andante, a (Sonatine)	?1818	1888	ix/3, 180; i	
968a	Introduction, 4 variations on an original theme and finale, Bb [formerly 603]	?1824	1860, op.82/2	ix/2, 216; i	
968b	2 marches caractéristiques, C [formerly 886]	?1826	1830, op.121	ix/1, 94; i	

SONGS

86ff

The following list includes duets, melodramas and works for or with unison chorus or incorporating brief passages for four-part chorus; all with pf acc. unless otherwise stated. SW nos. refer to vol. and p. in series 20, and NSA nos. to vol. and p. in series 4, unless otherwise stated. Incipits given where different from title.

D	Title	Incipit	Text	Key	Composed	Published	SW: NSA	
1a	Song sketch (no text)			c	?1810	1969	—; vi, 157	
5	Hagars Klage	Hier am Hügel heissen Sandes	C. A. Schücking	c	30 March 1811	1894	i, 1; vi, 3	4
6	Des Mädchens Klage (1)	Der Eichwald brauset	Schiller	d	1811 or 1812	1894	i, 16; iii	5
7	Leichenfantasie	Mit erstorbnem Scheinen	Schiller	d	c1811	1894	i, 22; vi, 22	5
10	Der Vatermörder	Ein Vater starb von des Sohnes Hand	G. C. Pfeffel	c	26 Dec 1811	1894	i, 40; vi, 46	
15	Der Geistertanz (1), frag.	Die bretterne Kammer der Toten erbebt	Matthisson	c	c1812	1895	x, 92; vii, 188	
15a	Der Geistertanz (2), frag.	Die bretterne Kammer der Toten erbebt	Matthisson	f	c1812	1895	x, 94; vii, 190	
17	Quell' innocente figlio version 1		Metastasio	F	c1812	1940	—; viii/2	
23	Klaglied	Meine Ruh' ist dahin	F. Rochlitz	g	1812	1830, op.131/3	i, 52; vi, 56	
30	Der Jüngling am Bache (1)	An der Quelle sass der Knabe	Schiller	F	24 Sept 1812	1894	i, 48; iv	
33	Entra l'uomo allor che nasce version 1		Metastasio	e	Sept–Oct 1812	1940	—; viii/2	
35	Serbate, o dei custodi version 3		Metastasio	C	10 Dec 1812	1940	—; viii/2	

D	Title	Incipit	Text	Key	Composed	Published	SW; NSA
39	Lebenstraum	Ich sass an einer Tempelhalle	G. von Baumberg	C	c1810	1969	—; vi, 171
42	Misero pargoletto (1)		Metastasio		?1813		
	version a, inc.			g		1969	—; vi, 180
	version b, inc.			g		1969	—; vi, 181
	Misero pargoletto (2)			g		1969	
				g		1895	x, 31; vi, 60
44	Totengräberlied (2)	Grabe, Spaten, grabe!	Hölty	e	19 Jan 1813	1894	i, 54; vi, 64
50	Die Schatten	Freunde, deren Grüfte	Matthisson	A	12 April 1813	1894	i, 58; vi, 68
52	Sehnsucht (1)	Ach, aus dieses Tales Gründen	Schiller	d	15–17 April 1813	1868	i, 62; ii, 241
59	Verklärung	Lebensfunke, vom Himmel entglüht	A. Pope, trans. J. G. von Herder	a	4 May 1813	1832	i, 68; vi, 73
73	Thekla: eine Geisterstimme (1)	Wo ich sei, und wo mich hingewendet	Schiller	G	22–3 Aug 1813	1868	i, 70; iv
76	Pensa, che questo istante		Metastasio				
	version a			D	7 Sept 1813	1969	—; vi, 184
	version b			D	13 Sept 1813	1871	x, 34; vi, 76
77	Der Taucher	Wer wagt es, Rittersmann	Schiller				
	version a			d	17 Sept 1813–5 April 1814	1831	i, 73; vi, 78
	version b [formerly 111]			d	by 1815	1894	i, 102; vi, 114
78	Son fra l'onde	Verschwunden sind die Schmerzen	Metastasio	c	18 Sept 1813	1895	x, 36; vi, 150
81	Auf den Sieg der Deutschen, with 2 vn, vc		?Schubert	F	autumn 1813	1895	x, 74; xiv
83	Zur Namensfeier des Herrn Andreas Siller, with vn, harp	Des Phöbus Strahlen		G	28 Oct–4 Nov 1813	1895	x, 72; xiv
93	Don Gayseros		F. de la Motte Fouqué		c1815	1894	
	1 Don Gayseros, Don Gayseros			F			i, 132; vii, 167
	2 Nächtens klang die süsse Laute			F			i, 137; vii, 173
	3 An dem jungen Morgenhimmel			Eb			i, 141; vii, 177
95	Adelaide	Einsam wandelt dein Freund	Matthisson	Ab	1814	1848	i, 169; vii, 3
97	Trost: an Elisa	Lehnst du deine bleichgehärmte Wange	Matthisson	a	1814	1894	i, 154; vii, 6
98	Erinnerungen (1)	Am Seegestad	Matthisson				
	version a			Bb	autumn 1814	1968	—; vii, 167
	version b			Bb	c1814	1894	i, 166; vii, 8
99	Andenken (1)	Ich denke dein	Matthisson	F	April 1814	1894	i, 144; vii, 11

	Title	Incipit	Poet	Key	Date	Pub.	References	
100	Geisternähe	Der Dämmrung Schein	Matthisson	E♭	April 1814	1894	i, 147; vii, 14	
101	Erinnerung	Kein Rosenschimmer leuchtet	Matthisson	e	April 1814	1894	i, 151; vii, 18	
102	Die Betende	Laura betet	Matthisson	B	autumn 1814	1840	i, 156; vii, 21	
104	Die Befreier Europas in Paris	Sie sind in Paris!	J. C. Mikan					
	version a			G	May 1814	1968	—; vii, 180	
	version b			G	May 1814	1968	—; vii, 182	
	version c			G	16 May 1814	1895	x, 76; vii, 24	
107	Lied aus der Ferne	Wenn in des Abends letztem Scheine	Matthisson					
	version a			E	July 1814	1894	i, 158; vii, 26	
	version b			D	?July 1814	1968	—; vii, 29	
108	Der Abend	Purpur malt die Tannenhügel	Matthisson	d	July 1814	1894	i, 161; vii, 31	
109	Lied der Liebe	Durch Fichten am Hügel	Matthisson	B♭	July 1814	1894	i, 163; vii, 33	
111	Der Taucher [see 77]							
113	An Emma	Weit in nebelgrauer Ferne	Schiller					
	version a			F	17 Sept 1814	1894	i, 172; iii	
	version b			F	c1814	1821	i, 174; iii	
	version c			F	c1814	1826, op.58/2	i, 176; iii	
114	Romanze	Ein Fräulein klagt' im finstern Turm	Matthisson					
	version a			g	Sept 1814	1902	—; vii, 36	
	version b			g	29 Sept 1814	1868	i, 178; vii, 42	
115	An Laura, als sie Klopstocks Auferstehungslied sang	Herzen, die gen Himmel sich erheben	Matthisson	E	2–7 Oct 1814	1840	i, 183; vii, 48	
116	Der Geistertanz (3)	Die bretterne Kammer der Toten erbebt	Matthisson	c	14 Oct 1814	1840	i, 186; vii, 52	
117	Das Mädchen aus der Fremde (1)	In einem Tal bei armen Hirten	Schiller	A	16 Oct 1814	1894	i, 189; viii	
118	Gretchen am Spinnrade	Meine Ruh' ist hin	Goethe	d	19 Oct 1814	1821, op.2	i, 191; i, 10	8, 30, 78, 86
119	Nachtgesang	O gib vom weichem Pfühle	Goethe	A♭	30 Nov 1814	1850	i, 197; vii, 55	
120	Trost in Tränen	Wie kommt's dass du so traurig bist	Goethe	F	30 Nov 1814	1835	i, 198; vii, 56	
121	Schäfers Klagelied	Da droben auf jenem Berge	Goethe					
	version a			e	Nov 1814	1894	i, 203; i, 194	
	version b			c	30 Nov 1814	1821, op.3/1	i, 200; i, 20	8, 22
122	Ammenlied	Am hohen, hohen Turm	M. Lubi	g	Dec 1814	1872	i, 224; vii, 59	
123	Sehnsucht	Was zieht mir das Herz so?	Goethe	G	3 Dec 1814	1842	i, 206; vii, 60	

D	Title	Incipit	Text	Key	Composed	Published	SW; NSA	
124	Am See	Sitz' ich im Gras	Mayrhofer					9, 10
	version a			g	Dec 1814	1968	—; vii, 194	
	version b			g	7 Dec 1814	1885	i, 210; vii, 65	
126	Szene aus Goethes Faust (Dom), with 4vv	Wie anders, Gretchen, war dir's	Goethe					9
	version a			c	Dec 1814	1873	i, 215; vii, 196	
	version b			c	12 Dec 1814	1832	i, 219; vii, 71	
134	Ballade	Ein Fräulein schaut vom hohen Turm	J. Kenner	g	c1815	1830, op.126	ii, 198; vii, 77	
138	Rastlose Liebe	Dem Schnee, dem Regen	Goethe					12, 30
	version a			E	19 May 1815	1821, op.51	iii, 198; i, 35	
	version b			D	1821	1970	—; i, 208	
141	Der Mondabend	Rein und freundlich lacht der Himmel	J. G. Kumpf	A	1815	1830, op.131/1	ii, 20; vii, 86	
142	Geistes-Gruss	Hoch auf dem alten Turme	Goethe		1815 or 1816			
	version a			E♭/G♭		1895	iii, 189; v	
	version b			E♭/G♭		1885	iii, 190; v	
	version c			D/F		—	—; v	
	version d			E♭/G♭		1895	iii, 191; v	
	version e			E♭/G♭		—	—; v	
	version f			E/G	rev. ?1828	1828, op.92/3	iii, 192; v	
143	Genügsamkeit	Dort raget ein Berg	F. von Schober	c♯	1815	1829, op.109/2	iii, 230; vii, 88	
144	Romanze, unfinished	In der Väter Hallen ruhte	F. Graf zu Stolberg-Stolberg	E	April 1816	1897	Rev. 46; vii, 201	
149	Der Sänger	Was hör' ich draussen vor dem Tor	Goethe					
	version a			D	Feb 1815	1894	ii, 41; vii, 90	
	version b			D	1815	1829, op.117	ii, 33; vii, 97	
150	Lodas Gespenst	Der bleiche, kalte Mond	Ossian, trans. E. Baron de Harold	g/B♭	17 Jan 1816	1830	ii, 21; vii, 105	
151	Auf einen Kirchhof	Sei gegrüsst, geweihte Stille	F. von Schlechta	A	2 Feb 1815	c1850	ii, 1; vii, 119	
152	Minona	Wie treiben die Wolken so finster	F. A. Bertrand	a	8 Feb 1815	1894	ii, 6; vii, 124	
153	Als ich sie erröten sah	All' mein Wirken	B. A. Ehrlich	G	10 Feb 1815	1845	ii, 15; vii, 135	

No.	Title	Version	Incipit	Author	Key	Date	Publication	Reference
155	Das Bild		Ein Mädchen ist's	Schiller	F	11 Feb 1815	1862, op.165/3	ii, 19; vii, 140
159	Die Erwartung	version a	Hör' ich das Pförtchen	Schiller	Bb	May 1816	1968	—; vii, 141
		version b			Bb	1816	1829, op.116	ii, 47; vii, 153
160	Am Flusse (1)		Verfliesset, vielgeliebte Lieder	Goethe	d	27 Feb 1815	1894	ii, 58; xiii
161	An Mignon	version a	Über Tal und Fluss getragen	Goethe	g#	27 Feb 1815	1894	ii, 59; i, 249
		version b			g	1815	1825, op.19/2	ii, 60; i, 129
162	Nähe des Geliebten	version a	Ich denke dein	Goethe	Gb	27 Feb 1815	1894	ii, 62; i, 276
		version b			Gb		1821, op.5/2	ii, 63; i, 40
163	Sängers Morgenlied (1)		Süsses Licht! aus goldenen Pforten	Körner	G	27 Feb 1815	1894	ii, 64; viii
164	Liebesrausch (1), frag.		... Glanz des Guten	Körner	G	March 1815	1928	—; viii
165	Sängers Morgenlied (2)		Süsses Licht! aus goldenen Pforten	Körner	C	1 March 1815	1872	ii, 66; viii
166	Amphiaraos		Vor Thebens siebenfach gähnenden Toren	Körner	g	1 March 1815	1894	ii, 68; viii
169	Trinklied vor der Schlacht, for 2 unison choruses		Schlacht, du brichst an!	Körner	C	12 March 1815	1894	ii, 76; iii/3
170	Schwertlied, with unison chorus		Du Schwert an meiner Linken	Körner	C	12 March 1815	1873	ii, 78; iii/3
171	Gebet während der Schlacht		Vater, ich rufe dich!	Körner	Bb	12 March 1815	1831	ii, 80; viii
172	Der Morgenstern (1), frag.		Stern der Liebe	Körner	Gb	12 March 1815	—	—; viii
174	Das war ich	version a	Jüngst träumte mir	Körner	G	26 March 1815	c1842	ii, 84; viii
		version b, frag.			D	cJune 1816	1897	Rev, 16; viii
176	Die Sterne		Was funkelt ihr so mild mich an?	J. G. Fellinger	Ab	6 April 1815	1872	ii, 86; viii
177	Vergebliche Liebe		Ja, ich weiss es	J. K. Bernard	c	6 April 1815	1867, op.173/3	ii, 88; viii
179	Liebesrausch (2)		Dir, Mädchen, schlägt	Körner	G	8 April 1815	1872	ii, 90; viii
180	Sehnsucht der Liebe		Wie die Nacht mit heiligem Beben	Körner	G	8 April 1815		ii, 90; viii
182	Die erste Liebe	version a	Die erste Liebe füllt das Herz	Fellinger	G	8 April 1815	1894	ii, 92; viii
		version b, frag., lost			G	July 1815	—	—;
	Die erste Liebe				C	12 April 1815	1842	ii, 94; viii

D	Title	Incipit	Text	Key	Composed	Published	SW; NSA	
183	Trinklied, with unison chorus	Ihr Freunde und du gold'ner Wein	A. Zettler	G	12 April 1815	1887	ii, 97; iii/3	
186	Die Sterbende	Heil! dies ist die letzte Zähre	Matthisson	Ab	May 1815	1894	ii, 100; viii	
187	Stimme der Liebe (1)	Abendgewölke schweben hell	Matthisson	F	May 1815	1894	ii, 98; viii	
188	Naturgenuss (1)	Im Abendschimmer wallt der Quell	Matthisson	Bb	May 1815	1887	ii, 99; viii	12
189	An die Freude, with unison chorus	Freude, schöner Götterfunken	Schiller	E	May 1815	1829, op.111/1	ii, 102; iii/3	
191	Des Mädchens Klage (2) version a / version b	Der Eichwald brauset	Schiller	c / c	15 May 1815 / 1815	1894 / 1826, op.58/3	ii, 104; iii / ii, 106; iii	
192	Der Jüngling am Bache (2)	An der Quelle sass der Knabe	Schiller	f	15 May 1815	1887	ii, 108; iv	
193	An den Mond	Geuss, lieber Mond	Hölty	f	17 May 1815	1826, op.57/3	ii, 110; iii	
194	Die Mainacht	Wann der silberne Mond	Hölty	d	17 May 1815	1894	ii, 112; viii	
195	Amalia	Schön wie Engel	Schiller	A	19 May 1815	1867, op.173/1	ii, 113; viii	
196	An die Nachtigall	Geuss nicht so laut	Hölty	f#	22 May 1815	1865, op.172/3	ii, 116; viii	
197	An die Apfelbäume, wo ich Julien erblickte	Ein heilig Säuseln	Hölty	A	22 May 1815	1850	ii, 117; viii	
198	Seufzer	Die Nachtigall singt überall	Hölty	g	22 May 1815	1894	ii, 120; viii	
201	Auf den Tod einer Nachtigall (1), frag.	Sie ist dahin	Hölty	f#	25 May 1815	1970	—; x	
204a	Das Traumbild, lost		Hölty		May 1815		—	
206	Liebeständelei	Süsses Liebchen, komm zu mir!	Körner	Eb	26 May 1815	1872	ii, 122; viii	
207	Der Liebende	Beglückt, beglückt, wer dich erblickt	Hölty	Bb	29 May 1815	1894	ii, 123; viii	
208	Die Nonne version a, frag. version b [formerly 212]	Es liebt' in Welschland	Hölty	Ab / Ab	29 May 1815 / 16 June 1815	1897 / 1895	Rev, 19; viii / ii, 124; viii	
209	Der Liedler	Gib, Schwester, mir die Harf herab	Kenner	a	Jan 1815	1825, op.38	ii, 184; ii, 144	
210	Die Liebe (Klärchens Lied)	Freudvoll und leidvoll	Goethe	Bb	3 June 1815	1838	ii, 130; viii	
211	Adelwold und Emma	Hoch, und ehern schier von Dauer	Bertrand	F	5–14 June 1815	1894	ii, 132; viii	12
212	Die Nonne [see 208]							
213	Der Traum	Mir träumt', ich war ein Vögelein	Hölty	A	17 June 1815	1865, op.172/1	ii, 158; viii	12

D	Title	Incipit	Author	Key	Date	Publication	Refs	
214	Die Laube	Nimmer werd' ich, nimmer dein vergessen	Hölty	A♭	17 June 1815	1865, op.172/2	ii, 159; viii	
215	Jägers Abendlied (1)	Im Felde schleich' ich still und wild	Goethe	F	20 June 1815	1907	—; i, 198	
215a	Meerestille (1)	Tiefe Stille herrscht im Wasser	Goethe	C	20 June 1815	1952	—; i, 197	
216	Meerestille (2)	Tiefe Stille herrscht im Wasser	Goethe	C	21 June 1815	1821, op.3/2	ii, 160; i, 23	
217	Kolmas Klage	Rund um mich Nacht	Ossian, trans. Kenner	c	22 June 1815	1830	ii, 161; viii	
218	Grablied	Er fiel den Tod fürs Vaterland	Kenner	f	24 June 1815	1848	ii, 166; viii	
219	Das Finden	Ich hab' ein Mädchen funden	L. Kosegarten	B♭	25 June 1815	1848	ii, 167; viii	
221	Der Abend	Der Abend blüht	Kosegarten	B	15 July 1815	1829, op.118/2	ii, 178; viii	
222	Lieb Minna	Schwüler Hauch weht mir herüber	A. Stadler	f	2 July 1815	1885	ii, 168; viii	
224	Wandrers Nachtlied	Der du von dem Himmel bist	Goethe	G♭	5 July 1815	1821, op.4/3	ii, 170; i, 34	12, 88
225	Der Fischer version a / version b	Das Wasser rauscht	Goethe	B♭ / B♭	5 July 1815 / c1815	1970 / 1821, op.5/3	—; i, 208 / ii, 171; i, 42	
226	Erster Verlust	Ach, wer bringt die schönen Tage	Goethe	f	5 July 1815	1821, op.5/4	ii, 172; i, 44	12
227	Idens Nachtgesang	Vernimm es, Nacht	Kosegarten	B♭	7 July 1815	1885	ii, 173; viii	
228	Von Ida	Der Morgen blüht	Kosegarten	f	7 July 1815	1894	ii, 174; viii	
229	Die Erscheinung	Ich lag auf grünen Matten	Kosegarten	E	7 July 1815	1829, op.108/3	ii, 175; v	
230	Die Täuschung	Im Erlenbusch, im Tannenhain	Kosegarten	E	7 July 1815	1862, op.165/4	ii, 176; viii	
231	Das Sehnen	Wehmut, die mich hüllt	Kosegarten	a	8 July 1815	1865, op.172/4	ii, 177; viii	
233	Geist der Liebe	Wer bist du, Geist der Liebe	Kosegarten	E	15 July 1815	1829, op.118/1	ii, 180; viii	
234	Tischlied	Mich ergreift, ich weiss nicht wie	Goethe	C	15 July 1815	1829, op.118/3	ii, 182; viii	
235	Abends unter der Linde (1)	Woher, o namenloses Sehnen	Kosegarten	F	24 July 1815	1894	ii, 204; viii	
237	Abends unter der Linde (2)	Woher, o namenloses Sehnen	Kosegarten	F	25 July 1815	1872	ii, 206; viii	
238	Die Mondnacht	Siehe, wie die Mondesstrahlen	Kosegarten	F♯	25 July 1815	1894	ii, 208; viii	
240	Huldigung	Ganz verloren, ganz versunken	Kosegarten	E	27 July 1815	1894	ii, 210; viii	
241	Alles um Liebe	Was ist es, das die Seele füllt?	Kosegarten	E	27 July 1815	1894	ii, 212; viii	
245	An den Frühling [see 587b]							
246	Die Bürgschaft	Zu Dionys, dem Tyrannen	Schiller	g	Aug 1815	1830	iii, 11; viii	

D	Title	Incipit	Text	Key	Composed	Published	SW; NSA	
247	Die Spinnerin	Als ich still und ruhig spann	Goethe	b	Aug 1815	1829, op.118/6	iii, 44; viii	
248	Lob des Tokayers	O köstlicher Tokayer	Baumberg	B♭	Aug 1815	1829, op.118/4	iii, 66; viii	
249	Die Schlacht (1), frag.	Sie konnte mir kein Wörtchen sagen	Schiller	b	1 Aug 1815	—	—; iii/2	
250	Das Geheimnis (1)		Schiller	A♭	7 Aug 1815	1872	iii, 2; xiii	
251	Hoffnung (1)	Es reden und träumen die Menschen	Schiller	G♭	7 Aug 1815	1872	iii, 4; iv	
252	Das Mädchen aus der Fremde (2)	In einem Tal bei armen Hirten	Schiller	F	12 Aug 1815	1887	iii, 10; viii	
253	Punschlied: im Norden zu singen	Auf der Berge freien Höhen	Schiller	B♭	18 Aug 1815	1887	iii, 30; viii	
254	Der Gott und die Bajadere	Mahadöh, der Herr der Erde	Goethe	E♭	18 Aug 1815	1887	iii, 32; viii	
255	Der Rattenfänger	Ich bin der wohlbekannte Sänger	Goethe	G	19 Aug 1815	c1850	iii, 34; viii	
256	Der Schatzgräber	Arm am Beutel, krank am Herzen	Goethe	d	19 Aug 1815	1887	iii, 35; viii	
257	Heidenröslein	Sah ein Knab' ein Röslein stehn	Goethe	G	19 Aug 1815	1821, op.3/3	iii, 37; i, 24	12, 30
258	Bundeslied	In allen guten Stunden	Goethe	B♭	4 or 19 Aug 1815	1887	iii, 38; viii	
259	An den Mond (1)	Füllest wieder Busch und Tal	Goethe	E♭	19 Aug 1815	c1850	iii, 40; ix	
260	Wonne der Wehmut	Trocknet nicht, trocknet nicht	Goethe	c	20 Aug 1815	1829, op.115/2	iii, 42; viii	
261	Wer kauft Liebesgötter?	Von allen schönen Waren	Goethe	C	21 Aug 1815	c1850	iii, 43; viii	
262	Die Fröhlichkeit	Wes' Adern leichtes Blut durchspringt	M. J. Prandstetter	E	22 Aug 1815	1895	iii, 64; ix	
263	Cora an die Sonne	Nach so vielen trüben Tagen	Baumberg	E♭	22 Aug 1815	1848	iii, 50; ix	
264	Der Morgenkuss version a version b	Durch eine ganze Nacht	Baumberg	E♭ C	22 Aug 1815 c1815	1872 1850	iii, 51; ix —; ix	
265	Abendständchen: An Lina	Sei sanft wie ihre Seele	Baumberg	B♭	23 Aug 1815	1895	iii, 52; ix	
266	Morgenlied	Willkommen, rotes Morgenlicht	Stolberg	F	24 Aug 1815	1895	iii, 54; ix	
270	An die Sonne	Sinke, liebe Sonne	Baumberg	E♭	25 Aug 1815	1829, op.118/5	iii, 56; ix	
271	Der Weiberfreund	Noch fand von Evens Töchterscharen	A. Cowley, trans. J. F. von Ratschky	A	25 Aug 1815	1895	iii, 57; ix	
272	An die Sonne	Königliche Morgensonne	C. A. Tiedge	E♭	25 Aug 1815	1872	iii, 58; ix	

No.	Title	Incipit	Text	Key	Date	Year	Reference
273	Lilla an die Morgenröte	Wie schön bist du, du güldne Morgenröte		D	25 Aug 1815	1895	iii, 59; ix
274	Tischlerlied	Mein Handwerk geht durch alle Welt		C	25 Aug 1815	1850	iii, 60; ix
275	Totenkranz für ein Kind	Sanft wehn, im Hauch der Abendluft	Matthisson	g	25 Aug 1815	1895	iii, 61; ix
276	Abendlied	Gross und rotentflammet	Stolberg	A	28 Aug 1815	1895	iii, 62; ix
278	Ossians Lied nach dem Falle Nathos	Beugt euch aus euren Wolken nieder	Ossian, trans. Harold		?Sept 1815		
	version a, frag.			E		1897	Rev, 34; ix
	version b			E		1830	iii, 108; ix
280	Das Rosenband	Im Frühlingsgarten fand ich sie	F. G. Klopstock	A♭	Sept 1815	1837	iii, 72; ix
281	Das Mädchen von Inistore	Mädchen Inistores	Ossian, trans. Harold	c	Sept 1815	1830	iii, 110; ix
282	Cronnan	Ich sitz' bei der moosigten Quelle	Ossian, trans. Harold	c	5 Sept 1815	1830	iv, 21; ix
283	An den Frühling (1)	Willkommen, schöner Jüngling!	Schiller	F	6 Sept 1815	1865, op.172/5	iii, 68; xi
284	Lied	Es ist so angenehm	?Schiller	G	6 Sept 1815	1895	iii, 69; ix
285	Furcht der Geliebten (An Cidli)	Cidli, du weinest	Klopstock				
	version a			A♭	12 Sept 1815	1895	iii, 70; ix
	version b			A♭	c1815	1885	iii, 71; ix
286	Selma und Selmar	Weine du nicht	Klopstock				
	version a			F	c1815	1895	iii, 74; ix
	version b			F	14 Sept 1815	1837	iii, 75; ix
287	Vaterlandslied	Ich bin ein deutsches Mädchen	Klopstock				
	version a			C	14 Sept 1815	1895	iii, 76; ix
	version b			C	c1815	1895	iii, 77; ix
288	An Sie	Zeit, Verkündigerin der besten Freuden	Klopstock	A♭	14 Sept 1815	1895	iii, 78; ix
289	Die Sommernacht	Wenn der Schimmer von dem Monde	Klopstock				
	version a			C	14 Sept 1815	1895	iii, 80; ix
	version b			C	c1815	1895	iii, 82; ix
290	Die frühen Gräber	Willkommen, o silberner Mond	Klopstock	a	14 Sept 1815	1837	iii, 84; ix
291	Dem Unendlichen	Wie erhebt sich das Herz	Klopstock				
	version a			F	15 Sept 1815	1895	iii, 85; ix
	version b			F	c1815	1831	iii, 90; ix
	version c			G	c1815	1895	iii, 95; ix
292	Klage [see 371]						

90

D	Title	Incipit	Text	Key	Composed	Published	SW; NSA
293	Shilric und Vinvela	Mein Geliebter ist ein Sohn des Hügels	Ossian, trans. Harold	B♭	20 Sept 1815	1830	iii, 100; ix
295	Hoffnung	Schaff, das Tagwerk meiner Hände	Goethe			c1816	
	version a			F		1872	iii, 193; ix
	version b			E		1895	iii, 194; ix
296	An den Mond (2)	Füllest wieder Busch und Tal	Goethe	A♭	c1816	1868	iii, 195; ix
297	Augenlied	Süsse Augen, klare Bronnen!	Mayrhofer	F	?1817		
	version a			F		1895	iii, 168; ix
	version b					1850	—; ix
298	Liane	Hast du Lianen nicht gesehen?	Mayrhofer	C	Oct 1815	1895	iii, 165; ix
300	Der Jüngling an der Quelle	Leise, rieselnder Quell	J. G. von Salis-Seewis	A	c1817	1842	vi, 208; ix
301	Lambertine	O Liebe, die mein Herz erfüllet	J. L. Stoll	E♭	12 Oct 1815	1842	iii, 112; ix
302	Labetrank der Liebe	Wenn im Spiele leiser Töne	Stoll	F	15 Oct 1815	1895	iii, 114; ix
303	An die Geliebte	O, dass ich dir vom stillen Auge	Stoll	G	15 Oct 1815	1887	iii, 116; ix
304	Wiegenlied	Schlumm're sanft!	Körner	F	15 Oct 1815	1895	iii, 117; ix
305	Mein Gruss an den Mai	Sei mir gegrüsst, o Mai	Kumpf	B♭	15 Oct 1815	1895	iii, 118; ix
306	Skolie	Lasst im Morgenstrahl des Mai'n	J. L. von Deinhardstein	B♭	15 Oct 1815	1895	iii, 120; ix
307	Die Sternewelten	Oben drehen sich die grossen	U. Jarnik, trans. Fellinger	F	15 Oct 1815	1895	iii, 121; ix
308	Die Macht der Liebe	Überall, wohin mein Auge blicket	J. N. von Kalchberg	B♭	15 Oct 1815	1895	iii, 123; ix
309	Das gestörte Glück	Ich hab' ein heisses junges Blut	Körner	F	15 Oct 1815	1872	iii, 124; ix
310	Sehnsucht (1)	Nur wer die Sehnsucht kennt	Goethe		18 Oct 1815		
	version a			A♭		1895	iii, 126; iii
	version b			F		1895	iii, 128; iii
311	An den Mond, frag.			A	19 Oct 1815	—	—; ix
312	Hektors Abschied	Will sich Hektor ewig von mir wenden	Schiller		19 Oct 1815		
	version a			f		1895	iii, 130; iii
	version b			f	c1815	1826, op.58/1	iii, 36; iii
313	Die Sterne	Wie wohl ist mir im Dunkeln	Kosegarten	B♭	19 Oct 1815	1895	iii, 142; ix
314	Nachtgesang	Tiefe Feier schauert um die Welt	Kosegarten	E♭	19 Oct 1815	1887	iii, 144; ix
315	An Rosa I	Warum bist du nicht hier	Kosegarten	A♭	19 Oct 1815	1895	iii, 145; ix

No.	Title	Incipit	Poet	Key	Date	Pub.	Vol.	Refs
316	An Rosa II		Kosegarten					
	version a	Rosa, denkst du an mich?		A♭	19 Oct 1815	1895	iii, 146; ix	
	version b			A♭	c1815	1895	iii, 147; ix	
317	Idens Schwanenlied	Wie schaust du aus dem Nebelflor	Kosegarten					
	version a			f	19 Oct 1815	—	—; ix	
	version b			f	c1815	1895	iii, 148; ix	
318	Schwangesang	Endlich stehn die Pforten offen	Kosegarten	f	19 Oct 1815	1895	iii, 150; ix	
319	Luisens Antwort	Wohl weinen Gottes Engel	Kosegarten	b♭	19 Oct 1815	1895	iii, 152; ix	
320	Der Zufriedene	Zwar schuf das Glück hinieden	C. L. Reissig	A	23 Oct 1815	1895	iii, 154; ix	
321	Mignon	Kennst du das Land	Goethe	A	23 Oct 1815	1832	iii, 155; ix	
322	Hermann und Thusnelda	Ha, dort kömmt er	Klopstock	E♭	27 Oct 1815	1837	iii, 159; ix	
323	Klage der Ceres	Ist der holde Lenz erschienen?	Schiller	G	9 Nov 1815–June 1816	1895	iii, 171; ix	
325	Harfenspieler (1)	Wer sich der Einsamkeit ergibt	Goethe	a	13 Nov 1815	1895	iii, 187; i, 218	
327	Lorma (1), frag.	Lorma sass in der Halle von Aldo	Ossian, trans. Harold	a	28 Nov 1815	1928	—; x	
328	Erlkönig	Wer reitet so spät	Goethe					12, 13, 16, 17, 26, 29, 30, 46, 87
	version a			g	?Oct 1815	1895	iii, 202; i, 173	
	version b			g	1815	1868	iii, 214; i, 180	
	version c			g	1815	1895	iii, 208; i, 187	
	version d			g	1815	1821, op.1	iii, 219; i, 3	
329	Die drei Sänger, frag.	Der König sass beim frohen Mahle	F. Bobrik	A	23 Dec 1815	1895	x, 97; ix	
330	Das Grab (2) version a [for version b see 'Male voices']	Das Grab ist tief und stille	Salis-Seewis	c	28 Dec 1815	1895	iii, 231; iii/3	
342	An mein Klavier	Sanftes Klavier	C. F. D. Schubart	A	c1816	1885	iv, 138; x	
343	Am Tage aller Seelen (Litanei auf das Fest aller Seelen)	Ruhn in Frieden alle Seelen	J. G. Jacobi		Aug 1816			
	version a			E♭		1831	v, 126; x	
	version b			E♭		—	—; x	
344	Am ersten Maimorgen	Heute will ich fröhlich, fröhlich sein	Claudius	G	c1816	—	—; x	
350	Der Entfernten (2)	Wohl denk' ich allenthalben	Salis-Seewis	E♭	?1816	1885	iv, 69; x	
351	Fischerlied (1)	Das Fischergewerbe gibt rüstigen Mut!	Salis-Seewis	D	?1816	1895	iv, 70; xi	
352	Licht und Liebe (Nachtgesang), S, T	Liebe ist ein süsses Licht	M. von Collin	G	?1816	c1847	iv, 253; iii/2	

135

D	Title	Incipit	Text	Key	Composed	Published	SW; NSA
358	Die Nacht	Du verstörst uns nicht, o Nacht!	J. P. Uz	Ab	1816	c1849	iv, 127; x
359	Sehnsucht (2)	Nur wer die Sehnsucht kennt	Goethe	d	1816	1872	iv, 200; iii
360	Lied eines Schiffers an die Dioskuren	Dioskuren, Zwillingsterne	Mayrhofer	Ab	1816	1826, op.65/1	iv, 221; iii
361	Am Bach im Frühlinge	Du brachst sie nun, die kalte Rinde	Schober	Db	1816	1829, op.109/1	iv, 230; x
362	Zufriedenheit (1)	Ich bin vergnügt	Claudius	A	1815 or 1816	1895	iv, 244; xi
363	An Chloen, frag.	Die Munterkeit ist meinen Wangen	Uz	G	1816	—	—; x
367	Der König in Thule	Es war ein König in Thule	Goethe	d	early 1816	1821, op.5/5	iv, 202; i, 45
368	Jägers Abendlied (2)	Im Felde schleich' ich still und wild	Goethe	Db	?early 1816	1821, op.3/4	iv, 203; i, 25
369	An Schwager Kronos	Spude dich, Kronos!	Goethe	d	1816	1825, op.19/1	iv, 204; i, 121
371	Klage	Trauer umfliesst mein Leben	Stolberg-Stolberg	b	Jan 1816	1872	iv, 5; x
372	An die Natur	Süsse, heilige Natur		F	15 Jan 1816	1895	iv, 2; x
373	Lied	Mutter geht durch ihre Kammern	Fouqué	g	?15 Jan 1816	1895	iv, 3; x
375	Der Tod Oskars	Warum öffnest du wieder	Ossian, trans. Harold	c	Feb 1816	1830	iv, 7; x
376	Lorma (2), frag.	Lorma sass in der Halle von Aldo	Ossian, trans. Harold	a	10 Feb 1816	1895	x, 102; x
381	Morgenlied	Die frohe neubelebte Flur		C	24 Feb 1816	1895	iv, 29; x
382	Abendlied	Sanft glänzt die Abendsonne		F	24 Feb 1816	1895	iv, 30; x
388	Laura am Klavier	Wenn dein Finger durch die Saiten meistert	Schiller				
	version a			E	March 1816		iv, 41; x
	version b			A	c1816		iv, 46; x
389	Des Mädchens Klage (3)	Der Eichwald braust	Schiller	c	March 1816	1873	iv, 52; iii
390	Entzückung an Laura (1)	Laura, über diese Welt	Schiller	A	March 1816	1895	iv, 54; x
391	Die vier Weltalter	Wohl perlet im Glase	Schiller	G	March 1816	1829, op.111/3	iv, 56; x
392	Pflügerlied	Arbeitsam und wacker	Salis-Seewis	C	March 1816	1895	iv, 58; x
393	Die Einsiedelei (2)	Es rieselt, klar und wehend	Salis-Seewis	A	March 1816	c1845	iv, 60; xi
394	An die Harmonie	Schöpferin beseelter Töne!	Salis-Seewis	A	March 1816	1895	iv, 62; x
395	Lebensmelodien	Auf den Wassern wohnt mein stilles Leben	A. W. von Schlegel	G	March 1816	1829, op.111/2	iv, 72; x
396	Gruppe aus dem Tartarus (1), frag.	Horch, wie Murmeln des empörten Meeres	Schiller	c	March 1816	1975, op.111/2	—; ii, 171

16, 47, 88

D	Title	Incipit	Poet	Key	Date	Pub.	Ref.
397	Ritter Toggenburg	Ritter, treue Schwesterliebe	Schiller	F	13 March 1816	1832	iv, 31; x
398	Frühlingslied (2)	Die Luft ist blau	Hölty	G	13 May 1816	1887	iv, 97; x
399	Auf den Tod einer Nachtigall (2)	Sie ist dahin	Hölty	a	13 May 1816	1895	iv, 98; x
400	Die Knabenzeit	Wie glücklich, wem das Knabenkleid	Hölty	A	13 May 1816	1895	iv, 100; x
401	Winterlied	Keine Blumen blühn	Hölty	a	13 May 1816	1895	iv, 102; x
402	Der Flüchtling	Frisch atmet des Morgens lebendiger Hauch	Schiller	B♭	18 March 1816	1872	iv, 35; x
403	Lied, version a	Ins stille Land	Salis-Seewis	g	27 March 1816	1845	iv, 66; x
	version b			a	April 1816	1895	iv, 67; x
	version c			a	March 1816	—	–; x
	version d			a	Aug 1823	—	–; x
404	Die Herbstnacht	Mit leisen Harfentönen	Salis-Seewis	F	March 1816	1885	iv, 61; x
405	Der Herbstabend, version a	Abendglockenhalle zittern	Salis-Seewis	f	April 1816	1895	iv, 68; x
	version b			f	1816	—	–; x
406	Abschied von der Harfe	Noch einmal tön, o Harfe	Salis-Seewis	e	March 1816	1887	iv, 80; x
409	Die verfehlte Stunde	Quälend ungestilltes Sehnen	A. W. von Schlegel	f	April 1816	1872	iv, 70; x
410	Sprache der Liebe	Lass dich mit gelinden Schlägen	A. W. von Schlegel	E	April 1816	1829, op.115/3	iv, 78; x
411	Daphne am Bach	Ich hab' ein Bächlein funden	Stolberg-Stolberg	D	April 1816	1887	iv, 81; x
412	Stimme der Liebe, version a	Meine Selinde	Stolberg-Stolberg	E	1816	—	–; x
	version b			D	c1816	1838	iv, 82; x
413	Entzückung	Tag voll Himmel	Matthisson	C	April 1816	1895	iv, 84; x
414	Geist der Liebe (1)	Der Abend schleiert Flur und Hain	Matthisson	G	April 1816	1895	iv, 87; x
415	Klage	Die Sonne steigt	Matthisson	C	April 1816	1895	iv, 88; x
416	Lied in der Abwesenheit, frag.	Ach, mir ist das Herz so schwer	Stolberg-Stolberg	b	April 1816	1925	–; x
418	Stimme der Liebe (2)	Abendgewölke schweben hell	Matthisson	G	29 April 1816	1895	iv, 90; x
419	Julius an Theone	Nimmer, nimmer darf ich dir gestehen	Matthisson	g	30 April 1816	1895	iv, 95; x
429	Minnelied	Holder klingt der Vogelsang	Hölty	E	May 1816	1885	iv, 103; x
430	Die frühe Liebe, version a	Schon im bunten Knabenkleide	Hölty	E	May 1816	1895	iv, 104; x
	version b, lost			E	c1816	—	—

81

62

D	Title	Incipit	Text	Key	Composed	Published	SW; NSA
431	Blumenlied	Es ist ein halbes Himmelreich	Hölty	E	May 1816	1887	iv, 105; x
432	Der Leidende	Nimmer trag' ich länger			May 1816		
	version a			b		1850	iv, 106; x
	version b			b		1895	iv, 107; x
433	Seligkeit	Freuden sonder Zahl	Hölty	E	May 1816	1895	iv, 108; x
434	Erntelied	Sicheln schallen, Ähren fallen	Hölty	E	May 1816	1850	iv, 109; x
436	Klage	Dein Silber schien	Hölty	F	12 May 1816	1850	iv, 95; x
	version a			F	1816	—	—; x
	version b [formerly 437]						
437	Klage [see 436]						
442	Das grosse Halleluja	Ehre sei dem Hocherhabnen	Klopstock	E	June 1816	c1847	iv, 110; x
	version a [for version b see 'Female or unspecified voices']						
443	Schlachtlied (1)	Mit unserm Arm ist nichts getan	Klopstock	E	June 1816	1895	iv, 112; x
	version a [for version b see 'Female or unspecified voices']						
444	Die Gestirne	Es tönet sein Lob	Klopstock	F	June 1816	1831	iv, 114; x
445	Edone	Dein süsses Bild, Edone	Klopstock	E♭	June 1816	1837	iv, 116; x
446	Die Liebesgötter	Cypris, meiner Phyllis gleich	Uz	C	June 1816	1887	iv, 118; x
447	An den Schlaf	Komm, und senke die umflorten Schwingen		A	June 1816	1895	iv, 120; x
448	Gott im Frühlinge	In seinem schimmernden Gewand	Uz		June 1816	1887	iv, 121; x
	version a			E	June 1816		—; x
	version b			E	cJune 1816	—	—; x
449	Der gute Hirt	Was sorgst du?	Uz	E	June 1816		iv, 124; x
450	Fragment aus dem Aeschylus	So wird der Mann, der sonder Zwang	Aeschylus, trans. Mayrhofer		June 1816	1872	
	version a			A♭	July 1816	1895	iv, 128; x
	version b	Zieh hin, du braver Krieger du!	C. F. D. Schubart	A♭		1832	iv, 131; x
454	Grablied auf einen Soldaten			c		1872	iv, 140; x
455	Freude der Kinderjahre	Freude, die im frühen Lenze	F. von Köpken	C	July 1816	1887	iv, 142; x
456	Das Heimweh	Oft in einsam stillen Stunden	K. G. T. Winkler	F	July 1816	1887	iv, 144; x
457	An die untergehende Sonne	Sonne, du sinkst	Kosegarten	E♭	July 1816–May 1817	1827, op.44	iv, 134; iii

D	Title	First line	Poet	Key	Date	Publ.	Ref	
458	Aus Diego Manazares (Ilmerine)	Wo irrst du durch einsame Schatten	F. von Schlechta	A♭	30 July 1816	1872	iv, 146; x	
462	An Chloen	Bei der Liebe reinsten Flammen	Jacobi	A♭	Aug 1816	1895	iv, 149; x	
463	Hochzeit-Lied	Will singen euch im alten Ton	Jacobi	E♭	Aug 1816	1895	iv, 150; x	
464	In der Mitternacht	Todesstille deckt das Tal	Jacobi	c	Aug 1816	1895	iv, 151; x	
465	Trauer der Liebe	Wo die Taub in stillen Buchen	Jacobi					
	version a			A♭	Aug 1816	1885	iv, 152; x	
	version b			A♭	c1816	—	—; x	
466	Die Perle	Es ging ein Mann zur Frühlingszeit	Jacobi	d	Aug 1816	1872	iv, 153; x	
467	Pflicht und Liebe	Du, der ewig um mich trauert	F. W. Gotter	c	Aug 1816	1885	x, 104; x	
468	An den Mond	Was schauest du so hell und klar	Hölty	A	7 Aug 1816	1895	iv, 148; x	
469	Mignon (1), 2 frags.	So lasst mich scheinen	Goethe	A♭	Sept 1816	1897	Rev, 86; iii	
473	Liedesend	Auf seinem goldnen Throne	Mayrhofer					
	version a			c	Sept 1816	1895	iv, 154; x	
	version b			c	Sept 1816	1833	iv, 159; x	
474	Lied des Orpheus, als er in die Hölle ging	Wälze dich hinweg	Jacobi					
	version a, inc.			G♭	Sept 1816	1895	iv, 164; x	
	version b			G♭	1816	1832	iv, 170; x	
475	Abschied (nach einer Wallfahrtsarie)	Über die Berge zieht ihr fort	Mayrhofer	G	Sept 1816	1885	iv, 176; xi	
476	Rückweg	Zum Donaustrom, zur Kaiserstadt	Mayrhofer	d	Sept 1816	1872	iv, 178; xi	
477	Alte Liebe rostet nie		Mayrhofer	B	Sept 1816	1895	iv, 180; xi	
478	Harfenspieler I (Gesänge des Harfners no.1) (2)	Wer sich der Einsamkeit ergibt	Goethe					16, 34, 89
	version a			a	Sept 1816	1895	iv, 181; i, 220	
	version b			a	1822	1822, op.12/1	iv, 189; i, 85	
479	Harfenspieler II (Gesänge des Harfners no.3)	An die Türen will ich schleichen	Goethe					16, 34
	version a			a	Sept 1816	1895	iv, 184; i, 224	
	version b			a	1822	1822, op.12/3	iv, 196; i, 93	
480	Harfenspieler III (Gesänge des Harfners no.2) (1, 2, 3)	Wer nie sein Brot mit Tränen ass	Goethe					16, 34
	version a			a	Sept 1816	1895	iv, 186; i, 291	
	version b			a	Sept 1816	1895	iv, 187; i, 226	
	version c			a	1822	1822,	iv, 192; i, 89	

16, 30, 87, 99

D	Title	Incipit	Text	Key	Composed	Published	SW; NSA
						op.12/2	
481	Sehnsucht (3)	Nur wer die Sehnsucht kennt	Goethe	a	Sept 1816	1895	iv, 198; iii
482	Der Sänger am Felsen	Klage, meine Flöte	C. Pichler	e	Sept 1816	1895	iv, 200; xi
483	Lied	Ferne von der grossen Stadt	Pichler	E	Sept 1816	1895	iv, 212; xi
484	Gesang der Geister über den Wassern (1), frag.	… dann zur Tiefe nieder	Goethe	G	Sept 1816	1895	x, 594; xi
489	Der Wanderer	Ich komme von Gebirge her	G. P. Schmidt von Lübeck				
	version a			c♯	Oct 1816	1895	iv, 214; i, 200
	version b [formerly 493b]			b	c1816	1970	—; i, 204
	version c [formerly 493a]			c♯	c1816	1821,	iv, 217; i, 26
						op.4/1	
490	Der Hirt	Du Turm! zu meinem Leide	Mayrhofer	F	Oct 1816	1895	iv, 220; xi
491	Geheimnis	Sag an, wer lehrt dich Lieder	Mayrhofer	B♭	Oct 1816	1887	iv, 223; xi
492	Zum Punsche	Woget brausend, Harmonien	Mayrhofer	d	Oct 1816	1849	iv, 226; xi
493	Der Wanderer [see 489b–c]						
495	Abendlied der Fürstin	Der Abend rötet nun das Tal	Mayrhofer	F	Nov 1816	1868	iv, 227; xi
496	Bei dem Grabe meines Vaters	Friede sei um diesen Grabstein	M. Claudius	E♭	Nov 1816	1885	iv, 234; xi
496a	Klage um Ali Bey	Lasst mich! lasst mich! ich will klagen	Claudius	e♭	Nov 1816	1968	—; vii, 84
497	An die Nachtigall	Er liegt und schläft	Claudius	G	Nov 1816	1829,	iv, 238; v
						op.98/1	
498	Wiegenlied	Schlafe, schlafe, holder süsser Knabe		A♭	Nov 1816	1829,	iv, 239; v
						op.98/2	
499	Abendlied	Der Mond ist aufgegangen	Claudius	B♭	Nov 1816	1885	iv, 240; xi
500	Phidile	Ich war erst sechzehn Sommer alt	Claudius	G♭	Nov 1816	1895	iv, 242; xi
501	Zufriedenheit (2)	Ich bin vergnügt	Claudius		Nov 1816		
	version a			E		1895	iv, 246; xi
	version b			G		—	—; xi
502	Herbstlied	Bunt sind schon die Wälder	Salis-Seewis	G	Nov 1816	1872	iv, 248; xi
503	Mailied (3)	Grüner wird die Au	Hölty	G	Nov 1816	—	—; xi
504	Am Grabe Anselmos	Dass ich dich verloren habe	Claudius	e♭	4 Nov 1816	1821,	iv, 236; i, 56
	version a					op.6/3	
	version b			e♭	c1816	1970	—; i, 216
507	Skolie	Mädchen entsiegelten	Matthisson	G	Dec 1816	1895	iv, 249; xi
508	Lebenslied	Kommen und Scheiden	Matthisson	C	Dec 1816	1845	iv, 250; xi

D	Title / version	Incipit	Author	Key	Composed	Published	Vol. refs
509	Leiden der Trennung	Vom Meere trennt sich die Welle	Metastasio, trans. H. von Collin		Dec 1816		
	version a, frag.						
	version b			g		—	—; xi
510	Vedi quanto adoro		Metastasio	g	Dec 1816	1872	iv, 251; xi
513a	Nur wer die Liebe kennt, sketch		Werner	E♭	?1817	1895	x, 40; xi
				A♭		1974	—; xi
514	Die abgeblühte Linde	Wirst du halten, was du schwurst	L. von Széchényi	a	?1817	1821, op.7/1	v, 29; i, 59
515	Der Flug der Zeit	Es floh die Zeit im Wirbelfluge	Széchényi	A	?1817	1821, op.7/2	v, 33; i, 63
516	Sehnsucht	Der Lerche wolkennahe Lieder	Mayrhofer	C	?1816	1822, op.8/2	vi, 386; i, 73
517	Der Schäfer und der Reiter	Ein Schäfer sass im Grünen	Fouqué		April 1817		
	version a			E		1972	—; i, 191
	version b			E		1822, op.13/1	v, 6; i, 95
518	An den Tod	Tod, du Schrecken der Natur	Schubart	B	1816 or 1817	1824	v, 130; v
519	Die Blumensprache	Es deuten die Blumen	? E. Platner	B♭	?1817	1867, op.173/5	v, 25; xi
520	Frohsinn	Ich bin in lockerem Schlage	Castelli		Jan 1817		
	version a			F		1895	v, 2; xi
	version b			F	c1817	1850	—; xi
521	Jagdlied	Trarah! Trarah! wir kehren daheim	Werner	F	Jan 1817	1895	v, 3; xi
	version a [for version b see 'Female and unspecified voices']						
522	Die Liebe	Wo weht der Liebe hoher Geist?	G. Leon	G	Jan 1817	1895	v, 4; xi
523	Trost	Nimmer lange weil' ich hier		c♯	Jan 1817	1885	v, 5; xi
524	Der Alpenjäger	Auf hohen Bergesrücken	Mayrhofer		Jan 1817		
	version a			E		1895	v, 12; i, 233
	version b			D		1970	—; i, 236
	version c			F		1822, op.13/3	v, 16; i, 104
525	Wie Ulfru fischt	Der Angel zuckt	Mayrhofer		Jan 1817		
	version a			d		1970	—; i, 269
	version b			d		1823, op.21/3	v, 18; i, 158
526	Fahrt zum Hades	Der Nachen dröhnt	Mayrhofer	d	Jan 1817	1832	v, 20; xi

D	Title	Incipit	Text	Key	Composed	Published	SW; NSA	
527	Schlaflied (Abendlied; Schlummerlied) version a version b	Es mahnt der Wald	Mayrhofer	F F	Jan 1817	1975 1823, op.24/2	—; ii, 193 v, 24; ii, 20	
528 530	La pastorella al prato (2) An eine Quelle	Du kleine grünumwachs'ne Quelle	C. Goldoni Claudius	G A	Jan 1817 Feb 1817	1872 1829, op.109/3	x, 46; xi iv, 232; xi	19, 30, 41
531	Der Tod und das Mädchen	Vorüber, ach vorüber	Claudius	d	Feb 1817	1821, op.7/3	v, 35; i, 66	
532	Das Lied vom Reifen, frag.	Seht meine lieben Bäume an	Claudius	A♭	Feb 1817	1895	v, 36; xi	
533	Täglich zu singen	Ich danke Gott und freue mich	Claudius	F	Feb 1817	1895	v, 38; xi	
534	Die Nacht	Die Nacht ist dumpfig und finster	Ossian, trans. Harold	g	Feb 1817	1830	v, 39; xi	
535	Lied, with small orch	Brüder, schrecklich brennt die Träne		g	Feb 1817	1895	x, 78; iii/1	
536	Der Schiffer version a version b	Im Winde, im Sturme	Mayrhofer	E♭ E♭	?March 1817	1970 1823, op.21/2	—; i, 263 v, 24; i, 152	
539	Am Strome	Ist mir's doch, als sei mein Leben	Mayrhofer	B	March 1817	1822, op.8/4	v, 54; i, 82	
540 541	Philoktet Memnon	Da sitz' ich ohne Bogen Den Tag hindurch nur einmal	Mayrhofer Mayrhofer	b D♭	March 1817 March 1817	1831 1821, op.6/1	v, 56; xi v, 59; i, 46	19
542	Antigone und Oedip	Ihr hohen Himmlischen	Mayrhofer	C	March 1817	1821, op.6/2	v, 62; i, 50	
543	Auf dem See version a version b	Und frische Nahrung	Goethe	E E♭	March 1817	1895 1828, op.92/2	v, 66; v v, 70; v	
544	Ganymed	Wie im Morgenglanze	Goethe	A♭	March 1817	1825, op.19/3	v, 75; i, 132	17, 47, 90
545	Der Jüngling und der Tod version a version b	Die Sonne sinkt, o könnt ich	J. von Spaun	c♯ c♯	March 1817	1895 1872	v, 80; xi v, 82; xi	
546	Trost im Liede	Braust des Unglücks Sturm empor	Schober	d	March 1817	1827; 1828 as op.101/3	v, 84; v	

D	Title	Poet	Incipit	Key	Date	Published	Refs	
547	An die Musik	Schober	Du holde Kunst					19, 88
	version a			D	March 1817	1895	v, 86; iv	
	version b			D	c1817	1827	v, 87; iv	
548	Orest auf Tauris	Mayrhofer	Ist dies Tauris	E♭	March 1817	1831 op.88/4	vi, 118; xi	
549	Mahomets Gesang (1), frag.	Goethe	Seht den Felsenquell	c♯	March 1817	1895	x, 110; xiii	19
550	Die Forelle	Schubart	In einem Bächlein helle					
	version a			D♭	c1817	1895	v, 132; ii, 194	
	version b			D♭	c1817	1895	v, 135; ii, 202	
	version c			D♭	Feb 1818	1895	v, 138; ii, 198	
	version d			D♭	c1820	1820; 1827 as op.32	v, 141; ii, 109	
	version e			D♭		1975	—; ii, 206	
551	Pax vobiscum	Schober	Der Friede sei mit euch!	F	Oct 1821	1831	v, 88; xi	70
552	Hänflings Liebeswerbung	F. Kind	Ahidi! ich liebe					
	version a			A	April 1817	1970	—; i, 260	
	version b			A	c1817	1823, op.20/3	v, 90; i, 145	
553	Auf der Donau	Mayrhofer	Auf der Wellen Spiegel	E♭	April 1817	1823, op.21/1	v, 92; i, 148	
554	Uraniens Flucht	Mayrhofer	Lasst uns, ihr Himmlischen	D	April 1817	1895	v, 99; xi	
555	Song sketch (no text)	—		a	?May 1817	1934	—; xi	
558	Liebhaber in allen Gestalten	Goethe	Ich wollt', ich wär' ein Fisch	A	May 1817	1887	iii, 46; xi	
559	Schweizerlied	Goethe	Uf'm Bergli bin i g'sässe	F	May 1817	1885	iii, 48; xi	
560	Der Goldschmiedsgesell	Goethe	Es ist doch meine Nachbarin	F	May 1817	1850	iii, 49; xi	
561	Nach einem Gewitter	Mayrhofer	Auf den Blumen	F	May 1817	1872	v, 116; xi	
562	Fischerlied (3)	Salis-Seewis	Das Fischergewerbe gibt rüstigen Mut!	F	May 1817	1895	v, 118; xi	
563	Die Einsiedelei (3)	Salis-Seewis	Es rieselt, klar und wehend	C	May 1817	1887	v, 120; xi	
564	Gretchen im Zwinger (Gretchen; Gretchens Bitte), frag.	Goethe	Ach neige; du Schmerzensreiche	b♭	May 1817	1838	x, 116; xi	
565	Der Strom		Mein Leben wälzt sich murrend fort	d	?June 1817	1876	v, 123; xi	
569	Das Grab (4), for unison chorus	Salis-Seewis	Das Grab ist tief und stille	c♯	June 1817	1895	v, 122; iii/3	
573	Iphigenia	Mayrhofer	Blüht denn hier an Tauris Strande	G♭	July 1817	1829, op.98/3	v, 127; v	
577	Entzückung an Laura (2)	Schiller	Laura, Laura, über diese Welt					
	frag. a			A	Aug 1817	1873	x, 119; x	
	frag. b			D♭		1895	x, 120; x	

D	Title	Incipit	Text	Key	Composed	Published	SW; NSA	
578	Abschied (Wiegenlied)	Lebe wohl! lebe wohl!	Schubert	b	24 Aug 1817	1838	x, 80; xi	
579	Der Knabe in der Wiege	Er schläft so süss	A. Ottenwalt					
	version a			C	autumn 1817	1872	v, 180; xi	
	version b, frag.			A♭	Nov 1817	1897	Rev, 70; xi	
579a	Vollendung [formerly 989]	Wenn ich einst das Ziel errungen habe	Matthisson	A	?Sept–Oct 1817	1970	—; xi	
579b	Die Erde [formerly 989a]	Wenn sanft entzückt	Matthisson	E	?Sept–Oct 1817	1970	—; xi	
582	Augenblicke im Elysium [see 990b]							
583	Gruppe aus dem Tartarus (2)	Horch, wie Murmeln des empörten Meeres	Schiller	C	Sept 1817	1823, op.24/1	v, 144; ii, 13	19, 26, 92
584	Elysium	Vorüber die stöhnende Klage!	Schiller	E	Sept 1817	1830	v, 149; xi	
585	Atys	Der Knabe seufzt	Mayrhofer	a	Sept 1817	1833	v, 159; xi	
586	Erlafsee	Mir ist so wohl, so weh'	Mayrhofer	F	Sept 1817	1818; 1822 as op.8/3	v, 164; i, 78	19
587	An den Frühling (3) version a	Willkommen schöner Jungling!	Schiller	A	Oct 1817	1885	iii, 8; xi	
	version b [formerly 245]			B♭	c1817	1895	iii, 6; xi	
588	Der Alpenjäger	Willst du nicht das Lämmlein huten	Schiller					
	version a, frag.			E♭	Oct 1817	1897	Rev, 66; ii, 236	
	version b			C	c1817	1825, op.37/2	v, 168; ii, 138	
594	Der Kampf	Nein, länger werd' ich diesen Kampf	Schiller	d	Nov 1817	1829, op.110	v, 171; xi	
595	Thekla: eine Geisterstimme (2)	Wo ich sei, und wo mich hingewendet	Schiller					
	version a			c♯	Nov 1817	1895	v, 177; iv	
	version b			c	c1817	1827, op.88/2	v, 178; iv	
596	Lied eines Kindes, frag.	Lauter Freude fühl' ich		B♭	Nov 1817	1895	x, 122; xi	
611	Auf der Riesenkoppe	Hoch auf dem Gipfel deiner Gebirge	Körner	d	March 1818	c1850	v, 184; xii	
614	An den Mond in einer Herbstnacht	Freundlich ist dein Antlitz	A. Schreiber	A	April 1818	1832	v, 188; xii	
616	Grablied für die Mutter	Hauche milder, Abendluft		b	June 1818	1838	v, 194; xii	
619	Vocal exercise, 2vv, figured bass (no text)		—	C	July 1818	1892	ser. xix, 95; viii/2	

						Composed	Published	
620	Einsamkeit	Gib mir die Fülle der Einsamkeit!	Mayrhofer	B♭	July 1818	1840	v, 196; xii
622	Der Blumenbrief	Euch Blümlein will ich senden	Schreiber	D	Aug 1818	1833	v, 213; xii
623	Das Marienbild	Sei gegrüsst, du Frau der Huld	Schreiber	C	Aug 1818	1831	v, 214; xii
626	Blondel zu Marien	In düstrer Nacht	Schreiber	e♭	Sept 1818	1842	v, 218; xii
627	Das Abendrot	Du heilig, glühend Abendrot!	Schreiber	E	Nov 1818	1867, op.173/6	v, 220; xii
628	Sonett I	Apollo, lebet noch	Petrarch, trans. A. W. von Schlegel	B♭	Nov 1818	1895	v, 225; xii
629	Sonett II	Allein, nachdenklich, wie gelähmt	Petrarch, trans. A. W. von Schlegel	g	Nov 1818	1895	v, 228; xii
630	Sonett III	Nunmehr, da Himmel, Erde	Petrarch, trans. J. D. Gries	C	Dec 1818	1895	v, 234; xii
631	Blanka (Das Mädchen)	Wenn mich einsam Lüfte fächeln	F. von Schlegel	a	Dec 1818	1885	v, 236; xii
632	Vom Mitleiden Mariä	Als bei dem Kreuz Maria stand	F. von Schlegel	g	Dec 1818	1831	v, 238; xii
633	Der Schmetterling	Wie soll ich nicht tanzen	F. von Schlegel	F	c1819	1826, op.57/1	iii, 225; iii
634	Die Berge	Sieht uns der Blick gehoben	F. von Schlegel	G	c1819	1826, op.57/2	iii, 227; iii
636	Sehnsucht (2)	Ach, aus dieses Tales Gründen	Schiller		c1821		
	version a			b		1975	—; ii, 250
	version b			b		1895	vi, 23; ii, 258
	version c			b		1826, op.39	vi, 29; ii, 165
637	Hoffnung (2)	Es reden und träumen die Menschen	Schiller	B♭	c1819	1827, op.87/2	vi, 36; iv
638	Der Jüngling am Bache (3)	An der Quelle sass der Knabe	Schiller				
	version a			d	April 1819	1895	vi, 40; iv
	version b			c	c1819	1827, op.87/3	vi, 36; iv
639	Widerschein		Schlechta		c1819		
	version a	Fischer harrt am Brückenbogen		D		1820	—; v
	version b [formerly 949]	Tom lehnt harrend auf der Brücke		B♭		1832	ix, 130; v
645	Abend, frag.	Wie ist es denn	L. Tieck	g	?Jan 1819	—	—; xii
646	Die Gebüsche	Es wehet kühl und leise	F. von Schlegel	G	Jan 1819	1885	vi, 1; xii

D	Title	Incipit	Text	Key	Composed	Published	SW, NSA	
649	Der Wanderer	Wie deutlich des Mondes Licht	F. von Schlegel	D	Feb 1819	1826, op.65/2	vi, 5; iii	
650	Abendbilder	Still beginnt's im Hain zu tauen	J. P. Silbert	a	Feb 1819	1831	vi, 7; xii	
651	Himmelsfunken	Der Odem Gottes weht	Silbert	G	Feb 1819	1831	vi, 14; xii	
652	Das Mädchen version a	Wie so innig, möcht ich sagen	F. von Schlegel	A	Feb 1819	1842	vi, 16; xii	
	version b			A	cFeb 1819	—	—; xii	
653	Bertas Lied in der Nacht	Nacht umhüllt mit wehendem Flügel	Grillparzer	e♭	Feb 1819	c1842	vi, 18; xii	
654	An die Freunde	Im Wald, im Wald da grabt mich ein	Mayrhofer	a	March 1819	c1842	vi, 20; xii	
658	Marie	Ich sehe dich in tausend Bildern	Novalis	D	?May 1819	1895	vi, 53; xii	
659	Hymne I	Wenige wissen das Geheimnis	Novalis	a	May 1819	1872	vi, 42; xii	
660	Hymne II	Wenn ich ihn nur habe	Novalis	b♭	May 1819	1872	vi, 49; xii	
661	Hymne III	Wenn alle untreu werden	Novalis	b♭	May 1819	1872	vi, 50; xii	
662	Hymne IV	Ich sag' es jedem	Novalis	A	May 1819	1872	vi, 52; xii	
663	Der 13. Psalm, frag.	Ach, Herr, wie lange	trans. M. Mendelssohn	D♭	June 1819	1927	—; xii	
669	Beim Winde	Es träumen die Wolken	Mayrhofer	g	Oct 1819	1829	vi, 54; xii	
670	Die Sternennächte	In monderhellten Nächten	Mayrhofer	D♭	Oct 1819	1862	vi, 56; xii	
671	Trost	Hörnerklagen rufen klagend	Mayrhofer	E♭	Oct 1819	1849, op.165/2	vi, 60; xii	
672	Nachtstück version a	Wenn über Bergen der Nebel sich breitet	Mayrhofer	c♯	Oct 1819	1975	—; ii, 225	24
	version b	Wenn über Berge sich der Nebel breitet		c	c1819	1825, op.36/2	vi, 62; ii, 125	
673	Die Liebende schreibt	Ein Blick von deinen Augen	Goethe	B♭	Oct 1819	1832; 1862 as op.165/1	vi, 68; xii	
674	Prometheus	Bedecke deinen Himmel, Zeus	Goethe	g	Oct 1819	1850	vi, 70; xii	24, 34
677	Strophe aus Die Götter Griechenlands version a	Schöne Welt, wo bist du?	Schiller	a/A	Nov 1819	1895	vi, 76; xii	24
	version b			a/A		1848	vi, 78; xii	
682	Über allen Zauber Liebe, frag.	Sie hüpfte mit mir auf grünem Plan	Mayrhofer	G	c1820	1895	x, 123; xii	
684	Die Sterne	Du staunest, o Mensch	F. von Schlegel	E♭	1820	1850	vi, 102; xii	
685	Morgenlied	Eh' die Sonne früh aufersteht	Werner	a	1820	1821, op.4/2	vi, 104; i, 30	

D	Title	First line	Poet	Key	Composed	Published	Reference	
686	Frühlingsglaube	Die linden Lüfte sind erwacht	Uhland					37, 89
	version a			B♭	Sept 1820	1970	—; i, 252	
	version b			B♭	1820	1970	—; i, 256	
	version c			A♭	Nov 1822	1823, op.20/2	vi, 108; i, 141	
687	Nachthymne	Hinüber wall' ich	Novalis	D	Jan 1820	1872	vi, 372; xii	
688	Vier Canzonen				Jan 1820	1871		
		1 Non t'accostar all'urna	J. A. Vitorelli	C			x, 48; xii	
		2 Guarda, che bianca luna	Vitorelli	G			x, 50; xii	
		3 Da quel sembiante appresi	Metastasio	B♭			x, 52; xii	
		4 Mio ben ricordati	Metastasio	b♭			x, 53; xii	
690	Abendröte	Tiefer sinkt schon die Sonne	F. von Schlegel	A	March 1823	1830	vi, 94; xii	
691	Die Vögel	Wie lieblich und fröhlich	F. von Schlegel	A	March 1820	1865, op.172/6	vi, 86; xii	
692	Der Knabe	Wenn ich nur ein Vöglein wäre	F. von Schlegel	A	March 1820	1872	vi, 88; xii	
693	Der Fluss	Wie rein Gesang sich windet	F. von Schlegel	B	March 1820	1872	vi, 91; xii	
694	Der Schiffer	Friedlich lieg' ich hingegossen	F. von Schlegel	D	March 1820	1842	vi, 98; xii	
695	Namenstagslied	Vater, schenk' mir diese Stunde	A. Stadler	A	March 1820	1895	x, 81; xii	
698	Des Fräuleins Liebeslauschen (Liebeslauschen)	Da unten steht ein Ritter	Schlechta	A	Sept 1820	1832	vi, 113; xii	
699	Der entsühnte Orest	Zu meinen Füssen brichst du dich	Mayrhofer	C	Sept 1820	1831	vi, 121; xii	
700	Freiwilliges Versinken	Wohin? O Helios!	Mayrhofer	d	Sept 1820	1831	vi, 124; xii	26
702	Der Jüngling auf dem Hügel	Ein Jüngling auf dem Hügel	H. Hüttenbrenner	G	Nov 1820	1822, op.8/1	vi, 126; i, 68	
707	Der zürnenden Diana	Ja, spanne nur den Bogen	Mayrhofer		Dec 1820			46
	version a			A		1895	vi, 133; ii, 210	
	version b			A♭		1825, op.36/1	vi, 141; ii, 113	
708	Im Walde (Waldesnacht)	Windes Rauschen, Gottes Flügel	F. von Schlegel	c♯	Dec 1820	1832	vi, 149; xii	26
711	Lob der Tränen	Laue Lüfte, Blumendüfte	A. W. von Schlegel		1818			
	version a			D		1970	—; i, 229	
	version b			D		1822, op.13/2	v, 10; i, 100	
712	Die gefangenen Sänger	Hörst du von den Nachtigallen	A. W. von Schlegel	G	Jan 1821	1842	vi, 164; xiii	
713	Der Unglückliche	Die Nacht bricht an	Pichler		Jan 1821			
	version a			b		1895	vi, 168; iv	
	version b			b		1827, op.87/1	vi, 173; iv	

D	Title	Incipit	Text	Key	Composed	Published	SW; NSA	
715	Versunken	Voll Locken kraus ein Haupt	Goethe	A♭	Feb 1821	1845	vi, 178; xiii	100
716	Grenzen der Menschheit	Wenn der uralte heilige Vater	Goethe	E	March 1821	1832	vi, 185; xiii	29, 55, 92
717	Suleika II	Ach um deine feuchten Schwingen	? M. von Willemer	B♭	?March 1821	1825, op.31	vi, 201; ii, 97	46
719	Geheimes	Über meines Liebchens Äugeln	Goethe	A♭	March 1821	1822, op.14/2	vi, 183; i, 118	29, 34
720	Suleika I version a	Was bedeutet die Bewegung?	?Willemer	b	March 1821	1970	—; i, 239	
	version b			b	c1821	1822, op.14/1	vi, 194; i, 108	
721	Mahomets Gesang (2), frag.	Seht den Felsenquell	Goethe	c♯	March 1821	1895	x, 125; xiii	
725	Linde Lüfte wehen, Mez, T, frag.		Goethe	b	April 1821	1929	—; iii/2	
726	Mignon I (1)	Heiss mich nicht reden	Goethe	b	April 1821	1870	vi, 189; iii	
727	Mignon II (2)	So lasst mich scheinen	Goethe	b	April 1821	1850	vi, 191; iii	
728	Johanna Sebus, frag.	Der Damm zerreisst	Goethe	d	April 1821	1895	x, 128; xiii	
731	Der Blumen Schmerz	Wie tönt es mir so schaurig	J. Mayláth	e	Sept 1821	1821; 1867 as op.173/4	vi, 210; v	
736	Ihr Grab	Dort ist ihr Grab	K. A. Engelhardt	E♭	?1822	1842	vii, 4; xiii	
737	An die Leier	Ich will von Atreus Söhnen	F. S. Ritter von Bruchmann, after Anacreon	E♭	? 1822 or 1823	1826, op.56/2	vii, 42; iii	
738	Im Haine	Sonnenstrahlen durch die Tannen	Bruchmann	A	? 1822 or 1823	1826, op.56/3	vii, 46; iii	
741	Sei mir gegrüsst	O du Entrissne mir	F. Rückert	B♭	between end 1821 and autumn 1822	1823, op.20/1	vi, 214; i, 137	32, 37, 60
742	Der Wachtelschlag	Ach! mir schallt's dorten	S. F. Sauter	A	1822	1822; 1827 as op.68	vii, 2; iii	
743	Selige Welt	Ich treibe auf des Lebens Meer	J. C. Senn	A♭	?autumn 1822	1823, op.23/2	vii, 14; ii, 6	
744	Schwanengesang	Wie klag ich's aus	Senn	A♭	?autumn 1822	1823, op.23/3	vii, 16; ii, 8	
745	Die Rose version a	Es lockte schöne Wärme	F. von Schlegel	G	1822	1822; 1827 as op.73	vii, 18; iii	
	version b			F		1895	vii, 21; iii	
746	Am See	In des Sees Wogenspiele	Bruchmann	E♭	? 1822 or 1823	1831	vii, 74; xiii	

749	Herrn Josef Spaun, Assessor in Linz (Sendschreiben an den Assessor Spaun in Linz)	Und nimmer schreibst du?	M. von Collin	c	Jan 1822			x, 84; xiii
751	Die Liebe hat gelogen		A. von Platen-Hallermünde	c	by 17 April 1822	1823, op.23/1	34	vii, 28; ii, **4**
752	Nachtviolen	Im kalten rauhen Norden	Mayrhofer	C	April 1822	1872		vii, 6; xiii
753	Heliopolis I		Mayrhofer	e	April 1822	1826, op.65/3		vii, 10; iii
754	Heliopolis II	Fels auf Felsen hingewälzet	Mayrhofer	c	April 1822	1842		vii, 14; xiii
756	Du liebst mich nicht	Mein Herz ist zerrissen	Platen-Hallermünde		July 1822			
	version a			g♯		1895		vii, 24; iii
	version b			a		1826, op.59/1		vii, 26; iii
758	Todesmusik	In des Todes Feierstunde	Schober	G♭	Sept 1822	1829, op.108/2		vii, 30; v
761	Schatzgräbers Begehr	In tiefster Erde ruht ein alt Gesetz	Schober		Nov 1822			
	version a			d		1823, op.23/4		vii, 35; ii, 10
	version b			d		1895		vii, 187; ii, 189
762	Schwestergruss	Im Mondenschein wall' ich auf und ab	Bruchmann	f♯	Nov 1822	1833		vii, 38; xiii
764	Der Musensohn	Durch Feld und Wald zu schweifen	Goethe				34	
	version a			A♭	Dec 1822	1895		vii, **48**; v
	version b			G	c1822	1828, op.92/1		vii, **51**; v
765	An die Entfernte	So hab' ich wirklich dich verloren?	Goethe	G	Dec 1822	1868	92	vii, **54**; xiii
766	Am Flusse (2)	Verfliesset, vielgeliebte Lieder	Goethe	D	Dec 1822	1872	34	vii, **56**; xiii
767	Willkommen und Abschied	Es schlug mein Herz	Goethe		Dec 1822			
	version a			D	Dec 1822	1895		vii, **58**; iii
	version b			C	c1822	1826, op.56/1		vii, **64**; iii
768	Wandrers Nachtlied	Über allen Gipfeln ist Ruh	Goethe	B♭	by July 1824	1827, 1828 as op.96/3		vii, **70**; v
770	Drang in die Ferne	Vater, du glaubst es nicht	K. G. von Leitner	a/A	early 1823	1823; 1827 as op.71		vii, **91**; iii

D	Title	Incipit	Text	Key	Composed	Published	SW; NSA	
771	Der Zwerg	Im trüben Licht verschwinden schon die Berge	M. von Collin	a	? 1822 or 1823	1823, op.22/1	vii, 95; i, 160	86
772	Wehmut	Wenn ich durch Wald und Fluren geh'	M. von Collin	d	? 1822 or 1823	1823, op.22/2	vii, 102; i, 168	
774	Auf dem Wasser zu singen	Mitten im Schimmer der spiegelnden Wellen	Stolberg-Stolberg	A♭	1823	1823; 1827 as op.72	vii, 106; iii	
775	Dass sie hier gewesen	Dass der Ostwind Düfte	Rückert	C	?1823	1826, op.59/2	viii, 2; iii	39, 92
776	Du bist die Ruh		Rückert	E♭	1823	1826, op.59/3	viii, 4; iii	39, 91, 97
777	Lachen und Weinen		Rückert	A♭	?1823	1826, op.59/4	viii, 7; iii	87
778	Greisengesang version a version b	Der Frost hat mir bereifet	Rückert	b b	by June 1823	— 1826, op.60/1	—; iii viii, 10; iii	
778a	Die Wallfahrt	Meine Tränen im Bussgewand	Rückert	f	?1823	1969	—; xiii	93
785	Der zürnende Barde	Wer wagt's, wer wagt's	Bruchmann	g	Feb 1823	1831	vii, 71; xiii	
786	Viola	Schneeglöcklein, o Schneeglöcklein	Schober	A♭	March 1823	1830, op.123	vii, 76; xiii	
788	Lied (Die Mutter Erde)	Des Lebens Tag ist schwer	Stolberg-Stolberg	a/A	April 1823	1838	vii, 104; xiii	
789	Pilgerweise	Ich bin ein Waller auf der Erde	Schober	f♯	April 1823	1832	vii, 108; xiii	
792	Vergissmeinnicht	Als der Frühling sich vom Herzen	Schober	A♭	May 1823	1833	vii, 114; xiii	
793	Das Geheimnis (2)	Sie konnte mir kein Wörtchen sagen	Schiller	G	May 1823	1867, op.173/2	vii, 125; xiii	
794	Der Pilgrim version a version b	Noch in meines Lebens Lenze	Schiller	E D	May 1823 c1823	1895 1825, op.37/1	vii, 130; ii, 229 —; ii, 132	
795	Die schöne Müllerin		W. Müller		Oct–Nov 1823	1824, op.25		38, 39, 41, 54, 55, 93ff
	1 Das Wandern	Das Wandern ist des Müllers Lust		B♭			vii, 134; ii, 21	
	2 Wohin?	Ich hört' ein Bächlein rauschen		G			vii, 136; ii, 23	88
	3 Halt!	Eine Mühle seh' ich blinken		C			vii, 140; ii, 29	86
	4 Danksagung an den Bach	War es also gemeint		G			vii, 143; ii, 34	
	5 Am Feierabend	Hätt' ich tausend Arme zu rühren		a			vii, 147; ii, 36	94
	6 Der Neugierige	Ich frage keine Blume		B			vii, 149; ii, 42	94
	7 Ungeduld	Ich schnitt es gern in alle Rinden ein		A			vii, 152; ii, 46	89
	8 Morgengruss	Guten Morgen, schöne Müllerin		C			vii, 154; ii, 50	

No.	Title	First line	Author	Key	Date composed	Publication	References	
9	Des Müllers Blumen	Am Bach viel kleine Blumen stehn		A			vii, 155; ii, 52	
10	Tränenregen	Wir sassen so traulich beisammen		A			vii, 156; ii, 54	
11	Mein!	Bächlein, lass dein Rauschen sein		D			vii, 158; ii, 57	
12	Pause	Meine Laute hab' ich gehängt		B♭			vii, 162; ii, 63	94
13	Mit dem grünen Lautenbande	Schad' um das schöne grüne Band		B♭			vii, 165; ii, 68	94
14	Der Jäger	Was sucht denn der Jäger		c			vii, 166; ii, 70	
15	Eifersucht und Stolz	Wohin so schnell		g			vii, 168; ii, 72	94
16	Die liebe Farbe	In Grün will ich mich kleiden		b			vii, 172; ii, 76	
17	Die böse Farbe	Ich möchte ziehn in die Welt hinaus		B			vii, 174; ii, 78	
18	Trockne Blumen	Ihr Blümlein alle, die sie mir gab		e			vii, 178; ii, 83	
19	Der Müller und der Bach	Wo ein treues Herze in Liebe vergeht		g			vii, 181; ii, 87	94
20	Des Baches Wiegenlied	Gute Ruh', gute Ruh'		E			vii, 184; ii, 90	
797	Romanze zum Drama Rosamunde (3b)	Der Vollmond strahlt auf Bergeshöhn	H. von Chézy	f	autumn 1823	1824, op.26	—; ii, 94	
799	Im Abendrot	O, wie schön ist deine Welt	K. Lappe	A♭	1824 or Feb 1825	1832	viii, 30; xiii	88, 97
800	Der Einsame version a	Wann meine Grillen schwirren	Lappe	G	early 1825	1825	viii, 36; —	88
	version b			G	c1825	1827, op.41	viii, 41; ii, 172	
801	Dithyrambe	Nimmer, das glaub mir	Schiller	A	by June 1826	1826, op.60/2	viii, 14; iii	
805	Der Sieg	O unbewölktes Leben!	Mayrhofer	F	March 1824	1833	viii, 16; iii	
806	Abendstern	Was weilst du einsam an dem Himmel	Mayrhofer	a	March 1824	1833	viii, 18; xiii	
807	Auflösung	Verbirg dich, Sonne	Mayrhofer	G	March 1824	1842	viii, 20; xiii	87, 90
808	Gondelfahrer (1)	Es tanzen Mond und Sterne	Mayrhofer	C	March 1824	1872	viii, 26; xiii	
822	Lied eines Kriegers, with unison chorus	Des stolzen Männerlebens schönste Zeichen		A	31 Dec 1824	1842	viii, 32; iii/3	
827	Nacht und Träume version a	Heil'ge Nacht, du sinkest nieder	M. von Collin	B	by June 1823	1975	—; ii, 267	88, 89
	version b			B		1825, op.43/2	viii, 32; ii; 184	
828	Die junge Nonne	Wie braust durch die Wipfel	J. N. Craigher de Jachelutta	f	early 1825	1825, op.43/1	viii, 62; ii, 178	46, 47, 55, 87
829	Abschied, melodrama	Leb wohl, du schöne Erde	A. von Pratobevera	F	Feb 1826	1873	x, 136; xiii	
830	Lied der Anne Lyle	Wärst du bei mir im Lebenstal	A. MacDonald, trans. ? S. May	c	?early 1825	1828, op.85/1	ix, 78; iv	64

D	Title	Incipit	Text	Key	Composed	Published	SW; NSA	
831	Gesang der Norma	Mich führt mein Weg	Scott, trans. S. H. Spiker	f	early 1825	1828, op.85/2	ix, 82; iv	64
832	Des Sängers Habe	Schlagt mein ganzes Glück	Schlechta	B♭	Feb 1825	1830	viii, 46; xiii	
833	Der blinde Knabe	O sagt, ihr Lieben, mir einmal	C. Cibber, trans. Craigher					
	version a			B♭	April 1825	1895	viii, 54; v	
	version b			B♭	April 1825	1827; 1828 as op.101/2	viii, 58; v	
834	Im Walde	Ich wandre über Berg und Tal	E. Schulze	g	March 1825	1835, op.93/1	—; v	61
	version a					1828, op.93/1	viii, 96; v	
	version b			b♭	c1825	1828, op.90/1	viii, 96; v	
837	Ellens Gesang I	Raste, Krieger, Krieg ist aus	Scott, trans. D. A. Storck	D♭	April–July 1825	1826, op.52/1	viii, 70; iii	
838	Ellens Gesang II	Jäger, ruhe von der Jagd!	Scott, trans. Storck	E♭	April–July 1825	1826, op.52/2	viii, 78; iii	
839	Ellens Gesang III (Hymne an die Jungfrau)	Ave Maria! Jungfrau mild!	Scott, trans. Storck	B♭	April 1825	1826, op.52/6	viii, 90; iii	48
842	Totengräbers Heimwehe	O Menschheit, o Leben	Craigher	f	April 1825	1833	viii, 50; xiii	
843	Lied des gefangenen Jägers	Mein Ross so müd in dem Stalle	Scott, trans. Storck	d	April 1825	1826, op.52/7	viii, 92; iii	
846	Normans Gesang	Die Nacht bricht bald herein	Scott, trans. Storck	c	April 1825	1826, op.52/5	viii, 82; iii	
851	Das Heimweh	Ach, der Gebirgssohn	J. L. Pyrker von Felsö-Eör		Aug 1825			49
	version a			a		1895	viii, 112; iii	
	version b			a		1827, op.79/1	viii, 120; iii	
852	Die Allmacht (1)	Gross ist Jehovah, der Herr	Pyrker		Aug 1825			49, 55, 62
	version a			A		—	—; iii	
	version b			C		1827, op.79/2	viii, 120; iii	
853	Auf der Bruck	Frisch trabe sonder Ruh	Schulze		March or Aug 1825			61
	version a			G		1835, op.93/2	—; iii	
	version b			A♭	c1825	1828, op.90/2	viii, 106; iii	
854	Fülle der Liebe	Ein sehnend Streben	F. von Schlegel	A♭	Aug 1825	1830	viii, 132; iii	88
855	Wiedersehn	Der Frühlingssonne holdes Lächeln	A. W. von Schlegel	G	Sept 1825	1842	viii, 136; xiii	
856	Abendlied für die Entfernte	Hinaus, mein Blick!	A. W. von Schlegel	F	Sept 1825	1827, op.88/1	viii, 138; iv	

857	Zwei Szenen aus dem Schauspiel Lacrimas		C. W. von Schütz		Sept 1825	1829, op.124
	1 Lied der Delphine	Ach, was soll ich beginnen		A			viii, 146; xiii
	2 Lied des Florio	Nun, da Schatten niedergleiten		E			viii, 143; xiii
860	An mein Herz	O Herz, sei endlich stille	Schulze	a	Dec 1825	1832	viii, 154; xiii
861	Der liebliche Stern	Ihr Sternlein, still in der Höhe	Schulze	G	Dec 1825	1832	viii, 160; xiii
862	Um Mitternacht	Keine Stimme hör ich schallen	Schulze		Dec 1825		
	version a			Bb	Dec 1825	1827,	—; iv
	version b			Bb	?March 1826	op.88/3	viii, 212; iv
863	An Gott, lost		C. C. Hohlfeld	—	by 1827	—	—
864	Das Totenhemdchen, lost		E. von Bauernfeld	—	after 1824	—	—
865	Widerspruch version b [for version a see 'Male voices']	Wenn ich durch Busch und Zweig	J. G. Seidl	D	?1826	1828, op.105/1	ser. xvi, 93; v
866	Vier Refrainlieder		Seidl		?summer 1828	1828, op.95	51, 64
	1 Die Unterscheidung	Die Mutter hat mich jüngst gescholten		G			viii, 240; v
	2 Bei dir allein	Du sagtest mir es, Mutter		Ab			viii, 243; v
	3 Die Männer sind méchant	So mancher sieht mit finstrer Miene		a			viii, 248; v
	4 Irdisches Glück			d			viii, 250; v
867	Wiegenlied	Wie sich der Äuglein kindlicher Himmel	Seidl	Ab	?1826	1828, op.105/2	viii, 252; v
868	Das Echo [see 990c]						
869	Totengräber-Weise	Nicht so düster und so bleich	Schlechta	f#	1826	1832	viii, 198; xiv
870	Der Wanderer an den Mond	Ich auf der Erd', am Himmel du	Seidl	g/G	1826	1827, op.80/1	viii, 234; iv
871	Das Zügenglöcklein	Kling die Nacht durch, klinge	Seidl		1826		51, 87
	version a			Ab		1979	—; iv
	version b			Ab		1827, op.80/2	viii, 237; iv
874	O Quell, was strömst du rasch und wild, frag.		Schulze	G	?Jan 1826	1974	—; xiv
876	Im Jänner 1817 (Tiefes Leid)	Ich bin von aller Ruh geschieden	Schulze	e	Jan 1826	1838	viii, 164; xiv

D	Title	Incipit	Text	Key	Composed	Published	SW; NSA	
877	Gesänge aus Wilhelm Meister		Goethe		Jan 1826	1827, op.62		49, 55, 56
	1 Mignon und der Harfner (5), S,T	Nur wer die Sehnsucht kennt		b			viii, 166; iii	
	2 Lied der Mignon (2)	Heiss mich nicht reden		e			viii, 169; iii	
	3 Lied der Mignon (3)	So lasst mich scheinen		B			viii, 172; iii	
	4 Lied der Mignon (6)	Nur wer die Sehnsucht kennt		a			viii, 174; iii	
878	Am Fenster	Ihr lieben Mauern hold und traut	Seidl	F	March 1826	1828, op.105/3	viii, 176; v	
879	Sehnsucht	Die Scheibe friert	Seidl	d	March 1826	1828, op.105/4	viii, 179; v	
880	Im Freien	Draussen in der weiten Nacht	Seidl	E♭	March 1826	1827, op.80/3	viii, 184; iv	
881	Fischerweise version a version b	Den Fischer fechten Sorgen	Schlechta	D D	March 1826	1895 1828, op.96/4	viii, 190; v viii, 194; v	62
882	Im Frühling	Still sitz' ich an des Hügels Hang	Schulze	G	March 1826	1828, op.101/1	viii, 202; v	51
883	Lebensmut	O wie dringt das junge Leben	Schulze	B♭	March 1826	1832	viii, 206; xiv	
884	Über Wildemann	Die Winde sausen am Tannenhang	Schulze	d	March 1826	1829, op.108/1	viii, 216; v	51
888	Trinklied (Come, thou monarch of the vine)	Bacchus, feister Fürst	Shakespeare, trans. F. M. von Grün- bühel and Bauernfeld	C	July 1826	1850	viii, 227; xiv	51
889	Standchen (Hark, hark the lark)	Horch, horch! die Lerch	Shakespeare, trans. A. W. von Schlegel	C	July 1826	1830	viii, 228; xiv	51
890	Hippolits Lied	Lasst mich, ob ich auch still verglüh	F. von Gerstenberg	a	July 1826	1830	viii, 230; xiv	
891	Gesang (An Sylvia; Who is Sylvia?)	Was ist Silvia	Shakespeare, trans. Bauernfeld	A	July 1826	1828, op.106/4	viii, 232; v	51, 58, 89
896	Fröhliches Scheiden, sketch	Gar fröhlich kann ich scheiden	Leitner	F	autumn 1827– early 1828	1920	—; xiv	
896a	Sie in jedem Liede, sketch	Nehm ich die Harfe	Leitner	B♭	autumn 1827– early 1828	—	—; xiv	
896b	Wolke und Quelle, sketch	Auf meinen heimischen Bergen	Leitner	C	autumn 1827– early 1828	—	—; xiv	

No.	Title	Incipit	Poet	Key	Composed	Published	Reference	
902	Drei Gesänge				1827			64
	1 L'incanto degli occhi (Die Macht der Augen) (2)	Da voi, cari lumi (Nur euch, schöne Sterne)	Metastasio	C		1827, op.83	x, 54; iv	
	2 Il traditor deluso (Der getäuschte Verräter) (2)	Ahimè, io tremo! (Weh mir, ich bebe)	Metastasio	e			x, 58; iv	
	3 Il modo di prender moglie (Die Art, ein Weib zu nehmen)	Or sù! non ci pensiamo (Wohlan! und ohne Zagen)		C			x, 65; iv	
904	Alinde	Die Sonne sinkt ins tiefe Meer	Rochlitz	A	Jan 1827	1827, op.81/1	iv, 257; iv	
905	An die Laute	Leiser, leiser, kleine Laute	Rochlitz	D	Jan 1827	1827, op.81/2	iv, 262; iv	88
906	Der Vater mit dem Kind	Dem Vater liegt das Kind im Arm	Bauernfeld	D	Jan 1827	1832	viii, 261; xiv	
907	Romanze des Richard Löwenherz	Grosse Taten tat der Ritter	Scott, trans. K. L. M. Müller		?March 1826			64
	version a			b		1979	—; iv	
	version b			b		1828, op.86	viii, 220; iv	
909	Jägers Liebeslied	Ich schiess' den Hirsch	Schober	D	Feb 1827	1828, op.96/2	viii, 264; v	
910	Schiffers Scheidelied	Die Wogen am Gestade schwellen	Schober	e	Feb 1827	1833	viii, 267; xiv	
911	Winterreise		Müller		Feb–spring 1827	1828, op.89		54, 59, 64, 69, 79, 80, 81, 84, 93ff, 102
	Book 1:							
	1 Gute Nacht	Fremd bin ich eingezogen		d			ix, 2; iv	97
	2 Die Wetterfahne	Der Wind spielt mit der Wetterfahne		a			ix, 6; iv	
	3 Gefrorne Tränen	Gefrorne Tropfen fallen		f			ix, 8; iv	86
	4 Erstarrung	Ich such im Schnee vergebens		c			ix, 10; iv	97
	5 Der Lindenbaum	Am Brunnen vor dem Tore		E			ix, 16; iv	59, 97
	6 Wasserflut	Manche Trän' aus meinen Augen		f♯			ix, 20; iv	
	version a			e			—; iv	
	version b			e				
	7 Auf dem Flusse	Der du so lustig rauschtest		e			ix, 22; iv	
	8 Rückblick	Es brennt mir unter beiden Sohlen		g			ix, 26; iv	
	9 Irrlicht	In die tiefsten Felsengründe		b			ix, 30; iv	

155

D	Title	Incipit	Text	Key	Composed	Published	SW: NSA	
	10 Rast	Nun merk ich erst						
	version a			c			ix, 32; iv	
	version b			d		1895	ix, 34; iv	
	11 Frühlingstraum	Ich träumte von bunten Blumen		A/a			ix, 36; iv	95
	12 Einsamkeit	Wie eine trübe Wolke						
	version a			b			ix, 40; iv	
	version b			d		1895	ix, 42; iv	
	Book 2:							
	13 Die Post	Von der Strasse her ein Posthorn klingt		Eb	begun Oct 1827		ix, 44; iv	
	14 Der greise Kopf	Der Reif hat einen weissen Schein		c			ix, 48; iv	88
	15 Die Krähe	Eine Krähe war mit mir		c			ix, 50; iv	
	16 Letzte Hoffnung	Hie und da ist an den Bäumen		Eb			ix, 53; iv	
	17 Im Dorfe	Es bellen die Hunde		D			ix, 56; iv	
	18 Der stürmische Morgen	Wie hat der Sturm zerrissen		d			ix, 60; iv	97
	19 Täuschung	Ein Licht tanzt freundlich		A			ix, 62; iv	80
	20 Der Wegweiser	Was vermeid ich denn die Wege		g			ix, 64; iv	97
	21 Das Wirthaus	Auf einen Totenacker		F			ix, 68; iv	
	22 Muth	Fliegt der Schnee mir ins Gesicht						
	version a			a			—; iv	
	version b			g			ix, 70; iv	
	23 Die Nebensonnen	Drei Sonnen sah ich						
	version a			A			—; iv	
	version b			A			ix, 72; iv	
	24 Der Leiermann	Drüben hinterm Dorfe						
	version a			a		1895	ix, 74; iv	
	version b			b			ix, 76; iv	
916a	Song sketch (no text)			C	?May 1827		—; xiv	
917	Das Lied im Grünen	Ins Grüne, ins Grüne	J. A. F. Reil	A	June 1827	1829, op.115/1	ix,85; xiv	57
919	Frühlingslied (2)	Geöffnet sind des Winters Riegel	A. Pollak	Ab	?early 1827	1897	ser. xxi, 325; xiv	
922	Heimliches Lieben	O du, wenn deine Lippen	K. L. von Klenke					58
	version a			Bb	Sept 1827	1895	ix, 92; v	
	version b			Bb	c1827	1828, op.106/1	ix, 97; v	

D	Title	First line	Poet	Key	Composed	Published	Vol.	Op.
923	Eine altschottische Ballade	Dein Schwert, wie ist's von Blut so rot	anon. Eng., trans. Herder					
	version a, 2vv			g	Sept 1827	1862, op.165/5	ix, 104; xiv	58
	version b			g	c1827	1895	ix, 402; xiv	
	version c, 2vv			g	c1827	1971	—; xiv	
926	Das Weinen	Gar tröstlich kommt geronnen	Leitner	D	autumn 1827–early 1828	1828, op.106/2	ix, 106; v	
927	Vor meiner Wiege	Das also, das ist der enge Schrein	Leitner	b	autumn 1827–early 1828	1828, op.106/3	ix, 108; v	
931	Der Wallensteiner Lanzknecht beim Trunk	He! schenket mir im Helme ein!	Leitner	g	Nov 1827	1835	ix, 112; xiv	
932	Der Kreuzzug	Ein Münich steht in seiner Zell	Leitner	D	Nov 1827	1832	ix, 114; xiv	62
933	Des Fischers Liebesglück	Dort blinket durch Weiden	Leitner	a	Nov 1827	1835	ix, 116; xiv	
937	Lebensmut, frag.	Fröhlicher Lebensmut	L. Rellstab	B♭	?summer 1828	1872	x, 134; xiv	
938	Der Winterabend	Es ist so still	Leitner	B♭	Jan 1828	1835	ix, 118; xiv	62
939	Die Sterne	Wie blitzen die Sterne	Leitner	E♭	Jan 1828	1828, op.96/1	ix, 125; v	
943	Auf dem Strom, with hn/vc obbl	Nimm die letzten Abschiedsküsse	Rellstab	E	March 1828	1829, op.119	x, 2; xiv	62
945	Herbst	Es rauschen die Winde	Rellstab	e	April 1828	1895	x, 90; xiv	
949	Widerschein [see 639b]							
955	Glaube, Hoffnung und Liebe	Glaube, hoffe, liebe!	C. Kuffner	E♭	Aug 1828	1828, op.97	viii, 28; v	
957	Schwanengesang				Aug–Oct 1828	1829		67, 68
	Book 1:							
	1 Liebesbotschaft	Rauschendes Bächlein, so silbern	Rellstab	G	Aug 1828		ix, 134; xiv	
	2 Kriegers Ahnung	In tiefer Ruh liegt um mich her	Rellstab	c			ix, 139, xiv	87
	3 Frühlingssehnsucht	Säuselnde Lüfte wehend so mild	Rellstab	B♭			ix, 144; xiv	
	4 Ständchen	Leise flehen meine Lieder	Rellstab	d			ix, 148; xiv	
	5 Aufenthalt	Rauschender Strom, brausender Wald	Rellstab	e			ix, 151; xiv	
	6 In der Ferne	Wehe dem Fliehenden	Rellstab	b			ix, 156; xiv	

157

D	Title	Incipit	Text	Key	Composed	Published	SW; NSA	
	Book 2:							
7	Abschied	Ade! du muntre, du fröhliche Stadt	Rellstab	E♭			ix, 160; xiv	
8	Der Atlas	Ich unglückselger Atlas	Heine	g			ix, 167; xiv	67, 89, 90
9	Ihr Bild	Ich stand in dunklen Träumen	Heine	b♭			ix, 170; xiv	91
10	Das Fischermädchen	Du schönes Fischermädchen	Heine	A♭			ix, 172; xiv	
11	Die Stadt	Am fernen Horizonte	Heine	c			ix, 175; xiv	
12	Am Meer	Das Meer erglänzte weit hinaus	Heine	C			ix, 178; xiv	
13	Der Doppelgänger	Still ist die Nacht	Heine	b			ix, 180; xiv	67, 87, 90 91
14	Die Taubenpost	Ich hab' eine Brieftaub	Seidl	G	Oct 1828		ix, 182; xiv	68
965	Der Hirt auf dem Felsen, with cl obbl	Wenn auf dem höchsten Fels	Müller, ?H. von Chézy	B♭	Oct 1828	1830, op.129	x, 16; xiv	68
965a	Die Taubenpost [see 957/14]							67
989	Vollendung [see 579a]							
989a	Die Erde [see 579b]							
990	Der Graf von Habsburg	Zu Aachen in seiner Kaiserspracht	Schiller	G	?1815	1853	—; xiv	
990a	Kaiser Maximilian auf der Martinswand	Hinauf! hinauf! in Sprung und Lauf	H. von Collin	B♭	?1815	1853	—; xiv	
990b	Augenblicke in Elysium, lost [formerly 582]		Schober		?		—	
990c	Das Echo [formerly 868]	Herzliebe gute Mutter	Castelli	B♭	?	1830, op.130	viii, 258; xiv	
990d	Die Schiffende, lost	Sie wankt dahin!	Hölty	—	?	—	—; iv	
990e	L'incanto degli occhi (1) ?frag.	Da voi, cari lumi	Metastasio	B♭	? ?	1933	—; iv	
990f	Il traditor deluso (1), ?frag., lost	Ahimè! io tremo!	Metastasio	—	?	—	—	
991	[part of 323]							
AJ/30	Mein Frieden	Ferne, ferne flammenhelle Sterne	Heine	E♭	?1815	1840	—	

Abend, 645; Abendbilder, 650; 'Abendgewölke schweben hell', 187, 418; 'Abendglockenhalle zittern', 405a–b; Abendlied, 276, 382, 499, 527a–b; Abendlied der Fürstin, 495; Abendlied für die Entfernte, 856; Abendröte, 690; Abendständchen: An Lina, 265; Abendstern, 806; Abends unter der Linde, 235, 237; Abschied, 578, 829, 957/7; Abschied (nach einer Wallfahrtsarie), 475; Abschied von der Harfe, 406; 'Ach, aus dieses Tales Gründen', 52, 636a–c 'Ach, der Gebirgssohn', 851a–b; 'Ach, Herr, wie lange', 663; 'Ach, mir ist das Herz so schwer', 416; 'Ach! mir schallt's dorten', 742; 'Ach, neige, duSchmerzensreiche', 564; 'Achumdeinefeuchten Schwingen', 717; 'Ach, was soll ich beginnen', 857/1; 'Ach, wer bringt die schönen Tage', 226; 'Adel du muntre, du fröhliche Stadt', 957/7; Adelaide, 95; Adelwold und Emma, 211; 'Ahidi! ich liebe', 552a–b; Ahimè, io tremo!', 902/2, 990f; Alinde, 904; 'Allein, nachdenklich, wie gelähmt', 629; Alles um Liebe, 241; 'All' mein Wirken', 153

'Als bei dem Kreuz Maria stand', 632; 'Als der Frühling sich vom Herzen', 792; Als ich sie erröten sah, 153; 'Als ich still und ruhig spann', 247; Alte Liebe rostet nie, 477; Amalia, 195; Am Bach im Frühlinge, 361; 'Am Bach viel kleine Blumen stehn', 795/9; 'Am Brunnen vor dem Tore', 911/5; Am ersten Maimorgen, 344; Am Feierabend, 795/5; Am Fenster, 878; 'Am fernen Horizonte', 957/ 11; Am Flusse, 160, 766; Am Grabe Anselmos, 504a–b; 'Am hohen, hohen Turm', 122; Am Meer, 957/12

Ammenlied, 122; 'Amoretten seh ich', 577b; Amphiaraos, 166; Am See, 124a–b, 746; 'Am Seegestad', 98; Am Strome, 539; Am Tage aller Seelen, 343a–b; An Cidli, 285a–b; An Chloen, 363, 462; An dem jungen Morgenhimmel, 93/3; An der Frühling, 283, 587a–b; Andenken, 99; An den Mond, 193, 259, 296, 311, 468; An den Mond in einer Herbstnacht, 614; An den Schlaf, 447; An den Tod, 518; 'An der Quelle sass der Knabe', 30, 192, 683a–b; An die Apfelbäume, wo ich Julien erblickte, 197; An die Entfernte, 765; An die Freude, 189; An die Freunde, 654; An die Geliebte, 303; An die Harmonie, 394

An die Laute, 905; An die Leier, 737; An die Musik, 547a–b; An die Nachtigall, 196, 497; An die Natur, 372; An die Sonne, 270, 272; 'An die Türen will ich schleichen', 479a–b; An die untergehende Sonne, 457; An eine Quelle, 530; An Emma, 113a–c; An Gott, 863; An Laura, als sie Klopstocks Auferstehungslied sang, 115; An mein Herz, 860; An mein Klavier, 342; An Mignon, 161a–b; An Rosa, 315, 316a–b

An Schwager Kronos, 369; An Sie, 288; An Sylvia, 891; Antigone und Oedip, 542; 'Apollo, lebet noch', 628; 'Arbeitsam und wacker', 392; 'Arm am Beutel, krank am Herzen', 256; Atys, 585; Auf dem Flusse, 911/7; Auf dem See, 543a–b; Auf dem Strom, 943; Auf dem Wasser zu singen, 774; 'Auf den Blumen', 561; Auf den Sieg der Deutschen, 81; Auf den Tod einer Nachtigall, 201, 399; 'Auf den Wassern wohnt mein stilles Leben', 395; 'Auf der Berge freien Höhen', 253; Auf der Bruck, 853a–b

Auf der Donau, 553; Auf der Riesenkoppe, 611; 'Auf der Wellen Spiegel', 553; Auf einen Kirchhof, 151; 'Auf einen Totenacker', 911/ 21; Aufenthalt, 957/5; 'Auf hohen Bergesrücken', 524a–c; Auflösung, 807; 'Auf meinen heimischen Bergen', 896b; 'Auf seinem goldnen Throne', 473a–b; Augenblicke im Elysium, 990b; Augenlied, 297a–b; Aus Diego Manazares, 458; 'Ave Maria! Jungfrau mild!', 839; 'Bacchus, feister Fürst', 888; 'Bächlein, lass dein Rauschen sein', 795/ 11; Ballade, 134; 'Bedecke deinen Himmel, Zeus', 674; 'Beglückt, beglückt, wer dich erblickt', 207

Beidem Grabe meines Vaters, 496; 'Bei der Liebereinsten Flammen', 462; Bei dir allein, 866/2; Beim Winde, 669; Bertas Lied in der Nacht, 653; 'Beugteuchauseuren Wolkennieder', 278a–b; Blanka, 631; Blondel zu Marien, 626; 'Blühtdennhieran TaurisStrande', 573; Blumenlied, 431; 'Braust des Unglücks Sturm empor', 546; 'Brüder, schrecklich brennt die Träne', 535; Bundeslied, 258; 'Bunt sind schon die Wälder', 502; 'Cidli, du weinest', 285a–b

Come, thou monarch of the vine, 888; Cora an die Sonne, 263; Cronnan, 282; 'Cypris, meiner Phyllis gleich', 446; 'Da droben auf jenem Berge', 121a–b; Danksagung an den Bach, 795/4; '. . . dann zur Tiefe nieder', 484; Daphne am Bach, 411; 'Da quel sembiante appresi', 688/3; Das Abendrot, 627; 'Das also, das ist der enge Schrein', 927; Das Bild, 155; Das Echo, 990c; Das Finden, 219; 'Das Fischergewerbe gibt rüstigen Mut!', 351, 562; Das Fischermädchen, 957/10

Das Geheimnis, 250, 793; Das gestörte Glück, 309; Das Grab, 330, 569; 'Das Grab ist tief und stille', 330, 569; Das grosse Halleluja, 442; Das Heimweh, 456, 851a–b; 'Da sitz' ich ohne Bogen', 540; Das Lied im Grünen, 917; Das Lied vom Reifen, 532; Das Mädchen, 631, 652a–b; Das Mädchen aus der Fremde, 117, 252; Das Mädchen von Inistore, 281; Das Marienbild, 623; 'Das Meer erglänzte weit hinaus', 957/12; Das Rosenband, 280; 'Dass der Ostwind Düfte', 775; Das Sehnen, 231 'Dass ich dich verloren habe', 504a–b; Dass sie hier gewesen, 775; Das

Totenhemdchen, 864; Das Traumbild, 204a; Das Wandern, 795 1; Das war ich, 174a–b; 'Das Wasser rauscht', 225a–b; Das Weinen, 926; Das Wirtshaus, 911/21; Das Zügenglöcklein, 871a–b; 'Da unten steht ein Ritter', 698; 'Da voi, cari lumi', 902/1a–b, 990e; 'Dein Schwert, wie ist's von Blut so rot', 923a–c; 'Dein Silber schien', 436a–b; 'Dein süsses Bild, Edone', 445; 'Dem Schnee, dem Regen', 138a–b; Dem Unendlichen, 291a–c; 'Dem Vater liegt das Kind im Arm', 906; 'Den Fischer fechten Sorgen', 881a–b

'Den Tag hindurch nur einmal', 541; 'Der Abend, 108, 221; 'Der Abend blüht', 221; 'Der Abend rötet nun das Tal', 495; 'Der Abend schleiert Flur und Hain', 414; Der Alpenjäger, 524a–c, 588a–b; 'Der Angel zuckt', 525a–b; Der Atlas, 957/8; 'Der bleiche, kalte Mond', 150; Der blinde Knabe, 833a–b; Der Blumenbrief, 622; Der Blumen Schmerz, 731; 'Der Dämmrung Schein', 100; 'Der Damm zerreisst', 728; Der Doppelgänger, 957/13; Der 13. Psalm, 663; 'Der du so lustig rauscht-est', 911/7; 'Der du von dem Himmel bist', 224

'Der Eichwald braus(e)t', 6, 191a–b, 389; Der Einsame, 800a–b; Der Entfernten, 350; Der entsühnte Orest, 699; Der Fischer, 225a–b; Der Flüchtling, 402; Der Flug der Zeit, 515; Der Fluss, 693; 'Der Friede sei mit euch', 551; 'Der Frost hat mir bereifet', 778a–b; 'Der Frühlingssonne holdes Lächeln', 855; Der Geistertanz, 15, 15a, 116; Der getäuschte Verräter, 902/2; Der Goldschmiedsgesell, 560; Der Gott und die Bajadere, 254; Der Graf von Habsburg, 990

Der greise Kopf, 911/14; Der gute Hirt, 449; Der Herbstabend, 405a–b; Der Hirt, 490; Der Hirt auf dem Felsen, 965; Der Jäger, 795/14; Der Jüngling am Bache, 30, 192, 638a–b; Der Jüngling an der Quelle, 300; Der Jüngling auf dem Hügel, 702; Der Jüngling und der Tod, 545a–b; Der Kampf, 594; Der Knabe, 692; Der Knabe in der Wiege, 579a–b; 'Der Knabe seufzt', 585; Der König in Thule, 367; 'Der Königssaas beim frohen Mahle', 329; Der Kreuzzug, 932; Der Leidende, 432a–b; Der Leiermann, 911/24a–b

'Der Lerche wolkennahe Lieder', 516; Der Liebende, 207; Der liebliche Stern, 861; Der Liedler, 209; Der Lindenbaum, 911/5; Der Mondabend, 141; 'Der Mond ist aufgegangen', 499; 'Der Morgen blüht', 228; Der Morgenkuss, 264a–b; Der Morgenstern, 172; Der Müller und der Bach, 795/19; Der Musensohn, 764a–b; 'Der Nachen dröhnt', 526; Der Neugierige, 795/6; 'Der Odem Gottes weht', 651; Der Pilgrim, 794a–b; Der Rattenfänger, 255; 'Der Reif hat einen weissen Schein', 911/14; Der Sänger, 149a–b

Der Sänger am Felsen, 482; Der Schäfer und der Reiter, 517a–b; Der Schatzgräber, 256; Der Schiffer, 536a–b, 694; Der Schmetterling, 633; Der Sieg, 805; Der Strom, 565; Der stürmische Morgen, 911/18; Der Taucher, 77a–b; Der Tod Oskars, 375; Der Tod und das

Mädchen, 531; Der Traum, 213; Der Unglückliche, 713a–b; Der Vater mit dem Kind, 906; Der Vatermörder, 10; 'Der Vollmond strahlt auf Bergeshöhn', 797(3b); Der Wachtelschlag, 742; Der Wallensteiner Lanzknecht beim Trunk, 931; Der Wanderer, 489a–c, 649

Der Wanderer an den Mond, 870; Der Wegweiser, 911/20; Der Weiberfreund, 271; 'Der Wind spielt mit der Wetterfähne', 911/2; Der Winterabend, 938; Der Zufriedene, 320; Der zürnende Barde, 785; Der zürnenden Diana, 707a–b; Der Zwerg, 771; Des Baches Wiegenlied, 795/20; Des Fischers Liebesglück, 933; Des Fräuleins Liebeslauschen, 698; 'Des Lebens Tag ist schwer', 788; Des Mädchens Klage, 6, 191a–b, 389; Des Müllers Blumen, 795/9; 'Des Phöbus Strahlen', 83; Des Sängers Habe, 832

'Des stolzen Männerlebens schönste Zeichen', 822; Die abgeblühte Linde, 514; Die Allmacht, 852a–b; Die Art, ein Weib zu nehmen, 902/3; Die Befreier Europas in Paris, 104a–c; Die Berge, 634; Die Betende, 102; Die Blumensprache, 519; Die böse Farbe, 795/17; 'Die bretterne Kammer der Toten erbebt', 15, 15a, 116; Die Bürgschaft, 246; Die drei Sänger, 329; Die Einsiedelei, 393, 563; Die Erde, 579b; Die Erscheinung, 229; Die erste Liebe, 182; 'Die erste Liebe füllt das Herz', 182; Die Erwartung, 159a–b

Die Forelle, 550a–c; 'Die frohe neubelebte Flur', 381; Die Fröhlichkeit, 262; Die frühe Liebe, 430a–b; Die frühen Gräber, 290; Die Gebüsche, 646; Die gefangenen Sänger, 712; Die Gestirne, 444; Die Herbstnacht, 404; Die junge Nonne, 828; Die Knabenzeit, 400; Die Krähe, 911/15; Die Laube, 214; Die Liebe, 210, 522; Die liebe Farbe, 795/16; Die Liebe hat gelogen, 751; Die Liebende schreibt, 673; Die Liebesgötter, 446; 'Die linden Lüfte sind erwacht', 686a–c; 'Die Luft ist blau', 398; Die Macht der Augen, 902/1

Die Macht der Liebe, 308; Die Mainacht, 194; Die Männer sind méchant, 866/3; Die Mondnacht, 238; 'Die Munterkeit ist meinen Wangen', 363; Die Mutter Erde, 788; 'Die Mutter hat mich jüngst gescholten', 866/1; Die Nacht, 358, 534; 'Die Nacht bricht an', 713a–b; 'Die Nacht bricht bald herein', 846; 'Die Nachtigall singt überall', 198; 'Die Nacht ist dumpfig und finster', 534; Die Nebensonnen, 911/23a–b; Die Nonne, 208a–b; Die Perle, 466; Die Post, 911/13; Die Rose, 745a–b; Die Schatten, 50; 'Die Scheibe friert', 879

Die Schiffende, 990d; Die Schlacht, 249; Die schöne Müllerin, 795; Die Sommernacht, 289a–b; 'Die Sonne sinkt, o könnt ich', 545a–b; 'Die Sonne sinkt ins tiefe Meer', 904; 'Die Sonne steigt', 415; Die Spinnerin, 247; Die Stadt, 957/11; Die Sterbende, 186; Die Sterne, 176, 313, 684, 939; Die Sternennächte, 670; Die Sternenwelten, 307; Die Taubenpost, 957/14; Die Täuschung, 230; Die Unterscheidung, 866/

1; Die verfehlte Stunde, 409; Die vier Weltalter, 391; Die Vögel, 691; Die Wallfahrt,778a; Die Wetterfahne, 911/2; 'Die Winde sausen am Tannenhang', 884

'Die Wogen am Gestade schwellen', 910; 'Dioskuren, Zwillingssterne', 360; 'Dir, Mädchen, schlägt', 179; Dithyrambe, 801; Dom, 126a–b; Don Gayseros, 93/1; 'Dort blinket durch Weiden', 933; 'Dort ist ihr Grab', 736; 'Dort raget ein Berg', 143; Drang in die Ferne, 770; 'Draussen in der weiten Nacht', 880; Drei Gesänge, 902; 'Drei Sonnen sah ich', 911/23a–b; 'Drüben hinterm Dorfe', 911/24a–b; Du bist die Ruh, 776; 'Du brachst sie nun, die kalte Rinde', 361

'Du, der ewig um much trauert', 467; 'Du heilig, glühend Abendrot', 627; 'Du holde Kunst', 547a–b; 'Du kleine grünumwachs'ne Quelle', 530; Du liebst mich nicht, 756a–b; 'Durch eine ganze Nacht', 264a–b; 'Durch Feld und Wald zu schweifen', 764a–b; 'Durch Fichten am Hügel', 109; 'Du sagtest mir es, Mutter', 866/3; 'Du schönes Fischermädchen', 957/10; 'Du Schwert an meiner Linken', 170; 'Du staunest, o Mensch', 684; 'Du Turm! zu meinem Leide', 490; 'Du verstörst uns nicht, o Nacht!', 358; Edone, 445

'Eh' die Sonne früh aufersteht', 685; 'Ehre sei dem Hocherhabnen', 442; 'Eifersucht und Stolz, 795/15; 'Ein Blick von deinen Augen', 673; Eine altschottische Ballade, 923a–c; 'Eine Krähe war mit mir', 911/15; 'Eine Mühle seh' ich blinken', 795/3; 'Ein Fräulein klagt' im finstern Turm', 114a–b; 'Ein Fräulein schaut vom hohen Turm', 134; Einheilig Säuseln', 197; 'Ein Jüngling auf dem Hügel', 702; 'Ein Licht tanzt freundlich', 911/19; 'Ein Mädchen ist's', 155; 'Ein Münich tanzt in seiner Zell', 932

Einsamkeit, 620, 911/12a–b; 'Einsam wandelt dein Freund', 95; 'Ein Schäfer sass im Grünen', 517a–b; 'Ein sehnend Streben', 854; 'Ein Vater starb von des Sohnes Hand', 10; Ellens Gesang, 837, 838, 839; Elysium, 584; 'Endlich stehn die Pforten offen', 318; Entra l'uomo allor che nasce, 33; Entrückung, 413; Entzückung an Laura, 390, 577a–b; 'Er fiel den Tod fürs Vaterland', 218; Erinnerung, 101; Erinnerungen, 98; Erlafsee, 586; 'Er liegt und schläft', 497; Erlkönig, 328a–d; Erntelied, 434; 'Er schläft so süss', 579a–b; Erstarrung, 911/4

Erster Verlust, 226; 'Es bellen die Hunde', 911/17; 'Es brennt mir unter beiden Sohlen', 911/8; 'Es deuten die Blumen', 519; 'Es floh die Zeit im Wirbelfluge', 515; 'Es ging ein Mann zur Frühlingszeit', 466; 'Es ist doch meine Nachbarin', 560; 'Es ist ein halbes Himmelreich', 431; 'Es ist so angenehm', 284; 'Es ist so still', 938; 'Es liebt' in Welschland', 208a–b; 'Es lockte schöne Wärme', 745a–b; 'Es mahnt der Wald', 527a–b; 'Es rauschen die Winde', 945; 'Es reden und träumen die Menschen', 251, 637; 'Es rieselt, klar und wehend', 393, 563

'Es schlug mein Herz', 767a–b; 'Es tanzen Mond und Sterne', 808; 'Es tönet sein Lob', 444; 'Es träumen die Wolken', 669; 'Es war ein König in Thule', 367; 'Es wehet kühl und leise', 646; 'Euch Blümlein will ich senden', 622; 'Fahrt zum Hades, 526; 'Fels auf Felsen hingewälzet', 754; 'Ferne, ferne flammenhelle Sterne', Al/30; 'Ferne von der grossen Stadt', 483; 'Fischer harrt am Brückenbogen', 639a; Fischerlied, 351, 562; Fischerweise, 881a–b; 'Fliegt der Schnee mir ins Gesicht', 911/ 22a–b; Fragment aus dem Aeschylus, 450a–b

Freiwilliges Versinken, 700; 'Fremd bin ich eingezogen', 911/1; Freude der Kinderjahre, 455; 'Freude, die im frühen Lenze', 455; 'Freuden sonder Zahl', 433; 'Freude, schöner Götterfunken', 189; 'Freudvoll und leidvoll', 210; 'Freunde, deren Grüfte', 50; 'Freundlich ist dein Antlitz', 614; 'Friede sei um diesen Grabstein', 496; 'Friedlich lieg' ich hingegossen', 694; 'Frisch atmet des Morgens lebendiger Hauch' 402

'Frisch trabe sonder Ruh', 853a–b; 'Fröhlicher Lebensmut', 937; 'Fröhliches Scheiden, 896; Frohsinn, 520a–b; Frühlingsglaube, 686a–c; Frühlingslied, 398, 919; Frühlingssehnsucht, 957/3; Frühlingstraum, 911/11; 'Fülle der Liebe, 854; 'Füllest wieder Busch und Tal', 259, 296; Furcht der Geliebten, 285a–b; Ganymed, 544; 'Ganz verloren, ganz versunken', 240; 'Gar fröhlich kann ich scheiden', 896; 'Gar tröstlich kommt geronnen', 926; Gebet während der Schlacht, 171; 'Gefrorne Tränen, 911/3; 'Gefrorne Tropfen fallen', 911/3

Geheimnis, 491; Geist der Liebe, 233, 414; Geheimnis, 719; Geistes-Gruss, 142a–f; Genügsamkeit, 143; 'Geistermähe, 100; 'Geöffnet sind des Winters Riegel', 919; Gesang der Geister über den Wassern, 484; Gesang der Norma, 831; Gesänge aus Wilhelm Meister, 877; Gesänge des Harfners, 478a–b, 479a–b, 480a–c; 'Geuss, lieber Mond', 193; 'Geuss nicht so laut', 196; 'Gib mir die Fülle der Einsamkeit!', 620; 'Gib, Schwester, mir die Harf herab', 209; '. . . Glanz des Guten', 164; 'Glaube, hoffe, liebe', 955

Glaube, Hoffnung und Liebe, 955; Gondelfahrer, 808; Gott im Frühlinge, 448a–b; 'Grabe, Spaten, grabe!', 44; Grablied, 218; Grablied auf einen Soldaten, 454; Grablied für die Mutter, 616; Greisengesang, 778a–b; Grenzen der Menschheit, 716; Gretchen, 564; Gretchen am Spinnrade, 118; Gretchen im Zwinger, 564; Gretchens Bitte, 564; 'Grosse Taten tat der Ritter', 907a–b; 'Gross ist Jehovah, der Herr', 852a–b

'Gross und rotentflammet', 276; 'Grüner wird die Au', 503; Gruppe aus dem Tartarus, 396, 583; 'Guarda, che bianca luna', 688/2; Gute Nacht, 911/1; 'Guten Morgen, schöne Müllerin', 795/8; 'Gute Ruh', gute Ruh'', 795/20; 'Ha, dort kömmt er', 322; Hagars Klage, 5; Haltt, 795/3; Hänflings Liebeswerbung, 552a–b; Harfenspieler,

325, 478a–b, 479a–b, 480a–c; Hark, hark the lark, 889; 'Hast du Lianen nicht gesehen?', 298; 'Hätt' ich tausend Arme zu rühren', 795/5 'Hauche milder, Abendluft', 616; Heidenröslein, 257; 'Heil! dies ist die letzte Zähre', 186; 'Heil'ge Nacht, du sinkest nieder', 827a–b; Heimliches Lieben, 922a–b; 'Heiss' mich nicht reden', 726, 877/2; Hektors Abschied, 312a–b; Heliopolis, 753, 754; Herbst, 945; Herbstlied, 502; Hermann und Thusnelda, 322; Herrn Josef Spaun, Assessor in Linz, 749; 'Herzen, die gen Himmel sich erheben', 115; 'Herzliebe, gute Mutter', 990c; 'He! schenket mir im Helme ein', 931; 'Heute will ich fröhlich, fröhlich sein', 344; 'Hier am Hügel heissen Sandes', 5

'Hie und da ist an den Bäumen', 911/16; Himmelsfunken, 651; 'Hinauf! hinauf' in Sprung und Lauf', 990a; 'Hinaus, mein Blick!', 856; Hippolits Lied, 890; 'Hinüber wall' ich', 687; 'Hoch auf dem alten Turme', 142a–f; 'Hoch auf dem Gipfel', 611; 'Hoch, und ehern schier von Dauer', 211; Hochzeit-Lied, 463; Hoffnung, 251, 295a–b, 637; 'Holder klingt der Vogelsang', 429; 'Horch, horch! die Lerch', 889; 'Horch, wie Murmeln des empörten Meeres', 396, 583; 'Hör' ich das Pförtchen', 159a–b; 'Hörnerklänge rufen klagend', 671; 'Hörst du von den Nachtigallen', 712

Huldigung, 240; Hymne, 659, 660, 661, 662; Hymne an die Jungfrau, 839; 'Ich auf der Erd'', 870; 'Ich bin der wohlbekannte Sänger', 255; 'Ich bin ein deutsches Mädchen', 229; 'Ich bin ein Waller auf der Erde', 789; 'Ich bin von lockerem Schlage', 520a–b; 'Ich danke Gott und freue mich', 533; 'Ich denke dein', 99, 162a–b; 'Ich frage keine Blume', 795/6; 'Ich hab' ein Bächlein funden', 411; 'Ich hab' eine Brieftaub', 957/14
'Ich hab' ein heisses junges Blut', 309; 'Ich hab' ein Mädchen funden', 219; 'Ich hört' ein Bächlein rauschen', 795/2; 'Ich komme vom Gebirge her', 489a–c; 'Ich lag auf grünen Matten', 229; 'Ich möchte ziehn in die Welt hinaus', 795/17; 'Ich sag' es jedem', 662; 'Ich sass an einer Tempelhalle', 39; 'Ich schiess' den Hirsch', 909; 'Ich schnitt es gern in alle Rinden', 795/7; 'Ich sehe dich in tausend Bildern', 658; 'Ich sitz' bei der moosigten Quelle', 282; 'Ich stand in dunklen Träumen', 957/9; 'Ich such im Schnee vergebens', 911/4
'Ich träume von bunten Blumen', 911/11; 'Ich treibe auf des Lebens Meer', 743; 'Ich unglückselger Atlas', 957/8; 'Ich wandre über Berg und Tal', 834a–b; 'Ich war erst sechzehn Sommer alt', 500; 'Ich will von Atreus Söhnen', 737; 'Ich wollt', ich wär' ein Fisch', 558; Idens Nachtgesang, 227; Idens Schwanenlied, 317a–b; Ihr Bild, 957/9; 'Ihr Blümlein alle, die sie mir gab', 795/18; 'Ihr Freunde und du goldner Wein', 183; Ihr Grab, 736; 'Ihr hohen Himmlischen', 542; 'Ihr lieben Mauern hold und traut', 878

'Ihr Sternlein, still in der Höhe', 861; Ilmerine, 458; Il modo di prender mogile, 902/3; Il traditor deluso, 902/2, 990f; Im Abendrot, 799; 'Im Abendschimmer wallt der Quell', 188; Im Dorfe, 911/17; 'Im Erlenbusch, im Tannenhain', 230; 'Im Felde schleich' ich still und wild', 215, 368; Im Freien, 880; Im Frühling, 882; 'Im Frühlingsgarten fand ich sie', 280; Im Haine, 738; Im Jänner 1817, 876; 'Im kalten rauhen Norden', 753; 'Im Mondenschein wall'ich auf und ab', 762; 'Im trüben Licht verschwinden schon die Berge', 771; Im Walde, 708, 834a–b; 'Im Wald, im Wald da grabt mich ein', 654
'Im Winde, im Sturme', 536a–b; 'In allen guten Stunden', 258; In der Ferne, 957/6; In der Mitternacht, 464; 'In der Väter Hallen ruhte', 144; 'In des Sees Wogenspiele', 746; 'In des Todes Feierstunde', 758; 'In die tiefsten Felsengründe', 911/9; 'In düstrer Nacht', 626; 'In einem Bächlein helle', 550a–e; 'In einem Tal bei armen Hirten', 117, 252; 'In Grün will ich mich kleiden', 795/16; 'In mondterhellten Nächten', 670
'In seinem schimmernden Gewand', 448a–b; 'Ins Grüne, ins Grüne', 917; 'Ins stille Land', 403a–d; 'In tiefer Ruh liegt um mich her', 957/2; 'In tiefster Erde ruht ein alt Gesetz', 761a–b; Iphigenia, 573; Irdisches Glück, 866/4; Irrlicht, 911/9; 'Ist der holde Lenz erschienen?', 323; 'Ist dies Tauris', 548; 'Ist mir's doch, als sei mein Leben', 539; Jagdlied, 521; 'Jäger, ruhe von der Jagd', 838; Jägers Abendlied, 215, 368; Jägers Liebeslied, 909; 'Ja, ich weiss es', 177; 'Ja, spanne nur den Bogen', 707a–b; Johanna Sebus, 728

Julius an Theone, 419; 'Jüngst träumte mir', 174a–b; Kaiser Maximilian auf der Martinswand, 990a; 'Keine Blumen blühn', 401; 'Keine Stimme hör ich schallen', 862a–b; 'Kein Rosenschimmer leuchtet', 101; 'Kennst du das Land', 321; Klage, 371, 415, 436a–b; Kluge der Ceres, 323; 'Klage, meine Flöte', 482; Klage um Ali Bey, 496a; Klaglied, 23; Klärchens Lied, 210; 'Kling' die Nacht durch, klinge', 871a–b; Kolmas Klage, 217; 'Kommen und Scheiden', 508
'Komm, und senke die umflorten Schwingen', 447; 'Königliche Morgensonne', 272; Kriegers Ahnung, 957/2; Labetrank der Liebe, 302; Lachen und Weinen, 777; Lambertine, 301; La pastorella al prato, 528; 'Lass dich mit gelinden Schlägen', 410; 'Lasst im Morgenstrahl des Mai'n', 306; 'Lasst mich! lasst mich! ich will klagen', 496a; 'Lasst mich, ob ich auch still verglüh', 890; 'Lasst uns, ihr Himmlischen', 554; 'Laue Lüfte, Blumendüfte', 711a–b; Laura am Klavier, 388a–b; 'Laura betet!', 102; 'Laura, Laura, über diese Welt', 577a; 'Laura über diese Welt', 390
'Lauter Freude fühl' ich', 596; 'Lebensfunke, vom Himmel erglüht', 59; Lebenslied, 508; Lebensmelodien, 395; Lebensmut, 883, 937 Lebenstraum, 39; 'Lebe wohl! Lebe wohl!', 578; 'Leb wohl, du schöne Erde', 829; 'Lehnst du deine bleichgehärmte Wange', 97; Leichenfantasie, 7; Leiden der Trennung, 509a–b; 'Leise flehen meine

Lieder', 957/4; 'Leise, rieselnder Quell', 300; 'Leiser, leiser, kleine Laute', 905; 'Letzte Hoffnung, 911/16; 'Liane, 298; 'Licht und Liebe, 352; 'Liebe ist ein süsses Licht', 352; Liebesbotschaft, 957/1; Liebeslauschen, 698; Liebesrausch, 164, 179

Liebeständelei, 206; Liebhaber in allen Gestalten, 558; Lieb Minna, 222; Lied, 284, 362, 373, 403a–d, 483, 535, 788; Lied aus der Ferne, 107a–b; Lied der Anne Lyle, 830; Lied der Delphine, 857/1; Lied der Liebe, 109; Lied der Mignon, 877/2–4; Lied des Florio, 857/2; Lied des gefangenen Jägers, 843; Lied des Orpheus, als er in die Hölle ging, 474a–b; Lied eines Kindes, 596; Lied eines Kriegers, 822; Lied eines Schiffers an die Dioskuren, 360; Liedesend, 473a–b; Lied in der Abwesenheit, 416; Lilla an der Morgenröte, 273; L'incanto degli occhi, 902/1, 990e; Linde Lüfte wehen, 725

Litanei auf das Fest aller Seelen, 343a–b; Lob der Tränen, 711a–b; Lob des Tokayers, 248; Lodas Gespenst, 150; Lorma, 327, 376; 'Lorma sass in der Halle von Aldo', 327, 376; Luisens Antwort, 319; 'Mädchenentsiegelten', 507; 'Mädchen Inistores', 281; 'Mahadöh, der Herr der Erde', 254; Mahomets Gesang, 549, 721; Mailied, 503; 'Manche Trän' aus meinen Augen', 911/6a–b; Marie, 658; Meeresstille, 215a, 216; Mein!, 795/11; 'Meine Laute hab' ich gehängt', 795/12; 'Meine Ruh' ist dahin', 23; 'Meine Ruh' ist hin', 118 'Meine Selinde', 412a–b; 'Meine Tränen im Bussgewand', 778a; Mein Frieden, Al/30; 'Mein Geliebter ist ein Sohn des Hügels', 293; Mein Gruss an den Mai, 305; 'Mein Handwerk geht durch alle Welt', 274; 'Mein Herz ist zerrissen', 756a–b; 'Mein Leben wälzt sich murrend fort', 565; 'Mein Ross so müd im dem Stalle', 843; Memnon, 541; 'Mich ergreift, ich weiss nicht wie', 234; 'Mich führt mein Weg', 831; Mignon, 321, 469a–b, 726, 727; Mignon und der Harfner, 877/1; Minnelied, 429; Minona, 152; 'Mio ben ricordati', 688/4; 'Mir ist so wohl, so weh'", 586

'Mir träumt', ich war ein Vögelein', 213; Misero pargoletto, 42/1a–b; 42/2; 'Mit dem grünen Lautenbande, 795/13; 'Mit erstorbnem Scheinen', 7; 'Mit leisen Harfentönen', 404; 'Mitten im Schimmer der spiegelnden Wellen', 774; 'Mit unserm Arm ist nichts getan', 443; Morgengruss, 795/8; Morgenlied, 266, 381, 685; Mut, 911/22a–b; 'Mutter geht durch ihre Kammern', 373; Nach einem Gewitter, 561; 'Nach so vielen trüben Tagen', 263; Nächtens klang die süsse Laute, 93/2; Nachtgesang, 119, 314, 352; Nachthymne, 687; Nachtstück, 672a–b

'Nacht umhüllt mit wehendem Flügel', 653; Nacht und Träume, 827a–b; Nachtviolen 752; Nähe des Geliebten, 162a–b; Namenstagslied, 695; Naturgenuss, 188; 'Nehm ich die Harfe', 896a; 'Nein, länger werd' ich diesen Kampf', 594; 'Nicht so düster und so bleich', 869; 'Nimm die letzten Abschiedsküsse', 943; 'Nimmer, das glaub mir', 801; 'Nimmer lange weil' ich hier', 523; 'Nimmer, nimmer darf ich dir gestehen', 419; 'Nimmer trag' ich länger', 432a–b; 'Nimmer werd' ich, nimmer dein vergessen', 214; 'Noch einmal tön, o Harfe', 406

'Noch fand von Evens Töchterscharen', 271; 'Noch in meines Lebens Lenze', 794a–b; 'Non l'accostar all'urna', 688/1; Normans Gesang, 846; 'Nun, da Schatten niedergleiten', 857/2; 'Nunmehr, da Himmel, Erde', 630; 'Nun merk ich erst', 911/10a–b; 'Nur euch, schöne Sterne', 902/1; Nur wer die Liebe kennt, 513a; 'Nur wer die Sehnsucht kennt', 310a–b, 359, 481, 877/1, 877/4; 'Oben drehen sich die grossen', 307; 'O, dass ich dir vom stillen Auge', 303; 'O du Entrissne mir', 741; 'O du, wenn deine Lippen', 922a–b

'Oft im einsam stillen Stunden', 456; 'O gib vom weichen Pfühle', 119; 'O Herz, sei endlich stille', 860; 'O köstlicher Tokayer', 248; 'O Liebe, die mein Herz erfüllet', 301; 'O Menschheit, o Leben', 842; O Quell, was strömst du rasch und wild, 874; Orest auf Tauris, 548; 'Or sù non ci pensiamo', 902/3; 'O sagt, ihr Lieben, mir einmal', 833a–b; Ossians Lied nach dem Falle Nathos, 278a–b; 'O unbewölktes Leben!', 805; 'O wie dringt das junge Leben', 883

'O, wie schön ist deine Welt', 799; Pause, 795/12; Pax vobiscum, 551; Pensa, che questo istante, 76a–b; Pflicht und Liebe, 467; Pflügerlied, 392; Phidile, 500; Philoktet, 540; Pilgerweise, 789; Prometheus, 674; Punschlied: im Norden zu singen, 253; 'Purpur malt die Tannenhügel', 108; 'Quälend ungestilltes Sehnen', 409; 'Quell'innocente figlio, 17; Rast, 911/10a–b; 'Raste, Krieger, Krieg ist aus', 837; Rastlose Liebe, 138a–b; 'Rauschender Strom, brausender Wald', 957/5

'Rauschendes Bächlein, so silbern', 957/1; 'Rein und freundlich lacht der Himmel', 141; Ritter Toggenburg, 397; 'Ritter, treue Schwesterliebe', 397; Romanze, 114a–b, 144; Romanze des Richard Löwenherz, 907a–b; Romanze zum Drama Rosamunde, 797 (3b); 'Rosa, denkst du an mich?', 316a–b; Rückblick, 911/8; Rückweg, 476; 'Ruhn in Frieden alle Seelen', 33a–b; 'Rund um mich Nacht', 217; 'Sag an, wer lehrt dich Lieder', 491; 'Sah ein Knab' ein Röslein stehn', 257; 'Sanftes Klavier', 342; 'Sanft glänzt die Abendsonne', 382

'Sanft wehn, im Hauch der Abendluft', 275; Sängers Morgenlied, 163, 165; 'Säuselnde Lüfte wehend so mild' 957/3; 'Schad' um das schöne grüne Band', 795/13; Schäfers Klagelied, 121a–b; 'Schaff, das Tagwerk meiner Hände', 293a–b; Schatzgräbers Begehr, 761a–b; Schiffers Scheidelied, 910; 'Schlacht, du brichst an!', 169; Schlachtlied, 443; 'Schlafe, schlafe, holder süsser Knabe', 498; Schlaflied, 527a–b; 'Schlägt mein ganzes Glück', 832; Schlummerlied, 527a–b; 'Schlumm'm're sanft!', 304; 'Schneeglöcklein, o Schneeglöcklein', 786 'Schöne Welt, wo bist du?', 677a–b; 'Schön im bunten Knabenkleide',

430a-b; 'Schön wie Engel', 195; 'Schöpferin beseelter Töne!'. 394; Schwanengesang, 744, 957; Schwangesang, 318; Schweizerlied, 559; Schwertlied, 170; Schwestergruss, 762; 'Schwüler Hauch weht mir herüber', 222; Sehnsucht, 52, 123, 310a-b, 359, 481, 516, 636a-c, 879; Sehnsucht der Liebe, 180a-b; 'Seht den Felsenquell', 549, 721; 'Seht meine lieben Bäume an', 532; 'Sei gegrüsst, du Frau der Huld', 623

'Seigegrüsst, geweihteStille', 151; 'Seimirgegrüsst, 741; 'Seimirgegrüsst, o Mai', 305; 'Seisanftwieihre Seele', 265; Selige Welt, 743; Seligkeit, 433; Selma und Selmar, 286a-b; Sendschreiben an den Assessor Spaun in Linz, 749; Serbate, o dei custodi, 35; Seufzer, 198; Shilric und Vinvela, 293; 'Sicheln schallen, Ähren fallen', 434; 'Siehe, wie die Mondesstrahlen', 238; 'Sieht uns der Blick gehoben', 634; 'Sie hüpfte mit mir', 682; Sie in jedem Liede, 896a; 'Sie ist dahin', 201, 399; 'Sie konnte mir kein Wörtchen sagen', 250, 793

'Sie sind in Paris!', 104a-c; 'Siewankt dahin!', 990d; 'Sinke, liebe Sonne', 270; 'Sitz' ich im Gras', 124a-b; Skolie, 306, 507; 'So hab' ich wirklich dich verloren?', 765; 'So lasst mich scheinen', 469a-b, 727, 877/3; 'So mancher sieht mit finstrer Miene', 866/4; Sonett, 628, 629, 630; Son fra l'onde, 78; 'Sonne, du sinkst', 457; 'Sonnenstrahlen durch die Tannen',738; 'Sowirdder Mann, der sonderzwang', 450a-b; Sprache der Liebe, 410; 'Spude dich, Kronos', 369; Ständchen, 889, 957/4; 'Stern der Liebe', 172

'Still beginnt's im Hain zu tauen', 650; 'Still ist die Nacht', 957/13; 'Still sitz' ich an des Hügels Hang', 882; Stimme der Liebe, 187, 412a-b, 418; Strophe aus Die Götter Griechenlands, 677a-b; Süsse, 717, 720a-b; 'Süsse Augen, klare Bronnen', 297a-b; 'Süsse, heilige Natur', 372; 'Süsses Licht! aus goldenen Pforten', 163, 165; 'Süsses Liebchen, komm zu mir', 206; Szene aus Goethes Faust, 126a-b; Täglich zu singen, 533; 'Tag voll Himmel', 413; Täuschung, 911/19; Thekla: eine Geisterstimme, 73, 595a-b

'Tiefe Feier schauert um die Welt', 314; 'Tiefer sinket schon die Sonne', 690; Tiefes Leid, 876; 'Tiefe Stille herrscht im Wasser', 215a, 216; Tischlerlied, 274; Tischlied, 234; 'Tod, du Schrecken der Natur', 518; Todesmusik, 758; 'Todesstille deckt das Tal', 464; 'Tom lehnt harrend auf der Brücke', 639b; Totengräberlied, 44; Totengräbers Heimwehe, 842; Totengräber-Weise, 869; Totenkranz für ein Kind, 275; Tränenregen, 795/10; 'Trarah! Trarah! wir kehren daheim', 521; Trauer der Liebe, 465a-b; 'Trauer umfliesst mein Leben', 371; Trinklied, 183, 888

Trinklied vor der Schlacht, 169; Trockne Blumen, 795/18; 'Trocknet nicht', 260; Trost, 523, 671; 'Trost: an Elisa, 97; 'Trost im Liede, 546; Trost in Tränen, 120; 'Über allen Gipfeln ist Ruh', 768; 'Über allen

Zauber Liebe, 682; 'Überall, wohin mein Auge blicket', 308; 'Über die Berge zieht ihr fort', 475; 'Über meines Liebchens Äugeln', 719; 'Über Tal und Fluss getragen', 161a-b; 'Über Wildemann, 884; 'U f'm Bergli bin i g'sässe', 559; 'Um Mitternacht, 862a-b; 'Und frische Nahrung', 543a-b; 'Und nimmer schreibst du?'. 749

Ungeduld, 795/7; Uraniens Flucht, 554; 'Vater, du glaubst es nicht', 770; 'Vater, ich rufe dich!', 171; Vaterlandslied, 287a-b; 'Vater, schenk' mir diese Stunde', 695; Vedi, quanto adoro, 510; 'Verbirg dich, Sonne', 807; 'Verfliesset, vielgeliebte Lieder', 160, 766; Vergebliche Liebe, 177; Vergissmeinnicht, 792; Verklärung, 59; 'Vernimm es, Nacht', 227; 'Verschwunden sind die Schmerzen', 81; Versunken, 715; Vier Canzonen, 688; Vier Refrainlieder, 866; Viola, 786; Vollendung, 579a

'Voll Locken kraus ein Haupt', 715; 'Vom Meere trennt sich die Welle', 509a-b; Vom Mitleiden Mariä, 632; 'Von allen schönen Waren', 261; 'Von der Strasse her ein Posthorn klingt', 911/13; Von Ida, 228; Vor meiner Wiege, 927; 'Vor Thebens siebenfach gähnenden Toren', 166; 'Vorüber, ach vorüber', 531; 'Vorüber die stöhnende Klage!', 584; Waldesnacht, 708; 'Wälze dich hinweg', 474a-b; Wandrers Nachtlied, 224, 768; 'Wann der silberne Mond', 194; 'Wann meine Grillen schwirren', 800a-b

War es also gemeint', 795/4; 'Wärst du bei mir im Lebenstal', 830; 'Warum bist du nicht hier', 315; 'Warum öffnest du wieder', 375; 'Was bedeutet die Bewegung?', 720a-b; 'Was funkelt ihr so mild mich an?', 176; 'Was hör' ich draussen vor dem Tor', 149a-b; 'Was ist es, das die Seele füllt?', 241; 'Was ist Sylvia', 891; 'Was schauest du so hell und klar', 468; Wasserflut, 911/6a-b; 'Was sorgest du?', 449; 'Was sucht denn der Jäger', 795/14; 'Was vermeid ich denn die Wege', 911/20; 'Was weilst du einsam an dem Himmel', 806

Was zieht mir das Herz so?', 123; 'Wehe dem Fliehenden', 957/6; 'Weh mir, ich bebe', 902/2; Wehmut, 772; 'Wehmut, die mich hüllt', 231; 'Weine du nicht', 286a-b; 'Weit in nebelgrauer Ferne', 113a-c; 'Wenige wissen das Geheimnis', 659; 'Wenn alle untreu werden', 661; 'Wenn auf dem höchsten Fels', 965; 'Wenn dein Finger durch die Saiten meistert', 388a-b; 'Wenn der Schimmer von dem Monde', 289a-b; 'Wenn der uralte heilige Vater', 716; 'Wenn ich durch Busch und Zweig', 865b; 'Wenn ich durch Wald und Fluren geh', 772; 'Wenn ich einst das Ziel errungen habe', 579a; 'Wenn ich ihn nur habe', 660 'Wenn ich nur ein Vöglein wäre', 692; 'Wenn im Spiele leiser Töne', 302; 'WennindesAbendsletztemScheine', 107a-b; 'Wennmicheinsam Lüfte fächeln', 631; 'Wenn sanft entzückt', 579b; 'Wenn über Bergen der Nebel sich breitet', 672a; 'Wenn über Berge sich der Nebel breitet', 672b; 'Wer bist du, Geist der Liebe', 233; Werkauft Liebesgötter?', 261;

'Wer nie sein Brot mit Tränen ass', 480a–c; 'Wer reitet so spät', 328a–d; 'Wer sich der Einsamkeit ergibt', 325, 478a–b; 'Wer wagt es, Rittersmann', 77a–b; 'Wer wagt's, wer wagt's', 785; 'Wes' Adern leichtes Blut durchspringt', 262

'Who is Sylvia', 891; 'Widerschein, 639a–b; 'Widerspruch, 865b; 'Wie anders, Gretchen, war dir's', 126a–b; 'Wie blitzen die Sterne', 939; 'Wie braust durch die Wipfel', 828; 'Wiedersehn, 855; 'Wie deutlich des Mondes Licht', 649; 'Wie die Nacht mit heilgem Beben', 180a–b; 'Wie eine trübe Wolke', 911/12a–b; 'Wie erhebt sich das Herz', 291 a–c; 'Wiegenlied, 304, 498, 579a–b, 867; 'Wie glücklich, wem das Knabenkleid', 400; 'Wie hat der Sturm zerrissen', 911/18; 'Wie im Morgenglanze', 544

'Wie ist es denn', 645; 'Wie klag ich's aus', 744; 'Wie kommt's, dass du so traurig bist', 120; 'Wie lieblich und fröhlich', 691; 'Wie rein Gesang sich windet', 693; 'Wie schaust du aus dem Nebelflor', 317a–b; 'Wie schön bist du, du güldne Morgenröte', 273; 'Wie sich der Äuglein kindlicher Himmel', 867; 'Wie so innig, möcht ich sagen', 652a–b; 'Wie soll ich nicht tanzen', 633; 'Wie tönt es mir so schaurig', 731; 'Wie treiben die Wolken so finster', 152; 'Wie Ulfru fischt', 525a–b; 'Wie wohl ist mir im Dunkeln', 313; 'Willkommen, o silberner Mond', 290

'Willkommen, rotes Morgenlicht', 266; 'Willkommen, schöner Jüngling', 283, 587a–b; 'Willkommen und Abschied', 767a–b; 'Will sich Hektor ewig von mir wenden', 312a–b; 'Will singen euch im alten Ton', 463; 'Willst du nicht das Lämmlein hüten', 588a–b; 'Windes Rauschen, Gottes Flügel', 708; 'Winterlied, 401; 'Winterreise, 911; 'Wir sassen so traulich beisammen', 795/10; 'Wirst du halten, was du schwurst', 514; 'Wo die Taub in stillen Buchen', 465a–b; 'Wo ein treues Herz', 795/19

'Woget brausend, Harmonien', 492; 'Woher, o namenloses Sehnen', 235, 237; 'Wohin?, 795/2; 'Wohin? O Helios!', 700; 'Wohin so schnell', 795/15; 'Wohlan! und ohne Zagen', 902/3; 'Wohl denk' ich allenthalben', 350; 'Wohl perlet im Glase', 391; 'Wohl weinen Gottes Engel', 319; 'Wo ich sei, und wo mich hingewendet', 73, 595a–b; 'Wo irrst du durch einsame Schatten', 458; 'Wolke und Quelle, 896b; 'Wonne der Wehmut, 260; 'Wo weht der Liebe hoher Geist?', 522; 'Zeit, Verkündigerin der besten Freuden', 288; 'Zieh hin, du braver Krieger du!', 454

'Zu Aachen in seiner Kaiserpracht', 990; 'Zu Dionys, dem Tyrannen', 476; 'Zufriedenheit, 362, 501a–b; 'Zum Donaustrom, zur Kaiserstadt', 476; 'Zu meinen Füssen brichst du dich', 699; 'Zum Punsche, 492; 'Zur Namensfeier des Herrn Andreas Siller, 83; 'Zwar schuf das Glück', 320; 'Zwei Szenen aus dem Schauspiel Lacrimas, 857; 'Song without title or words', 1a, 555, 916a

MISCELLANEOUS

(published in NSA viii/1–2 unless otherwise stated)

D	
16	7 contrapuntal studies, nos.1–4, g, nos.3–7, a, ?vv, ?1823, ed. in Orel (1940/R1977)
25	2 contrapuntal studies, a 2–4, frags., begun 18 June 1812
25a	2 contrapuntal studies, a 4, frags., ?sum. 1812
25b	15 contrapuntal studies, a 3, frags., ?sum. 1812 (part facs. in Landon, 1969)
AI/3	Fugue, C, str qt, frag., va only, ?1812
AI/14	Waltz, 'Kupelwieser-Walzer', G, pf, 17 Sept 1826 (Vienna, 1970)
AI/23	Lebenslied, TTB/TTBB, 2nd T only, 1815 or 1816 (Kassel, 1974) [? part of lost Lebensbild, 425]
AI/28	Klage, song, c1817 [formerly 512]
AI/32	Figured bass exercises, before 1812 [formerly 598a]
AII/1	arr. of ov. to Gluck's Iphigénie en Aulide, pf 4 hands, frag., ?early 1810
AII/2	arr. of W. Matiegka's Notturno op.21, fl, va, vc, gui, 26 Feb 1814 (Munich, 1926) [see also 96]
AII/3	arr. of 2 arias from Gluck's Echo et Narcisse, 1v, pf, March 1816
AII/4	arr. of M. Stadler's Psalm viii, S, 2 ob, 2 cl, str, timp, org, 29 Aug 1823 (Vienna, 1960)

DOUBTFUL AND SPURIOUS WORKS

D	
AI/4	Str qt, G, frag. [formerly 2]
AI/7	March, 2 pf 8 hands. Nov 1825, lost [formerly 858]
AI/12	7 leichte Variationen, G, pf, ?1810
AI/15	Minuet and trio, D, pf [formerly 336]
AI/17	Tantum ergo, Bb, frag., S only
AI/25	Drum Schwester und Brüder, 1v, chorus, insts, frag., Oct 1819
AI/26	Sturmbeschwörung, ? trio/qt, mixed vv, frag., S only
AI/29	Kaiser Ferdinand II, song
AIII/6	Offertory: Clamavi ad te, frag., ?Nov 1813, by J. Preindl [formerly 85]
AIII/11	Lass immer in der Jugend Glanz, canon, 2vv, after Mozart [formerly 92]
AIII/12	Selig alle, die im Herrn entschliefen, canon, 2vv, after Mozart [formerly 127]

Bibliography

BIBLIOGRAPHIES

O. E. Deutsch, ed.: *Franz Schubert: die Dokumente seines Lebens und Schaffens*, ii/1: *Die Dokumente seines Lebens* (Munich, 1914, enlarged 2/1964, Neue Ausgabe sämtlicher Werke, viii/5, with a selective list of Deutsch's writings on Schubert, p. 616; Eng. trans., 1946/R1977, as *Schubert: a Documentary Biography*)

W. Kahl: *Verzeichnis des Schrifttums über Franz Schubert: 1828–1928* (Regensburg, 1938)

A. H. King: 'Bibliography', *Schubert: a Symposium*, ed. G. Abraham (London, 1946/R1969, 2/1952)

CATALOGUES

G. Nottebohm: *Thematisches Verzeichnis der im Druck erschienenen Werke von Franz Schubert* (Vienna, 1874)

O. E. Deutsch with D. R. Wakeling: *Schubert: a Thematic Catalogue of his Works* (London, 1951) [preface, p. ix, lists and discusses all previous catalogues; corrections and addns to catalogue in *ML*, xxxiv (1953), 25]; Ger. trans., rev., enlarged, by W. Dürr, A. Feil, C. Landon and others, Neue Ausgabe sämtlicher Werke, viii/4, as *Franz Schubert: thematisches Verzeichnis seiner Werke in chronologischer Folge von Otto Erich Deutsch* (Kassel, 1978) [reviews: R. Klein: 'Der neue "Deutsch" und andere Schubert-Publikationen', *ÖMz*, xxxiii (1978), 573; E. Sams: 'Schubert and OED2', *MT*, cxx (1979), 577]

R. van Hoorickx: 'Thematic Catalogue of Schubert's Works: New Additions, Corrections and Notes', *RBM*, xxviii–xxx (1974–6), 136

DOCUMENTS

O. E. Deutsch, ed.: *Franz Schubert: die Dokumente seines Lebens und Schaffens*, ii/1: *Die Dokumente seines Lebens* (Munich, 1914, enlarged 2/1964, Neue Ausgabe sämtlicher Werke, viii/5; Eng. trans., 1946/R1977, as *Schubert: a Documentary Biography*)

——: *Franz Schuberts Briefe und Schriften* (Munich, 1919, 4/1954; Eng. trans., 1928/R1970)

——: *Franz Schuberts Tagebuch* (Vienna, 1928; Eng. trans., 1928) [facs. and transcr.]

H. Werlé, ed.: *Franz Schubert in seinen Briefen und Aufzeichnungen* (Leipzig, 1948, 4/1955)

H. Müller von Asow: 'Unbekannte Briefe der Familie Schubert', *ÖMz*, xiii (1958), 317

R. Klein: *Schubert-Stätten* (Vienna, 1972)

C. Landon: 'Ein neuer Schubert-Brief', *ÖMz*, xxxii (1977), 545

R. van Hoorickx: 'An Unknown Schubert Letter', *MT*, cxxii (1981), 291

ICONOGRAPHY

A. Trost: 'Franz Schuberts Bildnisse', *Berichte und Mittheilungen des Alterthums-Vereines zu Wien*, xxxiii/2 (1898), 85

O. E. Deutsch, ed.: *Franz Schubert: die Dokumente seines Lebens und Schaffens*, iii: *Sein Leben in Bildern* (Munich, 1913)

O. E. Deutsch: *Die historischen Bildnisse Franz Schuberts in getreuen Nachbildungen* (Vienna, 1922)

A. Orel: *Franz Schubert, 1797–1828: sein Leben in Bildern* (Leipzig, 1939)

R. Petzoldt: *Franz Schubert: sein Leben in Bildern* (Leipzig, 1953)

O. E. Deutsch: 'Rieders Schubert-Bildnis', *ÖMz*, xiv (1959), 1

F. Novotny: 'Zu einem Bildnis Franz Schuberts', *Musica*, xv (1961), 57

E. Hilmar and O. Brusatti, eds.: *Franz Schubert* (Vienna, 1978) [exhibition catalogue]

E. Badura-Skoda: 'A Schubert Life Mask', *MT*, cxx (1979), 575

MANUSCRIPTS, SOURCES

M. Friedlaender: 'Fälschungen in Schuberts Liedern', *VMw*, ix (1893), 166

E. Mandyczewski, ed.: *Revisionsbericht*, Franz Schuberts Werke: kritisch durchgesehene Gesamtausgabe (Leipzig, 1897/*R*1969)

J. Mantuani: 'Schubertiana: ein Beitrag zur Schubertforschung', *Die Musik*, i (1901–2), 1374 [Schubert autographs found in St Peter's, Vienna]

E. Decsey: 'Aus Josef Hüttenbrenner's Schubert-Nachlass', *Die Musik*, xi (1911–12), 297

R. Lachmann: 'Die Schubert-Autographen der Staatsbibliothek zu Berlin', *ZMw*, xi (1928), 109

J. G. Prod'homme: 'Les manuscrits de Schubert à la Bibliothèque du Conservatoire de Paris', *ReM*, xii (1928), 209

Internationaler Kongress für Schubertforschung: Wien 1928 [contains essays by R. Haas, J. Wolf, G. Kinsky, M. Friedlaender, on Schubert collections and source material]

M. J. E. Brown: 'Recent Schubert Discoveries', *ML*, xxxii (1951), 349

F. Racek: 'Von den Schuberthandschriften der Stadtbibliothek', *Festschrift zum hundertjährigen Bestehen der Wiener Stadtbibliothek, 1856–1956* (Vienna, 1956), 98

M. J. E. Brown: 'New, Old and Rediscovered Schubert Manuscripts', *ML*, xxxvii (1957), 359

——: 'Schubert's Manuscripts: some Chronological Issues', *MR*, xix (1958), 180

——: 'Schubert: Discoveries of the Last Decade', *MQ*, xlvii (1961), 293

W. Suppan: 'Schubert-Autographe im Nachlass Weis-Ostborn', *SM*, vi (1964), 131

M. J. E. Brown: 'Two Schubert Discoveries', *MT*, cix (1968), 801 [Albumleaf, 1821; *Die Wallfahrt* D778a]

A. Feil and W. Dürr: 'Kritisch revidierte Gesamtausgaben von Werken Franz Schuberts im 19. Jahrhundert', *Musik und Verlag: Karl Vötterle zum 65. Geburtstag* (Kassel, 1968), 268

O. E. Deutsch: 'Eine merkwürdige Schubert-Handschrift', *Musa-mens-musici: im Gedenken an Walther Vetter* (Leipzig, 1969), 283 [Schubert's arr. for voice and orch of Stadler's Psalm viii, ᴀII/4]

A. Feil and W. Dürr: 'Die neue Schubert-Ausgabe: über einige Probleme des Herausgabens von Musik', *ÖMz*, xxiv (1969), 553

R. van Hoorickx: 'About some Early Schubert Manuscripts', *MR*, xxx (1969), 118

I. Kecskeméti: 'Neu entdeckte Schubert-Autographe', *ÖMz*, xxiv (1969), 564

C. Landon: 'Neue Schubert-Funde', *ÖMz*, xxiv (1969), 299; Eng. trans., *MR*, xxxi (1970), 200

A. Orel: 'Schubertiana in Schweden', *Musa-mens-musici: im Gedenken an Walther Vetter* (Leipzig, 1969), 297

R. van Hoorickx: 'Two Essays on Schubert, I: Schubert's Variations, op.10, II: Ferdinand and Franz Schubert', *RBM*, xxiv (1970), 81

M. J. E. Brown: 'Schubert: Discoveries of the Last Decade', *MQ*, lvii (1971), 351

A. Weinmann: 'Zwei neue Schubert-Funde', *ÖMz*, xxvii (1972), 75 [version *a* of *Mut* D911, no.22; 4th setting of *Das Grab* D569 for chorus]

R. van Hoorickx: 'The Schubert Manuscript D.966', *ML*, liv (1973), 385
——: 'A Schubert Manuscript Identified', *MT*, cxv (1974), 127 [D966]
——: 'Un manuscrit inconnu de Schubert', *RBM*, xxviii–xxx (1974–6), 260 [*Über Wildemann* D884]

F. G. Zeileis: 'Bemerkungen zur Erstveröffentlichung einer bisher unge-druckten Komposition aus Franz Schuberts Studienzeit', *Beiträge zur Musikdokumentation: Franz Grasberger zum 60. Geburtstag* (Tutzing, 1975), 493

R. van Hoorickx: 'Some Unknown Schubert Manuscripts', *MT*, cxviii (1977), 1001

O. Biba: 'Einige neue und wichtige Schubertiana im Archiv der Gesellschaft der Musikfreunde', *ÖMz*, xxxiii (1978), 604

G. Brosche: 'Der Schubert-Autographen der Österreichischen National-Bibliothek', *ÖMz*, xxxiii (1978), 611

E. Hilmar: *Verzeichnis der Schubert-Handschriften in der Musiksammlung der Wiener Stadt- und Landesbibliothek* (Kassel, 1978)

R. Winter: 'Schubert's Undated Works, a New Chronology', *MT*, cxix (1978), 498

CONTEMPORARY ACCOUNTS

R. Bright: *Travels from Vienna through Lower Hungary, with some Remarks on the State of Vienna during the Congress in the year 1814* (Edinburgh, 1818)

J. C. von Zedlitz: 'Nachruf an Schubert', *Wiener Zeitschrift für Kunst und Literatur* (25 Nov 1828)

J. Mayrhofer: 'Erinnerungen an Franz Schubert', *Neues Archiv für Geschichte, Staatenkunde, Literatur und Kunst*, i/16 (1829), 23

L. von Sonnleithner: 'Biographie des Franz Schuberts', *Monatsberichte der Gesellschaft der Musikfreunde des österreichischen Kaiserstaates*, i/2 (1829), 19

J. Mailáth, ed.: *Leben der Sophie Müller* (Vienna, 1832) [diary references]

A. Schindler: 'Erinnerungen an Franz Schubert', *Niederrheinische Musikzeitung für Kunstfreunde und Künstler*, v (1857), 73, 81

H. von Chézy: *Unvergessenes: Denkwürdigkeiten aus dem Leben, von ihr selbst erzählt* (Leipzig, 1858), 259ff

I. F. Castelli: *Memoiren meines Lebens*, iv (Vienna, 1861), 123f

H. Hoffmann von Fallersleben: *Mein Leben: Aufzeichnungen und Erinnerungen*, ii (Hanover, 1868), 50ff

E. von Bauernfeld: 'Einiges von Franz Schubert', *Signale für die musikalische Welt*, xxvii (1869), 977, 993, 1009, 1025; Eng. trans., *Musical World* (15 Jan, 19 Feb 1870)

A. Fareanu: 'Leopold Sonnleithner: Erinnerungen an Franz Schubert', *ZMw*, i (1918–19), 466

J. von Spaun: *Neues um Franz Schubert: einige Bemerkungen über die Biographie Schuberts von Herrn Ritter v. Kreissle-Hellborn* [1865] (Vienna, 1934)

G. Schünemann, ed.: *Erinnerungen an Schubert: Josef von Spauns erste Lebensbeschreibung* [1829] (Berlin and Zurich, 1936)

O. E. Deutsch, ed.: *Schubert: die Erinnerungen seiner Freunde* (Leipzig, 1957, 3/1974; Eng. trans., 1958)

BIOGRAPHY

C. G. von Leitner: *Anselm Hüttenbrenner* (Graz, 1868)

C. von Würzbach: 'Schubert', *Biographisches Lexikon des Kaiserthums Oesterreich*, pt.32 (Vienna, 1876), 30–110

G. Grove: 'Schubert, Franz', *Grove 1*; repr. in *Beethoven, Schubert, Mendelssohn* (London, 1951)

L. Herbeck: *Johann Herbeck: ein Lebensbild von seinem Sohne* (Vienna, 1885), 162ff

M. Friedlaender: *Beiträge zur Biographie Franz Schuberts* (Berlin, 1887; Leipzig, 1928, as *Franz Schubert: Skizze seines Lebens und Wirkens*)

O. E. Deutsch: *Schubert-Brevier* (Berlin, 1905)

M. Vancsa: 'Schubert und seine Verleger', *Jahresbericht des Schubertbundes Vienna, 1905*, 47

E. Mandyczewski: *Geschichte der k. k. Gesellschaft der Musikfreunde*, suppl. (Vienna, 1912)

R. Schmekal: 'Grillparzer und die Gesellschaft der Musikfreunde in Wien', *Der Merker*, v (1915), 447

W. Schweisheimer: 'Der kranke Schubert', *ZMw*, iii (1921), 552

N. Flower: *Franz Schubert: the Man and his Circle* (London, 1928, 2/1949)

K. Kobald: *Franz Schubert und seine Zeit* (Zurich, Leipzig and Vienna, 1928; Eng. trans., 1928)

A. Orel: *Der junge Schubert: aus der Lernzeit des Künstlers* (Vienna, 1940/R1977)

F. Walker: 'Schubert's Last Illness', *MMR*, lxxvii (1947), 232

H. Goldschmidt: *Franz Schubert: ein Lebensbild* (Berlin, 1954, 5/1964)

M. J. E. Brown: *Schubert: a Critical Biography* (London, 1958/R1977, 2/1961; Ger. trans., 1969)

——: 'Schubert and Salieri', *MMR*, lxxxviii (1958), 211

——: 'Schubert's Early Association with the Kärntnertor-Theater', *MT*, c (1959), 261

——: 'Schubert: Discoveries of the Last Decade', *MQ*, xlvii (1961), 293

F. Hüttenbrenner: 'Anselm Hüttenbrenner und Schuberts H-moll Symphonie', *Zeitschrift des Historischen Vereines für Steiermark*, lii (1961), 12

O. E. Deutsch: 'Der "Mutwille" in Hütteldorf', *ÖMz*, xx (1965), 95

——: 'Ein Scherzgedicht aus der Schubertkreis', *ÖMz*, xxi (1966), 49

P. Ronge: 'Franz Schubert: der Mensch, Geschwister, Vorfahren, Lebenslauf: ein Beitrag zur Genealogie', *Genealogie*, xvi (1967), 721; see also xviii (1969), 534

M.-L. Kupelwieser de Brioni: *Une grande amitié: F. Schubert et L. Kupelwieser* (Paris, 1968)

P. Ronge: 'Katarina Laca a Franz Schubert', *SH*, xii (1968), 261

K. Stekl: 'Schuberts Aufenthalt 1827 in Graz', *Mitteilungen des Steirischen Tonkünstlerbundes*, xli (1969), July–Sept, 3

M. J. E. Brown: 'Schubert: Discoveries of the Last Decade', *MQ*, lvii (1971), 351

O. E. Deutsch: 'Schubert und die Königin Hortense', *ÖMz*, xxvii (1973), 121

H. J. Frölich: *Schubert* (Munich and Vienna, 1978)

H. Osterheld: *Franz Schubert: Schicksal und Persönlichkeit* (Stuttgart, 1978)

E. Sams: 'Schubert's Illness Re-examined', *MT*, cxxi (1980), 15

MUSICAL STYLE

G. Abraham, ed.: *Schubert: a Symposium* (London, 1947/R1969)

M. J. E. Brown: *Schubert's Variations* (London, 1954)

H.-W. Berg: *Schuberts Variationswerke* (diss., U. of Freiburg, 1958)

E. G. Porter: 'Schubert's Harmonies', *MR*, xviv (1958), 20

H. Goldschmidt: 'Die Frage der Periodisierung im Schaffen Schuberts', *BMw*, i/2 (1959), p.28

H. Truscott: 'Organic Unity in Schubert's Early Sonata Music', *MMR*, lxxxix (1959), 62

F. Braun: *Studien zur Dynamik in Schuberts Instrumentalmusik* (diss., U. of Tübingen, 1960)

H. Hollander: 'Zur Psychologie des Spätstils in Schuberts Musik', *Musica*, xiv (1960), 565

R. Rhein: *Franz Schuberts Variationswerke* (diss., Saarlandes-U., 1960)

E. Norman-McKay: 'The Interpretation of Schubert's *Decrescendo* and Accent Markings', *MR*, xxii (1961), 108

F. Eibner: 'The Dotted-quaver-and-semiquaver Figure with Triplet Accompaniment in the Works of Schubert', *MR*, xxiii (1962), 281

L. Misch: 'Ein Lieblingsmotiv Schuberts', *Mf*, xv (1962), 146

E. Seidel: *Die Enharmonik in den harmonischen Grossformen Franz Schuberts* (diss., U. of Frankfurt, 1962)

K. P. Bernet Kempers: 'Ganztonreihen bei Schubert', *Organicae voces: Festschrift Joseph Smits van Waesberghe* (Amsterdam, 1963), 7

R. Cox: *Choral Texture in the Music of Franz Schubert* (diss., Northwestern U., 1963)

E. Norman-McKay: 'Rossinis Einfluss auf Schubert', *ÖMz*, xviii (1963), 17

M. Chusid: 'Schubert's Cyclic Compositions of 1824', *AcM*, xxxvi (1964), 37

A. Feil: *Studien zu Schuberts Rhythmik* (Munich, 1966)

W. Riezler: *Schuberts Instrumentalmusik* (Zurich, 1967)

M. Boyd: 'Schubert's Short Cuts', *MR*, xxix (1968), 12

Yu. Khokhlov: *O poslednem periode tvorchestva Shuberta* [The works of Schubert's last period] (Moscow, 1968)

M. K. Whaples: 'On Structural Integration in Schubert's Instrumental Works', *AcM*, xl (1968), 186

R. Bruce: 'The Lyrical Element in Schubert's Instrumental Forms', *MR*, xxx (1969), 131

H. Keller: 'Schuberts Verhältnis zur Sonatenform', *Musa–mens–musici: im Gedenken an Walther Vetter* (Leipzig, 1969), 287

A. Whittall: 'The Sonata Crisis: Schubert in 1828', *MR*, xxx (1969), 124

E. T. Cone: 'Schubert's Beethoven', *MQ*, lvi (1970), 779

D. Schnebel: 'Auf die Suche nach die befreiten Zeit: Versuch über Schubert', *NZM*, cxxxi (1970), 498

M. J. E. Brown: 'Schubert and some Folksongs', *ML*, liii (1972), 173

D. Coren: 'Ambiguity in Schubert's Recapitulations', *MQ*, lx (1974), 568

M. K. Whaples: 'Style in Schubert's Piano Music from 1817 to 1818', *MR*, xxxv (1974), 260

W. S. Newman: 'Freedom of Tempo in Schubert's Instrumental Music', *MQ*, lxi (1975), 528

L. M. Griffel: 'A Reappraisal of Schubert's Methods of Composition', *MQ*, lxiii (1977), 186

W. Gray: 'Schubert the Instrumental Composer', *MQ*, lxiv (1978), 483

ORCHESTRAL WORKS

R. Schumann: 'Die 7. Symphonie von Franz Schubert', *NZM*, xii (1840), 81

J. F. Barnett: 'Some Details concerning the Completion and Instrumentation of Schubert's Sketch Symphony in E', *PMA*, xvii (1890–91), 177

F. Weingartner: *Ratschläge fur Aufführungen klassischer Symphonien*, ii (Leipzig, 1919), 1

A. B. Smith: *Schubert*, i: *The Symphonies C major and B minor* (London, 1926)

E. Laaff: *Franz Schuberts Sinfonien* (Wiesbaden, 1933)

O. E. Deutsch: 'The Riddle of Schubert's Unfinished Symphony', *MR*, i (1940), 36

T. C. L. Pritchard: 'The Unfinished Symphony', *MR*, iii (1942), 10

M. J. E. Brown: 'Schubert's Unfinished Symphony in D', *ML*, xxxi (1950), 109 [D615]

O. E. Deutsch: 'The Discovery of Schubert's C major Symphony', *MQ*, xxxviii (1952), 528

A. Carse: 'Editing Schubert's Unfinished Symphony', *MT*, xcv (1954), 143

J. Reed: 'The "Gastein" Symphony Reconsidered', *ML*, xi (1959), 341

E. Laaff: 'Schuberts grosse C-dur-Symphonie: erkennbare Grundlagen ihrer Einheitlichkeit', *Festschrift Friedrich Blume* (Kassel, 1963), 204

M. J. E. Brown: 'Schubert's Italian Overtures', *MR*, xxvi (1965), 303

H. Hollander: 'Die Beethoven-Reflexe in Schuberts grosser C-dur-Symphonie', *NZM*, cxxvi (1965), 183

S. Kunze: *Franz Schubert: Sinfonie h-moll: Unvollendete* (Munich, 1965)

H. Truscott: 'Franz Schubert', *The Symphony*, ed. R. Simpson (Harmondsworth, 1966–7, 2/1972), i, 188

P. Hamburger: 'Schuberts "Ufuldente": kendsgeminger og formodninger' [Schubert's 'Unfinished': facts and assumptions], *Dansk musiktidsskrift*, xl (1967), 37

M. J. E. Brown: *Schubert Symphonies* (London, 1970)

G. Abraham: 'Finishing the Unfinished', *MT*, cxii (1971), 547

R. Weber: *Die Sinfonien Franz Schuberts im Versuch einer Strukturwissenschaftlichen Darstellung und Untersuchungen* (diss., U. of Münster, 1971)

P. Andraschke: 'Die Retuschen Gustav Mahlers an der 7. Symphonie von Franz Schubert', *AMw*, xxxii (1975), 165

J. Reed: 'How the "Great" C major was written', *ML*, lvi (1975), 18

E. Hilmar: 'Neue Funde, Daten und Dokumente zum symphonischen Werk Franz Schuberts', *ÖMz*, xxxiii (1978), 266

P.-G. Langevin: 'La vraie "Septième" de Schubert et sa résurrection', *SMz*, cxviii (1978), 133, 197

B. Newbould: 'Schubert's Other "Unfinished"', *MT*, cxix (1978), 587

C. Perret-Gentil: 'Le point sur les symphonies inachevées de Schubert et leurs diverses réalisations', *SMz*, cxxi (1981), 76

CHAMBER WORKS

A. B. Smith: *Schubert*, ii: *Quartet in D minor and Octet* (London, 1927)

O. E. Deutsch: 'The Chronology of Schubert's String Quartets', *ML*, xxiv (1943), 25

H.-M. Sachse: *Franz Schuberts Streichquartette* (Munich, 1958)

H. Truscott: 'Schubert's D minor String Quartet', *MR*, xix (1958), 27

——: 'Schubert's String Quartet in G major', *MR*, xx (1959), 119

M. Chusid: *The Chamber Music of Franz Schubert* (diss., U. of California, Berkeley, 1961)

A. A. Abert: 'Rhythmus und Klang in Schuberts Streichquintett', *Karl Gustav Fellerer zum 60. Geburtstag* (Cologne, 1962), 1

M. Chusid: 'Schubert's Overture for String Quintet and Cherubini's Overture to *Faniska*', *JAMS*, xv (1962), 78

J. A. Westrup: *Schubert Chamber Music* (London, 1969)

M. J. E. Brown: 'Schubert's D minor Quartet: a Footnote', *MT*, cxi (1970), 985

H. Hollander: 'Stil und poetische Idee in Schuberts d-moll-Streichquartett', *NZM*, cxxxi (1970), 239

R. A. Coolidge: 'Form in the String Quartets of Franz Schubert', *MR*, xxxii (1971), 309

K. Marx: 'Einige Anmerkungen zu Schuberts "Forellenquintett" und Oktet', *NZM*, cxxxii (1971), 588

M. Chusid: 'Concerning Orchestral Style in Schubert's Early Chamber Music for Strings', *Zur Aufführungspraxis der Werke Franz Schuberts: Wien 1974*

J. Gillett: 'The Problem of Schubert's G major String Quartet (D.887)', *MR*, xxxv (1974), 281

R. van Hoorickx: 'Schubert's Guitar Quartet', *RBM*, xxxi (1977), 111

M. Willfort: 'Das Urbild des Andante aus Schuberts Klaviertrio Es-dur D.929', *ÖMz*, xxxiii (1978), 277

K. Geiringer: 'Schubert's Arpeggione Sonata and the "Super Arpeggio"', *MQ*, lxv (1979), 513

PIANO WORKS

L. Scheibler: 'Zur Datierung von Schuberts Klaviersonate in A-dur, op.120'; 'Zur Datierung von Schuberts "Letztern Walzer", op.127', *ZIMG*, viii (1906–7), 485; 487

H. Wetzel: 'Schuberts Werke für Klavier zu vier Hände', *Die Musik*, vi (1906–7), 36

W. Kahl: 'Das lyrische Klavierstück Schuberts und seine Vorgänger seit 1810', *AMw*, iii (1921), 54, 99

H. Költzsch: *Franz Schubert in seinen Klaviersonaten* (Leipzig, 1927/*R*1976)

M. J. E. Brown: 'An Introduction to Schubert's Sonatas of 1817', *MR*, xii (1951), 35

W. G. Hill: 'The Genesis of Schubert's Posthumous Sonata in B flat major', *MR*, xii (1951), 269

L. Nowak: 'Das Autograph von Schuberts Rondo in D-dur, op.138', *ÖMz*, viii (1953), 325

H. Truscott: 'The Two Versions of Schubert's op.122', *MR*, xiv (1953), 89

P. Mies: 'Der zyklische Charakter der Klaviertänze bei Franz Schubert', *Kongressbericht: Wien Mozartjahr 1956*, 408

H. Truscott: 'Schubert's Unfinished Sonata in C major', *MR*, xviii (1957), 114

A. Weinmann: 'Eine Plagiatsbeschildigung gegen Schubert', *ÖMz*, xii (1957), 19 [Trauerwalzer]

M. J. E. Brown: 'Schubert's "Trauer-Walzer"', *MMR*, xc (1960), 124

P. Mies: 'Die Entwürfe Franz Schuberts zu den letzten drei Klaviersonaten von 1828', *BMw*, ii/3 (1960), 52

P. Badura-Skoda: 'Unbekannter Eigenschriften bekannter Schubert-Werke', *NZM*, cxxii (1961), 502 [4 Impromptus D935]

A. Brendel: 'Die beiden Versionen von Schuberts "Wanderer-Fantasie"', *ÖMz*, xvii (1962), 56

M. J. E. Brown: 'Eine unbekannte Schubert-Handschrift', *NZM*, cxiv (1963), 92

——: 'Schubert: Three Dance-music Manuscripts', *Festschrift Otto Erich Deutsch* (Kassel, 1963), 226

A. L. Hanna: *A Statistical Analysis of some Style Elements in the Solo Piano Sonatas of Franz Schubert* (diss., Indiana U., 1965)

P. Radcliffe: *Schubert Piano Sonatas* (London, 1967)

F. Bisogni: 'Rilievi filologici sulle sonate giovanili di Franz Schubert (1815–17)', *RIM*, ii (1968), 453

M. J. E. Brown: 'Schuberts Fuge in E-moll', *ÖMz*, xxiii (1968), 65

R. van Hoorickx: 'A Schubert Autograph at the Brussels Conservatoire', *RBM*, xxii (1968), 109 [6 Polonaises op.61, D824]

——: 'Two Schubert Dances', *MT*, cix (1968), 532

M. Hughes, L. Moss and C. Schachter: 'Analysis Symposium', *JMT*, xii (1968), 184–239; see also *JMT*, xiii, (1969), 128, 218 [Moment musical op.94 no.1 D780]

R. Klein: 'Schuberts "Kupelwieser-Walzer": Information zu seiner Überlieferung', *ÖMz*, xxiii (1968), 79

A. Tyson: 'Schubert and *Terpsichore*', *MT*, cix (1968), 812

D. A. Weekley: *The One-piano, Four-hand Compositions of Franz Schubert: Historical and Interpretative Analysis* (diss., Indiana U., 1968)

K. Stekl: 'Zur Auffindung eines unbekannten Klavierwerkes von Franz Schubert', *Mitteilungen des Steirischen Tonkünstlerbundes*, xxxix (1969), Jan–March, 1 ['Grazer Fantasie' D605a]

W. Dürr: 'Eine unbekannte Fantasia von Schubert', *ÖMz*, xxiv (1969), 569

R. van Hoorickx: 'Franz Schubert (1797–1828): List of the Dances in Chronological order', *RBM*, xxv (1971), 68

K. Stekl: 'Zwei wiederaufgefundene Schubert-Ländler', *Steirische Sängerzeitung*, xli (1971), 1 [D679]

J. P. Vogel: 'Die "Grazer Fantasie" von Franz Schubert', *Mf*, xxiv (1971), 168

K. M. Komma: 'Franz Schuberts Klaviersonate a-moll op.posth. 164 (D537)', *Zeitschrift für Musiktheorie*, iv/2 (1972), 2

K. Musiol: '"Sieben leichte Variationen in G-Dur", ein verschollenes Jugendwerk von Franz Schubert', *Mf*, xxviii (1975), 202

F. Bisogni: 'Rilievi filologici sulle sonate della maturità di Franz Schubert (1817–1828)', *RIM*, xi (1976), 71

W. Dürr: '"Sieben leichte Variationen in G" – von Schubert?' *Mf*, xxix (1976), 175

E. Sams: 'Schubert's Piano Duets', *MT*, cxvii (1976), 120

SACRED WORKS

E. Prout: 'Franz Schubert's Masses', *MMR*, i (1871), 2, 13, 26, 39, 53, 69, 84

O. Wissig: *Franz Schuberts Messen* (Leipzig, 1909)

M. J. E. Brown: 'Schubert's Settings of the "Salve regina" ', *ML*, xxxvii (1956), 234

K. Pfannhauser: 'Zur Es-Dur-Messe von Franz Schubert', *NZM*, cxix (1958), 435

A. Bamer: 'Franz Schuberts Messen', *Singende Kirche*, viii (1960), 172; also in *Musica sacra*, lxxx (1960), 41

R. van Hoorickx: 'Schubert's "Pastoral" Mass', *ML*, xlii (1961), 53

R. S. Stringham: *The Masses of Franz Schubert* (diss., Cornell U., 1964)

K. J. Nafziger: *The Masses of Haydn and Schubert: a Study in the Rise of Romanticism* (diss., U. of Oregon, 1970)

F. Burkhart: 'Franz Schuberts "Deutsche Messe"', *ÖMz*, xxxi (1976), 565

D. Finke-Hecklinger: 'Franz Schuberts Messe in As', *ÖMz*, xxxiii (1978), 185

R. van Hoorickx: 'Schubert and the Bible', *MT*, cxix (1978), 953

STAGE WORKS

F. Liszt: 'Alfonso und Estrella', *Gesammelte Schriften*, iii/1, trans. L. Ramann (Leipzig, 1881), 68

R. Krott: *Die Singspiele Schuberts* (diss., U. of Vienna, 1921)

M. J. E. Brown: 'Schubert's Two Major Operas', *MR*, xx (1959), 104

E. Norman-McKay: 'Schubert's Incidental Music to "Rosamunde"', *MR*, xxi (1960), 8

——: 'Publisher's Errors in Schubert's Overture to "Die Zauberharfe"', *MR*, xxiii (1962), 128

——: *The Stage-works of Schubert, considered in the Framework of Austrian Biedermeier Society* (diss., U. of Oxford, 1962–3)

F. Racek: 'Franz Schuberts Singspiel "Der häusliche Krieg" und seine jetzt aufgefundene Ouvertüre', *Biblos*, xii (1963), 136

E. Norman-McKay: 'Schubert's Music for the Theatre', *PRMA*, xciii (1966–7), 51

M. J. E. Brown: 'Schubert's *Fierrabras*', *MT*, cxii (1971), 338

M. J. Citron: *Schubert's Seven Complete Operas: a Musico-dramatic Study* (diss., U. of North Carolina, 1971)

W. Szmolyan: 'Schubert als Opernkomponist', *ÖMz*, xxvi (1971), 282

G. R. Cunningham: *Franz Schubert als Theaterkomponist* (diss., U. of Freiburg, 1974)

R. van Hoorickx: 'Les opéras de Schubert', *RBM*, xxviii–xxx (1974–6), 238

P. Branscombe: 'Schubert and his Librettists – 1', *MT*, cxix (1978), 943

O. E. Deutsch: 'Schuberts "Rosamunde" im Theater an der Wien', *ÖMz*, xxxiii (1978), 179

E. Forbes: 'Schubert's "Claudine"', *Opera*, xxix (1978), 1168

CHORAL WORKS

V. Keldorfer: 'Schuberts Chorschaffen', *ÖMz*, xiii (1958), 257

P. Mies: 'Interessantes Schubertfragment aufgefunden: "Die Allmacht" für gemischten Chor', *Lied und Chor*, li (1959), 139

A. Niemeyer: 'Franz Schuberts "Lazarus"-Fragment und seine Beziehung zur Textdichtung', *GfMKB, Leipzig 1966*, 300

R. van Hoorickx: 'Schuberts Trio "Die Advokaten"', *RBM*, xxv (1971), 46

A. Weinmann: 'Eine österreichische Volkshymne von Franz Schubert', *ÖMz*, xxvii (1972), 430

SONGS

H. de Curzon: *Les Lieder de Franz Schubert* (Paris, 1899)

L. Scheibler: 'Franz Schuberts einstimmige Lieder nach österreichischen Dichtern', *Musikbuch für Österreich*, v (1908), 3–35

M. Bauer: *Die Lieder Franz Schuberts*, i (Leipzig, 1915) [only 1 vol. pubd]

H. G. Fiedler: 'Schubert's Poets', *ML*, vi (1925), 68

O. E. Deutsch: *Die Originalausgaben von Schuberts Goethe-Liedern* (Vienna, 1926)

R. Capell: *Schubert's Songs* (London, 1928/*R*1977, rev. 3/1973 by M. Cooper)

P. Mies: *Schubert der Meister des Liedes* (Berlin, 1928)

E. G. Porter: *The Songs of Schubert* (London, 1937)

E. Schnapper: *Die Gesänge des jungen Schubert vor dem Durchbruch des romantischen Liedprinzipes* (Berne and Leipzig, 1937)

E. Schaeffer: 'Schubert's "Winterreise"', *MQ*, xxiv (1938), 39

G. Mackworth-Young: 'Goethe's "Prometheus" and its Settings by Schubert and Wolf', *PRMA*, lxxix (1952–3), 53

M. J. E. Brown: 'Some Unpublished Schubert Songs and Song Fragments', *MR*, xv (1954), 93

T. G. Georgiades: '*Das Wirtshaus* von Schubert und das Kyrie aus dem gregorianschen Requiem', *Gegenwart im Geiste:' Festschrift für Richard Benz* (Hamburg, 1954), 126

H. Haas: *Über die Bedeutung der Harmonik in den Liedern Franz Schuberts* (Bonn, 1957)

H. Brandenburg: 'Die "Winterreise" als Dichtung: eine Ehrenrettung für Wilhelm Müller', *Aurora*, xviii (1958), 57

M. J. E. Brown: 'Schubert's "Wilhelm Meister"', *MMR*, lxxxviii (1958), 4

A. E. F. Dickinson: 'Fine Points in "The Erl King"', *MMR*, lxxxviii (1958), 141

J. Mainka: *Das Liedschaffen Franz Schuberts in den Jahren 1815 und 1816: Schuberts Auseinandersetzung mit der Liedtradition des 18. Jahrhunderts* (diss., Humboldt U., Berlin, 1958)

J. L. Broeckx: 'Het vraagstuk van de tekstbehandeling in Schuberts Winterreise', *Antwerpen jb 1959*, 51–81

J. Kramarz: *Das Rezitativ im Liedschaffen Franz Schuberts* (diss., Free U. of Berlin, 1959)

E. G. Porter: *Schubert's Song-technique* (London, 1961)

J. Kerman: 'A Romantic Detail in Schubert's *Schwanengesang*', *MQ*, xlviii (1962), 36

V. Levi: 'Le arie e ariette di Schubert su testo italiano', *SMw*, xxv (1962), 307

G. Spies: *Studien zum Liede Franz Schuberts: Vorgeschichte, Eigenart und Bedeutung der Strophenvarierung* (diss., U. of Tübingen, 1962)

W. Gerstenberg: 'Schubertiade: Anmerkungen zu einigen Liedern', *Festschrift Otto Erich Deutsch* (Kassel, 1963), 232

P. Hauschild: *Studien zur Liedmelodie Franz Schuberts* (diss., U. of Leipzig, 1963)

A. Holschneider: 'Zu Schuberts "Frühlingsglaube"', *Festschrift Otto Erich Deutsch* (Kassel, 1963), 240

A. C. Bell: *The Songs of Schubert* (Lowestoft, 1964)

M. E. Grebe: 'Estudio analítico de "Der stürmische Morgen": un enfoque metodológico', *Revista musical chilena* (1964), no.18, p.87

M. J. E. Brown: 'Die Handschriften und Frühausgaben von Schuberts "Die Forelle"', *ÖMz*, xx (1965), 578

E. Seidel: 'Ein chromatisches Harmonisierungsmodell in Schuberts "Winterreise"', *GfMKB, Leipzig 1966*, 437; see also *AMw*, xxvi (1965), 285

J. M. Stein: 'Schubert's Heine Songs', *Journal of Aesthetics and Art Criticism*, xxiv (1966), 559

G. Baum: 'Schubert–Müllers *Winterreise* – neu gesehen', *NZM*, cxxviii (1967), 78

M. J. E. Brown: *Schubert Songs* (London, 1967)

T. G. Georgiades: *Schubert: Musik und Lyrik* (Göttingen, 1967)

P. Hamburger: 'Reprisebehandlingen i den Schubert'ske lied', *Dansk musiktidsskrift*, xliii (1967), 163, 196

F. D. Stovall: *Schubert's Heine Songs: a Critical and Analytical Study* (diss., U. of Texas, 1967)

M. J. E. Brown: 'The Therese Grob Collection of Songs by Schubert', *ML*, xlix (1968), 122

R. van Hoorickx: 'Notes on a Collection of Schubert Songs copied from Early Manuscripts around 1821–5', *RBM*, xxii (1968), 86

I. Kecskeméti: 'Eine wieder aufgetauchte Eigenschrift Schuberts', *ÖMz*, xxiii (1968), 70 [*Die Nacht* D534]

D. C. Ossenkop: *The Earliest Setting of German Ballads for Voice and Clavier* (diss., Columbia U., 1968)

L. E. Peake: *The Song Cycle: a Preliminary Inquiry into the Beginnings of the Romantic Song Cycle and the Nature of an Art Form* (diss., Columbia U., 1968)

E. T. Simpson: *A Study, Analysis and Performance of the Schwanengesang of Franz Schubert D.957* (diss., Columbia U., 1968)

D. Berke: 'Zu einigen anonymen Texten Schubertscher Lieder', *Mf*, xxii (1969), 485

J. Chailley: 'Le "Winterreise" et l'énigme de Schubert', *SM*, xi (1969), 107

J. P. Larsen: 'Zu Schuberts Vertonung des Liedes *Nur wer die Sehnsucht kennt*', *Musa–mens–musici: im Gedenken an Walther Vetter* (Leipzig, 1969), 277

E. Schwarmath-Tarján: *Musikalischer Bau und Sprachvertonung in Schuberts Liedern* (Tutzing, 1969)

H. H. Eggebrecht: 'Prinzipien des Schubert-Liedes', *AMw*, xxvii (1970), 89

D. B. Greene: 'Schubert's *Winterreise*: a Study in the Aesthetics of Mixed Media', *Journal of Aesthetics and Art Criticism*, xxix (1970), 181

G. Maier: *Die Lieder Johann Rudolf Zumsteegs und ihr Verhältnis zu Schubert* (diss., U. of Tübingen, 1970)

E. Brody and R. A. Fowkes: *The German Lied and its Poetry* (New York, 1971)

G. Estermann: *Die Klavierbegleitung im Sololied bei Schubert und Schumann* (diss., U. of Innsbruck, 1971)

D. Fischer-Dieskau: *Auf den Spuren der Schubert-Lieder: Werden, Wesen, Wirkung* (Wiesbaden, 1971; Eng trans., 1976)

W. Gray: 'The Classical Nature of Schubert's Lieder', *MQ*, lvii (1971), 62

W. Wiora: *Das Deutsche Lied* (Wolfenbüttel and Zurich, 1971)

W. Gerstenberg: 'Der Rahmen der Tonalität im Liede Schuberts', *Musicae scientiae collectanea: Festschrift Karl Gustav Fellerer* (Cologne, 1973), 147

B. Kinsey: 'Schubert and the Poems of Ossian', *MR*, xxiv (1973), 22

H. Lowen Marshall: 'Symbolism in Schubert's *Winterreise*', *Studies in Romanticism*. xii (1973), 607

S. Sorensen: 'Baek-motiver i Schuberts sange', *Festschrift Gunnar Heerup* (Egtved, 1973), 217

J. H. Thomas: 'Schubert's Modified Strophic Songs with Particular Reference to *Schwanengesang*', *MR*, xxiv (1973), 83

J. Armitage-Smith: 'Schubert's *Winterreise*, Part I: the Sources of the Musical Text', *MQ*, lx (1974), 20

M. Flothuis: 'Franz Schubert's Compositions to Poems from Goethe's *Wilhelm Meisters Lehrjahre*', *Notes on Notes: Selected Essays* (Buren, 1974), 87–138

M. and L. Schochow, eds.: *Franz Schubert: die Texte seiner einstimmig komponierten Lieder und ihre Dichter* (Hildesheim and New York, 1974)

J. Chailley: *Le voyage d'hiver de Schubert* (Paris, 1975)

A. Feil: *Franz Schubert: Die schöne Müllerin, Winterreise* (Stuttgart, 1975)

G. Moore: *The Schubert Song Cycles* (London, 1975; Ger. trans., 1975)

A. Spirk: 'Theorie, Beschreibung und Interpretation in der Lied-Analyse', *AMw*, xxxiv (1977), 225

J. Reed: '*Die schöne Müllerin* reconsidered', *ML*, lix (1978), 411

E. Sams: 'Notes on a Magic Flute: the Origins of the Schubertian Lied', *MT*, cxix (1978), 947

W. Szmolyan: 'Schubert als Singspiel-Komponist', *ÖMz*, xxxiii (1978), 215

R. van Hoorickx: 'A Schubert Song Rediscovered', *MT*, cxxi (1980), 97

C. S. Brauner: 'Irony in the Heine Lieder of Schubert and Schumann', *MQ*, lxvii (1981), 261

A. Walker: 'Liszt and the Schubert Song Transcriptions', *MQ*, lxvii (1981), 50

GENERAL STUDIES

R. Schumann: *Gesammelte Schriften über Musik und Musiker* (Leipzig, 1854, 5/1914/R1969)

H. Kreissle von Hellborn: *Franz Schubert* (Vienna, 1865; Eng. trans., 1869)

A. Reissmann: *Franz Schubert: sein Leben und seine Werke* (Berlin, 1873)

H. F. Frost: *Franz Schubert* (London, 1881, 2/1923)

A. Dvořák: 'Franz Schubert', *Century Magazine*, lxviii (1894), 341

R. Heuberger: *Franz Schubert* (Berlin, 1902, rev. 3/1920 by H. von der Pforten)

W. Klatte: *Franz Schubert* (Berlin, 1907)

W. Dahms: *Schubert* (Berlin, 1912)

O. Bie: *Franz Schubert: sein Leben und sein Werk* (Berlin, 1925; Eng. trans., 1928)

D. F. Tovey: 'Franz Schubert', *The Heritage of Music*, ed. H. J. Foss, i (Oxford, 1927), 82–122

P. Stefan: *Franz Schubert* (Berlin, 1928)

R. Bates: *Schubert* (London, 1934)

W. Vetter: *Franz Schubert* (Potsdam, 1934)

B. Paumgartner: *Franz Schubert* (Zurich, 1943, 2/1947)

A. Hutchings: *Schubert* (London, 1945, rev. 4/1973)

A. Einstein: *Schubert* (London, 1951/*R*1971; Ger. orig., 1952)

W. Vetter: *Der Klassiker Schubert* (Leipzig, 1953)

P. Mies: *Franz Schubert* (Leipzig, 1954)

T. Marek: *Schubert* (Kraków, 1955)

F. Hug: *Franz Schubert: Leben und Werk eines Frühvollendeten* (Frankfurt am Main, 1958)

H. Wagemans: *Schubert* (Haarlem, 1958)

M. Erdelyi: *Franz Schubert* (Budapest, 1962)

L. Kusche: *Franz Schubert: Dichtung und Wahrheit* (Munich, 1962)

J. E. van Ackere: *Schubert en de romantiek* (Antwerp, 1963)

K. Kobald: *Franz Schubert* (Vienna, Munich and Zurich, 1963)

A. Kolb: *Schubert* (Gütersloh, 1964)

J. Bruyr: *Franz Schubert: l'homme et son oeuvre* (Paris, 1965)

F. de Eaubonne and M.-R. Hofmann: *La vie de Schubert* (Paris, 1965)

M. J. E. Brown: *Essays on Schubert* (London, 1966/*R*1977)

W. Marggraf: *Franz Schubert* (Leipzig, 1967)

J. Reed: *Schubert: the Final Years* (London, 1972)

R. van Hoorickx: 'Old and New Schubert Problems', *MR*, xxxv (1974), 76

——: 'Schubert's Reminiscences of his Own Works', *MQ*, lx (1974), 373

O. E. Deutsch: 'Schubert und Grillparzer', *ÖMz*, xxxii (1977), 497

P. Badura-Skoda: 'Fehlende und überzählige Takte bei Schubert und Beethoven', *ÖMz*, xxxiii (1978), 284

O. Biba: 'Franz Schubert in Niederösterreich', *ÖMz*, xxxiii (1978), 359

O. Brusatti: 'Desiderata der Schubert-Forschung', *ÖMz*, xxxiii (1978), 295

R. Klein: 'Begriff und Geschichte der Schubertiaden', *ÖMz*, xxxiii (1978), 209

E. Badura-Skoda and P. Branscombe, eds.: *Schubert Studies: Problems of Style and Chronology* (Cambridge, 1982)

COMMEMORATIVE

Die Musik, vi/7–8 (1906–7)

'Die intime Schubert', *Die moderne Welt* (Vienna, 1 Dec 1925) [Schubert suppl.]

Internationaler Kongress für Schubertforschung: Wien 1928

A. Weiss: *Franz Schubert: eine Festgabe* (Vienna, 1928)

MQ, xiv/4 (1928)

ML, ix/4 (1928)

ReM, x/1–3 (1928–9)

Ars (Buenos Aires, 1961), no.92

ÖMz, xxvii/4 (1972) [on Schubert interpretation]

ÖMz, xxxiii/6 (1978)

ÖMz, xxxiii/11 (1978)

MT, cxix/11 (1978)

19th Century Music, iii/2 (1979)

Index

Abraham, Gerald, 35, 81
Albert, Prince Consort, 73
Altstadt, 1
Aristophanes, 80
Artaria, 47, 50
Atzenbrugg, 30, *31*
Austria, 56, 75

Bach, Johann Sebastian, 84
Barbaia, Domenico, 33, 34, 39
Bärenreiter, 73
Barnett, John Francis, 32
Barth, Joseph, 49
Bauernfeld, Eduard, 32, 42, 45, 49,
  50, 51, 54, 57, 63, 69, 71, 75
Beethoven, Ludwig van, 4, 15, 20,
  33, 41, 54, 55, 58, 71, 76, 84, 86,
  87, 93, 99, 100
Berlin, 45, 46, 55, 64, 72, 75
Bocklet, Karl von, 50, 59, 61, 62
Bogner, Ferdinand, 41
Böhm, Josef, 62
Brahms, Johannes, 85, 103
Breitkopf & Härtel, 17, 40, 50, 73
Breslau, 39, 49, 65
Brüggemann, Karl, 65

Capell, Richard, 94, 96
Cappi & Co., 47, 49
Cappi & Diabelli, 30, 37
Carinthia, 50
Castelli, Ignaz, 37, 80
Charlemagne, 38
Collin, Matthäus von, 25
Czerny, Carl, 50

Dale, Kathleen, 18

Deutsch, Otto Erich, 73
Diabelli, Anton, 16, 47, 50, 55, *56*,
  64, 68, 72, 103
Dialer, Josef, 71
Dickens, Charles, 32
Dietrichstein, Count Moritz, 25, 30
Döbling, 57
Doppler, Josef, 11, 51
Dornbach, 56
Dresden, 17, 20, 37, 46
Dumba, Nicolaus, 73
Dürr, Walther, 74

Eisenstadt, 68
England, 47, 75
Esterházy, Count Johann, 20
Esterházy, Princess Caroline, 20,
  44, 63
Esterházy, Princess Marie, 20
Esterházy family, 21, 25, 43
Eybler, Joseph Leopold, 3

Feil, Arnold, 74
Florian, St, monastery, 48
France, 75
Frankfurt, 49, 55, 75
Fries, Moritz von, 30
Fröhlich, Anna, 26, 57, 62, 71
Fröhlich, Barbara Franziska, 26
Fröhlich, Josefine, 26, 62
Fröhlich, Katharina, 26

Gahy, Joseph von, 19, 49, 61
Gastein, 47, 48
Germany, 56, 65, 75
Gmunden, 46, 47, 48, 63, 67
Goethe, Johann Wolfgang von, 8, *9*,

11, 12, 13, 16, 19, 22, 26, 29, 34, 43, 49, 86, 87, 90, 93, 95
Gosmar, Louise, 57
Graz, 23, 57, 58, 61, 67, 72
Grillparzer, Franz, 26, 57, 62, 63, 71, 83
Grob. Therese, 8
Grove, Sir George, 21, 40
Gymnich, August von, 26

Halberstadt, 65
Hartmann, Franz von, 39, 53, 54, 96
Hartmann, Friedrich von, 39
Hartmann, Fritz von, 39, 96
Hartmann, Philipp Karl, *31*
Haslinger, Tobias, 55, 64
Hatwig, Otto, 15
Haydn, (Franz) Joseph, 4, 68, 75, 100
Heine, Heinrich, 61, 67, 68, 89, 90
Hellmesberger, Johann, 75
Hentl, Friedrich von, 33
Herbeck, Johann, 76
Herder, Johann Gottfried, 5
Hérold, (Louis Joseph) Ferdinand, 30
Hietzing, 46
Hofmann, Georg von, 22, 24
Holz, Karl, 62
Holzapfel, Anton, 2
Holzer, Michael, 2, 4, 8, 16
Hummel, Johann Nepomuk, 68
Hüttenbrenner, Anselm, 23, *27*, 29, 35, 36, 55, 58, 61, 71, 72
Hüttenbrenner, Josef, 11, 23, 55, 61
Hüttenbrenner family, 36

Italy, 49

Jäger, Franz, 22
Jenger, Johann Baptist, *27*, *31*, 57, 58, 61, 67, 71

Klein, Rudolf, 25
Kleyenböck, Anna [Schubert's step-mother], 6

Klopstock, Friedrich Gottlieb, 12
Körner, Phillip, 3
Körner, (Karl) Theodor, 11
Kotzebue, August von, 5, 6
Kreiner, Josef, 61
Kremsmünster, monastery, 48
Kupelweiser, Josef, 38
Kupelweiser, Leopold, 30, *31*, 42, 43, 49, 53, 100

Lablache, Luigi, 64
Lachner, Franz Paul, 41, 61, 68, 69
Laibach (now Ljubljana), 12
Landon, Christa, 74
Lang, Innocenz, 3, 4
Lászny, Katherina von, 46
Leidesdorf, Marcus, 64
Leipzig, 17, 20, 49, 50, 55, 64, 65, 73
  Gewandhaus, 73
Lewy, Josef, 62
Liechtental, 2
Linke, 59, 62
Linz, 30, 38, 42, 47, 48, 57
Liszt, Franz, 25, 75
Ljubljana: *see* Laibach
London, 53, 73
Lutz, Johanna, 53

MacDonald, Andrew, 64
Mainz, 55, 65
Märisch-Schönberg, 1
Matiegka, Wenzel Thomas, 8
Matthisson, Friedrich von, 5
Mayrhofer, Johann, 10, 11, 12, 19, 20, 22, 23, 26, 29, 34, 38, 42, 58, 61, 71, 78, 79
Mendelssohn (-Bartholdy), (Jakob Ludwig) Felix, 73
Metastasio, Pietro, 5
Menz, Ignaz, 68
Milder-Hauptmann, (Pauline) Anna, 45, 46, 68, 72

Moscheles, Ignaz von, 29
Mosel, Ignaz Franz von, 25, 37
Mosewius, Johann Theodor, 65
Mozart, (Johann Chrysostom)
    Wolfgang Amadeus, 4, *14*, 15,
    71, 75, 86
Müller, Sophie, 46
Müller, Wilhelm, 38, 54, 59, 93,
    94, 97
Munich, 55, 57, 64

Nägeli, Hans Georg, 49
Neudorf, 1
Niemeyer, August, 24

Ochsenburg, 32
Ossian, 12
Ottenwald, Anton, 48, 54

Pachler, Dr & Frau, 57, 58, 67
Paganini, Nicolò, 63
Paris, 66, 73, 75
Passini, J. H., 49
Paumgartner, Sylvester, 23
Pennauer, 47, 49
Pest, 68, 69
Pope, Alexander, 5
Pritchard, T. C. L., 35
Probst, H. A., 50, 65, 66, 68
Pyrker, Ladislaus (Patriarch of
    Venice), 26, 30, 49

Randhartinger, Benedikt, 29, 69
Reed, John, 48, 94, 97
Rellstab, Johann Carl Friedrich,
    67
Rieder, Wilhelm August, *44*, 49
Rinna, Ernst, 67, 69
Rochlitz, (Johann) Friedrich, 64
Röner, Franziska, 61
Rossini, Gioachino (Antonio), 18,
    34, 63, 101

Rückert, (Johann Michael)
    Friedrich, 32, 39, 95
Rudolph (Johann Joseph Rainer),
    Archduke of Austria, 41
Růžička, Václav (Wenzel), 3, 4, 12

Salieri, Antonio, 3, 4, 5, 6, 7, 11,
    23, 30
Sams, Eric, 68
Sauer & Leidesdorf, 37, 47
Schickh, Johann, 65
Schiller, (Johann Christoph)
    Friedrich von, 5, 12, 19, 22, 87
Schindler, Anton Felix, 55, 68
Schlechta, Baron, 71
Schlegel, Friedrich von, 26
Schnabel, Artur, 76
Schober, Franz von, 12, 13, 16,
    18, 19, 20, 30, *31*, 32, 33, 37,
    39, 40, 42, 43, 45, 49, 51, 53,
    54, 56, 59, 61, 69, 70, 71, 87
Schönbrunn: *see* Vienna
Schönstein, Baron von, 25, 41, 44
Schott, 65, 66
Schröder-Devrient, Wilhelmine,
    13
Schubert, Ferdinand [Schubert's
    brother], 1, 2, 5, 8, 21, 33, 43, 48,
    67, 68, 69, 70, 72, 73
Schubert, Franz Theodor Florian
    [Schubert's father], 1, 2, 5, 6
Schubert, Ignaz [Schubert's
    brother], 1, 2, 5, 83
Schubert, Josefa [Schubert's
    stepsister], 69
Schubert, Karl [Schubert's
    brother], 1, 61
Schubert, Karl [Schubert's uncle],
    1
Schubert, Maria Elisabet
    Katherina [Schubert's mother],
    1, 5

Schubert, Maria Theresa
[Schubert's sister], 1, 2
Schulze, Ernst, 26, 51
Schumann, Robert (Alexander),
65, 68, 72, 75, 103
Schuppanzigh, Ignaz, 41, 59, 61
Schuster, Vincenz, 45
Schwind, Moritz von, 29, 32, 40,
41, 42, 43, 45, 49, *52*, 53, 54, 57
Scott, Sir Walter, 47, 64
Sechter, Simon, 69
Seidl, Johann, 51, 67
Shakespeare, William, 32, 51
Slavík, Josef, 60, 62
Sonnleithner, Ignaz von, 22, 26
Sonnleithner, Leopold von [son of
Ignaz], 15, 22, 30, 54, 57
Spaun, Anton von, 33
Spaun, Josef von, 3, 4, 10, 12, 13,
25, 30, *31*, 38, 42, 48, 51, *52*,
53, 55, 58, 59, 61, 69, 75
Spina & Co., 72
Stadler, Albert, 11
Steyr, 23, 38, 47
Steyregg, 47
Storck, P. Adam, 47
St Pölten, 32
Strauss, Richard, 53
Sweden, 16

Teltscher, Josef, *27*
Tietze, Ludwig, 62
Tomášek, Václav Jan Křtitel, 59
Traun, Lake, 47
Traweger, Ferdinand, 67
Trieste, 13
Troyer, Ferdinand, Count, 41
Tübingen, 73

Vering, Josef von, 69
Vienna, 1, 12, 16, 20, 21, 22, 23, 29,
31, 32, 33, 34, 38, 39, 43, 44, 46,
47, 49, 51, 58, 63, 65, 67, 69, 72,
75, 76, 94

Annagasse, 7
Conservatory, 26, 41, 46
Erdberggasse, 14
Gesellschaft der
Musikfreunde, 57, 62, 63
Gundelhof, 22
Himmelpfortgrund, 1
Kaiserlich-königliches
Stadtkonvikt, 3, 7
Kärntnertor-Theater, 5, 22, 24,
29, 30, 33, 46, 53
Kettenbrückengasse, 67
Leopoldstadt, 1
Liechtental Church, 8
Margareten suburb, 70
Müllers Hall, 22
Musikverein, 36, 46, 71
Neue Wieden, 67, 69
Nussdorferstrasse, 1
Ringstrasse, 1
Rossau, 19, 20, 21, 37, 45
Säulenstrasse, 2
Schönbrunn, 46
Spiegelgasse, 32
St Augustine's Church, 8, 71
St Joseph's Church, 70
St Stephen's Cathedral, 7, 51
Theater an der Wien, 22, 24, 33
Wieden, 45
Wipplingerstrasse, 10, 22, 29
'Zum grünen Anker' inn, 51,
53
'Zum römischen Kaiser' res-
taurant, 20
'Zum roten Igel' inn, 62
'Zum roten Kreuz' inn, 69
'Zum Schloss Eisenstadt', inn,
54, 56
'Zum ungarischen Krone' inn,
39, 43
'Zum Wolf, der den Gänsen
predigt' inn, 57
Vietz, Maria Elisabet Katherina:

see Schubert, Maria Elisabet Katherina

Villach, 50

Vogl, Johann Michael, 16, 17, 22, 23, 24, 25, 29, 30, 33, 34, 38, 42, 45, 46, 47, 48, 52, 53, 59, 62

Volkert, Franz, 29

Während, 51, 55, 70

Walcher, Ferdinand, 83

Weber, Carl Maria (Friedrich Ernst) von, 33, 37, 39, 65, 87

Weigl, Josef, 5, 23, 54

Weigl, Thaddeus, 50, 64

Weimar, 13, 75

Weingartner, Felix, 32

Werfen, 47

Wildbach, 58

Windsor, 73

Winter, Peter von, 5

Wisgrill, Johann, 69

Witteczek, Josef, 13, 46

Zelter, Carl Friedrich, 13, 86

Zseliz, 20, 21, 43, 45

Zuckmantel, 1

Zumsteeg, Johann Rudolf, 86

Zurich, 49